Helio Tropez

By C.M. Rieger

Praise for Helio Tropez

A richly imagined world filled with intriguing characters. From the first chapter, I was hooked. If you like visionary fantasy, it's definitely worth a read.
   - Joanne Taylor, Booksprout Reviewer

I loved it! A hard sci-fi story involving time travel, a Matrix-like villain, and strong alien family support brings together one epic story! I couldn't put it down.
   - Sarah Anderson, Reedsy Reviewer

From the very first chapter, it had me enthralled. The journey of Hadden and Tia through the different timelines and flashbacks was truly intriguing. I particularly enjoyed the subtle but very clear references to the real situations which are damaging the human race as we know it. I'm looking forward to reading more books from this author. [Advanced Reader]
   - Christine Azzopardi

The characters are wonderful, the story is compelling. Highly creative throughout. I also love how the book weaves in a commentary on our present-day world with incredible insights on how to address issues so we can live better lives. [Advanced Reader]
   - Catherine Berris

C.M. Rieger's ability to reveal just enough to intrigue is amazing. The story draws you in with surprising twists and turns. Resolutions are hard won and beautifully human with all of the flaws and surprising, bright insights that lift us out of the ordinary.
   - Catherine Steele

Copyright

Get Access

Due to popular demand, we are offering FREE access to something called, **A Book Appendix** that goes with Helio Tropez. Some people find it useful to keep track of terms and characters as they read.

To that end, just use the QR Code or link below. It includes:

- A Glossary of Terms
- The TEVAS Aptitudes Quiz
- Family Tree Character Charts

https://GoldenAgeTimeline.com/Book-Appendix-Intro/

Prologue

<u>Hawaii – December 21, 1960</u>

I f Hadden Violetta had learned anything in life so far, by the ripe age of twenty, it was to act on his intuition...even if he risked losing everything. That day, stealing a plane felt worth the risk.

The sun had just edged over the horizon, a mere sliver of golden light in the sky. His face was tanned from afternoons of working out on the beach. The smell of cheap mulled wine hung around him, following him like a curious shadow but always half a step behind. Leaning against a blackened ironwood tree, he took a shaky breath to compose himself. Wiping the sweat from his brow, he bounced on the balls of his feet, rolled his shoulders, and broke into a sprint through the underbrush.

Emerging from the shade, the trees spat him into the muggy, petrol-filled air of the air force base. He darted from shadow to shadow before taking cover behind a discarded container. Peering around the corner, Hadden watched as the ground crew finished preparing the plane and huddled to chat amongst themselves. Right on schedule, a truck arrived at the entrance with a new shipment of supplies. As predicted, the ground crew left the plane unattended to help unload the shipment. With a skeleton crew left to cover the morning's shift, most of the crew were still sleeping off the Christmas party hangover. Those still on their feet either hadn't slept well or hadn't slept at all.

The F-100 Super Sabre now stood alone, its canopy open. Hadden looked in both directions, then broke cover. He sprinted across the runway, hoisted himself into the cockpit, sealed the canopy shut, and donned the pilot's helmet. Even without a photographic memory, he'd have known what to do. The countless hours of training had made the process of running checks a second nature, his hands moving from switch to button without so much as a hesitation. As the engines roared to life, the ground crew looked up, startled. The pilot emerged from the latrine with a confused expression, his eyes darting to and fro between the ground crew and his no-longer-idle aircraft.

As Hadden thundered down the runway, the crew ran for the airfield, waving their arms. The jet lifted him into the air and the base disappeared into the background. He breathed a sigh of relief. Once he entered the cloud cover, Hadden activated the cloaking device in his amethyst, but he couldn't tell if it was working. To be on the safe side, he deactivated the radio signal. No one could stop him now.

In the distance, the Makapu'u lighthouse jutted majestically against the azure sea. A humpback whale breached in the sea below, and Hadden barrel-rolled in response before dropping low over the water. The whale breached again, splashing down in great plumes of foam. Hadden smiled. He felt free, even if just for a few rare moments. He began a gentle climb until he reached five thousand feet, then veered north-east, leaning hard towards the Big Island. The jet engine vibrated in his chest as he leveled out the plane.

As he cruised through the atmosphere, faces appeared, as they often did, in clouds and seascapes. Today, his mother's star-drenched eyes appeared in the swirls of indigo below him. Their last conversation haunted him, still echoing in his ears. His decision to join the air force had torn the family apart, but this meeting could change all that and undo any wrongs against his family and those he loved.

His hands trembled on the controls, and he shifted, taking a breath to calm down. He searched through his memory banks for the story he needed – a tale about his father flying through a vortex that warped time, blurring the edges of one reality with another. It was a story that felt so real it was as though he'd experienced it himself.

Few people in the Air Force ever talked about these anomalies. Places like the Bermuda Triangle remained an unsolved mystery as far as civilians were concerned, but Hadden knew better. All those from where his father had come from knew about the places where you could travel between timelines and dimensions. A well-kept secret in one world was common knowledge in another.

He scanned the horizon until he saw it: the tubular cloud that marked an underwater volcano with a stargate. As he neared, the instrument panel became increasingly erratic, dials leaping like fleas. Instead of pointing to the magnetic north, it spun before locking on to the true north. His breath quickened as he unfolded the handwritten note. It contained four images, a date, and a set of numbers.

For four nights in a row, he dreamt the contents of that note. The first night was an image of the tubular-shaped cloud near Kilauea Volcano, also known as the Hawaiian vortex, with the date 21 December 1960 – the winter solstice. On the second night, he saw a city with skyscrapers and a tower that had a flying saucer on top of it. In the distance, a snow-capped mountain had towered above that city. On the third night, he dreamt of a house with a dome. It stood near a miniature Statue of Liberty. On the fourth night, he'd seen the time-space coordinates. The realisation had jolted him awake, covered in sweat. If this mission proved successful, it went against all-time travel regulations that had ever existed, but he had to do it anyway.

Gripping the controls tightly, he held the jet steady, pushing it to max speed, then plunged into the centre of the great cylinder. The cloud swallowed the aircraft whole. Inside, flashes of fork lightning erupted all around him. Thunder shook his ribcage. Swirling black clouds formed a tunnel ahead of him. As the propellers strained against the magnetic pull, sparks flew from the engine. Still, the plane glided forward as if on a frozen lake. His hands clenched the steering shaft, the plane shuddering so hard that metal plates started to separate. When the tailpiece erupted in a fireball, his breathing caught in his chest. He pressed his neck against the headrest, tucked his chin to his chest, brought his elbows in close and yanked the ejection lever.

The canopy flew off, and the charge beneath the seat fired, launching him clear of the plane. Seconds later, the chair fell away as his parachute thankfully opened. He watched in anguish as the jet flew into the distance, trailed by a cloud of black smoke. As he fell into the abyss, his stomach churned. Wind screamed in his ears, and sodden clouds engulfed him in the pitch dark. Hadden prayed for a soft landing.

When the clouds parted, the moon hung full in a starry sky. A landmass covered in silver skyscrapers sparkled in the twilight, most of them standing taller than anything he'd seen before. One looked like a flying saucer on top of a tower, just like in his dream. He manoeuvred his parachute away from the buildings and towards a nearby beach park. In the distance, the white cap of Mount Rainier looked on over his hometown. He recognised it, but Seattle had exploded in size, sprawling as well as stretching skyward.

Yet, despite the immensity of the city, it seemed quiet, the roads void of cars. He splashed down into Puget Sound, fifty meters from Alki Beach Park. Freeing himself of the chute, he swam to the familiar beach with the miniature Statue of Liberty. Crawling out of the water, he looked down both ends of the shoreline. Not a soul.

Dripping wet, he hiked up the rocky beach to a picnic bench. On the table, a newspaper was wedged between slats. Hadden held it up to the moonlight, squinting to see the date. He let out a breath and ran a hand through his hair. "It worked…" he muttered, spinning around in a circle, trying to see what this new century looked like. "2010. That's… that's unbelievable." A few blocks away was the house with the dome. He shook himself off and started heading towards it. It's why he'd come, after all. He'd been called, summoned to the future to meet someone, and that's where he'd find them – the person who had sent him the message.

His seventy-year-old self.

CHAPTER 1

Seattle – July 18, 2010

At 1:11 a.m., Tia Violetta ended her Skype call. This client was a tough one. The old woman preferred her sessions late at night when everyone in her house had gone to bed.

Breathing a sigh of relief, she flopped onto the four-poster bed, rubbing her forehead. She dimmed the lights and poured three drops of lavender into a diffuser. Indigo fabric canopied either side of the bed, helping her feel safe again. Her client lived in a prison of luxury, surrounded by vulturous and violent family members. Although she had spent the entire session complaining about the gardener, Tia knew what was really going on. She would need to spend days helping the woman process the unacknowledged anxiety and protect her from the possible death threats. After each session, Tia imagined the woman's fear burning like logs in a fire, and she erected a fortress of light to surround her night and day.

Her apartment stood separate from the rest of the estate where her father lived, which, she told herself, made it okay to live at home, even if she was twenty-nine. She had decorated her space in lush shades of lavender and magenta, accented with gold tapestries. Matching Ming vases, always brimming with violets, adorned each bedside table.

After seven clients in a row without a break, Tia was hungry. A kitchenette filled one wall of the apartment. On her way there, she caught a glimpse of her gaunt face, then grunted. Sleep wasn't as frequent an option as she'd have liked.

Normally, she chose not to eat – a side effect of a life encountering allergy after allergy. On this night, however, she was famished. Bowl in hand, she entered an indoor greenhouse next to the kitchenette. Shelves of hydroponically grown plants glowed in the pink LED lights, such as alfalfa sprouts, lettuce and basil. She harvested some of each, returned to the kitchenette and set her newly gathered ingredients on the counter. Beside it, a multi-tiered food dehydrator housed other plants from the greenhouse. From the top shelf, she took a flax seed cracker she'd made the day before.

Fetching a jar of cashew spread, she took a seat at a tiny kitchen table next to the window. A pink placemat shared the surface with a vase of purple roses and a matching napkin rolled in a silver ring. After placing the napkin in her lap, Tia inhaled the food as she looked out over Puget Sound.

To passers-by, her apartment looked like her father's mansion came from the future. With its curved walls of stainless steel and large round windows, it spilt out over the buff above the West Seattle beach. She'd often seen people on the shore pointing up, discussing the unusual sight.

As she sat back and patted the corners of her mouth with a napkin, the digital clock on the table flipped to 1:11 a.m. *That's strange. I thought it was 1:11 at least fifteen minutes ago.* Too tired to investigate the anomaly, she yawned and cleaned up her dishes. At her vanity table, she removed the seventeen pins that held her hair in place, then uncoiled each French braid before brushing out her hip-length hair. Once her routine was complete, she could only laugh at her reflection. Before going to bed, she often looked like Cousin It from the Addams Family. Fortunately, only her father had ever seen her like that, but he made enough playful jokes to compensate for those who missed out.

A series of thumps shuddered from below, and Tia groaned. This usually meant her father needed help with something downstairs. He'd taken to thumping the ceiling with his cane to get her to venture down. Wearily, she climbed back out of bed and put a headband on to keep her hair out of her eyes before bracing herself. The descent down the spiral staircase would lead her to the chaos of her father's world, so she took a breath to steel herself. Once the jewel of architectural magazines, the mansion now lay in disrepair, clutter reigning in whichever room her father chose to haunt.

A maze of decades-old newspapers, mouldy books, broken-down appliances and electrical cords ran haywire in all directions. It made a fine haven for spider webs and dust bunnies. Cobwebs ran from light fixtures down to dead houseplants while piles of old books choked the already narrow hallway. Dust and mould filled the air as she carefully avoided stepping on anything, moving with well-rehearsed precision. As she neared, the cacophony of three television sets grew louder. Floor-to-ceiling windows looked out over the ocean, but tattered curtains and untended trees blocked a million-dollar view.

When she entered the living room, her father was lying stuck in the 'feet up' position in his reclining chair. His domed head gleamed in contrast to the fringe of long, frizzy grey hair.

"I'm uh... well..." he looked at himself, assessing his situation, then looked back to Tia.

"Stuck?" she offered.

"Exactly! Did I wake you? I'm sorry if I did. I wouldn't have if it had been anything else, you know."

"I know, Dad. It's fine, I was still awake. "

Earlier that week, she'd taken him to visit the doctor's office – against his will, it should be noted. It was clear that he was overweight. But when the scales had reported a figure well over three hundred and fifty pounds and the doctor had to stop for a glass of water while listing his many maladies, the nurses had called him "a walking miracle."

"I'm going to push from behind the chair," Tia said, rolling up her sleeves. She heaved, but to no avail. After several attempts, she slumped exhausted in a nearby chair, awaiting the next instructions. Her father said nothing. He only squeezed his eyes shut.

"Maybe I should call that Care Centre," she suggested in a thin voice. "Remember a flyer was left in our mailbox recently? Maybe it's a sign. You know, how you like to talk about synchronicities..."

"No! Try again," he growled. "That could be an artificial sync."

Whatever that means, she thought.

"I can't do it, Dad. I'm not strong enough."

The corners of his mouth sagged downward. He blinked a few times as though trying to piece something together in his mind. "Someone is outside the house, trying to get in."

"Haven't I told you not to pay attention to visions like that? They just make you lose sleep."

"But I'm often right!"

"I don't remember any of them being right."

"But you need to believe me…"

She stopped. *Are we really having this conversation again?* she thought. After a few moments of tension, she mustered her courage and said, "You need help to get out of that chair. They'll only be here for a few moments."

He scowled. "Ten minutes, and ten minutes only."

She nodded and let out a low, slow breath. Searching in a hidden box, Tia found the flyer she'd stashed there. After dialling, however, the phone rang at least ten times. She was about to hang up when a cheerful woman answered.

"SRA Home Care!"

"Hi, um… my name is Tia Violetta, and we have a bit of a situation."

"What kind of situation?

"My seventy-year-old father is stuck in his reclining chair, and I can't get him out. We're going to need someone quite strong to help out."

"Your father is a big one then?"

"Uh-huh."

"Okay, then. We'll send our on-call nurse, Mary."

"I'm sorry," Tia said quickly, "but I think we might need a man in this case."

"It's okay. Mary used to be a bodybuilder."

"Got it."

As they waited, Tia peered into her father's fridge. The vegetables she had put in there were now turning new colours. Instead, TV dinners and fast-food containers filled every shelf. She walked back into the living room but paused when glass crunched underfoot. Amidst shattered glass and a fallen curtain

16

rod, a photo lay on the floor. Removing the glass shards, she studied the image.

"Your magazine cover is broken, Dad!"

He hummed his acknowledgement. "I dropped it by mistake and couldn't pick it up again," he said, keeping his eyes closed but moving his hands in front of him in Tai Chi type movements, quite unconcerned.

On the cover, eight-year-old Tia stood beside her father on the lawn of the Violetta mansion. The Seattle Magazine caption read: Genius Investor Builds Space Age Home. She smiled at the memory and made space for the frame on the counter as she swept up the glass. On the mantelpiece were three other photos of Tia at various ages but no other family members.

As he watched her cleaning, her father cleared his throat and said, "You know that you don't need to keep doing that therapy work, honey. I'm going to put another 10K into your account tomorrow..."

"You don't need to do that, Dad. I make okay income. And it's called performance coaching, actually. I like doing it."

"These people you work with, they rob your energy and hardly pay you anything."

"Yes, I know what you think about all that... it's fine, okay?"

"Still, I worry. It seems hard on you being on a computer with clients all day, every day."

"I'm in demand. By the way, I just got asked to speak at a conference for people in the coaching industry."

"What?" he said, that familiar facial tick that appeared whenever he got anxious. "Where?"

"Los Angeles."

"You're not thinking of going, are you?" His face was now in full twitch mode.

Tia felt a jolt of energy in her solar plexus. "It's an honour to be asked. How could I turn them down?"

Going against her father often brought on a headache. When she did leave the house to buy items that couldn't be shipped, a head pressure accompanied her the whole trip. Now her throat ached, too.

"My community wants to hear about the techniques I've developed. I have a full practice based on referral alone. I thought you'd at least be proud of me."

"I am proud of you!" he said with a force that startled both of them. They glared at each other, unable to speak for a few moments. He took a breath and looked down. "I just know they will try to…"

"Harm me? Who would try to do that? Why would they try to do that?"

A rapid clicking sound echoed through the old estate. The doorbell hadn't worked for years, and her father didn't want it fixed. Instead of a chime, it sounded like someone trying to start a car with a dead battery. Tia sighed and opened the door just as a woman lifted her fist to pound on it. A stocky woman in a blue oversized caregiver's uniform stood squinting at her. She looked like she'd hit her mid-fifties hard.

"I'm Mary Redus from SRA Home Care." Exhaustion rolled off the edges of her Bostonian accent. The dark circles under her close-set eyes spoke of burdens too painful to tell.

Mary brushed past her, leaving Tia to stare as the home care worker darted around stacks of rubbish, down the long hallway and into the main living room. *How does she know where to go?*

Tia caught up as Mary planted herself in front of Hadden, assessing the problem. He looked away.

She tilted her head and drummed her fingers on her elbow with a scowl.

"I'm Mary, Mister Violetta, and we're going to set you free in no time."

She summoned Tia's help, and together they took a running leap at the rocker. They hit the chair simultaneously, the force knocking him free. He winced as he staggered to his feet, flailing unsteadily. Grabbing his two canes, he stilled himself, but when the two women rushed to help him, he pushed them away.

"I'm fine!" he insisted, stalking off to the bathroom, cursing in a foreign tongue.

"What's that language he's speaking?"

Tia shrugged. "I've only ever heard him speak English… Well, until recently."

Mary looked intrigued. "Where is he from?"

"I don't know. Maybe born here, in Seattle?"

"I'm sorry. I thought you were his granddaughter."

"His daughter, actually."

"Oh... really?"

Tia nodded, knowing she looked more like a teenager with her tiny frame and Rapunzel length hair.

"Lately, he's been mumbling these strange words. When I ask him what he's saying, he either ignores me or says it's the Matrix language."

"Matrix? Like in the movie?"

"Maybe...?"

They both stifled a laugh.

Mary cleared her throat, growing serious. "With his physical limitations and growing dementia, he needs to be in a care facility. A skinny thing like you can't possibly give him the help he needs."

"Try telling that to him."

Mary surveyed the unkempt mess and raised her eyebrows.

"I try to tidy things," Tia explained, "but he stops me. He used to be fanatically tidy, but now he's gone in the opposite direction. I try to help, but he prefers to be alone."

"He needs to be in a well-equipped senior care facility," Mary repeated.

"I know, but he made me promise I would never put him in a home."

"It's not good for him here. This house is a fire trap. That said, the only place that could take a man of his size is where I work, SRA, but it's not cheap."

"We have the money. It's just that he would hate it there."

Mary raised her eyebrows. "Oh, yes. He's the owner of Violetta & Burres Investments. I remember reading about him. He's some kind of genius?"

Tia nodded, feeling that familiar discomfort of being seen as the weird father and daughter cloistered away in the UFO house.

Mary leaned in closer. "Are there any relatives who can help?"

"No."

"Your mother also passed away?"

"I don't know where my mother is. She left when I was a child and did not keep in touch."

"What kind of mother would abandon her own daughter?"

Tia stayed silent, giving the caregiver a look that told her to mind her own business.

Mary looked sideways and cleared her throat. "So you've lived here your entire life?"

"I live in the upstairs apartment. It's a totally separate living space, but I need to be close by, given his situation."

"Neighbours or friends?"

She shook her head. "As I said, he likes his privacy."

"So, there's no one else that can help you?"

"Listen, I understand you are trying to help, but my father would be upset if he knew I talked to you about all this."

Mary handed her an in-home caregiver leaflet from SRA. "I just want to be helpful, but only in a way that works for you. If you hire someone like me, I can clean this place up, make it safe for him, ensure his every need is taken care of so that you can focus on your life again."

"He won't allow anyone else in the home except me unless it's an absolute emergency."

Mary sighed. "It's your home, too. This is as much for you as it is for him."

Tia busied herself, clearing cobwebs from a door frame, unsure what to say. An inner pressure that had been building up over many years swelled.

The bathroom door opened, and he weaved his way towards the stair lift at the base of the grand staircase. "Thanks for your help," he grumbled. "You can go now."

They watched as he lost his balance part way there. Mary lunged forward like a defensive linebacker, righting him before he could topple. She guided him towards the stair lift, buckled him in and took him to the top. Maybe he felt too exhausted to resist, or maybe Mary was the kind of person he would finally 'let in'. Nevertheless, as she followed, Tia marvelled at how he softened under her care. Mary found his walker at the top of the stairs and led him to the bedroom door, where he stopped.

"Thank you. I'm good from here."

Mary nodded and followed Tia back down the stairs, down the central corridor to the front door.

"Call SRA," Mary said, stepping onto the front porch. "You don't have to do this alone."

Tia looked down at the ground and nodded, not trusting her voice to speak past the lump in her throat. Mary opened her umbrella and headed out into the damp night air.

Tia lingered, watching the woman walk away while enjoying the fresh air and contemplating her options. Hiring Mary would mean she could go out more, attend events or even, God forbid, date.

As she walked towards the door, a crash came from behind. She reeled around to see a man stumbling from the bushes. Tia jumped back and screamed.

He held his hands up. "My apologies, Miss, I didn't mean to scare you," he said. "I may have the wrong house. I'm looking for a Mister Hadden Violetta."

Tia backed up towards the door and pulled her sweater around her. What she had assumed was a man looked more like a teenager. He wore a helmet, military jumpsuit, and a bewildered expression.

"What are you doing here? Leave before I call the police."

"No, wait. Please. My name is... um... Addy. Does a man named Hadden Violetta live here? He would be... I guess seventy years old by now."

The man shivered, water dripping from his jumpsuit.

Tia opened the front door and stepped inside the landing, pausing, poised to slam the door. "There's no one here by that name. You have the wrong house. Now, leave!"

She slammed the door shut and double-locked it.

"What happened? What's going on?" Hadden shouted out from the bedroom.

Tia tiptoed upstairs and peered inside his bedroom. "This time, you were right. Someone is outside. A strange man jumped out of the bushes and scared the hell out of me. Maybe one of those weird fans of yours. He wore a helmet and jumpsuit, and he was all wet!"

21

"What did he say?"

"He asked if you lived here, but I said no."

His eyes grew wide. "Did he give his name?"

"Um... I think he said Addy."

"Addy? Bring him in! Now!"

Tia stared at him. "But you hate having strangers in the house..."

"He's not a stranger. Let him in."

"I – Okay..."

"Bring him into the living room. I'll meet you down there shortly. And if he's wet, bring him some of my old clothes from the hall cupboard."

Tia hadn't seen her father get so riled up about a visitor in a long time. She padded downstairs again and unlocked the front door. The man stood shivering in the cold night air, looking lost. "Come in. My father says he knows you."

"Thank you," Addy said, visibly relieved. He climbed the stairs, his helmet swinging from a finger. "You're his daughter? That's... amazing."

"Why is that so amazing?"

"It's just that..." he stammered, looking away then down at her hair that now frizzed out in all directions. "You have the same kind of hair as my mother's."

"Really? How exactly do you know my father?"

"I'll let him talk about that."

Tia stared at him for a moment, then led him into the living room. All the while, Addy looked around, awestruck.

"This is quite the place. Mister Violetta has done well for himself."

Tia narrowed her gaze but said nothing. Perhaps he's a con man, she thought. He stopped in front of the flat-screen TV and ran his hand over the top.

She noticed a puddle of water forming around his feet. "I'll get you a towel and some dry clothes. My father will be down in a few minutes."

As Tia gathered a tracksuit for him, she couldn't help but notice that he looked like a family member. In fact, he could even be her brother given their similar facial features.

"Try these," she said, holding out the clothes and pointing to the bathroom. "There's a towel on the shelf."

"Much obliged, Miss."

"You can just call me Tia."

"Tia," he nodded, "copy that."

When he emerged from the bathroom, he looked bemused, holding his arms up as he assessed his new attire. "This is quite the space-age outfit."

"Yes... right."

Maybe he comes from a rural part of the world and doesn't get out much. He stopped at the mantelpiece and held up the magazine cover image.

"This is him?"

She looked at him uncertainly. "Yes. Sorry, but how long has it been since you've last seen him?"

He hesitated before answering. "A very long time."

"Want some hot cocoa?"

"That would be mighty fine, Miss... Tia."

As she boiled the water, Tia peered at him from the kitchen, concerned he might steal something. He picked up the TV remote and studied it closely, then put it back down. Next, he looked behind the flat-screen TV.

"Here you go!"

"Thank you," he said, taking the mug and sipping from it. He hummed contentedly. "So good."

"Did you want to turn it on?"

His eyebrows lifted.

"The TV."

"That's a television set?"

She nodded.

"Sure."

She picked up the remote and on came a TV show. He jumped back, mesmerized by the images of starships fighting in space.

"Are these in your atmosphere now?" he said, sounding panicked.

"What? This is a TV show... Ever heard of *Battlestar Galactica*?"

"Oh! A TV show. Copy that."

One of the actors in the show spoke, and Addy looked to the left as if expecting to see someone there.

"It's surround sound."

"Surround sound?"

Tia nodded once and knitted her brow. "The audio doesn't come from the TV. We've got separate speakers for it."

"Pretty nifty."

Her father hobbled into the room with his two canes. Tia helped ease him into the chair, and Addy sat across. The two men nodded to each other but said nothing for a few moments.

Tia tapped her fingers on her knees, looking from one to the other. "How do you know each other?"

Her father cleared his throat and looked sideways. "It's a long story, Tia. I'll tell you later. Addy and I just need to have a chat..."

Tia nodded, but she couldn't help feeling left out. "Of course. I'll let you two catch up. Just call up if you need anything."

As she backed out of the room, Addy stood up and nodded to her as she left. *How old-fashioned*, she thought and smiled back at him.

"Don't go to sleep just yet, honey," her father called out. "I'll call you back down in a bit."

Puzzled by the request, Tia shrugged. "Ok. See you soon."

Maybe Addy needs a ride to the airport. Closing the door behind her, she climbed the spiral staircase to her apartment. She lay on her bed for a while, staring at the ceiling, but the curiosity gnawed at her. *Who was this stranger who had stumbled onto their property in the middle of the night? What made him so special that her father had let him into the house?*

Unable to bear it, she tiptoed to the floor radiator and placed an ear against the grate. As she strained to hear, they seemed to be speaking in a

24

strange language. Frustrated, she crawled back onto the bed and thumbed through a magazine, half concentrating and her heart drumming faster and faster.

CHAPTER 2

Hadden leaned forward on his cane, his corpulent mass spilling out over his knees. "Speak in Matrix."

Addy nodded and closed his eyes, looking for the words in his mother tongue. After several moments, he shook his head. "I can't seem to remember..."

"I forgot they took out your amethyst already," Hadden tutted.

"What do you mean?" Addy said, feeling behind his ear. "It's gone!"

"The SIM agents did it at night, a few days ago in your timeline, and then wiped your memories. But don't worry, I've got another one. They're a bastard to make, but it comes in handy to have a few spares," he said as he sifted through the old food containers that had piled up on the coffee table.

Addy kept feeling around on his skull. No wonder he couldn't cloak the plane. In the past few days, he'd felt so out of sorts – like he'd lost a vital organ. High-intensity energies pummeled his body, and even just dragging himself out of bed in the morning had become an effort.

"In addition to losing your amethyst, it's the time jump of fifty years," Hadden said as if reading his mind. "Back in 1960, wireless technologies were just getting going, but now they're thousands of times more intense. It's like we're frogs in hot water, slowly being boiled to death. With the time jump and losing your amethyst, you must be feeling pretty strange."

Addy nodded, rubbing his forehead.

Lifting away a stack of books, Hadden uncovered a gold-plated container, inside of which were five tiny gold boxes. "Each of these contains an amethyst. One is for you. I must warn you that once you re-activate it, your soul frequency may show up on their radar. We'll upgrade the SPS, but if they're looking at this time, the amethyst won't hide you. It'll buy time if nothing else." He closed his eyes and, holding up both hands, then started making intricate patterns in the air.

"An SPS?" Addy asked, recalling his classes as a boy. "I haven't set a Secure Protective Space for years."

"It's okay. I'll do it."

"Whose radar would I be on?"

"Those in the psychic warfare project. The ones that discovered you."

"What do you mean, discovered me?"

He sighed, failing at keeping his patience. "Remember when you did those district-wide tests at school? Of course, as a Voyent-Vision, you scored in the top one percentile on photographic memory and clairvoyance. That's why they recruited you."

"They recruited me to be a pilot, not to use my psychic abilities."

Hadden dismissed his statement by waving his hand. "A ruse. There is a hidden group, unbeknownst to most US Air Force people, except those at the top. They target people like you. They knew how much you wanted to fly. Why make it harder than necessary to recruit you?" Gnarled, swollen fingers handed Addy one of the boxes. "The box acts as a Faraday shield. I've never taken them out, just in case, but it's about time."

Addy examined the tiny box. "You made this?"

"It's based on the blueprint they give to people on the mission, except that this is an upgrade. Instead of masking your abilities to fit into the population, it enhances them. There's a map of our next stage of evolution embedded within it."

Addy remembered the day his mother showed him the blueprint for the amethysts. His photographic memory had captured it without effort, knowing it would come in handy one day.

"We need to converse in Matrix. So go ahead, put it on. We should be safe – for the time being, at least. Place it in the same spot as your last one, next to your upper left earlobe. Remember how to do it?"

Addy shook his head.

"Balance it on your index finger, then hover it over that area. It will magnetize to the correct part of your skull."

After placing it behind his left ear, a buzzing roared throughout Addy's skull. Closing his eyes, he waited as a protective shield emerged around him, and the pressure eased. Soon after, the words rushed back to his consciousness like water breaking through a dam. "It's working!"

"Good. Keep that on, no matter what," the old man warned in Matrix. "Addy…" he added as a smile touched his face. "I haven't heard that nickname since I was a kid."

"I hoped you wouldn't forget," Addy grinned back. He closed his eyes and sat in silence for a few moments, adjusting to the new frequencies running through his system. The Matrix language allowed them to exchange much more than words—it included intricate patterns of metaphors, feelings, impressions, symbols and information, each penetrating one's consciousness in multi-dimensional ways.

"I feel so much more like my old self now. Thank you."

"You're welcome."

"It's so amazing to be here. You know, my plane fell apart as it went through the anomaly. I had to eject. I barely made it."

"I thought that might happen. Thank you for your courage."

They laughed the same baritone chuckle. *Some things never change*, Addy mused.

"I didn't know whether you'd interpret my message correctly. You did well. Although I wasn't expecting you until tomorrow night."

"Your imagery helped. I guess I misinterpreted the time-space coordinates… but luckily only by a day. It's when I saw the number 111 or 1111 three times this morning, so I knew there was a glitch in the timeline and I'd better act."

"I saw that, too," the old man nodded.

"So, what's with that tower with the spaceship on top? The one in the downtown area."

"The Space Needle. It's now a landmark for Seattle. It hadn't been built yet in 1960. It will be part of the World's Fair in '62."

Addy smiled and took a sip of cocoa. "So, I end up looking like Santa Claus?"

"Yes," he mused, patting his stomach. "Only a hundred pounds heavier."

Addy wrinkled his brow and looked down at his own athletic body, comparing it to what he saw across from him. "So what happened?"

"I like food?" Hadden offered as he smiled for a moment, then the corners of his mouth turned down again. "Actually, it's been a hard life, and food has been my solace."

"But you obviously had a family, and you're wealthy..."

"All at great cost." A look of pain filled his swollen face. "They made me build Violetta Investments to fund their black projects. I'm the frontman, but Leo Burres and his family control everything."

"The Burres Family control you?" Addy asked, clenching his fists.

"Yes."

"How?" he growled.

Hadden grunted. "On the outside, I might seem a wealthy, successful man living a life of luxury. But the whole company is just a front. We launder money, use it to fund wars, assassinations, and crimes against humanity. I've been a slave to SIM my entire life up until the last few years. As you can see, it's taken its toll. That's what the CM does to you – cognitive modification. It was the price that I had to pay to keep my family safe."

A strangling sensation engulfed Addy's neck. He leaned forward and remarked, "So that's why you summoned me here... to change the timeline?"

Tears filled the old man's crinkled eyes. "Yes... I'm sorry, Addy. You're the only one I could call on. Listen, you have to pay attention, okay? I'm not going to last long. There's a fatal disease eating away at me, and the clock is ticking. I've protected Tia her whole life, but my strength is weakening. Once I'm gone, SIM will take her and try to weaponize her, just like they did with me."

"I've got protection against SIM – all of us in the Quinary Mission do."

Hadden smiled sympathetically. "They outwitted us years ago. Look, when you go back, you need to avoid any more CM."

Addy scoffed, unable to believe that what Hadden was telling him.

"Soon, they will take you at night, and the deep CM will start. They'll split your personality into two; the light and dark side. One won't know that the other exists. Then they'll wipe your memory to convince you that you're just this regular, good guy, but from time to time, you'll wake up with bad nightmares and strange bruises all over your body."

Addy's skin crawled. "When does that all start?"

"Soon. That's why I chose December 21st. It's the only date in the calendar that works because it's after I—I mean, you—become a pilot and before the deep CM starts."

A cold creeping feeling uncoiled in Addy's stomach. "Why did you wait to contact me now, fifty years later? Why not do it, say, one year later when I'm 21?

"It's taken me fifty years to heal enough from the CM to recover my abilities. My powers were tied to their agenda. I had to first build the protection grid, then rebuild my amethyst to help me re-access my capabilities."

"Isn't this time travel experiment forbidden by the Temporalia? I mean, you're never supposed to encounter yourself in a future or past timeline. It tears a hole in the quantum. At least, that's what father taught me."

"I know, but I was desperate. Maybe it won't cause too much damage."

A creaking sound above grabbed Addy's attention, making him sit straight as he pricked up his ears.

"It's Tia upstairs. She's restless. Addy, you must take her back home."

Addy frowned. "You realise I've never even *been* home?"

"Look, most everyone in the Quinary Mission disappeared in 1961, all because of me joining the air force."

"How did that happen?"

"They mapped my mind to find their whereabouts."

"Is that why Mum and Dad were so against me joining...?"

"...Of course. They knew that could happen."

"But I have protection from that..."

"SIM was smarter than I thought."

Addy's throat tightened up, thinking he had caused such harm to people he loved. "What happens to them in my future?"

"I'm not totally sure. The only people I saw from Quinary after that were Daphne and Annika. They also got pulled into working for SIM. Daphne and I tried to go home, but they blocked us from entering."

As he considered what the old man had confided in him, a burning feeling filled his chest. The names Daphne and Annika seemed familiar. "But now that I've left that timeline to come and see my future self, maybe it will all change."

"I hope so. When you go back to your timeline, you must escape the SIM agents, protect Quinary, and ensure the twins are born. With these amethysts in their possession, they might be able to do it."

"Twins?" Addy asked in a high-pitched voice.

"Tia has a twin sister, named Metta, but she doesn't remember her. I didn't want to explain why they had to leave. It would open a big can of worms. I don't even know if Metta and Daphne are still alive. If they are, then Tia needs to bring them these amethysts to dial up on their abilities. Please, you must help them."

"Why can't you help them? You seem to have developed powers I don't have."

"There's a suicide program in my mind. If I use my powers to help humanity or try to reconnect with my family or any other members of Quinary, I will drop dead within a second. But I'm going to die soon, so you're my last-ditch effort to make things right again. They will soon discover that I contacted you and kill me anyway."

Addy's stomach twisted into a knot.

Hadden cleared his throat, his voice becoming more instructional. This was no longer idle conversation. "There's a man who leads the psychic warfare project named Loman."

"I've met him already. He took me out for lunch."

"That's right. He'll be your good friend for a while until he gets what he wants. He is connected to the Burres family. In retrospect, it's quite obvious that the Burres family arranged my marriage to Daphne for the genetic pairing."

31

"You don't mean *the* Daphne?"

"Yes... of the House of Zuris."

"I get to marry her?"

"SIM lured her into one of the black projects, so you must help her escape as well."

The mounting assignments made Addy's hands tremble.

"When the twins were three years old, SIM agents tried to take them away from us. We pleaded with them, and eventually, they agreed to let them be as long as we met their conditions. We had to separate them forever and never let them come in contact. I took Tia, and Daphne took Metta. I don't even know where Daphne and Metta went, but that was twenty-seven years ago."

Addy leaned back in his chair and took a deep breath. "Why did you have to separate them?"

"They're the last two members of Pentada. I've seen the signs."

"Really? I end up being the father of the last two members?"

"Yes, and that's why SIM wants to keep all five members apart."

"Because if the next generation of Pentada reconnects...."

"It would be game over for SIM."

Addy let out a sigh. The responsibility weighed heavy on his young shoulders. "And Tia knows none of this?"

"She only knows about the three-dimensional world. It's for her own safety. If she knew, I'm afraid it would *dial up* her powers. They have a tracking device on her, so they'd know right away."

"Then how will I be able to protect her and get her home? Have you ever been back to Helio Tropez?"

"They wouldn't let me. Probably because my choices led to the failure of the Quinary Mission. I am hoping the first generation made it home, but they could have died or something much worse. You still have a chance to protect them."

Addy shifted in his chair, half regretting his decision to time travel to the future.

"Daphne and I added something to the amethysts that Tia and Metta gave us when they were still children. They just called it their MindStory game, but we soon saw its brilliance. It's a code in a double helix, like DNA, only it is structured in a story sequence."

"What does it do?"

"It's like the operating system you need to ascend to the next density level. I imagine that's what this next generation of Pentada are programmed to do – to give us the new operating system. After Daphne left, I tried thousands of times to map and encode it into the amethyst. Despite it being my life's work, there are still some missing parts, but I can only take it so far. I suspect it has to have the input of all five Pentada to complete the sequence. That said, anyone wearing it will have more protection against SIM than they did before, at least. Let me explain how it works."

They talked in detail about the capacities of the amethyst and his plan for redemption. Old Hadden transferred the mental photographs of his plan to the mind of his younger self. Once complete, Addy stood up and paced the room, unsure how to take in all this new information. Suddenly, his foot caught the edge of a bag sitting under the table, and a gadget fell out of it. Picking it up, he marveled at the device. "What's this?"

The old man donned his glasses to see. "It's just a smartphone."

"With all these space-age gadgets now... surely there's some way."

"Those *gadgets* are not a good thing. That smartphone, in particular, has managed to cognitively control masses of people."

Addy hastily put the phone on the table and recoiled his hand. "What does it do?"

"One thousand times more things than a computer from your era. Still, it's just a fraction of what is available in Helio Tropez. But it won't solve our problems now."

Addy studied the old man. The trauma in those hooded eyes filled his heart with dread.

"Where did you find this, by the way?" Hadden asked as he reached for the phone.

"It fell out of this bag," Addy said, pointing to a black handbag. "I'm sorry, I didn't mean to pry into your daughter's personal things. It just fell out."

Hadden straightened, frowning, then sharply said, "Give me that bag." He snatched it from Addy and upended it. A brush and a notepad with SRA letterhead tumbled onto the floor. "Shit!"

He picked up Addy's cup of cocoa and poured it over the phone. The screen flickered, then went black.

"Why did you do that?" Addy said, jumping to his feet.

"It's not my daughter's. It belongs to the home care worker who just left. The one time I let someone else in," Hadden tutted, cursing himself as he scanned the air with his hand. "Listen, Addy. She's a SIM agent. That device just spied on our conversation. I see a breach in the SPA. As far as I know, they can't decipher Matrix, but they know you're here. We have to move fast," he panicked, thrusting the gold boxes towards him. "Guard these amethysts with your life. They are *only* for Tia, Metta, Annika and Daphne."

"You mean Daphne's twin sister, Annika?"

"Yes. She's Pentada as well. All five are in the same bloodline. Three generations from the House of Zuris."

A rush of energy ran up Addy's spine as he placed the four boxes inside his coat pocket.

The old man heaved himself up on wobbly legs. "I have an idea how you can get Tia home, but it's not going to be easy."

CHAPTER 3

Upon hearing her father's cane on the ceiling again, Tia crept bleary-eyed down the spiral staircase. At the bottom of the steps, the clicking doorbell sounded again. *Seriously? What could be so urgent that it couldn't wait until a sensible hour?* Heading for the front door, Addy appeared out of nowhere and stepped in front of her.

"Don't open it," he said, his voice hushed.

A Bostonian accent pierced the quiet. "It's Mary! I left my bag there. So sorry!"

"She just needs her bag…"

Addy pulled her away from the door and whispered, "Your father says she's dangerous. We need to leave now. He says there's a secret back entrance?"

"Leave? You do know that my father is a paranoid man with growing dementia, right?"

"He's not! He's right about this. We *need* to go," he said, pulling her by the arm down the hallway.

Looking back, Tia saw her father near the front window holding up his hands, doing his crazy arm movements, eyes closed in a kind of trance. A second set of footsteps sounded on the front porch. Gunshots pinged against the front door lock, and shock waves pulsed through her body. She ran to her father, but Addy yanked her back.

"He wants me to protect you from whoever's behind that door. Leave him there to protect us. Here are your car keys, coat, handbag. We're leaving, now!"

Tia resisted Addy until her father turned and shouted, "Get out of here!"

Her eyes filled with tears and her heart pounded in her chest. Addy ran downstairs, dragging her behind him to a concealed back door.

"Wait! I forgot to get the contents of his safe! Where's his office?"

"The office is right there, but my father doesn't have a safe."

"Apparently, he does," he replied, stepping into the basement hallway. A drilling sound screeched from the front door, and they broke into a run until they reached a locked room. Addy unlocked it, picked up the set of jeweller's tools lying on the desk at the centre of the room, then enlisted Tia's help to move a bookcase aside. To her surprise, a safe lay embedded into the wall. After only a few seconds, Addy opened it.

"Your father gave me the code," he explained, pulling out three large, padded envelopes. He shoved them in her satchel.

"What are these?"

"I'll tell you later. We need to get to the company plane."

"Why?"

"It's the only way. Now stop asking questions and move."

"I hate going on that tiny plane. I get sick and panic ..."

"Your options are to get sick or die. Take your pick."

The door upstairs crashed open, and a man's voice shouted, "Where is she?"

Adrenaline pumped through her veins. "We need to help him!"

Addy took her by the shoulders, forcing her to look him in the eye. He spoke quickly. "Your father begged me to take you to safety and to leave him here. He's doing all of this for *you*. Don't make all his years of sacrifice mean nothing."

Her heart ripped apart as he dragged her to the back entrance. A black Jaguar sat gleaming in the low light. Addy jumped into the driver's seat, set the engine roaring, and took off at high speed down the back lane, taking side streets until they got onto the highway.

This has to be a dream. I'll wake up soon. Nothing like this happens in real life.

"Your father has a protection system on the house, the car and you. We should be okay until we get to the plane. He can take care of himself."

"He's a fragile old man," she rebutted.

"He's a lot stronger than you think."

Tia blinked. "Wait, what do you mean that there's a protection system? We don't have one."

"It's not electronic. Don't ask how, but it's done with the mind," Addy explained, yanking the wheel and manoeuvring between slower cars. "Ever wondered why he never wanted you to move out?"

Tia's eyes narrowed.

"They want to use your powers for their own agenda. He's spent the last thirty years doing everything he could to protect you, and we're not about to put all of that to waste."

"I don't have any powers," Tia said, clutching the handle on the roof. "And protect me from who?"

"The Burres Family."

"You mean Leo Burres, my father's business partner?"

"Yes."

"Not possible."

"Who do you think was at the door?"

A flood of emotions drowned Tia's thinking capacities as the voice at the front door echoed in her memory. *It can't be.* "But what kind of powers are you talking about?"

"Let's just get to the plane first."

Her hands trembled. The streetlights were skipping past. She didn't even dare glance to see at what speed they were going. "Make a left onto Elliot Avenue."

"I know the way."

Again, she reminded herself, *All this is just a crazy dream.*

"How far to the airfield?" he asked, peering out of the back window.

"You *just* said you know the way. Do you even know how to fly a plane? Because I don't!"

"Older planes, sure," he nodded. "I'll figure it out."

"What?" Tia's shouted, her knuckles aching from the tight grip. "You're just going to *figure it out*? You're crazy!"

"Crazy or not, you're going to have to trust me. Your father wants me to take you to his family. It's the only place you'll be safe."

The tyres screeched as he pulled a hard right. "Anything is better than driving in a car with you."

Addy grinned. "Just wait until you get on a plane with me."

"Not helping. Look, my dad doesn't have a family. My grandparents died when he was a kid. There isn't anyone else."

"That's what he told you?" Addy rolled his eyes.

A creeping sense of betrayal caught in Tia's throat. *Did he have a secret family somewhere?*

She glanced over at the man white knuckling the steering wheel. He definitely looked like a family member, but she had no idea that she had any cousins. "So, are you going to tell me who you are?"

"If I told you, you wouldn't believe me."

She narrowed her eyes at him. "Give it a try. I'm about to get in a tiny plane with you to God knows where, so call it a token of good faith."

He opened his mouth, then closed it again, seemingly thinking better of it. He tutted to himself, then stated, "My name is Hadden Violetta. I'm your father, just fifty years younger than the one you know."

Tia burst out laughing. "Right, and I'm the Queen of England, only fifty years younger." But when she looked over at Addy's face, he wasn't smiling, and she abruptly stopped laughing.

"No way..."

His jaw tightened, and he nodded. Inhaling a deep breath, she held her stomach. She was feeling nauseous, but it wasn't from the terrible driving. Although it seemed logically impossible, some part of her knew it was the truth. The whole evening replayed in her mind: his old-fashioned behaviour, his voice, his face. In fact, his whole demeanour utterly spoke of her father. He pointed to the mole on his left cheek in the exact same place. "See?"

"How? I... *How?!*"

"When I woke up this morning, it was 1960, and I was training as a pilot in Hawaii. The week before, your father telepathically transmitted a message to me, showing me how to time travel here. It almost killed me, by the way, but you can thank me later. Now he's asked me to get you to safety, after which I need to go back to my timeline and make different decisions so that I don't end up like him. But it can't be *that* different because you still need to be born, I still need to marry your mum, and I still need to get filthy rich and buy a big mansion. I'm not sure how to do any of this, so if you could chill out, you'd really be doing me a massive favour." He took a shaky breath, and Tia noticed his locked jaw and clenched shoulders.

Tia frowned, feeling the weight of all this bizarre new information. "You said you're taking me home. Where's that?"

"Again, you wouldn't believe me, and it's going to take too long to explain. Suffice to say, it's called Helio Tropez, and it's supposed to be a pretty nifty place where you live on cloud nine. At least for most of the time. You'll get to meet my parents, who, I guess, are your grandparents. I'm just hoping they'll let us in...."

At a stoplight, Tia slapped her cheek in the hopes of awakening from this dream, but it didn't help either—nothing did. Seeing that fighting didn't seem to be helping, she decided to go with it.

Addy glanced at her. "I know it's all hard to believe. Even though you're one of us, you've been raised like a surface person. The programming is deep. Scepticism is actually a SIM program designed to activate whenever there's a glitch in their control matrix."

Tia resisted shaking her head. She remembered a can of mace in her bag. *This is ridiculous – it's gone far enough. Once at the airfield, I'm macing and taking the car.*

Despite the appeal, doubt writhed at the back of her mind. *But where would I go? I'm being hunted. Someone wants me, and it doesn't sound like they have a tea party planned.*

She swallowed, biding her time. *An opportunity will come, and when it does, I need to either trust this maniac claiming to be my twenty-year-old father*

*supposedly taking me to someplace safe or make my own way into this world
that my seventy-year-old father has kept hidden from me.*

CHAPTER 4

For the second time in twenty-four hours, Addy found himself planning how to break into an airfield. A line of private jets rose out of the mist as they drove along the embankment. Once the car was tucked into a dark corner in the parking lot, Addy pulled a gold box out of his jacket pocket.

"Your father wants you to wear this. It's called an amethyst and is programmed to enhance your natural intuitive abilities, overriding the cognitive programming you've been subjected to since childhood. You install it just behind your ear, and it will help with the... scepticism... among other things."

"I'm not *installing* anything... and I don't even know what you mean by install."

"It's a consciousness technology. Look," he said, tilting his head and pointing behind his ear. "I've got one. This one apparently contains a map that you gave him as a child."

"A map?"

"A MindStory roadmap or something?"

Tia tutted and said, "MindStory was just a game I played as a child. I dreamed about it once, that's all. It was nothing special."

"Apparently, it's very powerful, and it's embedded into this amethyst crystal as a new operating system. We can use it as a cloaking device as well, which I need you to use soon."

Tia could barely see the crystal in the dim light. "What does 'consciousness technology' mean?"

"It's technology from the human SANA-based consciousness as opposed to most of the technology on the surface, which is synthetically-based and comes from SIM."

"Yeah, you're going to have to tell me what all of that means."

"Let's just say SANA is good and SIM is bad. I'll tell you more later."

Tia knitted her brow.

He sighed, "Look, all your computers and phones are SIM technology. Everything those technologies can do, you can do with your own mind. SIM wants you to rely on their tech to capture your energy so they can feed off it."

Tia shuddered, wondering if she was sitting next to one of those crazy conspiracy theorists that thinks evil people rule over the Earth. *What if he's abducting me, and the crystal will knock me out? But then, Dad obviously trusts him...*

"Place it on the tip of your finger like this and hold it just behind your ear. It's easy. I promise."

"I'm not doing that."

"Your whole world will look different once you do."

"So it's some kind of mind altering drug? No, thank you."

"On the contrary. It enhances your mind's capacity – you'll be able to remember your other lives and why you're here."

"My other lives? I don't believe in that kind of thing."

"Again, that disbelief is a SIM program. Once you install the crystal, you'll see past all the programming, slowly at first so as not to overwhelm you. It will enhance your aptitude, which your father says is Sentient-Attention, *The Inspirator.* You'll be able to help people dislodge stuck emotions and inspire their true potential."

"I do that every day when I coach people."

"Great! You'll be even better at it with this."

"Big deal."

Addy was starting to run out of patience. "Okay, how about this? You'll be able to read people's minds within certain parameters. I'll prove to you that I can do it. Think of something that I'd never be able to guess in a million years, like an image of something."

She remembered a snow leopard she had recently seen in a photo.

He sighed. "A snow leopard."

A prickling feeling arose on the back of her neck.

"You can also turn invisible for a few minutes, like this." In a blink, he disappeared without even leaving a single hint of his presence behind. Tia gasped, reaching out to see if he really was still there. "I'm still here, but I'm like The Invisible Man." After he reappeared, he said, "Wouldn't you like to do all that?"

Tia spread her hands across her chest and gulped. "Okay, that's pretty amazing. I just don't see how placing a gem on my skull will do anything."

"Try it and see."

Holding it between her thumb and index finger, she placed it on the middle finger of her left hand, pulled back her hair, and held the gem near to where he'd shown her. The amethyst jumped off her finger and magnetised onto her scalp. She turned her head to show him.

He nodded. "That's the place."

She paused, then said, "Nothing's happening."

"Give it a minute."

Seconds later, energy flashed through her body from head to toe, and a warmth cascaded over her nervous system, calming her down and making her feel more in control.

"Wow," she breathed.

"Amazing, right? Your eyes are flashing all these colours, which shows that it's connecting to your body-mind-soul system. The good news is that your powers will start coming back more and more and the SIM Cognitive Modification programs will lessen, but it will happen slowly so that your system can handle them. The bad news is that SIM will find out very soon and, once they do, they will come after both of us. That's why we have to cloak and get on the move.

He made to get out of the car, then looked back. "By the way, I have three other amethysts. You'll need to get them to your mother, aunt and sister."

What are you talking about?" she called after him as he got out. When he didn't respond she jumped out of the car to follow him.

"Your father hopes that they're still alive and that you can find them."

"I don't have a sister or an aunt. And my mother left, like, decades ago."

"You apparently have a twin sister who left *with* your mother."

"A twin sister!? Other family?! There's no way."

"You can remember now that you have your amethyst. Ask yourself to remember. Her name is... Metta, I think."

"Metta?" Memories of an imaginary friend flooded into her vision. Then her mother's face flashed before her. Tears stung her eyes as more fragmented images tumbled into her consciousness.

"I know it's a lot to take in, and as I said, it will all get explained to you. Your father needed to keep you in the dark to protect you. But now, you will have more and more access to all that information. Can we please get to the plane now?"

"Did I tell you that I hate flying?"

"Objection noted. Tia, I need you to cloak now, so you're going to need to concentrate. Just *will* your amethyst to do it. It requires a lot of focus, so beginners usually can only do it for a few moments. That's why we have to move quickly."

She took a steady breath, glancing around the empty parking lot.

"Ready?"

Addy's body disappeared into the darkness. His invisible arm then guided her towards the airfield as she asked the amethyst to cloak her, but nothing seemed to happen.

"Focus on your intent," he whispered.

Tia stopped for a moment and held up one hand in front of her face, willing herself to go invisible. Suddenly, it faded away in the misty air.

"I did it!" she said triumphantly, but as soon as she spoke, her hand popped back into visibility.

"Keep it up," Addy said. She could hear his smile in his voice. "Remember, as soon as you lose your focus, it'll stop working."

Damp sea air from Puget Sound filled her nostrils. One security guard sat nearby, scrolling through his phone, the light casting a garish shadow on his tired face. They darted past him and tried the back door to the office only to find it locked.

Addy pulled out the jewellery smith tools again and nodded to the guard. "Keep an eye on him, will you?"

Tia frowned but nodded, scurrying back to keep an eye on the guard. She glanced between him and Addy, then a metallic chink sounded as the lock popped open. The guard didn't even stir.

Inside the office, Tia spotted the keys to the company plane and unhooked them. Dropping them into her coat sleeve, she clicked the door shut, and they crept down the steps. Laying low, they turned back to see if anyone had noticed, but the security guard remained absorbed in Facebook.

With a run-up, Addy leapt over the eight-foot fence and landed with ease on the other side, then opened the gate to let her in.

Tia stopped mid-stride and stared at him. "Another superpower?"

"Indeed it is," he whispered.

The company plane stood as part of a line of other twin-engine jets. Addy ran his hand along the exterior as she unlocked the hatch. Tia winced. The last time her father had taken her flying, the weather had turned mid-flight. Winds had rocked the tiny plane so badly that they were forced to make an emergency landing. That day, Tia had sworn to herself that she'd never get in a tiny plane again.

"Come on!" Addy urged, ushering her in.

Maybe it was the power of the amethyst or his insistence, but whichever it was, it pushed her to climb into the co-pilot's seat. Addy donned the aviation headset and grabbed a tattered pilot's handbook. That's when Tia knew for sure. She watched as he took a mental snapshot of each page, blinking as if to "save" what he read, then promptly started the engine. Only her father ever did that.

Tia grimaced as the engine guttered to life. The security guard appeared in the doorway, a flashlight shining their way, but Addy paid him no mind. As he taxied down the runway, Tia snapped in her seat belt, donned her own headset, and prayed that he knew how to fly this thing.

Once airborne, Tia started to breathe again and looked over to see Addy checking all his gauges. He grinned, clearly proud of his feat. Tia hadn't met this unencumbered side of her father before. The man she had grown up with seemed to be constantly at war with himself: furtive and vigilante of unseen attackers.

The full moon cast a pinkish hue on the snow cap of Mount Rainier, the dormant volcano towering over the city, which often had layered clouds in a funnel shape over its crater. Addy levelled out the plane and made a direct trajectory for the peak. The propellers roared in her eardrums as he pulled the plane up. Below, the city faded into the background, and the foothills of the mountain came into view.

"That's where we're headed," he shouted, pointing at the summit. "Inside that mountain!"

"What?" she shouted back, feeling confusion and panic at the same time.

"There's an entrance, but it's camouflaged and guarded with a force field. I'm going to fly around in circles, calling out for them to let us in."

"And if they don't?"

Addy shrugged. "We'll think of plan B when we get there."

Before they came too near, he started chanting strange words like the ones her father spoke, but no entrance seemed to appear. They circled once, twice, then a third time. Still, nothing.

He flew closer to the crater, and Tia's stomach tightened. The funnel shaped clouds drew in around them, making visibility even tougher.

"You need to help," he shouted. "Ask for them to let you in. Just think about it, and they will be able to hear you. They'll know who you are."

"Who am I asking?"

"Your grandparents. Your entire family. Anyone who'll listen at this point!"

Tia doubted it would work, but as the alternative seemed less appealing, she repeated the words, "Please let us in", underneath her breath over and over again.

Addy touched her sleeve and pointed up. Following his gaze, a helicopter hovered overhead, almost shadowing them.

"That's the company helicopter! Maybe it's my father!" Just as she said that, a bullet tore through the hull of their plane.

"And maybe not. Hold on, I'm going in!"

He dive-bombed for the middle of the crater. Tia screamed, covering her face in her hands. She braced for impact but knew it wouldn't make much difference – all she could do was pray for a quick and painless death.

They plunged into the funnelled clouds, swallowed whole as it engulfed them. Just when it looked like they would smash against the rocks, Tia screamed, and everything went blank.

CHAPTER 5

Tia awoke from a strange dream, shocked at how real it had felt. Opening her eyes, she found herself suspended in warm salt water with only her face above the waterline. The chamber was small and narrow, its see-through domed roof only inches above her. On either side, her mane of hair floated out in all directions. Still in her yoga pants and sweatshirt from last night, the wet fabric clung to her limbs. She closed her eyes again, willing herself back to sleep. *Clearly, still a dream. I'm safe here. It's okay.*

A few moments later, a turquoise ball pulsing with light passed in front of her face, hovering just in front of her nose. It lingered for a moment, then moved towards her feet, emitting waves of heat along the way. Visions of the aeroplane dive-bombing into the crater filled her mental landscape, and her heart skipped faster. The turquoise ball pulsed quicker. Maybe she had somehow landed in her father's 'home'.

On the ceiling above her, images and patterns were displayed on a monitor, morphing into various sacred geometric patterns. A humming sound resonated in the room every time a new pattern emerged on the monitor. Although unnerved by this new environment, each new pattern and hum helped her feel more centred, light and peaceful.

A voice came from somewhere outside the chamber, but it was muted and distant. Tia strained to hear what it was saying. "She's awake. Vital signs look good."

Another voice spoke, but the words were unclear.

Suddenly, the first voice came through again, but this time, she could hear it, as though its owner was inside the chamber with her. It was a feminine voice, resonant and self-assured.

"How do you feel?"

Tia looked around. "Are you speaking to me?"

"Yes, but not in your native language of English. We are communicating telepathically."

"We are?"

Tia realised her mouth wasn't moving and the conversation existed solely in her mind.

"I'm okay, I guess."

"We're glad you're finally awake," it said, calmly but obviously in control. "What's your name?"

"Tia Violetta. My father is Hadden Violetta. Maybe you know him?"

"The man you came with says he's Hadden, but he's younger than you."

"That's supposedly him as a young man. My father is actually seventy."

Now she heard a man's voice ask, "You're from the future, then?"

"I have no idea. Where am I?" She tried sitting up, but her body ignored her, refusing to move. She tried rolling over. Nothing. She seemed trapped in a supine floating position. Her heart thumped loudly, and her throat constricted.

"Please, calm down and stay still. You are being scanned and purified of SIM programs, so it's best not to move. Who are you really?"

"As I said," she tutted, growing impatient, "I'm Tia Violetta. I live in Seattle with my father, who is seventy." The chamber walls loomed closer, and she struggled to breathe. "Addy said he was bringing me here to be safe. He said you were family."

"We are not of the House of Violetta. Why do you have a forged amethyst?"

"I don't know what you mean! Addy knows about the amethysts."

Tia lay motionless, waiting for a response for several minutes.

49

"The man you call Addy is still unconscious. He looks like Hadden Violetta, but he has no soul signature either and has another forged amethyst. We're assuming he's a clone, so he will be destroyed once we have confirmation. If you don't start telling the truth, the same will become of you."

The panic in her chest swelled, and she stammered. "My father supposedly made the amethysts himself."

A deep chuckle came from outside the chamber. "That just proves you're a SIM agent who stole the technology since Hadden Violetta died in 1961. The man you're calling your father died before you were even born. So, we suggest you start telling us who you really are before it's too late."

Tia's head pounded. Her father had been in the public eye for years. How could they think he'd died? "Addy says he's from the year 1960."

She waited. Silence.

"Are you still there?"

The pulsing ball returned, hovering above her head and pausing there as she looked at it. Before she could react, it pounced a beam of light at her head, sweeping her back to unconsciousness.

CHAPTER 6

Addy found himself in a stasis chamber when he awoke. Warm water with pulsing waves surrounded him; it smelled of saline and ozone. He could see through the chamber walls to a circular white room. Patterns of light danced on the wall. The symbols of the Matrix language glowed in response to his vital signs.

"You're awake!" A baritone voice boomed from somewhere behind him.

"Yes. Who's there?" Addy responded in Matrix.

"You speak Matrix? Good," the voice said, switching to the Matrix language. "English was never my strong suit. My name is Meraton of Zuris."

"Daphne's father? I remember you! I'm Hadden Violetta. We met at the Fete of Tropez that time in 1948. I'm the son of Trace and Rand."

"So you say, but we can't verify your identity. Your soul signature is blocked or non-existent. So, you could be a clone, and we don't allow clones here."

"I'm not a clone," he said, realising at that exact same instant that that's precisely what a clone would say. "I didn't realise that SIM removed my soul signature and my amethyst, but the older Hadden gave me a new gem. It's here behind my ear."

"That's not your original one."

"He made it from memory, apparently."

"Unlikely."

He breathed in sharply and water caught in his throat, making him cough and splutter. Meraton drained the chamber and released him. After drying off, Addy sat down, and Meraton handed him a green drink.

"This will rebalance your cell salts."

They sat in silence as Addy sipped the mint flavoured liquid. The time and density jump to Inner Earth had taken its toll on his energy. Meraton appeared to have a kind of protective light around him, probably as a precaution against him.

Addy remembered the first time he had met Meraton, his wife Cassandra and their two daughters, Annika and Daphne. Everyone envied those in the Zuris bloodline as they emanated a stronger light than most. Back then, Meraton had been clean-shaven with short hair to fit in with surface dwellers.

Now he wore the style of Heliotropans, with a long, plaited beard. His straw-coloured hair also lay plaited down his back, interwoven with gold. Piercing turquoise eyes peered out from under bushy eyebrows. He looked about thirty-five years old, but Addy knew he was far older – he hadn't aged since the Fete back in the 1940s. The giant man stepped closer, and a white wolf emerged from behind him. It yawned, displaying a set of sharp teeth before curling into a ball at his feet.

"Is that a wolf?" Addy asked, shuffling away slightly.

"She's my Jenio. Harmless, unless you mean me harm."

"I don't mean you any harm. I heard about Jenios from my parents, but I've never met one."

Meraton studied the young man's face. "I'm going to test your memory, recollections a clone won't have. At the Fete of Tropez, there was an accident. What was it?"

Addy scanned his memories, but only for an instant until he found the right one. "Your mate, Cassandra, was attacked by Blanche Carbone. She cut her hand from a distance somehow. A groundskeeper saw the blue-green blood, so my father erased his memories."

Meraton studied him and turned to the Matrix symbols on the monitor. After a few minutes, his face softened. "Good. It's the real you," he said, patting Addy's shoulder. "You were just eight years old back then. Look at you now!"

"It's been such a long time. I can't wait to see my parents again. Are they here?"

The giant man froze, glancing at Addy. "Your parents? I'm so sorry, son, you don't know...?"

Addy shook his head.

"Of course not. You're from the past. Most of the first generation Quinary never made it. We thought they died, but maybe, like you, they just lost their soul signature." He sat back and breathed out slowly.

"They aren't here with you in Helio Tropez?"

"Only Cassandra and I made it back."

"Everyone else just disappeared?"

"Yes. They could still be alive on the surface, but we have no way to tell. We lost all communication."

"When did that happen?" Addy asked, a sense of dread growing in his chest.

"1961."

"That's one year after the timeline I just left."

"Yes."

Addy shut his eyes tight as if to push the information away. His recklessness will cause their disappearance. The weight of this new information nauseated him, and somehow, he felt responsible, even though it hadn't happened yet.

Meraton looked him up and down. "But it turns out that you survive The Great UnDoing of 1961 and have a daughter?"

"That's what my older self told me."

"Did he tell you who the mother is?"

A knot grew in Addy's stomach. "It's actually... Um..." He braced himself. "Your daughter, Daphne. And Tia has a twin sister."

53

"Daphne! She becomes *your* mate? The Hall of Records couldn't access her soul signature after the Great UnDoing. We assumed she died along with all the others, including our other daughter, Annika. All of the Quinary have just disappeared from the Hall of Records."

They sat in silence for a moment, brooding on the weight of the information. Meraton stood and paced the chamber, his Jenio following him behind, emitting a low rumble.

"I can't believe she survived," Meraton said. He stopped in his tracks, and his eyes fixed on a console in front of him.

"What blocked the capacity of the Hall of Records to accurately read a person's soul signature on the surface?"

He typed something onto the console, and Matrix symbols appeared in the air in front of his face. "You must go back to your timeline and make things right."

Addy sighed, getting tired of hearing that sentence. He took a sip of his drink. "But how?"

"We'll send you back to your timeline in 1960 through our stargate. Escape from SIM before they cognitively reprogram you. You can warn us all to come home to Helio Tropez right away. We didn't know until 1961 that SIM knew about us and had plans to hunt us down. Now it's up to you to change the timeline and save those on the Quinary Mission."

"But then the whole mission is aborted. All those years of planning and sacrifice..."

"It must be done."

"But..."

"Think of your parents. You'll be saving their lives."

He looked down at the swirling patterns on the floor and nodded. His father, Rand, had gathered the volunteers and led the mission to the surface. He always said they would turn the tides of human evolution... or die trying...

"Where's the plane we flew in on? I lost consciousness before we hit the crater."

"We opened the portal long enough for your plane to enter while distracting the helicopter chasing you. Our tractor beam landed you down safely. You'll find the plane at our starship base, but as I said, you'll go by stargate back to your timeline, not plane."

His shoulders relaxed. "My father told me stories of all your advanced technology but experiencing it all is… is just amazing."

He smiled knowingly. "I imagine it's quite a shock to those of you born on the surface." Meraton dismissed the symbols with a wave of his hand. "But I doubt the Elders will let you stay very long."

"But what about Tia?"

"The woman in the plane with you?"

"As I said, Daphne is her mother. She's your granddaughter."

"Maybe, but she has no soul signature either, although we have determined she's not a clone."

"If all the Quinary members come back here in 1961, that means Daphne will marry her SANA mate, Rafael."

"That's correct."

Addy sighed. "But…"

"The pairing between you and Daphne was orchestrated by SIM and not sanctioned by SANA. It's a corrupted match."

"But then Tia and her sister…"

"Will never be born," he finished. "That's as it should be."

"But both girls are next-generation Pentada."

"The woman you came with is Pentada?"

"Yes."

Meraton sat back, looking puzzled. "That can't be true."

"That's why SIM wanted the two girls separated."

Meraton frowned and stared at the floor. His Jenio nuzzled the carpet near his feet. "I must take this matter to the Elders."

CHAPTER 7

The next time Tia awoke, she lay on a silken bed, pillows high around her shoulders, the walls curving much like her apartment's. A thin silver dress covered her, a mystifying softness she'd never experienced before. On a chair nearby sat her clothes, all dried out and folded, along with her satchel.

A handwritten note in English said *I am Amelia, your Integration Counsellor. If you need help, just press the green square.* A green button glowed next to the bed. She sat up, feeling free to move again. Swinging her feet to the side of the bed, she stood up and noticed a lightness to her, an ease of step. *Perhaps the gravity is weaker here*, she thought. The air smelled fresh, as if she was sitting outside in a rose garden.

On one side of the room, a window looked out on the scene outside, and Tia found herself glued against the glass, taking it all in. Clearly, she was in a high rise, about ten stories up. Tall structures jutted up from the ground like skyscrapers, only they were spiral-shaped and narrow, glimmering as if lit from inside by blue light. Off in the distance, three pyramids glowed a violet light through the mist. A phosphorescent brightness arose from the trees and bushes below. Birds that Tia had never seen before flew by, rainbow-coloured pelicans with huge wingspans and green flamingos soaring effortlessly over the city.

Looking up, she saw a crimson-blue mist instead of the sky. Rock pillars rose a mile high. Flying cars flew in orderly lines going one way or the other. Higher up, an airport seemed to float in mid-air. In addition to the smaller flying cars, larger kite-shaped spacecraft came and went from the airport, but instead of flying down to the city, they disappeared into the mist above. She remembered accounts of people spotting similar crafts flying near Mount Rainier.

Far off in the distance, a lake shimmered, reflecting light from above. *Where did the light come from?* Peering up, she saw no particular source. A river of turquoise weaved its way around this cavernous city. *What a dream!* Turning around, she saw her reflection in a mirror. Her hair frizzed out in all directions, so she pulled her mane to one side and French-braided it. As she did, she noticed that her skin glowed, and her eyes sparkled. The calm, peaceful feeling in her stomach remained.

Sacred geometric patterns adorned the walls, ceilings and floors. A trifecta latticework pattern ran from the floor to the ceiling. Under her bare feet, the floor felt cool and spongy, like walking on grass, although the green was too luminescent to be real grass.

No door led out of the room, so she ran her hands across the curved wall to see if she could feel a line or latch. Nothing. One pattern in the wall glowed in green. As she ran her hand past it, a door slid open, revealing a curved hallway heading in both directions, presumably leading to other apartments. She thought of venturing out but didn't know if she'd need a key to lock the room. Back inside, she ran her hand across the green pattern again, and the door slid closed.

Bringing her belongings to the bed, she decided to look for proof of her identity in the envelopes Addy had found. The satchel still contained the padded envelopes, although they'd clearly been unsealed. Sitting cross legged, she spread them out in front of her.

The first envelope included financial information for Tia, like where to access his cryptocurrency investments if she ever got stuck back on the surface again. *What are cryptocurrencies?* Another envelope was for Addy, like stocks to invest in that will do well in the future. *That would certain give him an advantage over the decades if he goes back to 1960.* A third envelope included a photo of her father, her mother and two girls about three years old. A shockwave of recognition ran through her. She ran her fingers over the photo. Her mother and sister looked alike with their red ringlets and green eyes. In contrast, Tia looked more like her father with his dark wavy hair.

Clearly, they were fraternal twins, not identical. A well of mixed emotion rose in her throat until tears tumbled down her cheeks as memories of being in her mother's arms and laughing and playing with her sister resurfaced.

Tia jumped when she heard a pinging on the far side of the room. A screen lit up with a woman's face.

"Hello, again! I've come for a visit," the woman said in English.

Tia tiptoed over to the screen. "Who are you?"

"I may be a family member."

Tia looked closer at the screen sceptically. "Sure, I guess you can enter."

The woman laughed. "Thank you. You just need to press the purple button to open the door."

"Um... sure. Here you go."

The door slid open, and the woman walked through, then bowed while holding one hand on her heart. As she did, Tia thought she had seen angelic wings on her back.

In English, she said, "I apologise for the intense purification ritual. It happens to any newcomers, especially unexpected ones. I'm Cassandra of Zuris."

The woman's presence mesmerised Tia. Large green eyes blinked at her, framed by a flowing golden river of hair that streamed below her hips. On her shoulder stood a tiny blackbird, tilting its head from side to side as if assessing her.

"You claim to be my granddaughter?"

Confused, Tia said nothing. The woman looked to be in her thirties.

"We don't age like you do on the surface, but it's still rude to ask about someone's age," she said with a wink.

Tia's mouth hung open. They stood looking at each other for a few moments, Cassandra clearly bemused.

"Don't worry, if you stay, we'll teach you how to guard your mind. May I sit?"

"Of course. I'm so sorry. I would get you something, but..."

"You have a replicator over there, above the row of pink lights," she said, pointing to the wall. "It will make anything you want."

"Like in Star Trek?"

"Is that a place?"

"It's a science fiction show."

"We lost connection with the surface after 1961, so maybe it aired after we left. Probably similar."

Tia frowned and moved over to the wall. She waved her hand over the pink lights, excited to see how the replicator worked. Cassandra stood behind her. A panel lifted, and a glass box about two feet wide and one foot deep slid forward.

"Cool!"

"What would you like?"

"What is on the menu?" She craved some French fries but didn't want to seem too uncouth, so she said, "I'll have what you're having."

"Verdant water and two flower bars. You can have French Fries, but you'll feel better if you have the water and bar."

Tia flinched, remembering that Cassandra seemed able to read her thoughts.

"It's okay. You'll get used to telepathy soon enough. We don't have too many secrets from each other here. That said, you can protect some thoughts with a little focus."

Confusion washed through her as she wondered how to do that, and Cassandra smiled pleasantly again.

"Watch, I'll demonstrate the power of intention." Cassandra stood before the replicator with closed eyes until two glasses of green water and two plates appeared with a small, round cake in the middle, shaped like a flower.

"You just intended the Replicator to do that?"

Cassandra nodded.

"Amazing!" Tia exclaimed.

They took their glasses and plates to the sitting area. Tia gulped the water, not realising until then how thirsty she was. The flower bar smelled like lilac, but it tasted like chocolate, so she inhaled the whole thing in three bites. Meanwhile, Cassandra performed a blessing over her food.

"Sorry," she said meekly. "I didn't realise how hungry I was."

Cassandra took one bite, savoured it, then put the plate down. Tia sat in silence until she was finished, unsure what to say.

"This may sound like a strange question, but how do I clean up the dishes and deal with refuse? I like keeping things clean and tiday."

"Just give it all back to the replicator for recycling. It's along the side of the device. We're a zero-waste city."

"Amazing."

"Can I see?" Cassandra said, gesturing to the photo.

Tia handed it to her, and Cassandra studied the image, running her fingers across it.

"This is you, your sister and your parents?"

Tia nodded, feeling tears well up again.

"And you've never seen this image before?

Tia shook her head, still awestruck and intimated by the woman's regal presence.

"I believe you now. They must have removed or blocked your soul signature. I'm so sorry that happened to you."

A wave of conflicting emotions overcame her at that moment; grief, hurt, joy, awe, and other emotions she didn't recognise.

"You just recently installed your amethyst?"

"Apparently, my father didn't want me to have it until he was sure that Addy could get me to safety. I don't really know what it does."

"It's unleashing your full capabilities. Members of the Quinary mission receive them. They work as both protection and masking. But this one is different."

"Members of the Quinary...?"

"You were born into the Quinary Mission, but you don't realise it. I'm sensing that your dominant power is Sentience tempered by the principle of Vision."

"Addy said something about everyone having a dominant power."

"Sentience is a natural ability that all humans possess but has been blocked in surface humans. It's where you can sense the emotional state of others. For example, you can sense mine at this moment."

She focussed for a moment, feeling both excitement and joy from the woman. Tia nodded. "I guess so, but I wasn't sure."

"In the beginning, it's easy to get mixed up and not know what you're sensing: your emotions or someone else's. Soon, you'll be able to differentiate and know how to better use these healing skills. I imagine people feel emotionally better just being in your presence? You know exactly what to say and how to help them feel better?"

Tia nodded with wide eyes. "People have told me they feel very calm around me."

"It's going to happen more now. Also, the aspect of Vision allows you to think in Visionary ways. That combination makes you a good counsellor and public orator. You can sense the emotional needs of people and inspire them with an empowering vision of the future."

Those words lit up Tia's solar plexus, and longing filled her heart. Cassandra glided across the room and stood near the window. A light glowed around her, and it almost was too much for Tia to take in. Outside, a cigar-shaped craft flew by the window. It looked like a floating bus.

"Where am I? What is this place?" Tia asked, getting closer to the window.

"It's the subterranean city of Helio Tropez, and it's the home of your ancestors."

"I've never heard of it before."

"It's kept secret from surface dwellers, for our protection and yours."

"Why did my father call this place... home? And where is Addy?"

Cassandra didn't say anything. Instead, she whispered something to the tiny bird on her shoulder. It was only now that she was closer when Tia noticed it had a red tuft of feathers on its chest. She watched in amazement as it made a trilling sound, flew towards the wall, and disappeared through it.

"Am I dreaming?" Tia had to ask.

"This is very real."

The bird flew back through the wall and onto Cassandra's shoulder, cawing and pacing on the spot as if whispering something to her.

61

"This is my Jenio, Lival. I know you don't get to have those on the surface. Lival keeps me informed. Young Hadden Violetta is alright. He finished his purification and identification process. Although, unlike you, he still needs containment."

Tia doubted that a bird could talk to her but didn't want to say anything. "Why does he need containment?"

"He has stronger CM than you."

"CM?"

"Surely your father told you about all the Cognitive Modifications SIM does to the population on the surface?"

Tia shook her head.

She looked troubled but explained regardless, looking out over the cityscape. "They use it in large doses to control people with enhanced capacities like Addy. Although with him, it has just started. According to your father, he will get a combination of electro-shock, sensory deprivation, isolation, technology, drugs, torture, autosuggestion and hypnosis to fully enslave him to SIM."

Tia shivered at the thought of her father having gone through that.

Cassandra tapped a device on her wrist, and a list of holographic symbols appeared. "Switch to English," she instructed it. Suddenly, the symbols turned into words. "Here's a list of the typical CM programs that whole populations get embedded with, such as the Gender Misery, Idolization, Cataclysm, Inferiority and Money Slave programs. You have all those. They come through education, media, popular culture, food, frequencies, and even in your tap water."

"How would you know I have these?"

"We checked your Galactic Record. Most people on the surface have them. You think it's normal to have gender and class wars, to idolize celebrities and to feel a sense of scarcity around money, time, love, support. In advanced civilizations, none of those exists."

She enlarged one area of the screen, "But now, Addy has extra cognitive modification. SIM likes to harness the superpowers of Heliotropans for their nefarious projects. Some of us can resist it, but Addy never fully took the oath."

"The oath?"

62

The bird hopped down onto the table and started pecking at crumbs. Cassandra minimized the hologram and sat back, her green eyes sparkling with wonder. "We all come into this life with a purpose, and we make an oath to serve that purpose. His soul waffled in his commitment even before birth. That gave SIM easier access to him. You, on the other hand, showed a clear oath to SANA from day one. That's your Pentada soul lineage."

"Pen...what?"

"Pent-ada," She said slowly. "You've been reincarnating as a specific kind of soul in many lifetimes, known as Pentada. Your unique frequency in harmony with the other four Pentada act as an anchor for our ascension."

Although none of that made logical sense, something familiar stirred in her, hearing that term...Pentada. "Who are the other four?"

"Me, your mother, Daphne, your aunt, Annika, and sister, Metta. Three generations in one matrilineal line...as it usually is."

As it usually is? She thought. So much to try and comprehend. "My father told Addy that his whole life was dedicated to protecting me. So he seemed at least committed to that," Tia said, thinking about how paranoid her father became whenever she left the house.

"That was you."

"But I didn't even know who I truly was..."

"Once he connects with Daphne and has two Pentada daughters, his oath will be activated. Until then, Addy has no North Star."

"My father always seemed to have a lot of inner conflict. But you must be happy to be reunited with your son!"

"He's not my son. As I said, we are related through your maternal lineage. Your mother, Daphne, is my daughter."

"Oh! But Addy said I was coming to meet *his* parents."

"His parents were born here and went to the surface on the same mission as us. During that time on the surface, Addy was born. However, after The Great UnDoing, they disappeared from our Hall of Records. We assumed that they died along with your parents in 1961. Obviously, that didn't happen. At least, not to your parents."

"So my mother is from here as well?"

"Daphne is full Zuris, of Heliotropan lineage, but she was born on the surface. Over the centuries, many Heliotropans have tried to help surface humans in our genetic experiment evolve, but only a few made any difference. Mostly, it's a suicide mission. We were advised to have children born on the surface. Unfortunately, they all got taken over by SIM, which meant that our mission was compromised."

Tia blinked, still not fully comprehending the term SIM.

Reading her mind, Cassandra said, "SIM is short for Simulated Reality. It is a multi-dimensional entity that was tasked by SANA to create a Simulated Reality where souls could experience duality and an inversion of the natural order of things. This allowed them to learn and grow more effectively. However, many players got lost in the game and ended up bonding their souls to SIM, unwittingly renouncing their organic SANA nature. SIM is now an entity upon itself, having taken on the life force energy of the lost players."

Tia's mind raced, trying to make sense of everything Cassandra had said. The thought of humans being a genetic experiment made her stomach tighten. She wrapped her arms around her waist. "So we on the surface are all just like lab rats to you?"

"Not you. You're part of our team. The Quinary Mission came to take back the control of the experiment. But, yes, we were tracking a certain genetic marker. But we love the humans in our experiment and would never hurt them. That's not always true with other genetic farmers. Some of them experiment in hurtful ways."

"Others? You mean more places like this exist in Inner Earth?"

"Thousands of outposts, settlements and cities, both on and off-planet."

"Meaning on other planets?"

"Other planets, planetoids, ships, stations in this galaxy."

"So, you're saying extra-terrestrials control humans on earth?"

"There have been on-going battles for controls through the ages, between many groups. That's because the earth's surface is a rare kind of laboratory."

Tia stifled a laugh. It all sounded so crazy.

Cassandra's face softened into compassionate concern, "SIM teaches surface humans to ridicule anything like aliens, psychic abilities or inter-dimensional beings. It's how they keep people from the truth."

Panic rose in her throat at the idea of everything paranormal being real and not imagined. On the other hand, why would there be so much detailed information about it all?

"In school, I was taught that the centre of the Earth is solid rock or molten lava, not full of cities."

"That's false information fed into the school systems by SIM, so much false science."

"False?"

"You'll learn the true science of how the universe works here. SIM wants to disconnect you from your SANA nature so they can control you."

"What is this thing called SANA?"

"Your father taught you none of this?"

Tia shook her head.

Cassandra sighed and pulled her hair over one shoulder. "SANA goes by several names on the surface, such as God, Goddess, the Great Creator, only it's much more than what surface religions and spiritual groups teach. It's the source of all life. SANA decided to terminate the SIM game as too many players had become addicted to it. Unfortunately, by that time, having absorbed the life force energy of the lost players, SIM had become an entity unto itself. It's now a force to be reckoned with against SANA and is doing all it can to avoid termination."

Tia slumped back in her chair, still trying to process this entirely new worldview.

Cassandra touched the top of Tia's hand, and it surprisingly calmed her nervous system. "I know. It's a lot to take in. You'll learn more about the whole thing at the SANA Rosa Academy."

"The what?"

"Our school. We'll enrol you. You'll need to learn our ways if you're going to stay."

Tia wasn't sure she wanted to stay. It was a lovely place, but it was so foreign.

"Would you like to meet your grandfather?"

"Of course," she said nervously, not sure what to expect.

"I'll let him know. He's just outside."

A moment later, a baritone voice filled the room.

"Tia! May I enter?"

"Please, come in," she said, a flutter in her chest as she pressed the purple button.

The door slid open, welcoming a bulk of a man who towered over her.

"Hello," Tia said sheepishly, trying to sound calm.

"I'm Meraton of Zuris," the great man said. He had kind eyes and a warm smile. Tia would have guessed that he was in his thirties – far from grandfatherly. His long yellow beard sparkled gold. As he stepped forward, a white wolf appeared, making Tia gasp. She froze as the great canine sniffed at her feet, then wandered away to inspect the rest of the room, seemingly uninterested in the long-awaited meeting taking place.

"And this giant furball is Ulwag, my Jenio," Meraton gestured with an open palm.

Tia eyed the wolf as it settled on its haunches, panting. Her heart quickened. "Good to meet you," she said, holding out her hand.

Instead of shaking it, her grandfather bowed and held his hand on his heart while holding eye contact. That seemed to be the customary greeting. As he bowed, she saw a similar etheric shape of wings on his back.

A moment of silence filled the space as they both struggled for words.

"I don't mean to be rude, but what is that on your back?"

"These? Oh, just wings," he said with a broad smile. He stepped back so he could spread them wide. "All humans here have them. They come out when we are in higher vibrational states and disappear when we go into lower ones. SIM keeps surface humans in lower vibrational states, so you never see them. The fact that you can see them now shows your vibratory level is rising already."

Tia felt around on her back for vestiges of wings. Nothing.

"I understand your father kept you completely in the dark about all this, apparently for your own protection?"

Tia shrugged. "I guess so."

"Addy says you are next-generation Pentada."

"I'm not fully understanding this Pentada thing," Tia admitted.

"It's a big subject. We should probably verify your identity before going much further. I suggest the three of us go to The Hall of Records – it can give us a little more clarity. At the same time, you'll be able to learn a little more about who you are and who we are."

"I agree," Cassandra added. "Let's visit with Malinah – if anyone is able to find the information we're after, it's her. She's the Librarian here."

Tia nodded and grabbed her satchel and clothes. "Okay. Maybe I should go and change. Is there a bathroom?"

"Just touch the pink coloured panel, and the door will open. Take the satchel, but you may want to keep on the crystal garment. It's very healing and will help you fit in more."

"Oh, I thought it was, like... pyjamas," Tia said, running her hand across the sleeve and studying the fabric. "People wear things like this outdoors?"

Meraton chuckled, a twinkle in his eye. "We all wear the same fabric. We know pyjamas, though, because we used to live on the surface." He then turned to his wife with a childish grin. "I had pyjamas with the stripes, remember? I think I miss them."

"Let's just say some things are better left on the surface..."

Tia smiled, then looked outside, trying to decipher the season. "Is it cold out?"

"You don't need a coat if that's what you're asking. Here, it tends to stay at 73 degrees Fahrenheit all year-round."

"Okay. So I'll just stay in this outfit?"

"We think it's best."

Meraton opened the door, and they walked out into the hallway. The door slid closed.

"How will I get back in?"

"Hand scan here," he said, pointing to a monitor next to the door.

Tia nodded, wide-eyed. They walked down the curved hallway until they arrived at a six-foot-wide pillar of light. They all stepped inside the circle, and Tia waited for something to happen, suspecting it was like an elevator. She blinked, and suddenly, they were at the entrance of a large, violet pyramid.

"What just happened?" she said, looking around stunned.

"Teleportation," Meraton simply said, setting off. "Come on, Malinah's just inside."

CHAPTER 8

A ddy looked out over the multi-coloured city of Helio Tropez, and a longing to explore it grew inside of him. Outside the door of his lodging, two men called Protectors stood guard. He felt more like a prisoner and wanted to somehow win back the trust of the people here. His room stood at the top of a spiral structure, maybe forty stories high.

When he looked closer to the ground, he didn't only see buses and cars fly by - he also saw people flying. They had wings, something he vaguely remembered his parents telling him about, but he thought they'd just been teasing him.

The round room consisted of a circular bed that floated off the floor, two floating chairs and a floating table. After pressing all the coloured panels, he discovered the bathroom, a replicator, and a console.

Although his parents were born here, he had never visited Helio Tropez before. They'd only told him stories about it all. He'd longed to come here when he was a boy, especially to fly.

The members of Quinary were given camouflage programming in their amethysts before venturing to the surface, making them seem like regular surface humans by masking their wings and other higher capacities. At least, that's what they believed. According to his older self, SIM had found a way of detecting Quinary members and other higher density beings like them. School tests, blood tests, career tests – they all showed markers.

Once they detected you, you were abducted at night, experimented on for hours, then time travelled back to your bed to the exact time you left but with an erased memory and dialled down capacities if they were low or irrelevant to their agenda. In some cases, they even killed the person, if they could get away with it.

According to his older self, when they discovered his aptitude and photographic memory, the SIM agents were thrilled. That's when the cognitive modification began. Someone with a photographic memory and the ability to see people's true intentions made for an excellent spy.

What puzzled him was their reaction here in Helio Tropez. The CM hadn't started yet for him in 1960, or had it? Why did they keep him isolated? As he lay there feeling sorry for himself, a pinging sound came from the console.

"Hello, Hadden. I am Halia of The House of Violetta. Do you remember me? I'm your grandmother," a woman said in Matrix.

"Um. My grandmother?"

"May I enter?"

"Of course."

"Just hit the purple button, and the Protector will let me in."

When she entered the room, a feeling of recognition washed over him. She wore a flowing silver robe and radiated a strange kind of violet aura. Although she didn't look much older than her mid-thirties, she carried herself with dignity and self-assuredness beyond her years.

Looking at him with wise eyes, she asked, "May I sit down?"

"Please," he said, gesturing to the table and chairs that hovered nearby. He took a seat across from her. They smiled at each other, and his cheeks reddened. He wondered what the social niceties were in Helio Tropez. "May I get you something?"

"Some tea would be lovely."

He stood in front of the replicator, not quite sure what to do. He remembered learning that you just had to think about what you wanted. His mum had made him practice willing things for when they could return to Helio Tropez, but it never came to pass. He frowned, willing two cups of mint tea to appear. Within a few seconds, two steaming mugs presented themselves.

"Amazing!" he said as he brought them over to the table. "Is this okay?"

70

"Perfect. You don't have these on the surface?"

"No. You have to do everything yourself. It's a lot of work," he chuckled.

They sat down together at the table and sipped the hot liquid. Halia gently blew across her tea. "Sometimes, I make things by hand. There's something therapeutic about it. I find that putting in the effort to get something can make it even better."

He considered it for a moment, but she spoke again before he could reply.

"Did your mother ever talk about me?"

"Always. I loved the stories about you and grandpa Triol. I feel like I've known you all my life."

"In many ways, you have. When I heard you arrived in Helio Tropez, I was so excited to see you!"

"Apparently, my older self tried to come back here with Daphne and the girls, but the Elders wouldn't let them in. Do you know why?"

Halia looked down at the floor, her eyes full of pain.

"When the Quinary left, they were instructed to sever contact with us. Otherwise, they'd be detected by SIM. We were told that if Quinary tried to contact us, it could be clones sent by SIM, trying to infiltrate us."

"Why did they let our plane in yesterday?"

"The Elders denied entry, but something happened to the cloaking system. The Progenitors overrode it somehow."

"The Progenitors? You mean our ancestors on the home planet?"

"Precisely."

"So Tia and I would be dead..."

"You have to understand. It was very hard on everyone to lose so many family members. Only two returned, and we never found out what happened to the rest. We heard that SIM agents got to you and inside your mind, which led them to all the Quinary members on the surface. Your name has been... unpopular here ever since. The Hall of Records couldn't detect any of your soul signatures, so we assumed you were dead. It's amazing that you survived and that I'm getting to meet you. I just knew that Trace and Rand had borne a child. Just you, correct?"

"Just me."

Halia smiled and touched his forearm. "You know, I sensed the day you were born."

Addy raised an eyebrow.

Halia nodded. "Your soul came to me. I remember the day well. I was sitting in the Garden of Jephsonite, tending to my beloved Azalias. A blue orb came down from the upper world and sat next to me. I knew my daughter had given birth to a boy that day. Later, I went to the Hall of Records and found your Potentiality Card. It's a record of the potential of a soul. Want to know what it said?"

He nodded, intrigued.

"It said that the offspring of my daughter, Trace, and her SANA mate, Rand, would be a male, Voyent-Action. His life purpose? A fly school instructor, helping people learn how to use their wings to travel vast distances. That's actually a highly coveted role here in Helio Tropez. That would have been your profession here… working with people who had strong flying capacities. You would start out in that role yourself and later become a teacher to others. We call those people SANA Eagles, with Eagle eyes. They fly to other dimensions and realms, bringing back the news."

"Maybe that's why I wanted to become a pilot."

"That's what you did on the surface of the planet?"

"I was in training." He paused and sipped some tea, frustrated that he hadn't been raised here. They sat in silence for a moment, but it didn't feel awkward. He felt safe with her. "Grandmother Halia, you seem very familiar to me. I remember you from my dreams as a child."

"I hoped you would remember me," she said, leaning forward with sparkling eyes. "I always felt a calling to help you, right from the time you were born."

Flashes of dreams rose to the surface, of a kind lady singing to him, guiding him as a young child. In his teenage years, he lost connection to those dreams, but he still remembered the bond they possessed.

Halia continued, "Now that we meet in person, I know that I am your protector and mentor. Many people here are angry at what you do in your future timeline, but I'm not one of those people. I am here for you, no matter what. I just want you to know that."

A lump formed in his throat, but she took his hand, and a calming sensation filled his heart.

"If you have to leave here, I want to make sure that you and I stay connected. I can come to you in your dream state and guide you, but we have to strengthen our SANA bond. Let me take you to the Garden of Jephsonite. We'll work with the stone frequencies there, so you'll always have some connection to me here."

He nodded and stood up.

"You're not allowed to leave this room, but we can travel there cognitively..."

Sitting back down, she took his hands, and they both closed their eyes. His mother often did these kinds of rituals with him growing up, so he knew what to do. They sat in silence for a moment, and then, an image of Halia beckoning him into a park appeared. Orchards of trees blossomed with multi-coloured fruits. They walked side by side, the natural beauty mesmerising him. They wove their way up a winding path flanked by pink rose bushes bestowing a calming scent in the air. At the top of a hill, they came to a grassy opening. A majestic oak spread its branches over new saplings. Something about this huge tree called to him like a long-lost friend. A pond stood nearby, and a small waterfall ran down. Waterfowl in pink, blue and green played in the water.

Off to the left, he saw a Spanish-style building constructed of hewn timbers and grey stone. A sign read, "Meditation Pagoda." Small groups of people sat on the veranda in deep conversation. No one could see them walk by. On the far side of the grassy area sat a wishing well with a bench in front of it. Sounds of splashing water echoed from the base. A basket with a lid held two violet coloured stones, and Halia handed one to him.

"These are Sugilite gemstones. They should help you remember your soul's purpose and give you the power to pursue it. It also helps with lucid dreaming and provides psychic protection. It's the gemstone of the Violetta family lineage. I want you to hold this stone near your heart and fill it with your essential energy. I will do the same with my stone. Then, we will dip the stones in the well together. This will symbolize our bond that transcends time, dimensions and space. Keep it with you always."

"I will."

"I emphasise this because when you left your childhood, you stopped paying attention to your dreams, breaking our connection. I need you to return to that so that I can help, even when you're on the surface. Okay?"

Addy nodded, and together they dropped the stones into the bucket before lowering it into the water. It splashed when it hit the surface, somewhere below, and Halia pulled the basket back up. They dried the stones and took one each. Then Addy placed the Sugilite stone safely in his pocket.

Halia watched him, joy radiating from her. "Don't forget, you have to ask for help. It's the prime directive. Hold the violet gemstone and say, Halia-jia, and I will be there for you. You have a photographic memory, so store this moment forever, no matter what happens to you."

In his lessons with his parents, he recalled that people in Helio Tropez often added the letters *jia* to the end of a grandparent's name as a sign of affection.

Halia looked troubled as she watched others in the park, and she sighed. "The city is in turmoil about your presence here with your future daughter. But it's all part of a great alchemical process." She squeezed his hand, and he opened his eyes to find himself back in the room.

They spoke for a while longer before she excused herself, reluctant to leave so soon. After she had left, Addy couldn't stop smiling. He had a grandmother – another family member. The rest of the city could hate him for all he cared. Someone out there loved him, wanted him to succeed, and for now, that was enough.

CHAPTER 9

The Hall of Records covered five square miles of terrain with vast storage vaults of records, such as Galactic Records and Potentiality Cards of each individual soul. As Tia entered the main pyramid, she walked between two pillars. A white beam of light scanned across her forehead.

"Contained within these walls is a storehouse of all experiences in the galaxy, housed in crystalline form," Cassandra explained.

The sloping walls glowed in shades of blue. A harmonic hum vibrated through Tia's chest, creating a sense of peace and groundedness in her body. Her footsteps echoed on the translucent floor as they ascended a staircase leading to a raised platform. Above their heads, hovering below the domed ceiling, a green orb pulsed energy through the room. It looked like a clock face, only with straight lines and symbols around the exterior. Tia tilted her head back to take it all in.

Meraton nodded to the great sphere. "That's the Abracadabra Orb, given to us by the Progenitors for healing, manifestation and dimensional shifting – a gift to help in our mission on Earth. As you can see, the crystals in the walls come in all shapes, colours, and sizes, each with its own frequency to best represent and express the information it holds. It's all a duplicate of the temple that resides in the physical body, within your field of consciousness."

Tia nodded but didn't fully absorb what he meant.

"We even collect books from the surface. I'm a big fan of Tolkein's *Lord of the Rings*. Most of those characters are from Inner Earth. Many have read his books. It's funny. The Orcs really don't appreciate how he portrayed them."

A woman materialised on the platform as they came closer. Tia bowed in unison with her grandparents.

"I am Malinah of Fae-Fair. I understand you are Tia of Zuris. I welcome you with an open heart."

"Zuris?" Tia asked, glancing at Cassandra. "I thought I was a Violetta?"

"The family name gets passed down by the maternal line. In our society, you are the House of Zuris, not Violetta, even though you use your father's name on the surface," Cassandra explained.

Tia nodded, feeling a strange loss of identity at the idea of giving up her last name.

Meraton stepped closer. "We seek information on the Progenitors, the Quinary Mission and Pentada."

"Certainly. Please, take a seat."

Three floating chairs materialised next to the platform. As they sat, a racoon appeared from behind Malinah's leg and sniffed the air in their direction. Tia thought of racoons as late-night scavengers in the alleyways of Seattle, not as beloved Jenios. That said, this animal had an intelligence about it that all the Jenios seemed to have – an intelligence well beyond that of the common dumpster diving animal of her hometown. She wondered if she would ever have one herself.

Malinah waved her hands across a see-through screen that hung in mid-air. Soon, characters and landscapes appeared on a holodeck platform.

"Enjoy," Malinah said, dimming the lights.

A holographic image of a man appeared, the title *Narrator* circling his feet. The words *The History of Helio Topez* appeared in mid-air then dissolved away.

The narrator began talking as images appeared and disappeared behind him. "The Progenitors of our race started a genetic experiment on planet Earth, sanctioned by SANA. Helio Tropez, the city, started out as a simple subterranean science lab. We were genetic farmers, here to help evolve a certain kind of humanoid species. We seeded them and have been studying them for thousands of years. Other off-world groups also reside in subterranean bases, performing genetic experiments both similar and dissimilar to our own. Some of them work with us, some against us."

Tia wondered which humans were in their experiment.

The Narrator paused, then resumed, as if rewriting his script. "Our surface humans carry a certain marker in their blood, but since SIM took over, they've interbred with other humans with different markers. Alas, we lost control of the experiment, once SIM started using our humans as an energetic food source."

"SIM can only survive by being a parasite of source-based SANA beings. To do this, they trick surface humans into disconnecting their minds from their hearts, thus creating soulless aggression and a hunger for power over others. They install beliefs in surface humans that they are born bad and worthless, which compels them to act out victim-villain-saviour roles. All that suffering provides energetic fuel for SIM."

Tia thought about all the senseless wars and cruelty humans had shown towards each other, animals and the environment. Something about this description made sense. However, to think it was all a manipulation, that those on the surface were at an entity's mercy, put a knot in Tia's stomach that she could not shift.

"SIM infiltrates non-organic entities such as computers and smartphones and uses them as a conduit into the minds and souls of organic entities. Yet, there is a catch. They can only infiltrate organic entities like humans with the permission of the host. That is the Law of Fair Warning, one of the Universal Laws that they must abide by. That said, they look for loopholes. They find planets like Earth, where the inhabitants are easy to manipulate; those that are still maturing. They convince humans that they need their SIM technology to have better, more convenient lives, but anything a computer can do, the human consciousness can do better."

Shifting in her floating chair, Tia didn't fully believe that could be true.

The narrator paused and continued, "They trick organic beings, like humans, into giving permission subconsciously, relinquishing their sovereignty. This is done through CM or Cognitive Modification, a subtle process orchestrated through devices, food, water and frequencies beamed down on the planet. Certain humans are specifically trained to keep others in order. Their endgame is to turn humans into full SIM slaves to keep feeding their system. Otherwise, SIM will die. Right now, humans are only partially enslaved. As soon as a human seizes back control of their body-mind system, they can remove the SIM infestation and create a firewall. This is our aim as we are approaching the harvest of souls."

Tia winced. "Harvest?"

"Explain 'harvest'," Malinah instructed.

The holographic stage filled with images of apple trees in an orchard and people choosing the good ones to bring to market.

"Heliotropans are like these apple growers. They discovered that many of the apples or souls, in this case, are infected with a pest known as SIM, making them unsuitable for harvest."

Tia paused the show and turned to Meraton. "Are you saying that we, as surface humans, are like apples to be eaten or thrown away?"

"No. Firstly, you're not a surface human. Secondly, the harvest is not like that. Let's continue with the presentation. You will understand shortly."

The narrator resumed his story. "A soul ready for harvest here on Earth is one that can hold the light of SANA in a 3rd density world. It's not impossible, but highly uncommon. Those that do, can then move as souls to other galaxies and inhabit the lower density worlds without being consumed by darkness. It's an important evolution in this sector of universe."

Tia nodded to Meraton, now understanding that the word 'harvest' was not a reaping but an evolution that brought light in a dense reality.

"Our evolution is tied to our surface humans. But when no other Pentada incarnated, Rand of the House of Violetta proposed The Quinary Mission. He'd heard a prophecy that the rest of Pentada would be born on the surface. Five couples were chosen to infuse the higher frequency colours into the collective consciousness of surface humans."

An image of ten people appeared before them, standing on a platform.

"That's the day we left. See there on the left. Rand and Trace are your father's parents. That's us on the far right."

"Wow! Those are my other grandparents? Addy said I looked like his mother, now I see what he means."

"Yes, she was a very beautiful person, inside and out." Cassandra smiled wistfully.

A lump formed in Tia's throat, thinking she would never meet them. Changing the subject, she asked. "Why does everything here come in fives?

Cassandra held up a five-pointed star on a pendant she wore. "Five has a sacred geometry that evolves life. Whereas geometry based on four is static. Four represents dispersal in all four directions, or exile. But five represents redemption, freedom and bringing light into physical form... that's our job here. Think about it. Hands have four fingers, and a fifth thumb that allows us to create."

She nodded, still not sure whether she understood. "I notice sacred geometry in everything you build here. I read about that on the surface and designed my apartment at home in the same patterns based on five. How could I have known?"

"It's in your ancestral memories stored in the subconscious. Call it instinct if you like. Also, sacred geometry is the language of the Universe and the substructure of all forms in creation. In other words, 'SANA is math'. And SANA code created this virtual reality."

"When you say... virtual reality... do you mean like a computer game with goggles and gloves?"

Meraton chuckled. "They do that on the surface now?"

Tia nodded.

"Heavens no," Cassandra said. "That would be based on artificial intelligence. The virtual reality on the surface was originally based on SANA source code, but SIM wants to turn it into AI, to keep people reincarnating without growth. That's the battle at play."

"So you're saying I was living in a false reality on the surface?"

"Not false. Just different."

"Okay. I've wondered about reincarnation in the last few years, but before that I thought it was impossible."

Cassandra tutted. "That's just a CM program. SIM wants surface humans to think they have just one life, after which they dissolve into nothingness. Therefore, people think their actions in this life don't matter. But in truth, the Law of Karma governs all your lives, and so you reap what you sow, in this life or another."

Meraton scratched the ear of his Jenio. "That said, sometimes, SIM tricks surface humans at the soul level to pay for the Karma that isn't theirs. SIM agents then shirk the responsibility of their own Karma, allowing them to live without consequence. But that's another matter..."

79

Cassandra pressed 'play'. "Let's continue with the holodeck presentation."

The narrator materialised again, "About 25,000 years ago, a new virtual reality matrix was established here on Earth as a playground for souls to explore. It was source based. All went well at first, but then some people in our genetic experiment needed help to evolve quicker. So, about 20,000 years ago, the first generation of Pentada were born so they could work telepathically with surface humans from here. They acted as teaching aides for those who needed it. That made a difference, but a small one, and progress was slow. The harvest looked to be poor. That's when the Progenitors sent in the second generation of Pentada about 15,000 years ago. But then, somehow, SIM started to take control away from SANA, and the Virtual Reality matrix became inverted."

Tia felt an ache in her midback and sat forward. *I wonder what he means by inverted.*

"All systems turned the opposite of what they promised. Health care created sickness. The justice system created injustice. The financial system turned people into debt slaves. It became an inorganic versus organic substructure where duality consciousness ran amok. The software known as *ego* installed itself into the entire collective of surface humans to slow evolution to a trickle. Karmic loops kept people making the same mistakes over and over again, lifetime after lifetime. Surface humans couldn't connect telepathically anymore because SIM masked their pineal gland.

"The third wave of Pentada went to the surface of the planet to help approximately 10,000 years ago. Within a few years, they were captured and tortured for information. When they wouldn't submit, SIM agents put them to death.

The fourth generation, about 5,000 years ago, had some initial success. They started a secret movement of spiritual seekers. But SIM infiltrated the movement and corrupted it, which broke it apart. All five Pentada were killed in the process."

Either this Pentada thing is beyond dangerous, or we've sucked at our job, Tia thought as she fidgeted with a loose strand of hair.

The narrator winked at her, "It was a dangerous job, but each generation made greater headway, learning as they went. Since then, however, Heliotropans decided to remain here, to heal from the trauma and focus on their own evolution. After all, another group from inner Earth made progress

80

freeing surface humans from SIM. Starting five hundred years ago, a group of red-haired giants built a highly evolved empire across the Northern hemisphere. Unfortunately, SIM corrupted them, and dissolved the empire just three hundred years later; erasing them from history."

Tia scanned her memory banks. *I don't remember hearing about a race of giants that lived on the surface in recent history.*

The narrator paused and turned to Tia, "There's evidence of the giants, but those who brought it forward were ridiculed."

Grand architecture in three-dimensional form came up on the screen, that Tia recognized as iconic buildings on the surface. The narrator continued. "These are just some of the remains of their advanced civilization. Mostly gone though. After that our people just wanted to give up and go back to Anatol, the home planet. The Progenitors denied our return, saying our bodies could no longer function properly on Anatol. We were now tied to the frequencies of Earth and her evolution. That's when they granted us one last generation of Pentada to help in our role. Around the turn of the 20th century, Cassandra from the House of Zuris was born. It harkened the return of another generation of Pentada, which activated us to take action once more. With the Precession of the Equinoxes nearing, Pentada had one last chance."

"What's the Precession of the Equinoxes?" Tia said out loud this time in English.

The narrator stopped to translate her question. "We are now at the end of a 25,000-year cycle, where large numbers of souls can ascend all at once. Pentada is key in preparing our genetic experiment to be ready."

If he hears my thoughts, I guess this isn't prerecorded, Tia thought.

The narrator looked a tad impatient. "My information interacts with the mind-body system of the listeners, to give just the kind of information needed."

Tia's eyes grew wide. *Amazing.*

"I shall now continue. Cassandra went to the surface alone at the beginning of the 20th century. She trained a group of young women in Central Europe to reconnect with their psychic powers. They formed a larger group dedicated to bringing Heliotropan values into everyday life. It went well, so Cassandra turned the project over to them and returned here. But in the late 1930s, surface time, SIM infiltrated and corrupted the entire project. All we could do was help just a few advanced souls ascend to a 5D reality. To our knowledge, they appear to be thriving there."

Tia willed her question to the narrator. *What is a 5D reality?*

"It's a reality like Earth, but in 5th density that operates beyond duality."

She nodded slowly, her head throbbing. *I wonder what he means by 'surface time'.*

"On the surface, SIM creates false constructs when it comes to measuring time. Things happen at a different pace in places like Helio Tropez where we follow natural time. To continue, we decided that more than Pentada needed to go to the surface this time. That's when five families from each of the five Houses went to the surface. They settled separately in Seattle, Montreal, London, Rome, and Sydney. It was the biggest project to date. They made little headway, though. The closer to the Precession of the Equinoxes, the more SIM dialled up on their enslavement tools. We couldn't keep up with their advancements. By 1961, SIM infiltrated our ranks, and only Cassandra and Meraton returned to Helio Tropez."

Cassandra turned off the holodeck. "That's when the Elders decided never to reach out to surface dwellers again."

"Hall of Records," addressed Meraton. "Can you identify who is part of the next wave of Pentada?"

A disembodied female voice resonated through the hall, "Only one remains alive, and she is sitting here today."

"Are you saying that Daphne, Annika, Tia and Metta are no longer alive?"

"Confirmed."

"But Tia is sitting right here."

"We detect no soul signature."

"You told us back in 1961 that Hadden and Daphne died, and yet, they lived decades after that."

"Again, we detected no soul signatures at that time and still do not."

"But Tia's physical form is right here," he said, pointing to her. "Could it be that her soul signature is just masked or has her soul actually disengaged from her body and she is possessed by SIM or she is a clone or...?"

"Let us investigate. Please, instruct the mind-body-soul system to step onto the platform."

Tia pointed at herself, and Meraton nodded. She stepped onto the platform, and a silver light spiralled around her in a tall cylindrical shape. Rays of energizing light scanned up and down about three feet on either side of her body. A series of symbols and numerals appeared in holographic form in front of her, one of which glowed yellow, drawing attention to itself.

"It appears as if a masking substance covers the feet, pineal gland and spleen of this mind-body-soul system. Would you like us to remove it?"

Tia glanced at her grandparents. "Will it hurt?"

Cassandra gave her an encouraging smile. "Only a little, but you'll feel stronger afterwards."

She took a breath, then nodded, addressing the hologram, "Yes, please."

Heat surged in the middle of her brow, and shots of energy ran up and down her body. Light poured out of her palms and the soles of her feet. Contrastingly, shivers ran up and down her spine. Her breath quickened, as a musical tone chimed through her core, resonating deep and filling her with lightness.

Once the lights faded, Tia stumbled as though suddenly catching the weight of her own body. Cassandra quickly reached out to help Tia off the platform and into a floating chair. Cassandra's touch on her shoulder helped her go from dizzy and uncomfortable to clear and calm.

"Hall of Records," asked Meraton. "Can you identify who is Pentada?"

A resonant voice answered, "Yes, but only two remain alive, and they are both sitting here today."

Tears welled up in Tia's eyes, and Cassandra and Meraton bundled her into a tight hug.

Malinah brought Tia a glass filled with green liquid.

"This is an Essence Elixir that will help rebalance you."

Tia sipped the liquid, a soothing cool mint flavour easing the heat in her throat and stomach. As she adjusted to the room, her senses grew more alive than ever. The green of the drink glowed with renewed intensity, the texture of her silver robe seemed more detailed, the woven fibres more clear and intricate. She heard the internal hum of the giant hall in a way she hadn't heard before, and her telepathic connection with the others in the room took on a surreal sensation. Emotions even had more nuance.

Tia looked up as the three of them gathered around her. "What would help make the Heliotropans change their mind? How can we convince them to turn back and actually help the people on the surface?"

Cassandra's eyes dimmed, and Malinah looked at the floor.

Meraton looked around the Hall of Records, searching for an answer with a sigh. "We have trauma to heal and need to find out how to fully protect ourselves. When we go to the surface, SIM either takes control of us or kills us. We threaten their agenda, and they threaten our lives. Until we have the upper hand, we can't do anything."

Cassandra added, "We did try to help them remotely through telepathic communication. But we realised that most surface humans had a masked receptor, like you did on your pineal gland, so they couldn't hear us. Those who could hear us got a lot of interference from SIM without realising it. People came forth to others with our message. On the surface, they were called gurus or empowerment teachers, but the message was distorted. SIM learned how to infiltrate the messenger, finding their weakness, inflating their sense of entitlement, feeding them with untruths mixed with truth. This sent the listeners off in the wrong direction. Therefore, the teachings never healed the collective consciousness of surface humans enough to dissolve their addiction to SIM."

Tia took a long, slow breath. Her brain was working faster, reaching conclusions with fewer steps and at greater speed. The rapid learning took her breath away.

"You are Cassandra's lineage," Malinah said, studying the air above Tia's head. "The Zuris aura surrounds you. Fascinating. It wasn't there before. This means that all of the next-generation Pentada are now born, right?"

Cassandra's eyes were filled with pride. "Yes, me, our daughters, Daphne and Annika, and Daphne's daughters, Tia and Metta. It was prophesized that most would be born on the surface, but I'd never imagined I'd be the only one born here."

Tia dug inside her satchel for the photo. "This is my mother and sister," she said, handing it to Malinah.

The three of them studied the image, then Meraton sighed, his eyes glassy. "We haven't seen Daphne in a very long time."

"Neither have I. Not since I was three years old, apparently. I would love to find her, and my sister and my aunt, too!"

The giant man lowered himself into a chair with a grunt. "We haven't seen our daughters in…"

"Since when…?" Tia asked.

"They were just teenagers. They left to explore their careers and ended up working for SIM."

"How?" Tia asked, a pain striking in her chest. She might never have known her mother and aunt, but they were family, and if there was any chance she could save them, she'd take it.

"As a teen, Daphne loved fashion magazines. One day, she was at a restaurant, and I think a photographer invited her to audition as a model. Something like that. Annika was playing music in our back yard around the same time, when a neighbour heard her play. He worked for the local symphony, and soon she was lead violinist in the local orchestra. They both left home against our wishes, wanting to explore their talents in the world. We understood, yet we knew the dangers."

Cassandra bit her lip, regret sitting deep within her eyes. "We took immense precautions to avoid their involvement in activities like that. Being born on the surface made them easier targets. Several others from that generation of the Quinary mission were also targeted. We don't know of any that weren't corrupted."

Meraton took his partner's hand. "All these years, we thought both our daughters were dead. Now we learn Daphne had two daughters who are thirty years old! She would be… what? Sixty-eight years old by now?"

They sat in silence, trying to absorb the information. A stabbing pain filled Tia's chest, making it hard to breathe.

Malinah glanced at Tia, then knelt on the ground in front of her. "You're Sentient-Attention, just like me. You're feeling our pain as well as your own. You don't need to process our pain for us. Just let that go. It's not your job. It's a weakness of our aptitude: use your aptitude to amplify empowering emotions, but don't be a vessel for disempowering ones." Malinah took her hand. "Imagine a shield of silver light around you. The silver light shield is something you learn in more detail at the SANA Rosa Academy, but for now, it will protect you from other people's emotional baggage while allowing you to see, understand and help them. Does that make sense?"

Tia shrugged meekly.

The librarian gave her a sympathetic look before addressing Cassandra and Meraton. "I suggest you enrol her in the academy as soon as possible so she can have a stronger grasp of her abilities."

Cassandra nodded.

A musical sound emanated from a band wrapped around Malinah's wrist. She tapped it once, then tapped her earlobe, and began talking in Matrix.

Malinah said, "The Elders would like to meet you and the young man you arrived with. A gathering in the Congress has already begun."

CHAPTER 10

Addy stood inside the entrance of a pyramid, flanked by two men called Protectors, though whether they were protecting him or everyone else, he hadn't decided. They'd not spoken a word to him, carrying out some apparent order while acting as if he didn't exist. Part of him wanted to run just to force them to acknowledge him, but his presence had irked enough people here, and he didn't want to add further notoriety to his name.

Tia, Meraton and Cassandra entered the pillared entrance of the Hall of Congress. Cassandra looked just as she did when he was a child. She must now be over a hundred years old. In fact, everyone looked youthful, healthy and vibrant, unlike the people on the surface. The longer he stayed here, the more he wished to never go back.

People bowed towards Cassandra as she passed by, but no one seemed to do that with Meraton. The tall man shadowed behind her, almost like a bodyguard. Addy wondered if she was their Queen given her Pentada status, and he was just her consort.

When she spotted him, Tia hurried towards him and his heart filled with gratitude, glad to see a friendly face in this alien place. They hugged each other and expressed their relief that the other was okay. She summarised what she had learned at the Hall of Records, and although he had learned some of the history of Helio Tropez from his parents, what Tia said piqued his curiosity further.

They entered the hall to see three concentric circles of people seated in floating chairs. They ushered Tia and Addy to the innermost circle towards four chairs. Cassandra and Meraton sat on either side of them.

Joining them in the innermost circle were six people - three men and three women - who looked older but still had a youthful glow. Addy whispered to Tia that most of them were well over 500 years old.

The room buzzed with conversation that echoed into the high, sloping walls of the chamber. An Elder acting as Speaker stood up. She introduced herself as Yeelay, her blonde hair spiralling six inches overhead and shaped into a cone. She turned and faced the outer circles, holding her arms out like a conductor. As she lowered them, the talking died down until the only sounds left were those of shifting feet and the occasional clearing of someone's throat. A balcony of onlookers leaned forward in their seats as though a great performance were about to begin. Addy took a breath and tried to ignore the number of eyes scrutinising him.

His older self had clearly caused much grief to this community, and he wondered if he could plead that he was a different person, that this future person was someone that didn't have to exist – he could become someone else. Despite it, questions circled his mind. *Would they allow him to stay? Would they send him back to the surface? Would they eliminate him entirely from the timeline?*

Yeelay spoke, and her voice seemed to be amplified, although Addy couldn't see a microphone anywhere in the room.

"We are here to understand the events that have led to the man calling himself Hadden of Violetta to be here at this time with a woman who claims to be his future daughter, also the daughter of Daphne of Zuris, and therefore granddaughter to Cassandra and Meraton of Zuris. As far as anyone has known for the last fifty years, the body-mind-soul complex known as Hadden Violetta has been dead since 1961." Yeelay turned to him and continued, "This is your opportunity to testify to our community the events that led to your presence here in Helio Tropez. If you are truly Hadden of Violetta, then I'd need not remind you that lying is futile. We are reading your auric field and energy frequencies as I speak, and any falsity will be plain to everyone in this room. Is that understood?"

Addy and Tia nodded solemnly.

"Who would like to begin?"

They looked at each other, and Tia gestured to Addy, who cleared his throat and rose to his feet. Without needing to project his voice, he explained how his seventy-year-old self had asked him to time travel from 1960 to 2010 and what he had learned from him about his life during those fifty years. He reported that at the end of the year 1960, SIM cognitively modified him to serve their interests until he tried to escape in 1985 to protect his family. After he finished, the Elders started talking amongst themselves.

Yeelay stood up to speak, narrowing her eyes at him. "You do realise that the Temporalia forbids this kind of time travel? You've created a rip in the time-space quantum!"

Addy nodded and looked down. A few murmurs rippled around the gallery.

The Elders looked at one another, communicating in coded telepathy. Eyes jumped from face to face within the group, and by watching their eyes, Addy could tell who was speaking and when, though that was his only clue.

Yeelay nodded to the Elders and stood up. "We have decided that this version of Hadden of Violetta is not yet fully owned by SIM and speaks the truth. We also believe that he and Daphne of Zuris survived The Great UnDoing of 1961, which may suggest others survived as well."

Conversation erupted in Matrix within the auditorium as voices strove to be heard over others. The Elders went on to discuss theories about why the Hall of Records would mistake so many members of Quinary as deceased. Even without soul signatures, it should still detect their life force energy. Addy sat and listened, trying to follow a single conversation for more than a few moments. After a time, he grew tired of everyone discussing him. He stood, his chair floating backwards soundlessly.

"You're all speculating when you have two people who have been born and raised on the surface. Why not use us, hey?" He looked around the auditorium, and when no reply became apparent, he continued. "Compared to how I feel here, living on the surface dials down on your energy frequency to the point of feeling lifeless at times. It's possible that SIM is inhibiting the population's life force to such an extent that the Hall of Records can't detect them, even if they're still alive."

The Elders nodded and resumed talking amongst themselves again. Hadden scowled at those in the room, feeling like an amusing distraction rather than someone with information. He decided not to tell them what had happened to Daphne and the life that SIM made her lead. He sensed that the loss of so many Quinary members had caused suffering they hadn't experienced in a very long time.

The Elders called for calm again, and Yeelay requested that Tia give her testimony. After explaining as much as she knew, the community voted unanimously. Tia was judged truthful as well. They called a man forward from the outer circles, holding a device similar to a flashlight in his hands. He asked Tia to remove her shoe and lift up her left foot. The man then shined a violet light on her foot and moved close to inspect. He stood up and nodded to the Elders. Cries of delight mixed with gasps of despair filled the hall. Those nearby came around to get a closer look, and Tia looked panicked, reminding Addy of a zoo animal. Cassandra moved beside her and removed her shoe, putting her foot next to Tia's. The violet light showed that she had the same pentagonal marking, confusing Tia.

The man with the light explained, "This device can detect your pentagonal birthmark – the sign of a Pentada. We have been waiting for you for many generations."

In unison, thousands of people stood in the gallery and bowed in reverence to her and her grandmother. Some people, however, chose not to bow. The dissension, Addy sensed, came from Tia's heritage – a life dominated by SIM.

An Elder stood to address the auditorium. "I grasp your discomfort with this situation, but remember, the Pentada females can only be 'service to others' oriented, not 'service to self'. Even if SIM tries to control Pentada as they have in the past, they always fail."

Another Elder stood, her chin raised. "We must reunite all five Pentada. Otherwise, everything we have worked for will be lost."

"Three of them are missing on the surface, or maybe even transitioned out of their bodies," Cassandra reminded her.

The man with the unmasking light asked Tia, "What age are you now?"

"I will be thirty in two weeks."

More gasps from the crowd. Tia's eyes grew wide, unsure why her ageing could cause such upset.

"If she's activated here, we are all at risk. She must be terminated!" shouted one of the Elders.

"Or at least returned to the surface," another called.

Cassandra stood to address the crowd, holding up both hands. "Thirty is only the age of activation if all five of us are together, consciously in union and in union with our SANA mates. Nothing happened when I turned thirty as no other Pentadas existed yet."

An Elder nearby nodded. "Pentadas deactivate if they get under SIM control. It's a failsafe built into the program."

People sat back in their chairs, mulling on this last comment. During the last generation of Pentada, Addy remembered hearing that SIM had tried to turn them against the other Heliotropans, but in the end, it had failed because the women lost all their powers.

A woman called out from one of the back rows. "She cannot be true Pentada since the coupling of Daphne and Hadden was orchestrated by SIM."

"We aren't sure of that," another Elder countered.

The Elders turned to look at Addy to explain his coupling with Daphne.

"That hasn't happened for me yet," he said with a shrug. Addy turned to Tia and asked, "What year were you born?"

"1980."

"That's another twenty years in my future. I don't even know if I'm their true father."

Meraton interjected. "We have just done a reading of Tia from the Hall of Records. The scan shows that her true parents are Daphne of Zuris and Hadden of Violetta."

The hall erupted again, and this time, it took Yeelay longer to calm down the uproar.

Addy re-iterated that his older self had made a last ditch effort to change the timeline by calling him forth from the past to protect Tia and change the course of history. The Congress continued to debate for hours. Some argued that Addy should go back to 1960 and ensure Quinary members come home safely. That way, Daphne would couple with Rafael to create the true Pentada children, meaning that Tia and her sister would no longer exist. Others argued that maybe Daphne and Rafael would not produce a Pentada child.

Addy finally stood up in frustration. "Why do you say I can't produce a true Pentada child? Can you prove Rafael is her true SANA mate and not me?"

91

Yeelay conferred with the Elders before speaking. "Verification of a true, ah, SANA mate is, how shall we say? A complex process. It's really up to the two individuals."

"So you don't have a light device that can verify my SANA mate status?"

"No."

"Consider this. If we ended up together and produced two Pentada daughters orchestrated by SIM, wouldn't that still prove that we are SANA mates? SIM wouldn't pair two people who are not. Besides, would the children be Pentada if it wasn't meant to be?"

An expectant pause filled the air as people considered the logic of his argument. Addy remembered hearing about the long-term animosity between the Houses of Zuris and Violetta, making him think that, maybe, they just didn't want him to mate with Daphne.

Cassandra and Meraton remained quiet, but he sensed their discomfort. After all, he remembered the two of them pushing Daphne towards Rafael when they were children. Burning anger arose in his chest at the thought that they didn't want their daughter connected to the House of Violetta – that somehow, he wasn't good enough. When he and Daphne had met, it was clearly fireworks for both of them, or so he'd thought.

Once Yeelay had regained order, she looked about the room, tired. "Our only choice is to call upon the Progenitors and see if they can help us in this matter."

The entire assembly settled into a resounding silence. A woman in the back row began singing, and the others gradually joined in. The harmonies echoed in the pyramid, calming and raising the vibration. She called out in song to the Progenitors over and over again, and a chorus of people echoed her words. Addy listened, his heart racing with each rise and fall of the melody. After what felt like an hour of singing, the songstress ended the lyrics and sat back down, exhausted.

Yeelay stood, looking defeated. "I suggest we reconvene tomorrow and see if they come to us in our dreams. If not, I encourage you all to meditate on the matter at hand. Perhaps we will come to an epiphany in solitude."

Just as people rose out of their seats to head for the exit, a light pierced the room by the doorway. People froze, looking on, but nothing appeared or moved, apart from a shifting spotlight.

From somewhere in the room, the songstress' voice returned, announcing their arrival. "The Progenitors are here!"

CHAPTER 11

Tia swivelled her head to see two beings materialise underneath the spotlight. She recognised one of them as the man from the hologram in the Hall of Records. A woman stood beside him, scanning the room, taking them all in. They wore robes of white and gold, their long hair plaited ornately down their backs. They didn't fully materialise into the room. Instead, they shimmered against the crystalline walls of the pyramid.

For a few moments, they stood in silence, seemingly to absorb all information in the assembly. Finally, the woman stepped forward and fully materialised into the room. She walked towards Tia, the audience members bowing in reverence as she walked by. No one spoke, and mouths hung open.

Cassandra whispered to Tia, "Some people have never seen a Progenitor in person. It's been hundreds of years."

"I am Waleya. Thank you for calling me here. Please, Tia of Zuris, join me."

She led Tia by the hand to a place in the centre of the pyramid, her hand trembling in the woman's palm. All rows of concentric chairs swivelled to face them, and people leaned down over the balcony to get a closer look. Tia's face flushed as she looked up at all the faces staring down at them. Waleya now held both of Tia's hands and closed her eyes. After a few minutes, she looked up, let her hands go, and addressed the assembly.

"I have assessed Tia of Zuris, and I can confirm she is genetically manipulated by the SIM."

A roar of voices rang out across the hall.

An Elder shouted out, "I told you she would be trouble!"

The Progenitor looked down at Tia, beaming love as if to protect her from the dissenting Elders.

Yeelay asked, "Where lies her allegiance? To SIM or to SANA?"

Cassandra stood up and approached. "Her allegiance is to SANA."

Waleya cushioned her hands to calm down the crowd. Immediately, the roar died down in the Congress.

Cassandra faced the Progenitor. "The Hall of Records removed a masking on Tia's soul signature, and now she can be detected. Am I correct?

"Indeed. It's a very clear signal, sourced by SANA, but her parents were under SIM control by the time she was born."

A woman from the second row spoke in a harsh tone, "It's our custom to prune such progeny from our family tree."

"Yes!" another man called out. "Even more so for the young man!"

The Progenitor turned her attention towards Addy and held up her hand, calling for silence. As she did, a forcefield appeared around him. She addressed those in the balcony and said, "He is infected with Artificial Intelligence. Your purification system couldn't detect all of it. SIM is getting smarter. I suggest you study everything this young man knows, everything about his system, his AI infestations, along with the envelopes he got from his older self. You have an opportunity. Do not squander it."

Tia sat down next to Addy, his face ashen.

"Can you give us a map of where to find and clear out the AI?" Yeelay asked.

Waleya shook her head. "Your role is to upgrade your systems. Our role is only to point out where the original experiment has gone off course and guide it back on course. At the beginning of this project, 25,000 years ago, we told you that your evolution is deeply tied into the evolution of the humans on the surface. All the genetic farmers on this planet have a responsibility towards their creations. Abandon them, and you are abandoning yourselves."

"We tried to help many times, but SIM made it impossible," Yeelay interjected.

"Was it truly impossible, or did you just lack the necessary vision?"

The crowd grew restless in their floating chairs.

"Perhaps it was all meant to be...Heliotropans born on the surface of the planet, pulled into SIM, but that is up to you to discern."

Disbelief rang through the Hall of Congress.

The Progenitor continued. "We tasked the Quinary Mission with finally bringing this genetic experiment to full fruition any way they could. That's what they chose."

Yeelay looked about the room, lost. "We don't understand."

The Progenitor turned to face Addy.

"This young man broke a time travelling law by meeting himself in the future. If he goes back to his timeline and changes events, it nullifies the experiment. Everything you've been working towards for all these centuries falls apart. The only solution is to erase his memory and return him to the original timeline. Everything must play out exactly as it did."

Despair washed through Addy's heart.

Waleya turned to face him. "May I inspect the amethysts created by your older self?"

Addy nodded and turned his head to the side, exposing the gem. The Progenitor held her hand a few inches away from his head, and the amethyst magnetised into her hand. She scanned it with her other hand.

"Excellent work," she murmured, turning to face the crowd. "I suggest your Gemsmiths study this amethyst and upgrade it as much as possible. While you've been cut off from the surface, SIM has evolved, but you have not. Learn what you can, and do not let yourselves fall to corruption again. Share your discoveries with those here and advance the technology. The harvest you've worked so long and hard for is on the horizon." She held up her hand, and the amethyst magnetised back onto Addy's skull.

"But... this wasn't our understanding of the original assignment," Yeelay stammered. "SIM is a parasite. How can their involvement help us achieve our mission?"

"You seem to have forgotten that even SIM is a part of the oneness."

The Hall remained silent. People shuffled in their chairs.

"Unify and activate Pentada," she said as she rejoined her partner. As they began to dematerialize, she assessed the room a final time, her gaze lingering on Tia and Addy. "I have left this in your hands. I trust that you will do the right thing."

CHAPTER 12

The next day, Hadden, in quarantine, prepared to leave Helio Tropez and return to his timeline on the surface. The Gemsmiths and programmers worked with him through the comm system, studying the envelopes from his future self, the photographic memories he had downloaded from Older Hadden, and scanned his system to learn as much as they could. Although he kept reassuring himself that it was for the best, sadness, fear and regret haunted him. What was the point of even knowing all this when it would all be removed from his memory?

Several Heliotropans came to visit him the morning of this departure. Maddox of Viridis came first: a man from the same lineage as Rafael. He appeared on Addy's comm.

"Thank you for talking with me. I heard what the Progenitors said, but you must warn all the Quinary members so they can get home safely. If you do, all of you born on the surface can come back here and lead far more peaceful lives. Daphne can be with Rafael, and you can be with *your* true SANA mate." He opened a wrist device, and a small 3D image of a young woman materialised above his hand.

"I checked with our Oracle. She predicts that your SANA mate, Nina. She is a highly sought-after girl from the House of Liven."

"She's beautiful," he said, her image striking a sense of wrongness in Addy's heart. Daphne still seemed like his true SANA mate.

"These two daughters you might have with Daphne are not the real Pentada, and you know that."

"Tia is worthy of saving. The Progenitors have spoken. I am sorry, but your requests are selfish. I cannot heed them."

The man looked away and slumped his shoulders. "You are right. I'm sorry." After a moment, Maddox stole a gaze again. "But please, consider what it must be like to have a life back here, with your family alive and well, staying youthful for hundreds of years. You could become a SANA Eagle, married to Nina."

Hadden couldn't help but compare that life to the life he was destined to live on the surface. A pang of sadness engulfed him.

Maddox sighed. "You don't have to take my advice, but the least you can do is listen. They plan to give you *The Milk of Nepenthe* to erase your memories. Although it's powerful, you are Voyent-Action. It's very hard to completely wipe the memory of someone like you. My aptitude is Ecrivent-Reprogram, and if you want, I've written a code you can activate to override the memory wipe. I can't guarantee it will work, but I can download it into your mind now. To activate it, just say the following before you go under – *Activate Huperzia*. It will activate the Huperzia plant receptors in your DNA, which is an organic antidote to Nepenthe. Please, all I ask is that you consider it."

Addy shook his head. "I can't. I made an agreement – a promise!" He'd be betraying his people and his future daughter. Not to mention that the Progenitors would know.

"You don't have to use it. It's just there in case you change your mind. It's entirely your choice. Do you want it or not?"

"As I said… no."

"Okay. I tried. I'll leave you in peace now."

Just as the man was about to sign off, an impulse seized him. He didn't know what the Heliotropans were planning. As far as they were concerned, he was better off dead. *It can't hurt to have it there, can it? I don't have to use it. I could use it only if things turn ugly.* "Wait! Okay, look. I'll take the program, but I'm not saying I'll activate it."

Maddox smiled and nodded. He placed his palms towards Addy's face, and with telepathic permission, the code entered his mind like a piece of software downloading into his applications folder.

"I have it now. Thank you. That said, it's very unlikely I will use it."

Maddox looked disappointed but nodded before leaving. As he sat looking out over the city, Addy mused at how many people lost family members in The Great UnDoing and that he could become their saviour by bringing them back. He didn't want to lose his parents and turn out like his seventy-year-old self. If he never mated with Daphne and warned everyone to escape, so much pain could be avoided. He could live out his days here in Helio Tropez, marry Nina, and not have to endure the harsh conditions of the surface – the manipulation and torture that SIM would put him through. On top of that, the Heliotropans wouldn't hate or imprison him – he'd be one of them. Yet, going rogue against the Progenitors remained a great unknown. What would happen if Tia never lived?

As he packed up his meagre belongings, he thought about how all of the memories of the past few days would soon disappear. Or would they? Would his photographic memory override the Milk of Nepenthe? Would the Huperzia code stop the process?

Just then, a pinging noise emanated from the comm. The screen showed an image of Tia. He asked the Protector if she could enter, and he agreed.

Tia rushed in. "I'm so glad you haven't left yet! I wanted the chance to say goodbye. I'm beyond grateful to you. You saved my life, not just as the young Addy, but as the old man, too. In fact, you gave me life. These last few days of getting to know the true Hadden Violetta before they broke him... felt so important to me."

Her eyes stung, but she blinked the tears back.

His throat tightened, and he squeezed her hand. Over these last few days, the bond with his future daughter had grown strong. The inner conflict chafed at his heart. He wanted his daughters to live and not be wiped from the timeline. The Progenitors wanted them to live out their true Pentada potential. If he messed with the timeline again, maybe the entire genetic experiment – thousands of years of work and sacrifice – would all be for nought.

As Tia watched him wide-eyed, he sensed that she could read his dilemma.

"You'll remember anyway, won't you?"

He shrugged. "I don't know. And if I do, I don't know if it will make any difference. There are people here who want me to keep my memories and to get everyone back to safety."

"I understand," Tia said quietly, "but I do hope you will do the right thing, which is whatever your heart tells you to do."

"Let's hope we will meet again when I am an old man, and things will be different... in a very good way."

They held hands, wrist to wrist, a gesture of eternal and mutual support. Standing in silence for a few minutes, darkness pressed on his heart. An Elder arrived to escort him to the stargate. Touching his amethyst, Addy took a step back and erected an SPS.

"Oh my gosh, I saw my father do those arms movements. What exactly is that about?"

He finished the SPS and touched his amethyst again, "I'm creating a Secure Protective Space for going back to my timeline."

"Actually, you must leave behind your amethyst," the Elder tutted, to protect the original timeline."

Addy pursed his lips and squeezed his eyes shut. "Right..." With one hand he demagnetized the crystal from his skull and put it back in the gold box. The Elder snatched it from him. Suddenly, Addy's entire energy system weakened. With a heavy heart, he hugged Tia. As he did, she slipped a box into his pocket, and when Tia pulled away, she gave him a knowing look.

The stargate portal stood majestic against the purple-blue haze of the Heliotropan sky. Although he felt like an outcast here, the place enlivened him; it felt like home. Now he would be leaving Helio Tropez behind forever and live a future that didn't look promising.

The Elder left him alone for a few minutes while he keyed in the stargate entrance code. Inside his pocket was another box, shaped exactly the same as the one he'd just given to the Protector. *Another of the amethysts*, he realised.

Although he appreciated the gesture, the risk that SIM might notice it back in his old timeline was too great. *On the one hand, it will give me an easier life. The gold box did act as a shield against SIM. Maybe they won't be able to detect it. On the other hand, if they did detect it, they'll kill me, or worse.*

Once inside the lab, the man ushered him to a table and instructed him to lie down. As a technician prepared the Milk of Nepenthe, conflict roiled within him.

"By the way, he is Voyent-Action," explained the technician, watching a monitor.

"Double the dose, then," the Elder instructed. He turned to Addy and inserted an IV into his arm.

"This will put you under, then the technician will take you to the stargate. We programmed it to take you back to the morning of December 21 of the year 1960, to a time before you woke up. You'll remember nothing and carry on with your day as usual. Are you ready?"

Addy nodded, and as the Elder turned away, he muttered under his breath. "Activate Huperzia." At the flick of a switch, his veins started to fill with a thin white liquid, and all went blank.

CHAPTER 13

After Addy left, aloneness surrounded Tia's heart. At least, they had been outcasts together. Now, she was the only person raised on the surface among them. Many of the Heliotropans didn't trust her, watching her with wary eyes, making Tia wonder how many of them would happily vote to destroy her, wiping her from this timeline and any other. *Well, if Addy does change the timeline, maybe they'll get their wish.*

Cassandra and Meraton came to collect Tia from her room. As they walked towards the elevator, Tia asked, "Who were the Temporalia that people talked about?"

Meraton knitted his thick brows. "They monitor and regulate time travel in this area of the galaxy. Hadden knew the rules and broke them anyway. You should never make physical contact with another version of yourself in the past, present or future. It is incredibly complicated to correct it, and The Temporalia will now have quite the headache on their hands. If they don't correct it, the natural timeline will disappear."

Tia took a sharp breath and nodded. *And I'd never be born*, she thought.

As they walked through the city, Tia was in awe of every sight and smell around her. The Palace of Zuris, as they approached, had an ethereal glow to it, reminding her of the Taj Mahal. The white twin domes were lit from below with a rainbow of lights dancing on the white marble. Paintings adorned the arched entrance. Tia's eyes grew wide as they got closer.

Cassandra smiled. "These paintings include heart-expanding mind code, similar to what some of the great Renaissance painters like Da Vinci did."

The images filled Tia with a sense of peace.

"Each House has its own Palace," Cassandra explained. "They serve the community's needs. Here, we serve those in the matrilineal line of the House of Zuris and their partners. Most people in the House of Zuris live nearby, but if you're an Elder of that House, like us, you live inside the Palace."

Six Protectors flanked the walkway like guards at Buckingham Palace. They each wore golden helmets and carried a crossbow. As Tia entered, a beam of light scanned her face. Signs in Matrix pointed to various locations, such as a Healing Bay, a Library, a Clothes Maker, a Gem Smith, and a Repair Centre for various pieces of technology. They entered a room labelled *High Council of Zuris*. Inside, six chairs sat waiting. Two of the chairs were marked for Meraton and Cassandra, the other two for Geata and Renolo. Two extra seats were nameless. They ushered Tia into one of the unmarked chairs while taking their seats.

After they arrived, Geata and Renolo entered from another sliding doorway, their respective Jenios following behind them – a brown marmot and a green tortoise. Geata stood as tall as Meraton, her silver hair flowing well below her waist. She was the first woman Tia had seen with wrinkled skin. *She must be several hundred years old,* Tia thought.

Renolo was shorter than Geata by a foot and had long, brown hair pulled into a bun. Another woman, wearing a Zuris Palace emblem on her gown, entered the room and sat next to Tia. Her Jenio, a large butterfly, buzzed nearby and settled on her shoulder. One entire wall displayed holographic images of flowers morphing from one to another, such as lilacs, then roses. The scent of each flower seemed to fill the room as the images came on the screen.

Geata tapped on a ceremonial bowl, and a resonant tone filled the air. "Welcome, Tia, to our council meeting. I am Geata, and this is Renolo. We are Elders of Zuris along with your grandparents. Since you are House of Zuris, it's up to us to oversee your integration here. Amelia, next to you, is your Integration Counsellor. She integrates people who immigrate to Helio Tropez. Although we haven't received anyone for decades, she's had lots of experience with people from other parts of Subterranean Earth. Whenever you need to talk or need a vital sign check, that's her job. It's a big transition to move from third to fourth density."

Renolo scooped the marmot off the floor and onto his lap. "I know the Progenitors want you to go back to the surface, but we don't think you're ready yet. You need to learn how to manage your Pentada powers and build your protection field."

Tia nodded, feeling relieved. Trying to just stabilise her energy after the unmasking at The Hall of Records was enough to deal with. Even though she wanted to find out what had happened to her father, the thought of going back to the surface unnerved her.

Meraton said, "I don't think it's a good idea for Cassandra to go. She is 105 years old, and if her energy system started to align with surface dwellers, it could start a rapid ageing process."

"Yes, we do need to consider that," Geata nodded.

The thought of going back alone only added to the terror brimming within her. *How am I supposed to find three people on an entire planet? Not to mention doing it without attracting attention from SIM.* She didn't say anything, but they all sensed the panic thrashing within her. Cassandra touched her shoulder, calming her.

"I suggest you stay here at least for a year to work on mastering your aptitude and Pentada powers."

Renolo waved his hand across the monitor. The nature images dissolved, Matrix symbols taking their place. "We need to ensure Pentada are back here, purified of SIM programming and activated as a unit before the next solar flare. That's in July 2012. We only have two years maximum."

"Solar flare?"

Renolo looked at her as if she'd just asked what gravity was. "It's complex, but I can speed up your learning if you like."

Tia nodded. "Sure, if it'll help..."

He waved his hand in front of her eyes as if to pull aside a veil. "Solar flares happen every 25,000 years or so to signal the end of a genetic experiment on a planet like Earth. We either ascend with our harvest and keep advancing, or we have to go somewhere else and start from the beginning, restarting another 25,000-year cycle."

Tia absorbed what he shared at a rapid pace. "What happens to all your surface humans if you don't ascend?"

Geata looked sideways at Renolo and took a deep breath, "They go back to the source."

"They die?"

Geata furrowed her brow. "Their bodies die, but their souls don't. They just take on another form in another dimension, realm or planet, or go back to SANA. Does that make sense?"

"Yes," Tia said, now able to comprehend more unspoken context. "In short, this ascension thing is a big deal."

"You could say that." Meraton scrolled through the pages on the screen until he found what he needed. "If three Pentada, maybe four, get trapped on the surface, then we won't make it in time for the harvest of souls. And it could mean that SIM gets access to this new MindStory Code that seems to be coming through the next generation of Pentada."

"And if SIM has the code, they can steal the harvest," Geata said.

All closed their eyes as if to meditate on the situation. Tia looked from one to the other, wondering when they would 'come back'. Amelia also had her eyes closed, so after a while, Tia did the same.

Finally, Cassandra said, "We need to accelerate Tia's learning and form a team to support her from here during the rescue mission. I volunteer to head up the team. There can be no mistakes, or it could prove fatal to all of us."

While the Zuris Elders nodded in solemn agreement, Tia emitted a long, slow, silent exhale. At least she had their support.

After the meeting, Cassandra and Meraton joined her on the walk back to her room. They stopped on a glass bridge between the palace and the spiral high rise to look out across at the city, Taking it in at ground level captivated all her senses.

"Why is there a glass wall around the city?"

"Raptors," Meraton said simply.

"What's a raptor?" You mean like a kind of dinosaur?"

"Yes, we have many breeds of dinosaurs here."

"But they went extinct..."

"No, some were saved in Inner Earth. The raptors once roamed the surface of the Earth as a genetic experiment of a reptilian race of beings. Just before one of the cataclysms that destroyed all life on the surface, the genetic farmers saved a few in Subterranean Earth. Over the last few million years, they grew in numbers and now live in caves in certain mountainous regions. They have their territory, and we have ours. We generally respect that boundary, but the mountainous region you see in the distance borders on raptor territory."

Cassandra's Jenio flew down from a tree and onto her shoulder. Nearby, small groups of people walked by, all with their Jenios. They seemed headed for large green buildings."

"What about those green pentagonal structures?"

"That's where we grow some of our food," Meraton explained. "It's an advanced form of hydroponics. Instead of electricity, oil or wind, we power everything with zero-point, free energy generated by our pyramids. We ban all Artificial Intelligence and only allow consciousness technology."

"Right..." Tia said, pretending to understand. "Also, there are pentagons everywhere, including on my foot. I always thought the pentagon shape had something to do with evil and witchcraft."

The wolf looked at her sideways as Meraton and Cassandra smiled at each other, making her cheeks grow warm.

"It's okay. You were never taught these things. Symbols and numbers are neutral, but it's the intention behind them that makes a difference. SIM agents know the power of five, so they invert its powers for their own purposes. The geometric shapes we use here are the opposite of what they use on the surface. SIM makes surface dwellers believe that the natural laws of the universe are evil and any inherent powers such as telepathy, clairvoyance or psychometry impossible. If you demonstrate them, you get ridiculed or disposed of."

Tia remembered witnessing that kind of scepticism and ridicule. "And the flying cars and spaceships?"

"They run via Anti-Gravity instead of fossil fuels. We travel by many methods, including teleportation, stargates and a bullet train that runs between many of the subterranean cities."

"Why doesn't everyone just teleport to everywhere?"

"Teleportation lines are only available between each person's private apartments to the Hall of Congress and the Library. We use the flying buses and flying cars to go from one short distance to another, as you might do to go shopping on the surface. We will show you how to use the Volabus later on so you can explore the city at your own pace. We have a Vola car we can take you in sometimes, but it requires special licensing to drive. You'll be able to apply once you're more integrated here."

"That would be wonderful. And the stargates?"

"We use stargates to go from one density, dimension, timeline or galaxy to another. The bullet trains take large groups of people and cargo to the other cities in a short period, providing it's within the same density level."

Tia nodded in amazement as she noticed a man walking towards them on the bridge, holding up his hand and talking to a 3D image of a person between his thumb and index finger.

"As you can see, we use 3D holographic imaging instead of phones," Cassandra said, opening her hand to activate her personal communication device. "We'll get you one, if you want?"

Tia nodded, but there were too many questions bubbling away at her. "What about this body of water?" she asked, pointing to the waterway flowing beneath the bridge.

"This is the Tourmaline River that comes down from the Riala mountain range and runs through the city," Cassandra explained.

The phosphorescent turquoise mesmerised her, as did the glowing green of the weeping willows and the fuchsia of the flowers adorning the banks. A gold winged creature went from one flower to another, giving it something. Tia squinted at it.

"Is that a butterfly or..."

"Just a fairy."

"Fairies are real?"

Cassandra laughed. "I forget that SIM tells you that fairies are make-believe. They're very real, along with many other types of elementals. They keep the plants and Earth energies thriving. In fact, some of our citizens are part fairy, like Malinah."

Tia's chest pounded in excitement.

Back at her lodgings, Tia looked at Cassandra's hair and realised that she didn't think she'd seen a woman with short hair since she'd arrived. "I notice that most of the women here grow their hair very long compared to women on the surface," Tia remarked. "I never cut my hair, and it just kept growing until it went down to below my hips. People thought I was a freak, but here it looks… normal?"

"It's good you listened to your instincts to grow it long. As you may notice, even the men wear their hair long. It enhances our intuitive abilities."

"How so?"

"SIM creates mind programs and food that weaken a person's hair follicles to block the intuitive powers of surface humans. Luckily, that didn't happen to you. You must have eaten a good diet."

"Mostly organic foods and purified water."

"Did your father teach you that?"

"Yes, but later in life, he gave all that up. He started eating the horrible fast food. And now that I think about it, he lost most of his hair like many older men on the surface. It looks like none of the men loses their hair here."

"It's very rare."

"I remember that Daphne fed me that way when I was young, too."

"Good. We taught her that way," Cassandra smiled. "That's what gave her a radiant energy that people in the entertainment industry wanted to capitalize on. The magazines and television on the surface feed young people with vanity programs and the need for adoration. Unfortunately, Daphne fell prey to that."

"She is uncommonly beautiful,"

"Yes, like you."

Tia grimaced. "No. I look more like my father."

"A combination of both, but he was a very handsome man."

"Metta and I used to play this game we called MindStory as small children, which started as a dream we both shared. We even used to draw this diagram of it. Strange."

Cassandra gave Meraton a knowing look. "That's because you are both Pentada. Each generation of Pentada gets downloaded with the latest MindStory Code that runs the collective human mind of our genetic group. I had the same dream as a child. Although, like you, I didn't know what to do with it other than turn it into a game I played with anyone who would listen.

When Daphne and Annika were born, they had the same kind of dream. That's when I knew it was related to being Pentada."

"That's fascinating. But what exactly is a MindStory?"

The blackbird leapt off Cassandra's shoulder and onto the floor. They watched as he hopped over to Meraton's wolf, who lay sprawled out on the floor, asleep. The bird pecked at the wolf's snout until she opened her eyes in a daze. Tia expected the wolf to snap at the little thing, but instead, she curled her paw around the bird, and they snuggled close. Tia shook her head in amazement.

Cassandra didn't seem to notice the odd animal behaviour. It seemed as if their camaraderie was an everyday occurrence. "A MindStory is an actual energetic mass in the body-mind-soul system. The brain takes a snapshot of any experience a person has, especially an intense one. That snapshot might be called a long-term memory, but it is more complex than that. We call it a MindStory. It includes images, sounds, archetypal characters, plots, themes, motivations, and so on. We tell ourselves stories about what happens to us and what they mean, so each experience creates a MindStory which becomes encrypted as a holographic package of information in the neural networks of our brains.

When Daphne and Annika got older, we could discuss parts of the MindStory Code, but we all felt like something was missing. We suspected we only had two-thirds of the code and wondered when the next two Pentada would show up. You and Metta were clearly needed so that the code could finish downloading."

"So if we all have all these shared experiences, does it mean that we all have the same aptitude?"

"No, everyone's is different. That's on purpose."

"What's yours?"

"Mine is Tangent-Vision, meaning *The Soul Healer*. I do physical healing on the body by accessing soul records. My hands access the cellular information needed to bring the damaged cells back to the optimal state. Shall I show you? Maybe I can heal that bruise on your arm...with your permission, of course."

Tia nodded and held out her forearm remembering smashing it against the plane console as they dive bombed the crater.

Cassandra hovered her hand over the bruise, and within a few moments, it disappeared.

She touched the previously bruised area. "That's amazing!"

Meraton smiled. "We all have important lessons to learn with our aptitudes. Your greatest strength can be your greatest weakness. If you lack maturity or integration, you can cause destruction to yourself and others through your aptitude. For example, mine is Sentient-Reprogram, *The Emotional Engineer*. I can help engineer a profound emotional reconfiguration in a group. The dark side of this aptitude is emotional manipulation. When I was younger, I used to play a game that is similar to rugby on the surface. I found that if I manipulated the opposing team's confidence, we would win. For months afterwards, I had no confidence in myself at all. If I helped their confidence grow, so did mine. But the same also applies the other way around. You reap what you sow. In other words, only use your aptitude in service to others."

"What is the dark side of your aptitude, Cassandra?"

Cassandra frowned, "I can cause physical injury to others just with my mind."

Tia nodded. "And the dark side of my aptitude?"

"You absorb people's emotional energy, making yourself sick, or you can use your aptitude to fill someone else's mind with a negative feeling about the future."

Tia remembered feeling exhausted after many coaching calls with clients. She also suspected that she let her own worries for the future get embedded in other people's minds.

"Daphne's aptitude was Voyent-Reprogram, *The Magician*. This meant she could create visual illusions in the minds of others, which is maybe why she was attracted to modelling and acting. Here, those who camouflage the entrance to Helio Tropez are *Magicians*.

Annika was Audient-Action, that's *The Musician*. She could pick up any musical instrument quickly and hear people's true intentions, which she could reflect back to them musically. In Helio Tropez, people with her aptitude often take on the role of Exo-Communicators. They communicate with beings in higher realms where music is the common language."

"I'm guessing that would leave Metta as Ecrivent-Acceptance," Meraton added. "That is the aptitude of *The Poet*. Here, she would take on a role such as a Retorica, who writes poems, songs and stories that reflect truths that help others heal from the past.

Renolo, the Zuris Elder you met, is Ecrivent-Attention or *The Spellcaster*. He cast a spell to increase your mind's ability to comprehend the cycles of ascension. Because his devotion is to SANA, he asked permission first of your Higher Self. Many SIM agents with that aptitude on the surface get put into positions of political power so they can cast mind spells over large groups of people."

Tia breathed deeply to try and process it all, but confusion reigned. *And I thought my exams were hard...*

Meraton and Cassandra laughed, and Tia blushed, forgetting they could read her thoughts. Her grandfather put a hand on her shoulder.

"It's okay that you find it frustrating. All this information is kept hidden from surface humans. We have been studying the TEVAS-AVARA aptitudes here for thousands of years, and parts of it still remained a mystery. Let's give a quick example. Everyone has all of the TEVAS-AVARA aptitudes, but each of us has a dominant one. These are like archetypal programs within the human psyche or the roles we explore to build the MindStories of our lives."

"Addy says my aptitude is *The Inspirator*?"

Meraton waved his hand, and a screen appeared in front of them. "According to our sensors, you are indeed *The Inspirator*, or Sentient-Attention. It's the last one on the scale."

"The scale?"

"There are twenty-five aptitudes on an ascending scale, not dissimilar to a musical scale. You are the 25th which is the highest frequency. That means you can cross to other densities and dimensions more easily than others." He turned the screen towards her and said, "As The Inspirator, your top learning style is through emotions. As a Clairsentient, you emotionally inspire others to meet their greatest potential. You're very emotionally sensitive to others, but the negative side of this aptitude is that you can easily take on other people's emotional states and can undermine yourself and others by activating dark emotions that stunt growth. Emotions fuel all our actions, so by helping people envision a positive emotional state, you compel them forward towards a good outcome. Many great motivational leaders have this aptitude."

Tia thought about how all that seemed true, especially in relation to how she worked with clients. "What about my father?"

Meraton scrolled through the aptitudes until he got to another kind of Vision aptitude. "He is Voyent-Action, also known as *The Eagle Eye*. They have photographic memories."

"That makes sense," Tia murmured as she started to realise there were twenty-five aptitudes in total, five times five. *All those fives, again.*

"I believe the five Pentada together will offer the final understanding," Cassandra added. "You and Metta clearly had a piece to add to the puzzle, which your father installed in the amethyst. But the physical unification of Pentada will be the final activation we need for ascension."

She cast an uncomfortable glance at Meraton as she said, "I also believe the Progenitors were correct in saying that our next stage of evolution involved the integration of SIM and SANA rather than overpowering them. I know some people don't see how that could be true, but even from a young age I had the inkling..."

Meraton opened his mouth to say something, then seemed to think better of it and remained silent.

Tia was relieved to hear Cassandra felt that way, although she suspected that Addy might not follow the advice of the Progenitors. The thought she might just disappear at any moment chafed at her nerves.

Cassandra continued, "Some citizens of Helio Tropez disagree with the Progenitors, but not that many. You are safe here. We must hold the vision that Addy will do the right thing."

A tightness filled her throat as she tried to stifle tears. The experience in the Hall of Congress haunted her. She'd always longed for a place to call home, to feel like she belonged. Maybe she would survive and could find community with at least some of the people here.

"Your parents are heroes," Meraton said. "I know people blame them for leading SIM agents to the Quinary Mission members...but..." he looked at Cassandra then back at Tia. "Maybe the Progenitors *are* right. It was all meant to be. And, as Cassandra said, you and your sister contributed missing pieces of the new MindStory code. Your father somehow downloaded it into this amethyst. All four of you are heroes."

Tia basked in the idea that it was all meant to be, that all her father's years of sacrifice and struggle would one day pay off. An image of his lifeless body appeared in her mind. "In my time period, he's no longer alive. I can feel it." She swallowed hard to avoid crying.

Cassandra sat down next to her. "Let yourself feel the grief. It's very important to process your emotions. Don't let them stay stuck in your heart, in your throat, or anywhere in your body. This is your creative life force energy wanting to express itself."

Tia tried, but she couldn't do it. Her father had never liked displays of emotions.

"Your father was Voyent. They are more analytical than emotional."

Tia looked up and shrugged.

"You likely shut down your aptitude to appease him. May I help you?"

Cassandra held her hand a few inches above Tia's heart to help the healing process. "Perhaps a metaphor will help. Imagine these feelings like fuel that hasn't been processed yet, like wood for a fire. Put the wood in the fire using your power of attention. By letting yourself actually feel them now, you start an alchemical process whereby they begin to transform into creative fuel."

"That's so interesting. I tell my clients to do that," Tia murmured, her eyes closed.

At that moment, a burning feeling filled her chest, making her gasp. Cassandra's energy helped her keep a steady attention. A cauldron of energy started to move. It overwhelmed her at first, but she sensed they didn't judge her. Their compassion helped her melt the resistance, and the emotions lightened and dissolved into a state of quiet acceptance.

"That's good. Whenever you feel a build-up, and it gets too much, just practise with the metaphor. It's a simple technique but effective. As a Sentient-Attention, you need to process emotions regularly. Otherwise, you become a magnet for people's negative emotions. Once you are clear, you can intuitively sense those emotions in others, but you don't have to keep them in your system. Just learn to let them go. On the surface, people block emotions, which creates diseases. It's one of the ways SIM keeps people under control, and the negative energy feeds them.

"How long will it take to get me ready to face them?"

"That depends," Cassandra said, waving her hand across a nearby wall. A 3D screen filled with symbols and numbers appeared. "The results of our scan show that you've got embeds of cognitive modification at the physical, mental, emotional, spiritual and etheric levels. We'll need to help you remove those and start the activation of your Plasma Coded Matrix."

"My what?"

"Your original human genetic code is designed to manifest twelve strings of DNA, which allow inter-dimensional travelling and existence without the deterioration of the biological form. We are all in the process of activation, but yours need a lot of repair.

Once activated, it allows you to transfigure, transmigrate and translocate, which earns you cosmic citizenship. As a cosmic citizen, your consciousness will no longer be identified with Earth. You see, SIM entities consider people born on the surface as their property. As a cosmic citizen, they don't own you anymore. That's the goal."

"What does it mean to transfigure and all that?"

"You'll learn all that soon," Cassandra assured her. "We've enrolled you in the upcoming semester of the SANA Rosa School."

Tia wondered what they taught in a place like that.

"They will teach you how to work with energy and build on your aptitude."

She tried not to grimace. Having her private thoughts amplified and on show to everyone was starting to wear on her.

"The nourishment here will help rebuild your light body as well," Meraton said as he activated the replicator. Three plates appeared on the tray with round cakes filled with what looked like phosphorescent flowers. He brought them to a nearby table along with steaming cups of liquid."

"Please, let's eat."

Hunger pangs and a dry mouth compelled her to grab for the cake.

"Blessings first," Cassandra said, holding her hands over the food and drink. "Beloved presence of SANA, please bless all those who provided this nourishment. Open all light fibres in our being to be fully connected with the living light code so that this sustenance allows us to serve in the highest way possible."

Meraton and Cassandra bowed, holding their hands over the food. Tia tried to mimic them. She'd never been taught to bless the food, nor had she experienced any religious kind of practice. So she was left feeling both awkward and intrigued. The norms of these people were so foreign and complicated, making her feel more alien than ever. *Perhaps I'll never really fit in here.*

"You will learn," Meraton said encouragingly. "This is your true lineage, your true home."

Tia nodded, but the lack of privacy even in her own mind left her feeling exposed, like an open book for any passer-by to read.

Cassandra shifted in her seat. "You can block certain thoughts from others. Just intend for them to be private. We forget you don't know how yet. If someone is sharing their thoughts, it usually means the person wants them to be heard, so we pay attention. But the next time a thought comes up that you want to keep private, just intend it that way."

She nodded glumly and looked down at the cake, her mouth watering.

"Please, eat."

It looked like a delicate sponge cake but smelled more like roast turnips. As she took a bite, a taste of bitterness filled her mouth. She wanted to spit it out but thought that it might look rude. This time, she purposely marked that thought as private. She looked up to see if they had realised how she felt about the food. They didn't seem to notice. She chomped down on the rest of the cake, and a more pleasant taste filled her mouth.

"What is this?"

Cassandra smiled. "It's made of Lily of the Lake. Highly nutritious. We love them."

"Question. Did you telepathically pick up that I felt like spitting it out a moment ago?"

"No," she laughed. "You marked that thought private?"

Tia nodded and smiled with full cheeks. She swallowed. The spongy mixture filling her empty stomach. Soon, a wave of euphoria raced through her bloodstream. The steaming drink tasted like a latte and also seemed to nourish every cell in her body.

"Your taste buds will soon recalibrate to our sustenance," Cassandra reassured her. "Tomorrow, we will enrol you in the Academy."

After the meal, they bid her goodbye and disappeared through the teleportation device down the hall. Tia sat near the window, staring out at the glowing lights of the city. The room hummed soothingly. Even though the food soothed her stomach at first, she now felt the familiar indigestion and hives that plagued her life. It must be the stress of all the change, she thought. Crawling onto the bed, she wanted to look at more of her father's information so propped herself up on one elbow. Before she could reach for an envelope, however, heavy eyelids made her lie back on the unbelievably soft pillow. The intensity of the day melted away until she fell into a deep sleep.

CHAPTER 14

Hawaii – December 21, 1960

The sound of snoring jolted Addy awake. A hand hung right in front of his face. He tugged at it, startling awake his bunkmate, Trevor.

"What? What's happening?"

"You sound like a backhoe," Addy grunted.

"Too much to drink last night," he grumbled, rolling over and immediately resuming snoring again.

Addy kicked the mattress above him.

"Hey!" Trevor squawked. "Cut it out. My head feels like a vice."

Addy smirked, drifting back into a half-sleep in the hopes of returning to his dream. He dreamed of being in Helio Tropez for the first time, meeting his future self, and helping his future daughter escape. *So weird.*

A buzzer pierced his eardrums, and the men clambered out of their bunk beds, throwing on their fatigues and making their way to the latrine.

"What date is it, Trevor?"

"Date? You *must* have had a lot to drink last night. We head home for Christmas tomorrow. Can't call it a holiday, but it beats this place."

"So it's Christmas tomorrow?"

Trevor frowned, looking at him with concern. "Tomorrow's the 22nd, dumbass."

"Right," he said. "I knew that."

"Are you still planning on staying here, or are you going back to Seattle?" Trevor asked.

"Actually, I'd love to see my parents. I had a dream that they died... It was rough."

"Yikes. My dad isn't well, so I'm heading out first thing in the morning for Nebraska. This might be the last time I see him."

As Addy went about his morning routine, flashes of his intense dream kept filling his mental landscape. It all seemed so real. After his shower, he made his bed and tidied his possessions in anticipation of inspection. Amongst his possessions lay a duffel coat with strange fabric. He frowned. *This isn't mine.* Addy looked through the pockets for a wallet. Instead, he found a small gold box and a violet gemstone. It looked like Sugilite, the gemstone of the House of Violetta. He opened the gold box and inside lay a tiny twinkling amethyst. Puzzled, he looked around at the men busying themselves with preparations for the day. Flashes of his dream came back. In the dream, his future self gave him an amethyst to replace the one he'd lost. He ran his hand along the back of his skull, near his left ear. Nothing there. What about the Sugilite? An image of his grandmother, Halia, giving it to him at a wishing well came to mind.

Was he supposed to replace the amethyst with this one? What was the Sugilite for? He hurried into a bathroom stall and opened the gold box to fully examine the amethyst. In the dream, he remembered how to install it. He placed it on his finger like a contact lens and held it above his skull behind the left ear. It leapt off his finger and magnetised into place. An alert energy fizzed through his fingers. He went back to his bunk area, taking in the new sensations the amethyst had granted him.

He went about his chores for the day, but as more of them were ticked off, more and more pieces of the dream came back. Fragments at first, followed by whole sections. Only at the end of the day, as he was sitting on the edge of his bed, was he able to give each piece the attention it needed, lining them up to make a whole story. Once the last few pieces fell into place, he fell back on his bunk bed, reeling from the information.

Maybe his photographic memory overrode the Milk of Nepenthe, or maybe the Huperzia did, or the amethyst, or all three. He almost wished he didn't remember because now, the inner war started to eat him up. On the one hand, he needed to inform everyone in the Quinary Mission to go back to Helio Tropez. On the other hand, he needed to let the natural timeline play out. But now, he'd already changed the timeline by remembering. *And, what if the SIM agents can detect the amethyst once outside the box. Do I take it off? If I do, will I forget everything again?* Gritting his teeth, he decided to remove it from his skull and put it back in the box before hiding it in his locker along with the Sugilite stone.

He ran towards the mess hall to find the payphone just outside the back entrance. At the entrance, he nearly bumped into Col. Loman.

"Son, how are you doing today?"

Addy's eyes widened. This was the man his future self had told him to avoid. "I'm good. How are you?"

"Excellent. My wife and I are expecting you tonight for our little soiree. Ty Richards will be there."

Ty was an ace pilot that Addy had looked up to ever since he joined as a recruit. He desperately wanted to meet him and be like him one day. However, this was the night when the cognitive modification started. Once inside his mind, the SIM agents would begin to form a map of the exact location of all the Quinary members around the globe.

"I'd love to, sir. Just give me the address."

"I'll just come get you at around 6:30 PM. Wait for me out front here."

"Yes, sir! Thank you, sir."

The Colonel strolled off, lighting a cigarette as he headed towards his 1959 Chevrolet convertible.

A million thoughts raced through his head. *If I don't meet the Colonel at 6:30 PM, they will come looking for me. It's 2:30 PM. That gives me four hours. The next flight from Hawaii to Seattle leaves in three hours and won't arrive for another six hours. If I put the amethyst on, it could help me, but SIM agents could locate me more quickly. With the amethyst activated, I could cloak myself and more easily sneak onto one of the upcoming flights. Better yet, I could steal a plane again and fly home.*

Maybe I should call and warn them all... My parents could tap into the entire Quinary network and get the process rolling. I just don't want them to leave without me. Maybe I could steal a plane and go through the Hawaiian vortex again, but this time, go back to Helio Tropez. They don't want me back, though, and they wouldn't let me in. Or would they...

His head spun, and he had to sit down on the grass. He looked up at the payphone across the parking lot and decided he would call home. Even if they left without him, it would be better than not warning them. He jogged to the phone and realised he had no change. He called the operator and asked her to place a collect call to his parents in Seattle. As soon as they accepted the charges, he sighed with relief.

"Hadden?" his mother's voice said.

"Mom? You're okay!"

"Of course! Are you okay? You sound upset about something."

"No, I'm good."

"That's good to hear. We're just so sad you can't make it home for the holidays. You said they wouldn't let you leave... has something changed?"

Addy remembered how he cancelled going home and made other plans for the holidays to stay on the base and attend the local events. They were upset that he had joined the military, and he imagined being with them over Christmas would feel awkward.

"Yes, things have changed. I'd like to come home. I'll try to catch the first flight out."

"That's fantastic! Your father will pick you up at the airport. Just call us back with the time. We would have missed you so much not being here. By the way, could you bring home some of those macadamia nuts? We just can't find them here."

"Sure, mom. Sure. I'm looking forward to seeing you!"

"Me, too, darling. See you tomorrow!"

Just as she was about to hang up the phone, he said, "I have something important to tell you...."

"What?"

He hesitated for a moment because he wasn't sure if SIM could listen in on a phone conversation. Maybe he should tell them in person.

"You need to get..." The line went dead. "Mom? Mom!"

He called the operator again.

Due to high call volumes right now, we cannot connect your call. Please, try again later.

He hung up the receiver in frustration and searched his pockets again for change. Nothing. A staff sergeant walked by. "Excuse me, do you have any change?"

"No, sorry, mate." He was British and was one of the less stern sergeants on the base.

The dorms were ten minutes away. *Maybe there's change in my locker...* He set off at a jog, but it seemed to take forever until he eventually broke out into a sprint across the green. He stepped into the dorm to the sound of metal against metal. A soldier was prying open his locker with a crowbar.

"There he is!"

Two soldiers came towards him, and as he turned to escape, he bundled into the short, British staff sergeant. "You're not going anywhere, mate."

His dorm mates gathered to watch as they handcuffed him, and Col. Loman entered the dormitory. He held the gold box in his right hand. "This young man was caught with marijuana in his locker. We don't take kindly to that here. Take him away. Let that be a warning to the rest of you."

CHAPTER 15

On her first day of class, Cassandra showed Tia how to use the Volabus to get to the Academy. From the top floor of her building, they took a walkway to a platform high above the city streets. Matrix symbols indicated when the next bus would arrive. Cassandra pointed up as a flying bus swooped down from above and hovered in front of them. No fee was required to enter. Inside, people sat on floating chairs, carrying bags, all of them with a Jenio. The bus lurched back into the sky, giving Tia an entire view of the landscape below.

The city glittered against a backdrop of vivid green pastures, and mountains were enshrouded in mist. The sky glowed in hues of pink, blue and purple, but she detected no single source of light. It was like being in a room with continuous lighting from one end of the ceiling to the other. Looking up, she could see the faint outline of volcanic rock in a honeycomb shape with the occasional tunnel that spacecraft moved in and out of.

"There is daytime and nighttime here, but I don't see a sunrise or a sunset."

"We create artificial night and day through our technology to mimic the surface so that people's circadian rhythms remain balanced."

"Interesting. And are people on this bus going to work? No one seems rushed or stressed like they do on the surface."

"Not work as they define it on the surface. As a child, you discover your main creative calling, but you also have a calling to contribute to the well-being of society. For example, that man works about ten hours a week as a groundskeeper, which he loves. Another ten hours or so, he devotes to his creative calling, which is music and poetry. Being well versed in many of the arts is highly valued here. The rest of the time, he meditates and works on soul growth or goal manifestation. Today, he's meeting with friends where they engage in philosophical conversations."

Tia nodded slowly, a longing arising in her chest. "Sounds divine."

The SANA Rosa Academy stood in the centre of the city: a violet coloured pyramid that pulsed like a beating heart. The bus swept down to a station near the pyramid. Several people disembarked. Cassandra led Tia into a silent, see-through elevator that took them down sixty stories to the ground level. Weaving through the metropolis, each turn seemed more wondrous than the next. One shop prescribed gems, flowers and minerals for medicinal purposes. Another had fruits and vegetables in colours and shapes that Tia had never seen before. A third displayed harmonic healing devices and songs. A rainbow of flowers exploded from every nook and cranny.

Above the entrance of the pyramid, a giant symbol lay embedded in the crystalline structure. It looked like a cross with a circle on top. *I wonder what that's for*, Tia thought.

Cassandra just smiled. "The ankh provides power for the building."

Tia said nothing, nodding in amazement. As they entered the Academy, both excitement and dread filled her heart. She wore a silvery-green robe with her hair tied back in multi-coloured braids in the style of Helio Tropez, which helped her fit in. They entered into a foyer full of tropical birds like parrots and love birds, as well as squirrels, rabbits and other strange, small animals.

"Those are the Jenios of Heliotropans who are still too young," Cassandra said as she walked by without pausing. "They play and talk to the spirit of the child until he or she is ready to receive them."

A waterfall cascaded into a pool of floating lotus flowers, and the smell of Night Blooming Jasmine filled the air. Although Tia wore the traditional Heliotropan garb, people seemed to stare and whisper anyway.

"It seems like people are talking about me."

"They can read your energy as that of a surface dweller. We don't get many here, not for several hundred years. You also lack a Jenio, and they notice that."

"If I were born here, would I have my own Jenio?"

"Once you reach puberty, your Jenio finds you. I'm sorry you missed that experience as they provide great comfort and insight."

Disappointment pulled at her chest. A companion like that seemed wonderful.

They climbed a spiral staircase, and everyone stopped to watch them. Inside a circular room, they met a woman named Ostara. She invited Tia to step into a cylinder. It hummed and spun for a minute while Tia closed her eyes, feeling her pulse quicken. Once the process finished, Cassandra and Ostara studied the results, which appeared on a wall lit up with numbers and symbols. They conversed in Matrix.

"Ostara is placing you at Novice Level 3," Cassandra announced. "I'm happy about that. I thought you might be a pre-beginner, but you are more advanced than that."

The woman gave Tia a purple bracelet with Matrix symbols indicating her level to wear.

Next, they went to a man who sat at a high table with jeweller's tools. He removed Tia's amethyst from behind her ear and studied it. Two other Gemsmiths came over to look, obviously fascinated at what they saw. Cassandra and the man whispered to each other, then he put the jewel inside an enormous quartz crystal behind him. A humming sound filled the room, and the man stood up to operate a three-dimensional display hovering in mid-air, adjusting numbers until the process began.

"He's making a copy so that he can reproduce it for others," Cassandra explained. "He's also dialling up on your ability to speak Matrix and understand telepathy," Cassandra said, tying back one of Tia's misplaced braids. "Not many people here like to speak English. Using Matrix and telepathy will allow you to better connect with others."

Tia nodded, excited at the prospect. The man placed the newly recalibrated amethyst on an oyster shell and handed it back to Tia. He bowed his head in reverence with his hand on his heart, so Tia bowed back in the same way, unsure of the customs. Cassandra lifted up her hair as Tia hovered the jewel behind her ear. It magnetised to the same spot as before. Cassandra held her hand over it as if in blessing, making Tia soften under her motherly care. At that moment, loneliness and isolation dissolved, even if just for a short time.

"Let's get you started. Telepathy class is down the hall."

As they walked towards the room, Matrix words flew from her tongue as naturally as English. The language allowed her to more easily comprehend the intricate complexity of life in Helio Tropez in a whole new way, filling her eyes with tears of joy. "I love this!"

Cassandra said, "It's opened up your right brain. People on the surface read and write from the left brain, which disconnects them from SANA. We use Matrix when there is less intimacy between people or when addressing a group. Once you get to know a person individually, you can converse through telepathy. This first class that you're enrolled in will give you the basics of both."

As they walked down the hall, Tia became aware of the thoughts of some others nearby. Some were curious, and others felt invasive as if they were trying to pry into her mind. Tia put her hands over her ears.

Cassandra pulled her into an alcove. "If it's too much for you, just dial down on your receiver," she said as she placed her palm on Tia's forehead and closed her eyes. Soon, the noise died down. "Did you notice how I did that for you?"

Tia nodded. A metaphoric soundboard filled her mind, and Cassandra moved the volume up or down as needed.

"Now, you try it."

Tia imagined herself moving the telepathy volume down and back up again. She breathed a sigh of relief, grateful to have control over something in her new surroundings. They continued down the hall, and Tia kept the volume on low. As they entered the classroom, everyone turned to look. Students sat in floating chairs around the circular room, all of them looking under ten years old.

"It's just children in this class?" Tia telepathically asked Cassandra, keeping the thought private.

"They look like children do on the surface, but many of them are the same age as you in years. Since we live much longer lives here, our bodies mature at a much slower pace. People stay in school for up to seventy years."

126

"Seventy years?"

Cassandra grinned and nodded.

A teacher stood in the middle, using hand gestures to pull up and take down holographic images. She looked up at them and smiled.

"Everyone, this is Tia of Zuris, granddaughter to Cassandra and Meraton," the teacher announced, her long, blond hair sparkling as she tilted her head.

"Welcome!" they all responded in unison.

"Thank you. Carry on," Cassandra said, a gentle hand guiding Tia further into the room.

Anxiety rose in Tia's throat as Cassandra bid her goodbye. She settled into the child-size floating chair, and it tipped sideways. Tia grabbed the edge to steady herself, making the children burst into laughter.

A girl next to Tia, blue eyes glowing phosphorescent, showed her how to operate the chair for maximum comfort and stability.

"Tia has been brought up on the surface, so I'll ask you all to be patient with her. We'll start at the beginning, and even though many of you know all this, it will be a good recap. Telepathy is an umbrella term used to describe the ability to mentally receive and transmit information from one mind to another without any physical vocalisation. Right now, I'm using the Matrix Language because that is best in a group. Telepathy is a natural human skill, but SIM disconnected that ability in surface humans to better control them. That's why it's new to you, Tia."

Several of the children looked at her with sympathy.

"This next piece of information, I'm only going to send to Tia telepathically."

All heads swivelled again to see if she could 'get it'.

"You can communicate telepathically while awake, asleep, dreaming or through hypnosis." The meaning of this sentence entered into Tia's mind, not through her ears but from a deep inner knowing.

The teacher asked Tia out loud, "Can you repeat back in Matrix what I said to you telepathically?"

Tia cleared her throat, uncomfortable about being put on the spot and still amazed by her ability to form sentences in this new language. "Telepathic communication can take place while awake, asleep, dreaming or through hypnosis?"

"Exactly. Well done."

The children put their hands in the air, palms towards her, tilting them back and forth like a Queen waving at her subjects.

"That's our way of showing you appreciation and support," the teacher explained with a smile. "It's like what surface humans would call *applause*."

Tia nodded and forced a smile.

"The Matrix Language is the native consciousness language inherent within all of humanity throughout the galaxy. It is present within every atom, found in every element in the physical world. This is the language of our soul that communicates with all other levels of our spiritual bodies, and it naturally communicates with the consciousness of others. It includes thoughts, mental imagery and sounds, conveyed through spoken words that are translated into electromagnetic instruction sets that affect our light body, which helps us co-create our reality."

Tia struggled to comprehend what all that meant.

As if picking up on her confusion, the teacher turned her eyes on Tia. "SIM took away Matrix from surface humans because it unifies human consciousness and reconnects them to their galactic family. Instead, SIM created separate languages to better divide and conquer. Simplistic languages like English, or Japanese, or Russian create abstractions instead of allowing a 'felt' experience of life. You will find Matrix much richer to use."

Tia turned to look around the room. All eyes were on her. Finally, the teacher turned back to the hologram images, and Tia breathed a sigh of relief.

"Telepathy is easiest with your family members and your SANA mate; it's hardest with beings who are very different from you."

Tia had heard the term SANA mate several times now and wanted to know more.

The teacher nodded and smiled directly at her. "Once you are ready, you will become aware of who your SANA Mate is. Not everyone has one, but most do. This is a relationship that is very important for your evolution. When consummated in the right way, both souls evolve, and this synthesis of souls helps the collective consciousness evolve too. If you mate with someone who isn't your SANA Mate, it can impede your growth. One of your soul evolution goals is to become a synthesis of your parents' yet unexpressed purpose. We progress as far as we can in our lives, much like a relay race. You pass along your yet-to-be-developed potential to your children."

Tia thought about how they said her parents were not SANA mates and that SIM had a hand in her birth.

"Another name for a SANA coupling is a Hieros Gamos Union. It means the embodiment of the union between the human being and the divine. In Hieros Gamos Couplings, both agree to be of service to SANA's divine plan. Right now, these unions are particularly important to restore the natural ascension process on Earth. The coupling starts by activating the inner unification of masculine and feminine. When this happens, it triggers ascension, and the third type of being, called a Hermaphrodite, emerges."

Tia had always thought a Hermaphrodite was someone with characteristics of both genders. The teacher displayed Matrix symbols for the feminine and masculine principles. The image intertwined the two in a sacred geometric pattern.

"On the surface, when a child is born with features of both genders, they are considered deformed. This is not how we see it here. In some cases, those babies are actually in an evolved state. A Hermaphrodite is the union of Hermes and Aphrodite from Greek Mythology, or Mercury and Venus from Roman Mythology, the first and second planet from the sun. Their union forms an evolved consciousness known as Gaia-Sofia or Earth, the third planet from the sun. Our planet here is supposed to be a Hermaphrodite, but SIM blocked that process to maintain control. Since then, SIM has been trying to absorb the aptitudes of as many surface humans as possible, which puts those humans on a false ascension timeline. As the harvest of souls approaches," her teacher continued, "SIM wants to fool surface humans into artificial Hermaphroditism. This kills off the engine of organic evolution. Souls get harvested into the AI hive mind. In other words, we lose all the work we've done for thousands of years to perfect human genetics that can stay embodied in higher densities."

The teacher paused and stared directly at Tia again. Panic rose in her throat, and she wondered if they thought she was somehow responsible for the behaviour of SIM on the surface.

"One must also realise the difference between an *Activation* Mate and a SANA Mate. An Activation Mate has powerful chemistry and will help you grow spiritually, but you may have several Activation Mates that can be romantic or friendship in nature. In contrast, you only have one SANA Mate. It's a primary union between souls who have attained great insight through many lifetimes together."

Tia wondered if her parents had been just Activation Mates, not SANA mates. If their union was orchestrated by SIM, what did that mean for her life purpose? Was she being programmed on a subconscious level to help destroy the perfect human?

Contrasting images of Activation Mates versus SANA Mates danced in the holographic space above the students. Cassandra and Meraton said they were SANA Mates, and she envied their bond. *Did she have a SANA Mate here in Helio Tropez?* Faces of different men in Helio Tropez ran through her mind. She imagined herself with one particularly handsome man who worked as a builder, although he probably already had a mate.

"Be careful of false Activation Mates or SANA Mates – it's easy to project romantic fantasies onto them. Ask yourself: does your attraction come from an immature part of the self or from your higher self? On the surface, SIM continually tries to lure people away from their true couplings to block ascension."

Shame dampened her imagination, the handsome builder man completely dissolving from her mind.

"An Activation mate is there for your inner growth, and therefore, once the lesson is learned, the relationship often ends. A SANA Mate, on the other hand, is to provide value to the world. Once a SANA Mate relationship is in play, it's almost impossible to end or break it because you are brought together by divine purpose. Therefore, you only tend to meet them once you've matured and done enough of your inner work."

After the explanation, they moved on to discussing the nuances of telepathy and how the Matrix language was the diplomatic language of the galaxy. Once the foundations were explained, they practised for a short time. Tia was paired with a young boy who stared at her with a scrunched up face as he tried to share his thoughts; Tia was too distracted by his face to be able to receive his messages.

The teacher brought their attention back to the front of the room with the clap of her hands. "Alright, that's it for today, class. We'll meet again tomorrow."

As the children ran out of the auditorium, Tia followed behind and was last to leave. She walked in a dream state, mulling intensely on the lesson. Out in the city streets, she looked around, wondering if her true SANA Mate walked amongst them, but no one stood out.

I guess I just need to be patient, she thought with a sigh as she headed for the Volabus station.

CHAPTER 16

Seattle – 1948

"Addy, dinner!" Trace Violetta called from the front door. Wearing his Superman cape, he pretended not to hear and instead climbed higher up his favourite oak tree.

She tiptoed down the front steps barefoot. "Right now! It's getting cold."

He looked longingly up at the next branch, then back at his mother.

What to do?

She beckoned him again, and he grumbled under his breath. Reluctantly, Addy crawled along the branch then leapt onto the ground, landing on all fours. Grinning with glee, he put both hands in the air like an Olympic gymnast.

The next-door neighbour, Mr Blackwell, looked up from watering the lawn and gasped. "Are you okay, son?"

"Sure. Why?"

"That jump was about twenty feet! You could have broken a leg."

"It's no problem for someone like me!"

Mr. Blackwell pushed his spectacles up his nose and walked closer. "You're not hurt?"

Addy inspected the cleanliness of his cape. "Nope! Superman doesn't fall – he lands!"

Trace overheard the discussion and rushed over, ushering Addy into the house. Rand hurried down the front steps and made a B-line towards Mr Blackwell, reached out his hand.

"Glen! It's nice to see you." As he shook the man's hand, he kept his hold for a moment. "It's these new capes you can get; they slow down the landing."

He scoffed. "That doesn't make any sense."

Rand patted the man's back and laughed. "That's technology for you!"

Mr Blackwell's eyes went blank. Then he turned on his heel and went back to gardening.

Once back inside the house, Rand's easy-going smile fell as he turned to his son. "How many times do I have to tell you, Addy? You can't jump that far when the neighbours are around. You don't want to bring attention to yourself."

"I didn't know he saw," Addy sulked.

"You can do all the leaps you want inside the house with us but never in front of others."

Addy nodded and plodded into the dining room.

"You removed that experience from his memory?" Trace asked her husband.

"Yes, but his wife might have been watching us talk. You'll need to change the conversation in his head to, um…"

"…to rose pruning." Trace added. "I talked to him about that last week, so I'll just change it to a continuation of that conversation."

"Good. That'll work."

Trace peered at Mr Blackwell from the living room window with half-closed eyes. Addy untied his cape with great care and put it on the back of his chair. Trace finished her Audient Reprogram on the neighbour and disappeared into the kitchen before remerging a few minutes later with salad, soup and glasses of green water. As his father and mother said a blessing over the food, Addy remained silent. Trace glanced at him with pursed lips, so he joined them.

133

Addy slumped forward, holding his knife like a hunter while staring at the bowl of salad. "Why don't we ever have meat and potatoes like other people?"

Rand took a sip of the miso broth. "You know what those kinds of foods do to us. It pollutes our circuitry. Remember when you had some of Tommy's birthday cake and were sick for a week?"

Addy crossed his arms and sighed. "I guess."

"By the way, this evening, we have your Gem Smith lesson, which is very exciting."

"What? I said I would go to Simon's this evening. They just got a new television set!"

Trace poured the rejuvenation water into his glass. "No, we don't want you watching that thing. It's full of cognitive modification."

Addy knitted his brow and speared his salad with force.

His mother watched him but chose not to say anything.

"It's important that you learn a trade you can use to help us with our mission here. I know you want to play with your friends and be like them, but that's not what we signed up for," Rand explained.

"That's what *you* signed up for. I didn't sign up for anything!"

Trace and Rand looked at each other with concern.

Rand said, "You've always loved our lessons. Lately, you rebel against it all. What's going on with you?"

Addy shrugged. "Why did you come here if you aren't going to be with other people?"

"We do interact with people," Trace offered. "I volunteer at the orphanage, and your father works at Boeing. We talk with people all day long."

"But they aren't friends. You're just spying on them."

Rand glanced at Trace, and dropped his chin, "We're trying to help them make better choices. That's a very friendly thing to do."

"But, no one comes over here, we don't go to anyone else's, and I'm not at school like the other kids in the neighbourhood."

"We need to home-school you in our ways. The schooling here is not conducive with the way your brain is structured," Rand explained. "You would hate it."

134

"I'd love to at least give it a try. Please?"

"No, son."

"Maybe we should connect him more with the other children in the Quinary Mission?" Trace said to Rand.

"How? They all live in different continents, never mind different cities."

"Yes, but we connect with them telepathically. Many of their children are about Addy's age now. For several years, we've been talking about hosting a *Fete of Tropez* here in Seattle. Maybe it's time we tried it? It would be a rare opportunity to see each other face-to-face," Trace said, flashing her starry eyes at him.

Rand chewed the thought over with a mouthful of salad. "They warned us that could bring too much power together in one place, and SIM would notice."

"What if we go to Mount Rainier? Any anomalies might be seen as Heliotropan energies in the region rather than ours."

Rand nodded, not yet convinced.

They finished their meal, and the three of them cleaned up the kitchen.

Trace handed Addy a plate to dry. "I miss people, too. Especially our families back in Helio Tropez. But this is what we agreed to – it's a part of the sacrifice."

"What exactly did we sign up for?" Addy asked.

"We've told you this before. You forgot?"

"Maybe."

"Let's review it as part of your lesson."

Once the dishes were put away, Rand led Addy into the living room and sat him down on one of the couches. "A few years before you were born, the Elders chose five couples, one from every House, for the Quinary mission. It was a rigorous process, and only the strongest, most disciplined and committed were allowed to come."

Trace joined them, sitting beside Rand. "I remember when we stood waiting at the stargate portal to leave. It was so intense. The artisans of clothing and props buzzed around us, ensuring we were all set. Depending on what city we were going to, we received one piece of luggage with several sets of clothing of that era and geographic region. They programmed our amethysts with the language and accent necessary. For us, American English. We got our new driver's licenses, passports, clothing and toiletries. It all seemed so strange. For you, it's all normal because you were born here. But nobody needs identification in Helio Tropez."

"Why not?"

"Because we read each other's soul signatures. And the temperature is always just right, so we possess one or two pieces of clothing, and that's all we need. We don't need to brush our teeth because the food we eat cleans our teeth for us. The women don't put makeup on their faces because the air and the frequencies make everyone young and beautiful for hundreds of years. In the few years we've lived here, I'm getting grey hairs and wrinkles on my skin. When we go back, I'll look older than my own mother."

"When will we go back to Helio Tropez?"

"When the Elders tell us that our job is done."

"How will we know? Will they send a letter?"

"When Pentada activation happens. It was foretold that most of the Pentadas would be born on the surface. That's why so many of us are having children."

"Am I Pentada?"

"No, Pentada are always female. But Cassandra and Meraton have twin daughters who are both Pentada. Their names are Daphne and Annika, and they're close to your age. You will meet them if they come to the Fete of Tropez."

A flutter of excitement tickled Hadden's chest. The thought of other children his own age – children who were like him – seemed almost foreign. With people in Seattle, he had to pretend that he couldn't read people's minds or memorise the contents of an entire book in ten minutes or jump twenty feet from a tree without sustaining any injury. "So that makes three Pentada in one family, right?"

"Yes, Cassandra and both her daughters are Pentada. According to the Hall of Records, all Pentadas are often all born within one bloodline. The last generation of Pentada was all Violetta, like us, but this time, they seem to be all Zuris."

Addy sensed resentment in his mother's voice. "Is that how they chose the couples to send to the surface – based on their potential for creating Pentada children?"

"I guess that was part of the plan."

"Were you disappointed when I was born?"

"Not at all," Trace said, circling her arms around him. "The five Pentada have a central role in our mission, like the geese who fly at the front of the V-shaped. They create a corridor for the others to follow, but it's a much harder path."

Rand smiled. "Being a SANA mate is just as important. Pentada cannot activate without them. Maybe you will be a mate to one of those Pentada girls."

Addy wrinkled his nose, and Trace laughed. He never liked it when they talked about SANA mates.

Trace stood up and smoothed her floral dress, "I'll leave you two to the lesson."

Rand pulled out a portable hi-tech device from their safe behind a bookshelf. After firing it up, he pulled up the lesson plan onto the screen. "Where did we leave off last time? Oh, yes. Here we go. There are amethysts you get in Helio Tropez when you are born that help you better manage your aptitude, but we were given specially outfitted ones on the day we left for the surface. Can you remember how they are different?"

"They protect us from surface radiation and hide our wings and stuff," Addy said quickly, his excitement adding volume to his words.

Rand put his finger to his mouth and nodded. "And if you take off your amethyst?"

"SIM agents might see me on their radar scans and take me away," he said in a triumphant whisper.

"Exactly. And how do you tell if someone is a SIM agent?"

"They are from a SIM family."

"But what is a SIM family?"

"People who have sold their soul to SIM."

"Why did they do that?"

"Um, I don't know... Why?"

"For power, wealth, fame... to alleviate the pain of losing their connection to SANA."

Addy stood up. "Right!"

"And what do they do for SIM?"

He paced in front of the sofa to think. "They are vampire slaves!"

"Vampire slaves?"

"You know, like in my comic book series. Slaves who get the victims for the vampires."

Rand tilted his head from side to side. "I guess so, then. Similar to a vampire's assistant. They must keep feeding SIM with the life force energy of surface humans. Why?"

"Cause they aren't connected to SANA anymore."

"Good. So they must steal the SANA energy from those who are still connected to the source. But why would surface humans let them do that?"

"Cause they're dumb?"

"No, Addy. Because they are tricked into consent. Do you remember that, in your comic book, a vampire must be invited in before it can bite you?"

"Yes!"

"They trick people at the subconscious level to give up their power. And do you remember how they do that?"

"Um, the food, water, school... and..."

"And radio, television, music, movies, books, newspapers. They also send out frequencies that people are unaware of that disempower them. That's why we only want you listening to music using the Solfeggio Frequencies. They align you with the resonances of Gaia and SANA."

"But that music is kinda boring – just all floaty. What about Swing? You know... you can dance to it...the Jitterbug, the Jive!" Addy jumped up and showed off his dance moves across the wooden floor.

Rand couldn't help but smile. "Yes, that music is fun. But, there's plenty of upbeat music in the right hertz and frequencies. We have many options here. Just have a look."

Addy turned his head upside down, facing the sofa. "But no one else listens to that here."

"They would if they heard it. We try to introduce it to people at our work. The 12-Tone modern scale and 440 Hz in the popular music here creates boxed-in thinking and fear at the subconscious level. Not good."

Addy sunk back into the sofa with a grimace.

Rand beckoned him to sit back up straight. "All that said, you can ban SIM from cognitively modifying you. That's a universal law: if you don't want them there, you can resign from the programming. Your amethyst is programmed to help you do that."

"Okay, got it. When are you going to invite the other Quinary families here?"

"I actually don't think it's a good idea. We are only supposed to get together in the case of an emergency."

Trace overheard the conversation and stepped back into the living room. She sat down next to Rand and scrolled through to another site on the screen. "True, but let's just send out a message on the encrypted comm system. I sense that some of them are struggling and need support. Getting together could regather our strength and inspiration. It is a kind of emergency if we're *all* struggling."

Rand rubbed the back of his neck. "You can send out the message, but you better tell everyone to use cloaking while travelling. Maybe the energies at Mount Rainier will camouflage us once there."

"Agreed," Trace said, then typed furiously in Matrix and hit *send*. "I'll also send out the message telepathically and see if we can come to a consensus."

An hour later, Trace checked the comm again. "The other four families have all agreed to meet in July for the Fete! That's so exciting! Addy, you'll get to meet Daphne, Annika, umm... who else?"

"Forsel and his sister, Nancy," Rand pitched in. Although he had been opposed to the idea, the excitement was already building.

"Miriam and her brother, Michael, and then Rafael. There, seven other children your age that you can play with."

Addy sat back on the sofa and smiled. He'd seen pictures and heard about the other children, but he'd never met them. His mother didn't yet trust him using the comm device, but maybe after the Fete, she would let him keep up with them. He would finally have some friends with whom he could just be himself.

CHAPTER 17

For the first few months of being in Helio Tropez, Tia loved it there. People wanted to know about life on the surface, especially since they had lost contact a few decades back. She was learning quickly and embracing the culture she now found herself in. Life was so different, and she was keen to experience as much of that new place with an open mind.

Then one day at the Academy, all that changed. The teacher had chosen the topic of *emotions*. As a Sentient-Attention and a well-trained Life Coach, this was her area of expertise.

At one point, the teacher explained, "You should reject any form of negative emotion and stay in the lighter emotions at all times."

Tia raised her hand.

"You have a question?"

"A comment, actually. While I understand the benefits of positive emotions, the negative ones are there for a reason. If you process them, then you create the fuel for creative renewal. If you ban negative emotions, you can end up suppressing them, making them grow below your awareness, owning you and stagnating your creativity. You say that everyone here has a radiant, clear aura, but I see dark areas."

Tia heard audible gasps from the other students. The teacher's eyes narrowed. "That may be true on the surface because you have to negotiate around SIM, but here, we don't need that. You only see the darkness that is within you."

Tia's cheeks coloured as anger rose in her voice. "It might be a projection, but maybe not. Don't get me wrong, I love that Helio Tropez is beautiful, harmonious, safe and clean, with no homelessness. No one is starving here like on the surface, but, compared to the surface, there is blandness here, a lack of progression, and an underlying feeling of repression of the other side of human nature. The colours here are all in the higher frequencies, so there is no shadow, no contrast. From my perspective, it looks like a child's colouring book, without depth or the ability to propel someone forward on their soul journey."

Murmurs of disapproval spread through the auditorium and out into the telepathic airwaves like a virus. Suddenly, the teacher received a private message through her comm. After studying it, she looked at Tia and said, "End of discussion. I'll see everyone tomorrow. Have a lovely afternoon!"

That same afternoon, the Zuris Elders called her in for a meeting at the Palace. When Tia arrived with Amelia, Matrix symbols filled the screen containing a forum of comments about what had happened in Tia's classroom.

Geata turned to her and called the meeting to order. "Let us sit. Beloved SANA, please fill this space with the divine essence of righteous action so that we may resolve this situation in the light of wholeness, goodness and service to the one source. And so it is."

The white wolf at Meraton's feet emitted a low growl and flashed her blue eyes at Tia.

Meraton exhaled slowly. "What motivated you to say such a thing in class?"

Cassandra placed a hand on Meraton's knee as if to reign him in. "It's okay. You're Pentada. You see things… differently."

Tia looked from face to face, trying to choose her words carefully. "It's… it's… just that's my area of expertise. You know, emotions. I thought the teacher was leading people down the wrong path…"

Geata sat forward leaning towards her. "You don't fully understand our ways here yet to make such a comment."

"Maybe not, but it seems like there's no freedom of speech here. Do you never allow opposing opinions? How can you grow as a society if you don't? I mean…"

Meraton interrupted, "…of course we do. It's just that in this matter, we have our ways. Ones that have worked for a long time."

Cassandra placed a hand on Meraton's forearm. "Our ways don't always work. We must remember that Tia brings a fresh outlook to a society that has closed itself off for decades. She's *Pentada* after all."

Meraton pulled his arm away. "What do you mean by that?"

Cassandra stood up and paced the room, trying to calm herself down. Coming to a standstill at the head of the table, she looked around the table. "I mean…that I know what she's talking about. Every generation of Pentada incarnates to push the envelope of our society. I've felt at odds with many of the ways of Helio Tropez since I was young. I've just never chosen to say anything, waiting until more Pentada would incarnate so that… I don't know… they could back me up."

Meraton opened his mouth to say something, then thought better of it.

Renola crossed his arms. "So you think we should allow the negative emotions?"

"If they are experienced within the right container, I feel it's vital."

Geata and Renolo looked at each other, sharing a private telepathic conversation. Meraton frowned and focused his attention on retying a loose braid in his beard.

Finally, Geata turned to face them. "The Head of the Academy suggests we remedy Tia's point of view."

"Suggests or orders you?" Amelia asked.

Tia's blood pressure rose.

The blackbird danced on Cassandra's shoulder, whispering in her ear. She nodded and said, "I suggest that, instead of retracting your comment, you leave the Academy. I've been thinking about this for a while. We'll get you a private tutor. Malinah, the Librarian at the Hall of Records, has already volunteered. And, of course, I will offer some lessons from the Pentada perspective as well. Amelia can continue to help you with the cultural aspects of integration."

A slow smile crept across Tia's face. The three people she'd grown to love the most would be her teachers.

The Elders reluctantly agreed, and Tia left the meeting feeling a new sense of expansion and lightness in her chest.

In the following weeks, Amelia and Tia met up on the high street and walked together to The Hall of Records to talk and share ideas each day. This helped build her confidence before embarking on her studies for the day with Malinah.

One day, Tia and Amelia passed a sign that said *Niklana – Oracle*.

Tia stopped and looked up at the domed dwelling that looked like a miniature turquoise mosque. "I've been walking by this sign for months. Do you think Niklana could predict our SANA mates?"

Her Jenio butterfly, the size of a small bird, sat on Amelia's shoulder and whispered something in her ear. "Gyal says we shouldn't go in. She's not always correct in predicting SANA mates, so you could end up chasing after the wrong person. You are supposed to use your *own* intuition."

"What's the harm in just asking her?" Tia said.

"Maybe a SANA mate isn't part of our destiny."

"It is for me. I sense that he exists, but I just don't seem to ever meet him."

"Maybe he doesn't want to be found."

Tia frowned and looked at her. "What do you mean?"

"The men here are a bit afraid of you."

"They're afraid? I thought they just looked down on me."

"Maybe that, too, but that's just their ignorance. I know how great you are."

A sharpness grabbed at Tia's chest as she noticed luminescent flowers running alongside the walkway. While the beauty of the surroundings in Helio Tropez amazed her, she felt socially isolated. "As much as I love your counselling and friendship, you don't have to hang around with me at social gatherings. It might be blocking your chances of finding your mate."

"I don't think that's the problem," Amelia said with a sigh.

"Then what?"

"I'm not meant to have a mate. I might be destined to be a Sanasta. Maybe you are, too."

144

"Do you mean one of those women in the blue gowns who pray all the time?"

"Yes," Amelia said, sitting down on a low wall made of stones. "They use all their creative energy in partnership with SANA to grow the collective spirituality of the society as opposed to using their creative energy to give birth and grow children."

Tia sat down next to her and smelled one of the flowers. "That's not for me. It's my understanding that I actually can't fully activate as Pentada without my SANA mate. I also *want* to have children."

"I kind of want that too..."

"Let's find out," Tia said, pulling Amelia by the hand until they reached Niklana's front door. Before Amelia could argue, Tia had already pressed the comm button, and a face had appeared on the console. Niklana looked kindly and slightly rotund, unlike most of the svelte women of Helio Tropez.

"Niklana? Hello. So, good to meet you. We were hoping −"

"I know why you are here," she said briskly, cutting her short. "Please, enter."

The door opened, welcoming them into a patio area looking over a garden of violets with lush ferns and a pond filled with blue-green ducks and a school of fish that swam in gentle circles. She welcomed them silently and gestured for them to sit with her on chairs next to the pond. A creature looking like a miniature polar bear jumped up onto the woman's lap and curled up in a ball to sleep.

Niklana wore her silvery hair in a high spiral cone, like many of the Elder women. At the tip of the cone, she had a silver beacon used to enhance her Voyent-Vision aptitude, also known as The Divinator. Holographic images of people, young and old, floated in a circle overhead. Tia swivelled her head to look at them.

"Those are my family members. At least 600, all descended from me. Imagine? That's what happens when you get to the ripe old age of 844." She reached towards a nearby replicator, and a bowl filled with treats appeared. Then she placed it on a low table in front of them. "Please, have a Bemint cup."

Tia had grown to love the food in Helio Tropez, particularly the Bemint cup, which was the closest thing to an ice cream sandwich. The two young women savoured the exotic treat that tasted like a combination of carob and liquorice. After they finished, Niklana waved her hand in the air, and a pyramid-shaped crystal about the size of a basketball appeared before her. She touched the top of her cone and half-closed her eyes as she focused on the crystal.

"Amelia, I sense you are destined for the life of a Sanasta, as you suspected. You *can* mate with someone, but as a Sentient-Acceptance or The Therapist, your greatest gift is unconditional love. When you take your vows and give that love to SANA, your devotion is so powerful that you don't look back. That's why many people with your aptitude have taken their vows."

The young woman slumped back in her patio chair. "I thought so."

"My great-great-granddaughter became a Sanasta when she was even younger than you. She never regretted it, not even for one single day."

They talked for a while about the daily life of a Sanasta, and Tia thought it actually sounded appealing. By the end of the discussion, Amelia seemed to have softened to the idea.

"All that said," Niklana added, "you must meditate on this yourself and talk with your family before making a decision."

She nodded and appeared relieved to have more background on the whole process.

"Respite Tea!" Niklana said to the replicator. Three steaming bowls of blue liquid materialised on a nearby counter. She moved with the grace and ease of a young person. Most Heliotropans remained fit for hundreds of years, doing a combination of conscious breathing, martial arts, callisthenics, yoga and qigong. They called it Tangency.

"Are you two young ladies going to the Fete of Tropez?"

"Yes, our House of Zuris team has been rehearsing our dance for weeks," Amelia said.

Tia couldn't participate in the flying part of the festival because she had no wings, at least not until she fully activated her ability to operate in 4th density consciousness. Since she grew up on the surface, it could take a while.

"I'm part of the ground crew. And you?" Tia asked.

"I'm one of the judges."

They talked for a while about past festivals: who had won, who had lost, and past themes. Finally, Niklana said, "Thank you so much for coming to visit. I must now prepare for Tangency."

"What about me?" Tia asked, alarmed. "Do I have a mate here in Helio Tropez?"

"I'm so sorry, dear. I'm not very good at reading surface dwellers."

Tia furrowed her brow.

Niklana sighed and closed her eyes for a moment. "I sense your primary SANA mate has no soul signature. He has passed on to another dimension. I am so sorry."

"Maybe he lives on the surface without a soul signature?"

"Perhaps. If he is a descendent of a Quinary family…"

Niklana entered a trance for a good five minutes. Finally, she drew glowing symbols in mid-air that Tia recognised as an aptitude, a family lineage and a birth date.

"What I can tell you is that he is Audient-Reprogram, from The House of Indicum, born on August 10, 1980."

Tia seared that information into her memory banks. "Anything else?"

"If he has survived without his soul signature and is living by his aptitude, he will be involved in a profession using sound to reprogram mind codes. I'm afraid I can't give you any further answers; anything else would be speculation."

Amelia shifted in her chair. "Remember, in the end, you and your SANA mate both need to decide for yourselves and not go by birthdates."

"Agreed, although I'm almost always correct," Niklana said as she ran her fingernails between the ears of the small bear on her lap. It made a happy grumbling sound that made the woman chuckle.

Tia watched the fish, wondering if she had any chance of ever meeting her partner. "It seems like most people here meet their SANA mate as children."

"Our intuitive abilities are the highest before eight or nine. They often meet on the playground and just know."

"So they get married as children?"

"Goodness, no. In fact, they are encouraged to date others after puberty, but by their thirties or forties, if they want to have children and want to ensure a smooth ascension, they need to couple with their SANA mate."

"Women can have children in their forties here?"

Niklana gave a knowing glance to Amelia and chuckled, "Of course. Women here give birth well into their four hundreds."

"Four hundred years old? Does that mean they have hundreds of children?"

"Oh no. SANA tells you how many children to have, if at all. It's not usually more than three, all birthed a few years apart."

Relief washed over Tia, knowing that if she stayed in Helio Tropez, the window of opportunity for having a child was hopefully far greater than on the surface.

Another miniature polar bear hopped up onto an empty chair and sat blinking at Tia.

"Goodness! What are *you* doing here?" Niklana said. "This is Wimba's brother, Bimini. He normally lives in the woods, and I rarely see him. He comes down every few months, but it's been a long time since I last saw him." She offered her hand to the bear, but it ignored the elderly woman. Instead, the bear clambered into Tia's lap and padded in a circle before dropping heavily and began grooming his paws. Tia stared at the bear, her hands held in the air before she glanced at Niklana and Amelia. The two women burst into laughter.

"Well," Niklana said, "Say hello to him!"

Tia gently lowered her hand and stroked the back of his neck. "Um, hello Bimini. It's nice to meet you…" His fur was soft as silk, and she relaxed into the touch. Bimini settled with his chin on his paws and began to purr. She didn't know bears could purr.

Niklana slapped her knee and stared. "He's never done that before!"

"What do you mean?"

"Sat on a human's lap."

Amelia stroked Bimini's head. "Are you Tia's Jenio?"

Niklana shook her head. "Unlikely. Jenio connections rarely happen past the age of six or seven."

Tears stung her eyes, but she quickly blinked them away. Not having one made her stand out. "I don't really understand why people have Jenios..."

Niklana looked into Wimba's round shimmering eyes and smiled. "Your Jenio gives you access to Earth-based wisdom. Jenios operate in the 2nd density world and bring back important information that we can't sense. For example, changes in weather, ley line frequencies and Earth vortexes can all be picked up on by our Jenios. They protect our souls and understand the emotional nature of a situation at a deeper level than we usually can."

Amelia held her butterfly high in one hand. "You talk to them telepathically once you've established a bond. Gyal, show them how handsome you are." The butterfly fanned his wings to display phosphorescent blues and greens. "In many cases, your Jenio knows something isn't right before you do."

"How can I tell if this... Bimini... is my Jenio?"

"When you and your Jenio first meet, you both just know it at a gut level. It feels instinctually right."

Tears welled up in her eyes as she remembered a childhood memory. "My uncle gave me a white teddy bear that looked just like Bimini. I was bonded to that bear for years. Maybe he knew about Jenios. But... how could he?"

Amelia's butterfly fluttered onto her shoulder and whispered something to her. "Wasn't your father an only child? How come you had an uncle?"

"Leo Burres wasn't my real uncle, just my father's business partner."

"Burres? He's from a SIM family? I wouldn't trust any gift from him."

"It's strange because I do trust the gift, but I never remember him being kind to me or bringing me gifts until now. Why would I remember that now? Unless..."

"Unless?"

Tia's eyes widened at the sudden realisation. Addy must have changed the timeline after all, and that had positively affected her relationship with Leo Burres. Some of her other memories were changing, too, or maybe she was just imagining it. She didn't want to say anything to Amelia or Niklana since changing any timeline was highly controversial in Helio Tropez. "I don't know. Maybe it was just a dream."

Bimini looked up at Tia with glassy eyes, the connection ringing as true as the one with her childhood bear.

With closed eyes, Niklana said, "Bimini says he wants to be your Jenio. He sensed your presence his whole life, but somehow, you were not picking up on his messages."

"I was never told about Jenios on the surface, nor anything about Helio Tropez."

Amelia sipped her Respite Tea. "If you don't connect with a Jenio as a child, you usually never do for the rest of your life."

"Except for one visitor from the surface a few decades back," Niklana tapped her chin. "He found his Jenio here as an adult. Did you hear about that, Amelia?"

"No. Never."

She frowned, trying to recall the event. "He was a tribal elder living on the surface. He went into a deep trance while fasting on Mount Rainier, and his intuition led him through one of the lava tubes until he found us. He stayed here for about a year, then went back to the surface and became a shaman healer. I remember, a few months after he arrived here, a jackrabbit appeared at his feet one day and became his Jenio."

"Did the jackrabbit follow him back to the surface?" Tia asked.

"No, Jenios know better than to risk losing their soul to SIM."

Tia shivered at the thought.

Niklana patted Tia's hand. "There is a way to test it. Leave my home and see if he follows you."

Tia nodded and gingerly lifted the small bear and placed it down on the ground. He sat back on his haunches, sniffed the air and grunted. Amelia and Tia tiptoed to the front door and waved goodbye to Niklana and the two bears. Bimini looked at her crossly but never moved. As the door slid shut, Tia felt a wave of grief fill her heart. They ambled down the street in a daze at what they had just experienced.

"I guess he wasn't. That's too bad. He's so sweet."

They stopped at a crossroad to say goodbye to each other when Tia felt silky fur brush against her leg. Bimini looked up at her with big, round eyes.

"You followed me!" Tia whisked the bear into her arms, kissing him on both cheeks. "Are you my Jenio?"

Amelia tickled his ear. "I thought so! He just had to think about it for a moment, didn't you?"

The bear snuffled the air and dipped his chin in a curt nod.

"He knows what we're saying?"

Amelia laughed. "Of course. Jenios are not like pets on the surface. In fact, he will often know what you need long before you do. Also, they don't eat, so you don't need to feed them. They live off planetary Chi or life force energy."

"Amelia!" a young woman called out. "We need to rehearse for the Fete. Where have you been?"

"Oh, I'm sorry. Where is it?"

"In the Shamon Field."

Tia backed away from her. "Have fun."

"Come watch! You're on the ground crew, right?"

"That's what Cassandra said."

As they walked down the street, Bimini remained cradled in her arms. By having a Jenio, she finally felt like she fit in. Once they were at the field, Amelia skipped over to join her team as Tia took a seat on a bench with Bimini to watch.

Amelia came from the House of Zuris, so when her wings unfolded to full size, they sparkled white. The others unfolded their wings to reveal all the other colours of the rainbow, at least those in the upper frequencies. Each person loaded a pouch strapped to their hips with sparkling dust of their respective colour, which they would use to paint the year's theme in the air.

The choreographer, Helena of Liven, gave them a pep talk. "As you know, in the Heliotropan calendar, each year represents a different crystal gemstone. Last year, when we danced Flourite, the House of Viridis led the choreography. This year, it's Lapis Lazuli, so they chose me to lead the dance. Next year is 2012, the year of ascension, so it will be Amethyst. Fresco of Violetta will have the lead, but until then, you're stuck with me," she said jovially. "The air dance of Lapis Lazuli must invoke the spiritual growth necessary for ascension. We need to inspire open-mindedness and honesty to self and others this year. Let's say our blessing and explore what wants to be expressed."

151

They bowed in blessing and then shot off into the sky one by one. Tia sat back on the bench in amazement as they circled each other, creating patterns and symbols with their coloured dust, like Tinker Bell in the Disney movie. Tiny particles of colour sprinkled down onto the grass in precise formations. *How could they do that?*

A voice from behind made her jump. "I'm so sorry. You'll have to leave," Helena said.

Tia swung around to face her. "But I'm part of the ground crew. Shouldn't I watch?"

"We have enough ground crew. This is for people born here only."

"But I am a descendant of The House of Zuris. Cassandra is my grandmother."

"I honor Cassandra as Pentada. But you were born on the surface to parents mated by SIM, not by SANA. You don't belong here, and you're not welcome at my rehearsal. Please, leave."

"I've been purified."

"We don't know that for sure. SIM's corruption is not straightforward. You're a risk to every single one of us here, and while I'm the lead of this performance, these people are under my protection. I won't ask again. Leave!"

Tia bristled, and so did Bimini. The words stung. Despite herself, Tia turned on her heel with a snarl, not saying a word. As she walked back to her chamber, fury bubbling in her, Bimini tottered along behind her. He made a short barking sound, and Tia scooped him up and to her chest. Bimini snuggled into her neck, comforting her.

So much for open-mindedness, she thought. Going back to the surface now seemed more attractive, especially if it meant meeting her SANA mate.

Back in her chamber, Tia saw a message left by the Zuris Elders. They wanted another meeting right away. She walked over to The Palace with Bimini trundling along next to her. As she entered the room, all four Elders stood up and applauded in their Heliotropan way.

Geata closed her eyes and smiled, holding her arms wide. "Thank you, SANA, for reconnecting our beloved Tia with her Jenio. Today, we sing our praises for this reunion and welcome Bimini into our circle of wisdom."

The group chanted a song of gratitude that Tia now knew the words to, so she sang along. Meanwhile, Bimini purred on her lap, soaking in the good vibrations from the group.

After the final note, the group crowded around her to meet the new Jenio.

Renola patted his head. "You're a fine Piccolorsa."

"Piccolorsa?" Tia asked.

"That's the name for this breed of miniature bears. They used to live on the surface several thousand years ago but went extinct, except for the few we saved."

"Bimini, the Piccolosa."

Cassandra smiled. "We never thought you'd find your Jenio as an adult, so it's truly a blessing. He will help you in ways you cannot even begin to imagine."

Tia smiled, the unpleasant interaction with Helena starting to dissolve away. They took their places in the floating chairs that formed a semi-circle around the screen while Bimini wandered the room, sniffing and investigating.

Meanwhile, Cassandra pulled up a plan in Matrix symbols on the screen. "Let's begin our meeting. We've decided to create a Task Force to study the new MindStory Code and help people integrate it. It's the code downloaded by all of Pentada that your father put into the amethyst. You will be on the Task Force, Tia, along with me, Meraton, Malinah and Amelia."

Malinah pulled up Matrix symbols representing all five members of Pentada. "Its physical structure is incomplete without all Pentada physically united, but we need to consolidate what we have to prepare for that."

Cassandra looked at Tia. "What was it that you did on the surface? You called it *coaching* but not like an athletic coach, right?"

"It's like counselling, except we don't reinforce past stories of limitation like many psychologists and counsellors do. Instead, we help empower people to believe in their greatest potential. We help people break free of limiting beliefs so they can have better lives in many areas, like health, relationships, finance, career, business, and spiritual purpose."

Cassandra waved her hand over the screen until a new document appeared. "Doesn't that remind you of the telepathic interfacing work we used to do with surface humans a long time ago?" Cassandra asked the group, who nodded in reply.

"Why don't you do that, uh, 'telepathic interfacing' anymore?" Tia asked, surprised.

"We gave it up because no one seemed able to hear us or act on the message in a meaningful way."

Cassandra pulled up another set of records. "Ever since the Great UnDoing, it looks like no one tried interfacing with surface humans. We completely lost touch."

"As we learn more about the new MindStory Code, we can help people integrate it with this *coaching* thing practice of Tia's, not only with our citizens but with any of the surface humans who will listen."

"SIM will block that," Renolo warned.

"Previous generations got past SIM on several occasions. It helped many of our surface humans ascend to 5D, so it's worth trying."

"I wouldn't say *many*," Renolo corrected her.

"Okay, some did. But even if we only reach some, it's better than ignoring them completely."

"True."

"Let's call it The Coaching Task Force," Cassandra suggested. "Tia can help select and teach the volunteers how to do it."

The Elders agreed. Finally, having an important role in this subterranean society filled her with a sense of purpose.

Over the next three weeks, they set up interviews with potential coaches who would also act as researchers. They needed to find one representative from each aptitude. On the first day of interviews, Tia sat with Meraton, Cassandra, Amelia and Malinah at a round table in a conference room. Her hand trembled, not knowing how to assess people and not sure if the others would see her as a capable leader.

Jaya Livens entered wide-eyed and formally greeted them all by bowing and touching her hand on her heart. On the screen, Tia read that Jaya was an Ecrivent-Vision, which was also known as The Prophet. It made sense that she wrote editorials on future predictions for the Heliotropan News. Although she looked in her twenties, she was born in 1907. Tia peered at her discreetly, trying to see any signs of ageing in the woman who was over a hundred years old, but her face seemed flawless. Cassandra nodded to Tia to begin the interview.

A bead of sweat trickled down the back of her neck as she spoke, Matrix coming to her as naturally as though it were her first language. "Jaya, welcome. Thank you for applying. I think you know everyone here?"

"Yes. I'm so honoured to be here."

"I see you have travelled to the centre of the planet, to Agartha, on a few diplomatic trips."

Jaya nodded. One of Tia's classes had been on the structure of the Earth's crust; she was taught that the outer core of the Earth was structured in a honeycomb of caves, some as big as Texas. The interior of the planet was hollow and had a central sun, several continents and oceans. They called the interior Agartha. For thousands of years, Heliotropans regularly sent a diplomate to visit the various nation states to share ideas and keep the peace. Jaya held that role for thirty-four years before the Great UnDoing in 1961, when Helio Tropez cut themselves off from Agartha. Rumour had it that SIM had infiltrated certain groups in Inner Earth.

"I see you now write a beautifully poetic column in the news. It's about helping us see how the collective consciousness of humans on this Earth is evolving. Are you thinking of leaving your role to pursue this one as it will be a serious time commitment?"

"Yes, I would like to try something new. I think I'm ideally suited to this role on the Task Force since I've been monitoring our collective mind codes for several years now."

"Your record says you were born in 1917. Did you ever do any interfacing with surface humans before the Great UnDoing?"

"I did try, and I made some progress up until the Second World War. Both my humans died in battle. I was heartbroken to lose them as they showed such great promise. That's another reason why I want to be part of this Task Force. Those two souls have reincarnated into the same bloodline, into the same genetic experiment, and so it will be easier for me to make contact with them."

"We'll make a note of that on your file. Your psychological assessment shows that your telepathy skills are in the 90% range, which is important for this role."

"Yes."

Choosing Jaya gave Tia a sense of peace. "Do you have any questions for us?"

"Will we get any training for this role?"

"Yes, I will be leading the coaching training, along with Cassandra and Meraton, as we are the only ones with direct experience with surface humans. Malinah and Amelia will be heading up the research aspect. Do you have any issues with that?"

"Not at all. I respect everyone on the team."

"Even me?"

Jaya frowned and glanced at the Zuris Elders, "Yes, of course. I'm a big supporter of yours."

Relief filled Tia's heart. Although she telepathically felt the support of many Heliotropans, those who disliked her presence had affected her confidence lately, and it was reassuring to know that those on her team had her back and respected her.

As Jaya thanked the panel and bowed a final time before heading for the door, a flicker of excitement sparked in her chest. This was her team, and it was going to make a difference to the world. Pride swelled in her chest, and she looked to the others with a grin before welcoming the next candidate into the room.

Three months later, twenty-five members of The Coaching Task Force appeared before the Elders at the Hall of Congress.

Malinah stood at the centre of the stage. "As you know, we interviewed over 100 applicants before settling on a total of twenty-five people for The Coaching Task Force. We have one representative from all twenty-five aptitudes. Within our ranks, we have a representative of every House, almost all professions, and an equal gender balance. Tia of the House of Zuris has shown great leadership by inspiring our team to action. With the help of Cassandra and Meraton, she is teaching us how to handle almost every kind of surface human issue. We have built empathy and broken down our previous prejudices. Many people on the surface from our genetic experiment are waking up."

Yeelay interfaced with the other Elders, then took the spotlight. "That's all very good to hear, but our Hall of Records still doesn't record anything happening on the surface. How do you account for that? And how do you know that people are awakening? We are only months away from the Harvest."

"We don't know why the Hall of Records won't record surface human activity. It's strange. We have a good connection with approximately forty-four people."

"Only forty-four? There are probably hundreds of thousands of people in our genetic experiment. This will not go down well with the Progenitors."

"We hope these forty-four will become positive deviants."

Yeelay looked at the older Elders quizzically, then back at Malinah. "What is that?"

"Tia, why don't you explain?"

Tia took the spotlight, her heart racing. "Within any community, some people have uncommon abilities, helping others find better solutions to problems. Given the right circumstances, they can create a ripple effect in the collective consciousness of those in their genetic subset. These individuals are referred to as positive deviants."

"Do you have enough of these positive deviants yet to create the desired effect?"

"No, but they exist within separate communities. Once the ripple effect comes into play, it'll spread to other communities, and the rate at which it spreads will multiply rapidly."

"Would it help if more Pentada members were involved in the Task Force?"

Tia looked at Cassandra. They both knew that was the case.

Yeelay interfaced again with the Elders, and the group remained silent as they waited. "We've decided that Tia should return to the surface within two weeks to find the other three Pentada and bring them back here to complete the task."

Tia looked to Cassandra, suddenly panicked. The other Task Force members looked concerned, sharing whispers between them.

Yeelay continued. "You will formulate a plan for how she will locate them and how she will bring them back to Helio Tropez. The artisans in the Replicator shop will create the kind of identification documents they now use on the surface. You must know what those are, Tia of Zuris."

"Sure," she stammered. "Passport. Driver's License."

"Good. Choose a different name and ensure they provide you with enough currency for whichever country and period you're landing in."

Meraton stood up. "Do you really think she's ready?"

"We have no choice. Time is of the essence."

Lines wrinkled across his brow. "I suggest she doesn't go back to Seattle as too many people would recognise her. She could start in Montreal. That's where we lived, so we can direct her better around the city. Besides, the algorithm points to this city as having the best chance at reaching our goal. Is there a way to set up a comm system with the Task Force?"

Ramu, a Task Force member with Gem Smith training, said, "We could create a comm in her amethyst that can't be detected by SIM, but we're going to need to work around the clock to get it ready on time."

Meraton stood, suddenly too tense to remain seated, and started pacing in front of the Elders. "When we immigrated to the surface, the artisans made clothing and luggage for that era and geographic region. Do you know how you should dress for Montreal in 2011?"

Tia nodded. "It's probably no different from Seattle in 2010. I can tell them what to make me."

Two weeks later, The Coaching Task Force gathered around Tia at the stargate platform. Bimini wasn't allowed to go with her, so she handed him to Amelia, a look of concern etched across his fuzzy face. Three of the coaches flew up into the sky, painting the words, "We love you."

She swallowed past the lump in her throat as she hugged each person goodbye. None of them acknowledged it, but the worry was visible on their faces. They bowed to her in reverence as she stepped onto the platform. No one knew how or if she would ever return.

CHAPTER 18

The Fete of Tropez fell on the weekend of the Fourth of July, a highly celebrated date in their community. Tropez was the name of a Progenitor who had seeded their community on the interior of planet Earth, and as part of the celebrations, they revered him and thanked him for founding the city.

Being at the lodge near Mount Rainier allowed them more access to the energies from Helio Tropez. Trace decided they would do their own version of the festival by bringing large sheets of paper and watercolours so they could paint together.

Addy studied the guest list as his mother organised the details.

1. Cassandra and Meraton of Zuris with their two daughters, Daphne and Annika, from Montréal.

2. Bertrand and Magdalena of Liven with their son, Forsel and daughter, Nancy, from London, England.

3. Lorena and Ben of Indicum with their daughter, Miriam and son, Michael, from Sydney, Australia.

4. Maria and Bruno of Viridis with their son, Rafael, from Rome, Italy.

5. Trace and Rand of Violetta with their son, Hadden, from Seattle.

"It looks like there will be four of us boys and four girls. Do you think they'll like me, or will they think I'm strange like most people do?"

"I'm sure they face the same issues in their cities, and they will appreciate your uniqueness," his mother reassured him.

That night, he dreamt of flying and colouring the skyscape with his Heliotropan friends.

A few months later, all five families made the journey to Mount Rainier National Park to stay at a place called the Paradise Inn.

They were the first family to arrive, and as soon as the engine silenced, Addy was out of the door. He made a sweep of the grounds, noting the playground and picnic benches nearby. As his parents unpacked the car, Addy wandered further afield, exploring the forest nearby. Pine needles cushioned his feet as he stepped between trunks, peering up at the branches as he tried to see their peaks. *I like it here,* Addy thought to himself with a sigh, the scent of pines filling his lungs.

He was trotting back to the lodge when a hint of blue caught his eye. Crouching at the base of a fir tree, he picked up two stones and held them in his palm, each one as blue as the ocean on a clear day. They felt rough under his thumb, but as his fingers closed around them, he felt an energy coming from them like a gentle warmth pressing into his skin. A smile touched his lips, and he slipped the stones into his pocket, then carried on his way.

As he approached the inn, Trace was bustling about, darting back and forth between the car to the building, each time with a bundle of flowers or a basket of treats to leave in each room. Just as she was closing the trunk, another car rumbled into the car park.

Cassandra was out of the car before it had even stopped moving, and Trace bundled her into a hug. "I can't believe it's been ten years already!"

As they chattered, barely pausing to hear the other speak, Addy approached, his head ducked, hands buried in his pockets.

"And this must be Hadden?" Cassandra asked, peering around Trace's side, beaming pure love. "You've gotten so tall since the last photo I saw of you. And so handsome!"

Addy blushed and looked down at the pavement as his mum laughed. "And how are the girls? Addy has been desperate to meet them."

The car had just parked nearby, and Meraton had Rand in a tight embrace. Behind them, the doors flew open, and two girls shot out, tearing around the parking lot, screaming as one chased the other. Addy watched them wide-eyed until Cassandra called them over. They raced across and flanked their mother on either side, out of breath.

Annika had a pixie quality about her with a frizz of dark hair, round glasses and a button nose. Daphne, on the other hand, stood long and lean with auburn ringlets that fell down to her mid-thigh. Addy thought they looked more like neighbours than twin sisters. Something about Daphne made the breath catch in his chest. Her eyes gleamed a light turquoise like her father's; he sensed in her the aptitude of Voyent-Reprogram, *The Magician*. That's why her gaze penetrated him, a typical quality of Magicians and people from the House of Zuris. Addy was not sure whether he wanted to shy from it or challenge it.

As their parents went back to the car to begin unloading, Addy stepped towards them.

"Want to see something cool?" he whispered.

"I would!" Annika said, stepping in between them.

Daphne and Addy looked at each other and smiled, both several inches taller than tiny Annika.

Addy pulled out one of the stones he had found in the forest and turned to Daphne. "This is Azurite, the birthstone of the Voyents. I found two. I was going to keep them both, but since you are Voyent too, you could have the other one. You know, if you wanted?"

Daphne looked at the stone in wonder. "Thank you – Mum says they help us stay strong in hard situations. I lost the one she gave me. Thank you so much!"

Annika looked disappointed, and Addy scrambled for something to say.

"Audients are Ruby. I didn't find any Rubies around here, but we can look and see."

Annika smiled and blushed. He put the blue stone back in his pocket and ran off to greet the others as the third car pulled in to join the expanding group.

After settling into their rooms, Addy took the boys, Forsel, Michael and Rafael, for a tour of the games room. They played air hockey until dinnertime. Forsel and Addy beat the other two boys five games to zero.

Forsel high-fived Addy and announced to the other two, "We're the bomb!"

"You just won because you're both Voyent," Rafael complained in his Italian accent. "You can see where we're sending the shot before it happens. Neither of us can do that."

Michael slumped down on a nearby sofa. "Yeah, but Rafael and I could beat you two fatheads at word games without any problem."

Addy rolled his eyes. "Word games, how lame. Because you're both Audients? I doubt it."

Rafael ran to the recreation room shelf and pulled out a box with the title, *The Dictionary Game*. "Wanna bet? First team to finish wins."

Addy looked at Forsel and said. "You're on."

Over the next half hour, the boys worked in two teams, trying to outwit each other. In the end, Rafael and Michael beat them hands down. For the rest of the trip, Addy and Forsel were inseparable. Michael occasionally joined in with some of their games, but they kept away from Rafael, who was constantly challenging them at one thing or another.

In the dining hall, the ten adults sat around a large wooden oak table while the eight children sat around a smaller table nearby. Addy made sure he sat next to Daphne on one side and Forsel on the other. Despite sitting beside her, Daphne spent a lot of her time talking and laughing with Rafael, who sat on her other side. Still, the group of children joked and shared stories of what it was like to be a strange child in the world of surface humans. For once, Addy didn't feel so isolated and wished they could all stay together forever.

The next day, they hiked the various trails that spiderwebbed Mount Rainier in groups of three and four, catching up from all their years apart. Meanwhile, the children played "kick the can" in the nearby playground. Come afternoon, Trace had booked one of the meeting rooms for them to do their drawing and painting together. Each person wore a painting frock and painted with the colour of their lineage. Each year, they painted the symbology of the gemstone representing that year. For the year 1948, the gemstone was Rose Quartz. This gem helped to clear negativity, cleansing the heart of resentment. The children created their designs, and the adults created their own. They pasted the sheets on the walls and stood back to watch as the sacred geometric patterns activated a rebalancing process in their subconscious minds.

Addy relaxed into a deep state of peace, for a short time at least. It was sharply disrupted when he noticed Rafael and Daphne holding hands, an unusual feeling filling his chest. The Audients of the group took out their musical instruments while Rafael sang a song to the group, and Daphne harmonised with him. Rafael was Audient-Acceptance, *The Sound Healer*, so the group sat mesmerised by the performance.

After that, Trace stood up to tell a story, and as her aptitude was *The Storyteller*, the group was enraptured as she told a tale of when their ancestors first built Helio Tropez. Forsel used his *Detective* aptitude to guess what was in people's pockets. His sister, Nancy, *The Artist*, did brilliant cartoon sketches of people who asked. One by one, people shared their gifts with the group, but Addy didn't feel like showing off any of his skills. The group laughed and played until they stumbled back to their rooms, exhausted. In the meantime, Addy didn't sleep very well. All he could think about was Daphne and Rafael. Something about seeing them together made his stomach twist, and his heart beat a little faster. He wanted to break them apart, to put himself between them, but he knew he was being daft. Instead, Addy sulked and stared at the ceiling until sleep finally stole him away.

At breakfast the next morning, Bruno and Maria Viridis stood up with their son, Rafael, to make an announcement. "Rafael has confirmed what we suspected. Daphne of Zuris will be his future SANA Mate!"

The group waved their hands in recognition and applause.

Meraton and Cassandra stood up with Daphne. "And Daphne confirms that Rafael is *her* primary SANA mate as well!"

Everyone but Addy cheered.

"This is beyond fortuitous," Lorena Indicum said in her Australian accent. "The chance of a SANA coupling amongst such a small group."

Meraton held up a glass of green rejuvenation water as a toast "To the happy coupling!"

Trace saw the look of disappointment on her son's face, and after breakfast, she pulled him aside. "Your primary mate is likely in Helio Tropez, and you will meet her one day. Be patient, and it'll all be worth it, I promise." She gave him a reassuring smile, but Addy shrugged and followed the others.

The third day saw more people arrive at the Paradise Inn. As the children charged around the playground near the hotel entrance, three Ford Woody station wagons pulled up to the entrance. Several families stepped out of the vehicles and watched the Quinary group as they had their picnic. About an hour later, a boy and two girls walked onto the field and stood nearby on the grass, watching them play ball.

"Hey, can we play, too?" the boy asked.

The Quinary children knew how to read the energy of strangers and screen for intention. Voyents, in particular, could immediately see a person's aura. They were clearly children from SIM families with heightened powers.

"Your aura is brown," Daphne announced to the boy, narrowing her eyes at him. Annika elbowed her.

"What are you doing?" she hissed. "We're not supposed to tell anyone about our abilities!"

"Yours is white," he said back to her. "Maybe you can teach me how to lighten up."

"What are your names?" Daphne asked.

"I'm Leo, and those two are Josie and Irene."

Leo had the same aptitude as Addy: Voyent Vision. That meant he could implant a curse in someone's mind. Josie on the other hand emanated The Magician, just like Daphne. She could play visual tricks with your mind. Her chameleon eyes darted from one child to the other, reading their soul signature and aptitude. Irene was The Musician, which meant she could make a person hear negative frequencies. Addy raised the SIM shields taught to him by his mother. But Josie locked her eyes on Daphne and took a step closer.

"Get lost," Addy said, stepping between them. "We know who you are. We're in the middle of a game."

Leo laughed and turned his attention to the adults. Cassandra noticed the interchange as she was cutting a watermelon on a nearby picnic table. At that moment, a woman walked onto the field and stared at her, visibly concentrating. Without looking at her hand, Cassandra sliced the knife right into her thumb, letting out a yelp. Addy shoved past Leo, and he and Annika ran towards Cassandra to find out what had happened. When they arrived, they saw green-tinged blood spattered across the table. The biological differences between surface humans and Heliotropans meant they had to take care of their own injuries and avoid hospitals. Leo and the girls emitted a wicked laugh as the woman led them back towards the hotel entrance.

Soon, the Quinary group gathered around Cassandra, helping wrap the wound and wipe up the blood.

Meraton said, "Wasn't that Blanche Carbona?"

"Yes, she's the matriarch of the most powerful SIM family," Cassandra said, wincing from the pain. "Those two girls are her daughters."

"And the boy is the son of Lloyd and Thelma Burres. Another powerful SIM family involved in the military," Rand added. "I've seen their pictures on the comm."

"Any coincidence that they show up at the same hotel?" Lorena inquired.

"Blanche is Tangent-Vision, she caused that injury!" Meraton interjected.

A grounds person nearby noticed Cassandra's blood. His eyebrows raised, as he stepped in to get a closer look.

Addy stood in his sightline and whispered to his father, "That man saw."

As the man walked towards the hotel, Rand caught up with him. "My wife is a nurse. We have this handled," he said, tapping the man's shoulder.

Daphne watched, confused as the groundskeeper's face went from frowning to totally placid. "My Dad is a Tangent-Reprogram," Addy explained to Daphne.

"Cool. *The Shapeshifter*. So he just wiped that guy's memories by touching his back?"

"Yep. My mum will give him a new screen memory by giving him a whole new story about what happened."

Daphne puffed her chest up. "Wow! Well, my mum can heal any wound instantly. Just watch and see."

Once the man was out of sight, Cassandra held her hand over the wound. After a few moments and some muted grunts from Cassandra, the wound sealed up completely, but they kept the wound covered to maintain the disguise.

Annika sprang forward and sang the word "Abracadabra" while focusing on her mother's hand. The scar disappeared, and Cassandra kissed her head.

Addy whispered to Daphne. "Why did Annika say that? It seems stupid."

"I think mum just lets Annika do that to help her feel special. People give me more attention than her, so mum feels sorry for her."

Miriam overhead them and whispered, "It's not stupid. Annika is a sound healer, and that's an ancient incantation. It helps remove vibrational wounding. Surely you know that the Abracadabra Orb is one of the most powerful manifestation tools in the universe? Annika already understands how to use it at only eight years old. She's a genius."

"Whatever," Daphne said, turning away from her.

Miriam frowned at them, making Addy feel bad for ridiculing Annika. He nodded. "That makes sense."

Miriam smiled at him and walked over to Annika. The two girls hugged.

Forsel elbowed him, "You like Miriam, too?"

Addy rolled his eyes. "What? No! I mean, I think Miriam is cool. I just don't want to get on her bad side. She's a Tangent-Action."

"Yeah. *The Warrior*. She could knock out those SIM agents with one blow! I like girls like that."

"You like Miriam?"

"Yep, I bet she's my SANA mate."

"Do your parents know?"

"No. I don't want to tell them. They want me to be with a Zuris girl. Daphne's spoken for, so that leaves Annika. Ugh."

"She's a bit..."

"Intense, weird and more like a boy than a girl. I know."

"I can't tell if Miriam likes me, too. If only I were a Sentient..."

"She likes you. Anyway, we're supposed to choose our SANA mates, not have it done by our parents?"

"I know, right?"

Addy looked back and forth between Miriam and Forsel. She was tall, dark and muscular, and he was scrawny with white-blond hair and freckles. *They'd make an odd couple*, he thought.

The whole group formed a circle around a picnic table, not knowing what to do next. A maple leaf wafted down from one of the huge trees nearby and landed on the table. Instead of being brown, it was green. Addy looked to see where it had come from, but the only trees visible were a hundred yards away, and they were all pine. *Strange...*

"It's a sign from SANA," Meraton said, pulling Cassandra close. "We must leave at once. Our energy is magnified together – we're like a beacon for anyone who's looking. It's clearly how these SIM agents discovered us."

Trace asked, "Shouldn't we investigate who is here and what they want first? This is a green leaf, not a brown leaf. It's not autumn. No maple trees grow around here. How can we better interpret this sign?"

"Maple is a symbol of strength and endurance," Rand said, picking it up. "This is an opportunity for us to grow in strength and endurance, not run away."

"You can stay if you want," Ben Indicium announced. "But we're leaving."

"I think Rand is right. We need to stay and fight back, or they've won," Magdalena said. "Otherwise, we'll go back to our cities living in fear of them."

Bruno pulled his wife and son close to him. "They clearly planned this infiltration well. There's no way we can beat them."

Maria, pulled away. "I disagree. I can feel how afraid they are of our powers. I say we take them down."

As the adults discussed the issue in quiet but heated tones, the children gathered together to talk.

"Let's take them down!" Forsel announced.

"Yep. I'm with you," Addy agreed.

"Those people are too powerful. We'd lose," Rafael argued.

Addy elbowed Miriam. "Come on, you could cut them to shreds!"

Miriam and Annika had become fast friends, so the tiny girl stepped between them. "She's just a kid. I say we leave this place right away."

Daphne rolled her eyes and huddled close to Addy. The group now stood divided with half the children on one side with Rafael and half with Addy. Miriam and her brother, Michael, stood in the middle, undecided.

Rand approached the children and said, "We've agreed to stay and face them. Follow everything we tell you to do to the letter."

Addy high-fived Forsel and Rafael looked shaken. The group packed up the picnic and gathered in one of the meeting rooms. After setting their amethysts to high cloaking capacity, Rand led a planning session to assign tasks to each adult. Meanwhile, the children were supposed to play in the recreation room and act as though everything was fine. However, after a few minutes, Addy whispered to Daphne and Forsel to follow him. They tiptoed out of the recreation room as the other children continued playing Monopoly. They paused at the door of the meeting room, and Addy pressed his ear to the wood, beckoning the others to join him.

Rand was speaking amid the hushed discussion. "First, we needed to remote view the situation, so we need all the Voyents together."

Remote viewing was the aptitude of Voyents as they could send their inner sight to another geographical location or even dimension.

Addy turned the handle on the door and burst into the room with the other two children stumbling behind him. "All three of us are Voyents!"

The adults looked at each other, unsure about involving the children. Rand hurried them in, closing the door behind them. Just as he did, the other five children scurried down the hallway to find out what was happening. A heavy eye-roll later, all of the children were gathered in the room, grinning.

The adults looked at each other in brief telepathic conversation. Finally, Rand looked at the children. "Fine. We need as much help as possible, but only if you want to help, okay?"

The children nodded in earnest. The five Voyents sat in a circle, Addy, Forsel, Daphne, Ben and Magdalena, helping to magnify the power of their remote viewing. They closed their eyes, each set on the goal to get a piece of the puzzle, and then interweave each piece together. After ten minutes, they debriefed their findings. The SIM family members were gathered in the Alpine meeting room, discussing what to do. Rand thanked the Voyents and called on the Audients to eavesdrop on what they were saying. Trace, an Audient-Reprogram, sat in one of the centre chairs along with Lorena Indicum, an Audient-Vision. Just before they started, Daphne pushed her sister forward.

"Annika's an Audient-Action."

Annika was stunned, hugging her arms around her waist. Trace offered her hand, welcoming her and helping her into the adult chair. After a few minutes of meditation, the three of them triangulated their powers. Nearly fifteen minutes later, they reported that SIM was planning to create conflict between the members of Quinary, fragmenting the group.

Rand addressed the group. "So they plan to divide and conquer. We aren't going to let that happen. In fact, we need to make them forget what they saw here. Reprogrammers and Ecrivents, we need to do this quickly."

Those with the Reprogram or Ecrivent aptitude came forward. Together, they triangulated their efforts to wipe their memories of any knowledge of the Quinary families and re-write new screen memories. Meanwhile, the Sentients in the group, Maria, Meraton and Nancy, worked together to re-engineer the dark emotions growing amongst the SIM families, raising their frequency.

Suddenly, Maria gasped, her face contorted in pain. "They're fighting back. They know what we're doing!"

Moments later, the door burst open, and the members of the SIM family filed in. The Tangents in the SIM group led the way, energy pouring from the centre of their hands. Addy watched in horror as one person after another doubled over in pain and crumpled to the floor. He ducked under a table, but Leo had noticed, so he strode toward him. They shared the aptitude of Voyent-Action, The Eagle Eye, making them equally matched.

That said, Leo stood several inches taller than Addy. Leo dragged him out from under the table, pinning him down and focusing his right eye on the centre of Addy's forehead. He searched for a weakness in Addy's mind, but Addy's inner shield protected it. In the middle of their physical struggle, Addy forced his way into his opponent's mind, prying his way to find any unhealed wound he could press on. Then he found it. Leo felt rejected by a cold-hearted mother who regularly ignored his efforts for attention. He had never measured up to her expectations. It felt like a low blow, but Leo refused to back off. Addy was left with no other choice. He imparted a single, subconscious thought in Leo's mind, ensuring that all females in his life never thought he was good enough.

Upon implanting that curse, Leo's strength fell away, and Addy was able to break free, shoving Leo off. This caused a ripple effect whereby the other SIM family members were drained of their powers. The Quinary families now had an opportunity to regain their strength. The Voyents stood on the outer edges of the group, creating a shield around the SIM family members, penning them in. The Audients lulled them into a hypnotic state while the Ecrivents re-wrote the mind code of all the SIM family members, wiping any memory of ever seeing Quinary at the Paradise Inn. Then, the Reprogrammers installed a heavy sleep program. After all was said and done, the Sentients helped heal the trauma of the attack within their own group.

Before the SIM agents awoke, the entire Quinary clan had vacated the premises, scattering back to their various cities, promising to maintain their bond but vowing to remain physically separate throughout the rest of the mission.

Rand did one last reconnaissance, shapeshifting into a Falcon. He flew back to investigate the Paradise Inn where the SIM families remained. Shifting back into a human, he returned with good news; they were all still dazed and half asleep, all memory of what had happened forgotten.

Once back in Seattle, the Violettas were safe once again, but an unease grew within Addy as the years went by, though he could never place why. Even though he didn't know it yet, what had happened with Leo would haunt him for years to come.

CHAPTER 19

Montreal – 2011

Walking through the stargate felt like moving through jello. Yet, it made a splashing sound as if Tia just waded through a puddle of water. The air went from the pristine scent of Helio Tropez to the dirty, humid air of Montréal. Suddenly, she landed in the middle of a deserted street. A salty wind sailed along the sidewalk, fluttering chocolate bar wrappers around her feet. The density of the surface frequencies weighed heavy. She took a breath, trying to be courageous as she surveyed the area. Stairs in front of her led up to the shallow porch of an apartment block.

Cassandra's voice came through to her telepathically.

We lived at number five, 4379 Rue de Bullion. Do you see it?

Yes. I'm right in front of it.

Is anyone around?

Not a single soul.

The ghost-quiet street smelled of diesel and damp leaves. Parked cars sat waiting in silence under dim streetlamps. Tia tiptoed up the front steps and saw a list of names next to intercom buttons but decided against buzzing anyone so early in the morning.

The name on number five is A. Indicium.

That's amazing! The Indicium family were part of our Quinary mission, stationed in Sydney. I wonder if they're related.

Tia tiptoed back down the steps. *I'll come by again tomorrow in the daytime and see if anyone's home.*

Yes, you must get settled somewhere. There's a hotel on Rue St. Denis called Hôtels Gouverneur Montréal.

Rolling her suitcase towards Rue St. Denis, she spotted a few cars carrying late-night partiers home. Otherwise, she passed no one. Once at the hotel, the sleepy-eyed front desk clerk found her a room on the fourth floor. Inside the room, Tia barely unpacked before crawling under the covers for a few hours of sleep.

In the morning, a newspaper was slid under the door, dated July 29, 2011, almost a year after she had left the surface with Addy. Tia pulled out the family photo from 1983. *What would her sister look like now at thirty years old? Like a grown-up version of her three-year-old self? And what would her mother be like at sixty-eight?*

By midday, Tia's stomach growled every five minutes. She got dressed into long shorts and a pair of sandals before asking the clerk – a new, bright-eyed man - for suggestions where she could eat. The clerk recommended several restaurants. Tia chose one named Café Santropol - something about it appealed to her.

The humid summer air clung to her skin as she wandered down the street. Surface life now felt strange to her: the roaring of buses, the beeping of horns, the bustling bodies pushing past her, and the smell of industry. In Helio Tropez, the vehicles ran silently in the air, people walked with presence, and the aroma of roses often filled the air. While she missed the harmony of Helio Tropez, surface life felt more familiar. This is where she had grown up, and a part of her heart had remained connected to these people and places.

The hostess at the outdoor café found her a table under the trees. People nearby bit into thick sandwiches. Looking at the menu, the food portions appeared three times larger than in Helio Tropez. A waitress arrived to take her order, but Tia couldn't decide. As she waited, the waitress kept looking over her shoulder. Tia followed her gaze to a group of men in puffy white shirts.

"C'est le chanteur de Simla..." she whispered.

"I don't speak French, sorry," Tia answered, wishing she had installed the French language into her amethyst.

"The lead singer from Simla. You know, the band."

Tia shrugged.

"You really don't know them? They're playing at the Olympic Stadium tonight. It's been all over the news. I can't believe they're here in our restaurant!" She scarcely looked at Tia as she spoke, a dreamy look on her face, then she blinked, returning to herself. "Anyway, what would you like?"

"Just a bowl of the soup, thank you."

Two girls from a nearby table approached the band and asked for an autograph. One particular man stood up so they could take selfies with him. He noticed Tia watching and smiled at her.

Tia furrowed her brow. *Have I met him before?* He seemed familiar, but a scan of her memory found nothing. He looked like a character from a 17th century novel, with his long hair, his D'Artagnan beard and a pirate shirt. After finishing the photos, he sauntered over to her table, and her eyes widened. At the same time, the waitress arrived with her soup.

"Oh my God! You're Dax! I'm such a big fan."

"Brilliant. Lovely to meet you," he said in a London accent.

"Will you sign the back of my waitress pad?"

172

He smiled and obliged. The waitress blushed and scurried off in a tizzy of delight to tell her co-workers.

Turning his attention to Tia, he asked her, "We've met before, right?"

"No, I don't think so."

"Really? What's your name?"

Tia opened her mouth then remembered the name on her driver's license. "Linda Wright. And you?"

"Dax."

"Right, that's what the waitress called you."

"You've never heard of me?"

Tia shook her head.

"What a delight."

"Is Dax your real name?"

"Is Linda *your* real name?"

A robin hopped onto the table, looking for a handout. They looked at the bird, then back at each other.

"So you're in a band?"

"Yes. Are you from another country?"

"I'm from the States."

His pupils dilated, and his annunciation lagged at times. "We're huge all over the world."

"I don't get out much."

One of his bandmates called him back to the table, and Dax smiled, excusing himself.

Tia finished her soup and asked for the bill. The band stood up to leave, and as they did, Dax dropped two tickets on her table.

"You should check us out. Olympic Stadium. Tonight."

"Oh, I don't think I can... but thanks anyway."

He waved and slipped out of the back to avoid the paparazzi that had congregated at the entrance, somehow catching wind of the band's whereabouts. After he left, a wide smile formed across Tia's face. Walking back toward the hotel, the smile wouldn't go away for blocks.

Strange.

Just before arriving at the hotel, she spotted an electronics store where she could buy two cell phones. Across the street, she found an Internet café and settled in a booth. She typed in the name of the band, and a biography of the lead singer, Dax, popped up on the screen. He was born in London in 1980, and the band had been together since they were teenagers, though they'd only found fame recently. Most of the information about his family and history seemed false, except for his year of birth.

Conflicting thoughts swirled in her head after reading his bio. Niklana had said her SANA mate was born in 1980, but he was from the House of Indicum. The bio never mentioned a last name, but Dax could be a stage name. Yet, her connection with him was palpable and almost otherworldly. *What are the chances that I'd bump into my SANA mate in the first place I go to on the surface? Can SIM work that quickly to set something up?* If so, it meant she was in danger and should avoid the concert at all costs. Finally, she resolved to discuss it later with the Task Force.

After setting up the burner phone, Tia decided to try calling her father's home number. She still held a thread of hope that he had survived or that someone there could tell her what had happened. After dialling the number, an automated voice informed her that the number was out of service. So she called the number for Violetta & Burres Investments instead.

"I'd like to speak to Hadden Violetta."

"Oh, I - I'm so sorry, but he died about a year ago. Who is this?"

Despite the fact that she had been expecting it, the news felt like a punch to her stomach. Tia bit her lip and hung up the phone without another word.

Tears stung her eyes, and a pain grew in her chest. She searched the Internet for any relevant stories from a year ago. One headline read:

> *Hadden Violetta found dead in his own home alongside his business partner, Leo Burres. The police suspect foul play. Hadden Violetta's daughter, Tia, fled the scene. She is a prime suspect.*

Her stomach coiled in a knot. A photo of her appeared lower in the article. *How could I be a prime suspect? Why wouldn't they think I'd been abducted and held for ransom instead?* Clearly, SIM had manipulated the situation to enlist the help of others to capture her.

She looked around the Internet café, no longer feeling quite as inconspicuous. However, no one seemed to pay her any attention. Not wanting to push her luck, she paid her bill, then ducked into a nearby store, bought sunglasses and a ball cap, then headed back to the hotel. Back in her room, she braided her hair and wore it up, trying to differentiate herself as much as possible from the photo taken over two years ago. Clearly, Addy hadn't been able to change the timeline, and if she wasn't careful, it was going to come back and bite her.

CHAPTER 20

<u>Vancouver, Canada – 1979</u>

Leo Burres waved at Hadden as he entered *The Cave* nightclub. Handing his wet umbrella to the hat check girl, he weaved his way through the crowd and joined Leo and a young woman at a booth.

"I'm so glad you decided to join us, man!" Leo said, shifting over to make room. "Cindy, this is Addy, my partner at the Investment Firm. Cindy works at the deli across the street here. We just met."

"Nice to meet you, Addy," the blonde-haired woman replied with a smile. She had bright, round eyes that complimented the necklace sparkling around her neck.

"You can call me Hadden," he said, shaking her hand.

Cindy smiled and ran her fingers through her feathered hair. "I've heard a lot about you. I understand you've just made the list of... What was it? One of the top five investment firms in the country? Congratulations."

Hadden nodded sheepishly. "Just this week. Thought it was about time I let my hair down, or what's left of it," he chuckled.

Earlier that day, they'd met with a potential investor, one of the wealthiest men in Canada. The meeting had gone well, and Leo had insisted they stay overnight in Vancouver to celebrate by watching a show at *The Cave*.

"Hadden is one of Seattle's most eligible and interminable bachelors," Leo teased. "We have to help him get lucky tonight – God knows he needs a wingman!"

They chatted for a while over glasses of champagne, then the lights dimmed, and a Latin band took over the stage. Hadden struck a match to light his cigarette. As he inhaled, a crimson spotlight beamed down on a woman so stunning that he stopped breathing for a moment.

She stood illuminated in sequins, chiffon and a feathered headdress, her gloved hands held high above her head, eagerly awaiting the first note. Her high cheekbones framed sultry eyes as her full lips opened to emit the first note of the song. Waves of auburn ringlets shimmied down her back as she undulated to the melody. Hadden's heart fell in that moment, lost into an abyss of longing that he had never fully recovered from.

After the show ended, Hadden sat back in awe.

"He's lovestruck!" Leo said, elbowing Cindy.

"Why don't you go over and say hi?" she said with a twinkle in her eye.

"Naw...it's getting late." He looked at his watch. It said 11:11 pm. Something about that number jolted the back of his mind.

Cindy leaned and whispered, "Just tell her what you liked about her performance. Every singer likes to hear that."

Hadden thought for a moment, then nodded and gulped down his entire glass of scotch for courage. Breathing deeply, he approached her as she stood at the bar ordering a drink.

"Amazing performance! I just came over to let you know that was one of the best shows I've ever seen in a club."

"Thank you," she said, averting his eyes and stepping back.

"What a magnificent voice you have."

"That's very kind."

"Cigarette?" Hadden said, holding up a Marlborough.

She smiled and looked penetratingly into his eyes as if assessing his intentions. After a moment's hesitation, she accepted it. "I'm Daphne. And you?"

"Hadden."

She peered at him a little closer. "You seem familiar."

"You look familiar to me too, but I'm not sure from where."

"What's your last name?"

"Violetta. And yours?"

"Zuris."

They looked at each other, struggling to find the connection.

"I don't know," she said with a shrug.

"Me, neither."

Hadden ordered a drink, and they sat at the bar together, talking until the bar closed. Leo and Cindy left without saying goodbye, most likely not wanting to disturb Hadden. They only parted ways when her band manager insisted she got a good night's sleep.

Instead of going home the next day, Hadden extended his trip and showed up the next night to see her perform again. At the end of the night, he joined her again at the bar.

"Another fantastic performance. Okay, I have to ask. A beautiful woman like you must be married or have a boyfriend?"

"Recently divorced, actually. And you?"

"A bachelor."

They both smiled, and he moved in closer to steal a kiss. That's when he noticed the Azurite stone necklace hanging around her neck. The kiss and the energy of the stone triggered something buried deep within his subconscious: an image of Mount Rainier came to mind.

"Where did you get that necklace?"

"I don't know," she blushed. "I always loved this stone, so I had a jeweller turn it into a necklace."

Memories of the Quinary Mission, returning to Helio Tropez, meeting Halia, the trip to Mount Rainier, finding the Azurite stones – it all came flooding back.

"I gave that to you," he said, sitting back as the memories rushed through his mind.

"What? When?"

"When we were eight years old at the Paradise Inn. We were at Mount Rainier for The Fete of Tropez. Remember?"

She shook her head, looking confused.

Hadden's jaw tightened, and he turned to face her squarely. "Our parents knew each other. We were on a mission, the Quinary Mission. They were born in a place called Helio Tropez, in the Inner Earth."

Daphne took a step back, looking a little frightened. "I have no idea what you're talking about."

That's when Hadden noticed two women watching their every move. He recognised them as the band manager and the keyboardist. A flood of images of every interaction he'd ever had with a SIM family member filled his mind.

He rubbed his forehead and turned back to Daphne, whispering, "They took away your memories. Wiped your mind clean. They did the same to me, but... your necklace has just jogged something in my mind."

"Who? What do you mean?"

"Look at this Azurite stone I wear on my wrist. It's almost identical. I found them at Mount Rainier. I gave you one and kept the other. They are the birthstone of Voyents, like you and me."

Daphne laughed uncomfortably, glancing at the women by the stage before whispering back. "You're sounding a bit crazy. You do know that, right?"

A short, roundish woman joined their conversation. "Daphne, we're leaving. Say goodbye to your fanboy."

Daphne cleared her throat. "Hadden, this is my sister, Annika. He thinks we've met before.

"You were there, too, Annika. When we were all around eight years old."

Looking up at him, she pushed her glasses further up her nose to inspect, then shook her head. "Nope, never seen you in my life."

"Surely you remember, at Mount Rainier, near Seattle?"

Annika looked puzzled. "Neither of us have ever been there."

Hadden sighed and tried another angle. "Were you told that your parents died in a car accident?"

They looked at each other again and said nothing.

"That's only a story they told you. They're alive in Inner Earth."

Annika whispered something to her sister before shooting Hadden a dirty look. "That's a sick joke."

The band manager approached, putting herself between Hadden and the two women. "Maybe you should leave these ladies alone," she said in a Bostonian accent. The woman stood as tall as Daphne and wore a black bandana and a motorcycle jacket.

"And you are...?"

"Josie Carbona. Band manager. Come on, ladies, we're leaving."

The Carbona Family, Hadden thought. *It couldn't have been any of the other SIM families...* Hadden remembered meeting Josie and her sister, Irene, as children at Mount Rainier, and his blood boiled at the mere memory. Annika followed after Irene like an automaton, and although Daphne followed Josie in the same way, she looked back just once before exiting out the back door.

Back in Seattle, Hadden stayed home and avoided work. Nausea and headaches plagued him for weeks. He told Leo he had a bad flu, but in truth, he had no idea what it was. At first, his brain scrambled to find a logical excuse for these strange memories, but the more he tried to push them away, the more they kept tumbling out one after another. The most vivid memory was his seventy-year-old self contacting him in his dreams to time travel in a plane from 1960 to 2010, meeting Tia, the daughter he would later have with Daphne, and ending up in Helio Tropez.

Another vivid memory involved meeting his grandmother, Halia, and bonding with her using a violet Sugilite stone. The worst memory involved coming back to the surface and being caught with the amethyst. Horrors of the intense mind wiping rituals with all the drugs and torture made his heart thunder in his chest. They'd mapped his mind to find the other members of Quinary before locking the memories away in a deep, dark corner of his mind.

Clearly, he hadn't been able to change the timeline. They had destroyed the Quinary Mission, and his parents had died. The Burres Family had given him screen memories that all looked false now: parents named Ted and Julie, growing up in Portland, and going to Harding High School. None of that had ever happened. It was the grief and confusion of all that which kept him curled up in bed for days. His head hurt so badly that he had to lay as still as possible with an eye mask and earplugs on and the shades drawn. After several days of not eating, he felt dizzy and fantasies of revenge filled his mental landscape

– he indulged his imagination in all the possible ways he could destroy those who harmed him and his family.

But what would that serve? They'd destroy him and anyone else he loved.

More memories floated to the surface. When Halia had given him the Sugilite gemstone, she had said, "Photograph this memory forever, no matter what happens. Whenever you need me, you just have to ask. Hold the gemstone and say, Halia-jia, and I will be there for you."

The Sugilite gemstone! But what happened to it? I haven't seen it since the day I arrived back to the surface. They must have taken it as well.

He rolled over in bed and clutched a pillow as an emptiness descended onto his chest. Tears stung his eyes, and his breath grew ragged. After several minutes, he rolled over on his back, and an idea flashed to mind. He tumbled out of bed and crawled along the floor to the cabinet along the sidewall. The lower shelf contained a wooden box full of knickknacks. He pulled it out into the light and searched for anything violet.

All he could find were old key chains, champagne corks, ticket stubs from a Supertramp concert, Mexican pesos from his last trip to Acapulco, two quartz crystals, three buttons, and... *what was this?* A violet-coloured stone. He held it up to the window. *Was this the Sugilite stone my grandmother gave me? Maybe, maybe not. The one she gave me seemed bigger. It is worth a try anyway.*

He called out to Halia-jia with all his heart over and over again, clutching the violet stone tightly. Nothing happened at first, but he remained patient. He drew the blinds open, letting the sunlight fall on his face, softening the lines etched across his brow. A deep sigh bellowed from his chest. Tension drained away from his shoulders. In silence, we waited.

Nothing.

Maybe she's forgotten about me. He tried again, certain that his grandmother wouldn't have abandoned him. After two hours, he gave up for the night. The next day, he tried again. He chanted the name Hali-jia over and over again. Still nothing. He sighed, accepting it and setting his frustration aside. *After all, that interaction with her happened in the future, thirty years from now. She doesn't even know I exist.*

That's when a prickling of energy shot up his arm. An image of her face appeared. She seemed to exist in another dimension, one not controlled by SIM. Frequencies of peace and unconditional love whirled around his chest.

For several minutes, he let the tears melt his hardened heart. That's when the telepathic communication opened up.

I'm here. Oh, Hadden, I'm here. I've been trying to return your calls, but you've not been responding. It's like we have a bad connection.

I'm so sorry. My frequency has been very low.

Well, it's alright. We're connected now. It's wonderful to finally meet my grandson.

Do you know that I met you thirty years from now, in 2010? That's why I'm reaching out to you now.

You did? How? Time travel is forbidden.

Yes, I know. But my future self called me into the year 2010 to change the timeline. It caused a lot of trouble in Helio Tropez. I was only twenty years old, and the Elders sent me back to the surface in the year 1960. But before I returned, they wiped my memories. Only, recently I met Daphne of Zuris here on the surface, and it must have unblocked something in my mind. That's what made me reach out to you again. You and I had a deep bond in 2010. You took me to the Wishing Well, and we used the Sugilite Stones to deepen our connection.

That sounds like something I'd do... Thank you for sharing all that with me. It's amazing, but... I'm concerned. Maybe us talking like this, its changing the timeline in a way that's not sanctioned.

Possibly... I'm sorry. Do you want to end our communication?

Um. No. I'm not sure. Before the Great UnDoing, we used to reach out to people on the surface. I was one of the interfacers. We were trying to connect with the humans in our genetic experiment to help them evolve. After 1961, all that stopped. I don't think it was a good idea, and I don't like the thought of you alone up there with no support whatsoever.

Thank you.

I always sensed that my daughter, Trace, had a son and that it was my job to help you in the struggles you faced on the surface.

That's exactly what you said to me in 2010.

Truly? Well, that's what I've always felt. I wasn't allowed to connect with you, not even when you were born. The Elders were afraid of SIM intercepting the message. But I knew right away when you were born. Let me guess, it was February 10, 1940?

Exactly!

So, now in the surface year 1979, you must be already thirty-nine years old.

Yes.

I'm sure it hasn't been easy so far. Well, I will help in whatever way I can, but please, know that I cannot tell anyone else here in Helio Tropez that I'm connecting with you. They will cut it off.

I understand. But does that mean you can't help me get back to Helio Tropez?

I would love to. I will see what I can do. I may need to go over the heads of the Elders and connect with one of the Progenitors on the home planet. The Elders are not letting anyone come here from the surface, even if they were in the Quinary Mission. They let Cassandra and Meraton return, but they regretted that.

Why?

The Elders believe that they polluted things here.

What do you mean? From SIM? I thought Helio Tropez had purification processes to protect from that.

They do, but things changed after they came back. The resonance meters showed a lower level of vibration in the collective consciousness of Helio Tropez. But I believe that the lower vibration is from the fear of SIM. We lost so many Quinary members, and no one truly dealt with its trauma. They don't like negative emotions here. But I believe my purpose is to ...

The line between them faded. Hadden sat up straight and dropped his chin to strengthen the connection. *Your purpose is to what?*

After several moments of silence, a panic arose in his throat.

...to help you.

She was loud and clear now.

Thank you so much! The Progenitors told me I need to keep to the original timeline so that all Pentada can be born. My future twin daughters are the last two Pentada. But my life has been under SIM control, and that goes on for decades. Daphne and Annika are also Pentada and totally under SIM control.

It's horrible. Is there any way you can help me stick to the right timeline but find freedom from SIM at the same time?

I will do whatever I can, but I need to go now. I just need to figure out a way to mask that fact that I'm interfacing with a surface dweller. I think I know a way.

A day later she thankfully reached out to him again. *I'm masking our telepathic coordinates. I've got a window of time right now that I can help.*

I'm so grateful...

It's okay. It's on purpose for me. I just know that. I suggest we try to reverse as much cognitive modification as possible without alerting SIM to what we're doing. Can you remember what they did to you? And who did it to you?

I've been totally under the control of the Burres Family.

That makes sense. Somehow, the House of Violetta and the House of Burres are karmically linked.

Something happened with Leo when we were children at Mount Rainier. One night, Leo tried to kill me. I fought back by giving him a curse so that he would end up emotionally disconnected from females his entire life. It took hold and was far more powerful than I had anticipated. Leo's mother continued to ignore and abuse him. No relationship ever lasted more than a few weeks – they all just used and abused him. I have to admit that I get this savage pleasure knowing that Leo suffered, too. I mean... I've been under the control of Leo and the Burres family for almost twenty years now.

That curse is keeping you locked in with Leo in a bad way.

You think it's the curse, or they'd do this to any Heliotropan they could get their hands on, or anyone with psychic gifts for that matter?

The curse is part of your inability to get out. How do they have you controlled?

They programmed me to run this investment firm with Leo, helping SIM launder money used for drugs, arms and human trafficking. They got me addicted to drugs, bad food, alcohol and cigarettes. I often wake up in the morning with bruises and cuts from doing who knows what in the middle of the night.

Let's start there. We will go back in your timeline and heal the trauma.

We can do that?

I think we need to do that.

Okay. Good. At some point, I think they split my personality. One personality isn't aware of the other. At night, I have an alter personality that does the SIM's biddings.

Let's remote view one particular experience and see what we can do.

I don't know. I don't think I can face that.

I will be with you, keeping you from being re-traumatised. It's important.

Hadden sat back and covered his face with his hands. *What if I did something unspeakable?*

Nothing is beyond forgiveness if you're willing to learn from it.

I am. I am willing to learn. Okay. There was one particular experience a few weeks ago where I woke up with a huge lump on my forehead and track marks on my arm. Something intense must have happened that night.

Let's go back to the day before. I'll be with you the whole way.

He closed his eyes and travelled back in time with Halia by his side like an angel looking down on his body, moving about the office at Burres & Violetta Investments. It was the end of the workday. Leo came into his office and just said the words, "Railspur Tidings." It was a CM trigger. His daytime self disappeared, and the well-trained spy took over his consciousness.

Leo laid out the plan, and Hadden's alter followed orders without question. He went to a corporate office down the street and entered an elevator. It wouldn't work without his thumbprint and iris scan. Once that was done, it took him down twenty-three floors to a deep underground military base. Knowing exactly where to go, this alter personality walked two long corridors until he came to a door that, again, only opened with a thumb and iris scan.

The dour, grizzled face of Leo's father, Lloyd Burres, studied a monitor with still intent. The alter came up beside him. On the monitor, a man sat tied up, a black cloth bag over his head. He looked eight feet tall with bluish skin.

"Reporting for duty, sir."

"I needed you an hour ago. This man is an off-planet corporate spy working for our competitor. He wants to start an operation near our base on Ganymede. You need to become one of his, act like another prisoner and find out their agenda."

185

Hadden remote viewed his alter self from a few feet away, like watching an actor in a movie. Sweat formed on his upper lip. Shapeshifting for that long a time took its toll on his powers. It wasn't his dominant aptitude like it was for his father, Rand, who could physically shapeshift into any form. For a Voyent, it was just a visual trick for a short period of time. These SIM agents seemed to think all Heliotropans could shapeshift.

"How long would you like me to stay in the cell with him?"

"As long as it takes, but time is of the essence. Use everything you've got."

Lloyd looked very similar to his own father, Rand. Both had impossibly wide shoulders and penetrating gold eyes. In fact, they even had the same *Shapeshifter* aptitude, Tangent-Reprogram.

"You do know I'm Voyent-Action, not..."

"Didn't your father teach you anything?"

"You know my father?"

Lloyd flipped through a clipboard of papers. "The outfitters will provide you with a prison jumpsuit. Report back as soon as possible."

Watching his alter, Hadden wondered if Lloyd had captured his father. The thought filled him with grief and regret. *No, impossible. I warned my parents so they could make it back to Helio Tropez in time... or did I not get the chance?*

In the outfitter's room, a guard handed him a huge prison jumpsuit. The alter used all his mindpower to shapeshift into an eight-foot-tall alien man with bluish skin. Because the visual illusion faded in and out at first, the guard waited. When it seemed locked into place, he led the alter into the same empty cell and chained him to the wall. A few minutes later, they returned with the off-planet prisoner and chained him up nearby. When they took off his black hood, the foreigner was shocked to see another prisoner of his species.

"Where are you from?" he asked telepathically.

Hadden had to tell the truth without giving away his agenda. "I'm from Inner Earth." He knew that several alien groups with blue skin had bases in Inner Earth.

The man squinted his eyes, looking him up and down. Hadden suppressed his intentions and dialled up on the frequency of compassion and empathy. Much to his relief, the man closed his eyes and nodded off. A moment later, Hadden dropped the shapeshifting.

In a Theta brain wave state, between sleep and waking, he could enter a person's mind more easily and retrieve the information he wanted. His alter never asked SANA for permission, which added to Hadden's karmic debt. He cringed as he watched the alter download every conversation the man had with his superiors and imprint it using his photographic memory. Once complete, he called out telepathically to the guard to be let free. Back in the outfitters room, he collapsed on a gurney.

All the late nights, the drugs and alcohol were impairing his natural aptitudes. A security guard with a snake tattoo coiled around his neck stood nearby, cracking his knuckles, staring at him. Hadden's alter dragged himself up, and the man escorted him to a room where Lloyd Burres and one other man waited.

"What did you get?

Hadden conveyed the messages he had downloaded, most of which were about mundane matters.

"This is useless to us," Lloyd Burres scowled. He inhaled his cigar and butted it out on the edge of the table. "You used to dig so much deeper, jumping from one mind to another. Why didn't you get into the mind of his superior?"

Hadden's voice cracked. "It's... it's... just that there seemed to be some kind of firewall."

"There never used to be a firewall. I don't think that's the problem. We've heard too many reports lately. In the last few months, your work is getting slow and sloppy."

"I don't think that's what..."

"Don't lie!"

The man with the tattoo smacked him across the brow.

Hadden clutched his forehead. "Honestly, I'm trying my best."

"Maybe you're just getting too old. What are you now, almost forty?"

Hadden's alter nodded. A lump was already growing on his forehead.

"I don't think we can trust your skills anymore," the other man said, glancing at Lloyd. "Not much use keeping him around. We might as well terminate him."

Hadden knew that meant either death or completely wiping his mind, taking away all his worldly possessions and leaving him homeless. "No, please. I can do so many things. You've barely touched my skill set. I can do... ah... make you extra income."

Hadden had an epiphany to send his alter a memory. It was about the information his older self put in the envelope; pages of information about what stocks will go up and down in the future. Addy's photographic memory 'saved' all of it.

"Like, I can... I can know...or I mean... *create* the conditions that would make a stock go up or down exponentially faster. So, I'll bet on the good ones, and short the bad ones, and literally triple the Burres family stock portfolio in no time. Please, just let me try."

The Burres patriarch lifted his chin to the tattooed man, who then dragged Hadden out of the room and pinned him against the wall. As he waited for the man to break his neck, the door opened again.

"We'll give you two weeks," Lloyd barked. "If you can double our portfolio, we'll keep you on, but only so long as you can keep that performance up."

Hadden nodded, feeling sweat roll off the tip of his nose.

"In the meantime, Grigor, take him to Room 660."

Hadden's heart faltered. Room 660 was where they reinforced your CM programming. "No, you don't need to do that. I'm completely on board with this."

"Just to be on the safe side," Lloyd smiled.

Terror coursed through Hadden's veins as Grigor dragged him down six more floors to Room 660. As they moved along the hallway, he caught a glimpse inside a room labelled A113. Cages and pods held children, though what was happening to them, Hadden couldn't tell. All he knew was that they were all silent.

He'd heard rumour of the horrors that SIM did to children. The gifted ones served as agents like him, but the ungifted ones faced a kind of torture and death he couldn't even bear to think about. Because of their parasitic nature, SIM and their agents fed off the life force energy of SANA based humans – the purer, the better. The rumours were that they drank the blood of children, but Hadden had never thought there was much truth to it.

He fetched himself up against the wall, suddenly dizzy, but a jab to the ribs had him stumbling on again. *There's no saving me, but the children? They barely know how to spell their own name...*

Inside the CM room, a group of lab technicians dressed in white lab coats hovered over several victims strapped to gurneys. Howls and cries echoed against the stark metal walls of the sterile room. Two attendants strapped Hadden's alter onto a gurney, and as they prepared the drugs, his alter actually prayed to SANA for protection for the children in the nearby room. Something about helping the children made this alter break free from the programming, even if just for a moment. Halia gave Hadden clear instructions about how to protect himself.

Bring your light body and local memories over to me in the 4D for safekeeping while they do their work.

I don't understand.

It's like doing a backup of your computer on an external drive for safekeeping while a technician wipes your hard drive.

Okay.

Using his Voyent powers, he imagined this entire consciousness of the body strapped to the gurney below, moving to the safety of Halia in 4D, where she filled him with frequencies of peace and unconditional love.

He watched as the attendants used a combination of psychoactive drugs, chemicals, and electroshocks on his alter as a way to pry open his mind and traumatise his body. That allowed them to embed more cognitive modification commands through hypnosis, enhancing his aptitude in service to their agenda.

He paid close attention to the commands so that he could appear to still be under their control during day-to-day life. After they finished, Halia performed healing rituals on his light body and physical body, removing the toxic chemicals, rebalancing his brain and soothing his nervous system. When he returned to his 3D body, his entire nervous system still felt frazzled, but the damage was far less severe than on previous occasions. After they unstrapped him, Grigor escorted his alter to the elevator and let him go. His alter stumbled home that night and fell into a deep sleep.

How was it to watch yourself go through that?

It was hard, but your presence and healing made a massive difference.

189

We must do that again. What happened after that incident? Did you keep your promise to Lloyd Burres?

Yes, my abilities seemed to dial back up again. I focused on two main stocks in the Burres portfolio. Within ten days, I'd tripled their portfolio. That's why they haven't terminated me yet.

Good for you. I will help you keep up that performance. Each night, we will do more healing work. By the way, I sense they will now try to invite you to special initiations and into their dark cult practices. Whatever happens, do not accept. I will help protect you. I suggest you create a room in your house protected from SIM, acting as a shield. You'll get instructions from us. For now, rest. That was a lot to deal with.

Thank you. I will.

She disappeared from his consciousness, and he opened his eyes. Hadden's head pulsed with pain, just reliving the torture he'd endured that night. Then an alarming thought came to mind: would the Burres Family know his CM programming broke down when he saw Daphne's necklace? Could they monitor him in that way? If so, they would subject him to more torture and more reprogramming. Maybe they would only know if Daphne and Annika told the Carbona's what he had said to them.

He tried to remote view but could get no information. His intuition told him that Daphne and Annika wouldn't tell their SIM handlers. With his reconnection to Halia, he decided to trust that intuition, even if it meant losing everything. As the days wore on, he continued to ignore phone calls and knocks at the door as he tried to integrate more lost memories and work with Halia.

Hadden's estate had two separate areas: a lower level with two bedrooms, a sunken living room, a huge kitchen and picture windows overlooking the ocean, and a second floor with more bedrooms and bathrooms. On one side of the house, he'd designed a circular dome that looked like a spaceship from outside. When anyone asked him why he had put a spaceship on his house, he just shrugged. But now, he remembered that the architecture in Helio Tropez looked just like that in many places.

Halia instructed him to redesign this dome as a space-time bubble they could use to communicate with each other. In the walls of the dome, he lay Faraday shielding so that SIM would not detect him when he re-structured his mind or communicated with Halia. Together, they erected several shields and reinforced the frequencies until it felt like an entirely different realm each time

190

he stepped into it. She gave him an advanced version of the SPS protocols, or Secure Protective Space shields. Using his mind, he surrounded the entire house. Each day, he practised the arm movements and Matrix incantations until he perfected the protocol.

After the whole shielding project felt complete, he asked Halia a question.

SIM got access to the amethyst back in 1960. I need to create something better than that to outwit them. Can you download all you can find about gem smithing in Helio Tropez and help me do that?

A week later, she sent him the most recent research about the amethysts. Hadden used his own intuitive skills to read the central mind of SIM as best he could to discover what they knew about Heliotropan technology. That began a process of reconstructing a better version of the amethyst that far outperformed any before it. It helped that Seattle had the top tools and research available in the country on microchip technology. Under the guise of upgrading his own work computer, Hadden employed a few microchip developers to help him. He set up a lab in the dome where he could do his work. After a week of trial and error, the first iteration of the amethyst provided at least some form of protection.

Once he felt safe enough from SIM, he and Halia began the process of rebuilding his strength, reconstructing his memories, and healing the trauma from the cognitive modification. Each day he got better, and their connection grew stronger.

After a couple of weeks of working together, Halia suggested they deal with the curse. They remote viewed the event with Leo back at Mount Rainier where he cast a spell. Halia then guided him to an incident that had happened while travelling back home from Mount Rainier. They were in the car, his father driving. Hadden sat in the back seat while his parents discussed what had happened with the SIM families.

Rand said, "It was so strange the way the tables turned so quickly. They had us completely overpowered, then it all shifted."

"That was me," Addy explained.

"I don't think so, son."

"I planted a vision in Leo's head. I saw his weak spot and made it grow bigger. Right after that, all the SIM agents lost their power. Pretty nifty, huh?"

Trace looked at Rand and frowned.

Rand glanced at him from the rear-view mirror. "You planted a curse?"

"Not a curse, really. Just a bad vision."

"What exactly did you do?"

"I saw that he felt bad about himself because his mother ignored him a lot, so I just imagined that bad feeling growing bigger in him."

Trace's face paled. "Addy, that's... Unless you remove that feeling, he will view the world from that place more and more as he grows older."

"So what?"

"It could mean that he blocks the affections of all females throughout his life. It could block his ascension."

"What do you care? He wouldn't *ascend* anyway. He's a SIM agent."

"Our job is to help anyone we can to ascend, not just the people we like."

"But he would have killed me! I needed to defend myself."

"We suggest you use your aptitude in wiser ways. Cursing is not sanctioned by SANA."

"But I saved everyone. We would have all been killed or taken over by SIM. How can you say that?"

"SANA saved the day, not you."

"It was SANA working through me."

"No. Addy, the way you used your aptitude today was the same way that SIM agents use their aptitude. You mustn't use it like that ever again, okay? If anyone saved the day, it was young Miriam. She used her Warrior aptitude to weaken everyone enough for us to bring our SANA energy forward. If you look inside your heart, you will see that SANA now wants you to reverse this curse."

"I don't get it. Why would you say that?"

"Because you've created a karmic bond with Leo. The curse you gave him will boomerang back at you until you take it away."

"Naw. I don't think that will ever happen. I'll make sure of it."

His mother turned to face him. "It's not up to you. That's a Universal Law. You must promise us that you will remove it. We'll show you how as soon as we get home."

Hadden nodded, but he didn't believe them.

Back home, they showed him the curse removal process. He promised them he'd do it later that day, but he never did. He didn't want Leo to be more powerful than him.

After the memory faded away, Hadden's chin dropped to his chest.

Halia's voice came through loud and clear. *Your parents were right. Do you see now how you allowed Leo full power over you because of this?*

Maybe. Not exactly.

You're karmically indebted to him now. I imagine many of your troubles over the last twenty years actually started with that curse.

If so, how can I remove it?

Halia helped him remember the curse removal process and watched over him as he did it. As he recited the prayer taught to him as a child, a tear formed in the corner of his eye. He hadn't cried in a very long time.

If I, Hadden Violetta, ever harmed myself, SANA or others because of having implanted a curse in Leo Burres, I humbly ask for forgiveness for myself, from SANA and any others who were affected by this. I humbly ask to forgive all errors, offences, blocks and attachments that I may have created, knowingly or unknowingly. From the bottom of my heart, I am truly sorry. Will you please forgive me?

Hadden waited in silence but heard nothing. Maybe SANA couldn't forgive him, or maybe he was so far removed from his SANA connection that he couldn't hear anymore. More tears rolled down his cheeks. Maybe what he had done could never be forgiven. He reached out to Halia telepathically.

You forgot to forgive yourself as well.

Forgive myself? I don't think I can.

Of course you can. We all make mistakes. You were young. You didn't realise what you were doing.

He sighed and said out loud, "I forgive myself for implanting the curse in Leo." When he said those words, they sounded inauthentic, ingenuine. He didn't actually *want* to forgive himself. All those times in his life when he had let pride, selfishness and fear dictate his decisions came creeping up. They became mirages in front of him, one after another, like ghosts coming up from the cellar. Halia encouraged him to let each ghost come forward. Each one kneeled before him, and he tried to forgive it. At first, it was hard, but he kept saying his prayer over and over again until his heart slowly started to thaw. Compassion ignited in his chest, and it grew.

Finally, he saw an image of Leo as a boy sitting in front of him on the grass at Mount Rainier. "I forgive you," Leo said with a genuine tone and loving eyes. Hadden shuddered inside, unable to let that forgiveness in.

Now you need to accept that forgiveness.

He would never actually forgive me. He hates me.

He is a part of you, and if you experience his forgiveness of you, it means it's a possible timeline. Focus on it, and it becomes a reality.

Alright. I allow myself to be forgiven. His hands trembled, and he let out a huge breath.

Good. Now do the last part of the curse removal process.

The words came through telepathically, and he recited them out loud.

"Holy SANA, please identify, locate, remove and repair any curse living in Leo Burres and myself. We release all spiritual, mental, emotional, physical, material, financial or karmic bondage between us. We affirm that, as of this moment, there is no holding on to the past. We pull out of all our memory banks, release, sever and remove any trace of resistance. And so it is forever."

This is good. Very good work.

I feel so different now.

Let's do more each night.

The next night, they worked on his first cognitive modification experience at twenty years old. After that, they went through as many situations from the past twenty years as possible, remote viewing, learning, releasing trauma, reconstructing the timeline and forgiving. After a week with Halia by his side, a lightness filled his body and a freedom expanded through his mind for the first time in years. That's when his connection with SANA returned, permeating him from head to toe. Waves of ecstasy ran through his entire nervous system until the tears of grief turned into tears of joy.

After those two and half weeks with Halia, Hadden slept for two straight days and awoke ravenously hungry and ready to return to work. He vowed to keep connecting to Halia, heal his own mind as best he could and keep that all hidden from SIM. Although he still couldn't fully forgive the Burres family

194

and Col. Loman for all the years of abuse, he could accept forgiveness from the boy named Leo.

After several weeks, he asked Halia telepathically, *May I now come home to Helio Tropez?*

As you know, you have to find Daphne and create a family with her on the surface. The whole mission needs the last two members of Pentada to transform the control situation with SIM. After that, we will look into whether we can bring you all home. If you don't, the Progenitors won't sanction your return.

I would love to find her again, but I think I scared her away.

Ask Leo Burres to help. As your future self told you, SIM actually orchestrated the pairing of you and Daphne. You might as well work with them, seeing as it'll get us where we want. Only this time, I will help you, Daphne and Annika to protect yourselves from SIM. Agreed?

How?

I'm not sure yet, but we'll figure it out together.

Later that day, Hadden went to the local Seattle library. He looked up anything he could find about Daphne Zuris. Her face appeared on the cover of several top fashion magazines. She was on the cast list of several plays and movies. In the people section, it said, "Career Politician, Rafael Viridis, to wed actress and model, Daphne Zuris." SIM agents must have known about Rafael and Daphne being SANA Mates. They wanted them to create Pentada children. Another article from six months ago said, "Rafael Viridis and Daphne Zuris divorce." No listing of children. She signed a prenuptial and walked away with very little while Rafael remained a multi-millionaire. *Why was that?*

Strangely enough, the next day at work, Leo called Hadden into his corner office overlooking Puget Sound. He poured Hadden a scotch. Although he no longer smoked or drank alcohol, Hadden pretended to sip.

"Whatever happened to that singer from the club in Vancouver that you liked?"

"We lost track. She's on the road all the time. Why do you ask?"

"It turns out that my father knows their band manager, Josephine Carbona. Dad is planning a party for my mother's 70th birthday. I recommended that her band played. It's happening at the Edgewater Hotel. You know, the one on the waterfront. What do you think?"

195

"Sure. Why not? It would be nice to see her again, but I don't think she liked me in the end."

"Why do you think that? Did you say anything weird to her?"

"No, of course not," he said, lying and fishing for information on what Leo knew about their last interaction. "I probably shouldn't have tried to kiss her so soon."

"That's probably it. She's fresh off a divorce from that politician guy."

"Rafael Viridis."

"Exactly. But that's over now. Let's give it a second try. You seem like such a lonely guy these days, not coming to parties anymore, keeping to yourself. I need you at your best, pal. We have some huge deals in the pipeline."

"Okay. I'll give it a try."

Hadden figured that anything he had said to Daphne or Annika that night had been erased from their memory banks. The Carbona family were a well-known criminal family, and Daphne stayed under tight control as one of their assets.

CHAPTER 21

Montreal, Canada – 2011

Back in her hotel room, Tia interfaced with Cassandra on the comm. The team had inputted facial and vocal information on Dax into their computers.

Dax might be the grandson of one of the other couples in the Quinary Mission, Lorena and Ben Indicium. We predict he's born in 1980. If he's full blood Heliotropan, there's a good chance he's been pulled into serving SIM in some way.

Tia shifted on the bed. *He seems to be on some kind of narcotic. It could be a trap if I go to the concert.*

The team is researching the situation, and they believe that you will be protected enough with your amethyst. I think you should go to the concert and use the frequency blocker to protect yourself. We believe SANA has led you to that restaurant – take that synchronicity seriously. It can't be a coincidence.

Tia reluctantly agreed, and later that day got a cab to the stadium. Her heart pounded as she walked through the gates. Niklana, the Oracle, said her SANA mate was from the House of Indicium, and born in 1980. An usher looked at the ticket and led her to a VIP area right upfront. Screaming fans crushed her on either side as an electric guitar boomed from the giant speakers, rattling her rib cage. The band members took to the stage, and the crowd roared even louder. When Dax stepped into the limelight, everyone rose to their feet.

"Bonjour, Montreal! Nous t'aimons!"

The roar of the crowd overwhelmed Tia. Dax pulled up a stool and started with a ballad. The first song had a melody she recognised, like something from her childhood, but she couldn't quite remember what. The lyrics, the melody, his voice, they all mesmerised her. The lyrics spoke of deep esoteric truths in code form that a source-based human would long to connect to. As the concert progressed, she noticed the crowd had fallen into a spell. Symbols appeared on a screen above the musicians, similar to those found in Helio Tropez, only in reverse. Above them, an invisible vortex acted like a siphon, pulling on the life force energy from the concert-goers, especially those in heightened states of emotion. That energy should be returned to the people, but instead, SIM took it from them.

As the concert ended, the band made their final bows, and the crowd went crazy, wanting them to come back twice more for encores. They loved Dax in a way she'd never seen a crowd love someone before, making her long to get close to him. After the final bow, Tia started following the crowd to the exit, but an usher led her through a side door and into a VIP after-party function. Celebrities, media personalities, concert bookers, groupies and friends of the band congregated, eating caviar and drinking champagne.

The band members made their entrance a few minutes later, and Tia hung in the background, watching. Dax was clearly looking for her, but in her glasses and hat, she looked quite different from when they had met in the cafe. Still, he weaved his way through the crowd, searching until he appeared in front of her.

"There you are. You wear a different disguise," he said with a smirk. "Very clever."

His smile dazzled, making her breath quicken.

"Are you trying to escape the paparazzi just like me?"

His Audient-Attention aptitude, *The Lover*, clearly made him an ingenious musician who could keep an audience in rapt attention, loving an entire audience back until they transcended their everyday life. She also knew that he could read between the lines of what someone said.

"No." She suddenly felt silly wearing a ball cap and sunglasses at night while inside.

"Then let me see your eyes."

She took off the hat and glasses, then looked up at him.

"I know I said this before, but you seem so familiar."

Tia stayed silent, again noticing his dilated pupils and rapid hand movements. Her amethyst detected a narcotic, like cocaine, in his system.

Dax stepped closer to be out of the earshot of his bodyguard. "I believe you know things about me and how we are connected. Why are you choosing not to tell me?"

"I don't know what you're talking about. I think you're mistaking me for someone else."

An older man joined them. A crocodile tattoo ran up one hairy arm, and bloodshot eyes peered at her from under bushy eyebrows. "Who's this lovely young thing?"

"Linda, this is JJ Redus, my agent!"

Tia reached forward a limp hand. "Nice to meet you,"

Swirls of red filled JJ's aura. Her amethyst detected his aptitude as Audient-Attention, just like Xander. The Redus family were SIM agents. His energy grabbed at her emotional centre, seeking to intimidate her, but the mirror shield made that energy boomerang right back at him. He took a step back and raised his eyebrows.

"The concert was fantastic," Tia said, ducking her head. "Thank you so much for the tickets. Now, I really have to get going. See you later." Smiling, she turned on her heel and fled for the entrance.

Dax caught up to her and said, "There's an after-party back at the hotel. I know JJ is a bit much, but hopefully, he's not going to be there. Several celebrities will, like Hugo B, Fabian Marxet, Metta Z., Crystal Edgemont..."

Tia stopped. "Did you say Metta Z?" *Maybe that was a stage name, short for Metta Zuris*, she thought.

"Yes, do you know her?"

Freezing for a moment, Tia had to think fast. As an Ecrivent-Acceptance, Metta must have a songwriting aptitude. "Ah... actually, I just know her music."

"Right! She wrote three of the songs that we sang tonight."

"Really?"

"Yes. For example, the opening song, *Shades of Light*. You can meet her face-to-face. I'll introduce you. We're both with the same record label."

"Okay. Sounds good."

"The party is at the Queen Elizabeth Hotel, room 822. I'll tell security to expect you. We're all headed there in a few minutes. Your name again... Linda...?

"Wright."

"Linda Wright. Promise you'll be there?"

"Umm... Yes. I'll try to."

"No try. Do or not do," he said, doing his best Yoda impression.

Tia returned a weak smile, knowing that was not only a Yoda quote but a Heliotropan philosophy. She slipped out the side door and ran breathless to find a cab.

"Take me to the Queen Elizabeth Hotel."

On the way, she had a telepathic conversation with Cassandra.

Should I go to this party or not? Metta might be there. It could be a trap. SIM knows I wouldn't miss the chance to reconnect with her.

We are running the possibilities through our timeline program. It could just be a SANA synchronicity. We did choose this time and location for you to come to Montreal based on our SANA timeline calculations...

Okay. How long will it take? I'm only fifteen minutes away from the hotel.

It's done now. We don't detect any SIM interference. They can't see who you really are.

Okay, thank you.

If anything goes sideways, remember, we can bring you back quickly through teleportation if you get into an enclosed space and create the shield. You remember the command?

Yes. Got it.

After paying for the cab, she entered the hotel's lobby, humming with fancily dressed people in party mode. In a restroom, she took off the ball cap and unravelled the braids pinned up on her head. As they fell down her back, she took a breath for courage and smoothed out any loose strands. Back in the lobby, she found the elevators and hit the button for the eighth floor. When the elevator doors opened, thumping music filled the hallways. A bodyguard stood near the doors to room 822. After showing him her ID with the name Linda Wright, he stepped back and let her in.

CHAPTER 22

<u>Seattle – 1979</u>

Floating over Elliot Bay, the Edgewater Hotel blazed in the setting sun. As Hadden's limo pulled into the entrance, he patted the inside pocket of his tux where the upgraded amethysts lay safely tucked away. As the valet opened his limo door, he noticed other guests arriving: executives from top companies, celebrities, media magnates, family and friends of the Burres Family.

He shook a few hands as he entered, smiling pleasantly. For years, Thelma's philanthropic work had made her a darling in the eyes of the media, but Hadden knew that some of her philanthropic projects were fronts for money laundering projects and human trafficking.

Until recently, making money had driven all the priorities in his life. Anything humanitarian, spiritual, compassionate or thoughtful didn't occur to him. The adjustment back to his true self felt shattering. His daily routine, ways of thinking and bad habits all came from a place of not caring about himself or others. On top of all that, the detox effects from quitting all the bad food, alcohol and drugs that had littered his system for years gave him a constant headache.

He wasn't looking forward to nursing a glass of water and eating salad while everyone else gorged themselves on cake and champagne. If not for Halia, he would never be able to attend an event like this while staying sober and protected.

There was still a chance that the upgraded amethysts might be detected by SIM, but his ingenious plan involved programming the amethyst to compartmentalise a part of the mind where SANA could thrive, while another part of the mind appeared enslaved to SIM. Light and dark would literally live within the same body, where the light was aware of the dark, but not the other way around. Usually, the game was played in reverse. Throughout human history, the suppression of the shadow caused it to grow. Now his plan served the opposite purpose.

He had arrived early to make sure to greet the band. A cab pulled up, and his breath quickened upon seeing Daphne again. She seemed happy to see him as if nothing unusual had happened between them. Annika, carrying her violin case, walked right by without looking up. Josephine barked orders at hotel staff to get things set up just right. Hadden surmised that Josephine acted as Daphne's CM handler. And he guessed that Irene Carbona, the keyboard player, acted as Annika's. Somehow, he had to get both women away from their handlers long enough to implant the gemstone.

As Josie checked the sound levels, Hadden pulled Daphne aside in a quiet alcove. He held the amethyst on one finger behind his back. She wore the Azurite stone necklace again.

"Can I have a look at the necklace?"

Daphne glanced sideways to see if anyone noticed. "Um, sure."

As he leaned in to touch the necklace, he pressed the amethyst into the indent behind her left ear. Her eyelids flickered rapidly, and her irises radiated a rainbow of colours as the frequencies settled. Her legs gave out below her, but Hadden caught her and ushered her to a table. *Maybe not the best idea when she's about to perform, but when else?*

With his telepathic vision, he watched her mind open up enough to download everything she needed to remember, know and pretend not to know so she could survive. Her face flushed red, and beads of sweat formed on her brow.

"Get ready for the show. We'll talk afterwards."

Obligingly, she stood up and walked in a daze toward the dressing room.

Hadden sighed. The trickier part would be Annika. He approached the petite woman as she tuned her violin. Irene looked sideways at them, and Annika furrowed her brow.

"You're that guy we met in Vancouver, right? The Daphne fanboy."

Hoping she still had a crush on him like she did at Mount Rainier, he whispered, "Want to smoke a joint outside?"

She looked over at Irene, who was bent over a soundboard. "A joint? No, I'm good."

Hadden sighed in frustration. "It's Acapulco Gold."

"No kidding? That stuff's rare around here. Alright, maybe one puff."

They slipped out the side entrance and onto a balcony. Peering over the edge, the waves slapped against the pier, and the wind whipped up her pixie haircut. He could see a place on her bare scalp to place the gemstone. Pulling a joint from his wallet, Hadden gave it to her and stood close so he could use his lighter. As he did, he reached behind her ear to implant the amethyst. She swatted him away, and it fell to the ground.

"Cut that out!"

"Sorry, I was just trying to protect you from the wind."

Panicked, he searched the balcony floor, praying the wind hadn't pushed it over the edge. She inhaled the joint and passed it back to him. He pretended to inhale, knowing he needed to stay clear-headed from now on.

"Did you drop something?"

"Yes, actually. I think my contact lens fell out."

"Bummer," she said, indifferent.

He crouched down and dialled up on his powers of detection. It lay stuck to the side of a bench. He retrieved it and breathed a sigh of relief.

"Got it!"

Annika's aptitude allowed her to detect nuances in sound and voices that most people never picked up.

She narrowed her eyes at him. "You want something from me..." She looked at him more closely as though trying to read him. "It can't be me. You're just trying to get to her."

"No. Nothing like that. I just like you. I think you're a musical genius. In fact, I know it. I just want to get to know you better."

"We just met. How would you know I'm some kind of genius? By the way, I'm not into men." Annika took a deep inhale of the joint and muttered under her breath as she exhaled, "...at least, not anymore."

"That's cool. I'm not trying to hit on you anyway. I saw you play in Vancouver. I know a brilliant musician when I see one. I feel like I've met you somewhere before. Ha! But maybe it was in another life." He winked.

She seemed about to scoff at the remark, but then her eyes looked up to the left as if she was remembering something. He placed the amethyst on his finger again and lunged forward, holding her head firmly with one hand and placing the amethyst behind her left ear with the other. She fought him off until the amethyst connected. Her eyes flashed an iridescent green, and she fell limp into his arms. He sat her down on a bench as the summer wind lashed at their faces.

"What's with you, man?"

"Sorry, I'm just trying to help you."

"I feel so strange. You were right about that pot. It's strong stuff."

He couldn't tell whether the amethyst properly implanted. Maybe the marijuana blocked her receptors. Irene called out from an open doorway, but he couldn't make out what she said.

"You better go in. Irene's looking for you."

Annika stumbled to her feet and weaved towards the doorway. He followed her inside and watched as she sat down at a table with Irene and the other musicians. Somehow, the process overloaded her system. While the others talked, Annika slumped forward and lay her head on the table, moaning.

"What the hell is going on with you?" Irene asked, grabbing her shoulder.

She just cradled her forehead and whimpered.

"You smell like pot. I told you never to do that stuff. It messes you up. I'm getting you some coffee. We're on in 30 minutes!"

Hadden stayed nearby, trying to help her stabilise with his mind. Soon, the Emcee came on the loudspeaker. After a short preamble, Thelma and Lloyd Burres approached the stage. Hadden shuddered just by looking at his face. She expressed her gratitude to everyone for attending. After a hollow speech from Lloyd and the head of the foundation, the Emcee said, "Let's welcome... The Latin Heart Club Band!"

The musicians, including Annika and Daphne, took their places on stage and began a popular Gypsy Kings tune. It got the party started, and people headed for the dance floor. Meanwhile, Hadden sat at a table in close proximity to the stage, and Leo came to join him.

"Did you get a chance to chat with Daphne?"

"Yeah, we're good. I'm going to ask her out after the set."

"Good, man. She's a total catch. I'm sure you'll help her get over that nasty divorce."

Annika seemed off her game. The other band members glared at her as she lost the rhythm of the song, and although the crowd didn't seem to notice, Irene did. During the break, she pulled Annika aside and started shouting at her. Hadden sent a telepathic message to Annika to dial up on her amethyst's protection field. As soon as he sent the message, Irene pulled away enough for her to escape back into the crowd.

Daphne came to join Hadden and Leo at their table. They chatted for a while about the music, then Leo winked at Hadden and excused himself.

He telepathically called Annika over, and she sat down with them. The others looked distracted enough, so he leaned forward, creating a cloaking shield around them.

"Do you remember meeting me when we were children, now?"

Both of them nodded slowly as though they weren't sure the memory was one they could trust.

Annika leaned forward and whispered, "You tried to tell us things in Vancouver..."

Daphne interrupted, "...about Mount Rainier, and about our parents being alive in Helio Tropez. But we thought you were crazy."

"Did you tell Josie or Irene what I said?"

"No, did you?" Daphne asked, looking at Annika.

"No. We wrote you off as another of Daphne's crazed fans."

"He's one of us, Annika. His family was in the Quinary Mission, too."

"I know that now. You freaked me out on the patio, though. What were you trying to do, and why do I feel so strange? All of these new... old memories, where did they come from?"

Hadden explained how he had installed an upgraded amethyst without their handlers detecting them. They asked several questions to better understand how to handle the transition, but he felt that his answers weren't helpful enough.

"Take my hand, but discreetly from under the table so that I can boost our connection and help you understand more."

As they pretended to make small talk, Hadden uploaded his entire game plan to free them from the cognitive modification so they could both get to Helio Tropez and be reunited with their parents. By the end of the break, they both looked more grounded.

The rest of the night flew by. As the last of the partygoers went home, he decided to invite Daphne and Annika to stay at his Seattle mansion. He would, of course, have to invite their handlers to avoid trouble. Hadden ran his idea past Leo, and luckily, Leo supported it.

Leo approached Josephine and, with money in hand, said, "I hear your next gig isn't for a week. Instead of staying here or some dodgy place in Portland, why don't you come on down to the Violetta estate? Hadden has lots of spare rooms. It's quite the space-age place overlooking the water."

Josie and Irene looked at each other, then over at their assets.

"We'd love to," Josephine said as she winked at Leo.

The next day, Daphne, Annika, Josie and Irene arrived in a van filled with luggage and music equipment. Hadden showed them around the house, then to their rooms. As they sat down for dinner, he showed them five bottles of a 1960 Chateau Palmer that he'd brought up from his wine cellar. He knew how much Irene Carbona loved her fine wines, and each bottle he possessed cost over $300. In the kitchen, he added two ground-up sleeping pills to the bottom of Irene and Josie's wine glasses before pouring them each a glass.

They spent the evening chatting, talking about past gigs and on-tour mishaps. By the time all of the plates were cleared, all of the glasses were empty.

Hadden feigned a yawn. "It's been a long day. I see that we're all quite tired. Let's call it a night and meet down here for breakfast at, say, 9 a.m. How's that?"

Josie and Irene nodded, so Daphne and Annika did too. The four of them thanked him and turned in for the night.

About forty minutes later, when Hadden was sure the handlers were fully asleep, he slipped a note under Daphne and Annika's door to meet him in the dome. He shielded the room before they entered, then raised the vibration. They spent that entire night and every night that week receiving healing and reconstruction of their damaged neural pathways, ensuring the proper recalibration, balancing and compartmentalization necessary to deprogram. He also taught them how to pretend like they were still programmed, the same way he had learned to do with Leo.

On their last day there, Leo joined the group for dinner. Hadden noticed Leo and Josie talking quietly between themselves at one end of the table. As the servants cleared the dishes away and they moved onto the patio, Leo whispered to Hadden, "So, how's it going with Daphne?"

"Good. I really like her a lot."

"So, uh, have you done it yet?"

Hadden feigned a smile, then turned away from him to give instructions to the staff. Later that night, Josie and Daphne appeared before him, linked arm in arm.

Josie sat Daphne down next to Hadden. "We love your futuristic house."

"Thank you. By the way, I love that movie you were in... that sci-fi."

Daphne swept her hair over her shoulder. "Oh, God. That one about Venusians?"

"Yes, Galactica III. You were amazing."

"Ugh, I thought I was so bad."

Josie backed away as she said, "You could just thank him for the compliment."

Daphne smiled in an obedient way. "Thank you for the compliment, Mr Violetta."

"Just call me Hadden."

Once Josie was out of earshot, Daphne whispered, "Leo and Josie are clearly trying to get us together. Do you know why?"

"They want us to mate and create Pentada children."

"They do? But you're not my SANA Mate."

His heart sank.

She penetrated his gaze and read his mind. "Although... I must say, we do have a strong connection."

"You actually think that?"

She fiddled with a stray length of hair, looping it around her finger. "Back at Mount Rainier, I did feel more connected to you than to Rafael... So maybe you are."

"I wasn't sure," he replied trying to sound aloof.

"Of course, but my parents wanted me to be with Rafael."

"Right. I get it. We were just kids. How could we know?"

She laughed in her alluring way and touched his forearm. Across the patio, Leo smiled at them.

Putting up extra shielding, he whispered, "I think it's time I tell you about my trip into the future. More specifically, from 1960 to 2010."

"Your what?"

"Let's talk in the dome. They are okay with us being alone anyway."

She nodded and followed him up the spiral staircase as the others continued chatting on the patio.

After clicking the door shut and dialling up the frequencies, he told her the story of meeting his future self and daughter and his trip to Helio Tropez. After he finished the story, Daphne leaned forward, holding her face in her hands.

"So your future self at seventy years old told you that we marry and have twin Pentada daughters?"

"Exactly."

She paced the room in her shimmering halter dress and stilettos, touching the wall of the dome on one side and then again on the other. "This is a lot to take in."

"I know."

She stopped at the window and looked out at the ocean, auburn ringlets swaying from side to side. "I was never really sure I wanted to bring children into this world or that I could ever be a good mother."

Hadden's chest tightened and said, "I never wanted to bring children into this world either."

"My mother predicted that Annika or I would have twin girls, both of whom would be Pentada. That was clearly SIM's plan for Rafael and me. They must have studied my memories and knew my parents wanted me to mate with him," she said with a wistful smile.

"You felt he was your SANA mate?"

"I don't know. My parents thought so, but I was only eight years old!"

"I think they didn't want you connected to the Violettas. Your parents and my parents never saw eye to eye."

"That's right! I forgot about that."

"Why didn't it work out with Rafael?"

"We tried, but we never could have children. We also didn't have a strong sexual connection."

He joined her at the window, placing his hand on the small of her back. A shock of longing ran through him. "Aren't SANA mates supposed to have a strong sexual connection?"

Her turquoise eyes glanced at him, shimmering with aliveness. "I suppose. I heard they give back to humanity in some way, so the bond needs to be strong to ensure they stay together."

"I thought that only SANA mates could produce Pentada children."

She turned to face him, pressing her forehead against his. "I guess my parents were wrong all along."

"What is your relationship with Rafael like now?"

"We're estranged. They won't let me contact him since the divorce is final. SIM didn't get what they wanted from the match, so that's it. Josie programmed me to create issues until he divorced me."

Hadden took a step back. "Like what?"

She turned away and lowered her eyes. "I'd rather not say."

A rush of warmth filled his chest. "I won't judge you. I've done all kinds of things that my true self would never do. I know it's the CM."

"Really? You'll have to fill me in," Daphne said as she hugged her waist. "Josie programmed me to be one of those women who seduce men in power until their whole life falls apart. SIM used me as a tool for revenge against whoever they wanted to take down. When Rafael found out, it destroyed him. I doubt he'll ever talk to me again."

"He probably loved you very much."

"I know. I was so upset with him through the whole divorce, but now that it's over and my mind is better, I remember how much we cared about each other. That said, it wasn't like the relationship my parents had. I longed for something like that, but we were both so damaged. We did the best we could given the circumstances."

Hadden hoped the same fate wouldn't befall the two of them. "I saw some articles in the news about you two."

She turned away from his embrace and crossed her arms. "Lots of horrible gossip. It's hard living your life in the public eye."

"If it's any consolation, I'm not much in the public eye. At least, not anymore."

"Good. I'm not nearly as big a celebrity as I used to be either, so hopefully, they will leave us alone."

He pulled her back into an embrace. "I can help us stay safe together."

She looked up at him, then asked, "But if we do have children, won't they just take them away?"

"I've seen the future. We can protect them."

"How?"

"At least, I am able to protect Tia. They made us separate when the girls were three years old, and you took the other twin, named Metta. Apparently, I never found out what happened to you and Metta."

"That's horrible..."

"I believe that we can change the timeline and get back to Helio Tropez, though."

"How would that be possible?"

"I can get help from Halia – my grandmother. I didn't have that connection in the first timeline."

"But you told me she cannot tell the Elders she's in contact with anyone on the surface."

The room below them erupted in laughter.

He stepped closer, "She thinks the Progenitors will allow her to help once the twins are born."

"Because the girls will be Pentada?"

"I assume so. Are you willing to do this with me? Get married... start a family? I know it's all very sudden, but Leo has been programming me to go in this direction ever since I met you at the Cave nightclub in Vancouver."

Daphne shook her head in disbelief. "That meeting at the nightclub was all orchestrated?"

"I guess so."

"Of course it was," she sighed. "I'm starting to be more and more aware of all the programming that Josie gives me, like matchmaking me with you."

"Do *you* want that? I mean, the true you, the deprogrammed part of you..."

She looked at him with kind eyes, sensing his insecurity. "Yes, of course I do. Even without the CM programming."

Hadden breathed a sigh of relief as he read the truth in her eyes.

Daphne sat back down on the chair and folded her arms around her waist. "That said, I'm nervous about all this. We barely know each other. What kind of mother will I be? I might mess them up."

"I know. The relationship I saw between my seventy-year-old self and Tia was... strained. But that's because he kept her trapped in this house all her

211

life, rarely letting her step foot outside. That is no life for someone as brilliant as a Pentada. And I got fat and depressed! We can't let that happen this time."

"You got fat?" she laughed. "How fat?"

"You don't want to know. Ever since I got my memories back that day in Vancouver, I've stopped all my bad habits and started exercising daily."

"I don't know if I could handle it – meeting my seventy-year-old self."

"It was tough, but it's given me the chance to make new decisions."

"I thought we're not allowed to change timelines?"

"Yes, I know, but my memories came back anyway. The Temporalia probably stitched the timelines back together. That's their job. We need to somehow keep our true memories, no matter what happens."

Daphne touched the Azurite stone on his wrist. "Why don't we use our Azurite stones as the trigger?"

He lay his hand across hers on top of the pendant. "Agreed. We always wear and program them to keep us lucid. We also have these upgraded amethysts and support from Halia. How could we not make it back to Helio Tropez this time?"

She turned away with an unfocused gaze, her luminous eyes searching inside for the truth. "The Progenitors must want us to unite all of Pentada back in Helio Tropez. They wouldn't want to keep us stranded here, would they?"

"No, of course not."

Daphne looked sharply at him this time, her Voyent aptitude assessing his capability to pull off the impossible. After a few moments, she relaxed her breathing. "Okay. Let's do it."

An expanded feeling filled his chest as he moved closer to her. "You know, this is our last night together before you leave."

"I know." She reached forward and pressed her full lips onto his. The kiss sealed the deal, sending shivers through every cell in his body. It created an oath between them to love each other through eternity and bring the last Pentada souls into the world. With that kiss, he carried her to a chaise in the corner of the room and untied the halter dress from behind her neck. As the dress slid off, he tore off his jacket and shirt. She ran her hands down his chest and helped him with the buckle of his belt.

Soon, they lay naked in each other's arms. The feeling of her silky skin against his chest sent him into ecstasy. As he entered her, the connection to SANA between them roared to an unprecedented zenith. All the lives they'd had together, all the love they shared, all the creativity that birthed from their union came racing to Hadden's mind, forming one poignant image after another. They'd loved and lost each other so many times. To finally find each other again meant everything to him. For the first time in a very long time, Hadden was finally happy.

Six weeks later, Leo sauntered into Hadden's office with a bottle of Dom Perignon and two flute glasses. "I hear you're going to be a father!"

Hadden leaned back in his chair and grinned. "Who let it slip?"

Leo raised his eyebrows. "Josie Carbona could tell. Daphne had that glow. So... that's amazing. And it happened quickly."

Hadden shrugged, although he knew that SIM had helped orchestrate it.

Leo poured the champagne and handed him a glass. "Well, the good news is that Josephine is letting Daphne out of the band contract."

Hadden pretended to sip, then placed the glass far away on the desk. He swivelled around to look out at the vista from his 43rd floor office. The Space Needle gleamed in the sunlight a few blocks away. "Yes, she's moving to Seattle at the end of the month."

"I heard." Leo came around to the window and sat on the ledge. "So, when is the wedding?"

"She wants to do it soon so that she can still fit into this wedding dress Josie bought her."

"Josie bought her a wedding dress already?" Leo guzzled his glass and poured another one. "I'll call the Edgewater Hotel. Let's do it there, where you reconnected."

"Sounds good. I was hoping Annika could move here too, but Daphne said that she's moving to Australia?"

"She's marrying Michael Indicium. Remember him? He's that tech genius."

Hadden remembered meeting Michael back in 1948 at Mount Rainier when they were all children, but he pretended not to know him. "I think you mentioned him before. Isn't he already married?"

"Recently divorced."

Hadden had suspected that SIM orchestrated all the marriages and divorces of Quinary family members, trying to get them to conceive high powered children. Michael and Annika had not been identified as SANA mates, yet SIM clearly wanted to see whether Annika could conceive Pentada children too. The fact that she would be moving halfway across the world troubled him, but he hoped that the upgraded amethyst would keep them all connected long enough to get back home together. Perhaps once the children were born, they'd let Annika visit.

CHAPTER 23

Montreal – 2011

As she entered the presidential suite, Tia scanned the room for SIM interference. A cacophony of voices, smoke and thumping rock music assaulted her senses. People zig-zagged their way from one group to another, eyes half-closed, looking for another fix. No one seemed to notice her. The amethyst clearly worked.

What would an adult version of Metta look like now? The waiter came by with a tray of glasses containing steaming red liquid. *Maybe it's mulled wine?* She declined and instead weaved her way through the crowd, scanning the eyes of every woman in the room. A bedroom door opened, and Dax stepped out. He caught Tia's eye and beckoned her over. She froze. All her senses went on high alert, looking for a potential trap.

Surely, a famous musician like Dax had a CM handler. She zeroed in on the man she'd met named JJ Redus. He sported a walrus moustache and wore a red velvet jacket, so was easy to spot. She snapped a picture with her mind and passed it along to the Task Force.

Can you run this image of JJ Redus and see if you get anything on him?

A few seconds later, Cassandra said, *The Redus family are SIM agents who target Indium family members due to the opposing colour frequency of red and indigo. The chance that Dax is actually the grandson of Ben and Lorena*

Indicum is now at 91%. We did a DNA match. The chance that JJ Redus is his handler is at 74%.

JJ watched Dax call her over. His eyes turned in her direction, and she ducked out of sight. When she noticed JJ turn away, Tia darted to the bedroom door and slipped inside.

Two other people sat in the room; a woman with a rocker mullet and another woman with auburn ringlets, hair falling to her thighs. That had to be her.

"Hey Metta, I met Linda here in the restaurant today. Remember I told you about her? She loves your songs."

Metta projected her hand forward with a limp wrist and a dazed expression. "Thanks... I try."

Tia shook the floppy hand and smiled. Metta scrutinized her over the top of tinted glasses.

"And this is Ruth Carbona."

Tia froze. The woman nodded absently and then went back to scrolling through her phone. The Task Force went to work scanning the images of both women.

The chance that Ruth Carbona is Metta's handler is 98%. She is Josie Carbona's daughter. Very dangerous. Tread carefully.

I've never met Ruth before, but I did go to school with her sister, Andrea. Can you scan to see if she recognizes me?

Negative. She thinks you're just another fan. The other woman is definitely your twin sister, Metta.

"We're just about to do some E. Care to join?" Dax asked, pulling out an envelope.

Tia assumed he meant a recreational drug. In a few seconds, the Task Force told her that E stood for Ecstasy, also known as "the love pill". It heightens colour, sound, touch, passion and empathy. Focusing in on Ruth's bloodstream, she detected no narcotics or alcohol. Although she looked bored and disconnected from the others, her auric field webbed into Metta's in a menacing way.

Dax handed everyone a pill and a glass of red wine. Metta downed hers instantly, as did Dax. From her peripheral vision, she saw that Ruth pretended to take hers and pocketed it instead. Tia did the same. Ruth's aptitude was Ecrivent-Acceptance, just like her twin sister. That meant she could hypnotize people using mind code and words. Clearly, as Metta's handler, she was doing that. Dialling up on her own protection shield, she sent an empowering mind code to Metta to override it. Metta's face instantly softened while Ruth's gnarled up in tension.

They talked about the concert, the crowd, their next gig and Metta's upcoming songwriting project for another band. Tia saw herself in Metta's gestures, voice and mannerisms, and longed to tell her, but maybe Metta didn't even know she had a sister. After all, Tia hadn't known until a year ago.

As the drug took effect, both Dax and Metta leaned closer and wanted to know more about Tia. She hadn't rehearsed much of a back story. Telepathically, she connected with Cassandra and the Task Force, asking for advice on how to handle the situation. In a few seconds, she received a download with a few suggestions.

"I'm from Illinois, just here for a conference."

"What kind of conference?"

"People from the coaching industry. I'm a performance coach for people in the arts."

"What does that mean?"

"I help people perform better as musicians, writers or artists by not letting limiting thoughts get in their way. It's similar to the kinds of coaching that pro athletes receive to perform well under pressure."

Dax slumped back on the sofa, glassy-eyed and grinning. "I could use a performance coach. My business manager tries to pump me up on tour, but he's crap at it. I should hire you!"

"Me, too," Metta laughed. "This music business is tough. So much rejection. Let's both hire her!"

Ruth wrapped her arm around Metta's neck and whispered something. Metta's brow furrowed, and she reached out to grab Dax, but Ruth pulled her off the sofa and led her out of the room.

"We gotta go. Mia Soulis should be here by now. She wants Metta to write her next song."

After they left the bedroom, Dax turned his attention to Tia, and she panicked. If he was her SANA mate, the coupling instinct would be strong. Dax moved closer, his bedroom eyes mesmerizing her.

How do I get out of this? Tia asked Cassandra.

Create a protection shield over the hara area. It's not the right time, and he's not in the right frame of mind. He's been programmed to seduce any woman he wants.

He circled his arm around her waist and kissed her neck. Her knees weakened. With all her willpower, she imagined a diamond-shaped shield over the body, from chin to knees, just like she'd been taught, weakening the magnetic current between them.

JJ entered the bedroom, taking in the two of them in a tired glance. "Dax, they're making a toast to you. Let's go!" he barked.

He quickly jumped up to his feet and followed JJ out of the room like an automaton.

In the main room, Tia watched as one of the sponsors made a toast to Dax and the band members. She took the opportunity to immerse herself in the crowd, weaving through it. An older woman whispered something to JJ making him look around the room. That's when a shock of recognition ran through her. She looked like the home care worker who came the night her father died. *What was her name? Mary...something...Mary Redus!* She took another mental snapshot and sent it to the Task Force.

Who is that woman next to JJ Redus?

A few minutes later Cassandra responded. *It's a relative, maybe his mother or aunt.*

I recognize her from the night my father died...she was there. I had no idea she was a SIM agent. What if she recognizes me?

Get out of there as soon as you can.

Tia weaved her way to the back of the room, to find Metta standing next to Ruth.

Cassandra warned her. *Remember, this mission is about installing Metta's amethyst, but you mustn't do it while she's on the drug. It will need to be at another time.*

How will I ever get Metta alone and sober?

Invite her somewhere...say... tomorrow.

When Ruth turned to talk to someone else, Tia took the opportunity to move in closer to Metta. "I had this MindStory that I would get to meet you face-to-face one day. Your music means a lot to me."

Metta's eyes grew wide and glassy. "Did you say a MindStory?"

"Yes."

"That's so funny. I used to play this game called MindStory as a child. I used to make up possible futures and turn them into stories. I didn't know anyone else used that term."

"It's become quite popular," Tia lied. "Did you have any brothers or sisters?"

"No. Just me and my mom. She left, though, and I ended up in foster care."

"What happened?"

"She just disappeared one day," Metta answered, glancing away.

"So you haven't seen her since you were...?"

"Maybe six or seven. I don't really remember."

"I'm so sorry to hear that."

"No matter," Metta shrugged, taking a sip from her glass.

"Listen," Tia said, taking a breath for courage. "Usually, I do what's called a discovery session with a potential client to see if my coaching is a good fit for them. If you're interested, we could get together tomorrow for, say, forty minutes? I'm only in town one more day."

"Oh. Ok. Um. That might be good... I'll have to ask Ruth...she takes care of all my scheduling. Do you have a phone number?"

Tia wrote down the number of her burner phone. "We could meet at Café Santropol, on St. Urbain? I'm free most of the day tomorrow. Just let me know." Tia gave her a smile. Metta looked dazed, as though her brain was trying to keep up with the events.

"Okay. Thanks. I have this big deal with a production company that I'm trying to negotiate. It *would* be great to have someone to talk to besides Ruth."

"Sounds great. I hope to see you tomorrow."

"What about Dax?"

Tia paused and turned to look back at Metta. "What about him?"

"He couldn't stop talking about you all day. Do you like him?"

Tia read Metta's mind at that moment and could tell that she was attracted to him, like many others in the room. Confused by the comment, Tia said, "I just met him. And, isn't he your boyfriend?"

"No. I'm not his type. Neither are you, for that matter. He doesn't tend to like tall, skinny white girls with freakishly long hair like ours."

"Oh really? What's his type?"

"He ends up with short, curvy girls with dark skin, like Genna over there."

A stunning East Indian woman nuzzled close to him.

"Okay, got it. She's beautiful. I'm not looking for a boyfriend right now, anyway, and I really need to go."

Every time Dax looked over at her, she noticed JJ sending CM trigger symbols to keep him in line. Clearly, his connection to Tia had created a new frequency...one that JJ felt threatened by. She tapped into her connection with Cassandra.

If Dax is a descendant of Quinary, shouldn't we try to rescue him too?

If you can do it without getting caught by SIM, go ahead, but Metta is our first priority.

Got it.

"Tell Dax to join us at the Café if he wants. Maybe there will be time to do some coaching with him, too."

Metta nodded and reached out to hug her. Memories of playing together as children filled her heart, and her eyes welled up with tears.

"You're crying! Do you really love my music that much?"

Tia laughed and wiped the tears. "Yes, very much. I hope to see you tomorrow. Bye!"

At 10 AM the next morning, she awoke to a beep from her burner phone. A text arrived from Metta: *Dax and I will meet you at the record label office at 2 PM. Our boss, Josie Carbona, wants to meet you too. Does that work?*

A dread crept into her chest. *Josie Carbona will recognize me! She was there at my sixteenth birthday party. But, wait, I never had a sixteenth birthday party. I never met Josie before. Argh! It's the two timelines confusing me again. Which timeline was Josie on?*

CHAPTER 24

"Sit closer together," Hadden said as Daphne pulled the girls onto her lap for the photo.

Hadden hit the timer and positioned himself on the sofa next to them.

"Perfect."

The nanny entered the room and asked, "Time for nap?"

"Yes, I want them to be well-rested for the birthday party," Daphne replied.

As the nanny took the girls to their room, Hadden beckoned her towards the dome. They entered and sealed the door shut, then dialled up on the frequency using their amethysts.

"Leo warned me the other day. They might come for the girls again around their third birthday...which is apparently what happened in the first timeline."

"But we masked their powers, so why would they?"

"Because they are still Heliotropan and might have dormant powers - ones that they can weaponize, just like they did with you and me."

"I can't believe Leo actually warned you. Is he growing a heart these days?"

"I think he's getting affected by the frequencies here. Although I appear to be the same CM drone from before, I do send a code that breaks down his SIM programming when he's not paying attention to me."

Daphne pressed both temples with her fingertips and leaned back against the sofa pillows. "This compartmentalization in my mind is still driving me crazy. The connected part of me watches the disconnected part get undermined by CM triggers. I fight with myself not to go there, but I have to. I have to spy on people, read their minds, and fill their heads with horrible visions. At least, I had no conscience before the upgraded amethyst. Now, I can't take it anymore. We need to try some other way to get back to Helio Tropez."

"I can't connect with Halia anymore. It's probably because I'm worried a lot, and my frequency is low. Their stargates are locked with codes I can't decipher. I've remote viewed all the volcanoes around the planet with entrances to Inner Earth. I even tried hiking at Mount Rainier. Nothing."

"But we have two Pentada daughters now. Surely, they will want to protect them. We *must* try again. I also want to find Annika and Michael and bring them with us."

"They won't let us connect with them."

Daphne paced the room like she usually did when trying to think. "I know. I sense they've done something even more terrible to Annika's mind. She needs our help, Hadden."

"If we get back to Helio Tropez, we can come back to rescue them." Hadden looked out at the peak of Mount Rainier and tapped his fingers on the windowsill. "Ok, let's try taking the company plane this time. The girls can't make the hike, and maybe, if they're with us, it'll make a difference. I got in there once before that way."

She wrapped her arms around his waist and furrowed her brow. "Yes, I guess… okay. We have that wedding to attend in Portland, so maybe we don't even need to come up with an excuse for using the plane!"

"Good idea."

The next morning at the office, Hadden said to Leo, "We're thinking of going to the Cartwright wedding on the 25th."

"Really?" Leo said. "Maybe I'll come with you. I'm dating that supermodel, Trina. You can tell me if she's worth my time or not."

"Sure, but I don't think there's room in the plane for all of us."

"You're taking the plane? Right. Hmm. Maybe I'll just take her to my place on Vashon instead."

Hadden breathed a sigh of relief as he left Leo's office. Leo guarded Hadden as his asset, and Josephine still guarded Daphne as hers. More and more, Hadden could navigate his way around Leo, but Josephine would be tracking their every move. *How can we manoeuvre past her?* Daphne had the Voyent-Reprogramming aptitude and could implant a screen memory of them staying at home in her head, but if they got caught, life could get uncomfortable and dangerous for the girls.

The night before they left, Daphne went to Josephine in her dreams and implanted a screen memory that would play out for 24 hours while they tried to enter Helio Tropez. The next problem involved duping the company pilot into letting Hadden pilot the plane himself. When they arrived at the airfield with the two girls, the pilot got the plane ready. Just before take-off, Hadden injected him with a tranquillizer.

As soon as he was unconscious, they carried him off the plane and left him propped up on a sofa in the office with a screen memory to cover their tracks. When he woke up, he only remembered that his assignment had been cancelled and he'd been given the day off.

As they gained altitude and flew toward the mountainside, both Daphne and Hadden went into prayer, reaching out to the Elders of Helio Tropez. Physical entrances were highly guarded and camouflaged, so the chances of getting in were slim, but they couldn't think of any other solution.

At least, if Halia, the Elders and the Progenitors knew that they had the girls with them this time, they might open it up. So they flew around the crater and called out for help. When Hadden finally connected with Halia, she told them that they were denying entry. They flew in circles until the girls grew tired and the fuel gauge fell too low, and they had no option but to turn around.

Back at the airfield, Daphne could barely contain her tears. They drove back to Hadden's mansion overlooking the water. Josephine Carbona sat waiting in their sunken living room, along with Col. Loman. Seeing him there made Hadden nauseous.

"You're back," Josephine stated, getting to her feet. "You remember Col Loman, right?"

Hadden nodded. The Colonel orchestrated the trauma-based CM on him 20 years earlier.

"I know what you did, darling. You forget that I know all these mind games and have protection against the likes of someone like you. Where did you go?" she demanded.

Neither of them said anything. Both girls started crying at raised voices, and Daphne instinctively picked up Metta while Hadden put Tia on his lap.

"It's okay," he whispered to her.

"We're going to test the girls," Col. Loman announced.

"No!" Daphne said, clutching Metta closer.

Hadden stepped towards them. "We showed you when they were born. They have no special powers. These two girls are just like any normal surface humans."

"Then you won't mind if we do the testing. Place both girls on the sofa here."

Neither of them moved.

"Do I have to come and get them myself?"

Hadden gave Daphne a knowing look, then brought the girls down to the sofa as they both used their powers to shield the girls from any detection. The risk involved their handlers finding out their deception. Col. Loman took a device out of his briefcase and held it three feet above the girls' heads in turn, taking readings on each of them. After several minutes of investigating, retesting and talking with Josephine in private, Col. Loman put the device back into his briefcase.

"I don't detect any special aptitudes. However, we're going to take them anyway."

Hadden was on his feet. "Why waste your resources on children that have nothing to offer your program? Can't we work out some kind of arrangement?"

Josephine and Col. Loman continued to whisper to each other. Meanwhile, Hadden took the risk of trying to read their minds. All he could detect was their fear of the readings being wrong. SIM's days were numbered if Pentada remained free and if all five reunited. Josephine turned to look at

Hadden. That's when a scorching pain tore through his skull. He slipped out of the room and rocked back and forth holding his temples until the throbbing subsided.

When he re-entered the living room, Col. Loman cast a stern look at Daphne. "If you don't want to lose the girls, then you have to separate them. One of them has to stay here with Hadden. And Daphne, you take the other. You must never have contact with each other again if you want them to remain alive. We are tracking you both, so we'll know."

Daphne kept her cool until they left, and until all four of them were safely in the dome upstairs. As soon as the door closed, she shouted, "How dare they? How did we let this happen? Why didn't Halia help us? Don't the Progenitors care about us?"

"Either they don't want to rescue the girls, or something has happened to Halia."

They called out to Halia several times. The girls continued to cry as Hadden held them both in his arms, and Daphne paced until she collapsed in a puddle of tears.

The thought of being apart from his family made Hadden's heart numb, but at least the girls would be with one of their parents and not with SIM. Daphne and Hadden made a plan about how to keep the girls safe and how they could someday find a way to reconnect. They weren't sure how, but they vowed to figure it out. The day Daphne kissed him goodbye while holding Metta in her arms was seared into his memory.

Night after night after they left, he tried to connect with Halia, but it was all for nothing. He suspected all the feelings of helplessness, frustration and anger were blocking the signal. It was only after a year of working through his grief that he finally received a message back from her.

You need to toughen up. While we do have compassion for what has happened, SIM is triggering you to feel disempowered. You are like the elephant who got chained up when it was young, but as a full adult, you can rip off that chain in one movement. The only thing keeping you chained up at this point is your mind. You were chosen for this role because the Progenitors believed you had what it takes.

Why do you say that? What are you asking me to do?

Remember who you really are. Strengthen your connection to SANA and let that connection guide you.

Hadden was frustrated by what she said and abruptly signed off. Feelings of abandonment and anger kept him in a loop at night, making it impossible for him to sleep. He lay in bed tossing, turning and ruminating. Finally, he sat up and looked out at the city lights and decided to pray to SANA. By morning, a new level of resolve had formed, and he met sunrise with a tight jaw and a determination not to be beaten down again.

CHAPTER 25

The text from Metta said: *Dax and I will meet you at the record label office at 2 PM.*

Clearly, SIM was on to her. After interfacing with Cassandra and the Task Force, she felt better about plan B that they had hatched together.

Just before heading out of the door, she responded to the text with, *Sounds good. Text me the address. See you then.*

After walking for a few blocks, Tia arrived back at #5 - 4379 Rue de Bullion. She rang the buzzer and waited. Nothing. She rang again, and as she stepped back to take the building in, she saw the curtains move. After a few more minutes, she rang a third time.

The door opened, and a tiny woman with a shaggy head of grey hair and thick glasses glared at her. "What do you want?"

"Are you related to Lorena and Ben Indicum?"

"Who's asking?"

"My name is Linda Wright. Friends of mine used to live in this building – in this suite, actually."

"I've owned this suite for longer than you've been alive. Whoever you're looking for, they don't live here."

Tia hesitated, not wanting to give away her identity. "I... um... they must be your neighbours and..." She squirmed, not sure where she was going with her line of thought.

The woman scrutinised her, then her face softened as if reading her mind. "You come from the House of Zuris?"

Tia's eyes widened. *How does she know? Is she a SIM agent or part of the Quinary Mission?*

Keep talking, Cassandra instructed. *Just feed us the details of the woman's face and vocal frequencies with your mind. We'll enter it into the Hall of Records and see if we get a match.*

"The House of Zuris, what's that?"

The woman's eyes narrowed. "You know exactly what it is."

Cassandra interrupted her thoughts. *We have a match! The system is ageing her features, just to be sure.*

Tia said nothing and looked sideways, feeling a growing discomfort in her stomach. The woman was just about to close the door in her face when Cassandra said, *It's Annika!*

Tia's heart skipped a beat, and she put her foot forward to block the door. "You're Annika."

The old woman grimaced, then held her finger to her mouth. "I told you, people, to leave me alone. You've bled me dry. I'm useless to you now."

"I'm not a SIM agent."

Suspicion clouded her features. "Then who are you?"

Tia asked Cassandra telepathically what to answer her. The team triangulated all possible outcomes to denying versus allowing the truth, and Cassandra finally said, *Admit who you are. The odds are in your favour. She doesn't appear to be under SIM control anymore, and besides, we don't keep secrets in this family.* Tia could hear the joy in her voice, even as it came through their connection.

"I *am* from the House of Zuris."

Annika smiled wryly. "I thought so."

"I'm your niece... Tia."

Annika pushed her thick glasses higher and leaned in to get a closer look. "Really? I thought they took you away into a SIM program."

"They did with my sister. I stayed with my father, and he protected me for as long as he could. My mother and sister left when I was three years old, and I haven't seen them since."

Annika nodded solemnly. "I heard they pulled your family apart." As she looked Tia up and down, she seemed to relax a little. "So, you're really Tia all grown up? What are you doing here?"

"I've been in Helio Tropez for the last year, and I'm here to take you back."

Annika's eyes crinkled shut. "That's a hard one to believe." She took off her thick glasses to reveal one eye covered in cataracts. With her good eye, she zeroed in on Tia, searching for the truth. "I can't quite read people's minds like I used to."

"It's true. I can prove it."

The old woman sighed and kicked the door open to let Tia inside. The room reminded Tia of her father's home: piles of clutter and hardly a place to sit. Annika pulled a stack of newspapers from a chair and ushered Tia to sit down. As she did, a cloud of dust puffed up around her. Annika pulled herself up on the sofa. At four-foot-five, her feet dangled several inches above the musty carpet.

"Chocolate?" Annika offered, handing her a plate with mostly unwrapped truffles.

"No, thank you."

"I never got to meet you or your sister. Not once. They separated us when Daphne was pregnant with you, sent me packing off to Australia."

"What happened?"

"Everything happened, but I'm not saying another word until you prove who you are."

Tia held one hand to her ear and telepathically said, "Okay. Just give me a moment."

"Who's listening in on us?"

Tia froze and dropped her hand to her lap.

"You're interfacing with someone. As I said, if you've become a SIM agent, I've got nothing left to give."

"I'm a sovereign being. No SIM control. My father, Hadden, helped me get back to Helio Tropez last year. When I was there, I met Cassandra and Meraton. They helped me heal, and I'm now on a mission to –"

"My parents? They died in 1961."

"They're very much alive."

Annika frowned, and she said, almost in a whisper, "That's what Hadden said, but I didn't believe him."

Tia paused for a moment as Cassandra instructed her on what to say next. "When you were a child, you and your mother said a word together to help her heal a wound?"

"Maybe. So you're saying that you're talking to my mother right now?"

"Yes. Cassandra is talking to me right now. She says the word is... Abracadabra?"

Annika looked sideways. "Daphne could have told you that."

Tia knitted her brow. "Daphne left when I was three. I have no memories of her."

Annika cleared her throat and sat up straighter. "Okay. When I was a child, I got laryngitis, and nothing worked to cure me, except for one thing. What was it?"

Tia closed her eyes and then opened them again. "The Lisella herbal tincture that they brought from Helio Tropez?"

The old woman took a sharp breath as her eyes turned glassy. "How are they doing down there?"

"Good. Very good. They're excited to reconnect with you."

Annika laughed and wiped away a stray tear. Tia saw a tissue box buried on the cluttered coffee table and handed her the box. "The Hall of Records said you died."

"I did die at eighteen. It's just that my body kept going. Please, tell them how sorry I am for leaving, even after they warned me."

"How *did* you get separated from your parents?"

A nostalgic smile crossed her face, and she gazed into a middle distance, reliving a memory. "Music. I could play any string instrument: violin, guitar, cello. We were home-schooled, but a neighbour heard me play in the backyard one day and introduced me to her friend in the symphony orchestra. They invited me for an audition, but I didn't tell my parents. I hadn't attended any music school, so normally, they wouldn't let me in, but the owner of the symphony made an exception. I joined them on tour and told my parents I would be back in the summer. When I came back, they were gone." She wiped her eyes and blew her nose, but the tears kept coming. "I've lived in regret because of that stupid decision my entire life."

Tia didn't know what to say and reached out to Cassandra for advice. She heard her grandmother's soft voice say, *Tell her that we forgive her.*

"Your mother and father say that they forgive you."

Annika nodded and pursed her lips, trying to stifle the tears. "The problem is... I don't forgive me."

"But you just wanted to follow your dream..."

"My dream turned into a nightmare. The police said they died in a car accident – such a bad accident that the bodies were unrecognisable. I attended their funeral along with Daphne. I wanted to stay with her, but I had this contract with the symphony, and she had a modelling contract. Just like that, our broken family was broken even more. I didn't see her for years. After a while, I realised they were taking me at night and conducting some kind of cognitive modification on me. I felt compelled to live by these instructions inside my head that went against everything that was good and right. At night, unbeknownst to my conscious self, I was part of this group that implanted destructive voices in the heads of SIMs targets."

Tia rubbed her eyes, itchy from all the dust. "How did you awaken from all the programming?"

The old woman dropped her chin and closed her eyes. "To be honest, and I've never told anyone this... SIM agents told me that I could become the top violinist in the world, but only if I took part in one of their black-hearted rituals. I won't tell you what goes on there because it would haunt you for days, like it did to me. They literally wanted me to sell my soul. In my CM stupor, I might have gone for it, but something made me say no. Some unseen force was looking out for me. That's when the programming started to break down."

Goosebumps covered Tia's forearms. "What kind of force?"

232

"I don't know... like some kind of guardian angel from another dimension?"

The Task Force went to work trying to figure out the identity of the guardian angel, but they couldn't get a read on it.

Tia settled back on the sofa. "Amazing."

"So, then my career magically disappeared," Annika said, waving her hand. "No more engagements, no more symphony. They mostly left me alone after that, but they still couldn't let me be totally free. I convinced them to let Daphne and I be in a band together. They agreed as long as our handlers were part of it too. She was the singer, and I played the violin. Then we reconnected with Hadden, your father, and he gave us this amethyst. See here... behind my ear?"

"He did?! What year was that?" Tia leaned forward.

"That was... I don't know, the late 70s? Before you were born, anyway. We were playing at a club in Vancouver, and he fell in love with your mum on the spot. It was only when he saw her Azurite stone that he'd given her when we were kids that he realised we'd met before. All his memories came back. He created an amethyst that compartmentalised the CM part of his mind from the free part of his mind. He gave one to Daphne and me, which saved our lives in many ways, but also made them harder in others."

Tia was beyond excited. "That means my father kept the memories of his time in Helio Tropez when he was twenty."

Annika shrugged. "I guess so. He told me his older self had called him into the future, but I didn't totally believe him back then."

"Tell me this. The news on the internet says he still died at the age of seventy... and the authorities blame me for it. I thought he would have changed all that?"

"I don't know. I lost touch because they separated us all, and I never pay attention to the news. It all seems so fake and manipulative."

"Why did they separate you and my mother?"

"Both Daphne and I were at the end of our childbearing years, and neither of us had created Pentada children yet. I was infertile, but they tried one more time by mating me with Michael of Indicium. They sent me off to Sydney. Meanwhile, they wanted Daphne to mate with Hadden. So that begs a very big question. Are either you or your sister Pentada?"

233

"Yes, I have the marking. And Metta also had the marking as a child, but our parents masked it to protect us from SIM."

Wonder crossed her face, and a disbelieving smile was not far behind. "So now all five Pentada are born and in adulthood?"

Tia nodded. "That's part of why I'm here. To bring everyone back to Helio Tropez so we can unite and create a plan for transforming this situation with SIM."

"Good luck with that."

"We have a lot in our favour that we've never had before, but all five of us have to be together. I've found Metta – she's here in Montréal right now. Did you know that?"

"No. I never even knew either of your names."

"She is a songwriter – a very successful one - but they have her drugged up most of the time. I'm supposed to meet her and the rock musician named Dax today. I think he might be a descendent of the Quinary Mission, too."

"What makes you say that?"

"We had a very strong connection, and I think he might be my SANA mate. An Oracle in Helio Tropez told me that my mate might be living on the surface, born in 1980 and from the House of Indicium."

Annika's eyes brightened as she searched her memory bank. "Your SANA mate, from the House of Indicum, born in 1980. I bet he's Miriam's son."

"Miriam?"

"I met her as a child at Mount Rainier, but then we lost contact after I got taken over by SIM. I heard she married Forsel. I also met him at Mount Rainier. He was a friend of your father's. They lived in the UK and had a son named Xander in 1980. I remember because it was the same year you were born."

"Xander?" She liked the name. It suited him far more than Dax. "According to his bio, he was born in the UK."

"I only know this because SIM mated me with Miriam's brother, Michael. I heard that SIM took Xander into one of their programs."

"I guess so. They took him into a band, stuck him front and centre. They tour the world, but he's still in there. They've given him this alter ego named Dax."

"That's what they like to do with those of us from the Quinary mission: turn us into agents of social engineering for the general public."

"Annika, listen, I need your help to rescue Metta and Xander, and then, hopefully, my mother. By the way, where is Daphne?"

"I have no idea what happened to her, which is strange because we're twins. We used to have such a strong connection, but I haven't felt anything from her for a long time. Not since the mid-80s."

"Metta told me that Daphne abandoned her in the mid-80s."

"They probably killed her so they could take Metta."

A wave of despair filled Tia's heart. "How can we know for sure?"

Annika sighed and shook her head. "Each time I tried to tap into her consciousness, I got a horrible headache. There's like a mental trap keeping us apart. After I didn't have any children, they mated Michael with another woman. I came back here because this apartment felt like home. I thought maybe Daphne would come here, too. It's where we grew up. But no one had heard from her. I got a job at the University, teaching music, and saved up enough money to buy this apartment. I've been here for a few decades now, living a very solitary life. I don't fit in with surface humans. I'm too…"

"Strange to others," Tia finished with a smile. "I know. I get it."

"And so, I mostly meditate and try to heal my mind. I'm eternally grateful to your father for at least giving me this amethyst."

"How are your powers these days?"

"Low, until you showed up on my doorstep. My telepathy, my extrasensory perceptions, they're dialled up somehow. Maybe it's the Pentada connection."

"Listen. I need to wrestle Metta and Xander away from their handlers long enough to get them back to Helio Tropez. Can you help me?"

"I'll do whatever I can. As I said, at this point in life, I don't have anything left to lose."

"Good. But before we get started, here's the most upgraded amethyst to replace the one you have."

"A better one?" she asked, her eyes lighting up.

Tia pulled out the gold box. "Of course! As soon as I open this box, we might get on the SIM radar. I'm going to create a cloaking shield around us both until it's installed and you activate the permanent cloaking setting that's in there. Ready?"

Annika nodded and clambered off the sofa, wincing as her swollen feet hit the floor. Tia envisioned a silver, circular forcefield around them both, then capped the top and bottom. As soon as the team in Helio Tropez reinforced the shield, Tia opened the box and helped Annika remove her amethyst and place the new one behind her left ear.

The team grounded her energetically as the amethyst re-calibrated her body-mind-soul system. Tia held Annika steady as her breathing became ragged, and her eyes flashed several different fluorescent colours.

When she could properly breathe again, Tia gently took off her glasses and put them down on the coffee table. Then she held Annika's forehead with one hand. "Now command permanent cloaking of the amethyst."

Annika nodded imperceptibly. After a few minutes, Tia could tell that the command was activated.

When Annika opened her eyes, they dazzled in the same turquoise way that Cassandra's did, all cataracts gone.

Annika's jaw dropped as she looked in all directions. "I can see again with both eyes!"

Tia explained all the things she could now do with her new amethyst, and Annika started experimenting with it immediately. She took dishes to the sink with her mind, levitating up to a high shelf in the kitchen without the use of a step ladder and listening to what her plants had to say.

"I feel alive again!" Annika smiled.

"I'm so glad to hear that. It sounds like it's been a rough journey."

"Rough is an understatement, but I never expected to reconnect with my parents, to meet you, or to get to go back to Helio Tropez. So, what can I say? You've made my day."

"I'm so glad I found you. It was Cassandra that told me to come to this apartment in Montreal."

"I guess a part of me hoped that what Hadden said was true, that they were alive in Helio Tropez and they'd come to find me one day, but as the years went on, I lost hope in that."

"They thought you died back in 1961."

Annika raised her eyebrows. "Right."

Tia could tell she didn't totally believe that, so she changed the subject. "What was my mother like?"

"Daphne? Everybody loved her. She was classy, elegant, beautiful, smart, wise... she looked a lot like you."

Tia laughed as her cheeks flushed.

"She could also be stubborn, competitive and a little too full of herself at times. Maybe less like you," she said with a sad smile. "If she's still alive, her life force energy is very low."

A wave of anxiety clenched at Tia's stomach. "We need all five Pentada to assure the Harvest goes well."

"Oh yes, The Harvest. That's coming up... what... next year already? God, how time flies. Yes, we need to find her too. I can't wait to see my parents again."

Tia nodded and closed her eyes. "They can't wait to see you again soon either."

"Okay, let's go get Metta and Xander and go home... finally."

"But if they're under SIM control, how are we supposed to do that? It's the last part of this puzzle. One that we haven't figured out."

Tia rolled out a parchment onto the kitchen table. It showed a circle with several intersecting lines, with Matrix symbols all over the page. "I brought a portable version of the Abracadabra Orb."

Annika put on her glasses, then quickly took them off because she could now see better without them. "I haven't seen one of these since I was a kid. Amazing." She ran her hands over the parchment and looked up at Tia. "I'm particularly good with the Abracadabra Orb."

"I heard," Tia smiled. "I'll explain the plan for extraction. We only have three hours to get ready."

CHAPTER 26

Seattle – 1988

Tia doled out her monopoly money. "Uncle Leo, I'd like to buy a hotel on Park Place."

"She's going to bankrupt us both," Leo laughed. "Look at all these hotels!"

Hadden smiled. "What can I say? She's a chip off the old block."

The wind and rain rattled the circular windows nearby. They sat huddled near the fireplace in the dome atop the Violetta estate, cherishing their regular Sunday afternoons playing games and watching old movies. Other than that, it was a lonely life for a child with no friends and two bachelors who mostly worked.

"I forgot to tell you. I got you something," Leo said, going over to a rolling briefcase he had left by the stairs. "I was on a business trip in Portland and walked by this magical shop where they made these!"

He pulled a white stuffed polar bear out of a bag and handed it to Tia.

"For me? He's amazing!" She cuddled the toy and ran her fingers over its well-crafted facial features. "Thank you, Uncle Leo."

After bankrupting the two bachelors, they curled up on the sofas to watch *It's a Wonderful Life*. Tia brought the box of tissues to Leo since he always seemed to need them. They passed around the buttered popcorn, and the bear took its new place between them on the sofa.

After Leo left and Hadden had put Tia to bed, he went back up to the dome for his regular reconnaissance with Halia. Since the dome acted as a meditation chamber for connecting to higher frequencies, it had a healing effect on those who spent time there. After sitting in meditation for twenty minutes, a telepathic connection came through.

Greetings, my beloved grandson. I come to you in love and light and send you my gratitude for continuing to connect with me.

Hadden breathed a sigh of relief and sent his love and gratitude back to her, knowing it strengthened their telepathic connection. *It's working, just like you said. Leo is softening.*

Halia's reassuring voice said, *Yes, we thought so. And having him as an ally will make your lives so much easier when dealing with SIM.*

I hope so.

Now, we need to talk about Tia's schooling.

I'm homeschooling her well enough. I teach her surface human studies that she might need to survive day-to-day, like English, math, business and computing skills – anything that won't put her on SIM's radar. But I'm avoiding the false or incomplete sciences like Newtonian physics, Darwinism, and the solid earth theory, for when she goes to Helio Tropez. What are you suggesting?

Being isolated from other children isn't good for her development.

I know.

Having met Tia first as a 30-year-old adult, he could tell that living such a sheltered life compromised her soul growth.

We will instruct you on how to rebuild your amethyst so that you can keep her shielded from SIM even when she interacts with people in regular surface life. Besides, as she grows older, her frequencies will rise, so she will need better protection anyway. This is an upgrade from the one you created before. SIM can't detect consciousness technology made in 5D and above. They only operate in 3D and 4D.

But how can you create that when you operate in 4D?

This is highly usual. We're connecting with our ancestors who've gone onto 6D already. There's only a few of us who can, so we keep it to ourselves. The

Elders don't know we're doing this because, in the past, those who connect to 6D got shunned by the others.

I thought Heliotropans were all about graduating to higher densities.

We thought so, too, but it seems to create some kind of discomfort, jealousy or cognitive dissonance when some people in the collective go there. The others instinctively want to pull them back. They fear we might get infiltrated by SIM, but we are very careful.

But you're all telepathically connected. How can you do that without them knowing?

We cloak with the help of the amethyst.

Isn't that lying?

No, this is sanctioned by SANA because, in any collective consciousness, you always find early adopters and late adopters. Think of a bell curve. The majority are in the middle. Usually, the late adopters don't like to change, so they will sabotage the early adopters. The only time they change is when the majority of the collective have gone through already.

That makes sense, he replied, scratching his head. *Okay. I'll get to work on it. I guess I'm an early adopter here on the surface, so I'll take any cloaking help that I can get.*

After that interaction, he spent many long hours working in the dome to perfect the next level of consciousness technology in the amethyst, as instructed by Halia. Just when he completed the project, a family moved in next door. When Hadden was in the dome experimenting on the crystal, he heard a scraping noise outside. Outside the window, he saw Tia scrambling over the fence. He went outside and peered over the fence to see her playing with the neighbour girl. His heart sank, recalling how lonely he'd felt as a child being homeschooled and without any siblings.

For the next week, Hadden sleuthed all he could about the family next door. They seemed harmless. The mother worked at a private girls' local school, and her husband worked in high-end real estate. They had one daughter named Valerie, the same age as Tia. One day, he waited out in the garden until Tia came running around the corner to climb over the fence.

"Dad!" she said, skidding to a halt, the colour suddenly draining from her cheeks. "What are you doing here?"

"I could ask the same of you. Are you going to visit your friend Valerie?"

She pulled on one wrist, "You know about that?"

"A little."

"I'm sorry. It's just that she invited me over one day to try the blackberries in their yard, and she has a whole swing set and sandbox and everything!"

"I can see that. Are you having fun?"

"Yes. Can I keep going over there?"

He folded his arms and sighed. "Only if I can meet her parents first."

"Sure! I can introduce you. They're very nice."

They walked around to the front door and rang the bell.

A short, roundish woman in her late thirties answered the door with a whale spout ponytail, a striped aerobics outfit and legwarmers. "Tia!" The woman said breathlessly." It's so nice to see you. Sorry, I was just finishing my workout."

"Hello, Mrs Weston. This is my father. He just wanted to... um... say hi."

He extended a hand and cordially introduced himself. "Pleased to meet you. I'm Hadden Violetta."

"Nice to meet you, too. Just call me Emily. We're new to the neighbourhood."

"Yes, I'm sorry I haven't dropped by to say hello sooner."

She opened the door wide and stepped to one side. "Please, come in. I just made some lemonade. Would you like some?"

He nodded, and the two of them went to the kitchen while Emily turned off her aerobics video. A well-worn sectional sofa surrounded a glass coffee table, resplendent with peonies. The carpet – a deep green – made the house feel welcoming. Emily padded into the living room and placed the lemonade on the table. "Please, sit."

Eight-year-old Valerie skipped into the room and planted herself on the carpet. "Hello, Mr Violetta. You have a way cool house."

"Thank you, Valerie. We'll have to give you and your mother a tour one day."

"I heard you designed it yourself," Emily said as she handed him a glass of lemonade.

He downed it in four gulps. "I did. It took nearly three years to build, but it was worth it to call a place home."

"It certainly stands out in the neighbourhood. We use it as a landmark for directions to people," she laughed. "We're right next door to the flying saucer house!"

Hadden looked down. A feeling of discomfort arose in his throat. "It's an eyesore indeed."

"No, I didn't mean it that way. According to my husband, it actually raises the real estate value in the area. People want to say they live in the neighbourhood with the flying saucer."

"Do they?"

Valerie stood up and grinned to reveal one missing front tooth. "Can Tia stay to play in the backyard?"

Emily and Hadden looked at each other. After years of distrusting the outside world, it was hard for him to relax in the company of strangers, but for the sake of Tia's wellbeing, he wanted to try. He forced a smile and said, "Of course."

As the girls ran to the back deck, Emily poured him some more lemonade. "I just got a job as Principal at the Lafayette School for Girls just down the road here. Do you know it?"

"Yes, I'm familiar with it. I hear it's very good."

"Does Tia go?"

"No, no," he said, shifting in his chair. "I actually... home-school her."

Emily took a sip of lemonade and coughed. "Really?" She dabbed her mouth with a napkin. "That's quite an undertaking for a busy man like you. Don't you run an investment firm?"

"Yes, but I can do it from home now with these new personal computers you can get."

"Oh, you have one of those? How exciting. Daniel, my husband, wants to get one of those ones from the Microsoft company. We'll have to get your recommendations."

Hadden nodded. "I prefer Apple computers."

"Oh, yes, that's another brand. Well, if you ever want to try enrolling Tia at Lafayette, I'm sure she'd get in. I'd certainly put in a good word. She seems very bright and so well behaved."

"Thank you. That's kind of you." His heart skipped a beat at thinking of sending Tia out into the regular world. Yet, the synchronicity of a girl's school Principal moving in next door seemed too important not to pay it any attention.

For the next fifteen minutes, she talked about the school and showed him a brochure. His reluctance softened, and he started to get a good feeling about it.

"Okay, I can at least start the application."

"Exactly. That's fantastic. Valerie loves it there. The deadline is Friday, so I'll get you an application right away."

Within the month, Tia was accepted. She could only go, however, if he got her to wear the amethyst. But how could he explain to her why she needed to have a crystal behind her left ear?

The problem was solved one day when Tia asked, "Can I get my ears pierced, Dad?"

He smiled, feeling relieved. "Let me think about it."

That evening, he connected with Halia. *Will the amethyst still work in her ear lobe?*

Yes, we can help you reconstruct it to work in both ear lobes, but you have to convince Tia to wear only your amethyst earrings and never take them off. We'll also show you how to pierce her ears yourself, as the way they do it on the surface is damaging to the meridians of the ear.

After downloading all the instructions from Halia and reconstructing the amethyst into two pierced earrings, Hadden put them in a gold faraday box.

When Hadden walked into her room where she was playing, Tia looked up, waiting for him to say something. "What?"

"Come with me."

At the top of the stairs, he said, "Close your eyes." Then he led her to sit down at his worktable.

When she opened her eyes, there sat the gold box, a bowl of ice, rubbing alcohol, cotton balls and a small mirror. "What's all this?"

243

He opened the gold box, and two tiny amethysts sparkled under the light.

"For me?

He nodded.

"They're for pierced ears only. You're going to let me get them done?" Tia asked.

"Yes."

"Thank you, Dad! You're the best," Tia said as she hugged him. Then she ran her fingers over the gems. "They're beautiful. When can I get my ears pierced?"

"I'm going to pierce your ears for you, right now."

Covering both ears, she looked at him, horrified. "What? Shouldn't I go to a professional?"

"I *am* a professional. I was trained as a medic in the air force. Those clerks at the earring shops are not trained medics."

"Oh, um, okay. Are you sure you know what you're doing?"

"Yes, I can do it so that it won't hurt a bit, but there's one condition. You have to wear this set of earrings only, and you must wear them all the time."

"Okay. Why?"

"It's just a family tradition, but it's very important. You have to promise me." He knew that Tia had a strong code of ethics about promising something.

"I don't know."

"Otherwise, I will have to say no."

Tia sighed and held the earrings up next to her face. "No hoops?"

"No, just these."

"For the rest of my life?"

"Until I make you a new pair."

Tia's eyes narrowed, and she crossed her arms. "What if the other girls at school hate them or make fun of me?"

"They'll envy you. Not everyone can wear amethysts, you know."

"Okay. But maybe you'll change your mind one day?"

"Not likely. At least, not until I make you a new pair. You can say no."

"I have to wear them night and day?"

"Yes. That's the deal."

She looked down at the earrings proudly, then back at him. "Okay. Let's do it."

Hadden felt guilty about lying to her, but it wasn't time for full disclosure yet. A week later, Tia started school. He worried the whole day, constantly monitoring her frequency on his detection devices. No huge up or down swings. When she came home, Tia seemed happy and excited. They treated her like a regular surface child and didn't know anything about her true powers.

He breathed a sigh of relief and decided to relax about it all. After all, with Tia gone part of the day, it freed up more of Hadden's time to do his work and focus on his most important project to date.

CHAPTER 27

Late one afternoon at the end of the school year, Hadden tinkered on his latest amethyst up in the dome. He wanted to finish Tia's next set of earrings in time for her sixteenth birthday. Looking up from his work, he saw Tia come up the driveway. Something seemed wrong. He went down the spiral staircase and opened the door just as she arrived.

"Hi, sweetheart."

Tia averted her eyes. "Hey, Dad."

"How was school?"

"Fine."

He frowned. "Doesn't seem like it was fine."

"It's nothing."

Tia never lied to him. He frowned and watched as she went down the hall to her room. Softening his focus, he picked up streaks of black running through her energetic aura. Someone wanted to lower her frequency. That night, he did a background check on students attending her school. He discovered that one of Josephine Carbona's daughters had just enrolled at

Lafayette Academy. The Carbona family liked to target people in the Zuris bloodline. Somehow, they had discovered her. A panic clenched at his throat.

At dinner time, he said, "I think one of the Carbona girls goes to your school, right?"

Tia's eyes narrowed, and she shrugged. "You mean Andrea? She just enrolled midterm."

"Her father is a client of ours."

"I figured."

"Something happened between you and Andrea?"

Tia shrugged and speared a piece of asparagus, sniffed it, then put it back on the plate.

Hadden poured a glass of green water for both of them. "Those Carbonas can be nasty at times."

"I'd say," she huffed.

"Is she tormenting you?"

Tia paused and measured her words. "I can handle it, Dad."

"Why don't you invite her over one day?"

"Here? She'd never say yes. Besides, I'd hate having her here, and you hate visitors in general. It's a stupid idea." She pushed her plate away and said, "I'm going to my room. I have a test tomorrow."

Over the next few weeks, Hadden checked in with Halia and her team several times.

You must help to forge a friendship between those two girls. Andrea is her shadow counterpart. It's not going to be easy, but try to bring her to the dome. It might help.

The next morning at breakfast, Hadden laid down a plate of his famous Eggs Benedict, Tia's favourite. "I think that if she knew my connection with her father, she would act differently towards you."

"She already knows, so I highly doubt it."

"What does she do or say that bothers you so much?"

247

"She's telling people that I'm an evil alien from another world because we live in the flying saucer house."

"And they believe that?"

"I don't know, probably not, but now that's my new name... the evil alien. No one wants to sit with me at lunch or be my partner in gym class. Even Valerie stopped inviting me over. She's inviting Andrea instead. I saw them in Valerie's backyard just yesterday with Andrea's cool friends."

"Let's invite her into the flying saucer so she can see for herself that it's just a room."

Tia snorted, "Not gonna happen."

That evening, as he meditated and connected with Halia, he shared his concerns.

Andrea can likely read our true energy signatures and the Heliotropan frequencies in the dome. She might ruin all my work here. It's not a good idea.

The frequency here is so strong now. She wouldn't be able to bring it down. Yes, she probably knows Tia is Heliotropan...

Yes! So she'll tell Tia and cause all sorts of trouble...

Not if you get her on your side.

Andrea won't go against her whole family. I don't see how this plan can work.

She needs as much time in the dome as possible. So you need to create an area where the two girls can, perhaps, study. Convince Tia to be Andrea's study partner.

I doubt she'll agree to that.

You must try. This is extremely important to the entire experiment.

What experiment?

To get you back to Helio Tropez and help surface humanity. Just like what's happening with Leo, it could happen with Andrea.

Hadden grumbled and ended the transmission.

The next day, he saw a girl leave Valerie's house. With black miniskirt, torn fishnet stockings and work boots, she looked more like a grunge groupee than a student at a prestigious girls' school. *That must be Andrea*, he thought, reading her energy. After the front door closed, Andrea pretended to leave but then hid behind a tree and turned her attention to the Violetta mansion. Observing everything, Hadden backed away from the window and went downstairs.

He peered from behind a curtain as the girl stared at the house. She was a Sentient-Attention, just like Tia. That meant she could implant a negative emotional feeling in another person's heart. As he raised the protective shield around the house, the directed energy coming from her mind bounced right back at her. She crumpled to the ground in pain, holding her chest. *This might be the right moment to bring her in.* By the time he got to her, Andrea was leaning against the tree, sobbing.

"You must be Andrea. I'm Tia's father. What's wrong?"

She tried to scramble to her feet to get away, but she could barely stand up. Tears streaked her face. Hadden helped her inside to the living room, then gave her a glass of water and a box of tissues. Her face softened, and she rubbed her forehead.

Tia walked in to find out what the commotion was about, but she came to an abrupt stop in the doorway. "Andrea, what are you doing here?"

"I'm… I'm… sorry. I'll be going in just a minute."

Hadden touched Andrea's shoulder. "It's okay. You can stay as long as you like."

Tia scowled at him and crossed her arms. "I thought you were at Valerie's this afternoon."

"I was but… I, um, hurt myself on the way out. I hurt my… wrist." Andrea cupped her left wrist and winced in pain. "And your father saw me crying." Andrea's left eye kept quivering.

"Is something wrong with your eye?"

"No, just a weird thing. Some kind of muscle spasm thing that I get sometimes."

She was clearly uncomfortable being there. Hadden inspected her wrist. It was fine. "I can wrap that for you. Take Andrea up to the dome, to the new sitting area. I'll bring the first aid supplies."

Tia shook her head. "Why go up there? Let's just wrap it here so she can go."

Hadden gave her a look. "All the supplies are up there."

"Okay, whatever."

The two girls went upstairs, and Hadden followed a few minutes later. They settled in a sitting area with a coffee table next to the window, upon which lay all of Tia's school books.

As Hadden wrapped Andrea's wrist, Tia looked through the stack of books on the table.

"Why are all my books up here?"

"I thought this would be a nice place to study."

"I guess. I have that huge algebra test on Friday."

"So do I," Andrea said, black bangs hanging over her eyes.

"Maybe you two should study together. It might make it easier."

Andrea stared at Hadden, trying to read his mind, but he had put up a shield so she couldn't gain access. Looking frustrated, Andrea stood up. "I prefer to study alone."

Tia picked up her algebra book and flipped through the pages. "Me too."

Andrea's smudged mascara made her look like a racoon. "It's not a big test anyway. I don't really care if I fail."

"It is a big test, Andrea," Tia scolded.

"I don't have time. My father needs my help setting up for one of his parties."

Hadden looked nervously from one girl to the other. "I'm sure your father would prefer if you passed the test,' he said. 'Maybe you should help, Tia."

They both scowled at him.

"Fine," Tia said with pursed lips. "I'll quiz you to assess how badly you're going to do."

"Or, maybe I should quiz you," Andrea snapped back.

"I think your wrist should be fine. I'll leave you, two girls, to it. See you later."

When Andrea left a few hours later, her aura looked lighter. Maybe this experiment would work after all. The next afternoon, Andrea showed up again to study and again the day after.

One morning at breakfast, Hadden asked, "So, how's it going with the studying?"

"Good. I think we're ready."

"Is she being nicer to you?"

"Actually, yes. I'm no longer the 'evil alien'. Thanks for helping out, Dad."

A weight lifted from his chest. "Good."

"In fact, she showed me Tarot cards and how to read someone's aura!"

"Really? Did she tell you why she wanted to teach you that?"

"She just said that her family all knows how to do it, so she wanted to share it with me."

As Tia washed her breakfast dishes in the sink, Hadden breathed a sigh of relief.

"She says mine is mostly white and violet. When I looked from my peripheral vision, like she suggested, I actually could see her aura too."

Trying to sound calm, Hadden asked, "Really? What did you see when you looked at hers?"

"I saw all kinds of colours. Yellow, orange, brown, black."

His heart skipped a beat. "Did she tell you what that meant?"

"She said that families like ours are in the upper frequencies of the colour wheel and that families like hers are in the lower frequency. That way, we complement each other quite well."

She rolled her eyes and started packing her knapsack with books.

Hadden handed her the lunch bag he had prepared for her. "Do you think that's true?"

She shrugged and stared at him with a knitted brow. "You're asking me a lot of questions about Andrea. You never showed this much interest in any of my other friends."

"It's just that I know her father and mother, and he can be—"

"A bit much, I know. I heard."

"Just be careful. Don't let them bring your energy down in any way."

"Ok, Dad. Chill out. It's all okay."

A few weeks later, Hadden finally reconnected with Halia.

The two girls are now inseparable. Every other sentence of Tia's is 'Andrea this' or 'Andrea that...' She got invited to a fancy dinner at the Carbona mansion on the weekend. Just yesterday, I caught her wearing a black miniskirt to go to a yacht party! This can't be a good thing.

It is a good thing.

I don't get it. Why won't you tell me more about this experiment?

Up to this point, we didn't feel you were ready, but now, we can't keep you in the dark anymore.

About what?

As we studied your relationship with Leo Burres, it led to a series of revelations that shocked everyone on the team. Through studying Leo's DNA and RNA, we discovered the true nature of the SIM families – Carbonas, Burres, Redus, Oranta and Saffron.

What do you mean by 'true nature'?

All the surface families who serve SIM came from the same star system as the people from Helio Tropez. The Hall of Records verified parts of our theory. Since Leo's soul signature had been removed, it was hard to trace, but by piecing together a variety of information, a picture of what had actually happened emerged. All we know so far is that the Burres family line is simply an annex of the Violetta family line.

An annex? So you mean we're related?

We're still working that out, but there's definitely a connection between the bloodlines. SIM can better feed off of a lower frequency person, so they latched onto these soul annexes. In other words, the annexed families have been enslaved to SIM for a very long time.

So you're saying that the SIM families are actually part of us? Heliotropan?

Exactly. Although they may have never stepped foot here, they're part of us. All our disowned and unprocessed emotional energy formed into soul counterparts, which then incarnated into physical bodies.

Hadden leaned forward, resting his head in his hands. *How could that be possible? I never learned about that.*

It's not laid out that way in the Hall of Records. We only figured it out by piecing together information that didn't add up at first.

Why would it not be there? The Hall of Records is supposed to have a record of everything since our arrival on Earth.

We don't know, but we intend to find out.

That's where the idea of the experiment came from, Hadden said telepathically, trying to figure out how all these fragments formed a whole.

You're the only one who has met with his counterpart and recovered from corruption.

Why do you say that?

Halia spoke slowly, as though laying the path before she walked on it herself. *You're the only Quinary member on the surface who is connected to Helio Tropez. We interface with you in secret. If the Elders knew, they would completely shut down our communication with you.*

But surely there are others?

I checked. You're the only one. The Elders don't trust anyone on the surface, and they particularly don't like anyone who tries to change the timeline.

But that's in the future. It's only 1996, and that doesn't happen until 2010. The Elders don't know I time travel yet.

We are concerned they might have access to technology that allows them to see probable futures.

Okay. Is that why it's so hard to reach you sometimes?

Exactly. It's a lot of work to create a Secure Protective Space here. As you know, we can't lie to the Elders. They just assume our communication is with others within Subterranean Earth. If they ask us directly, we can't hide it from them.

But you're saying this experiment could bring us back to Helio Tropez and help surface humans?

That's the intention, but we need to act soon. They're starting to get suspicious.

Okay, what do you suggest?

Bring as many SIM family members together as possible. Create a crucible into which higher and lower frequencies can integrate and transform into something altogether different, beyond control and separation. It has to be on your property.

Hadden paced the dome, thinking. *What if we had a garden party this summer? I could ask Leo to contact as many SIM family members as he can.*

Good, Halia said. *Meanwhile, our team can create a similar field in 4th density Helio Tropez. We will attempt to bridge the two fields. We've created a program to map out as many SIM and SANA counterparts as possible. For example, your counterpart is Leo, Tia's counterpart is Andrea.*

How will I convince Tia to be part of this? She wants to distance herself from me a lot more lately.

Make this gathering her 16th birthday party. Ask her to invite all her friends from school, especially descendants of SIM families. Many parents will attend as chaperones.

After a lot of planning, the day arrived, and people gathered in the garden. When Andrea's mother, Josie, arrived, Hadden bristled. He remembered how she had caused the separation of their family and had tormented Daphne for years.

Tia flitted between groups and greeted people as they arrived, accepting lavish gifts with a shy smile. Around the swimming pool, helium balloons wafted in the breeze and a table piled up with gifts as a catering team brought out buffet items. Some people knew each other and gathered in small groups to chat. Once the majority of people arrived, Halia and the team could see both fields side by side. They set up the counterparts in the exact locations where they stood on the surface.

Hadden watched from the sidelines, eyes darting from one group to the other, watching for signs of trouble while listening to Halia and trying to stay close to Leo. As the SANA energy dialled up, SIM energies went into resistance. It started with Josephine shouting at one of the servers for bumping into her. A mother and son got into an argument. A man looked at Hadden with fire in his eyes. Faces contorted in agitation.

Andrea turned to Tia. "You're doing some kind of energy attack on us!"

Tia looked around as the chaos spread. "What are you talking about?"

Andrea shoved her backwards. "You don't belong here. Go back to where you came from."

"Stop that!" Hadden said, lunging forward to protect his daughter.

Tia moved close to her father. "You know you sound crazy, right?"

Leo came up behind them, seething with rage. "This is a trap. Everyone, leave now."

People started murmuring amongst themselves and packing up to leave. All hell broke loose when both of Leo's grandparents fainted. Hadden immediately called 911. Meanwhile, Halia and her team increased the SANA frequency in hopes of keeping everyone calm. When the darkness and the light hit their zenith, the two energies seemed to cancel each other out. Both sides lost all their powers, and Hadden could feel his mind power extinguish completely.

At the same time, he saw a double rainbow above the horizon, something he'd never seen before. In fact, he saw a rainbow of light hovering over the garden. Neuro pathways in everyone's mind short-circuited, at least those with a counterpart in Helio Tropez. By the time the ambulance left with Leo's grandparents on life support, everyone had left the party. Tia looked at him, completely dumbfounded by what had just happened. But Hadden didn't know what to say, so he just told her to go to her room.

Hadden went up to the dome and tried to focus his mind to reach out to Halia. Nothing. He tried to read the minds of the Burres Family. Nothing. He tried levitating a cup with his mind. No power. The forcefield on the house no longer worked. Panic coursed through his veins as he felt vulnerable and utterly alone. His phone repeatedly rang with threatening messages on his answering machine. Things couldn't have gone worse. That night, he didn't sleep at all. Instead, he lay waiting for one of the Burres or Carbonas to assassinate them both.

CHAPTER 28

<u>Seattle – 2007</u>

The doorbell rang, and Hadden swivelled in his chair to scan the eight monitors mounted on the wall. CCTV footage captured all entrances outside the mansion. Javier, the security guard, stood at the front door with two boxes.

Tia peeked her head inside his office. "Can I let him in?"

"Just a second, sweetheart." Hadden continued to scan the other screens for hidden intruders. "Okay. It's just Javier. You can answer it."

She returned a few minutes later with two boxes of groceries and an envelope. "Here's your fabulous Pork and Mash dinners. Five of them," Tia said, feigning a smile.

"TV dinners are just easier. I don't have time to cook."

"I'll cook for you, Dad. I've said that many times."

"I don't want to bother you..."

"It wouldn't bother me."

He knew it would, though. Over the last eleven years, they had grown apart, only talking to each other when they had to, despite living in the same house. Other than Javier, he ensured no one entered the house. She still resented him for cutting her off from everyone after her 16th birthday party for no apparent reason. He had tried to explain how people in the Burres family would assassinate them both if they left the house, but she didn't believe him and called him paranoid instead. Maybe he was.

It pained him to see her locked away. Recently, he saw her watching a couple from the window as they walked down the street hand in hand. She sighed, and Hadden's chest tightened. He knew she felt imprisoned, but he had no other choice. When she was younger, he had modified the amethyst earrings, programming them to alert him if she ever left the house without his permission.

It worked. The first time it happened, he had rushed to the window. There she had stood, halfway down the driveway, suitcases set beside her. But she had turned around and came back to the house. The exact same thing happened a second time. Was it fear, programming, loyalty to him, or something else that kept her from leaving home?

The Burres family never talked to them anymore. Leo's grandparents died after Tia's party. The cause of death remained a mystery. Hadden had heard a rumour that both of them had literally dissolved into ash in the ambulance.

For the eleven years after that, Hadden and Tia lived in a fortress. She had to leave school and cut off all friendships. To appease her, Hadden fixed up the dome so she could live there. He added a kitchenette, an office and a bedroom area so that she could have some sense of autonomy from him.

"I'm going back upstairs. Need anything?" she asked in a monotone voice.

"No. I'm good. What's in the other box?"

With a flourish of her hand, she answered, "Fresh vegetables, fruits and supplements for me."

"Good. I'm glad you're eating that kind of food."

"Remember when we both ate that way?"

He nodded, but Tia's face spoke of disappointment, filling him with remorse and shame as it always did. He'd grown heavy around the middle, despite all his intentions. For years, he had home-schooled her on Heliotropan nutrition. He had even built what he called 'the Health Room', which consisted of a gym with weights, an elliptical machine, a Pulsed Electro-Magnetic Field mat, a portable oxygen bar, and a Ganzfield Healing Device. It provided for all their health needs.

After a year, he had stopped using it. Tia, on the other hand, spent hours a day in the room, burning off the frustration from a life of imprisonment.

He noticed an envelope under her arm. "What's that?"

"Don't know. It has no return address. Probably a promotion for a new credit card."

"Probably."

She tossed it in his wastebasket and went upstairs.

Later than evening, Hadden noticed the envelope was missing – he even rummaged through the wastebasket, but it was gone. *Maybe she wants her own credit card,* he mused. Perhaps this was her way of securing some sort of freedom from him. Still, he narrowed his eyes at the wastebasket. He had to know for sure.

The next day, when Tia was in the *Health Room*, he crept upstairs and found the envelope hidden under a stack of books. It was an invitation to a ten-year high school reunion from Andrea Carbona. Neither of them had seen any of the Carbonas for eleven years. The date was eight days from now, on Saturday, July 20, in the afternoon.

Hadden frowned at the envelope. *She can't possibly think of going, can she?* But the fact that the letter was hidden troubled him.

She had never returned to the Lafayette Academy after her party, and he had cut any contact with her friends there. *Why would Andrea invite her? They can't have taken her departure very well.* His face darkened.

The Carbonas want control of her.

The next day, Tia came to talk to him. He lay in his recliner holding three remotes for his different television sets, flipping from one channel to the next, glancing at the monitors from time to time.

"Dad?"

"Hmm... mmm," he said absently, lost in a malaise of painkillers.

"I think I need to see a dentist. I have a bad toothache. I'm going to call Dr Richards and set up an appointment."

"Who's Dr Richards?" The older he got, the more absent-minded he got. His razor-sharp memory was a thing of the past.

"The dentist you went to last year."

"Does he do house calls? I'll pay whatever he wants."

Tia sighed. "I'll ask."

She went into the kitchen and called Dr Richard's office.

"Do you do house calls? No? I didn't think so. That's okay. I'll see you on the twentieth."

She poked her head through the door. "No house calls."

"You have to go there? When?"

"Next Saturday."

He didn't say anything at first, trying to assess the risk level. Next Saturday was the day of her high school reunion. It broke his heart that she chose to lie to him, but he kept his expression clear because he couldn't confront her about it without admitting that he'd gone through her things.

"So? My tooth really hurts."

"Did you try the Ganzfield Device on it?"

She narrowed her eyes. "That thing only works on skin abrasions. Have you made any in-home dentistry devices lately?"

He feigned a smile, but her sarcastic tone stung. Didn't she realise he was trying to save her life? Hadden took and deep breath and answered, "Take Javier with you."

"Fine."

The rest of the week, Hadden noticed Tia smiling for the first time in a long time. Although his intuitive powers had greatly diminished the last ten years, he could often read Tia's thoughts and emotions. She cycled between excitement and fear about going to the reunion.

A hidden camera pointed at his office door, and another inside the room told him everything. Several times that week, he caught her poking around his office in the middle of the night.

Two days before the reunion, his computer alerted him that Tia was in his office again. This time, she tapped on the wall near his shelf, removed books from the shelf, then slid it over enough to reveal his wall safe.

Hadden leaned closer to the monitor. It was hard to see in the dark, and all she had was a flashlight, but it looked like she wanted to figure out how to crack the safe. After a few minutes, she tiptoed back upstairs to the dome, and he breathed a sigh of relief. A stiffness had grown upon him while he was glued to the monitor.

He sat back into a half-sleep only to be awoken again half an hour later to see Tia back in his office with a flashlight and a list of numbers on a piece of paper. She went down the list of combinations, trying one after the other, but the safe remained locked. As she persisted, his nervousness grew. Finally, the safe clicked. He must have taught her the sequence of numbers she had just keyed in. His favourite mathematical sequence was for a pentagonal shape which he often used in his inventions: 1-5-12-22-35-51-70.

Inside was the one thing he hoped she would never find: his journal of teachings from Halia. Tia spent the next few minutes poring over it and taking photos of each page with her phone. Carefully, she put it back in the safe as she had found it.

Hadden lay in his bed that night, his heart racing, but he couldn't do anything. The very thing he had set up to protect them, to protect her, was now working against him.

The next morning, Tia joined him in the kitchen. "Let's have tea together," she said without preamble.

Hadden's heart was in his throat. "Okay."

"Mint?"

"Sure."

They hadn't done that in years. As she busied herself making the tea, she talked about the weather and repairs needed around the house. Hadden hoped she wouldn't bring up anything about the safe or the journal. It wouldn't make sense to her anyway because it was all written in Matrix.

After settling into the breakfast nook with him, she asked, "Do we have a relative named Halia?"

Hadden nearly choked on the tea. Clearing his throat, he said, "What? Why do you ask that?"

"A woman named Halia came to me in a dream. She said she was my great grandmother."

Hadden paused, not sure how to answer. He gripped the table edge as a flush of adrenaline raced through his system. "Ah, yes. She's... um. I mean... that was the name of my mother's mother."

"Interesting. I've never had a dream as vivid as that."

"What did she look like in the dream?"

"She had long brown hair coiled up on her head in a cone shape with a silver cap on top. Very strange."

During the years of contact with Halia, that's exactly what she had looked like to him. However, ever since the party, he couldn't connect with her, no matter what or how hard he tried. Somehow, since finding the journal, Tia had been able to connect.

She took a sip of tea. "That would mean she lived sometime in the 1800s, but her clothing looked futuristic."

Hadden laughed nervously. "Maybe that's her spirit you're talking to… in the angelic realms… where they wear futuristic clothing."

"Uh huh," Tia said in a faraway voice. "She said some interesting things."

"Like what?" Hadden asked more forcefully than intended.

"I don't know. Like the fact that you already know I'm going to my high school reunion on Saturday and not the dentist."

Hadden's face flushed. Trust Halia to try and intervene between them. "Your reunion?"

"I know you looked at the invitation."

"Okay, I did – but only for your protection. Why did you lie?"

She smiled broadly and crossed her arms. "Would you have let me go if I'd told you the truth?"

"You don't understand the gravity of being outside the house."

"Maybe that's because you never explained why. It doesn't make sense."

His chest tightened. "I promised your mother I would keep you safe from the Carbonas. They target people from the Zuris bloodline."

"The Zuris bloodline?"

"Your mother's family."

"Why?"

Hadden frowned, not knowing how to answer. "It's complicated."

261

"You always say that," she said, becoming increasingly frustrated. "Why did you encourage me to be friends with Andrea in high school, then?"

He opened his mouth and shut it again as she looked at him expectantly. When he stayed silent, she huffed, took her cup to the sink, washed it, and headed for the spiral staircase. He felt torn about the situation. The only way out was to connect with Halia again, but it looked like he'd need to do that through Tia.

"Because Halia told me to," he said just before she reached the first step.

"What?" Tia stopped and turned back to look at him with quizzical eyes.

"Halia used to speak to me in dreams too."

She narrowed her eyes. "Say more."

"Halia wanted you to become friends with Andrea. I thought it had something to do with the idea to keep your friends close and your enemies closer."

Tia pursed her lips and took a deep breath. "So, it's not all in my imagination... Halia is a real ancestor trying to speak to me?"

"Yes, and I'm eager to reconnect with her. It's been eleven years."

"She says I should go to the reunion."

"She's talking to you now? I mean right at this second?"

"I think so."

Hadden scurried forward, his sore feet slowing him down. "You *think* so?"

"I'm hearing a voice in my head that sounds very different from my own voice, and I'm seeing her face."

Hadden smiled. "That's telepathic communication. It's her. Tell her I'm so relieved to reconnect."

Tia closed her eyes and sank into a rare stillness. "She says it's your own fault... that you lost connection with her. You didn't use the Sugilite?"

His throat tightened. "I know. I lost the Sugilite stone. I lost myself. I'm so sorry."

Tia's eyes became distant. "She says it's now time for you to tell me everything."

"Everything?" he asked, exasperated. "But that could put you on SIM's radar."

"I don't know what SIM is, but she says that I'm already on their radar, and the more I know, the more I can protect myself."

Hadden sighed. She was right.

"Best make another cup of tea. We might be a while."

Hadden spent the next two hours explaining everything to her.

Over the next few days, they continued talking, giving Tia time to digest the information before coming back with questions. He held nothing back, even his trip into the future from 1960 to 2010. By the day of the reunion, he felt much closer to her and so much better at not having to carry all this information by himself. He even helped her choose an outfit.

As she walked to the car, Hadden called after her. "Good luck at the reunion, but keep Javier close."

He watched them drive off, then hurried back to his office, where the feed was already coming through. Hadden had fitted Javier with a hidden microphone and camera, unbeknownst to Tia. He knew it might ruin the newfound trust between them, but he was worried. He watched on the monitor as Javier drove her to the Sheraton Hotel.

After parking the car, Javier opened Tia's door. She stepped out, then smoothed her hair and dress. "Okay. I'll be back in a few hours."

"Your father wants me to accompany you," he said timidly.

"Why? Bringing a bodyguard would look weird."

"Many of these people are from wealthy families and will have bodyguards."

"I don't think so. Just wait here."

Tia walked away, and Hadden panicked. On the comm, he said to Javier, "Follow her. But stay out of sight."

As Tia arrived at the meeting room, two young women sat behind a rectangular table registering guests for the afternoon mixer. Javier stayed a few feet behind.

"Tia! I never thought you'd come!" a woman said from behind the table.

"Valerie?"

"Yes! I know that I look totally different. New hair. Gained a bit of weight since you last saw me. But you look exactly the same. I mean... exactly."

They hugged. Valerie smiled in a sly way, then pointed to Javier, who was standing behind her. "And who's this?"

Tia looked over her shoulder and scowled at him.

He stepped forward and reached out his hand. "I am her... boyfriend. I'm Javier."

Valerie smiled at Tia with raised eyebrows. She hesitated a moment and smiled back at her. "Yes, indeed. Javier is my boyfriend."

"Nice to meet you, Javier."

She filled in a name tag for both of them. "It's been years. You just left school all of a sudden. I knocked at your door, and I called, but no one ever answered. I figured you moved away or something. What happened?"

"I'm so sorry we couldn't keep in touch. Yes, I had to move away, but I've just gotten back."

"Where have you been all this time?"

"I went to, ah, stay with my mother in Montréal. She needed me to be there with her... um... due to health reasons... I've been living with her this whole time. I'm so sorry I never told you. I'm not very good at keeping up with people," Tia laughed meekly.

Hadden frowned, wondering why she made up a story about being with her mother.

"Ok. Well, it's good to know you're still alive," she replied, hurt etched across her brow. "That's amazing that you were reunited with your mother..."

"Yes. Totally. So, what have you been up to over the last decade?"

Valerie patted her belly. "I run a pastry shop in Bellevue. Can't you tell?"

"Nice. You were always amazing in the kitchen."

"Tia! I can't believe it," Andrea said, giving her a huge hug. "I wasn't sure if you still lived with your father or not, but I had our butler hand-deliver the envelope to your mailbox."

Andrea looked very different. She no longer sported black bangs that covered half her face or torn black stockings with work boots. Instead, she

264

appeared like a successful businesswoman with hair pinned up neatly and dressed in a Ralph Loren dress suit.

"Hi, Andrea. I was just telling the others I've been away... um... living in Montréal. Sorry I never said goodbye. I was just telling Valerie I'm not very good at keeping up with people."

"No problem. So do you have a job, go to school, or did you get married?" Andrea asked, scrutinizing her and looking over at Javier.

"I'm, um, a... performance coach. And Javier is just my, ah, boyfriend. He lives in my neighbourhood."

"What's a performance coach?" Valerie asked.

"I know what that is," Andrea replied. "There's a performance coach for the top brass in our company. He supposedly helps people deal with the stress of their job and to handle the pressure. He's crap at it, but I bet you're good. That's a very cool profession. Who do you work with?"

"Actually, I just finished my training. I need to find some clients now."

"I'll be your client," Andrea grinned. "I mean it. I just got this new VP position in one of my father's companies, and I have no idea what I'm doing."

"That's great," Tia said, faking a smile. "I'd love to take you on."

"Thank you! Now let me get you both a drink. There's wine or sparkling water...?

"Sparkling water would be fine for both of us."

"Of course. You never even tried any of that vodka we snuck out of my Mum's cabinet. You were always such a good girl."

Tia winced, but they followed her into the room. Javier scanned the room so Hadden could see the layout of things. People milled around, some awkwardly standing with hands in their pockets or their faces buried in their phones, others stood in groups, reminiscing about stories from school and laughing about long-forgotten memories.

"Don't get me wrong," Andrea was saying, handing Tia and Javier a Perrier. "I loved that about you. You were a very good influence on me. That's why I was so sad when you stopped showing up at school."

Their last interaction was anything but cordial. Hadden was confused. What had changed? She must want to target Tia. Valerie joined them at the bar and downed a glass of wine in a few gulps.

Andrea laughed. "And you can work with Valerie too! She's trying to build her pastry shop."

"Please, Tia. I'd love your help. I eat and drink too much, and the stress of running a business is driving me crazy."

"Um. Okay... sure."

They found chairs nearby and chatted about their lives over the past eleven years. Javier made up a story about working at Violetta and Burres Investments as an analyst. A few old school friends joined them to trade stories, reminiscing about high-school scandals and laughing about classroom antics that had driven their teachers crazy.

After a few hours, Javier whispered to her, "It's time to go."

Tia shot him a disappointed look but said to the others, "I've loved reconnecting with all of you, but we really have to go."

Andrea jumped to her feet. "So soon? That's too bad."

Valerie smiled. "So, you're back in town for good now?"

"Yes, I'm living with my dad at the moment because he's not well."

Andrea took Tia's hand, which made Hadden nervous. "Yes, I heard he went a bit crazy a few years back. So sorry to hear."

"He's not crazy. He's just got diabetes and arthritis and can't move very well. That was just a false rumour."

"I wondered about that. Ever since your party, everyone just hated your dad, and I never really figured out why."

Something bubbled in Hadden, but he wasn't surprised that they hated him.

"I don't remember that party," Valerie said.

"You weren't invited. I'm not sure why," Andrea said, raising her eyebrows at Tia.

Valerie handed her a business card. "At any rate, here's my number. Let's set up an appointment."

"And here's mine," Andrea said, writing her phone number on a napkin.

"Good. Thank you. I'll call you both later."

On their way back, Tia said, "So you listened in the whole time, Dad?"

Javier glanced at her nervously and said nothing.

"Now all my friends think he is my boyfriend. What will his wife and children think of that?"

"Please, ma'am. I was only following your father's orders. He just wanted to keep you safe. He says he's sorry."

Hadden hadn't actually said that he was sorry but made a mental note to thank Javier for covering for him.

Tia scowled as she threw herself into the passenger seat. "I'd like to see him apologise to my face."

When they got home, Hadden waited for her in the kitchen. "I truly am sorry, Tia. I trust you. I just don't trust *them*. I don't think that coaching them is a good idea."

"Halia thinks it's a good idea."

"You're interfacing with her now?" He felt glad they had connected, but why would she interfere with his parenting?

Tia looked sideways. "Yes."

Hadden sighed and realised he needed to back off. "Okay. I'm going to trust that you and Halia can make this work. Only if Halia is guiding you."

"No problem. I'm still getting used to this interfacing thing."

"Keep me posted."

Later that week, Tia joined Hadden in the kitchen for an update. "Andrea and I had a session on Skype. Halia's presence was nearby."

"What happened on the call?"

"She said her father wants her to take the role of VP for one of their production companies in Florida. She doesn't feel qualified, and there are people with far more experience, so now she thinks they hate her. She's only twenty-seven and spent most of the last ten years just partying. Her first leadership meeting is on Monday, so I helped her to start changing the way she thinks so that she can be more confident."

"Good. That sounds good."

267

"I always thought of her as confident in school because she came from this powerful family and liked to boss people around, particularly me. She said that after my 16th birthday party, she lost all her confidence and all her intuitive abilities. And, no longer having me in her life really bothered her. Somehow, I made her a better person. Imagine that?"

"I can imagine that." He smiled. "Like I said, all the counterparts lost their abilities, you and I included. You do have a good effect on people, and I'm sorry if I haven't been more supportive of your choice to coach people."

Tia looked up, shocked to hear his apology. "Okay. Thanks. I'm glad to know I have your support. You know, all these years, I've felt like I've been working against you – it was draining. "

"Agreed. I'm fully on your side now. Really," Hadden promised, his eyes stinging with tears.

Tia's face softened, and she smiled. "Good. Me, too. No more lying and sneaking around."

They hugged, and Tia left the kitchen. When she was at the end of the hall, she called out, "By the way, Andrea has been referring me to other people. My roster of clients is filling up."

"Good!" Hadden called back, trying to sound enthusiastic.

The following week, Tia was scanning over some folders at breakfast. Hadden peered over her shoulder, intrigued at what might be keeping her so busy.

"So, are you still seeing lots of SIM family members as clients?" he asked.

"Total transparency between us, right? Here's my roster of clients," she said as she pulled out a list of names from a folder.

Hadden scanned the names at the top of each folder. "Almost all SIM family members. Impressive."

"I'm the only person they want to work with because they say I feel familiar to them. They know the dome provides a Secure Protective Space, which shields them from SIM interception. That way, they feel safe to confide in me. I had no idea of the ritualistic abuse they face as children. It's so horrible that I don't even want to repeat it to you."

Hadden's chest filled with pressure. "I know what happens to them," he said quietly. "That's how SIM controls. It's why your mother and I fought so hard to protect you from that."

"Did any of that happen to you too?"

Hadden nodded slowly.

"I can't imagine, Dad." She hugged him, and his chest trembled as the darkness began to break down under the light of her compassion.

She brought him a tissue. "Thank you for letting me know. It helps me understand you so much better and why we've lived like this."

Hadden tried to speak, but his throat tensed up.

"My clients tell me that anyone who tries to go to the authorities gets killed or put in a mental institute. I'm sworn to secrecy. I shouldn't even be telling you, but it's a hard burden to bear alone."

"Tell me about it," he said in a fretful voice. "It *is* dangerous that you know this information, but we are both protected here. Let me help you share the burden. I hope now that you understand why I've been so reluctant about you coaching them, even when Halia encouraged it."

"Halia and her team help me with each session. I know I'm healing them at a deep level. I can't just live this secluded life and not be doing something to help the situation."

Hadden smiled, pride bubbling within him. "That's so good, sweetheart. I'm very proud of you. I know I should be doing more too."

"You have done a lot already, Dad."

Hadden sighed, not sure whether he believed it. "How do you coach them? Maybe I could learn a thing or two."

Tia looked at the clock then checked her mobile phone. "I'm coaching Andrea very soon. Do you want to listen in?"

"Okay, if you think she'll be okay with that..."

"We'll ask her." Tia skipped up the stairs. "Come on."

Hadden huffed his way up the spiral stairs, clutching the rails on each painful step. She pointed to the swivel chair near her desk, and he collapsed down into it in relief.

"Just give me two seconds while I set up. By the way, Andrea's my toughest client. If I do well here, then you can be doubly impressed."

Hadden nodded, and Tia swept her hair over her shoulder before squaring her shoulders and taking a breath. Once composed, she opened Skype and dialed.

Andrea's face appeared on the monitor a few moments later. "Tia! You wouldn't believe what just happened, I–"

"Just before we begin, is it okay if my Dad listens in? He wants to learn how I work with people." Tia swivelled the webcam to face him. He gave an awkward wave, shrinking back into his chair.

"Mr Violetta! It's been such a long time. Um, I guess so. This is all confidential, right?"

"Absolutely," Tia and Hadden said in unison.

Andrea looked down, and her face flushed. "Right. Okay. Are you both coaching me or...?"

"No, just Tia. I'm learning from her. But I will help create a very safe space for you to get whatever you need." Hadden said as he dialled up on the shielding frequencies in the dome with this mind.

"Whew! Great. I need that. I sense you are doing that. Um... Thank you. So... where to begin... my mother has been driving me crazy..."

For the next few minutes, Andrea talked about a situation at work with her mother, also known as Josie Carbona, the matriarch of the Carbonas and Daphne's handler back in the 1970s. The issue involved one of the family companies and a merger with a smaller company. Andrea called it a hostile takeover and wouldn't sign it as one of the board members.

"Okay, thanks for that explanation," Tia said, scribbling copious notes on a pad. "That's a tricky situation. I'm going to use a combination of our typical processes and end with an audio, which you can use daily throughout the next week to anchor in the results we get. We've done all these before, so they'll be familiar to you."

"Sounds good. I need a result ASAP," Andrea said, looking over her shoulder.

Tia cleared her throat. "Okay. What meaning are you're giving to this situation? We're going to try and find the MindStory, the roles and scripts of this story."

Hadden was shocked to hear her use the word 'MindStory' as that indicated that she was now using her Pentada wisdom, albeit on SIM agents.

"The meaning... hmmm. I don't know," Andrea squinted.

"What does it mean to you, your mother, and life in general?"

Andrea's eyes widened. "Right. The meaning is that the only way to please my family is to take advantage of others, and if I don't, then I'll be punished. My mother is a witch. Life is unfair, and I'm trapped."

"Good. So if we could sum that up in terms of the archetypal role that you're playing, it would be...?" Tia shared her screen and showed a list of common archetypal roles people play in the MindStories that they create in life, along with the corresponding scripts.

"If I were to choose from one of these, it would be... The Slave, and my script is *I'm oppressed*."

"Right. And, as we've said before, these roles and scripts are arbitrary. You can change them like an actor changes costumes if you train yourself how. What's the opposite you see on the list?"

"Sovereign – *I'm free to create the life I want*. That sounds great. But how?"

"That's what we're going to work on now; strengthening this more empowering MindStory Archetype and Core Script."

For the next forty-five minutes, Tia worked in helping Andreas create a series of past, present and future stories to reinforce the Sovereign character who believes *I'm free to create the life I want*. Together, they extracted the lessons learned, which she could apply in the future.

"Good work. Now I'm going to take you through a blueprinting audio session. I'll record it for you to listen to afterwards. Listen to it at least 20 times between now and when we meet next. After it's done, we'll do our action steps."

"Got it."

Tia then took Andrea through a kind of guided self-hypnosis and mental rehearsal with brain wave entrainment music in the background. As she spoke, Halia helped Tia build a new neuropathway in Andrea's mind. It created an alternative, more empowered pathway for Andrea to take in any situation where she felt oppressed and taken advantage of. Once it was over, they brainstormed on different ways she could approach the situation and created an action plan. The session ended, and Andrea seemed imbued with clarity.

"Same time next week?" Tia asked, adding it to her digital calendar.

"Yes. Thank you so much! I'm heading into a meeting now. Wish me luck."

Tia signed off and turned in her chair to face her father. "So?"

"Exceptional work. I had no idea how talented you were. You created all these systems and processes?"

Tia grinned and leaned back in her chair. "That was just the tip of the iceberg of what I've learned to do with people, all with Halia's help, of course. She makes all the difference."

"It's excellent teamwork." Hadden pulled himself up and leaned against the wall to keep the pressure off his knees. "I forgot how great it feels to be up here in the dome." He closed his eyes, and positive frequencies calmed his brain waves. "One question. Do you ask permission from Andrea's Higher Self *before* doing the mind code work?"

"Um... yes, that's a universal law of SANA that Halia taught me. We did it on the first session, so I figured it would stick."

"Maybe. I hope so. The Carbonas don't like insurrection from within their ranks. Have you helped her deal with a situation in the company like this before?"

Tia shook her head. "Usually, we deal with her lousy communication skills, her endless bad romances or her many addictions."

He rubbed the back of his neck. Tia seemed so compassionate and skilled on the call, yet clearly she judged Andrea. Out of the corner of his eye, he sensed a presence near the window. "Let's both ask SANA for extra help on this one."

"Got it."

He limped towards the stairs and glanced back towards her. "I'm proud of what you do. Thank you for sharing it with me."

Tia beamed as he disappeared down the staircase.

A few weeks later, Hadden found Tia in the kitchen, reading a book on Performance Coaching.

"How's it going with Andrea?"

"It's weird. She hasn't shown up for the last couple of sessions and won't return any of my messages. I'm getting worried that something's happened."

A lingering unease built up again in his mind. "Any guess what it can be about?"

"No idea. I can't get a fix on it. Maybe she's just busy with work."

"Maybe." Hadden knitted his brow. He knew it was something more, but when he tried to read Andrea's mind, he just got a headache. A firewall, most likely. Something wasn't right.

"Did you try calling the main reception where she works?"

Tia shook her head and looked up the number online. After placing the call, she spoke to a receptionist for a few minutes, then hung up. "Apparently, she doesn't work there anymore, but they wouldn't tell me why."

"That's not good. I suggest we look into this." As soon as the words left his mouth, Hadden felt a sharp pain in his temples.

At the same time, Tia's cell phone pinged. "It's a text from Andrea." After reading it, she showed it to Hadden.

Sorry I haven't gotten back to you. I've left the company. Not really my thing. I'm excited to be travelling instead. I won't be needing any more coaching now that I don't have this stressful job to worry about anymore. All is good. Thanks for everything! Smiley Face. Heart Emoji.

"I guess all is okay," Tia shrugged, but a troubled look crossed her face. "I think the coaching series was successful. Sometimes it's just not needed anymore. Anyway, she was a handful. I'm a bit relieved to tell you the truth."

"A handful? The last session seemed to have gone very well."

"She was on good behaviour because you were there. Usually, she balks at my suggestions. I think she's critical of how I coach her. No other clients are like that. It affects my confidence. But she sends a lot of clients to me, so I put up with it."

Hadden nodded but wasn't convinced that everything was fine. "Does she openly criticise you?"

"No, it's more a Sentient thing that I pick up. She's more the passive-aggressive type."

"So you feel judged?"

Tia looked away and coiled her arms around her waist. "Yeah. Maybe, sometimes."

"You are both Sentient-Attention, the most highly tuned emotionally, but also the most sensitive. If you sense she is judging you, chances are she *knows* you judge her too. It might be a defense mechanism."

Biting her lip, Tia looked directly at him. "Right. Right. Makes sense. Yikes. Hopefully, she'll come back for more coaching since we did make a lot of progress."

The whole situation made Hadden uncomfortable, so he dialed up on their protection tenfold, praying to SANA for her safety and for theirs. After that, they never heard from any Carbonas for the next three years. Perhaps they were waiting for Tia's thirtieth birthday.

CHAPTER 29

*I*t's almost time for you to return to Helio Tropez.

Hadden awoke from a dream with Halia's words in the forefront of his mind. It was near Tia's birthday and the day his younger self time travelled to the year 2010. Only now, he was the old man and not the young one.

He reached out to Halia again. *What do you mean? Are they letting me come to Helio Tropez?*

Her voice rang loud and clear. *Yes, you've earned your ticket. However, before that happens, just make sure you send the messages to your younger self so that he time travels here from 1960.*

What? I thought that kind of time travel was forbidden.

Not any longer. Not for you. We need to close the loop on the timeline and ensure Tia gets back to Helio Tropez like she did before.

I don't get it. Why not just send us both via a stargate?

It doesn't work that way. Your route back is through Leo. He's coming to see you soon.

But the last time he came here was to kill me!

Hadden waited for an answer but couldn't sense any response. After a few minutes, he said, *Are you still there?*

You'll have to just trust me on this, was all she said.

Hadden sighed and thought of asking other questions, but she hung up the telepathic phone line before he could say anything. *Through Leo... Is this the experiment she tried all those years ago at Tia's party that went horribly wrong? I sure hope not.*

He lay in bed and sent the telepathic messages to his younger self, intending for him to receive the instructions loud and clear. After a few minutes, he remote viewed the situation and sensed that, at least, the first one was received. Each night, he'd send more messages until he was certain that his younger self had gotten all of them.

On the way to the kitchen, he looked in the mirror. Over the last three years, he'd adopted better lifestyle habits and had slimmed down. In fact, he looked in pretty good shape for a seventy-year-old. The tasteful and uncluttered decor of the living room also put him at ease. He didn't want his younger self to feel repelled by his life and lifestyle. That's what happened for him when he was a young man meeting himself in the future. Had it not been for Tia's rebellion, he might have ended up back where he had started. Her willingness to fight for the truth had set them both on a better path.

On that fateful night in July, he stayed by the window and waited for Addy. This time his million-dollar view was clear and worth every cent, especially on this night. The stillness of his well-loved oak, the beauty of the stars in the summer sky and the occasional hooting of an owl somewhere in the neighbourhood only seemed to emphasize the underlying tranquillity of his inner mind.

One good thought is all it takes to reconnect to the source of all things, but a single mistake can burn down the forest in your heart, hiding all the stars in all the skies.

This time, there would be no mistakes. No home care worker would try to stop them as he didn't need one anymore. He would spend longer with Addy and Tia to prepare them for what to expect. Tia now understood her whole heritage and was fully aware of what would happen on that day, so the shock wouldn't be so severe.

When Addy entered the driveway soaking wet in his jumpsuit and helmet, Hadden opened the front door and welcomed him with open arms. *He must be relieved to see a future version of himself that was less ravaged by time.*

Hadden handed him a towel and gave him some clothes that fit. When he emerged from the next room after he was done changing, Tia was waiting. The three of them sat in the living room together. She was fully cognizant of who Addy was and why he was there. They explained the situation until Addy understood his full assignment. Proudly, Hadden gave them both the latest versions of the amethyst, along with three others for Daphne, Annika and Metta. This version was well beyond the power of anything previous.

In a transcendent state, he told Addy how to fly the plane back to Helio Tropez. His last words to both of them filled his heart with longing. "I love you both. Now, go!"

Tia and Hadden embraced, knowing it would be their final time together, at least in this timeline. Once they left, Hadden unlocked the front door and went up to the dome to meet his fate with Leo. Within thirty minutes, he heard footsteps on the front porch. The person never knocked or rang the bell - the door just opened. Footsteps climbed the spiral staircase. Hadden sat in a swivel chair, facing the ocean, waiting for the inevitable to happen.

"Where is she?" a familiar voice asked.

He turned around to see Leo standing in the doorway with a gun in his hand.

"She's gone for good."

"Gone?"

Leo's eyes confronted him. Memories of all their past lives together flooded his mental landscape. A cascade of understandings churned inside him. It was now totally clear why they were there at that moment. His original soul had to separate into dark and light to learn in this inverted realm. Each trauma, loss, betrayal, challenge that he refused to learn from got buried away. Eventually, those buried energies took on a life of their own.

His soul created a partition to pretend he had nothing to do with it. A kind of alter personality grew unbeknownst to him. Without a connection to SANA anymore, this dark alter personality had turned to SIM, selling a part of his soul over and over again without even realizing it. Each lifetime of disowning this dark side increased its power and control. Finally, in this lifetime, the soul annex known as Leo Burres was one of the most powerful men on earth.

277

In fact, the majority of the Violetta bloodline must have done the same thing. The entire Burres bloodline existed as a separate entity due to all the unresolved trauma from every member of the Violetta bloodline. Leo no longer had access to SANA, so he had to steal energy from others. SIM grew from the disowned parts of all sovereign souls unwilling to face and process their own lessons on the path of evolution. Therefore, everything Leo did in all lives was Hadden's responsibility. All the acts of evil were his.

"She's left. You won't find her. It's over, Leo."

Leo gritted his teeth and thrust the gun up, pointing it at Hadden's face. "Where has she gone?"

"You're too late." The gun trembled in front of him, and Hadden closed his eyes. "Beloved SANA, please help heal us in whatever way is possible before I die. Help our souls integrate again." Although he'd said this before over the years, this time, he genuinely meant it, for he now understood in a way he never had before.

The message from SANA came back loud and clear. An unbridled download of universal love filled him with multisensory information. To free himself and save the entire experiment meant letting go of the resistance to Leo completely - all the negativity, fear, hurt, shame, guilt. It needed to burn in every cell in his body. As the burning intensified, he surrendered to death, waiting for the bullet.

But it never came. He opened his eyes as Leo stood there shaking, but he wasn't looking at Hadden.

Tia's white teddy bear sat dusty on a side table. Hadden leaned forward and tossed the stuffed animal towards Leo. It landed on the floor in front of him. Leo put the gun down and picked up the bear. Memories of Sunday afternoons playing games and watching movies filled Hadden's mind, and he sent those images to Leo. His eyes regained focus and filled with a glowing light.

He blinked several times. "Hadden? What am I doing here?" Leo asked, looking around.

"It's the CM."

"Always the damn CM," Leo said with a wry smile. He looked at the gun on the floor, the smile fading to a pleading frown. "I guess I was supposed to kill you and take Tia away?"

"Probably."

Leo slumped forward and put his face in his hands. "I'm tired of all this."

"Me, too."

Both men closed their eyes, their company enough, no words or communication needed. After a time, they slipped into a deep meditation. Halia appeared and showed them how to cut the karmic cords to all negativity, all agreements, oaths or vows to SIM from all lifetimes and all timelines. Some cut away easily, but some remained as strong as steel.

Halia pointed to a petrified mass of black energy holding some cords in place. They stemmed from a blackened place in his heart towards Leo. The truth is, Leo was the one who endured the worst torture, being cut off from SANA, being left empty inside. It took all Hadden's courage to feel compassion for him, but when he did, a melting process began. Halia's love formed a solid crucible for the alchemical process to occur. The blackness liquified until it looked like crude oil. He knew to focus his attention like a magnifying glass in the sunlight until the oil burst into flames and engulfed them both. Their bodies bubbled and boiled in the flames. Hellish emotions lashed at him, burning his flesh until only the ashes remained and an eerie stillness permeated his heart.

Relief settled upon him as the last of the cords finally severed.

Next, Daphne appeared before him, the love between them magnetizing him forward to another world where all the colours of the rainbow soothed his soul. As he surrendered to the love, Hadden and Leo merged back together. Once complete, he fell into an abyss of nothingness, which frightened him. No longer a separate entity, Hadden was finally whole again.

The next morning, the authorities found only ash from their two bodies and a gun on the floor. The coroner identified them as belonging to Leo Burres and Hadden Violetta, but no explanations could be surmised. The Burres family knew exactly what had happened and wanted to use it to find Tia. And so, the media plastered her face everywhere.

CHAPTER 30

Upon hearing the extraction plan, Annika took a breath, leaning forward on her knees. "Listen, kid, I've been dealing with these SIM families my entire life. They are far more powerful than you can imagine, even with these upgraded amethysts. If you think that they don't know that we are hatching a plan to take their assets away from them, you're sorely mistaken."

Tia sighed and slumped back on the ancient sofa. "Why haven't they taken us down yet then?"

"I don't know. I'm surprised." Annika stood up and started pacing the room, chewing her lip as she put her mind to work.

"Maybe we are more powerful than them," Tia suggested. "Is there any way we can test?"

She then interfaced with the Helio Tropez team, and Meraton said, *I suggest that Cassandra, Annika, and Tia try connecting with Daphne telepathically. With three Pentadas interfacing, it would normally show up on their radar, and some kind of SIM agent will be on your doorstep in minutes. If no one shows up, the cloaking is working. If they do show up, we'll extract you right away.*

Sounds like a plan. Annika agrees.

As Meraton readied the team to extract the two of them if necessary, Tia and Annika joined Cassandra in a meditative state. They concentrated their attention on Daphne. Although her soul signature was likely removed, there always remained a trace link to the person's actual soul, even if the person had completely sold their soul to SIM. It was like a digital footprint in the soul matrix.

Tia's heart danced at the idea of finally reconnecting with her mother. She sensed the triangulation of their psychic powers, creating a powerful vortex circling through the wormholes of time, sniffing out their target through multi-dimensions, times, spaces and realities. She saw streams of violet and white lights intertwining, soaring high and low.

After searching the entire surface and interior of the planet, they found no trace of her. A sadness welled up, but Tia cleared her throat, averting her gaze to the window. *How can we not even find a fragment of information?*

Cassandra sent a wellspring of compassion to them both. *At least, that didn't trigger any response from SIM. You are protected. Let's focus on rescuing Metta and Xander of Indicium. Once four of the Pentada are together, our power might be boosted up enough to find Daphne.*

The plan involved Tia meeting them at the record label, wearing her hair back and a pair of glasses. After all, Josie Carbona had only met her once or twice as a teen, so the disguise didn't have to be too elaborate. At the same time, Annika would create a teleportation field in an empty room in the same building. Somehow, they had to get Metta and Dax in that room alone for a few minutes. Then, Cassandra and the team could teleport the four of them to Helio Tropez.

Annika needed a disguise to enter and move around the record label unnoticed. A maid service car was parked across the street. Tia had an idea. When no one was around, she sneaked over to the car and tried the driver's door. To her relief, it was open. In the back seat, she found a maid's uniform and cleaning supplies. She gathered it all up and raced back to the apartment. The maid's dress was a bit too long for Annika, so Tia pinned it up with safety pins. They finished off the disguise by tucking her hair under a cap.

"I better not look anything like the Annika of yesteryear because the owner of that record label used to manage the band I played in back in the 1970s."

"Josie Carbona?"

Annika grunted. "She's a piece of work."

"I've heard. I'm sure you look different enough. That was aeons ago. Plus, you'll have the amethyst to cloak your aptitude."

Once they were ready, they left the apartment separately. Annika arrived at the record label several minutes before Tia. Luckily, the lobby was packed with people coming and going for lunch, so Annika snuck past the reception and onto the elevators without a second glance. Tia's meeting was to happen on the fifth floor, so that's where Annika got off. She surveyed the entire floor until she found an empty, unused office. Once inside, she had forty-five minutes to create the teleportation field as instructed by Tia and the Helio Tropez team.

Meanwhile, Tia set her frequency to that of a regular surface human and showed up for the meeting at 2 PM as planned. In Helio Tropez, a separate group focused their remote viewing on people rushing from one room to another, some spilling pages, others coffee. A receptionist greeted her, barely glancing up from her monitor to acknowledge Tia. While she perused her calendar for the appointment, Tia took in the contemporary furniture: square leather sofas sat beneath portraits of artists mid-performance; the carpet – a deep red – made the golden awards in the cabinets shine even brighter. The receptionist cleared her throat, drawing Tia's attention back to her.

"If you'll follow me, I'll take you to the boardroom." She tottered ahead in heels that made Tia wince at the blisters she'd have within minutes of wearing them. The receptionist paused by a door, opening it for her. "They're already waiting for you," she said with a forced smile.

Tia took a breath to compose herself, then stepped inside. Sat at a long table were Metta, Dax, Ruth, and an older woman that had to be Josie Carbona. She broke their conversation to look up. Dax was on his feet and across the room in moments, pulling Tia into a quick hug.

Metta jumped up to greet her as well. "Linda! So glad you could make it. You remember Dax and Ruth, of course, and this is Ruth's mother and the head of the record label, Josie Carbona. She wanted to meet you face to face."

"Linda," the woman said, standing and offering a hand. "So nice to meet you."

Josie gripped her hand like a sledgehammer. When she released her hold, Tia slipped into a seat beside Metta, massaging her hand under the table. After a few pleasantries, Josie cleared her throat and got the group down to business. "With the festival circuit about to start, Metta and Dax have got a

282

busy few months ahead of them. My question for you, Linda, is why do they need you? They've made it so far just fine."

Her stomach tightened. The last time she had seen Josie was on her sixteenth birthday. Even though that was eleven years ago, people often thought Tia still looked like a teenager. That said, before her father changed the timeline, she'd never even met the Carbonas.

Which timeline are Ruth and Josie on? Tia asked the Helio Tropez team.

We're working on it, but they have some kind of firewall that's making them hard to read.

Tia nodded, jumping into a well-rehearsed pitch she had used when she had lived with her father. She described how the coaching worked and the benefits of having a sounding board to help them make decisions. As the discussion went along, a thought must have come to Josephine, who started scrolling through her phone all of a sudden.

"My other daughter, Andrea, hired a woman she knew in high school who called herself a performance coach. That was a few years ago. What was her name?"

Ruth shrugged. "I don't remember."

Tia conveyed to the team. *They are clearly on the second timeline. She's met me...*

As Josie searched her phone, the Helio Tropez team gathered data from her face, voice and energy signature. All they could see was that Josie repeatedly tried to access Tia's energy field, but each attempt failed.

"Here it is!" Josephine said, lifting her phone. "Tia Violetta. Maybe you know her?"

Tia pretended to consider the name for a moment, then shrugged and shook her head.

"Right! And wasn't Tia Violetta wanted for murdering her own father?" Ruth asked.

"I believe so..."

"That's awful," Tia frowned.

You need to move fast, Cassandra said in her mind.

Straightening, Tia shook her head. "I don't know her. Over 5,000 people are registered as performance coaches in North America alone. Anyway, I usually like to run a trial session with new clients just to see if we're a good fit for one another. How about I do a practice session with them now, and we'll see how everyone finds it?"

Josephine didn't look up from her phone. "Go ahead. Metta, tell her one of your *many* issues."

Metta frowned and looked over at Tia, reluctant.

Tia gave her an encouraging smile. "I think it would be better if we could be in private. It might be easier for Metta to speak freely."

"Do you have something to hide, Metta?" Josephine asked coyly.

"No. But it would be nice to just talk one-to-one, without everyone watching. I'd feel more comfortable."

"Okay then. What do you suggest?"

"Is there a free spare room?" Tia suggested innocently.

"There's one down the hall. How long will you be? I'm a busy woman."

Tia tried to hide her relief. "In that case, I can work with Metta and Dax at the same time, so long as that's okay?"

The two looked at one another and nodded. Josephine shrugged, her eyes still fixed on her phone. "Whatever."

"We won't be long – just a quick twenty minutes."

The three of them got up and followed Ruth down the hall. As they left, Tia thought she had seen Josephine give Ruth a knowing look. The Heliotropan Task Force went to work, scanning both of them for subterfuge, but they didn't detect anything.

Tia hoped she would take them to room 511. Instead, Ruth let them into 509, a dark room with a small square window.

"I'll come back in twenty minutes," Ruth said and left them to it.

Tia stepped further into the room, then tutted. "No, this isn't right. We need a better environment than this. Let me just check next door," she said, then dipped out of the room and came back a moment later. Retrieving the others, she led them to room 511, cameras mounted on the wall swivelling to follow them. Tia knew the timer had started.

"I just like this room better," she explained, though it was laid out exactly the same as room 509, with a poster on the wall being the only difference. As they entered, Annika stood in the corner.

In a mock Quebecois accent, Annika said, "Sorry, I just have to empty da wastebaskets."

The heightened energy vortex in the room made the hair on Tia's arms stand on end, and she wondered if the others could feel it too. The team announced that Dax and Metta were clear of drugs and alcohol, enough to make the teleportation easier on their system.

"Take a seat so we can get started." Metta and Dax sat around a small meeting table. In the middle of the table lay the Abracadabra Orb in 2D form. Metta ran her fingers over the symbols as if she could psychically read the mind code. Tia stalled, asking questions about the next festival circuit.

Finally, the team gave her the word they'd locked onto their position using the Orb.

Under her breath, Annika muttered, "Abracadabra. Begin transmission."

Metta laughed, "Are we going to do magic tricks?

Dax's face turned ashen. "Begin what?"

Before Tia could answer, the Orb grew into a full three-dimensional hologram. Annika used her mind to program it to the time-space coordinates for Helio Tropez. Just as they started to dematerialize, Dax and Metta stood up from the table with shocked expressions. Metta reached for the door, opening it to reveal Josephine standing there. Tia panicked and instructed them to speed up the process. She blinked, and the meeting room disappeared around them. When they re-materialised in Helio Tropez, Tia scanned those standing with her. Dax looked like he was about to throw up, and Metta was crumpled on the floor. Annika leaned with her hands on her knees, groaning, but Tia did not lose any time calling out to the teleportation team.

"Did anyone else hijack their way in?"

The teleportation team leader checked all her controls, "No. Just the four of you."

As Tia sighed with relief, members of the team came rushing over, checking on the new arrivals. Annika waved them away, and Tia draped her arm around her aunt, grinning.

"Welcome to Helio Tropez."

CHAPTER 31

Helio Tropez – 2011

Once their vital signs were checked, familiar faces came forward to give Tia a hug. Amelia pushed through the crowd, carrying Bimini and placed him in her arms. Gratitude and joy rose up as she reconnected with her Jenio and everyone supporting her.

Metta and Dax, having been born on the surface without knowledge of their true origins, went into a state of shock. The stargate team were bustling around them, helping Metta to her feet while another gently guided Dax away to a decompression and purification chamber. Annika and Tia were also sequestered away soon after for purification.

Tia hoped the process would detect an energy signature from Josie Carbona. Before climbing into a chamber, she warned them about what she had seen, and so, the stargate staff performed a thorough scan of the entire area. Nothing. After a full twenty-four hours in the purification chamber, they released Tia.

She joined Cassandra and Meraton as they went to check in on Annika, who'd just been released from The Healing Bay. Upon entering her chamber, Annika was sitting in a swivel chair facing the cityscape, looking frail and shaken. As they hugged the daughter they had not seen for fifty-one years, Tia stood back.

"Your purification and healing process went so quickly," Meraton laughed.

"Did it? Maybe that's because I've spent about thirty years living alone, unravelling from all the SIM stuff," she smiled. "And that new amethyst from Tia made a huge difference too."

"Tia is our hero!" Cassandra said, wrapping her arm around Tia's shoulder.

Annika swivelled towards the window. "It's just like all the stories you used to tell us when we were kids," she said, scarcely taking her eyes off of the city. "It's so magical here."

Cassandra smiled. "We will take you on a tour as soon as you are feeling up for it."

"I want to stay here forever."

"In this room? You can have your pick of places to live."

"I mean here in Helio Tropez."

Meraton held her aged hand into his. "Of course. If we'd known you were alive, we would have brought you back years ago." He looked at Cassandra for a few moments, guilt rising in his eyes. "We barely escaped alive, and the Elders forbade our return. We looked for survivors through the Hall of Records, but we didn't know that SIM could remove your soul signature."

Annika leaned forward and looked at her reflection in the glass. "Look at me! I'm old, grey and wrinkled, and both of you look just like you did fifty years ago."

"We have technology here that can rejuvenate your cell structure. The surface of the planet is hard on the human body, but you will be amazed at how much more youthful you will be afterwards."

Annika looked up, almost scared to hope. "No kidding?"

"No kidding," Meraton laughed. "We have a plasma-based consciousness technology that uses dominant harmonic frequency resonance. The system scans your entire life to find a time when your cells were at their optimum. It then projects that perfect image over any damaged cells, making them want to conform to the perfect image. In other words, the technology doesn't heal you - it trains your body to heal itself. Without this kind of technology, a body often heals imperfectly, and that is why you get scars, or bones don't align properly after breakage on the surface."

"So, not only will my arthritis go away but the grey hair and wrinkles too?"

"Of course."

They stayed with her a while to share stories of their life in Helio Tropez, and she about her life on the surface. The hardships she had endured were hard to hear: trauma-based cognitive modification, forced to spy on people and breed with different men, one miscarriage after another, all her musical talent used in service to SIM instead of SANA. Again, Tia silently thanked her father for protecting her from all that. The more she heard, the more catastrophic thoughts of what might have happened to Daphne filled her with anxiety.

"Hadden told us that they mated you with Michael of Indicum? And that they mated Miriam with Forsel? Remember how we met them all as children in Mount Rainier? We didn't know that they were still alive after the Great UnDoing."

Annika smirked. "Is that what you call it here, The Great UnDoin??"

Cassandra looked away and paced the room. "Yes, we were the only ones to escape. What did Michael say happened to his parents, Ben and Lorena?"

"They died in a tragic car accident, like you did."

"I wonder if they are alive somewhere."

"I don't know. SIM programmed us to avoid contact with each other unless they had a purpose, like breeding. Although, they let Daphne and me play in a band together but that was nineteen years after not seeing each other at all. Then, as soon as they mated Daphne with Hadden, they took me away to Australia and wouldn't let me stay in touch. I only heard rumours that she had twin daughters."

Meraton stood next to Cassandra. "Tell us what you know about Daphne."

"She went to New York to be a model, as you know, but after the two of you were supposedly killed in a car accident, she came back to Montreal. We attended your funeral. We talked, cried, and vowed to stay in touch. Then I had to return to the symphony, and she got an acting job in Hollywood. We never did stay in touch, but in retrospect, I can see that they programmed us to behave that way. When I reconnected with her again nineteen years later, she told me they had tried mating her with Rafael, but it didn't work. These SIM families turned him into a political puppet doing their bidding. He had that magical 'Sound Healer' voice, remember? People got mesmerised every time he gave a political speech. At the same time, he was one of the most sensitive

289

among all of us in that generation. I think all the trauma damaged him in some way."

"And this man that they call Dax, is he the son of Forsel and Miriam?"

"Yes. His original name was Xander. I met him once when he was just a baby, but they took him away as a child and put him in a performing arts academy to eventually use his talents to help mind control the masses."

"He seemed to be on drugs quite often," Tia added.

Meraton scratched his jaw, thinking. "They will have to do a full detox of his system and rebuild his cell structure. Tia, I understand that you went to Niklana, and she predicted he is your primary SANA mate. Do you feel this is true?"

A heat grew on the back of her neck. "Um, I guess so. There's an intense connection between us, but I don't know what he's going to be like after his healing process. I think he's been through a lot."

"A true connection with your SANA mate is deeply healing," Meraton said, glancing over at Cassandra. "Your presence in his life will help immensely."

They talked late into the evening until Annika could barely keep her eyes open. The three of them left and walked Tia to her sleeping chambers. Bimini strolled along at her ankles, squeaking happily as they spoke as though part of the conversation too.

"We're so grateful to you for finding them all and bringing them home," Meraton said. "It took immense courage."

Tia nodded, proud of her own achievements, while also feeling the stress and the fatigue of the whole experience. She remembered when she had first arrived in Helio Tropez. It had taken her a long time to acclimatise. The energetic differences between the surface and subterranean worlds were vast. Once back at her room, she bid them good night and fell into a deep sleep.

The next day, Tia tried to visit Xander and Metta, but the rehabilitation team said it would be weeks before they were ready for visitors. They warned Tia that as his primary SANA mate, she needed to stay away until he had acclimatised and reconnected to his true self.

Dejected, she walked through Helio Tropez, content to refamiliarize herself with the vibrant colours and clean air. The swish of her silver garment against her skin revitalized her, and in contrast to the rough fibres she had worn on the surface, the clothes nestled around her like a weightless shawl. As the morning wore on, she came upon Amelia and Jaya sitting in a cafe by the river.

"Tia!" Amelia called out. "Come, sit with us."

The two women were relaxing on floating chairs as the turquoise waters of the Tourmaline River flowed by. Flamingos preened themselves on the shoreline. Ancient Banyan trees grew along the riverside and throughout the grounds of the café. In the middle of their floating table lay a replicator. As she neared them, a glass-bottom riverboat drifted by. Like a gondola in Venice, a man steered as two lovers lay in rapt attention to each other at the bow.

"We're having Jamushas and Rosadio. Want some?" Amelia asked.

Jamushas consisted of dates, nuts and berries wrapped in a sheet of mint jelly, whereas Rosadio was a pink ionizing liquid that gave you a buzz. No one drank alcohol in Helio Tropez as it lowered a person's frequency too much, but when they wanted to relax and raise their frequency, they had a Rosadio. Tia sat down in a chair next to their table. "Yes, please! I've missed these."

She popped a Jamusha in her mouth and washed it down with a sip of Rosadio. Her body craved the rich nutrients of the treat and the euphoria of the drink. Sitting back, her eyes followed the boat until it went out of view.

Jaya smiled slyly at Amelia. "She's dreaming of her SANA mate. Too bad he's under quarantine."

Amelia nodded. "It's amazing that your mate was on the surface, just like Niklana had foretold. What's he like?"

Tia blushed and stuffed another Jamusha in her mouth. "I don't know. He's quite a character."

"And quite handsome, I noticed."

They talked for the next hour about Xander, Metta, Annika, life on the surface and what it was like for them in the Task Force as Tia had been undertaking her intense mission.

A pinging sound from Tia's wrist alerted her to an event in her calendar. "I need to go. We have our meeting in fifteen minutes." The whole Task Force was scheduled to debrief at the Palace of Zuris.

291

Amelia stood up. "Right. Let's bring some extra Jamushas for the team. My Aeria is parked on the roof. We can go together."

They took a glass elevator up to a floating car park. Amelia scanned a key card across a floating screen, and a few minutes later, her aerial car pulled up in front of them. The hatch flew open, and they clambered inside, sitting in a semi-circle facing forward as the hatch slid back into place. Without touching any instruments, Amelia gave conscious instructions to the vehicle to take them to the Palace of Zuris.

The car rolled to the exit gate, and they took flight. The ten-minute trip took them over several glowing pyramids, spiral-shaped skyscrapers and lush, green parks. The Palace of Zuris was one of the few white structures in the whole city, so its Taj Mahal presence stood out against the other buildings. As the aerial car floated down to a soft landing in the car park, Tia noticed a glowing space beckoning the car to park itself there. They gathered their things and exited the vehicle.

A pathway led them down through gardens of Bougainvillia and lush smelling ferns. At the entrance of the palace, a receptionist directed them to the correct meeting room. The other members of the Task Force sat around a large boardroom table as Meraton went through the agenda. They were late, so the three women quietly slid into floating chairs.

Meraton finished going over the agenda and turned the meeting over to Cassandra, who said, "First item on the agenda: the possible presence of Josie Carbona here in Helio Tropez. All our scans show no interference, but we want to remote view the entire transfer again to see if we can detect anything at the etheric level."

After a complete re-enactment with the help of the most talented remote viewers in the group, Meraton announced, "We cannot detect any SIM presence."

"Good," Cassandra said, exhaling audibly. "We hear that the House of Indicum is taking care of their relative, Xander. We, in the Palace of Zuris, are taking care of my daughter and granddaughter. Let us all send them prayers for a speedy recovery."

Cassandra led the prayer. By the time it was over, the entire group was in a well-balanced and compassionate state of mind to deal with the next item on the agenda.

"My other daughter and final member of Pentada, Daphne, needs to be located. We've remote viewed the entire planet using our familial connection to locate her energy signature. No luck. We need other suggestions."

After an entire hour of researching and discussion, they felt no closer to a solution.

Tia sat up, clearing her throat. "Maybe Halia can help us?"

Isla, from the House of Violetta, asked, "Halia of Violetta?"

"Yes, my great-grandmother on my father's side."

Isla looked at the other members and then back at Tia. "She disappeared over ten years ago."

"What!?" Tia sat bolt upright. "Addy said he saw her here last year. They talked at length."

"No. Not here. He couldn't have."

Tia furrowed her brow. "Who was he interacting with, then?"

"Did you talk with Halia as well?"

"Not here in Helio Tropez. While living with my father on the surface, she came to me in a dream. I learned to interface with her telepathically. In fact, both my father and I did."

Cassandra raised her eyebrows. "I thought you said you had no contact with Helio Tropez and didn't even know it existed before you came here."

"Is that what I said last year?"

"Yes."

"I do remember being shocked when I first arrived and not knowing it existed. But these days, I'm remembering two timelines. My father and I interfaced with Halia regularly in the second timeline. He also chose to tell me about Helio Tropez."

Cassandra pulled up a resonance meter on the large screen that measured various frequencies in Inner Earth and Surface Earth. "Addy *did* change the timeline. You can see here that the measurements have improved ever since he returned to the surface."

"So that's a good thing?" Tia asked.

Cassandra pursed her lips. "It depends on who you ask. The Temporalia disavow changing the timeline, except in certain circumstances."

Meraton checked the Hall of Records data. "No one from Helio Tropez interfaced with surface humans before you arrived last year, so how could you have been in contact with Halia?"

"When were you in contact with her?" Isla asked.

"Starting in 2007 and up until 2010. But my father was in contact with her back in the early 1990s. When did she disappear?"

"According to our records, Halia and her mate Triol disappeared in 1996. The only thing left behind was ash which our system identified as their DNA."

"That was the same year as my sixteenth birthday party. My dad had set up a plan of some sort, but it went wrong. An elderly couple from the Burres family died. No one ever saw them again after they were taken into the ambulance. When the medics arrived at the hospital, there was only ash left behind."

Isla frowned and brought up some research on the large monitor. "Over the years, a few people here have disappeared in that way. This researcher suspected that's what happens when you ascend. It's the process of bringing your body to a higher density, but the council haven't approved the theory because we have no way to test it."

Tia leaned forward to read the screen. "I don't totally get it."

Meraton pointed to a diagram on the screen. "It's a spontaneous combustion process that dissolves the carbon-based body needed for the 3rd and 4th density and transforms it into a plasma wave body needed for the 5th and 6th density. We all need to do it by July 2012, or they will wipe out our experiment. Otherwise, we have to start from scratch with an entirely new experiment somewhere else." He shook his head and sighed. "Thousands of years of work for nothing."

Tia sat back in her chair, frowning. "July? That's in a few months."

"And we still have a lot to achieve," Cassandra said. "It's why we need Pentada back together. We have the power to create the rainbow bridge, which would allow huge numbers of souls to make the transition all at once."

Tia narrowed her eyes, chasing a memory. "Do you have any images of Halia and Triol?"

Isla pulled up an image of a kindly woman with long brown hair in a spiral cone, sitting next to a slender man with a dark beard and long plaited hair.

Both of them looked in their late 30's. "This is Halia and Triol, parents to Trace Violetta and grandparents to Hadden."

"That's her!" Tia exclaimed, moving closer to the screen. "She helped me when I was coaching SIM family members."

Cassandra folded her arms, giving her a stern look. "You've never mentioned you coached SIM agents."

Tia blinked, then shook her head. "In the second timeline, I did. Sorry, it's hard to know which past is the right one."

Meraton looked at her with a curious expression. "Why would she encourage you to interact with SIM agents? And where was she? This sounds like the work of SIM."

Cassandra studied Halia's chart. "Look, she was Tangent-Attention, *The Revolutionary*. Her main drive is to help people physically ascend. It makes sense. Triol's aptitude was *The Detective*, remember? He did all the investigations on missing people. When they went missing, it all seemed so ironic. Even their Jenios vanished, and since they were the only ones who everyone relied on to locate missing people, there wasn't anyone with enough experience to find them."

Meraton huffed, still not convinced. "Let me test something." He played with the image, putting an overlay that created a violet glow around Halia's image. "Did she look more like this in your interfacing?"

"You mean with the violet aura? Yes!"

Meraton grunted, looking at the others in the room before turning his focus back to Tia. "She did not speak to you from here but from the 6th density."

Tia widened her eyes. "6th density?"

"Those who successfully go through ascension move from the 4th density up to the 6th density. Or so we've been told. It's a shift in consciousness frequency – a natural progression, if you like. Tia, on the surface of the planet, you lived in the 3rd density, but when you arrived here, in Helio Tropez, you naturally moved to the 4th density.

"Before we ascend, we humans are technically Homo Sapiens, but the ascension process triggers an abrupt evolution unlike anything else in the natural world. Once we've transitioned to 5D and 6D, we become Homo Luminous, a new species with more connection to the Monadic Self."

Tia frowned, trying to piece the information together. "So Halia is a Homo Luminous being, although she looks like a regular Homo Sapien? Just more... well, I guess... luminous. I thought 3D referred to the third dimensional."

Cassandra nodded. "SIM likes to keep surface humans confused. You are probably familiar with these five dimensions: length, width, depth, time, space. There are many more dimensions, but in the 3rd and 4th density, we just work with those five. We're told that in higher densities, you can move more freely between many more dimensions. It's like switching between radio stations. People who try to do that in lower densities can end up going crazy."

Meraton pulled up a new holographic image. "There are a multitude of dimensions, but five dimensions we work with are tied to the AVARA nuance of our aptitude system."

1st dimension is HEIGHT or PAST [Acceptance]

2nd dimension is DEPTH or FUTURE [Vision]

3rd dimension is LENGTH or PRESENT [Action]

4th dimension is TIME or SYNCHRONICITY [Reprogram]

5th dimension is SPACE or ASCENSION [Attention]

"When surface humans organically ascend, they go from the 3rd density that's actually in the 4th dimension up to the 5th density that's in the 6th dimension. SIM hijacked the process for surface humans a few thousand years ago, and so, it's now referred to as "inverted 3D" as they are cut off from having control over the 4th dimension of time."

Tia furrowed her brow.

Even Isla scratched her head. "I'd forgotten how complicated this all gets, and I was taught this in school!"

Meraton chuckled. "I know it's complicated. In short, 4D humans in Inner Earth support 3D humans on the surface. And, 6D humans support 5D humans on the surface. It's always been that way. Each surface human is an aspect of someone in a genetic farmer group like ours. Our experiment here is to see if we could merge certain disparate DNA strands to help higher density consciousness operate in lower density realms. The only way to do that is for those running the experiment – everyone in Helio Tropez – to be one rung higher on the density ladder. As they ascend, they bring the lower rungs with them, so each evolution skips a step. Make sense?"

"Not totally," Tia admitted.

He thought for a moment to find a better way to explain it. "The higher the density level, the more refined and complex the vibrational frequency. It's like moving from kindergarten to elementary school to high school to university. Each density has its own lesson that must be learnt, and you can only progress once you have completed it."

Tia nodded, trying to absorb it all. "So if there is 3D, what are 1D and 2D?"

"1D includes the four elements - earth, air, fire and water - but they have no local focus. 2D is like the mass consciousness that you get in the animal kingdom. It's a more primal consciousness without the individuation. They don't think of anything beyond that moment or that day, living purely on instinct and necessity."

An image of a human on the surface arose on the hologram, as Meraton continued. "3D consciousness is where there's a sense of individuation, and the lesson is discernment, learning what's true and what's false. You enter 3D with no memories of your past lives or your galactic family. If you try to tap into that knowledge, you're ridiculed or shunned, so people start believing the false narratives to fit in. It's only when they trust their inner knowing that they are ready to ascend."

Another image of a human in Helio Tropez appeared. "4D is where you learn the lessons of love, service to others versus service to self. 5D is where you focus on growing your wisdom. 6D is where love and wisdom come together. In 7D, you go back to the intelligent infinity, your sense of individuation dissolves away, and you merge into the one consciousness."

Isla asked, "How did Halia and Triol move to 6D, then?"

Cassandra leaned on the table, her fingers interlaced. "I think it's related to that experiment they were doing in 1996, but they never said much about it."

Tia's eyes widened. "My father and Halia wanted to bring SIM families together with their shadow counterparts from Helio Tropez. That's when Leo's grandparents died."

"We met Leo Burres as a boy and his parents at Mount Rainier," Cassandra said. "Who were his grandparents?"

Meraton searched the Hall of Records and pieced together the puzzle. "That would be Tanda and Jeffrey Burres. Are you saying that SIM family members are shadow counterparts to people in the Violetta bloodline?"

Tia swallowed, trusting her memory. "That was Halia's theory."

"I can see why people shunned her back then. Heliotropans don't like that theory. Yet, their disappearance might be proving it true. If Leo's grandparents were the SIM counterparts to Halia and Triol, that's what allowed them to ascend."

A rush of recognition ran through Tia's body. It all made so much more sense now as if she had all the fragments of a smashed vase and was now able to see how they all fit back together.

Cassandra scrolled through more Matrix symbols on the screen. "We need as many people to ascend as possible. According to the Hall of Records, nearly everyone in Helio Tropez has a lot of work to do before they're ready, which means that if we aren't ready, the humans on the surface are even further behind." She took a breath. "People aren't going to like it, but it's up to us to merge the shadow counterparts of those who have them."

Everyone in the room shifted uncomfortably.

"Does everyone have a shadow counterpart?" Tia asked, trying to understand what this meant for her.

Cassandra frowned. "I don't know. The Hall of Records won't answer that question."

"It doesn't matter yet anyway. We can't even create the Rainbow Bridge unless Pentada is reunited," Meraton reminded them. "They are the anchors of this whole process. We could reconnect everyone in Helio Tropez, but without the Rainbow Bridge, it would be much more of a challenge."

"We have so much to do," Cassandra sighed.

A pang of worry lodged in Tia's chest. Cassandra had always been the strongest and the most determined of all of them. Seeing her waver reminded her that there was no guarantee that the mission would succeed.

"And to top it all off, we still can't find Daphne," Cassandra concluded.

Jaya put up her hand. "I have an idea. What about looking for her off-planet?"

The group went silent, puzzled by the suggestion.

"Off-planet? Why would we look for her anywhere but on Earth?" Amelia asked. "She's not an astronaut."

"I went on a secret diplomacy trip to Shambhala back in the 1930s."

Tia vaguely remembered that Shambhala was the capital of Agartha, in the interior hollow core of the Earth.

"At the time, they told me that SIM started sending humans 'off-planet' to help them grow their empire. Maybe that's where she is."

"But that involves interdimensional travel. Surely, we'd have know if SIM had sent our people off-planet," Cassandra argued.

"We didn't know about all those Quinary members who were still alive," Meraton reminded her. "We chose to cut ourselves off fifty years ago."

"True."

Meraton leaned back in his chair, his eyes full of curiosity. "We've never considered it before. I guess it's worth a shot."

Tia had no idea what they were talking about, but for the next hour, they explored how they'd go about an off-planet search. Helio Tropez had starships capable of interdimensional travel and often traded goods with others in the galaxy. That said, organizing a search party with all the crew would be complicated. They decided that Cassandra and Tia should enter the meditation chamber and remote view off-planet in search of Daphne to at least find a specific location first.

"Just so you know," Tia interrupted, "I only learned remote viewing basics at the Academy, and I was never very accurate."

"It's a pity that the Academy only teaches the Advanced Remote Viewing to Voyents but not the rest of us," Cassandra said. "But don't worry, as a Sentient, you'll actually be Remote Sensing. Using your emotional connection to her, you'll be searching for some sense of her. I will Remote Touch, meaning I will sense into our physical bond."

"Daphne was in your life for eighteen years. She was only in my life for three. I don't remember her at all."

"As a Sentient and her daughter, your heart energy is strong because of the mother-daughter bond. I have that with her as well. It stays with you your entire life."

Tia nodded but was still unsure what it meant to Remote Sense. They took a brief break to stretch their legs and prepare for the remote session, making sure they had plenty to eat and drink. While everyone else discussed the plans, Tia sat on her own, looking about the room, unsure whether she fit in at all. Despite feeling more at home in Helio Tropez, she still felt like an outcast. Up until recently, in fact, she thought anyone who believed in extra-terrestrials was a nut case. Now she was flying around different planets looking for them.

After a while, Cassandra got to her feet and gestured for Tia to follow. She led Tia into a room with floating chairs specifically designed for trance states. Scooting into it, the chair was surprisingly stable, giving her a sense of weightlessness, allowing her to forget any bodily distractions. She could focus entirely on her consciousness, enabling ease of access to the trance state. Once protective protocols were in place, Meraton instructed her on how to direct her emotional energy towards outer space, feeling the presence of Cassandra doing the same.

Within a blink, she had become an ethereal being, a blue orb of light next to Cassandra's. They sped towards Earth's atmosphere, and Tia laughed at the thrill of it, exhilarated. She swooped and spiralled among the clouds, Cassandra darting just ahead. Although they couldn't communicate, there was a connection between them, an understanding of intent.

In a heartbeat, they shot toward the very edges of Earth's gravity, breaking free from it. Cassandra pressed on, gaining speed, and Tia willed herself to keep up. Within an hour, they'd reached the moon. They scoured its surface, searching for anything that might pull them nearer, but all Tia felt was a strong SIM type of energy emanating from below the moon's surface.

Tia could tell Cassandra was growing impatient, accelerating even faster, speeding away from the moon like a bolt of lightning. Mars was their next stop, then the asteroid belt and then beyond, to Jupiter, Saturn, Neptune and Pluto. Nothing. Some time later, a bell rang, pulling her away from the distant planets in the solar system. Part of her didn't want to let go - she felt liberated, free of the problems that followed her on Earth.

Here, in this form, she could explore the cosmos, wander the constellations, free in every essence of the word. A hand gripped her. It felt distant, as though it was happening to someone else. Then the bell rang again, only louder this time, jolting her back to her body.

Tia lay on the chair, her heart racing. Meraton stood at her shoulder, and Cassandra was already sitting up, looking at her. "Be careful, Tia. Remote

Work is a wonderful experience, but your body is here. You must not lose yourself. It's partly why we have to specially train people for his, and even then, we often lose people. Their consciousness drifts, and if they ever come back, they're not the same."

Tia swallowed, nodding. She could see how easy it would be to forget the life she had on Earth.

"Was there any sign of Daphne?" Meraton asked hopefully.

"I didn't sense her anywhere," Cassandra said, swinging her legs over the side of the chair.

Tia grimaced, sitting up. "Neither did I."

"Take it slow," Meraton said, keeping a hand on her arm. "Disassociating from the physical form is not always an easy process, never mind coming back again."

Cassandra was already pacing the room, frowning at the floor as she walked. "I thought we'd find her on the moon. It's SIM's control centre for cognitively controlling surface humans – it's the only place she'd be if she wasn't on Earth."

"Maybe she's there, but we can't sense her," Tia suggested.

"I put protocols in place so that we could override SIM control. I think we need to brainstorm on this with the others."

Meraton helped Tia to her feet, keeping her steady. They returned to the other room where the others were waiting. Isla had fallen asleep, her head on the table, while Jaya and a few others played a game with floating discs.

"Daphne is not anywhere within this solar system," Cassandra announced once everyone was roused.

"We were talking about it," Jaya said meekly, "and there's one thing we haven't considered. She might have taken on a cosmic identity."

"What's that?" Tia asked, still feeling groggy.

Meraton helped Tia into a seat as Jaya explained. "It's when your consciousness is no longer identified with Earth. Your light signature traces you to your parents if they were born on Earth. However, once you develop cosmic citizenship, your foetal cells dissolve away. You may hold memories of being on Earth, but that means of detection disappears," Jaya explained.

"But we already know that SIM removed the soul signature of many Quinary members," Meraton countered. "It shouldn't make any difference."

"True, but they can't remove a person's light signature unless they've graduated into cosmic citizenship. Then it's considered an upgrade."

Tia gave up trying to understand all of it and started growing impatient. "Okay, let's say she has this cosmic citizenship. How do we find her?"

"The only thing left, in that case, is the mother-daughter umbilicus link," Jaya said. "Only Tia and Cassandra have that with her. I suggest we all work to help them strengthen that connection while they transfigure beyond the solar system."

"Isn't transfiguration something that's easy for Tangents but not for Sentients?"

"True," Cassandra said, pulling up a hologram depicting a graphic with the names Daphne, Tia and Cassandra with lines between them. "As you can see here, according to our sensors, you have a stronger bond with Daphne than I do. This will be important in leading us to her."

"But why? I don't even remember my mother."

"Again, it's your ability for a strong heart connection. Don't worry, I'll lead the transfiguration process, but we need both of our aptitudes to find her."

"If she is now a cosmic citizen, the first place to search is Anatol – our home planet," Jaya suggested.

That was where the Progenitors resided. Tia had heard about Anatol at the Academy, and the opportunity to go there and explore other galaxies was practically unheard of. She recalled a class at the SANA Rosa Academy on transfiguration. By definition, it allowed a person to shift a portion of their consciousness into, what they call a Merkaba light ship, and travel.

Instead of just an orb, their entire body travelled through time and space. It was more intense than astral projection because it involved the physical matrix, except the body was lighter in vibration. It was like a copy of the carbon-based body on Earth, a second skin that could be used temporarily.

Meraton turned to address the room. "I want everyone to go home and get some rest. Tia and Cassandra are going to be away for a while. I'll stay here to make sure everything's okay, but the rest of you go home, get some food and some sleep, and report back tomorrow. Hopefully, we'll have some updates for you by then."

Bleary-eyed nods circulated the room, and the rest of the team slowly filed out, those who were more awake gave them encouraging smiles as they left. Once they were alone, Meraton turned to his family. "Are you sure you want to do this today? You can rest for a bit."

Cassandra shook her head. "We're running out of time, and besides, we'll be in a meditative state. We'll practically be sleeping anyway." She kissed his cheek, and Tia felt a swell of pride towards her grandparents. She thought of Dax and wondered if she'd ever have something like that with her SANA mate.

"You get some rest, too," Cassandra said softly. "We'll be okay."

He nodded reluctantly. "I'll get some food, then I'll be right outside the door, okay?"

She cupped his face gently, communicating without any need for words.

Once they parted, Tia followed Cassandra down a long staircase and into a dimly lit, women-only meditation area, called the Raka Chamber. Gomala, the chamber operator, welcomed them. It was sparsely furnished and surprisingly warm. The air felt still, and the scent of roses hung in the air. Two beds lay carved into the rock, and when Tia brushed her fingers against the wall, she found that the rock was warm to the touch.

Inside the hollow, it was cushioned with a mutable plasma substance. On the overtop of the chamber, you could lower a glass covering that protected the meditator but also acted as a scanner to monitor their vital signs and brain wave frequencies. If anything was unusual, it would sound an alarm to call for assistance, and Gomala would work to bring them back.

The Raka Chamber held the Mother SANA frequency, whereas the one for men down the hall held the Father SANA frequency. To create anything in the universe, one needed to bring the Mother and Father frequencies together. But in other certain situations, those frequencies needed to be kept separate. For example, if a woman had female reproductive issues or needed to bond with someone in her mitochondrial DNA line, she would use this chamber.

Gomala helped them both settle inside their respective meditation pods. "You will hear a brain entrainment hum inside the pod to help elicit the Theta Brain Wave state that you need to transfigure. If at any time you need me to release you from the chamber, press this button on your left side."

She closed the glass coverings, and soon after, Tia fell into a deep trance. She floated above the pod and watched Cassandra do the same. Below, they saw their bodies lying in the pods. Gomala was monitoring their vitals, seemingly unaware of their presence. Floating higher, they passed right through the chamber's rock ceiling. For a while, they went through many layers of rock until they entered into a tunnel, leading to the upper atmosphere of Helio Tropez.

The solar-powered flying cars and SANA Eagles whizzed past, not noticing them. Wings emerged on Cassandra's back and then on Tia's. Some instinct spoke within her, helping her take to flying as though she'd been doing it since birth. As she relished the feeling of finally having her wings, she flapped them with her intention, helping her fly higher. Then, they flew through lava tubes until they emerged out of the volcanic crater at Mount Rainier.

They rose high above the landmass of Washington State until they were in the upper atmosphere of Earth. The velocity of speed made her feel like a hummingbird, the vibration shaking her from head to toe. Higher and higher they flew until the Earth appeared as only a blue and white orb in the dark of space. Once out into the solar system, they went towards the Bootes constellation, veering directly for Arcturus, an orange binary star. As they circled around the larger of the two stars, a planet with similar features to Earth came into view.

A magnetic draw tugged them both towards a northern region on the planet's surface. To Tia's surprise, they flew towards an ocean rather than a landmass. Upon hitting the ocean's surface, they dived deep down towards the ocean floor. She braced herself, unsure whether they could breathe underwater.

As if hearing her thoughts, Cassandra communicated to her. *In light body form, you don't need to breathe air, eat food or sleep. It's liberating.*

Tia said back to her, *I'd love to stay in this state forever.*

You will someday, but remember, it's easy to lose yourself. You'll come here eventually, but until then, know that this is waiting for you.

The drive to find Daphne and help everyone ascend grew stronger in Tia's heart. They continued deeper into the ocean, but she didn't feel any pressure like a person would from scuba diving on Earth. Soon, an entire underwater city appeared before them. It had one central glass dome connected to several smaller ones, forming a pentagonal shape on the ocean floor. An external hatch rolled open, and they flew through until they landed on a teleportation platform. Once she planted both her bare feet firmly on the platform, her wings disappeared, and her body turned from ephemeral to more solid.

A group of five humans wearing gold gowns stood in a semi-circle just beyond the platform. The female progenitor she'd met in Helio Tropez came forward to meet them. "I am Waleya of Ribos. Welcome to Anatol. We've been expecting you."

CHAPTER 32

Anatol

The intensity of her first transfiguration journey sent Tia into minor shock. Cassandra, on the other hand, seemed fine, as if she transfigured every other day. She stepped forward, bowing and holding her heart.

"Greetings. I am Cassandra of Zuris, and this is my granddaughter, Tia of Zuris." Tia followed suit, bowing in the same manner to Waleya and then moving on to the next person.

Adim, Waleya's partner, addressed the rest of the group. "These two reside on the Magite known as Gaia-Sofia."

Tia glanced at Cassandra, hoping for a telepathic download on Magites. She got it instantly. *A Magite is a planet or star that is a sentient being.*

Realizing her confusion, Adim said, "Gaia-Sofia is a fallen Magite, which contributed to a whole fallen star system surrounding her. We sent your ancestors to Gaia-Sofia thousands of years ago to set up the station known as Helio Tropez. We hoped they'd bring her back to wholeness, but it still hasn't happened. The whole galaxy needs to be clean slated. The Precession of the Equinoxes is the last opportunity."

Tia's eyes grew wide. "Why is it the last opportunity?"

"If a Magite cannot be rehabilitated, the other Magites believe termination is best."

"You mean Earth will die?"

"Just transposed back to the great ocean of oneness."

Cassandra interrupted, careful not to be rude. "You were expecting us?"

"Yes, we called you here."

"I don't remember getting your message, at least not consciously."

"Yes, the minds of the people on your Task Force remained closed off from our ideas, except for that of the one whom you call Jaya."

"She was the one who suggested we go off-planet to find Daphne and then to go beyond Gaia-Sofia's solar system to Anatol. You could only communicate with her?"

"Indeed."

"Why didn't you just come and visit us?"

"You didn't ask. You must always ask first."

Cassandra raised her eyebrows and nodded. "So is my daughter Daphne here? This is where we were led..."

"Indeed. She is in our healing bay."

A shock wave rippled through Tia's body.

Cassandra's eyes grew wide. "She's actually here?"

"We discovered her essence quite by accident not so long ago. Our team in the loading dock and healing bay managed to rescue her. We'll take you to her now."

Waleya glided down a giant hallway of gleaming metallic blue and beckoned them forward. With each step, Tia bounced a few inches into the air. At one point, she lost balance, and Cassandra had to help her stabilise. Maybe she was giddy at finally getting to be reunited with her mother, or maybe it was this planet or underwater city.

"Yes, the gravity here is half that of the Earth's surface." Waleye replied, reading her mind. "In addition, you're in a light body right now and not in your 4th density body," Waleya explained. "Please, take care. We will get you a gravity belt and elixir in a moment."

Tia nodded, trying to move more carefully. As if moving through water, she focused closely on each step. The hallway glowed with similar colours and geometric patterns as Helio Tropez, although the humans stood taller and leaner than on Earth.

They arrived at a dome-shaped room filled with pods. People floated in stasis chambers with golden light lines running from monitoring machines into their bodies, with devices beeping and charts displaying symbols and numbers. Waleya led them to an isolated chamber in a separate room, kept behind glass. There, an attendant fitted them each with a gravity belt and handed them each a glass with blue liquid.

"This elixir will help stabilise your molecular structure so you can adapt to the gravity and pressure," the attendant explained.

As Tia sipped the sweet liquid, she followed her gaze to a woman laying with her eyes closed. Long grey hair floated in a saline solution.

"Daphne!" Cassandra called out.

Daphne stirred as if hearing something in a dream.

Tia drew close to the glass, hoping her eyes would open, but they didn't. "She looks so old. What happened?"

"Life on the surface of Gaia-Sofia and in outer space was hard on her. We need to rebuild her body-mind-immune system and return her cells to optimum functioning."

Tia noticed a monitor with all her vital signs and the words 'Prodigal Find'. "How did she end up on here? It's so far from home."

"SANA works in mysterious ways." Waleya touched a replay button for a holographic video. It showed a ship landing in their cargo bay. "We occasionally trade with other planets. She worked on this cargo ship as a camouflager and navigator. Normally, they don't let navigators off the ship, but they had a system error. She was allowed to leave the ship to talk with one of our navigators. That's when we identified her as one of our bloodline, or a Prodigal Find. We managed to scan her and recognised a lineage traced back to the Helio Tropez experiment on Gaia-Sofia. SANA clearly brought her to us."

Cassandra knitted her brow. "We've been praying to reconnect with her. Maybe that helped."

"I'm sure it did." Waleya pulled up Daphne's chart as a hologram and pointed to red cubes in her brain stem area. "We detected artificial intelligence programs embedded in her system and pieced the puzzle together. She'd clearly been taken by SIM and used as an asset."

"How did you rescue her?"

Waleya frowned. "We made a tough decision and decided to give her a dose of potassium cyanide so that she temporarily appeared to have died from heart failure. After some negotiations, the captain of the ship agreed to let us handle her remains, and they left. As far as SIM was concerned, she no longer appeared as an asset in their database. Before bringing her back to life, we gave her cosmic citizenship so that SIM would no longer detect her as their property. We brought her back to life in the Healing Bay only yesterday."

Tia clapped her hands together. "Thank you for doing that. Jaya told us she thought Daphne might be a cosmic citizen and that it was why we couldn't detect her."

"Yes, but despite everything we've done to save her, she's still severely damaged."

Cassandra pressed her face against the glass of the pod. "In what specific way?"

"Signs of torture, cognitive modification, trauma, malnourishment. She appears much older than she really is."

Tia's stomach tightened in a knot. "When can we talk to her?"

"It's best that she remains unconscious until she gets back to Gaia. We must warn you that living in our submerged city of Telmores here on Anatol for any length of time is hard on people from your planet. Although your bloodline originated from Anatol, it was before we had to move under the ocean. It's no longer safe to live on Anatol's surface. In other words, you must take Daphne back to Helio Tropez soon. The rhythms here can cause heart attacks for beings born on Gaia."

"How long do we have?"

"The sooner you leave, the better. We have begun the rejuvenation process for Daphne. The process is quick, but it can disorientate the patient. Once she's ready, we will send you back, but in the meantime, please sit with me in the restoration chamber. You've made a long journey and have another ahead of you."

Obligingly, they followed Waleya into a round dome and sat in facing chairs. The floor pulsated a pearlescent light. Huge windows adorned one side where they could see the sea-life outside. The chairs sent healing frequencies into their light bodies, and soon, Tia relaxed and grew energized.

Cassandra turned to Waleya. "When you said that it will no longer be safe to live on the surface of Gaia, were you referring to the solar flare that our Hall of Records predicted hundreds of years ago?"

"Yes. All surface humans who have not yet ascended will be wiped out. In fact, your city of Helio Tropez is so close to the surface that it will also be wiped out. The solar flare will cause radiation and flooding, even into the external layers of the Earth's crust."

Waleya pulled up a monitor that floated in the centre between them. It showed calculations based on studying the solar maximum and minimums of the sun. "One could happen very soon with your star. As you may know, your permit to continue the genetic experiment is coming to an end. You have to ascend your experiment to the next level. Otherwise, they will get removed."

"If they die in the cataclysm, what happens to us?"

"Every human soul within your surface experiment is connected to a soul within Helio Tropez. At this point in Gaia's history, you have just over 50 million in your genetic experiment. And there are 50,013 Heliotropans. In other words, every Heliotropan is responsible for approximately 1,000 souls. If they don't make it, you don't make it either."

They sat in silence for a moment. The weight of one thousand souls felt heavy in Tia's heart.

Cassandra studied the monitor with great interest. "But what if we moved farther away from the earth's crust and closer to the centre of Gaia?"

"Yes, you will physically survive, but you will stay in 4D and not ascend to 6D. Your next chance to ascend will be in another 25,000 years from now."

Cassandra nodded. "Last year, you recommended that young Hadden be returned to his timeline with his memories erased so that the experiment could proceed on schedule. We believe he recalled his memories and changed the timeline. Will this cause the experiment to fail?"

"I'm glad you asked. We have been monitoring his progress. At first, the Temporalia kept stitching the timelines back together because that's the law of 3D, but the Galactic Alliance stopped it. We aren't sure why. He seemed to have a connection with souls from 6D, where they can manipulate the time-space continuum freely if done for a higher purpose."

Tia vaguely remembered that the Galactic Alliance was a coalition of off world civilizations working together for the harmonious existence of all life in this part of the galaxy. The Progenitors were members of this alliance. "So it won't make the experiment fail?"

"Time will tell. As you may know, many genetic farmers are in competition with each other to create the most ideal human for the next evolution of the species. Some are devoted to SANA, and some are infiltrated by SIM. The SIM groups seek to manipulate the timeline through cognitive modification of the collective consciousness of humanity. Once souls are trapped into the SIM hive mind, they are used as batteries to keep SIM alive."

"What happens when the 'batteries' run dry?" Tia asked, not sure she wanted to hear the answer.

"Once SIM has siphoned all their energy, they leave them to die, and just move on to another solar system. It's like a hive of locusts."

A wave of nausea made Tia lose her balance for a moment. *I must help stop this*, she thought.

On the screen, Waleya pulled up a diagram. "Here are our calculations of the two possible timelines - although there are more than these, the two front runners are in red and green here."

"The timeline we seek is where SIM gives up their separation and returns to a united consciousness. As you may know, SANA originally created SIM to help humans grow and learn. If they reintegrate back together, then the SIM separation has a purpose and contributes greatly to the wisdom and evolution of the collective. If not, the whole experiment fails."

"What can be done to ensure the right timeline wins?"

"As Pentada, you have incarnated many times over to help the experiment progress. Your generation is like the last runner in a relay race. It's up to you to win the race. We wanted the fifth generation of Pentada to incarnate from the House of Zuris and grow up on the surface. Although you thought the Quinary Mission ended fifty years ago, it's still in play from our perspective."

Cassandra's eyes narrowed. "Still in play?" She moved holographic images around with her hand to study hidden sections. "So we're all still changing the timeline?"

"So it seems," Waleya said, zooming in on the symbols representing all five members of Pentada along with corresponding numbers. "According to our records, the project is 73.4% complete."

Tia leaned forward and noticed that every generation of Pentada had these words following it: *Subjects Terminated Before Project Completion.* "Does this mean that every Pentada generation before us failed in their projects?"

Waleya expanded the section on Pentada, revealing a graph assigned to each generation. "We don't view it that way. Each generation of Pentada took the project a step further. Consider it progression rather than failure."

Tia's chest tightened. "So we may face the same fate?"

"Not necessarily. If you integrate all you've learned from the past incarnations, work together, and transcend the final duality of light and dark, evolution is still an option."

Cassandra sighed. "You mean Zuris versus Carbona is the final struggle?"

"Yes. As the House of Zuris, you've moved from green, blue, indigo, violet and now white. Your house includes the entire colour spectrum. You are also at a pivotal point where many endings are happening at the same time, as in the Precession of the Equinoxes, the solar flare, and the projected end date of the genetic experiment. If the experiment is successful, then your humans will have evolved enough to manage their own genetic evolution and animate lower density avatar bodies with a higher spiritual frequency. A huge accomplishment. They will get to self-govern on the new 5D Earth, and you get to ascend to 6D." Waleya then opened a folder of symbols representing SIM family members. "But you'd need to re-integrate the SIM family bloodlines."

Cassandra recoiled her hands. "We've become aware of that, but what do you mean exactly by integrate?"

"All of your problems with the genetic experiment spawned from choices made by Heliotropans who went to the surface throughout your entire history on Gaia-Sophia."

Cassandra turned away from the hologram and looked out the window at a school of golden fish swimming past. A fluorescent pink creature that looked like an octopus climbed along the exterior of the glass. Lime green seaweed swayed with the currents. "Why were we never taught any of this?"

she asked, keeping her frustration in check. "That information isn't found in our Hall of Records."

"Somewhere along the way, your Elders must have removed that information. Your records *should* be in sync with ours."

Cassandra stood up from the chair to pace the room. Her gait now looked more grounded due to the gravity belt. "So, you're saying that the Carbona family is key to our ascension?"

Tia sat up. "Halia suspected that, but no one in Helio Tropez would believe her. She told Hadden instead, but we've never been able to verify that information."

Cassandra snapped her head around, "How come you never said that to us when you first arrived in Helio Tropez, Tia?"

Tia opened her mouth and closed it again. "Because it only happened in my second timeline when Addy went back to 1960."

Waleya checked the monitor. "The reconnection with the Violetta and Burres bloodlines has started. That sets a precedent for the Zuris bloodline re-integrating with the Carbona bloodline. This is good news."

"I still don't fully understand," Cassandra said.

"Each SIM agent who tries to control a Heliotropan is simply an un-integrated soul annex."

Cassandra looked sadly out the window. "Is that why the Carbona family involves two generations of twins-like with our family?"

"Of course."

Moving back to the hologram, Cassandra launched the folder marked 'Quinary'. "Can your Hall of Records identify which members of the last Quinary Mission are still alive on the surface?"

"Of course."

"Out of the five couples that went to the surface, we are the only couple that returned to Helio Tropez in 1961. What happened to the others?"

Waleya pulled up the names from the Quinary mission and ran them through a search. "They are all still alive."

Cassandra leaned in to see the list. "How can that be? They would all be over one hundred years old, and most people on the surface don't live that long."

"They most likely do the same thing as the SIM families - harvest the blood of others to remain youthful."

"They would never do that," Cassandra objected as she closed her eyes, searching inside for a better answer. "Maybe they found a way to stay youthful organically."

Waleya looked down, and her face tightened.

Tia's breath quickened. "Our Hall of Records said they died. How could that be?"

Waleya searched in the cache for a history of deletions on auxiliary servers. "Our records show that the information got deleted in Helio Tropez in 1961."

Cassandra started pacing again, tapping her fingers against each other. "Only the Librarian at the time could have done that. Who was that?"

Waleya did another search, "According to our records, it was Malinah of Fae-fair."

"She's still the Librarian. Why would she do that?"

"Perhaps the Elders asked her. We suspect that they wanted to convince you that all of Quinary had died so that there would be no reason to go back."

"Of course. Several of them were against the mission in the first place. They know we would have gone back had we found some were still alive. The abuse that my daughters faced, the abuse they all must have faced, and we could have rescued them all this time?!"

Cassandra's eyes grew red with anger.

Tia leaned against the glass, staring out at the fish swimming by. A sense of betrayal welled up within her. *I thought Heliotropans couldn't lie to each other, but apparently, they can. How might my life have turned out had I been raised in Helio Tropez instead of Seattle? Although... if they had rescued Hadden and Daphne before my birth in 1980, maybe I wouldn't even exist.*

Waleya looked sombre. "You must go back to Helio Tropez. Bring truth and reconciliation back to your community. You have all veered far away from the mission since its first inception thousands of years ago. We are counting

314

on this 5th generation of Pentada to make it right. We will help you transport Daphne in physical form via our time travel portal, and I suggest keeping her in stasis until you get there. It will be easier for her body to heal on Gaia than here."

"Why a time travel portal?"

"In her time, she's only been gone a few years. But we don't want to send her back to the late 1980s on Earth. She needs to reunite with Pentada in Helio Tropez in the time you came from."

"She looks so old. Are you sure her body can handle it?"

"We will help restore her to the highest possible functioning. The scans show she's healing very well."

"So, when she wakes up, she'll think it's still the 1980s?"

"Yes."

The team at the Healing Bay transferred Daphne into a transportable stasis chamber and prepared her for departure. Meanwhile, Tia and Cassandra entered a different kind of stasis chamber to travel back to their bodies still lying in meditation in Helio Tropez.

Just before stepping into the chamber, Cassandra bowed deeply to their hosts. "Thank you, Waleya and everyone here, for helping to rescue my daughter, Daphne, and for teaching us about our true history."

As a response, she smiled and bowed back. "It is our pleasure to serve. Remember that humans are like imaginel cells in the body of Gaia. When you ascend, so does she. Pentada is the key on more levels than you realise."

Cassandra and Tia looked at each other, then back at Waleya.

"The soul of a Pentada is programmed to sacrifice herself for this cause, if necessary. It's what you agreed to before incarnating into this life. At the conscious level, you have probably forgotten that. A part of you will fight that sacrifice, but you must keep your eye focused on the bigger picture. Even if only two of you make the sacrifice, it won't work. All five of you need to do it."

"What do you mean by sacrifice? Sacrifice our lives or...?" Tia asked.

"Ask your heart what it means. Your soul will know."

Tia looked at Cassandra with concern. The stargate operator began inputting the space-time address for the Helio Tropez Stargate: 7.5.3.84.70.24.606.545: the year 2011, a few minutes after they had left.

Tia climbed into the stasis chamber, feeling ill at ease.

Cassandra paused before entering her own. "How can we make a sacrifice unnecessary?"

"Pray to SANA."

CHAPTER 33

Helio Tropez – 6D Helio Tropez

When Hadden awoke, he smelled oak leaves and sweet moss. It reminded him of the Garden of Jephsonite back in Helio Tropez, filling him with a melancholic longing. His body was light, pain-free and a sense of relief washed over him. Opening his eyes, he saw the blurry outline of a wishing well and an oak tree. He lay in a floating chair that cushioned him like a cloud, and the air in his lungs felt fresh. A soft hand touched his arm, and he looked over to see Halia looking across to him. She beamed, "You did it."

Hadden blinked, unable to fully comprehend what she meant.

"You made it to 6D. Your Graduation is complete."

Memories of his real life in the lower densities flooded back to him. It was like seeing the end of a movie and realising you're not in the story anymore, that you're just sitting in a cinema. He climbed out of the floating chair and noticed a violet glow around his hands. The oak tree in front of him looked smaller, or was he bigger?

The last thing Hadden remembered was his confrontation with Leo and their reconciliation. He looked down to see if Leo had somehow managed to attack him, but his skin showed no sign of harm. In fact, his skin looked youthful again. Touching the top of his head, he breathed a sigh of relief. His head of hair was full, thick and brown again. As he gazed at the oak tree, it looked crystal clear, not fuzzy, even though his glasses were nowhere to be found.

"What happened?"

"You integrated your shadow counterpart, and now, your two souls and aptitudes have merged. The entity known as Leo Burres was always just an aspect of your soul. You did it, Hadden. All your hard work has paid off. Well done."

He smiled, focusing his eyes on a flower nearby. Everything was crisp and clear; radiating life force energy. Residues of the emotional intensity he had gone through with Leo remained in his system, so he breathed a few times to clear it. At the same time, his entire body exuded a robust strength and flexibility that he hadn't experienced in a very long time. The skin on his hands glowed with youthful radiance. "I'm young again?"

"Of course. You bring your light body with you, and so your cells revert back to optimal levels before degeneration started."

He marvelled at the lightness, vigour and clarity of mind that he had dearly missed when living in a seventy-year-old body. "I'm back in Helio Tropez, then?"

"Yes, you are in a parallel reality of Helio Tropez in the 6th density. Above us, on the surface, it is now the 5th density Earth. Consider it like graduating from high school and moving onto university."

A hummingbird hovered four feet away as if to observe him. An aura of violet illuminated the field around the bird. All colours seemed brighter, the gravity felt lighter, and objects looked smaller and more etheric.

"Although you didn't realise it at the time, the experiment you tried in 1997 helped both Triol and I ascend. When Leo's grandparents supposedly died, they actually merged back into us. This helped you do it yourself thirteen years later."

Triol came forward from behind her. His hazel eyes sparkled, and, like Halia, he looked like a young man. Triol helped Hadden sit up and move to a standing position. All three of them glowed with a vibrancy he had never experienced before. They stood on the precipice of a hill at the top of the Garden of Jephsonite. Below them, the occasional flying car darted between two spiral buildings, and the violet pyramid glowed brightly against the blue mist.

"The city looks so much smaller."

"It's only inhabited by those who have achieved a rainbow body as we have, allowing them to ascend. We don't need to build a sprawling city like the one you might remember."

Hadden shifted from one foot to the other, amazed at his sense of balance. "You said I graduated, right? What's happened to my body?"

"Your body has shifted from carbon-based to crystalline plasma-based. You are now eternal until you choose to leave this form and go back to the source. Right now, only 10% of those who have ever lived in Helio Tropez have ascended into 6D. But we hope that changes soon."

As a boy, he had learned about how their genetic experiment would be like on the Earth in the year 2012. They either had to bring their experiment to full fruition or abandon it.

"Has a cataclysm happened on the surface of Earth yet?"

"No, not yet. But it's coming soon. There isn't much time, and they need our help."

Halia and Triol were downloading him with reams of information in what seemed like a much more complex version of the Matrix language. He completely understood what they were communicating, even though they didn't move their mouths or use vocal cords. As he organized the information inside his mind, all the memories of other lives, other multidimensional experiences in different bodies on different planets and in different timelines came online. He now fused all of those experiences into one, enabling a full remembrance of his soul journey. As soon as he did, a soothing sense of self-acceptance permeated every cell in his body.

"What's it like on the surface of the new Gaia now? And what year would it be?"

"5D is 500 years ahead of 3D Gaia. However, once in 5D, time-space is measured in coordinates, not years. Why don't we show you?"

She stepped towards a cliffedge overlooking the city, and beckoned him to follow. When they stood side by side, she took his hand and stepped off the ledge. At first, he let out a yelp and gripped Halia's hand tightly, but she only laughed.

"I thought you were supposed to be a pilot?"

"When I had wings!" he yelled, flailing in the air.

"Best you find some then," she said with a grin before letting him go.

As Hadden's grip slipped, he tumbled through the air. Screwing his eyes shut, he cried out, but after a few moments, a humming sound replaced the rush of air, and he felt oddly still. Cracking an eye open, he peeked out at the city below, expecting the ground to be close. He was still high in the air. Overhead, Halia and Triol were flying in circles clutching their sides with laughter.

Stunned, Hadden reached back to feel his wings had activated, instinctively keeping him hovering in midair.

"Come on," Halia called. "What are you waiting for?"

He laughed, thrilled, and hastened after his grandparents. They headed for a lava tunnel towards the surface, and several minutes later, they were soaring over what looked like Puget Sound near Seattle. They landed on top of a building and sat on the ledge, looking down.

The city of Seattle looked entirely different, much more like the city of Helio Tropez, with spiral buildings and greenery everywhere, no cars, flying aerial units, fresh air, far more sunshine and turquoise ocean water. All the colours vibrated and ran a much wider spectrum of frequency.

Near the horizon, two suns glowed in the sky; one above Mount Rainier, beaming yellow light across the foothills, and the other to the west hovering over the bay beaming more of silvery-blue light. "Two suns! We must have moved to another solar system."

"We are in the Andromeda galaxy," Halia said. "And this mirror reality of Gaia doesn't tilt on its axis like the old one, but she stands straight and strong."

SIM had caused the tilting of the axis, a sign amongst the Magite planets that Gaia was sick. She was now healed, restored to better health and moved to a better home, and just as 4D supported 3D, now 6D supported 5D Gaia.

A fervent yellow sunset poured through a rift in the clouds. "It's stunning. What about the population here?"

Triol smiled. "It's just the people who have ascended from 3D over the last 25,000 years. Hopefully, the numbers will increase soon."

He looked up into the sky. "And that's real space as opposed to the fake dome we see from the 3D flat Earth?"

Triol stood up and spread his wings. "We now live as cosmic citizens, trading with other worlds such as those from Antares," he said, pointing to a cargo starship flying across the sky. "We'll introduce you to some of your cosmic cousins soon."

A feeling of joy overwhelmed him as he realised that SIM had integrated back into SANA. The challenges of human slavery, mind control, pollution, hunger and violence no longer existed in this 5D future world. Like any civilization, they had their own challenges, but they now came in different, less intense forms.

"What is our role here?"

"In 6D, we act as guides to those in the lower density levels."

"Like those in 4D?"

"Exactly."

"Can we go to 4D Helio Tropez now? I'd love to see what's happening with Tia."

"Yes, but let's time travel to when she finally brought all of Pentada back together again. That's when they really start needing our help."

Using their intention alone, the three of them went to the Garden of Jephsonite but, this time, in 4D Helio Tropez. They stood by the wishing well, looking down at the city. The plants and people no longer had a violet aura, and the city looked ten times bigger than in 6D.

Hadden was on his feet, looking down keenly. "Let's go down and see what's happening."

Halia touched his arm. "I warn you that the majority of people will not be able to see you."

"But I saw you when you came to visit me in Helio Tropez."

"Yes, because you and I had an ancestral and karmic bond. *And* you had developed enough multidimensional consciousness by then."

"Did anyone else interact with you?" Hadden asked.

"No, you were the only one. Surprisingly, even though you grew up on the surface, you were ahead of many people here in Helio Tropez in terms of soul growth."

Hadden always thought of himself as inferior to the people of Helio Tropez. He now saw that his descent into darkness had actually helped build his capacity for light and the resulting unity consciousness.

Halia started down the path to the city, treading lightly as though she were on the moon. "We're on a reconnaissance mission to identify those who are ready to ascend."

"If they see us, we will have a violet tinge to our aura," Triol added. "People here understand that as opposed to most of those on the surface."

As they entered the city, several people passed by, walking right through them.

"I suggest we start with Tia and Daphne. You are closest to them, and they will arrive at the stargate very soon."

"Daphne is back in Helio Tropez?!"

"Yes," Halia said. "Daphne, Tia and Cassandra are about to land in Helio Tropez. Just tap into the telepathic conversation going on here in the city."

News of the return of the final member of Pentada had travelled throughout the city, and a crowd had gathered at the stargate. The whole story of Tia and Cassandra going to the home galaxy and finding her there amazed them all. No one from Helio Tropez had been granted access to Anatol for thousands of years.

Hadden, Halia and Triol made their way to the front of the crowd at the stargate, and still, no one seemed to notice them. Within a few minutes, three stasis chambers appeared on the platform. People rushed forward, but the Protectors kept them back as they wheeled the chambers into the decompression area.

Meraton held up both hands. "We will meet in the Congress tomorrow and explain everything," he assured the crowd.

Hadden and his grandparents flew above the crowd and watched as they brought Daphne's chamber into the Healing Bay at the Palace of Zuris. Meanwhile, the Protectors escorted the other two to the purification unit.

Over the next few hours, the three of them moved throughout the city, watching people and seeing if anyone noticed them. Everyone seemed oblivious, except a few who did a double-take as they went by. Each time, they took a note of that person's name and soul signature. Once they knew Tia would be released from purification, they flew up to the entrance of her room and waited until she arrived.

As she rounded the corner, they waved at her, but she walked right past them. Hadden felt disappointed, but he immediately remembered that her aptitude was Sentient. As she opened her door, he beamed love towards her. She stopped and turned around to face them. "Is someone there?"

"It's me. Your father," Hadden exclaimed.

"And Halia and Triol," Halia added.

Tia squinted. "Really? I haven't been able to connect with you ever since I left Seattle. How is that even possible?"

Halia said, "Perhaps we weren't supposed to connect until now. And you have clearly built greater multi-dimensional communication skills since coming back from Anatol."

"You know about my trip?"

"We saw you arrive at the stargate. We are here to walk amongst the people of 4D Helio Tropez, but we are actually from 6D Helio Tropez."

Tia paused a moment and cleared her throat. "Is this real, or am I hallucinating? Does transfiguration have any side effects?"

"It's real," Hadden reassured her. "Just after you escaped, Leo came to the house to kill me and take you away."

"So you did die? The papers accused me of killing you both."

"No. The two of us ascended and became one."

Tia closed her eyes and sighed. "I'm so relieved to hear that."

"You don't actually see us, do you?

"Not at first, but the more we talk, the more you're coming into view."

"Good. We are so relieved you can communicate with us," Hadden confessed.

"It's really you, Dad. You didn't actually die! Or is it Addy?" Tia asked, feeling her eyes tear up.

"No. I didn't die. I ascended. And I'm young again, like Addy, but I remember all my years of parenting you. That said, you can call me Addy. It goes better with my new youthful looks."

323

Tia laughed. "I'm so relieved. So, where exactly are you?"

"We're all in another higher density right now, looking into your density. It's similar here, but different. It's surreal."

"Oh! Okay..." Tia paused, the lump in her throat stopping her. "I- I thought you'd died, that you gave up everything just so that I could escape." She looked up, smiling. " But you're okay."

"Remember I told you we would meet again on a better timeline?"

"Yes!" Tia smiled, her eyes turning glassy.

She invited them into her chamber, noticing that those who walked by were giving her strange looks. Once inside, Hadden explained the whole integration of his shadow counterpart and that Leo no longer existed as a separate entity - they were unified. Halia went on to explain the nature of their reconnaissance mission in 4D.

After she heard them out, Tia explained, "Waleya told us that there is a short window of time this year when a number of people can ascend. She said that we have to help people get ready here in Helio Tropez because each one of us is responsible for not only ourselves but at least 1000 surface humans each."

Halia said, "Exactly. And hopefully, now that Daphne has returned, we can speed up the process. Pentada needs to finally come together." They shared with Tia the necessary steps for Pentada to anchor the process of building what's called a 'rainbow bridge' for people to ascend. "Each individual needs to do inner work first to manifest their own rainbow body before they can cross the bridge."

"Let me know what I can do to help."

"We will go to the Healing Bay now to see Daphne and then come back to you with the next steps." With that, they bid her goodbye and dematerialized out of her room, re-materializing in the Healing Bay.

The last time Hadden had seen Daphne, she was still in her early 40s, looking astoundingly beautiful. Now, she looked old and frail, skin weathered and spotted, fingers gnarled with ragged and grey hair. He tapped into her subconscious mind, and her higher power allowed him entry. Even though she lay unconscious, he was able to remote view the last thirty-five years they were apart. She had brought Metta to Montréal, but her amethyst couldn't protect them enough. SIM had pulled Daphne into a space program to keep her as far away from any other Pentada as possible. As a Voyent-Reprogram, she had been the perfect navigator of a consciousness-driven spacecraft. Without her mother, Metta had ended up in foster care in Montreal since SIM couldn't detect any psychic abilities. The masking had clearly worked, but Hadden's heart went out to both of them for the trauma they must have endured. The readings showed that Daphne's cells were rejuvenating, but there was still a lot more to go. He stayed nearby in meditation, sending prayers for her speedy recovery.

Hadden moved on to find Metta, who lay unconscious in the stasis chamber. She looked like a young version of Daphne. Hadden smiled, and memories of the three-year-old with red ringlets filled his heart. The two girls had been inseparable, and tearing their family apart had broken something inside of him. He hoped they could heal their bond soon. The readings on Metta's chart showed that she had experienced some kind of trauma. Knowing what SIM did to children on the surface made his stomach turn. To think that they had done that to his own daughter felt almost too hard to imagine.

That evening, at the Congress Hall, Hadden, Triol and Halia stayed near Tia in the centre circle. When her turn to describe what had happened came, she stood in the centre stage, taking Hadden, Halia and Triol with her.

"Please, stand if you can see my father, Hadden, and my great-grandparents, Halia and Triol, who have ascended to 6D Helio Tropez. They stand here right next to me."

The crowd murmured. Twenty odd people in the entire group stood up. Discussions ensued about how it was possible that only so few people could see into the next dimension.

"We don't believe you," Obar said. "What proof do you have?"

Halia interfaced with Tia so she could pass on important information to the Congress.

Tia announced, "Halia used to live amongst you. Obar, you and her worked on the stone circle at Morguise as children. That's when you kissed her behind the Sacred Mother Tree."

The Congress erupted in laughter. Obar's face turned crimson as he chuckled under his breath. "True. I lost her to that handsome young Triol."

"Are you convinced now?"

He shrank back in his chair and nodded.

Tia bit her lip to suppress her smile. "Ok, to continue. The role of this final generation of Pentada is to install the MindStory Code in the collective consciousness of our community, which we will then transfer to the surface humans that we represent. It's a kind of monomyth seeded into surface humans, but mostly at the subconscious level."

A holographic image appeared on the stage, where a spiral depicted how the MindStory Code operated at macrocosmic and microcosmic levels. Five core pillars of the story with smaller subsections within each pillar twirled around each other, each stage having its dark and light side.

"As you can see here, the original human DNA pattern has twelve base magnetic female codes and 12 base electrical or male codes. This holds the mathematical program for each double helix strand, which combine to form a set of twelve vector codes. One male code plus one female code is equal to one vector code. Only four of the vector codes have been active in surface humans since SIM rebelled from SANA. On the surface, they refer to the other eight strands as junk DNA."

The crowd buzzed with telepathic cross talk. On the one hand, people were incensed that SIM had deactivated eight DNA strands in their surface humans. On the other, they marveled at the ingeniousness of the new code.

A river of relief rushed through her. Feeling a rare sense of pride, Tia zoomed in on the cross-stitch at the centre of the code. "If you integrate each stage, your life journey evolves you. If you don't integrate them, it devolves you. Most people here have been devolving by cutting themselves off from the original experiment."

Amazement dissolved into shame as people started recognising the truth of the statement.

She took a breath to compose herself. "It's important that you remain compassionate and curious with your behaviour regarding SIM. If you let shame overtake you, you will be strengthening SIM's power. It was Hadden's descent into darkness that helped him create the force to ascend. The problem lies in staying in one extreme or the other – we all need to experience both."

Cassandra glided in beside her to speak. "Waleya told us their Hall of Records shows that the other Quinary members are still alive on the surface. Yet, our Hall of Records shows that everyone died in 1961. The only person who can change the records is the Librarian." A murmur rang around the Hall of Congress, and all the people turned in their seats to find her. "Malinah of Fae-fair, can you tell us why you changed the records fifty years ago?"

Malinah sat in the second rung of chairs from the centre. The light of amplification fell down on her, and she looked away. Although she couldn't directly lie due to the telepathic connection, she could still omit information.

She squirmed in her seat, face ashen. "The Elders ordered me to do it. If I made it look like they had perished, the Elders hoped the community wouldn't send any more task forces back to the surface."

Outrage erupted throughout the hall, cries of betrayal and disgust coming to voice as the depth of it sank into the hearts of the community.

Cassandra held a hand aloft, calling for silence. "Which Elders ordered this deletion?"

Malinah darted a glance at the inner circle of Elders and took a deep breath for courage. "Obar and Frenla led the initiative."

The light of amplification swivelled to the two elders in the centre circle, the light casting an eerie glow on their downturned faces.

Obar squinted under the glare and slowly rose to his feet. Turning to Cassandra, he cleared his throat. "I admit that I suggested it, Frenla seconded it, and then *all* the others agreed."

Another Elder, Tasma, stepped into the spotlight, holding up a hand. "I would never have agreed..."

"But I *did* ask for permission, and you all agreed."

Tasma faced him head-on. "Obar, we all know your aptitude is the Spellcaster. You hypnotized us into an agreement."

The Elders argued amongst themselves while disdain rained on them from the galleries.

Meanwhile, Yeelay scrolled through the dates on a holographic card catalogue until she reached the year 1961. Agreements amongst Elders were stored as symbolic pictograms. "We all signed this. Hypnotized or not, we are all responsible."

That's when the colour drained from Tasma's face. "I don't think..."

Yeelay interrupted, "At the subconscious level, you agreed to the spell cast by Obar. Fear ruled our minds at the time as we didn't want to lose more people to SIM."

Cassandra took the limelight, fire burning in her eyes. "Have you seen what happened to our daughters? The abuse they faced? And we could have rescued them all this time! Tia, Metta, Hadden, and all the others were forced to live in slavery!"

Taking a deep breath, Yeelay turned to face her. "We understand the pain that this has caused, and we take full responsibility for this choice. That said, the Progenitor said it all happened as it should have. Maybe we were also guided towards this choice by SANA rather than just fear. If Quinary had returned *before* The Great UnDoing, those two Pentada girls would have never even been born."

Tia stepped between them, her face stern. "Waleya said we must learn from this incident. Let go, forgive each other, and move on. We need to bring truth and reconciliation back to this community."

Cassandra nodded and sat down. Obar and Frenla followed. The three souls from the 6D Earth worked to create a container of empathy around the city of Helio Tropez, knowing that healing would take time. And without that healing, they would miss the 2012 window of opportunity to ascend.

CHAPTER 34

<u>Helio Tropez – 4D Earth – 2011</u>

After the Congress, Tia and Cassandra focused their attention on piecing together the MindStory Code. They wanted the Gemsmiths to upload the code into people's amethysts, but they needed to wait for Annika, Daphne, and Metta to be healed enough to join them.

They went to visit them at the Healing Bay in the Palace of Zuris. Annika's vital signs showed vast improvement from when Tia had brought her back to Helio Tropez. When they entered, they found her sitting in a chair next to an unconscious Daphne, who floated in a glass healing chamber. Annika looked decades younger: her hair had returned to dark brown, and her skin had smoothed out, regaining its elasticity. Her eyes looked alive and full of gratitude.

Tia pressed her face against the chamber to check on her mother. Daphne's hair had turned back to her red ringlets, and her skin looked youthful. Flashes of happy memories broke through into her consciousness; catching a ball and hearing her mother's laugh, resonant and playful, in her ears.

Suddenly, she felt a strange and strong urge to hold her mother's hand pulling at her, prompting her to lift the protection shield. As she did, a warning light came on the dash, and a beeping sound filled the air. Daphne's hand lifted, even though her eyes remained closed. Tia entwined her hands with her mother's, and immediately something felt wrong.

An attendant arrived on the scene. "You mustn't do that. She's not ready. If the process is interrupted, she might not return to us."

Tia let go and quickly closed the shield back down, her cheeks pale. "I'm sorry. I don't know what came over me."

She left the Healing Bay abruptly, feeling ashamed. Down the hallway, she discovered the room with Metta lying unconscious. The chart showed slow progress. Like the others, her mind had been compartmentalised, and many brain cells and heart cells needed to be rebuilt.

She had endured the typical torture that special assets received to force them under SIM's control. Tia recoiled from the images that surfaced, pushing them away. Now she understood more deeply what her father had fought so hard to protect her from.

SIM had discovered Metta's Ecrivent-Acceptance powers, The Poet. Artistry and music were the perfect vehicles for cognitive control. They had put her to work writing love songs that kept people locked in misery towards the opposite sex, which, of course, blocked ascension since the union of SANA partners drove the ascension process.

She sat next to Metta's stasis chamber and sent prayers of healing. The twin bond that Annika had talked about with Daphne stirred in her whenever she spent time with Metta – like finding a lost treasure that she'd been looking for all her life.

Later that day, while walking back to her room, one of the Elders approached Tia. She recognised the woman as Frenla of Indicum, the great grandmother of Xander. In her robes of indigo and white, and ringlets of white-blonde hair, she looked more like a 40-year-old would look on the surface.

"I've been meaning to speak with you, Tia, but shame has stopped me from doing it before. May I speak to you now?"

Tia nodded and took a breath.

"I led the charge back in 1961 to hide the fact that Quinary members were still alive on the surface. When my daughter, Lorena, and her mate, Ben, chose to join Quinary, I fell into shock. I grieved as if they had both died. I knew that if they ever came back, they might never be the same. Since I'd grieved their death once, I didn't want to go through that again. Yet, they had a daughter, Miriam, who had a son, Xander. Now that I've met him and have seen what they did to his mind, I'm confronted with my bad choices. I want to help him, to make amends to him, to you, and to all the others who suffered..."

She lowered her head and covered her face. Tia led her to a bench under a Banyan tree. They sat together, and she used her Sentient-Attention aptitude to examine the wound in the woman's heart. She poured light into Frenla's pineal gland as a way of accepting her apology. As the woman wept, Tia wrapped her arm around her shoulders, and they stayed there until the emotional wounds were processed. A light wind blew down the pathway, and Tia smelled the aroma of rose petals. The process was complete.

"I forgive you fully. As Waleya said, it was all meant to be."

Frenla looked at her through bloodshot eyes and whispered, "Thank you."

Tia smiled, and the bond between them deepened.

"You lived on the surface, but now you seem so whole. Is there a way you can help me help Xander?"

"My father protected me from a lot of the harm from SIM, and I've had a year here so far to heal."

"But you are necessary for his healing. You understand the world he came from, and you are his primary SANA mate."

"The Elders told me to keep away because of that."

"But I think that makes you the perfect person to help him. In fact, how you helped heal my heart just now, he could use some of that. We've removed many of his memory blocks, but in doing so, it revealed trauma. They took him away from Miriam at a very young age and placed him in a performing arts school. Even though he loved performing, they enslaved him to their agenda. They gave him drugs and used trauma-based cognitive control on him. I can see the scarring in his brain tissue and the wounds in his heart. It pains me to see this."

"If you think I can help, I will do what I can."

"Thank you! He is in the Healing Bay at the Palace of Indicum. Lately, he is showing signs of improvement. Now would be the perfect time. Please, come by tomorrow morning."

Tia agreed and went to sleep that night, asking for a dream about how to help Xander and speed up his recovery. The next morning, she awoke with a clear plan in mind.

The Palace of Indicum lay low to the ground, but from above, it looked like a five-petaled flower. A central hub glowed indigo, making it easy to find. As soon as she entered, Frenla greeted her and guided her to the Healing Bay. After the weeks that had passed, Xander now looked different. His eyes glowed with presence, and his energy field radiated the indigo current in alignment with his birth lineage.

Sitting on a cushion inside a circular chamber, he played an instrument that looked like a guitar, only more sophisticated. It had three fingerboard necks and a keyboard like the one on an accordion. He was playing one of Metta's songs that she had heard at the concert. His voice felt soothing and familiar as if she'd heard him in her dreams. Clearly, their souls had interacted in other lives, and, at that moment, their destined partnership rang true. He finished the song and looked up. Her heart pounded so loudly she could barely think. Putting down the instrument, he beckoned her inside. Then Frenla left them alone to talk.

She sat on a cushion next to him, her hands trembling. In English, she said, "That was beautiful, Dax. I remember hearing that song at the concert."

"Thank you," he said. "Call me Xander. That's my real name, and I feel more connected to it. This Ptafla instrument is amazing. I picked it up so quickly. It's like I've played it before."

"Maybe you did play it in another life in Helio Tropez."

"Perhaps. Although this whole scene and my supposed true lineage feel like a dream or some kind of Candid Camera show. I'm expecting a camera crew to come out from behind the corner, laughing and telling me that this whole thing is a weird publicity stunt for the record label."

Tia laughed nervously.

"Is it?"

"No. I'm afraid it's all very real. When I first arrived here, I felt sure that it was a dream. Seeing that everything I'd been taught was wrong put me through a whole identity crisis. Apparently, the Heliotropan de-programming protocols do ease the process."

"Indeed. I'm less in shock than when I first arrived. If it's all real... then brilliant! To know that I descended from this amazing group of people..."

"So you like being here?"

"As you say, this higher vibrational place is a shock to the system, but rebuilding my inherent skills and memories... that's mind-blowing. I feel like an entirely different person."

"Yes, if you grow up on the surface and then come here, it's quite the culture shock."

"Thank you for rescuing me. I would've stayed on the surface my entire life until I died of a drug overdose or liver cirrhosis or some other such dire end."

Beads of sweat formed on her upper lip. "You're welcome. It's amazing that I actually found you. I went to the surface, looking for my aunt, my mother, and my sister. Yet, I ran into you, and you brought me to Metta."

"Yes, I heard about Pentada... and how the five of you are the anchor point for this grand genetic experiment."

"Apparently so."

"I'm just trying to wrap my head around all these entirely new concepts of who I am, where we came from, what happened to me on the surface. I'm working with this chap, Tarom, the Integration Counsellor. He gave me access to The Hall of Records, where I can ask any question I want."

"Amazing, isn't it? It's like 1,000 times better than the Internet," Tia said, shifting on the pillow, feeling a strong attraction towards him. She felt embarrassed thinking about how he could maybe read her thoughts now. Although she'd dated a few boys in high school, her attraction to Xander was nothing like she'd ever experienced before. Every cell in her body wanted him. However, given his life as a rock star, surrounded by adoring groupies, he likely had far more experience with the opposite sex than her.

"I found out that you are my primary SANA mate," Xander said.

Tia laughed louder than she wanted to. "Apparently so!"

"And I've been learning to read thoughts telepathically."

Her cheeks burned.

"It's true that I have been with a lot of girls, but I'm not proud of it. And for the most part, it felt empty. I don't think I know what real connection is."

He looked down and furrowed his brow. She sensed his loneliness and the pain that Frenla talked about.

Changing the subject, she asked, "Did you find any information on your parents?"

"No."

"I found out that your grandparents, Lorena and Ben Indicum, are still alive on the surface."

He nodded, his gaze fixed on some empty part of the room. "Yes, I saw that they were part of the Quinary Mission and that they went to the surface with your grandparents."

"When I went to the home planet of Anatol, they had more accurate records than here. Apparently, both of them survived the Great UnDoing of 1961. Do you have any memories of them as a child?"

He shook his head, his attention drifting to the window. "No, my mother was separated from them in her late teens, just like your parents were. It would be amazing if they are all still alive."

"I'm hoping to make another trip to find more Quinary members and bring them back."

"I imagine that trip was dangerous for you. SIM lost two of their best assets – they're going to be on the lookout if you went back."

A coldness stabbed at her heart when she remembered looking into the eyes of Josie Carbona; the predatory darkness and rage that boiled within her.

He added, "I just had a vision of Josie Carbona. That's who you were thinking about just now, correct?"

Tia nodded.

"I had this dream that she was here, trying to get inside this chamber, along with JJ Redus. Remember him? But they couldn't get in, thankfully."

Tia looked around to check if she sensed her presence, but she couldn't. "You're safe here. And if you get the chance to go to the SANA Rosa Academy, they'll teach you about energetic shields. Those made a huge difference for me."

They talked for several hours about her life, his life, their hopes and dreams for the future until she noticed his energy fading.

"I'm going to let you rest now."

He nodded and said, "Thank you for coming to me in your dream last night. Whatever you did made a big difference. I feel more of a wholeness now. I knew that you were special from the very first moment I saw you in that restaurant. It was a true serendipity that we met."

Tia's eyes welled up with tears, and he reached for her hands. Currents of energy ran from his fingertips through hers, shuddering her body from head to toes. They hugged, and the passion engulfed her. Remembering his fragile state, she backed away and bid him goodbye.

That night, she barely slept. This reconnection with Xander reminded her of the time she had first heard about SANA mates. Every cell in her body commanded her to commit herself, heart, body, mind and soul to Xander, no matter what.

CHAPTER 35

Helio Tropez – 4D Earth – 2011

The next day, Cassandra asked the Ascension Task Force to go on a mission. Deeper within the Earth's crust lay an intersection of ley lines that could help them work on the code in more powerful ways. This time, they invited Annika, who was desperate to help them in any way she could. The amethyst Tia had given her on the surface had sped up the healing process, and now, she was ready to play her part. Having three out of the five Pentada on the mission could make a huge difference.

The twenty-five members met at a Volantabus platform. A private bus just for them arrived, and they piled onboard. It flew the group down through a narrow lava tube and out into an open pasture land deeper inside the earth. Off in the distance, a high-speed train whizzed by, heading towards a station.

The Volantabus arrived at the station just in time for them to catch the train. The train system connected over 100 cities throughout Agartha. It reminded Tia of the subways back home, only much more advanced, sleek and beautiful.

Inside the train, she sat in a row of three chairs facing each other with Cassandra and Annika across from her. As they travelled, Tia noticed humans from various races and cultures embarking and disembarking at different train stations. Some of them looked like Africans, some like Indians, others like the aboriginals of Australia, or even some like characters from fairy tales.

Many of them wore clothing like the flowing silvery robes and amethysts they wore in Helio Tropez. The train travelled in and out of gigantic caverns and tunnels. Sometimes, the caves included forests, lakes and mountain ranges. Then, the train silently whipped past settlements, towns and even cities.

As Tia peered out of the window, observing the changing scenery, Cassandra explained a lesson Tia had forgotten from one of her classes. "The outer edge of the Earth's crust is like a honeycomb of caves, some as big as the United States. In those cases, you don't think of yourself as in the cave, but you are. Once you get a few thousand miles below the surface, you reach an area known as the hollow centre or Agartha. There, you'll see a central sun. You can see beams from that sun on the surface near the poles. Surface humans call those lights the Aurora Borealis. That's where we're going today. It is a vast area of continents, oceans, mountains, rivers, valleys and cities. Some of the people are friendly with us, but some are less friendly. However, we asked for special dispensation to stay at Tinaghan for a few weeks."

"A few weeks?!" Tia said. "I didn't bring any overnight things."

She laughed. "You don't need overnight things here. You can replicate anything you need."

Annika overheard, and a wry smile crossed her lips. "She's not worried about overnight things... She misses Xander."

Tia blushed and looked away while the other two chuckled. Bimini nuzzled in closer on her lap.

Cassandra patted her knee. "He needs a few more weeks of acclimatization anyway before activating your SANA partnership."

Tia sighed. She didn't want to wait a few more weeks to see Xander again. "What do you mean by activating the partnership?"

Annika grinned, "It's not like a shack up... it's more like a..."

"Wedding," Cassandra smiled.

Tia sat upright. "A wedding? We barely know each other."

Cassandra's blackbird alighted on her forearm. "If he's your SANA mate, then it's for life. Why wait? You shouldn't 'shack up' before a SANA ceremony, is all I'm saying. I know they do that on the surface, but it can lead to problems if you don't perform the vows correctly first."

The thought of marrying Xander seemed both appealing and terrifying. *What kind of vows will I even make?* Before she could ask the question, Cassandra moved across the aisle to speak with another person.

Annika leaned in close to Tia and directed a private thought to her. *I have finally met my SANA mate.* Her eyes darted to a man sitting across the aisle from them, a few seats ahead.

Tia looked over to see Stavron of the House of Virids, one of their newly replaced Task Force members. He was a short man, part human and part dwarf, and as far as she understood, his orientation was to other men.

Tia returned a private thought to Annika. *Stavron is your SANA mate?*

Yes. That's what my mother thought, but I doubted it. He prefers men, and I prefer women. So I thought, what the heck is she thinking? I figured she was meddling, just like when she pushed Rafael and Daphne together. But that's all changed since I met him.

Stavron smiled at Annika from across the aisle, and she blushed.

Tia leaned closer, "Do tell."

"First off, he's amazing. And, since being here, I remember my past Pentada lives. I need a mate of the opposite gender to activate as a full Pentada. I want that, not just for me, but for all of humanity. I feel the calling."

"You don't feel like you're betraying your... true orientation...?"

She laughed so loudly that people nearby turned to look over at them.

Annika sank down in her chair. "Listen, I think we can all go back and forth on a spectrum of sexual orientation. I don't like to get stuck in any one *identity.* I used to have crushes on both genders when I was young. Not that any boys thought I was a great catch. But once SIM got control of me, Irene kept sending women my way to seduce me, so I went for it. They seemed to idolize me in a way that men never did. Anyhow, I got all identified with the lesbian community. Some women were amazing. Some were jerks. But once I broke free of the SIM trap, I saw how my controllers just wanted me to avoid Pentada activation. They knew I could go both ways, so they capitalized on that."

Tia pulled Bimini onto her lap and tickled his chin. "But you were married to Xander's uncle, right?"

The bear looked at Annika with watery blue eyes and held up a paw. Annika glanced at Tia and back at the bear with a surprised expression. She shook his paw, and he emitted a deep purr.

"So cute and so soft! The only reason they mated me with Michael Indicum was that Daphne and Rafael didn't produce any children. It was friendly between us but awkward. I fancied him, but not the other way around."

Tia elbowed her, "How is it with Stavron?"

"Strangely enough, we both seem to find each other attractive, fascinating and...something more. I've never experienced anything like it." At that moment, Annika was like a schoolgirl, a far cry from the old woman living alone in misery in Montreal.

"You're talking about me, aren't you?" Stavron asked, crossing the aisle and joining them. His cat-like eyes and long eyelashes made him look feminine, yet his strong upper body spoke of tremendous strength. His neatly braided hair and beard were interwoven with multicoloured ribbons.

He jumped up on the chair opposite her. Like Annika, his feet didn't touch the floor. "Annika and I met just two days ago, but we've covered so much ground since then. It's like we've known each other for centuries."

"Actually, we have!" Annika added. "Many lifetimes together. I can now remember them all."

They smiled at each other in that goofy, lovestruck way, and Tia's heart melted to see Annika youthful and happy again.

When Annika finally broke free of his gaze, she turned to Tia and said, "Stavron originally suggested we all come to Tinaghan because he's been there many times before."

"Exactly. My father is from there. My expertise is in ley line and earth grid reconstruction and how it affects the human mind. Tinaghan holds a very rare energy because of the intersection of three strong ley lines. That could help us access interdimensional intelligence to perform our upgrades." A striped chipmunk peaked out of his breast pocket. "Hey there. Riley is my Jenio."

"Nice to meet you, Riley." Tia smiled as the chipmunk dipped its chin in acknowledgement. "Interdimensional intelligences. That sounds otherworldly. I'm looking forward to it."

Bimini jumped onto the opposite chair to chat with the chipmunk.

339

"Soon, you will find your Jenio, just like Tia found hers."

Annika beamed. "That would be the icing on the cake, especially with everything else here that's rocked my world. I think I'd like a giraffe. Are there any miniature ones that fit on your lap here?"

"As a matter of fact, there are." Stavron laughed. "Over in the Manui Plains!"

His laugh was as uproarious as Annika's. The two of them could barely contain themselves, which made everyone turn to look and meet their laugh with infectious chuckles throughout the rail car.

The train arrived at Tinaghan in only thirty minutes, even though they had travelled thousands of miles. At the station, they disembarked along with the other members of the Task Force. Meraton led the way towards a hovercraft, soundlessly floating five feet off the ground, that seated all twenty-five of them perfectly. The Jenios gathered together in a secure kennel type structure. Meraton's white wolf, being the biggest of the animals, protected the smaller ones.

As soon as the doors closed, the tube-shaped craft sped off over the hillside, around the side of a mountain, and down a valley towards a lake. The lake sparkled aquamarine, and purple flowers adorned the embankment. They flew across the water while multi-coloured waterfowl took flight in all directions. Arriving at a dome-shaped building sitting on the water's edge, they were met by a rotund man, who stood only about three feet tall.

He looks like one of Snow White's dwarves, Tia said to Meraton.

"I've seen that Disney movie," said the tiny man, unsmiling.

To her embarrassment, she realised that she had forgotten to keep that thought private.

"We appear in your stories and myths. Sometimes, we steal some of those books and movies and have a good laugh," he frowned. "So little understanding of the true nature of our species. We are the best builders in Inner Earth. Your gemstone technology? Made by us – the original blueprint. Your best tools in Helio Tropez? Made by us. Your most captivating buildings? Originally created by us."

"Got it. Amazing." Tia smiled.

"These are your living quarters. Each of you has his or her own room. This is a sacred land, and so, most people stay in silence to connect with the interdimensional presence that's readily available here. We ask you to abide by that silence, not speaking using your vocal cords, but only telepathically."

They settled into their rooms. Tia's room was smaller than her room in Helio Tropez. Bimini sniffed each corner, as he often did, to suss out the energetic frequency of a place and clear any bad energy. The size of everything in the room befitted dwarf-sized people as the Tinaghan land was owned by dwarves. To accommodate taller people, one could turn dials to raise the bed, the toilet and the doorways. Her room jutted out over the water and contained an oval sleeping pod, a bathroom, a replicator and a comm system. The walls glowed a pearlescent pink and contained sacred geometry patterns like in Helio Tropez. Outside of the window, the lake rippled in the breeze. The plasma floors soothed her tired feet. Above her, the domed ceiling twinkled as if covered in stars.

Later that day, the Task Force members gathered outside on the lakeside to do Tangency together, where Cassandra led them through breathing exercises along with movements that reminded Tia of qigong. She loved graceful movements, and after they were finished, a re-invigorated, grounded feeling permeated her body. As they walked back to the meeting room, Annika and Stavron walked arm in arm. She sighed, imagining being in this beautiful place with Xander one day.

In the meeting room, they sat in meditative silence so they could tap into the higher wisdom available in the area. Each person on the team represented a different aptitude. Since there were twenty-five different aptitudes, they suspected that the MindStory Code had twenty-five stages. To explore the theory, Cassandra asked each person to call down the wisdom for their stage of the code. To that end, Tia held the space for the Sentient-Attention part of the code. The others went into a theta brainwave state quickly, but Tia lacked the mental discipline to get there with the same ease. Instead, thoughts of Xander filled her mind.

After several hours, Cassandra led them through a telepathic debrief of their experiences, and asked Meraton to map it. He started by creating a map of the code, the part of the puzzle they had solved so far. Each person added any wisdom they had garnered to the map. When it was Tia's turn, she had nothing to add. Annika elbowed her and winked. However, Tia gave them a blank stare as a feeling of heat arose on the back of her neck. Some Task Force members looked annoyed at her, while others smiled knowingly.

They continued mining the information over the next few days, and Tia's mind eventually settled down and connected to the right vibration. Once

341

connected, huge downloads of information came through. Throughout the ages of genetic upgrades on surface humans, each stage required a different operating system, which always came in the form of a story. The story consisted of characters, themes and plots just like a screenplay or novel. When it came time to share her experiences during the next meeting, she felt relieved to have something of value to contribute.

"On the surface, I spent years studying story writing and story structure, and now I know why."

Meraton said, "Sentient-Attention people in Helio Tropez often take on the role of *story shamans* to free individuals from limiting mindsets using stories."

"I guess that on the surface, we would call those people Narrative Therapists."

"Isla here is an Audient-Reprogram or *The Storyteller*. Those with that aptitude help free whole groups from limiting stories by creating empowering myths that get retold through the generations."

Tia's eyes lit up. "On the surface, those would be the novelists and moviemakers."

"Except that SIM now controls most of the stories that surface humans consume, which entrenches them in limiting MindStories. It's how they get around Universal Laws like the Law of Fair Warning."

Tia blinked. "The what?"

"SIM cannot manipulate humans without their conscious or subconscious consent. The Law of Fair Warning states that they must get surface humans to agree to be enslaved. For example, SIM uses metaphors, stories and symbols which speak to the subconscious versus the conscious mind, such as on TV, in movies, fiction, or through symbols in art or in company logos. Most people are not aware of how they get manipulated subconsciously, so they just pass it off as harmless entertainment."

Tia nodded as she remembered all the violence on TV and the neurotic behaviour depicted in movies. "Yes, of course. So, the next MindStory Code prepares people for moving to higher densities and integrates all 25 aptitudes in one individual?"

Stavron nodded. "I put the existing MindStory Code under my pillow last night to get more insight as I slept. I awoke with this," he said as he used his hand to draw a type of double helix surrounded by matrix symbols. Seeing mind code was a rare skill of people like Stavron, an Ecrivent-Reprogram, also known as *The Mind Coder*. The other Ecrivents nodded. It made no sense to Tia, but it was a language all Ecrivents seemed to share.

Meraton used his hand to add Stavron's helix to the map they were working on. "This is excellent. So it's like Pentada creates the five main turning points in the story. They are the TEVAS cornerstones. Amazing. Then, within each of the five segments are four smaller turning points, equalling a total of twenty-five turning points. Why didn't we see that before?"

With a sparkle in his eye, Stavron added more symbols to the map. "My insight comes from the creativity 'vortex' of all of us together on these sacred ley lines. I share this accomplishment with all of you. So, what I see is that each aptitude is responsible for one turning point, and Pentada anchors the five main turning points like this:

Cassandra = Part 1 of the story, Setting the Existing Platform,

Annika = Part 2 of the story, Tilting the Platform,

Daphne = Part 3 of the story, Consequences,

Metta = Part 4 of the story, Regaining Stability,

Tia = Part 5 of the story, Setting the New Platform."

Several people on the Task Force stood up and walked around the room to look at the 3D map of the double helix.

Meraton laced his fingers behind his back. "This is excellent work, everyone. It's the start of the blueprint. I suggest we break for the day and continue tomorrow."

Tia left the room feeling elated. During the evening meal, Ramu sat down next to Tia. His Jenio, a miniature leopard, jumped up onto his lap and nuzzled its head against her forearm.

"Who's this?" Tia laughed.

"This is Morvato, my Jenio. She likes you."

Bimini came up to Morvato and growled at her. The leopard blinked at him with an innocent expression until the bear calmed down.

"We haven't really gotten the chance to get to know each other. I'm Ramu of Viridis. I work as a gem smith."

Ramu was new to the Task Force, so they'd never spoken one-to-one. He usually wore a silver cap that covered his hair and half his face, but today, he wasn't wearing a hat, letting his long hair flow down and his violet eyes stand out.

Tia remembered hearing that he'd begged several members to help him get on the Task Force. This made Meraton and Cassandra reject his application before properly assessing him. Only after Ramu solved one of their biggest technical issues on his own time, and forced them to look at it, did the Task Force relent.

"I heard you're quite the talent, especially when it comes to weaving the old and new mindcodes together seamlessly."

"Yes, the existing circuitry in the amethysts is based on the Earth ley lines when the gem smiths first created them. Everything has shifted since then, and that's why you were all having issues with the new one. But luckily my workaround seems to have solved the problem. I guess this group didn't realize all these rare skills I can offer." He pulled up a list of his career accomplishments on his wrist device.

Tia's eyes grew wide as it went on for several pages. "That's amazing to, um, achieve so much at such a young age. I mean young as far as Heliotropans go..."

"Yes, that's because I'm one of the few here with Elven blood in my ancestry. Combine that with the fact that I'm the first one on the aptitude scale."

"First? Oh yes, you mean Tangent-Acceptance."

He nodded. "I'm the Earth Healer. You're the last one on the scale, The Inspirator. We hold the opposite ends. Very serendipitous." He closed down the screen and turned to face her. "I've been watching you lead people and inspiring them with this vision of the MindStory Code. You are truly living your aptitude."

Although Tia felt embarrassed by the compliment, she had learned to accept all praise. In Helio Tropez, they viewed compliments as more about the giver than the receiver. "Thank you. Having grown up on the surface, I feel at a disadvantage compared to the rest of you. I didn't get the kind of education you all did as children."

He nodded lost in thought about something as he arranged the string beans on his plate in perfect rows. "Maybe it's because you grew up on the

344

surface that you will teach us all something different and important. SANA works in mysterious ways."

They talked intently throughout the entire meal break, and Tia began to sense a look of devotion in his eyes. Either he put her on a pedestal as a leader, or he had an attraction to her, or both. Feeling increasingly uncomfortable, she ended the conversation and excused herself.

Over the next few days, she noticed him looking at her longingly. He made a point of sitting next to her at each mealtime. In fact, as a Tangent, he could bi-locate. Although he was only supposed to do so in emergencies, he often seemed to be in the meal area and in the meeting room at the same time. At one point, he touched her knee, and a shockwave of electricity ran up her leg. *Is the attraction mutual?* Tia shook her head. Only a few days before, she'd felt a complete devotion to Xander, but this connection with Ramu was confusing her.

"May I speak with you privately for a moment?" Ramu asked as they were leaving the meditation room one day. She nodded, and he led her into a private room.

"I think we both feel the bonding energy here. We are clearly primary SANA mates. Yet, I notice you seem to have some apprehension..."

"No, well, yes. I mean to say that yes, you are a very attractive man. But, no, I don't think we are primary SANA mates. My mate is Xander of Indicum, the man I just brought here from the surface."

"Strange. I've never felt this way with anyone before. And I know you feel it too."

"It's my understanding that you can feel attraction for others, but your feeling toward your primary SANA mate is entirely different. It's a past and future life connection. I don't think you and I have that. Besides, I've been here for a whole year, but we never connected before."

A look of disappointment crossed his face, and she couldn't help feeling guilty.

"I know you've been here for a year, but we just never had the chance to get to know each other until I joined the Task Force. I think I was just afraid of the intensity of our attraction. I suggest we do a test. "

"What kind of test?"

"Kiss me. If you still think this Xander is your mate, then I will leave you alone."

Tia stepped back. "I don't think so. We could end up blocking ourselves from our true SANA mates."

"Look, you are the only woman for whom I've ever felt this. There's something very particular about your energy that I know is important for me to pay attention to. Please, just give it a try."

He stepped forward and stood a few inches in front of her. His large brown eyes looked at her through long eyelashes, and she felt a rush of warmth run through her body. Indeed, she did fear kissing him, especially due to lack of experience. She had no idea what to do. If they felt that SANA bond, did that mean that Niklana was wrong? Amelia did warn her that, sometimes, her predictions were incorrect. He wrapped his arms around her waist and leaned in for a kiss. Just before his lips met hers, she heard a knock on the door.

"Tia. Are you in there? We're starting the next session," Cassandra's voice came from behind the door.

Tia pulled away, feeling that it was a sign not to kiss him. She excused herself and left the room. However, after that experience, she continued to feel distracted during the meditations, especially when she sensed Ramu's energy reaching out towards her. Her downloads and insights dwindled to nothing as she kept thinking about his eyes and lips and his hand on her back. Finally, one day, she noticed him walking by the lake alone. She followed him to a private spot by the water's edge.

"May we talk?" she asked.

He nodded, seeming apprehensive.

"I'm feeling distracted by this thing between you and me. I think we should do the experiment. If it's not meant to be, we stop sending our energy to each other and focus on the task at hand here. Agreed?"

"Agreed," he smiled.

She looked around. They were alone. Stepping towards each other, they embraced and kissed. Electricity ran through her system. Their kiss lasted a full minute, and during that time, she allowed her higher mind to get clarity. She sensed they had three past lives together, but only as a friend or acquaintance, not a primary partner.

Breaking free from the kiss, she said, "Okay. I get it." She took a step back and composed herself. "I sense that we are part of the same soul family, but we are not primary partners. What did you get?"

His brow wrinkled, and he sighed. "I didn't get that. Niklana said my primary mate was born into the House of Zuris and had your exact same birth date."

"You went to Niklana as well? She told me that my mate was from the House of Indicum and that his birthday was August 10, 1980. That profile fits Xander. When is your birthday?"

"It's February 28, 1980."

She looked out at the lake and allowed the passion to die down. A flash of illumination trickled into her mind's eye. "I think I know who your primary partner is."

"Who?"

"My twin sister, Metta."

CHAPTER 36

Helio Tropez - 6D and 4D Earth – 2011

N ear the well in Jephsonite Park, a trellis of purple Bougainvillaea bloomed with tiny Udumbara flowers growing around the edges. Hadden was amazed. The Udumbara flowers only bloomed during auspicious times in history, although maybe in 6D, it was more common. The energy emitted by the flowers sparkled gold. Today, he was practising shrinking his consciousness down to the size of an insect and standing on one of the Bougainvillaea petals. This ability to expand or shrink your light body came more naturally in the 6D, but not without practice.

Once comfortable, he started working on shrinking to the cellular level. Inside the cells of a petal, he could experience the balanced, electromagnetic impulses. In a thriving flower, those fired rapidly. In a wilting flower, they slowed right down. He practised on a wilting petal by rebuilding the impulses between the cells until the flower was vibrant and full of life again. After repeating the process a few times, he felt ready to move his light body down into 4D Helio Tropez.

There he turned all his attention to Metta's healing process. In prayer state, he asked SANA for permission to help her.

In 6D, you could not make selfish or ignorant choices without suffering from immediate repercussions. On the other hand, in the lower densities, the karmic consequences could take lifetimes to manifest. So, he only proceeded when he got a definite 'yes' from SANA.

Trauma in her entire nervous system needed dissolving. After he shrunk down, he travelled between the nerve cells, working with her higher self to dissolve the stuck emotion. In her brain, he found places where the receptor cells no longer communicated. The alcohol and drug use had stopped her body from naturally producing the hormones that created mental and emotional stability. In turn, it had made her fluctuate back and forth between elated while on the substances and re-traumatised once they wore off. And so, Hadden first worked on reconnecting the receptor cells and building the reserves of natural hormones needed for mental and emotional balance.

Unprocessed negative emotions appeared stuck in the hippocampus. Having healed his own body-mind system from torture, he could now detect similar issues in others. For example, he saw the pattern of abandonment trauma and ritualistic CM trauma stuck in the interior parts of her brain. SIM agents knew that neurons that fired together were wired together. To activate her aptitude for their own agenda, they had installed trigger words and symbols. They had used the same trigger phrase with her as Leo had done with him. Whenever she used the CM trigger "Railspur Tidings," her obedience to her handler activated.

As Halia surmised, many people who originated from Helio Tropez seemed to have a shadow counterpart on the surface. In Metta's case, this person was unsurprisingly Andrea's twin sister, Ruth, her handler He removed the activation trigger, then healed and sealed all entrances.

Energy blockages existed at various choice points in her life. He cleared the blockages where possible. In general, she couldn't connect with people in healthy ways. Hadden suspected this came from a lack of caring parental figures, which engulfed him in guilt. She latched on to people who showed her any sign of affection, and all too often, they used her for their own agenda.

Moving to the corpus callosum, scar tissue created a blockage between the left and right hemispheres of the brain, creating a learning disability. A blockage between the lower part and the upper part of the brain meant she had lived the majority of her life in a survival brain state. He healed the scar tissue, meaning that the nervous system could recalibrate and reconnect her to the whole brain functions. The last thing he checked was soul ownership. Had she sold her soul essence to SIM for fame and fortune? The silver cord

349

between the higher self and the physical body looked thin but intact. A huge relief. Once finished, her entire system seemed to stay balanced and efficient. This final part of the unification process would require conscious participation. Moving back to his place in the corner of the room, Hadden watched as two attendants entered to scan the readings.

"Look at this," one attendant said in amazement. "Her recalibration process is complete, weeks in advance. How?"

"It's her guardian angel."

"What?"

"I don't know who he is, but I sensed his presence in this room yesterday, and now he's back."

"You know, I can sense that as well." He looked around the room. "Whoever you are, thank you. Her scan looks amazing."

Hadden smiled and telepathically sent the message, *You're welcome.*

The attendants made arrangements for her awakening. They coordinated with various counsellors and healers to help her integrate into life in Helio Tropez. Once awake, the first integration counsellor, named Cinda, entered her room. She scanned her hand across one of the walls, and a window overlooking the entire city appeared. Fields and mountains resting in a crimson-blue mist sprawled into the distance. Eyes wide, Metta sat up and moved close to the window. Flying cars and kite-shaped spaceships weaved between tall, spiral buildings.

In English, the woman said, "I'm Cinda. Welcome to Helio Tropez. How do you feel?"

"Is this real or a dream?"

"It's very real."

"Where are we?"

"We are in a subterranean city several miles below an area you call the Pacific Northwest of North America."

"A subterranean city? I've never heard of it."

"Your schools on the surface tell you that the centre of the earth is solid. Correct?"

"I guess so. I never paid much attention in school. How did I get here?"

"Your sister, Tia, brought you here."

"What? I don't have a sister."

"Yes, you do. You just can't remember her. She's actually your twin sister, but you were separated at the age of three."

"Where is she now?"

"She's on a Task Force mission with your grandparents."

"My grandparents? My mother's parents?"

"Yes."

"The social worker told me I had no family. No grandparents, no father, no siblings. When my mother left, they had to put me in a foster care system. And this whole time, I had grandparents!"

"Yes, but they didn't know that you were alive."

"Where did my sister grow up?"

"In Seattle, with your father."

"My father?"

"Hadden Violetta, whose parents also came from here. You are a purebred Heliotropan, and that's why we are so glad to have you back. We realise this is all very strange to you, and it sounds as though your mother never told you about your true heritage."

"I barely remember my mother. She left when I was five."

"Then you'll be happy to see her again."

"Mum is here too?"

"Yes, she's not been here long, but you'll learn more soon. For now, just relax."

"This is all just too weird to me. One minute I'm sitting in a meeting room in Montréal, the next minute I'm here."

"I understand this might seem strange to you. We beamed you here from the surface."

"As in Star Trek, beam me up Scotty?"

"Yes, I think you mean the popular television show from the surface of the Earth."

"Okay, I get it. This is some kind of promotional event cooked up by the Carbonas, isn't it?" Metta asked as she wandered the circular room, looking for an exit. "It's very entertaining, but I'm on a PR tour right now, so I really need to get back."

"That's inadvisable. Several people put themselves at great risk to rescue you. We highly advise not going back to the surface."

"I just need to find Ruth. She must be around here somewhere."

"Who's Ruth?"

"Ruth Carbona, my PR person. We have a meeting."

"The Carbona family are dangerous SIM agents."

"SIM agents?"

Cinda sighed and sent a Matrix text on her wrist device. "Hi, Rainard. It's not going so well. I think it would help if you brought Xander of Indicum here. He's had more time to adjust to things, and he knows Metta from the surface."

As they waited, Metta caught a reflection of herself wearing the silver outfit common amongst people of Helio Tropez in the mirror. "Cool costume. I don't remember changing into this, though. Did someone drug me?"

"When someone first arrives from the surface, we put them to sleep until they've gone through decompression and purification processes."

"So I *was* drugged! This is getting creepier by the second."

The attendants ran several checks, updating charts and asking questions about how she felt. Twenty minutes later, Xander arrived with his integration counsellor, Rainard.

"Metta! So happy you are up and about. What a strange and wonderful world."

They hugged, and she wouldn't let go for several seconds.

"Xander, they drugged me, then dressed me up in this weird outfit," she whispered.

"Yes, they did the same to me. But it's okay. You're safe here. This is our ancestral home. I've learned that I am from the House of Indicum, and you are from the House of Zuris. And, that woman Linda who brought us here is your twin sister!"

"The performance coach? That makes no sense. I don't have a sister."

"Apparently, it's true."

Metta squinted and wrung her hands. "We don't even look alike."

"You do a bit."

They sat down on a sofa together, and she snuggled in next to him. The two integration counsellors stayed several feet back to let them talk. Xander explained about the Quinary Mission and how their grandparents were born in Helio Tropez but had gone to the surface to help eliminate SIM. After describing the genetic experiment, SIM and the true history of the Earth, Metta buried her head in his shoulder.

"This is all just too weird and way out there. Not only that, but I feel so strange inside... I don't feel like myself anymore."

"SIM agents did horrible things to us so we would obey their commands. That's what they're helping us heal from using these medical beds. It's the real you that is emerging."

"But I didn't choose to be here," she whispered. "I want to go home."

He wrapped his arms around her and explained how lucky they were to be there and how they removed all the damage from the CM, food, drugs, alcohol on the surface. After a while, the integration counsellors left them alone, deciding that Xander had the situation under control.

Hadden watched silently as Xander and Metta talked. An hour or so later, Xander left. When he saw Metta lay back down and fall asleep, he moved to Daphne's room and started the same healing process. She, too, needed to rebuild receptors, heal trauma, and recalibrate her system. The Gender Misery program needed removing. Although the medical bed removed chemicals from all food, drinks and drugs, it couldn't access a deeper level of trauma healing. From 6D, he could purify her at the higher energetic levels.

The same two attendants scanned Daphne's readings, and one shook her head with a smile. "It's happened again. Her recalibration process is complete, weeks in advance. Thank you, guardian angel!"

Various counsellors and healers at the Palace of Zuris came forward to awaken and integrate Daphne into life in Helio Tropez. Still in a daze, she settled into her quarters, and after a long night of sleep, Daphne met with an integration counsellor in a room overlooking the fountains next to the Palace. Hadden stayed nearby as she settled in.

A petite woman with long, black hair introduced herself in English. "Hello, Daphne. I'm Jimona, and I'm your Integration Counsellor. Welcome to Helio Tropez."

"You mean the place my parents came from?"

"Yes."

She shook her head, smiling gently. "It's everything I ever dreamed of. How did I get here?"

"The Progenitors on Anatol rescued you from the navigation ship."

"On Anatol?" She frowned. "I remember I had a job there. I had a shipment to drop off but had to fix my nav scanner before leaving."

"Anatol is our home planet. They recognised your energy signature as being a descendant of the original team that came to Earth."

"That's the home planet of Heliotropans, how did I not know that?"

Jimona squirmed. "Maybe your parents never told you?"

Daphne pulled her pony table over one shoulder inspecting her red locks. "Maybe. Anyway, I'm so grateful. I've been trying to get back to Earth for years, but SIM controlled my every move."

"We've removed the SIM programming in your system, purified your bloodstream, and rejuvenated your cell structure. You've also had a guardian angel helping move things along faster. Someone who is working from another dimension."

"Who?"

"We're not sure, but it's someone who loves you very much. They haven't left your side."

Daphne lifted her head and turned towards the side of the room where Hadden was hovering. "I wonder who it could be."

"They've been helping you heal ever since you arrived."

"Thank you, guardian angel," Daphne smiled.

You're welcome, Hadden replied, even though he doubted Daphne could hear him.

As Daphne looked down at her hands, shaking her head in disbelief. "My skin is so... amazing now." She looked out the window. "I always dreamed of coming here one day – my parents talked about it all the time. It's so beautiful, harmonious, and alive. I'm home in a way I've never felt before."

"Your parents are looking forward to seeing you soon."

"My parents?!"

"Cassandra and Meraton. They are here in Helio Tropez. We just wanted to give you a few days to integrate first."

She held up her hands. "I don't get it. Did I die, and now I'm in the next dimension?"

"Well, we're in the 4th density instead of the 3rd. But no, you didn't die."

"My parents died on the surface of Earth when I was a girl. You must be mistaken."

A wave of alarm shuddered through Hadden. In the second timeline, he had told Daphne about her parents being still alive. How could she be stuck in the first timeline?

Jimona shook her head with a smile. "They didn't. SIM orchestrated the lie, forged the records, and as far as anyone on the surface was concerned, they died. But in truth, they escaped. They were the only ones who did."

"I went to their funeral," Daphne said, becoming a little more erratic. "They died in a car accident. I saw the accident report."

"Cassandra and Meraton escaped The Great UnDoing of 1961, then came back here," Jimona said gently. "They've been here ever since."

"I don't believe you. They would have come and rescued us."

"They thought you were dead. The Hall of Records showed no soul signature after 1961. As far as we were concerned, you were dead, just as you thought your parents were."

Daphne sat down, trying to digest the idea of her parents being alive this whole time. She took a sip of water and stood up to pace the room.

"I've spent a lifetime feeling guilty for causing their death…"

"You didn't cause anything."

"I left home when they told me not to, and the next thing I knew, they had died, and I ended up a slave to SIM."

"You were a teenager wanting to explore the world. You did nothing wrong, Daphne."

355

"Well," she said with a sigh, but a smile crossed her lips. "It's a huge shock, but I'm glad they're alive, and I'm eager to see them. Although, they must be over 100 years old now."

"Yes, but I'm over 100 years old and look at me."

The woman looked to be in her 30s. Daphne looked her up and down, seeking signs that might betray the fact that she had walked the Earth for over a century. She saw nothing.

"I heard tales that people stayed youthful for hundreds of years here, but I never really believed them. How wonderful!"

Jimona reached for a hand mirror. "Have you looked in the mirror since you awoke? In surface years, you're 69 years old, but you don't look it."

"I'm not 69. I'm only in my forties." Daphne held the mirror close and touched her face. "Yes, my skin...and my hair... and all those wrinkles around my eyes... gone. Amazing. Is it really all this technology here?"

"Indeed. We reverted your cells to optimal functioning based on your body's quantum blueprint, which in women is usually around 25 years old."

"I'm 25 again? Halleluja!" Daphne laughed. "I'm liking this place more and more."

"Your sister is here, too."

"Annika? That's amazing!"

"And your two daughters, Tia and Metta."

Daphne sat down. "This is getting more unreal by the minute. I'd love to see them all now!"

"Soon. We know it's a lot to take in all at once, so we want to let you digest each piece of information one at a time."

"How did my sister and daughters get here? Did Annika rescue the girls?"

"No, Tia rescued Annika and Metta, actually."

Concern crossed her face. "How... How could she? Hadden was protecting her."

Hadden swallowed, thankful that she couldn't see him.

"It's a complicated story. But it started when Hadden called on his 20-year-old self to jump into the future, more specifically from 1960 to 2010. Then, young Hadden brought Tia here..."

"Wait… did you say it's 2010?!"

"In surface time, it's actually 2011."

"I left the surface in 1985, and I've only been gone for three years. How could I have lost twenty-six years?!"

"Time is different in outer space. Your ship must have left the galaxy and moved into another time-space continuum," Jimona explained.

Daphne sat down, wide-eyed, and counted on her fingers. "When you told me that my daughters were here, I expected to see eight-year-olds. That means they would be… what… thirty-one years old?"

"Yes, that's true, but safe and sound here…"

Daphne collapsed, burying her face in her hands. "I missed their entire lives?"

Jimona brought her a tissue and sat next to her. Hadden's chin started to tremble.

"What happened to my five-year-old Metta? I left her with a neighbour and told her I'd be back in a few days. The next thing I know, I'm on a starship out near Jupiter."

"It's likely they wanted to keep you away from other Pentada members."

Daphne folded her arms and sunk her head on the table. Jimona touched her back as she sobbed, rubbing small circles between her shoulder blades. After a while, Daphne sat up and wiped away her tears. "That is why you said I was 69 years old."

"As I said, we sent you through the rejuvenation process. Your sister went through it too. She looks just as youthful as you do."

Daphne turned to Jimona. "I haven't seen her in thirty years. Is she okay?"

"Yes, Annika is okay. She is on a Task Force mission with Tia and your parents. I heard she just met her primary SANA mate, Stavron. So I'd say she's happier than ever."

Daphne laughed through wet eyes. "That's good. What about my daughters? Are they okay?"

"Your daughter, Tia, has shown herself to be a true leader helping us get ready for graduation."

"Graduation?"

"The harvest of all the genetic experiments on Earth. She lived a highly protected life under her father's care, so when she came here, the damage from the surface was minimal. On the other hand, Metta endured quite a bit of damage, but we've managed to heal her quite well. She's just come out of the purification and re-stabilization process. Like you, she seemed to have a guardian angel speeding up the healing process."

"What about Hadden? He would be… what… 70 years old now?"

"We have reason to believe that he died trying to get Tia to safety."

Daphne's face turned pale. "He died?"

"We think so, but as I said, we lost track of the Quinary members on the surface."

Daphne squeezed her eyes shut and grabbed a tissue. This time, she sobbed so loudly that an attendant knocked on the door just to check in on them.

"She's okay,' Jimona called back. "She's just processing a lot right now."

Hadden felt her heart breaking, and he moved in energetically to support her.

"I loved him so much. Some part of me thought we'd find a way back to each other. Something in my heart believed we'd put our family back together again. For me, it's just been a few years… They broke us apart… in so many ways!"

Jimona stayed with her, listening and talking through all the feelings and implications. Finally, she said, "I think that's enough for now. I'm going to take you back to your room to rest, but if you need anything, all you need to do is ask."

Daphne wiped her eyes and nodded, thanking her. Hadden accompanied her back to her room. Once alone, she climbed into her bed and grabbed a pillow to her chest. She screwed her eyes shut and buried her face into it, and as Hadden sat on the bed beside her, her shoulders heaved and shuddered.

He wished he could comfort her, to hold her and stroke her hair, tell her that he was okay, that it would all be okay.

I'm here, Daphne. I'll always be here for you. I'll always be here for you.

CHAPTER 37

Helio Tropez – 2011

Hadden stayed by Daphne as she rested. He felt like a ghost in many ways but being in the same room as her gave him comfort. As she slept, he stood by the window and looked out over Helio Tropez. Her conversation with the counsellor troubled him. Daphne knew back in 1979 that her parents were still alive. *Why didn't she remember him telling her that? Maybe this Daphne came from the first timeline. Did the Progenitors erase his timeline, or were there two timelines that existed separately?*

Back inside her memory banks, he tried to figure it out. There, he saw both timelines sitting alongside one another like two sets of railroad tracks going in the same direction but separate, eternally parallel. All the healing he had done in the second timeline had never happened.

Why does her system operate from the first timeline when the second one is right there? He traced the timeline back to the first time they had met after the timeline split, back to the 1970s nightclub. There, he had discovered a switch in her body-mind system – like a railway switch – set to the first timeline. Either she had switched it, or her SIM controller had. After a prayer to SANA and getting the green light to proceed, he tried switching to the second timeline, but it didn't work. A numbness seized him, and he couldn't move towards the switch anymore.

That's when he felt her. The energy signature of Josie Carbona. Then he remembered Tia saying that she might have hijacked the transport from Montreal to Helio Tropez. He turned around and saw her there – directing malevolent energy towards him. Before he could defend himself, energetic chains engulfed him in fear and dread.

If you try to switch it back, I'll kill her, Josie told him telepathically.

Hadden narrowed his eyes. *If you kill her, you'll be killing yourself. It's not your place to control Daphne. She's a free agent now.*

No, she isn't. She's made a contract with us.

SIM agents, like Josie, had a way of tricking people into giving up their sovereignty. In Daphne's case, after losing her family, they had lured her into a modelling and acting career, promising her success if she let them 'take care of her.' This gave them a doorway into reprogramming her while she slept at night.

Even though the healers had removed harmful CM programs, SIM could reinstall the programs if the person still had a subconscious agreement to be controlled. Hadden had forgotten to check for 'booby-traps.' These were programs that automatically launched if the asset or someone else tried to remove them. Hadden shrunk down further and re-entered Daphne's brain stem. All the healing work he had done on her memory banks, neural networks and brain cells was gone. To his horror, all the old programs had been reinstalled.

Josie's voice came through loud and clear. *It's too late. She belongs to us. You have no authority here. This mind is our private property. Leave, or I will harm the asset.*

Since Hadden came from 6D, she couldn't kill him, but she could completely take Daphne over. He retreated from 4D to 6D, where Halia stood waiting for him by the Wishing Well. When he explained the situation, she suggested they bring it to the Elders in 6D Helio Tropez.

The Hall of Congress in 6D looked similar, only with less density of matter. The walls looked like see-through holograms. Souls inhabited their 6D bodies but were not limited to the laws of 6D physics - they could phase in and out of sight by changing their frequency, or levitate, or bi-locate at will. In fact, some of them could simultaneously work on a project in a lab while also attending the meeting.

The five Elders sat in a semi-circle in the middle of several semi-circles. Hadden approached and explained the situation in 4D Helio Tropez. The Elders and everyone in attendance meditated on the situation, cross-pollinating their wisdom with information held in the 6D Hall of Records.

After the exploration was finished, Nibel, the moderator, summarised their conclusions. "It seems as though the SIM agent known as Josephine Carbona concealed her identity by shapeshifting into a virus. She embedded herself into Tia's right hand. Anyone she has touched since she arrived back in Helio Tropez now has the virus."

Hadden's chest tightened. "So everyone on the Task Force is infected?"

"Depending on a person's level of soul development, they may be able to protect themselves from the virus. However, according to our research, it influenced the Task Force enough to search for Daphne off-planet. Clearly, Josephine wanted all five Pentada together so that SIM could hijack their power. The virus also compelled Tia to touch Daphne's hand before the purification process was complete. Since Josephine already had a connection with Daphne, this was the best place for her to start regaining control."

"What can we do? Josephine threatened to kill Daphne if I tried to heal her."

"Daphne must nullify any past agreements made with SIM."

Hadden doubted this could work. "But SIM has tripwires in place all over her mind. I can see them. If she tries to undo an agreement, she experiences severe emotional pain and agitation. It's like trying to get through an electrical fence. You feel like you will die."

"But she is much stronger than SIM. She attained cosmic citizenship on Anatol."

"I know, but she somehow doesn't realise that or be connected to it anymore. I can see it in her memory banks. Otherwise, she wouldn't have succumbed to SIM so easily. The only time she was strong was when we were together."

"She clearly needs her SANA mate for fuller activation of her power."

Halia stepped forward. "But he is in 6D, and she is still in 4D. And the SIM agent threatened him. How could that work?"

Everyone in the Hall of Congress meditated, discussed and researched any data they could find in the Hall of Records. After an exhaustive search, a man came forward onto the central platform next to Hadden. "There is one precedent. I was the brother of a Pentada SANA mate in a previous life. Does anyone remember?"

Hadden searched his past life memory banks, and an image of two brothers working side-by-side came to mind. "I think so."

"He was separated from his SANA mate in the same way, 4D and 6D. They had a talisman that reconnected them and helped her break free from SIM enough to continue with the mission."

"Daphne and I do have a talisman. Two Azurite stones. That might just work."

Halia asked, "But how will you negotiate around SIM?"

Hadden sighed. "I don't know."

"Do what you can as soon as possible," Nibel warred. "It's very important that you keep her from coming into any physical connection with the other four members of Pentada. She is infected now and could pass it on to others. Since Pentada anchor the consciousness of all Heliotropans, that could destabilize the entire city."

Hadden nodded. "Thank you. I will do my best."

When Hadden returned to 4D, he went to Daphne's room. Annika was there. *The Task Force must already be back from Tinaghan.* Much to his chagrin, they stood at the window with their arms around each other.

Annika was talking. "When Tia found me, I lived as a hermit in our old apartment in Montréal. All I had was that amethyst that Hadden had given us to protect me."

"What amethyst?"

"Remember when we met Hadden in the late 70s, he gave us each an upgraded amethyst that he had created?"

Daphne shook her head. "I don't know what you're talking about."

"You know, when he jumped the timeline in 1960 and saw the future?"

"He never said anything like that to me."

362

At that moment, Hadden realised that Annika lived by the second timeline, whereas Daphne lived by the first. After getting permission from SANA to enter Annika's mind, he scanned for the virus and found it. It had already entered through skin contact and moved through her bloodstream towards the brainstem. Instead of the energy signature of Josie Carbona, it was her sister Irene. That made sense, given that Irene used to be Annika's handler and understood how her mind worked. Now that Josie had a foothold, she let in other SIM agents as etheric level viruses to Helio Tropez.

In Annika's memory banks, he discovered the same two timelines running parallel, except that the switch pointed to the second timeline. He needed to move fast to remove the first timeline completely. That's when Irene came forward in full strength, removing the second timeline. This created a domino effect, undoing all the healing work on Annika's mind.

Irene said to him, *This asset belongs to us. You are a trespasser here. I will harm the asset unless you leave immediately.*

Hadden acknowledged the threat and left Annika's mind, retreating back to the corner of the room.

Annika held each temple, grimacing.

"What's wrong?"

"I have a horrible headache. I think I need to go lie down."

They hugged goodbye, and Annika left.

Hadden interfaced with Halia and the 6D Elders to discuss how to manage this rapidly deteriorating situation.

We need to create an anti-virus. In the meantime, keep Metta away from both Daphne and Annika.

When he went to check in on Metta, she was sitting next to Xander on a sofa. He seemed in good spirits.

"The healers at the House of Indicum are amazing. They told me that my aptitude is Audient-Attention. It's also known as *The Lover*. But SIM used my power for their agenda. By grooming me as a rockstar that fans would adore, they could steal people's energy during my concerts. I'm finally free of that! Everyone from Helio Tropez has a kind of superpower that can be used for good, so we need to find out what yours is."

"I just want to go home, Dax."

"This is your home. Your sister is here, and apparently, your mother has just arrived. Don't you want to see them?"

"I don't remember my mother or sister. They're strangers to me. You are the only person that's not a stranger. I think we should find a way to leave."

He pulled back from her, searching her face. "I don't want to leave."

Metta sighed and snuggled in closer. "Come on. Please, come with me. Please, help me."

Xander stood up. "Just give it some time."

They heard a trilling sound, and an image came up on her console with the name Daphne Zuris underneath.

Xander grinned. "It looks like your mother is here to visit you."

Hadden wondered how to stop the physical interaction between them. He reluctantly dialled up on a memory where Metta, as a child, realised that her mother wasn't coming back.

"I don't want to see her."

"You haven't seen your mother since you were five years old."

"Exactly. What would we say to each other?"

Xander pressed ENTER, and Daphne stepped into the room. They looked so similar with their long red ringlets and freckled skin. Daphne had glassy eyes as she reached out her arms.

"Metta! There you are. All grown up. I'm so sorry…"

Metta recoiled from the embrace. Hadden instilled in her a fear of touching her mother. In his haste, he forgot to ask for permission from SANA.

"Please, don't touch me."

Daphne flinched. "Metta, I've spent years trying to get back to you. In my timeline, it's only been three years, but in your timeline, it's been twenty-six years. I've been crying my eyes out. Please, I don't know what to say…"

"Then don't say anything." Metta's chin trembled. "Three years is still a long time to leave a five-year-old with a neighbour."

"They told me I would be back in a few days."

"Sure they did."

"You don't believe me?"

364

"It's hard to know what to believe. All this is… so bizarre."

Daphne sat on a chair opposite the sofa. "It's my fault. I never told you about SIM or about Helio Tropez…"

"I'll leave you two to talk," Xander said, backing out of the room.

"No, don't leave…" Metta said, clutching his arm.

He pulled away. "My mother was taken away from me too, but it wasn't her fault. You two need to talk." He tucked a strand of hair behind her ear. "Just listen and keep an open mind. I'll be back later, okay?"

Metta closed her eyes, her lip trembling, but she nodded. With that, the door slid closed. Mother and daughter looked down, stroking their hair in a very similar fashion.

Daphne leaned forward, and in a soft voice, asked, "What happened to you? Do you remember?"

"You want all the gory details?"

"Yes. I think so." Daphne said with a grimace.

Metta slumped on the far end of the sofa. "I guess the neighbour got tired of looking after me and gave me to a social worker. I went from one foster home to another. I ran away at fourteen because of all the beating, molesting and alcoholism my foster parents put me through."

Daphne's chin dropped. "Oh my God…"

"On the street, I met this girl named Ruth Carbona who brought me to meet a school headmaster. It was a school for performing artists and writers. They put a roof over my head, three square meals on my plate, and a place to get educated. I've been writing songs for them ever since. They were the first people to treat me half-decently."

"I was so afraid of that." Daphne squeezed her eyes shut. "Even as a baby, I knew you were a strong Ecrivent-Acceptance."

"I don't know what that means."

"We all have a special aptitude…"

"Yeah, Xander told me about 'superpowers.'"

"That man who just left? Who is he?"

"He's a musician friend. We used to sort of… date. Apparently, my sister rescued both of us. I didn't even know I had a sister. You never told me."

365

Daphne frowned. "Yes, you have a twin sister. I planned to tell you when you were older. SIM made us separate you, and I haven't seen her since she was three years old."

"I met her in Montreal. She called herself Linda, but she looks nothing like me."

"She always looked a lot more like your father." -

With flaring nostrils, Metta zeroed in on her. "And my father is...?"

"Hadden Violetta, but... he died trying to rescue Tia."

They both sat in silence for a few moments, looking away from each other.

Daphne swallowed. "Listen, I understand why you're angry. I never meant to abandon you. I just want you to know that. I'm so sorry all that happened, but I'm here now."

Metta looked off in the distance with a furrowed brow. "Thank you for saying that. I resented you for years, but it sounds like it wasn't your choice."

"Not at all. They held me captive."

Her face softened around the eyes. "That's a relief for me but horrible for you."

"Being a slave was a terrible life, but here, we can escape from that."

"Okay. Look, this is a lot to process. I'm not saying I forgive anyone or that I'm ready to throw my old life away, but I understand better now. Give me time, okay? I think I just need to rest for now."

"Of course. I'll go."

Metta stood up and lost her balance. As she did, Daphne lunged forward to help stabilise her. Before Hadden could move, he saw the virus pass from mother to daughter, and he let out a groan. Metta lay down on the bed, and Daphne kissed her forehead.

A Healing Bay attendant rushed in and examined the monitor. "Stand back, please. Her vitals are suddenly weak. I need to see what caused that."

"We just had a very emotional conversation," Daphne said in a ragged voice.

"Okay, we'll monitor her. You should probably go."

Daphne backed out of the room with a distant, empty stare.

Hadden saw the virus move into Metta's bloodstream and head for the brain stem. He sensed the energy signature of her handler, Ruth. Rather than go through the same confrontation and risk Metta's life, he backed out and left 4D entirely.

Hadden returned to Halia in 6D full of anxiety and defeat. "Now, all five of them are infected."

Halia turned on him. "What? How could you let that happen?!" Halia rarely got angry like that. "The entire 25,000-year project is at risk here."

Shockwaves ran through him. "I know."

"Hadden, you *need* to keep the five Pentada separate. If they physically connect, it could create the anchor effect that the Elders warned us about."

"I don't know how I can stop that. They've been looking for each other all their lives, and finally, they are in one place. I'm going to need help."

"We've been working on the anti-virus ever since you left. If SIM agents can transform themselves into viruses, we should be able to transform ourselves into anti-viruses, but we need to better understand the properties of the virus first before reconstructing our own energy signatures in anti-viral form," Halia said.

Triol frowned. His Voyent-Acceptance aptitude, now amplified in 6D, allowed him to see into the past. "Trying to become an anti-virus to a SIM agent has always been a suicide mission."

A realisation dawned on Hadden, and a surge of adrenaline coursed through his veins. "Up until now..."

Halia turned to look at him. "You know something... How can we find out more about the virus?"

"I will see if I can capture a sample and bring it back. If we can reverse engineer their process, we should be able to find a way to combat them."

She watched him with pursed lips, thinking. At last, she sighed. "Alright, but be careful."

CHAPTER 38

Helio Tropez – 2011

B ack at her apartment in Helio Tropez, Tia breathed a sigh of relief. Although she had loved Tinaghan, she'd had a strange headache the whole time. In fact, she'd had the headache ever since returning from the surface. *I'm just tired from all the intensity*, she thought. *Or, maybe I'm just lovestruck.* After a long nap, she opened her console and pulled up her copy of the MindStory Code.

By everyone's standards, the Task Force had achieved its goal of mapping out the code, but without the influence of the last two members of Pentada, the code lacked full integrity. Soon, they could remedy that. She closed her eyes and reached out to Hadden telepathically.

I'm back. Are you available to talk? After a few moments of silence, Tia sat in her chair overlooking the city and closed her eyes to change her frequency. Because of napping, her brain wave was still too much in the Delta range. She needed to be more in a Theta-Alpha brain wave state to connect with 6D. As she imagined the waveforms of Theta and Alpha increasing, her mind became more alert. All of a sudden, she heard Hadden say, *Tia, can you hear me? I need to share some urgent information.*

I'm here, but the connection is very static. What's happening?

I sped up the healing process for Daphne and Metta, and they're both awake now.

That's amazing!

It's good and bad. It's allowed a virus to activate.

What virus?

Josie Carbona. You were right – she's managed to get in. She hijacked her way to Helio Tropez by taking the form of a virus that entered your skin cells.

Dread crept up Tia's spine. *How? They scanned me. I didn't feel or notice anything.*

Clearly, SIM agents are far more sophisticated than we suspected. She influenced you and the Task Force to go looking for Daphne on Anatol. Then, she compelled you to touch your mother's hand and spread the virus.

Tia recoiled at the idea of a SIM virus in her system. *But they didn't even detect it on Anatol.*

We suspect that the virus stayed in your physical body, but didn't travel with your light body, maybe to avoid detection on Anatol.

Do I still have the virus, or did it leave me when it went to Daphne?

You may still have it.

Does that mean that anyone I've touched now has the virus as well?

It could be. Depending on a person's level of soul development, their system could kill off the virus.

Tia wrapped her arms around her waist, engulfed by guilt. *What is Josie's agenda?*

She established herself as Daphne's handler on the surface. That means Daphne has subconscious agreements in place for Josie to take back control. Although we tried to remove them, she managed to shift Daphne back to the original timeline before I changed things. Now, all the original CM programs have reinstalled themselves.

So all the good healing work is gone?

It's reverted back to full SIM control at the mind level.

So, where is she now?

She's awake, and she's already spread the virus to Annika and Metta. I tried to prevent it but failed. You are the only one able to communicate with me so far in 4D. That's why I've come to you.

What can I do?

Right now, the only Pentada free from the virus is Cassandra.

Tia's heart sank. *But I touched Cassandra several times since I've been back. We just hugged goodbye at the bus platform.*

Of course. I'm just hoping that at least one Pentada could kill off the virus.

How can we tell if I killed the virus or if it's still there?

I can check to see which timeline is active in your mind.

Go ahead.

After a few minutes, Hadden said, *I do sense the presence of the virus. It's in your system, but not it's activated. At least, not yet. Your second timeline is still in effect. Maybe that's because you had a better relationship with your SIM counterpart, Andrea, and that makes you immune.*

That's good if it's true. What can I do to help?

I don't completely understand the SIM agenda here. The Elders in 6D want to work on an anti-virus, but they need more information on how the virus operates. They suggest you get me a reading on your blood and DNA.

Tia grimaced, wondering how she would do that.

Hadden picked up on her discomfort and sent a calming frequency to her. *Go to the Healing Bay. But don't tell them what it's for. We don't want to cause a panic. In the meantime, you need to prevent contact between all five Pentada. That might be SIM's way of corrupting the whole city and the ascension project.*

Tia nodded, already heading towards the Healing Bay at The Palace of Zuris. As soon as she entered the lobby, she saw Daphne and Annika talking in the lounge area. Stopping dead in her tracks, Tia turned to face the other way. Beads of sweat formed on her brow. *How can I pass by unnoticed?* Otherwise, a physical reunion would be impossible to avoid. She ducked behind a pillar to watch, hoping they would leave soon. A few moments later, Cassandra and Meraton joined them.

"You're awake so much earlier than scheduled!" Cassandra said, reaching for a hug.

Daphne stood up and let both parents embrace her, although her face remained grim. Next, they turned to Annika, but she refused the hug. With a stern demeanour, she sat down and crossed her arms. *What happened to the lovestruck woman she had just witnessed at Tinaghan?* Tia thought.

They sat down together and started to talk.

"Daphne, have you re-connected with your daughters yet?"

Daphne's face stiffened. "Metta, yes. Tia, no,"

Cassandra looked around the lobby. "Tia must be around here somewhere. It's a miracle we are all finally back together."

They continued talking about her healing process and how well she was adjusting. Tia realised the conversation could go on for a long time. *Perhaps I could go to the Healing Bay at the Palace of Indicum*, she thought. *It would be a good excuse to reconnect with Xander.* As she ducked out of the entrance, she walked at a clipped pace. *If I could fly, this trip would be much faster*, she thought, looking up in the air at people flitting around the city with shopping bags. As she turned a corner, she ran into Ramu.

"Tia! I'm looking forward to meeting your sister. Do you know where she is? Maybe you can introduce us."

Ramu lunged towards her for a hug, but she side-stepped him. "Yes, once she's better acclimatised. They estimate it could still be weeks, though."

He looked down, trying not to look disappointed. "Okay. I understand."

"I've got to go. Sorry about that."

"Going to find Xander?"

"No. Well, yes. I have another pressing matter," she said, purposely choosing to hide her thoughts.

Just then, another voice behind her said, "Tia! It's nice to see you."

She swivelled around. "Niklana, nice to see you." Looking for an excuse to get out of talking to both of them, she said, "You may remember, Ramu. You predicted his SANA mate, and he thought it was me, but I suspect it's my twin sister."

She looked at Ramu. "Yes, of course I remember you. And yes, Tia's sister, Metta of Zuris, indeed. Let me think about that a moment." Niklana touched the silver tip on the top of her head, "I would need to meet Metta. But I don't see SANA mate energy between you and Tia. Although it can be confusing as the energy signature of twins is very similar."

"Right? Exactly," he said, staring at Tia.

Tia feigned a smile. "Totally understandable. I'm just in a hurry right now."

Niklana looked confused. Few people in Helio Tropez hurried anywhere. "Where are you going?"

"To the Palace of Indicium."

"I'm going there, too. I'll walk with you."

Tia nodded politely and turned to Ramu. "See you soon?"

He frowned. "Sure."

They started up the winding pathway to the Palace together.

"I just wanted to congratulate you. You found your SANA mate on the surface and brought him here."

"Yes. You were right about his birthdate and lineage. Thank you so much."

Tia looked over her shoulder and saw Metta coming towards them. She pulled Niklana into an alcove overlooking a waterfall.

"By the way, Niklana. I understand you also helped my aunt Annika with her SANA mate." Tia said, trying to find a justification for pulling the woman off the path.

Niklana looked confused. "Um... yes. Your mother came to see me not too long ago, wondering about Annika. She mentioned that her daughter romantically preferred women and was wondering if there was a way to have a SANA mate anyway, given she is Pentada. As you know, it's important that she has a SANA mate, not just for her, but for the entire harvest of souls."

Tia noticed Metta walk past and turned her attention back to Niklana. "I understand that ascension happens because of the marriage of the masculine and feminine principles within you, so does the gender of your mate really matter? "

"Well, yes and no. As you may know, the masculine body has a microcosmic orbit that spins in one direction, and the female body has a microcosmic orbit that spins in the opposite direction. Therefore, people of the same gender would just reinforce polarity and not create unity. They would have to find another way to ascend outside sexual union. It just seems like a lot of extra work."

Tia shrugged. "If you prefer the same gender, I guess you will just find another way."

"I suppose, but gender confusion has been used as one of SIM's tricks to keep people from ascending, if I'm not mistaken?"

Tia was growing annoyed by the limited beliefs of some older Heliotropans but didn't want to get into an argument. "I don't know."

Niklana's face lit up, "Unless they've already integrated. Has Annika integrated already?"

"Annika definitely seems like an old soul to me. Her masculine and feminine sides are probably well integrated."

"That's why Stavron is a good choice, because he's well integrated, too. All those challenging years being so different from the others here. It helps with the spiritual growth."

"So you're saying Annika and Stavron aren't SANA mates?"

"No, I think they are. I gave the birthdate and House to Cassandra, then she did the research and figured out it was Stavron. He was the only one with that combination. I bet that's why she invited him onto your Task Force."

"Only Annika will know for sure if he is the right one."

"Of course, dear. It's just that I am almost always correct on these things."

"I hope so. It does seem to be going well so far." Tia shifted from one foot to another. "Look, it's been great chatting with you, but I do have to go."

"Give my regards to your lovely man..."

Tia nodded, then ran down the path and entered through the doors of The Palace of Indicum. When she arrived at the Healing Bay area, she saw Xander and Metta in an intimate embrace. When she kissed him on the lips, Tia stepped back outside the entrance of the Healing Bay, wondering what to do next. Her heart went cold and nausea boiled up in her stomach.

She ran past Niklana, who was deep into discussion with the Palace Director. Tears stung her eyes. How could this happen? On the one hand, it made sense that Xander could be attracted to Metta—they were twins after all. That said, all thoughts of common sense seemed hard to access at that

373

moment. Instead, her body tremored, and the pounding in her ears made it difficult to even see the path before her.

In the Garden of Jephonsite, she found a quiet, private place by an oak tree and allowed herself to scream. She picked up a dead branch and hit it repeatedly against the tree trunk, shouting, "How dare she! I hate her! I hate him! I don't want to be here! I hate them all!"

Once she exhausted herself, she collapsed back down on a bench, breathing hard, sweat running down her temples. Since leaving the surface, she rarely succumbed to negative emotions. Maybe the virus had activated after all. She needed to get the test done. *But where?* There was a Healing Bay at the Palace of Violetta. She wiped the tears, resolved to focus on the task at hand.

The Palace of Violetta glowed like a purple heart rising six stories high. As she approached the attendant at The Healing Bay desk, her heart skipped a beat. "I'd like to get a blood and DNA sample."

"What's it for?"

"Just for my own research."

"Research into what?"

Tia took a deep breath and remembered that people in Helio Tropez could detect lying easily. "My father is from the House of Violetta and ..."

"...you want to look into your patrilineal markers? Got it." The man said without looking up from his console. "I did that once and it was so fascinating."

An hour later, she had the results. Their readings showed nothing out of the ordinary, no strange virus. She went back to her room and interfaced with Hadden. Using a data transfer process he taught her, Hadden then brought the results back to the lab in 6D Helio Tropez.

Rest reassured. We will get to the bottom of this. In the meantime, keep away from the others. I can see that the virus is trying to trigger your survival brain, especially with this Xander issue. Don't take the bait. I'll get back to you as soon as I can.

A rush of embarrassment overtook her. *Why was she so upset about Xander and Metta? She had kissed Ramu, who might be Metta's mate. Does it really matter? She hardly knew Xander anyway. Perhaps those two were better suited. Maybe the SANA mate predictions were wrong. She didn't have time to worry about romance at a time like this.*

Back at her console, Tia resolved to get back to work on the MindStory Code, but her mind started to wander again. *Maybe if Metta got to meet Ramu, she would lose her attraction for Xander.*

After scrolling through her comm to find Ramu's name, she sat looking at it for several minutes until finally hitting the 'call' button.

"Ramu! Good news. Metta is up and about. Do you want to meet her?"

"Sure. I hope she's as beautiful as you."

"Much more so. You'll love her. I'll meet you outside the Palace of Zuris in one hour."

Tia headed back to her room, took a shower, and straightened up her appearance. At the Palace, Ramu sat in his formal way on a bench near the fountain and jumped up upon her arrival. She hugged him, knowing that he may have the virus anyway. They went inside and hit the comm for Metta's room. No one answered.

"Let's go to The Palace of Indicum. She might be there visiting a friend."

On the way out, Annika appeared out of nowhere. "Tia! Your mother is awake."

"Yes, I heard."

"She's just over there and wants to meet you."

Cassandra sat with Daphne. Four out of five of Pentada in close proximity was not a good thing. "I'll go meet her in a little while. We were just in the middle of something..."

"It's not important," Ramu insisted. "You must go see your mother!"

Annika waved at them and then pointed at Tia. Daphne jumped up and ran over with her arms wide open.

"My baby girl, all grown up!"

Daphne bundled her into a hug, and Tia melted upon impact. Childhood memories came rushing back. The smell of her hair and her skin, the sound of her voice. Waves of love flooded through her. Tears flowed for both of them, and they held each other tighter. Annika and Cassandra joined them. Ramu and Meraton stood back as the four women embraced.

Tia knew it wasn't a good idea, but she didn't want to let go. As she was lost in the embrace, she did not immediately realise that Metta had entered the foyer and seen them there. That's when she joined the embrace. After a few moments, they looked up and laughed through wet eyes.

A shockwave of electricity ran up Tia's spine, until it hit her brain stem. Pulsations of terror burned in every cells. All of them seemed to feel the same thing as they all stood back from each other with looks of horror across their faces. Something evil vibrated through them.

Tia backed away, feeling as if she'd done something terrible to everyone. She ran from the Palace and back to her room to interface with Hadden. After several minutes in meditation, nothing happened. She couldn't calm her mind enough to connect. The world caved in on her. Curling up on her bed, a feeling of numbness blanketed her heart. After all, she had brought the virus to Helio Tropez. Her efforts to bring Pentada back together had led to the worst possible outcome. Torturous thoughts continued to swirl through the night. All the while, she prayed for an anti-virus that never came.

CHAPTER 39

At the Hall of Congress in 6D, the anti-virus Task Force sat in a centre circle facing the Elders, having requested a meeting.

A halo of light came down upon Hadden's face. A nervous energy coursed through him, causing his hands to tremble. "4D Helio Tropez faces a deadly virus. The SIM agent known as Josie Carbona restructured her consciousness as a virus and entered from the surface undetected."

The Elder, Moraira, asked, "How could that have happened?"

"Her consciousness appeared to be a benign human virus on Tia's skin. But when she touched Daphne, the virus activated. When all Pentada made physical contact, SIM went into full lockdown over the entire collective consciousness of 4D Helio Tropez."

A series of gasps arose from the auditorium. Hadden sat down with his head in his hands as they talked it through. As the voices got louder, Hadden sunk deeper into this chair.

Triol whispered to him, "Tell them what we found. They need all the information before they go overboard."

Hadden nodded and sat up straight, "Okay." He then stood up again, collecting himself. "We managed to get more data on the virus to see if we could create an anti-virus."

"That's good. What did you find out?"

"We don't see how to get it to work."

"Why not?"

"It's not a regular virus. As it is a creation of SIM, it's been genetically manipulated, designed solely for the person who has it. For example, Tia hosted the virus, which could only influence her to reach out to the person that it was originally designed for. In other words, it only fully activated upon skin contact with Daphne of Zuris."

"Because Josie Carbona was her SIM handler?" Nibel asked.

"More than that," Hadden added. "Josie is her soul annex."

The Elders nodded in solemn agreement as they understood the soul annex problem in 4D.

"How did SIM get so advanced to bypass the 4D sensors?"

"We are trying to discover that. The lack of involvement from 4D Helio Tropez might be part of the problem. They have entirely stopped monitoring the surface after the Great UnDoing."

Nibel hummed. "They lost proper stewardship of the experiment."

"That's true for us, as well," Halia said.

A shocked silence spread amongst the attendees, and Halia scowled at the room.

"Those of us in 6D are responsible too. We are all connected. The window for ascension is closing, so we must act soon."

The Elders talked amongst themselves again until Nibel took the spotlight. "We are divided on this topic, so we must ask the Progenitors."

They went into prayer and chanted for an hour until the same Progenitor couple materialised. Waleya stepped forward into the centre stage.

"We have been watching your situation. We understand that you would like us to intervene, but that goes against the prime directive. The inhabitants of 4D Helio Tropez need to become the anti-virus themselves. Many of them still need to process all their lifetimes of unresolved emotions. Karma needs to be addressed. This means facing mistakes, owning them, learning from them, forgiving others, and, most importantly, forgiving themselves. It's a personal, conscious choice."

The Congress talked amongst themselves for a few moments until Nibel summarised their thoughts. "What can we do to help them?"

"Start by helping them restore the Fascia Crystalline Network within the body. The trauma and negative emotions have embedded themselves there, but without guidance, they may not heal enough in time. Teach them how to do that. After that, the next steps will become clear."

With that, the Progenitors dematerialized. The Congress remained silent for a long time, absorbing the information and deciding how to proceed.

"How do we teach them?" Hadden asked Halia. "Anyone with the virus now has a weakened intuitive receptor. I tried with Tia, but it seems like she can't sense my presence anymore."

"They have to reach out to us," Halia replied.

The rest of the day, Congress explored what might work. They established a set of best practices for everyone to become familiar with. Soon, twenty people at a time started taking meditation shifts in the central pyramid. They sat in floating egg-shaped chairs to interface and coach anyone in 4D Helio Tropez who would listen.

Hadden joined the first shift to tap into Tia and Daphne, his closest connections. Tia still lay curled up on her bed, tortured by feelings of abandonment. Memories of her mother and sister leaving when she was three circulated in a loop in the hippocampus area of the brain. The meaning she had created was that she couldn't trust people to stay. Hadden himself had remained emotionally absent the majority of his daughter's life, and Xander now appeared to have left her for her own sister. Deep down, she felt unworthy of love. He sent her a positive memory to see if that would awaken her intuitive receptors.

She was seven years old, heading for the carnival rides, holding her father's hand.

"Let's ride the roller coaster!" he said.

"No, I don't want to. I get sick. Remember last time?"

"The trick to not getting sick is to let go of the handlebar. We're going hands-free the whole way!"

The cars pulled up, and they got in. Tia white-knuckled the handlebar and looked down at her feet.

"As soon as we get to the top of the first hill and start to going down, hold your hands up high like this and scream as loud as you can. This is going to be so fun!"

Tia frowned and held on tighter. As they went down the first hill, Hadden let go, but Tia held on, her face turning green.

"Let go, sweetheart! You can do it!"

As the ride came up the next hill, her hands loosened their grip and floated an inch off the handlebar.

"Good, now look up into the sky, not down at the tracks!"

As the ride reached the pinnacle of the next hill, Tia looked up at the brilliant blue sky. The G-force of the ride pulled her arms up high in the air. As the car sped up and thundered down the track, it pulled them both into a standing position. They roared with laughter as the ride went high again and then spiralled down a chute. The laughter at that moment changed her—she went from hating the ride to loving it... in an instant. When it ended, she wanted to go again, but this time, she went hands-free the whole way, laughing and enjoying herself.

Adult Tia's face softened, and her shoulders relaxed. He knew a door had just opened, so he sent her a message.

I'm here to help. We all are.

Dad?

Yes, sweetheart. I'm here.

Tears rolled down her cheeks, and she sat up straight. *Do you have the anti-virus?*

Yes and no. You are the anti-virus. I don't have an external one to give you. It's all part of the ascension process.

She frowned again, and he explained what the Progenitor had said and the best practices from 6D to move into unity consciousness. After a while, she thanked him and pulled herself together so that she could share the information with the other Pentada members.

I can only stay connected to you if you allow it. You'll know that I'm here when I send you a positive memory like I did of the rollercoaster ride. If you let that positive memory in, it changes your brain chemistry enough to open your intuitive receptors. That's the basis of why the MindStory Code works. Remember?

Of course. Got it. Will you come with me to these meetings? It could be hard without some help.

Yes, of course.

On the way to see Cassandra, people walked by with frowns and furrowed foreheads. The virus had clearly spread to everyone. She announced herself on the comm, and Meraton answered.

"It's not a good time, Tia. The Zuris Elders are in the middle of an important discussion," he answered, looking sullen on the comm.

"It's very important. I need to speak to you now."

He sighed in frustration but allowed her to enter. Inside their room, tension filled the air. She explained everything that had happened with Josie, the virus, finding Daphne, spreading the virus, and now, the corruption of Pentada. The group erupted into an argument.

Cassandra held her left hand out in front of her, eyes closed. A stabbing feeling grabbed at Tia's neck, making it hard to speak. The others in the group held their throats, wincing in pain.

"Stop the arguing. Clearly, we should have sent someone to the surface who was born here, not a surface dweller. Now the whole project is corrupted. We have so little time left before this last ascension window."

Geata struggled to say, "I told you we should never have let Tia and Hadden back into Helio Tropez. You used undue pressure to override the Elders because you are so..."

Cassandra interrupted. "Silence!"

Geata's face turned red, and nothing came out of her mouth.

"We had nothing to do with that override, and you know it!"

From 6D, Hadden surrounded the group in compassion. Once he received permission from SANA, he focused his consciousness down to the subatomic level and entered Cassandra's mind. Near the left amygdala, a shadow hovered nearby, triggering fear in her mind, ensuring that Cassandra interpreted all her experiences from a negative perspective. He masked his own energy signature to get closer. As he zeroed in on the shadow form, the image of Blanche Carbona, the matriarch of the Carbona clan, loomed into view. He remembered meeting her at Mount Rainier.

Travelling back in time through her many incarnations, he saw Cassandra splitting a part of herself right at the beginning of the genetic experiment. That rejection had created a separate soul annex, a shadow soul. As with the others, the annex had gotten cut off from SANA, forming its own identity. Like a sunflower left in the shade, the soul annex had wilted and attracted pests in the form of SIM. In this life, the soul annex was known as Blanche Carbone, yet her soul signature looked identical to Cassandra's, except the symbols were in reverse. No bond of love appeared between them. That's when he had an epiphany. The true antivirus didn't destroy the virus but integrated it instead.

To help them bond, Hadden sent Cassandra a calming frequency. Her eyes brightened for a moment, enough to release the grip she had on the others. The whole group scattered in different directions, to get away from her. Instead of staying with Cassandra, Hadden chose to follow after Tia, as he had promised to stay with her.

She ran to the Palace of Zuris holding her throat, still in pain from the encounter with Cassandra. In the lobby, Annika and Daphne sat in conversation. Annika looked like she'd been crying.

"May I join you?" Tia asked reluctantly.

They looked at her blankly and said nothing.

"What's wrong, Annika?" Tia asked, sitting down next to her aunt.

Daphne scoffed. "She's upset because Mr. Wonderful doesn't like her anymore. That's men for you."

"Stavron won't talk to me anymore," Annika sniffed. "We had a fight over …I don't know…over nothing. He said all these nasty things, and that triggered me to say nasty things. And now, we hate each other…I..I just don't get it. How did we lose what we had?"

Tia put a hand on her upper back. "It's just that everyone's got this mind virus. Those thoughts don't belong to him or you – they're part of the infection."

They looked at her and then back at each other, unable to process what she had said.

Daphne rolled her eyes and turned back to Annika. "Don't waste any more time on him. Move on."

Two men walked by, eyeing Daphne up and down, then whistled. Tia stared at them, shocked. Men in Helio Tropez never objectified women like that before. Clearly, the virus had installed SIM programs common on the surface of the planet. *The Gender Misery* program, in particular, caused men and women to objectify, hurt, disrespect and abandon each other. This helped SIM maintain control, stopping ascension.

Annika frowned. "It's easy for you to say. Men are always attracted to you. He's the only man I ever felt happy with."

"Grow up, Annika. You only just met him."

The two men stood near the entrance of the palace. Daphne shrugged and stood up before walking towards them with an alluring smile. Annika shook her head in disbelief.

Hadden drew back, finding the scene too painful to watch. He remembered all the years trying to help Daphne remove the Femme Fatale programs she had received from SIM. Now they were clearly back online.

Tia sat with Annika, trying to console her, but to no avail. After a few minutes, Annika rushed off in a flood of tears. Hadden telepathically suggested Tia go to Metta's room instead. After several tries with no answer on the comm, Tia went to the Palace of Indicum. As she was going down the steps towards the palace entrance, Metta came running up and flew past her.

"Metta!"

She ignored her and kept running. Tia caught up with her when she stopped to catch her breath. "What's going on? Why are you running?"

"Leave me alone!" Metta said, red-faced.

"Is this about Xander?"

"He's a jerk. I hate him!"

"What happened?"

"He's got every woman in that place fawning over him. I don't even know why I'm surprised – he's always been like that."

Tia stepped back and wrapped her arms around her waist. "I'm sorry to hear that. Have you met Ramu yet? He's your true SANA mate."

"My what?"

"We all have a true SANA mate who helps us ascend. Yours is Ramu. He's eager to get to know you."

"That guy with the weird silver cap and the needy energy? He's clearly in love with you, not me. He's got you on a pedestal, just like Xander does. Why, I don't know. Maybe the same reason our father chose you over me. I guess I just got stuck with the wrong parent. He didn't even come to find me when Daphne left."

"He wasn't allowed to have any contact with you. They programmed him that way with a suicide program! And, he never even knew what happened to you."

"Bullshit."

Tia's face froze trying not to react. "You just need some time with Ramu. Your true SANA mate is supposed to be an otherworldly experience ..."

Metta shook her head. "To him, I'm probably just another low life from the surface. I hate this place. I just want to leave."

"Listen, Metta, you have a mind virus. Almost everyone's got it, throughout the whole city. These angry thoughts aren't the real you."

Metta glared at her.

"Just sit down here with me and take some deep breaths."

She refused and stood looking away with arms crossed.

Tia continued, "I felt the same way when I first came here. People here just aren't used to surface humans. Plus, everyone's got this SIM virus now. It's not the truth of the situation. We can heal from this if we work together."

"Look, if our grandparents came to the surface on a mission and then returned without their own children, that's a sign. They don't want to stick together – they're just looking out for themselves. This place seems beautiful on the outside, but people here are just as selfish as people on the surface."

Tia stood back, took a deep breath, and said nothing. Hadden surrounded them both in compassion and returned to 6D with a heavy heart. In many ways, Metta's conclusion had plenty of truth to it, virus or not.

CHAPTER 40

Helio Tropez – 2012

Eight months after the virus had infected people, things only grew worse in 4D Helio Tropez. Most people's Jenios had fled back into nature, feeling unsafe in the presence of a human possessed by SIM. Most people blamed Tia for this change of events, and on the rare occasions when she ventured from her chambers, she donned a headscarf as a disguise.

Today, she felt the need to try again to bring people back to sanity. Setting out from her spiral building, she headed straight towards the Palace of Zuris.

"Please, go away," Cassandra said to her over the comm. "We're not interested in reinstating the Task Force. No one wants to. We just need to weather the storm until all the infected people get well or die off."

"Die off?" Tia said, aghast. "What happened to helping them?"

"It's their lack of evolution that's causing the problem – there's nothing we can do."

"There's lots we could do."

"We've tried."

"Have you? That kind of attitude shows that you've got the SIM virus too."

"I hardly think so. Look in the mirror."

Cassandra and Meraton now lived locked away in an upper wing of the Palace of Zuris along with the other Elders, all insisting that they were free of the virus.

Meraton got on the comm and said, "You've caused enough damage here, Tia. As we said many times before, those of you from the surface need to go back. If you don't go willingly, the Protectors will have to force you. I'm sorry, but you don't belong here."

He switched off the comm, leaving Tia frozen on the spot. A rage escalated in her heart. *They once supported me to stay in Helio Tropez. They were the ones who had suggested that I go on a dangerous mission to the surface to find other members of Pentada. Everyone knew about the risks. It wasn't my fault!* Going back to the surface meant being targeted by SIM and possibly getting tortured and turned into an asset. That said, SIM had now clearly flourished in the subterranean world too. There seemed to be no escape.

Back in the spiral tower, she called Annika. At first, there was no answer on the comm. After several tries, Annika appeared on the monitor looking bloated and overweight.

"What do you want?"

"To check in on you. How are you doing?"

"Not well. Just like everyone else."

"I just want to see if I can help. They want to teleport us – the people born on the surface – to go back there."

"I know. That's why I'm not leaving my room. I'm never going back there."

"Me either. But you can't just stay locked away in your room."

"It's working for me. Although, can you fix my replicator? It only gives me a small amount of food now."

"That happened to me too. I suspect the Elders are rationing everyone's replicators now."

Annika grimaced. "What! They can't do that!"

"Apparently, they can. I can't help you, but the people in 6D are here for us. Reach out to them."

"Yeah, yeah... all your ghosts in 6D. Can they fix my replicator?"

"They fixed mine."

"You know what, maybe I'll try speaking to your ghosts. How do I do it?"

"First, you have to be willing and agree to be helped so you can ascend."

"And they'll fix my replicator then? I don't need to ascend. I need to eat."

"If you don't reach out to them, you'll have to barter with others..."

"Like Daphne? That's the last thing I would do. Thanks for checking in, kid, but don't bother anymore."

Tia stood looking at the blank screen, feeling an icy constriction at the back of her throat. Walking towards the promenade, she went to check in on Metta. As usual, she was working with a small group of women growing and harvesting the Hepa plant.

Metta sat at a table, crumbling dried leaves and laying them flat on rolling papers for people to smoke. "Tia! Come join us." Speaking to her companions, she said, "You all remember my twin sister Tia?"

The other women looked at her through half-closed lids and nodded.

"I haven't seen you in months. Where have you been?" Metta asked.

"I stay home mostly," Tia said, taking a seat beside her.

"Why? We could use your help here. The demand for our cigarillos is far outnumbering our supply."

"Actually, Meraton wants us to go back to the surface, so I'm hiding out."

She grunted. "I heard about that, but the Protectors haven't come for us yet."

"Listen, I really suggest you reach out to our father, Hadden. He's already moved to 6D. He can help you get ready for ascension."

"I tried, like you suggested, but I don't really hear anything. I don't remember him at all. Anyway, I'm on a roll writing new songs – the Hepa plant helps me get creative."

The Hepa plant was only supposed to be used sparingly during sacred ceremonies to access higher frequencies. Overuse could cause the opposite effect.

"Smoking the Hepa plant is blocking your ability to ascend."

"I know you keep saying that, but I am kind of addicted now. I can't imagine life without my smoke."

"This is another one of SIM's tricks to keep you enslaved."

"I'm not so sure. Maybe this ascension thing is a trick. Why is it also called the Harvest? With a Hepa plant, you have to kill the plant to harvest it. Maybe SANA is the real enemy here, Tia." Metta snickered. "Maybe it just wants to kill us and smoke us."

"Ascension means a harvest of souls. We've reached a certain level of development, so now, we change form to serve SANA in a higher consciousness way."

"That's exactly what we're doing with the Hepa plants. They are changing form from alive plant to dead plant to raise our consciousness."

Tia sighed and stood up.

"Don't go. Help us roll. I'll give you one for your efforts."

"I don't want any, thanks."

"You are such a prude, Tia," a woman said.

Tia turned and resisted a gasp. "Amelia! I didn't know you were part of the group."

With a cigarillo hanging out of her mouth and a buzz cut, she looked very different. "I just joined. You should try one of these before you knock 'em."

"I thought you had become a Sanasta. Don't they renounce all these kinds of substances?"

"The Sanastas disbanded a while back. Nobody feels drawn to prayers and rituals anymore. I'm relieved, actually. It was all too rigorous for me."

Tia looked around the group and realised that several of the women were Sanastas or had left their SANA mates.

"Where is Sevo?" Tia asked Renate.

"We parted ways."

"What about you, Alma?"

"Same thing. All of us are single now. I think we're all done with men," Alma replied as she cut up leaves with a razor blade.

"My mate wants to be with many women, not just one," another woman said.

"My mate wants to be with many men, not just one," Renate added, and the rest of them burst into laughter.

They talked amongst themselves for a while, complaining about men, especially the groups of men who raided and stole from other groups.

Metta inspected the leaf of a Hepa plant, one side, then the other. "The whole SANA mate thing is just a lie, trying to enslave us."

"I think it's actually the other way around," Tia said. "You break free of enslavement by going through the Hierogamic Union with your SANA mate."

"You do realise that you are one of the very few people who still believe all that crap?" Amelia asked.

The women laughed in a way that reminded her of the mean girls in high school. Lowering her head, Tia walked away without saying goodbye. Daphne now also worked with a group of other women, not to make Hepa cigarettes but to service men sexually in one of the meditation pagodas that now acted as a brothel. All the SIM programs from the surface of the planet now grew strong in Helio Tropez.

The Gender Misery program blocked the Hierogamic union and compelled men and women to use each other or cause them misery. Since the Elders had reprogrammed the replicators to ration people's daily needs, people found other ways around that. The prostitutes exchanged sex for food. The men foraged their own food in the forests in gangs. After spending weeks in the forest, they came back to get their sexual needs met and then left again.

Daphne sat with two other women, Looma and Aspra, near the entrance of the pagoda. All three were dressed in revealing lingerie, making Tia feel embarrassed for them.

"Tia! Have you finally agreed to join us?" Daphne smiled.

"No!" she said more forcefully than she wanted. "I'm just checking in on you."

"Tia, you could charge a hefty fee with that lovely figure and alluring eyes," one of the women said. "I'd love to put some makeup on you. Will you let me?"

"Not right now, thanks."

"She's a puritan, Wilma. Leave her alone."

Tia flashed a false smile. "I just want to talk to my mother for a moment privately."

The two women smirked and sauntered inside the pagoda.

"Don't call me your mother around here. I know it's normal for people of different generations here to look the same age, but it could get in the way of business."

"Okay. I'll just call you Daphne." Tia sat down on the bench. A man walked up, covered in dirt and carrying a crossbow.

"Have you come for Looma?" Daphne asked.

"Whoever you have. What about her?" he asked, pointing his chin at Tia.

"No. I don't work here," she sneered.

Daphne laughed. "Looma's inside, waiting for you."

Tia wrinkled her nose and said, "Hadden reaches out to you, but you don't respond."

"I know, you keep nagging me about that. I just don't see him, and I wonder if you actually see him too. The bond between you two was strong on the surface. Maybe you're just imagining him."

"I don't think so. He's living in 6D, and he can help you get there, especially since he is your SANA mate. In fact, he's said he's willing to descend back into 4D to help you. It would be a big sacrifice because he might not be able to go back. But he will do it if you ask him."

Daphne shrugged and looked off into the distance with a vacant stare. Loss welled up inside. Her mother didn't seem to care about him the same way he cared about her.

Tia sighed, frustrated. "Look, I get it. You don't care anymore. But it will only work if you are willing. The ascension window is fast approaching, and hardly anyone has made any progress. As Pentada members, we have the biggest responsibility."

"Do you know that everyone here calls you *The Evangelist*? You should go and hang out with the other Evangelists."

"Who?"

"Those that see ghosts from other dimensions."

"There are others," Tia exclaimed, her mouth gaping.

"Oh, yes. They left the city to live in that pagoda up in the mountains."

The sound of shuffling gravel made Tia look up. Two Protectors came down the path, walking in their direction.

Tia panicked and said, "I gotta go. The Protectors want to send us back to the surface."

Daphne chuckled. "Those two come here all the time. They're customers."

"I don't want to take any chances. See you later."

She went back to her room and found that her passkey no longer worked. *They've shut me out!* Sitting in a nearby courtyard, she called on 6D. Nothing happened. Fear of homelessness lowered her vibrational state and blocked the connection. In an attempt to calm down, she headed to a nearby garden and sat on a bench. Down a hill, off in the distance, a group of people sat in a circle on the grass. One man sat in a throne-like chair speaking to them while a woman massaged his feet. She watched for a while, wondering about them. Then a woman brought each person a cup of liquid. They drank it and lay back on the grass. Curious, she moved closer to overhear their conversation. Finding a bench closer by and sitting there, she realised that the man was Xander.

She overheard him say, "This journey with Bejula will break you free from the pain that you feel and give you the power to ascend."

In the subterranean world, people knew about the hallucinogenic properties of the Bejula plant. Although it had started out as a medicinal plant to heal cuts and abrasions, or to calm an agitated heart, some people used it to seek visions. At first, it connected you to higher density realms, but later, it sank you into a hellish experience. The Hall of Records now labelled it as 'A Trick of SIM.'

After a while, the brew kicked in, and many people started writhing and howling in agony as the hallucinations took the form of dark entities taunting them. Every now and again, people crawled over to Xander. He touched their forehead and predicted their future, a beautiful place of serenity and empowerment. Then, he offered them more brew to go deeper towards Nirvana. Instead, the brew brought them farther away. After watching them for a while, Tia couldn't take it anymore and left.

Back at her chambers, she tried her passkey again. It still didn't work. She slumped against the wall just outside her room, feeling hopeless and despairing. Although she knew that this lower vibrational frequency would block a connection with 6D, she just couldn't shake it. Outside of the window, she looked down at a ragged woman pulling a floating wagon with a few belongings behind her.

The reality of no home and no replicator shocked her system enough to make her remember the work they'd been doing on the new MindStory Code. The body-mind system manifested things into reality based on vibration. The lower the vibration, the more you bring dense, hard, uncomfortable, painful realities into existence. The higher the vibration, the more you bring light, easy, comfortable, healing realities into existence. Also, the body-mind system couldn't tell between imagination and reality, so imagining a better reality changed your vibrational frequency. She decided to focus on a happy memory.

One day, Amelia had taken her to see the Cave of Christos Sophia within the Temple of Lions. They had teleported outside the city to the edge of the Nalia Valley and landed outside the entrance. Heliotropans had performed ceremonies inside the cave, such as fertility rituals, funerals and weddings. Multi-coloured stalactites had hung down, glowing violet, purple, turquoise, pink and green. Thousands of inscriptions had adorned the limestone walls, marking the purpose of each ceremony. Peacefulness and elation had descended upon her the moment she had stepped inside. Amelia had then pointed to one of the inscriptions marking the Wedding Ceremony of Halia and Triol.

Tia smiled as the memory took shape in her mind. Closing her eyes, she took a deep breath and felt the tension leave her body. A few moments later, she called out, "Halia-jia?"

A warmth spread through Tia's chest, easing a weight from her shoulders. *Yes, I've been here, waiting for you.*

Thank goodness. I'm locked out. You got my replicator working before. Can you help with the door?

Yes. Of course.

A few minutes later, Halia and her Task Force in 6D had reprogrammed the keycard, overriding the blocking mechanism installed by the 4D Elders.

Thank you!

Over the next few weeks, Tia stayed indoors. She committed to maintaining a good diet, a positive mindset and meditated regularly to keep the 6D connection strong. She worked with the 6D community to learn all twenty-five aptitudes on the MindStory Code. Each had its light and shadow aspect. Halia suggested she start with her dominant, Sentient-Attention. That meant looking at all the occasions when she had used this aptitude to control others or to punish herself. Each time she remembered one, she said a prayer to forgive herself and ask for forgiveness from anyone affected and from SANA.

One day, Hadden came to her telepathically and said, *You're improving a lot.*

I know, but I rarely leave this room. Few people will talk to me, let alone listen to my advice. The Elders want to teleport me back to the surface. Everyone blames me for what happened.

That's about them, not about you. Remember what Waleya said? This is all meant to be.

I wish that the 4D Congress would meet again and invite the Progenitors. But they don't even meet anymore. The Elders just isolate themselves.

Some people in 4D have reached out to us, and we are making progress, Hadden reassured her. *In particular, Xander of Indicum. I answered his call. He's listening now.*

What? He's using the Bejula plant with groups to supposedly spiritually awaken people.

I know. That's why he reached out. It backfired on him and his followers. He's now hit rock bottom. He needs you. I suggest you reach out to him.

Tia coiled her arms around her waist. *He's got plenty of women. He doesn't need me.*

All that behaviour comes from the virus, or in his case, the soul annex known as JJ Redus.

Yes, I met him on the surface. JJ was his manager and handler. Are you saying that he's ready to integrate him?

I believe so. You keep asking me if you're ready to ascend to 6D. This could be the last step in your journey since his soul and your soul have a bonded destiny.

Tia scowled. *He probably won't even talk to me.*

Like you, he's been ostracized now. He needs a friend.

Tia sighed and sat back, looking out at the city that looked drab now. Fewer cars and buses flew by because the Elders had cut off access to most people. The SANA Rosa Academy had shut down. The train station and teleport gate only worked for the Elders.

He's got a good soul, Hadden said gently.

Visions of seeing Xander and Metta together blocked her ability to feel anything for him.

Are you saying that I need to choose him as my mate?

Just reach out and see what's there.

She slumped back in her chair. *But where will I find him?*

He's on the move because he's been cast out. Use your intuition and synchronicity will guide you.

Okay, Dad. I will try

They both laughed. Hadden looked like a young man again. The father-daughter relationship seemed far away. They had since reawakened to past lives, one where she was the parent, and he was the child. She only called him 'Dad' now as a playful way of chiding him when he used the 'fatherly advice tone'.

CHAPTER 41

Helio Tropez – 2012

After two weeks of mulling on the situation, Tia finally made her way to the Palace of Indicum to find Xander. More Protectors than ever scoured the walkways, most of them carrying weapons. Before, Protectors had used their aptitudes to protect others from harm. Now, they sought to protect the Elders from everyone else. Pulling her headscarf closer, she scrolled through the list of residents. Xander's name no longer appeared. Near the entrance, she approached a man huddled under a tree, who looked homeless.

"I'm looking for Xander of Indicum. Do you know him?"

The man nodded, staring up at her with hollow eyes.

"He's not listed as a resident here. Do you know where he is?"

"They kicked him out, just like they did with me."

"Who did?"

"The Protectors."

"Where did he go?"

"I don't know, and I don't care."

"Why do you say that?"

"I joined one of his groups, but instead of helping me, that potion made me sick. The Protectors broke up the group and locked us out of our rooms. Now I have nowhere to go."

"I am so sorry to hear that," she said and sat down with him for a while. "If you reach out for help from 6D with an honest heart, you can get it."

"I tried, but… nothing."

He sat back against the tree trunk and closed his eyes. Tia called out to Halia and Hadden to help the man.

After sensing their presence, she said, "They're here now. Just allow them in."

With closed eyes, he nodded. Tia waited beside him for several minutes, and when a tear rolled down one cheek, she quietly left him in meditation.

In the Garden of Jephsonite, she tried connecting to Xander's spirit. *Where did he go?* Nothing appeared in her mental landscape. Helio Tropez now looked like the mean streets of Seattle. People huddled over, clutching their belongings, constantly vigilant against would-be thieves.

Power hierarchies replaced the collaborative spirit that once reigned. Those with access to resources chose to exclude those with less power. The Elders hoarded housing, food, water, transport and clothing for themselves and only those they approved of. Tia would be homeless, too, were it not for the help from 6D.

Others weren't so lucky. As she walked towards the main river, Tia saw a tent city under a bridge. Watching from afar, people milled about in ragged clothing. Things were worse than she had thought. Memories of the once lush and life-enhancing riverside flew through her visual landscape. The contrast shattered her sense of decency, and she clutched her heart as she felt talons of shame.

Like brown sand dunes, a mile of slums rolled away from the riverside and met the horizon with dirty heat-haze mirages. The miserable shelters were a pathetic ensemble of old robes, scraps of building materials, reed mats and bamboo sticks. They slumped together, attached one to another with narrow lanes winding between them.

Tia approached. Outside the first tent, a woman sat with two children: a boy about ten and a girl about five.

"I'm looking for Xander of Indicum. Do you know him?"

She nodded and scowled. "He stayed here a few days, but the people didn't trust him and asked him to leave."

"Do you know where he went?"

"I don't know. The mountains..." the woman pointed with vacant eyes.

Off in the distance, the Riala mountains glittered in the crimson-blue sky.

"Where in the mountains?"

"If I tell you, will you give me some food?"

Tia pulled out a bag of Gova berries and nuts. The mother gave it to her children, who devoured it all within seconds.

The woman breathed a sigh of relief and said, "Maybe try the Mountain Pagoda."

"Where's that?"

"Follow the trail leading out of the gate near the Hall of Congress."

Her son said, "Isn't that how Maeve and Ruman got eaten?"

Tia looked at the boy, then back to his mother. "What?"

The woman sighed and looked around. "There are raptors in the mountains. Three people tried to go to the pagoda, but two of them got killed. The one other barely escaped. They didn't have any protection, but if you want to make the trip, you'd better take a weapon and not go alone."

"What kind of weapon?"

"A Genfa maybe...?"

"What's that?"

The woman tutted, then muttered something underneath her breath. Tia caught the word 'surface.' "It's like a stun gun."

Tia nodded, gave the woman more food, thanked her, and headed back to her apartment. *Hadn't Daphne said something about the Evangelists going up to a mountain pagoda?* To her relief the key still worked. She fired up the replicator to produce a warm coat, a pair of hiking boots, a Genfa, a sleeping bag, water and nourishment for the journey.

After an hour of trying to figure out how to use the weapon, she sat down frustrated. According to the Hall of Records, it seemed to be like a taser to shock and subdue a threat long enough to get away. The only way to stun raptors was by hitting them in the face or neck. She tried firing at the floor, but nothing happened. The only alive thing to test it on was her beloved orchid, and she didn't want to do that.

After packing the replicator into a backpack, she headed for one of the gates that led outside the city. She stopped just outside the gate and fired at a purple Heliotrope flower. It wilted on the spot. *Okay, I guess it works.* The Heliotrope Flower was the emblem of Helio Tropez. Strangely the flowers grew in abundance around the outside walls of the city but, since the SIM virus, had died off completely inside the city.

Using her intuition and the occasional signpost as a guide, Tia followed the switchback trails heading into the Nalia Valley. The damp aroma of pine followed her as she climbed further into the foothills, each strange noise making her jump. She had vowed not to stop, but the path got steeper and steeper, and her lungs needed a break.

Sitting down on a rock, she drank some water and looked down at the vista below. The entirety of Helio Tropez lay in the valley between two mountain ranges. For the first time, she saw the sacred geometric design of the city. The causeways, gardens and waterways all interweaved to form a pentagram within a triquetra symbol. At the same time, the energetic ley lines that usually flowed in congruent patterns now looked blocked. Rubbish piled up.

Those who had once taken pride in waste removal had given up the role. Many other vital services to the city, such as cleaning, gardening and preparing goods, disappeared as people sought refuge from their pain in addictions. Once-beautiful areas fell into disrepair and attracted vermin-like rats. Disease and malnourishment sent people scurrying to the Healing Bays only to find no one there to help them. A pang of regret clenched at her throat. Comparing Helio Tropez to how it had looked a year before broke her heart. The colours were no longer all in higher frequencies— they were now in lower frequency ones too, with oranges, yellows, reds, browns and blacks scattered across the landscape.

She sighed, and, feeling more rested, she stood up to keep going. A rustling in the bushes caught her attention. A moment later, a jackrabbit leapt up onto a nearby rock. She breathed a sigh of relief and watched as it twitched its nose, sniffing the air. Its ears fell backwards. Something wasn't right.

A moment later, a roar came from the bushes, and a raptor trampled onto the trail, snatching the rabbit, tossing it into the air and swallowing it whole.

Standing over eight feet tall, blood gushed from its razor-sharp teeth as it devoured the jackrabbit. Tia backed away and pointed the Genfa at its head. It looked up at her and emitted a bloodcurdling scream. She fired the Genfa and missed. The beam ricocheted off a tree trunk. It screamed again, and she fired again. This time, she hit it halfway down its neck. It squawked, stumbled, and fell on the ground in a daze.

Her heart beat wildly in her chest. The raptor quivered on the ground, clearly shocked but not completely unconscious. She needed to move past it to get to the pagoda. After climbing through the brambles to avoid passing too close, she looked down to see scratches all over her legs. The smell of blood would only draw more of them. She fired again at the raptor's head, and it stopped moving. As she stepped over its head, however, it groaned, causing her to jump out of the way. As she did, the raptor snapped at her heels. She screamed and scrambled up the hill as fast as possible. Although there were gouge marks on her hiking boots, the teeth hadn't punctured her skin.

Going up the switchback trail with a heavy pack took its toll. After going strong for fifteen minutes, she was panting with exhaustion and had to stop. Looking back, nothing seemed to have followed her. That said, sometimes raptors travelled in groups. So she made sure to keep a keen eye and ear out for any other sounds. Adrenaline kept her moving fast for the next hour, praying at each corner that the pagoda would come into view.

After two more hours of hiking, she came upon a turquoise lake. At the opposite end of the lake stood a dwelling, shimmering in gold. It looked like a Buddhist temple: wide at the bottom with a circular dome reaching up over a hundred feet in the air, ending in a fine point. Two men dressed as Protectors stood near the entrance. Staying out of sight, she moved closer to observe. People came in and out of the front entrance, then went to another building or down to the lakefront. Another two Protectors stood near the other end of the lake with Genfa weapons, probably to keep the raptors away.

Would they turn her away or let her in? Gathering her courage, she came out of hiding and headed for the entrance. Just then, two women came out the front door. She recognised them both as the Elders, Frenla and Tasma. They seemed at odds with each other. Tasma put on a backpack and trudged down the path towards her, so Tia stepped back into the shadows. As she passed by, Tasma seemed perturbed. Had they forced her to leave? Maybe she could find out more by talking to her.

A thumping sound caught her attention. Looking back, a raptor appeared on the path. Tasma stopped dead in her tracks. It lunged towards her, and she tried to run. Tia fired the Genfa with a shaking hand but missed. It grabbed Tasma by the leg and pulled her down. The Protectors arrived and stunned the raptor, and it ran back into the forest, screeching. They carried Tasma, who was now bleeding from the leg, back to the pagoda.

Tia followed behind but stayed out of sight. She went around the back of the pagoda, shaking. A door opened, and a woman walked out to gather water from the lake. After she left, Tia slowly crept inside. A hallway led to several rooms, and Tia ducked inside one. She overheard voices and followed the sound down another hallway leading out of the room and onto the backstage area of a stage. From behind a curtain, she noticed a room full of people – about fifty of them – gathered in a circle. Frenla addressed the group.

She was the Elder who had deleted files about the Quinary Mission from the Hall of Records. As a Sentient-Vision with strong Social Activist tendencies, it made sense that Frenla was one of the first to come to the pagoda and bring together a group to help heal Heliotropans from SIM. Obar, her partner, sat nearby.

As she searched for familiar faces, she saw several people she knew like Ramu, Stavron, Meraton and Xander! He was here, just as the woman in the tent city suggested. Most of the others, she didn't recognise. But for some reason, Cassandra wasn't among them. *Why would Meraton be here without Cassandra?*

Frenla said, "I know many of you disagree, but Tasma can't be trusted. She's not one of us – she's a spy. The Elders want to undermine what we're doing here."

"She's injured now, so we have to keep her here until she heals," Meraton voiced. "How do you know she's a spy?"

"My aptitude is Sentient. I can read her heart. It's not pure."

Toran nodded. "Yes, I sense a double agenda. But Tasma, maybe you will come clean about your purpose here."

A Tangent member of the group used his healing powers to close the wound on Tasma's leg. She breathed a sigh of relief and sat up to address the group, still looking unsteady.

"You must all realise that my aptitude is Ecrivent-Action, *The Resource Builder*. I created the resource infrastructure at the Palace of Zuris that gets shared with the whole city. Together with the Zuris Elders, we cut them off. That's what happened, right Meraton?"

He nodded and looked down at the floor.

"That's when the other Palaces did the same. When I connected to 6D and broke free of the SIM virus, the horror was hard to face. All the people who've suffered because of our decision, it's a huge karmic burden to bear. What you sense is my shame. My purpose here is to make amends. Meraton and I can restore the resources, but we have to get the other three Elders who are still under the control of the virus. I can't do it alone. I need your help."

After she was finished, the group sat in silence, absorbing the full explanations on many levels. Tasma sat looking away, waiting.

Frenla spoke first. "I sense your truthfulness, but what exactly do you need from the other Elders?"

"It takes five hand codes to turn it back on... Meraton, Renolo, Geata, Cassandra and... me."

Meraton spoke quietly. "We need to go back to the city and get that done."

With pleading eyes, Tasma searched the faces of the group. "Please, forgive me. I came because I want to make this right."

Frenla reached out her arms to Tasma. "We've all made grave errors and need to forgive each other."

An audible sigh rippled through the room, and several people crowded around Tasma to welcome her into the group.

After the group settled down, Meraton stood up and said, "We have someone else to add to the group. Someone we've been waiting for a long time."

Tia peered through the curtain to see who he was referring to, but as she did, she saw him walking to the side of the stage. He opened the curtain, and Tia stood there, unmasked and shocked. Heat rose in her cheeks, and she gave a weak smile.

"Tia of Zuris has finally arrived," Meraton said.

Everyone stood up, and a loud cheer of applause filled the room.

When it died down, Meraton helped her off the stage, and she joined the circle. "I just got here. I'm sorry I didn't announce myself, but when I saw you expel Tasma, I thought you might do the same with me. I barely escaped a raptor myself."

Meraton asked, "You were attacked?"

"Almost. But I have a Genfa, so I protected myself."

"That's good. We are relieved and happy that you are finally here."

"I'm confused. The last time we spoke, you threatened to teleport me back to the surface."

Shame coloured his cheeks. "I was under the spell of SIM and the other Elders who living are in fear. I started to have dreams where Hadden spoke to me, which made me question why we were trying to control other people in Helio Tropez. When I voiced those concerns, the Elders threatened to kick me out. In my waking state, I reached out for help to SANA, and Hadden answered. He instructed me to find Ramu, Xander and Stavron, who all received the same instruction from Hadden, which was for us to connect. We needed a place outside of the city, so I suggested we come here. Several others chose to come with us."

"You're all connected to 6D now?"

Almost everyone in the room nodded in unison.

"I meditated just before our meeting today, and Hadden told me that you were on your way."

"So you don't blame me for what happened with the virus, like everyone else?" she asked, feeling a constriction in her throat.

"We know you were just the catalyst. This ascension process has been a long time coming," Meraton replied.

Ramu looked up and said, "We are actually grateful you're here."

Tia looked over at Xander, who sat isolated from the group, looking down at the floor. All the months of loneliness and isolation melted away as several people came up to hug her.

"You'll be thrilled to know that I have a working replicator," she said, pulling it out of her backpack.

Ramu smiled, "How did you get yours working?"

"Halia from 6D gave me the codes to not only fix it but to give me access to higher vibrational foods as well."

"That's amazing. The only replicator here doesn't work. We didn't think to ask for help from 6D."

"Yes, you do have to ask."

"We've been foraging for berries and nuts, and everyone is so hungry. Let's feast!"

Working as a team, they produced a feast of Heliotropans' favourite foods, along with new delicacies from 6D, such as the Lembutter stew. Tia still buzzed from the intensity of her trek up the mountain and seeing everyone there, but she felt famished. She loaded up her plate with food and looked around for a place to sit and eat. Xander had his plate of food already and was sitting alone.

Tia stood next to him and asked, "Can I sit with you?"

He looked up and shrugged. "Sure."

"I came here to find you, actually."

"Really?"

"Hadden recommended it."

"Yes, he recommended that I should connect with you too. But when I checked in with myself, I didn't get that you'd want to."

"I've changed my mind."

He looked down and pulled a blanket around himself.

"It's just that I saw you with my sister and later with all those other women. I was jealous. I thought we had something between us."

He nodded and rubbed his forehead. "Metta felt lost and just needed someone to feel close to. I didn't have the heart to reject her. We had a thing on the surface, but it never quite took off. I love her, but more like a sister."

Tia breathed a sigh of relief.

"Then I saw you in the park acting as a guru to all your followers and the Bejula plant. Quite frankly, your behaviour... scared me."

He smirked and looked away. "I get it."

"Also, Metta told me that I'm not your type."

"That's true. You're not."

They both laughed.

"She said you like short, curvy, dark-skinned women... not exactly me."

"What? Hardly. What gave you that idea?"

"That's what Metta said when I met you at that hotel in Montreal."

"Oh, that girl? That was JJ putting programs in my head to get me interested in whoever he wanted me to seduce. At that time, it was the daughter of a record producer with whom he wanted to cut a deal. I didn't care for her at all."

They sat in silence, eating the Lembutter stew. The food gave her renewed energy.

Xander devoured the last few bites. "This food is unbelievable. Thank you for bringing the replicator. I've hardly eaten anything for weeks."

He lay down on the floor and put a pillow under his head.

"I'll let you rest," Tia said, gathering her things.

"No, please stay. I like talking to you. I'm just weary from lack of food."

"When did you arrive?"

"Just last week. I hiked here with Meraton, Stavron and Ramu. We had to fight off a few raptors along the way, but we finally made it. I'm still recovering from the ordeal, though."

"Me too. I had a Genfa. What did you use to get away?"

"We each had a Genfa, but there were four raptors. I'd never used a weapon like that before and kept missing. Those raptors are fast. Two of them got stunned, and the others took off."

"That's good."

"I think we had help from 6D or SANA or something. It was weird how they just left."

He put another pillow next to him and patted it, then tossed her a blanket. "Let's recover together."

The thought of physical intimacy with him made her nervous, so she lay a few feet away from him. Around the room, others talked in small groups or cleaned up after the meal.

"Come closer."

"I'm good here."

"It's just kind of cold, and together, we'd be warmer."

"I don't want to be one more of your seductions."

404

"Really?" he said, shaking his head in disbelief. "After all I've been through lately, that's the last thing I'm looking for. It's been recommended that we connect, so that's what I'm doing."

She swallowed. "Ok, good. I just wanted to check."

She moved closer, and he spooned her as they lay on the floor. Her body melted into his, feeling calmed by his physical warmth. Visions of rainbow lights sparkled in her mind's eye.

"Plus, I want to make the others jealous," he joked.

"What?"

"All your secret admirers."

"I don't have any secret admirers."

"Believe me, you do. They couldn't wait for you to arrive, especially Ramu, Neals and Tagar, and probably several others."

She laughed nervously and looked over at them as they talked together in a group. Ramu glanced at her, and she quickly looked away. "So why am I not *your* type?"

"We're just so different."

"Let me guess. I'm too much of a prude?"

"Well... maybe."

"I've lived a totally sheltered life, and you've seen everything... done everything."

"I guess that's another big difference, but I think that the real issue is... that you seem to look down on me."

"What? I don't."

"When we first met, I saw pity in your eyes. It hurt. Especially when everyone else put me on a pedestal. I think that's what fascinated me about you."

"In Montreal, yes. I knew that you were programmed and far away from your true self. But not now."

"There's still pity in your eyes."

"That's not pity. It's compassion. I know what it's like to hit rock bottom and have to face all of your mistakes."

"You've made mistakes?"

"Plenty."

"From what I've heard, you're a saint. People have *you* on a pedestal."

"Maybe, but it only lasted until I brought the virus here."

"We all brought the virus. You, me, Metta, Annika. It's not all on you. And Josie Carbona would have found her way here one way or another."

Tia sighed, turning onto her back to look up at the dome of the pagoda.

"You saved my life, Tia. You saved Annika, Metta, Daphne. You led the charge on these expeditions where you risked everything."

Tears welled up in his eyes. She glanced at him, and her own heart melted.

"It's true. I would still be enslaved on the surface if not for you."

She allowed his words to soothe her as she sensed the truth in what he had said. *I will no longer beat myself up about what had happened*, she thought. Self-judgment, after all, was just another trick of SIM.

He rolled onto his back and folded his hands behind his head. "I've suspected that SIM implants a mind block to ensure you don't get connected to your SANA mate."

Tia looked at him. "That makes sense."

"But even under full SIM control in Montreal, I felt the attraction."

A smile touched her lips. "Me too."

"In Montreal? You seemed so standoffish."

"Attraction and fear at the same time. I was afraid of SIM trying to trap me there."

"I guess that makes sense. Again, very brave of you to come to my concert and the party at the hotel."

"It was amazing to see you perform. You're so talented."

"Thank you. I didn't know whether you'd like it. You had that look of aversion that you get."

"You get that look too, you know. You liked me, but you didn't."

Xander glanced at her. "I do? It's just that you looked so young when I first met you, as a kid almost. You've changed now, grown into more of a..."

"A woman? You mean that I now have a figure?"

He chuckled, "Yes, a lovely hourglass figure."

"I know. It's strange. Maybe it's the good nutrition here or...."

"...maybe it's meeting your SANA mate," he said with a sly smile.

Beads of sweat formed on the back of her neck. "Could be. I mean, on the surface, we get programmed with all these silly romantic movies and stories and songs that don't really show what true, mature, healthy relationships should be like. My parents and grandparents are SANA mates. They say it's a union that forces you to grow."

"And humans seem to have a natural resistance towards growth."

Tia nodded, remembering all her negative thoughts about Xander and how the SIM virus had tried to weaken the bond between them.

Xander wrinkled his brow. "Hadden's been so good to me, helping me find forgiveness in myself and dealing with all the darkness."

"Yes, he's been a true spiritual warrior for all of us."

They talked for the next few hours, sharing the intensity of their lives over the last few months, what they had learned, and what they had lost. Soon, everyone else crawled off to sleep, and they were alone. Although she felt like crawling into his arms and falling asleep right there and then, she decided against it. They still both were in a fragile state.

"I'm so tired. Is there a place where I can sleep? I literally ran up that mountain today," Tia said.

"Sure. You can choose any room. They're mostly empty. I'll show you if you like?"

He led her down a hallway to a room. It looked like the interior of a two-berth campervan, with a tiny bathroom, a fold-down desk and a floating plasma mattress that you had to pull down from the ceiling. "Here's one. There are instructions for how to use everything here on the console."

"Wow. Nice. Thank you."

They hugged goodnight, and he left. After figuring out how the bed worked, she lay curled up in a blanket, unable to fall asleep. Her feet, calves and shoulders ached from the intense hike. The events of the day replayed in her mind, all her thoughts seeking to be processed and integrated. After trying to reach out to 6D in prayer for a while, Tia gave up. *I must be too tired.*

It was only as she drifted off to sleep that Hadden appeared in her mind's eye, his baritone voice ringing sound waves through her mind. *The whole Task Force here is glad you made it to the pagoda safely.*

Tia's eyes opened wide. *You're here!*

We distracted several raptors away from you during your hike.

You did? Thank you!

Everyone who is working with 6D is together now, Hadden said. *It's been quite a task gathering you all in one place.*

I bet. Is it safe here?

The Task Force here needs your help to create a better protection shield around the property. I'll show you how in a moment.

Despite her tiredness, they worked together to create two kinds of shields around the pagoda and the lake. The first one was a 6D version of the SPS protocol, or Secure Protective Space shield, to keep out harm. The second one was a platinum light shield to raise the vibration and nourish the inhabitants. The pagoda already had protective energy, so they simply boosted the existing structures.

Once the shields were up, Tia relaxed again, though she could tell Hadden was keeping something from her. *What is it?*

I've decided I'm going to re-materialise back into 4D.

A sadness welled up inside her. *Even though you may get stuck here?*

Yes, it's necessary. I'm the only Pentada mate who's not in 4D.

Daphne definitely needs you...

I'll need your help to make it happen, Tia. You're the only one who seems to have the receptors for this information.

Whatever you need.

For the rest of the night, he downloaded her with instructions as she slept. By the time she awoke, the plan was complete for how to make it happen.

CHAPTER 42

Helio Tropez – 2012

"**W**e don't think it's a good idea," the Moderator said during the 6D Congress. "If you go back into 4D consciousness, you may never return. That's exactly what SIM wants. Why risk it? You are making progress with people from here."

Hadden replied, "Those in 4D can't make it without the full Pentada working together. Remember what Waleya said? Pentada have been hit the hardest. Their SANA mates are the key to turning things around. I've been working with the men, but it's hard doing it from here. Most importantly, Daphne is my mate, and she can't see or hear me. I need to go back and connect to her face-to-face."

"This could be a SIM tactic to infiltrate 6D."

"But SIM can't survive in this frequency."

"No, but as you go through the stargate, they could easily capture you and map your memories of 6D, thereby creating a false 6D timeline. They would re-route lower density people away from organic ascension."

Hadden sat back, and an image flashed into his mind. His twenty-year-old self was at the stargate in 4D Helio Tropez, about to go back to the surface. "Maybe you could wipe my 6D memories before sending me back."

The Elders looked at each other speechless for a few moments. They talked amongst themselves in a private telepathic conversation.

The Moderator turned to face him. "Then you could really get trapped there. How will you find your way back? And how would you help others?"

"I will ask the people that I connected to... to teach me what I taught them."

"Perhaps, but you wouldn't have access to any 6D resources,"

"True."

"Or any of your 6D capacities."

Hadden clasped his hands tightly in his lap. A feeling of sadness washed over him. But there were times that he'd regained memories that had been wiped on the surface of Earth. "Once I'm through the stargate, I'll use my photographic memory to rebuild my memories."

"Maybe, but you'll be in a devolved state. How helpful can you be then?"

"Tia can keep her connection to 6D, then re-feed the information back to me."

A silence descended upon the Congress. Sceptical eyes looked at him from all directions.

Hadden stood up and faced the whole Congress with arms wide. "We have to do something. It's only a few weeks until the ascension, and we can't leave them stranded."

They deliberated for a long while and finally put it to a vote.

It was close, but the majority voted in favour of Hadden—to send him back to 4D.

"On one condition," the moderator said. "We need as many people on the Task Force with Halia and Triol as possible. The more people we have working on this, the faster we will see the effects."

The Congress agreed without the need for a vote, and preparations began. Halia and Triol went to work training new members on the Task Force to bring them up to speed on how to connect with people in 4D.

On the day of the transfer, Halia said, "As a reminder, you won't remember your connections to any of us in 6D. You'll only have memories of those in 4D that you knew before you ascended. We can't let SIM discover how you made the transition. That safeguards your transfer process. Once you're there, the others can rebuild the information you lost. We will create a firewall around your mind where you can store that information. It doesn't guarantee safety from SIM, but it could slow them down."

Putting Hadden into a gentle sleep, they removed the appropriate memories, capacities and programmes from his mind. As they teleported him back to the precise location of the mountain pagoda in 4D, Hadden prayed to SANA that he would make it safely without any SIM interception.

He re-materialised standing next to a lake. A gold pagoda reflected its magnificence in the rippling waters in front of him. He vaguely knew that he had recently descended from 6D to 4D and that he needed to find Tia. Looking down at his hands, he was relieved to find that he still had a youthful body. As he moved towards the doors of the pagoda, two Protectors held up weapons, denying him entry.

"Who are you?"

"I'm Hadden of Violetta."

One went inside while the other kept his weapon up. A few minutes later, the door burst open.

"You made it!" Tia exclaimed, reaching out to hug him.

"Tia... you're here!"

"Yes, we've been waiting for you. Come in."

"What is this place, and why am I here?"

Inside the Pagoda, a group of people sat on cushions on the floor. As he approached, they stood up and went to greet him. The only one he recognised was Meraton.

"What's happening?"

Tia explained, "You agreed to come back here to help us, particularly Daphne. And you warned me that you wouldn't remember anything about your connections with us from 6D. We're all your resources to recall anything you might have given up to make the transfer."

"I agreed to come back?"

"Yes."

"Why?"

"We'll catch you up on everything. Let's get you settled in first," Tia said.

He had some time to rest in a private room. The 4D density weighed heavy on his bones. His *Eagle Eye* aptitude still mostly worked, but other higher abilities from 6D were now inaccessible. Meanwhile, the group sat in meditation to scan for SIM interference.

Once Hadden was rested, Tia gathered a group of people with a strong connection to Hadden in one of the smaller rooms. The five Pentada mates and several people from the House of Violetta gathered in a circle. One by one, they shared what he'd passed down to them from 6D. After an entire day of studying his mind, they created their own firewalls to protect the areas in their mind where they stored the information needed to ascend.

After that, Meraton announced, "We need a separate meeting of Pentada's SANA mates."

Hadden nodded. "Okay, they're all here?"

"Yes, on your instruction."

The five men found a separate room and gathered in a closer circle, sitting cross-legged on the floor.

Hadden cleared his throat. The dense air chafed. "I'll admit, I don't know what to do next. You are the mates of the Pentada women?"

"Well... supposedly," Ramu explained.

Hadden frowned at the wavy-haired man in the silver cap. "What's your name?"

"You don't remember me at all? You've been talking to me in meditation for months."

"I'm sorry. I know I've been connecting with all of you, but I only remember Meraton because we met before I went to 6D."

"Of course. I'm Ramu of the House of Liven. Tia thinks I'm the SANA mate of Metta, but I've never had more than one conversation with her, so..."

"Metta is here in the subterranean world?"

"Yes, but back in the city of Helio Tropez. She lives in a tent village with a group of women... we call them the Cigarillo girls."

"Why do you call them that?"

"They make the... Hepa cigarillos."

"From the Hepa plant?" Hadden asked, despair creeping into his voice.

"Yes. Many people in Helio Tropez are now addicted, despite the warnings," Meraton said.

Ramu furrowed his brow. "She's always smoking one. And all the women in her group hate men, so I didn't even bother trying to talk to her."

"You'll need to try again," Hadden said.

"I don't think that's going to work."

"Why?"

"I don't know. We're just so... different."

"In what way?"

"She has a whole 'tough girl' thing going on. I don't know how to relate to someone like that."

Hadden raised his eyebrows. "You do know you're talking about my daughter?"

"Right. Sorry. She just kind of scares me."

Stavron added, "I got to know my SANA mate, Annika. It was a huge soul connection, which was surprising for both of us, given our same sex orientation. Of course, that all turned sour ever since the SIM virus. We said hurtful things."

"I'm sorry to hear that. Are you talking about Daphne's sister?" Hadden asked.

"Yes."

Hadden nodded. "I know Annika. I met her several times on the surface."

Stavron nodded. "She's here now, but back in Helio Tropez as well. She isolates herself. I haven't seen her since the virus took hold of everyone."

Hadden sighed and looked over at Meraton. "You and Cassandra have been together for aeons... What happened?"

Meraton sighed. "She wants to keep separate from everyone else and agrees with the other Elders about hoarding resources. Since connecting with you, I just can't abide by that. So I left and came here instead."

Hadden nodded and turned to Xander. "That leaves you. You must be Tia's mate... your name?"

"Xander of Indicum. I just want to say you've made a huge difference for me, and I wish you could remember that."

"Yes, for me, as well," Stavron added.

The others nodded, and Hadden felt touched by their appreciation. "I hope I can continue to be helpful. I'm not in 6D anymore, so I probably don't have the same level of healing powers. We'll have to muster those up ourselves."

They remained in silence for a few minutes, looking at each other, unsure what to do or say next.

Finally, Meraton interrupted the silence. "It's important that you all sanctify your relationships with your mate. Cassandra and I did that at the Temple of Lions. I'm assuming Hadden and Daphne did not…"

Hadden put his hand up. "We knew enough to do our SANA vows in private before we consecrated our relationship…"

"Good." Meraton glanced at Xander, "Yes, ideally do this *before* you consecrate the relationship." Before Xander could protest, he added, "Xander grew up on the surface like you, Hadden. SIM made him into a big rock star."

"Really? Daphne and I were both put in the limelight too. It can be tough. So are you related to Miriam of Indicum in any way?"

"Yes, she was my mother," Xander said, still scowling at Meraton.

"Amazing. And your father?"

"Forsel."

Meraton smiled. "That makes sense. Your grandfather, Ben, announced those two were SANA mates at our Mount Rainier event." He slapped Hadden's knee. "Remember?"

"Yes, your father was my childhood friend. We only met once, but we became instant friends."

Xander's eyes turned glassy. "Brilliant. I didn't know that."

Hadden touched the young man's shoulder. "What happened to your parents?"

"Once I got my memories back, I remembered who my real mother was. At least I remembered her name. She is a well-known and high-ranking official in the military. Her husband, Forsel, whom I now remember is my real father, is with the British Intelligence."

"That makes sense. I remember Miriam was Tangent-Action, *The Warrior*. Of course, SIM would want her in the military. And Forsel was, um, Voyent-Acceptance, I think. That's *The Detective*. Perfect for intelligence work. What about Forsel's sister, Nancy? She was very artistic."

"My aunt Nancy does huge art installations in skyscrapers and city parks around the world. At first, her work was beautiful and inspiring, but unfortunately, her commissioned pieces now seem dark and ugly."

Hadden gave him a sympathetic smile. "She most likely got infiltrated by SIM. They use art and symbolism to reprogram people into their inverted ways. But tell me, how did you get into music? You're Audient-Attention, right? I think that's *The Lover* aptitude."

"Hah! The Lover – makes sense!" Ramu laughed.

Xander cleared his throat and ignored the comment. "They turned me over to the Redus family as a child. Essentially, they abandoned me and never kept in contact."

Hadden frowned. "You have to understand something. Those of us in that generation were forced to give our children over to SIM agents and lose touch. They didn't willingly abandon you. It was probably the hardest decision they ever made."

Xander nodded reluctantly.

"So no contact with them… They never came to watch you play music?"

Xander took a deep breath. "Nope. Not that I know of. I had screen memories of different parents, but they never came either."

He nodded remembering how SIM gave him false screen memories, too. "Of course. SIM does that to their young assets. So, how did you get here to Helio Tropez?"

"Tia came to the surface and rescued Metta, Annika and I."

"Amazing. How did all of that come to pass?"

Meraton explained the process of Tia going to Montreal, the transfer, the virus, and their lives since then.

"So, at least you and Tia are here together face-to-face," Hadden said to Xander.

"We've mostly been estranged until last night. We are coming back around to each other. It's not easy, though."

Ramu cleared his throat and touched Hadden on the knee. "Excuse me. I just thought I should let you know that I find it quite easy with Tia. I'm wondering if we've got it mixed up, meaning that Tia and I are SANA mates. Maybe Xander and Metta should be SANA mates instead."

Xander glared at him, but Ramu continued, "I'm just saying. After all, I saw you kissing Metta. Hardly seems like you're interested in Tia if you ask me."

"That was a mistake," Xander snapped. "I just didn't have the heart to reject her. Arriving here was terrifying for her. I was the only person she knew, but she's not my mate. She's more like a sister. I've known her for years on the surface. Underneath the tough girl act is a very creative, brilliant woman with a huge heart. Don't write her off just yet."

Ramu frowned.

"It's not always easy connecting with your SANA mate," Meraton said softly.

"But how does a person know who their *true* SANA mate is?" Ramu asked.

"You just know. You see the rainbow frequency when you are together. SANA mates are not just for this lifetime. You come back many times with the same mate to resolve your differences and evolve," Meraton explained.

Stavron nodded. "Interesting. I had that rainbow effect with Annika and past life memories."

"That's it. That's the sign. I have that with Cassandra. Your connection ignites the rainbow bridge that we all need for ascension."

They looked at Xander, but he avoided their gaze. The group turned to Ramu, and he shrugged. "I had that with Tia, but I've never had any physical contact with Metta."

Meraton turned to look at Ramu. "You had the rainbow effect with Tia?"

"Sort of," Ramu said, averting his eyes.

"It can't be 'sort of.' It's much different from any other connection you've had with others. You'd know."

"I'm trying to remember."

"You would remember," Meraton insisted. "Hadden, you told me that one of the main reasons why you came back to 4D is to reconnect with Daphne in person."

"I said that?" He thought about it for a moment, then shrugged. "Makes sense. We certainly both experienced the rainbow frequency when we physically connected. Is she in Helio Tropez as well?"

"Yes, Tia and Cassandra rescued her from off-planet."

"From off-planet!?"

They spent fifteen minutes updating Hadden on the rescue and Daphne's rehabilitation. As soon as they were finished, he asked, "So, how can I see her?"

"She's in the city."

"Why didn't she come here to the pagoda?"

"She thinks we're all *Evangelists* for ascension. SIM has her trapped back in old programs."

Ramu asked, "Are we talking about the Daphne who runs the whorehouse?"

Everyone looked uncomfortable.

Stavron slapped him on the kneecap. "Why? Have you been one of her customers?"

"No! There's just a lot of talk going around the city about how she enrolled all these women and…"

Meraton said, "Yes, she runs a brothel. Not something a father is proud to share."

"Daphne is Tia's mother?" Ramu asked.

Hadden said, "Yes, and Metta's mother."

"Right. They sure do look alike."

Hadden sighed. "It makes sense given the *Femme Fatale* programming they gave her."

Meraton shook his head. "Sex for personal gain corrupts your soul structure and blocks ascension. Of all the SIM tricks, it is the hardest to heal from."

"So… we have our work cut out for ourselves, then," Hadden said.

Meraton climbed to his feet and paced the room. "Let's start by helping Tia and Xander heal their relationship. They are the only two who are both here at the pagoda, so it should be the most straightforward. That way, we will have a template for the rest of us."

All nodded in agreement except for Xander and Ramu.

Meraton pulled out a small handheld device from his satchel and placed it in the middle of the circle. It projected a see-through blank page with a blinking cursor. "I suggest we use this to map our group results. We'll each use our aptitude to gather information. Luckily, we have all five TEVAS styles here. I'm Sentient, Hadden is Voyent, Xander is Audient, Ramu is Tangent, and Stavron is Ecrivent."

Meraton closed his eyes the others followed suit.

Xander interrupted a few minutes later. "What exactly are we doing here?"

"We are viewing your soul structure and assessing what needs healing. Then we create a course of action."

Ramu raised his hand tentatively. "What kind of action?"

"To remove a SIM virus, you need to identify, locate, remove and repair the bad code in the mind. We will start by helping Xander identify and locate the code."

"Identify and locate. Got it," he said with puzzled eyes.

Xander cleared his throat. "Just as a reminder, I'm the only one born on the surface here, and all of this is very new to me."

Hadden nodded. "I was also born on the surface, Xander. In some ways, our minds are the best to study so we can help Heliotropans break free from SIM. As an Audient-Attention, just listen for the harmony versus the discord in your soul vibration. Treat it like you would when listening to music. What is working and what isn't?"

He nodded with a grim face. Over the next hour, they sat in prayer and meditation to study Xander's mind. Using his Voyent aptitude, Hadden saw the damage in his soul structure from the CM, drugs and sexual promiscuity. At the end of the hour, they compared notes, and Hadden summarised.

"I want to reassure you that I had similar issues growing up on the surface. I healed many of them independently, so I know what to do. Like you, I received CM as a young man. Using the trauma and guilt of separation from my family, they could create portals into my energy system. They loaded me with all their prize programs: Superiority, Idolisation, Addiction, Victim-Victimizer, and Gender Misery. I was hooked on alcohol, drugs, food and sex.

Through the process of trauma-based mind control, they split my personality into a light side and a shadow side. At night, they would awaken the shadow side to go on corporate espionage assignments. By day, my light side used that information to create huge wealth for my SIM families. It all seemed above-board until the two parts of my personality realised what the other was doing. I just thought I was brilliant at knowing what stocks to pick in my investment company. I lived a life of wealth and recognition, but I was miserable. My handler, Leo Burres, controlled everything I did. I only broke free after I met Daphne, and we had a family together."

"Are you saying that they did something like that to me?"

"It looks like it. You've got all those same CM programs. Capturing someone with a Heliotropan lineage is a big win for them. We have abilities that people on the surface don't. The CM you received involved weakening your soul so they could control you. They used autosuggestion about your worthiness, amplifying the pain you felt at being separated from your parents so young. The drugs further weakened your soul matrix, allowing them to use your natural talents, such as your musical talent, magnetism, and ability to emotionally connect with an audience, for their own ends."

Xander sighed and pulled his long hair away from his face. "After they deprogrammed me here in Helio Tropez, it reminded me of when I was young, before SIM abducted me into the performing arts program. Metta and I were at the same school. They trained us to embed words, tones and chord progressions into songs that triggered certain brain chemicals for mass mind control of our listeners. For example, songs that made you feel like a victim to someone you once loved."

"That helps them embed the Gender Misery program. They need to keep the genders at war with each other. It's a form of 'divide and conquer.'"

Meraton explained, "During our time on the surface, we noticed they did that with anything they could – trying to instil race wars, religious wars, class wars, anything to keep the consciousness of humanity divided. SIM must reveal their true intentions towards their victims, and the victims must agree to it at some level. What we will do here is help you decode the tricks, games and symbology of SIM that came to you through direct CM, but also through the media, songs, movies, video games and various aspects of popular culture on the surface."

Meraton pulled up a holographic image in front of the group. "Here's the MindStory Code that the Task Force worked on. It shows the path to avoid being deceived by SIM. If you pass all the tests of your journey, you complete the alchemical process, where you turn the lead of deception into the gold of truth, which is the main lesson of the 3D reality.

The archetypes you lived by are like characters in your MindStory. SIM tries to activate the shadow side of each archetypal character, and SANA tries to activate the light side of each. Once both are activated and go through the alchemical process, you ascend."

"So you're saying that my music programmed listeners to be in a state of disharmony so that they could feed SIM?"

"Yes."

"Why would people love it so much then?"

"It's as you said, you are trained to create and perform the music in a way that triggers pleasure centres in the brain. People associate emotional pain, which SIM feeds on, with pleasure. It's a reversal of what's healthy for a human being."

Xander shook his head in disbelief and rubbed his temples.

Hadden looked around at the group, sensing the discomfort. "Let's get started. Then you'll see how it works and how freeing it can be."

After creating a protection field to ensure that they were protected from SIM, Hadden instructed the group on how to proceed in more detail. Forty minutes later, they summarised their findings.

Ramu curled his lip. "I'm getting that you slept with, like, ninety-seven women."

Stavron chuckled. "Yeah. Your hara complex has ninety-seven cords with other people."

Xander looked at them, shocked. "What are you talking about?"

Meraton added, "I saw the same thing. You cannot mate with Tia until these issues are resolved. She is a virgin. A person's first sexual experience can either empower or disempower them the rest of their life."

"She's a virgin at thirty years old?"

"Here, it's quite typical to remain a virgin until you've found your mate."

"But she grew up on the surface. It's not normal there."

Hadden looked off into the distance. "She was always quite tuned into the ways of Helio Tropez, even though I never told her anything about it. She dated a few boys in high school, but it was never anything serious."

"Did she tell you she was a virgin?"

Meraton nodded. "Yes, when she first arrived in Helio Tropez."

"It didn't help that I insisted she rarely leave the house," Hadden mused.

Xander shook his head. "Why do you think I will disempower her?"

"Each sexual connection creates an energetic cord. The sexual act allows them to access your creative hub in the sexual organs. People don't do it consciously, and the majority of the people you mated with had little or no connection to SANA. They are vampiric in nature, needing to feed off other people's energy to survive."

Xander grimaced. "Lovely."

Hadden squared his shoulders. "I dealt with the same thing. As a wealthy, powerful man in the surface society, women threw themselves at me. Not one of them cared about me—they just wanted to siphon off my energy."

A silence filled the room. The men born in Helio Tropez couldn't relate to their experience on the surface. Although they tried not to judge, a discomfort permeated the room.

Changing the subject, Hadden said, "Tia said she saw you play in front of thousands of people?"

Xander nodded and looked away.

"Oh, that's why Tia likes you so much," Ramu said. "It's all the fame."

Meraton frowned at him. "Unless you have something productive to contribute, Ramu, kindly keep your thoughts to yourself."

"So, lots of groupies?" Hadden asked.

"Of course. Now that I think of it, I usually felt completely drained the morning after."

Hadden watched him, concerned. "Many of them are still siphoning your life force energy. To enter into a union with Tia means exposing her to that. A person opens themselves up to all the energetic cording of any sexual partner that their existing partner has had."

"That can't possibly be true."

421

They all nodded.

"And you all knew this from a young age?"

They all nodded again.

"Why didn't anyone teach that to me?"

"It's not your fault. You were controlled by SIM agents and had no one to teach you the rights and wrongs when it comes to relationships. Part of the detachment process will involve learning your lessons and forgiving them."

"You expect me to forgive those bastards?"

"We can help you remove each cord, but they will re-attach unless you wholeheartedly forgive yourself and others. That's the only way to break all subconscious agreements."

Xander stared at them, his jaw gritted. He got to his feet and threw his shirt off before turning his back to them. It was laced with scars and welts, interwoven with dozens of lashes. Gasps circled the group. "That's the result of JJ Redus torturing me over and over again."

Ramu narrowed his eyes at him. "Hmm, ugly."

Meraton glared at Ramu.

"If celebrities don't play by their rules, they get tortured. Fans put them on a pedestal, but if people only knew what they had to endure..." Xander pointed to a scar down his side. "This is where JJ tried to kill me because I wouldn't participate in their sickening rituals."

"Rituals?" Ramu knitted his brow.

The other men looked at each other, surprised by his ignorance.

"What? No one ever taught me about this stuff."

Meraton shook his head, "We stopped talking about these things after the Great UnDoing. It was too painful." He looked over at Hadden, hoping he would explain.

Hadden cleared his throat and sat up straight, smoothing his tunic before addressing Ramu. "They try to get celebrities and powerful people to engage in heinous acts as a way of relinquishing their dedication to SANA. That way, they are forever bonded to SIM. If you don't do it, you lose everything important to you. Sometimes, they even kill you. In Xander's case, it's amazing that they allowed him to live. But maybe, like in my case, a divine presence intervened."

Xander retrieved his shirt and settled on the floor, clutching his knees to his chest. "Something saved me. He left me for dead, but then I woke up in the ICU. After I healed, they put me back on tour, but JJ Redus was… I don't know… less of a cretin."

"Somehow, those of us from the Quinary Mission were not completely abandoned. Even in our deepest despair, our souls stayed connected to SANA, to our sanity." Tears stung his eyes as the others nodded in sombre recognition of that fact. "We can hopefully heal you of those scars and help you detox of all the drugs and chemicals they gave you on the surface."

"I thought all that already happened at the Healing Bay. They said I had detoxed completely."

"Yes, but the SIM virus you succumbed to has caused the timeline to revert back to before you came to Helio Tropez."

"So I have to go through that whole process again?"

"Actually, that brings up an important point." Hadden spread out two ribbons on the floor to illustrate his point. "When I looked in your mind, I saw two timelines like these two ribbons. I suspect the SIM virus doesn't have the power to reconstruct an entire lifetime of CM, so it does the most efficient thing. It finds a time in your life when your soul matrix was the most damaged and sends you back in time to that moment. With you, Xander, that was just before you got here."

"And with others from Helio Tropez, it might be the lowest point in their life," Meraton said.

"Yes, exactly. That's good news for everyone. That means we just need to bring you to the timeline after your healing process completed and before the virus. That would speed up the process, but because you hadn't done a forgiveness process before, the SIM virus affected you. So, that's important now."

"Got it. Brilliant." Xander sat up straighter.

Meraton nodded, looking at each of them, pleased at their acceptance so far. "Let's take a break and get to work."

During the break, Xander kept to himself. He stood by a window, looking out over at the lake. Hadden cleared his throat as he stood by his shoulder.

"Do you mind if I join you?"

Xander tilted his head but didn't shift his gaze. "Sure."

"I know it seems like you've had it harder than the others from Helio Tropez, but it's all for a higher reason. You will be helping people on the surface. You're not doing it for the people here. It's for everyone on the surface who doesn't even know they need help. It's an important reframe on your life experiences. Those tough times forged you in the fire of wisdom to help others in the same position, but that's only if you allow the healing process to happen. Otherwise, it stays stored as trauma instead of wisdom."

He nodded. "Thank you. That helps."

Hadden pulled him into a hug. At first, Xander tensed, but as Hadden held him, it eased from his shoulders, and Hadden felt him let some of the weight soften. When they pulled away, Xander excused himself and headed for the door. As Hadden watched, he wondered how long it had been since someone had just held him in compassion and not to leech energy from him.

As soon as Xander left, Ramu came to talk privately with Hadden. "I'm a virgin, too, you know. I wouldn't corrupt your daughter the way he would."

Hadden sighed. "Listen, I want to talk to you about these comments you keep making. We're here to help Xander, but you keep comparing yourself to him. If Tia thinks that Xander is her mate and Metta is yours, I'm going to back her up on that. She's very intuitive. Listen to your heart, not your mind."

Stavron shuffled closer. "Sorry, I couldn't help but overhear. I agree. You need to let this thing with Tia go."

"But I can't. The minute I met her, I just knew. This thing with Xander just seems to be in the way. I'm as good looking as him, right? I mean, Stavron, you like men. Which one of us would you prefer?"

Stavron laughed. "Listen, I don't want to get into the whole comparison thing with you and him. I prefer a dwarf build on a man, short and stocky. So if you really need to know, you're both as ugly as underfed giraffes," he said with a cheeky grin. "Neither of you is my type, but I could certainly help you find a guy if you're looking."

Hadden chuckled to himself, deciding he quite liked Stavron. He was easy going and quick to diffuse a situation – something this group sorely needed.

The door slid open again, and Xander came back into the room. As he approached, Ramu continued explaining the situation to Hadden. "But I had that rainbow effect when I kissed Tia."

Xander stood behind him. "You kissed Tia? When?"

"At Tinaghan. We had a very powerful connection."

"I never heard about that."

Ramu turned to face him, chest puffed up. "That's because you were with Metta and all those other women!"

Xander's eyes narrowed. "I've had it with you trying to convince everyone that you're her mate. Back off."

"You don't care about her. You just care about yourself. She deserves better than that!"

Xander pushed him in the chest, causing Ramu to stumble backwards. He regained his footing and lunged back at him. They wrestled each other to the floor until Hadden and Meraton pulled them apart.

"How dare you say I don't care about her!"

Hadden forced himself between them, eyeing them both, then looked to Xander. "To be honest, maybe he's right. Sometimes, it seems like you don't care about her or this process. This is the first time I've seen you fight for your relationship with her. We need that from you. We're all going to need to fight for our mates."

"I do care! It's just …"

"What?"

Xander looked down still panting from the encounter. He wiped sweat from his brow. "I don't know."

Hadden's face softened. "You need to tell us what's really going on. Otherwise, we can't help you break free from the virus."

He pulled away from the group and stood near the door ready to bolt. "She judges me. She doesn't think I'm good enough for her. Maybe she *should* be with Ramu."

Hadden did agree that Tia could be quite judgmental. "Perhaps. But I think that you judge yourself too. You're putting yourself in your own way."

"I have so far to go in this whole spiritual growth thing…"

"We all do," Meraton said.

Hadden stood between Xander and the door. "We all need to feel good enough about ourselves before attempting to help Pentada. This process we're about to do will help that a lot."

Xander crossed his arms, looking doubtful.

"Ramu?" Hadden asked. "We have to be there for each other 100%, or this process won't work."

He nodded with stern eyes, massaging his shoulder where Xander had hit him. They formed a circle again, and Xander reluctantly joined them. After a few moments of silence, Hadden began guiding them through the process.

"We are helping Xander shift timelines, also known as a MindStory. It's like an entire operating system consisting of self-images, beliefs, feelings, and perceptions that make up your view of reality. Once you change it, reality changes for you. Let's begin."

As a Voyent, Hadden saw all the segments of Xander's life like ropes of light. The MindStory before he came to Helio Tropez looked red, the one after he arrived looked indigo, then went back to red after the virus infected him. As a team, they helped him disengage from the red MindStory and re-engage with the indigo one. Once intact, Hadden showed the others how to heal and seal any entrances that could turn the red one back on again. That helped the negative experiences from all MindStories leave the hippocampus part of the brain and move into the neo-cortex with a new vibration of wisdom versus trauma.

"Now, to lock into the SANA timeline and your purpose, Xander, the only thing remaining is the forgiveness process. We need a focal point, so I suggest directing it towards your shadow counterpart, JJ Redus."

"Why him?"

"He was your CM handler and now embodies the virus that's in your system. The Redus Family targeted anyone from the Indicum lineage on the surface."

Xander's eyebrows pinched together as he searched his memories for the truth of that statement.

"It's about looking at the old MindStory where you gave your power away to him. Now, instead of resenting him and pushing away from it, completely own it. It's an acceptance process where you come to peace with the past.

Ironically, this allows you to give it away because you can't give away something you don't own. Once you own it, you choose to give it back, to recycle it, to let it go and create space for the new MindStory. You were not a victim but a willing player at the soul level." He pulled up a hologram image. "This is a form of 'consciousness technology' that combines taking an oath of service to SANA and to forgiveness. That's the only way you will integrate your soul annex."

The hologram consisted of a five-pointed star representing all spiritual medicines and all five colour frequencies. Inside the star, two overlapping circles blazed. They symbolised the bi-wave architecture of the SANA and SIM polarity. As Hadden waved his hand across it, the two circles became three intersecting circles, representing the tri-wave. That integration of dark and light powered the ascension to the next density level.

"Through this process, you will move from a bi-wave to a tri-wave architecture within your mind-body system. Xander, I will give you the words that you need to repeat. At the same time, imagine being connected to your heart so that this no longer remains merely an intellectual exercise. Meanwhile, the rest of us will use our aptitudes to help strengthen the transformation from bi-wave to tri-wave."

"So we just focus on seeing Xander within the three circles?" Stavron asked.

"Yes, exactly."

An oath appeared inside the three circles. The tiny lettering grew larger.

Xander read the oath first and sighed, "I don't believe that."

"You have to manufacture the belief."

"Manufacture?"

"Believe without doubt, then it comes about."

"Come again?"

"It's whereby you imagine a timeline in which all this is true. Think of it this way, do you remember a time when you didn't think you could play music the way you do now?"

He nodded.

"But you kept going anyway, imagining the day you reach the level of mastery you have now."

"That's true."

"Same thing here. Imagine a future timeline where this oath is true as you say it. It helps write the code in your mind. This lays down the train tracks of the default thinking that you need. Then you can choose to direct your consciousness in that direction anytime you like. Before doing a process like this, the train tracks aren't there. Now you have means to travel."

He nodded with a puzzled look. "Okay."

The words appeared in English to him.

I, Xander, now fully own and accept all shadow counterparts and the SIM timeline I have reverted to. All experiences served a purpose as part of my growth so that I could realise my true purpose in this life. I give my full gratitude now for all the gifts that SIM gave me. And I now choose to fully integrate all those gifts and give that old timeline back to the universe for recycling. In doing so, I break all vows, agreements, oaths or contracts I have ever made with SIM in any lifetime, timeline or reality. All is dissolved in the Celestine Fire of Purification. I now reclaim my vessel as my own. So be it.

They sat in silence together, breathing and helping him fully release the story so that it couldn't take hold of him again.

If I, Xander, ever felt hurt, judged, offended, or abused by SIM through thought, word or action from any time, any life, any dimension or timeline… I now offer SIM and all SIM agents full forgiveness. I forgive all offences that were created knowingly or unknowingly.

Hadden saw trauma in Xander's hippocampus move to the neo-cortex part of the brain storing it as wisdom.

If I, Xander, have ever harmed myself because of going against my SANA nature in thought, word or action from any time, any life or any dimension, I humbly ask for forgiveness from myself.

Hadden said, "Once you receive a yes from your higher self, let us know."

Xander sat in silence with his eyes closed. Soon, tears rolled down his cheeks, and he nodded.

"Okay, next part."

If I, Xander, ever hurt others because of going against my SANA nature… through thought, word or action from any time, any life or any dimension or timeline… I now ask them all for forgiveness.

"Once you receive a yes from any that felt harmed by you, let us know."

"*All* of them?"

"Yes, imagine all of them at the soul level, forgiving you. All beings are connected. You are, in essence, giving and receiving forgiveness from yourself."

He sat in silence again for a long time. Hadden saw the cords fall away one by one, then several at once. The group helped clear them away and burn the cords of pain in a fire of purification.

If I, Xander, ever hurt my relationship with SANA via thought, word or action, I humbly ask for forgiveness. Will you please forgive me, SANA, and help me to learn from all these experiences?

Hadden said, "When you receive a yes from SANA, let us know."

A few minutes later, he nodded. The other men gathered around him, holding compassionate space for him to release any remaining stored trauma.

Hadden said a final prayer to end the process. "In all these instances, we acknowledge the connectedness of all beings, including this group here today. We release all spiritual, mental, emotional, physical, material or karmic bondage on behalf of this soul, our souls and all souls that are ready. We affirm that, as of this moment, there is no holding on to the past. We pull out of all our memory banks, release, sever and remove any trace of resistance. We cleanse, purify and transmute all these unwanted energies into the pure light of love. Let peace, balance, wisdom and understanding manifest in all our affairs. And so it is forever."

After they were done, the men sat in silence, letting the experience get absorbed into their systems. When all felt complete, they stood and hugged each other, moved by the experience. Xander could barely stand, so Ramu helped him to his room and to settle in. Any trace of animosity between them had vanished.

Xander slept for twelve hours, undisturbed and deeply. When he rejoined the group the next day, he was an entirely different man.

CHAPTER 43

Helio Tropez – 2012

When Xander returned to the meeting room, he walked with a straighter posture and more confidence in his stride. For the first time since meeting him, Xander looked comfortable with himself, and it gave Hadden hope for the rest of them. The bond between all of them felt palpable now, and he trusted that the rest of the healing would go more smoothly.

Stavron discovered floating chairs in a supply room and distributed five in a circle so that they didn't have to sit on the floor anymore.

Once they were gathered together, Hadden clapped his hands once, drawing their attention. "Today, we start by focusing on Ramu."

Ramu furrowed his brow and took a deep breath. "Or... we could try someone else?"

Hadden smiled and ignored the request. "Let's take an hour to sit in meditation and study his mind."

At the end of an hour, Hadden rang a bell. Each of the men brought his attention back to the room.

Hadden began, "Although you don't have the same kind of damage to your soul structure as Xander, I see an immaturity. Without intense growth experiences, a soul lacks the capacity to serve. While I understand that people in Helio Tropez wanted to remain safe and high vibrational, there was a clear cost."

Meraton cleared his throat. "What are you implying?"

"I get it," Stavron nodded. "I noticed that anyone born after 1961 is kind of a wuss."

Meraton looked puzzled.

Stavron looked at the group warily. "Any kind of change seems to rattle them."

Meraton glanced out the window, scanning his memories.

Ramu cleared his throat, "I wouldn't say…"

"Just listen for now, Ramu," Hadden said.

"I see what you mean," Meraton conceded. "I'd never really noticed it before you mentioned it, but you're right."

Ramu took a breath to speak, then glanced at Hadden and stopped.

Meraton continued, "I also see a superiority-inferiority program in you, Ramu. I probably have it too. People in Helio Tropez consider themselves as protected from SIM influence. Yet, 'feeling superior' is actually a SIM program. Before the Great UnDoing, we never used to see ourselves as better than others."

Stavron narrowed his eyes. "Feeling superior usually hides a feeling of inferiority?"

"True," Meraton nodded.

Ramu sank down in his floating chair.

Xander glanced at him. "When I listen to your soul structure, it's like a song in one chord with no melody. You've cut yourself off from the highs and lows to remain safe while trying to control others."

Stavron added, "Yes. I see it in terms of the matrix language code. It's all zeros and no ones. There's a one-sidedness to many aspects of your soul structure."

Ramu wiped sweat from his brow. "I didn't expect such bad news."

Hadden touched his arm. "It's okay. It's an understandable mechanism – you've done it to survive, to make your way in the most comfortable way

431

possible. It's kept you alive until now, but it's time to let go and let life take care of you more, especially to properly relate to Metta."

Xander nodded. "Metta and I were in the same school for music as teenagers. I saw her get used and abused by males over and over again. She's come to expect that and sets herself up as a victim."

Hadden felt guilty, wishing he could have done more for his daughter. "It could be easy for you two to get into a victim-villain relationship."

Ramu looked at him, hurt. "Wow... I would never do that."

"Of course you wouldn't consciously, but until she goes through a healing process, she could set you up like that."

"I think I need more motivation to make this SANA relationship with her work. I know she's very pretty and all, but is there anything you can tell me about her as a person beyond all her issues?"

Hadden looked at him, starting to understand the man more. While the immaturity was there, he was scared of committing to something that he was unsure of. He was logical, not wanting to hurt himself or someone else, and for that, he had Hadden's respect. "We all have issues, Ramu. That said, I only knew her as a toddler, but even then, she sparkled with creative energy. Her aptitude is Ecrivent, so her writing and reading developed far quicker than with Tia. In fact, she had the language skills of a nine-year-old at only three."

Xander added, "She's the most talented poet and songwriter I've ever met, and I've met a lot. When she is feeling good about herself, she's a mesmerising singer-songwriter and a loyal friend with a brilliant mind. Once we all go through this healing process, you won't believe your luck in having such a partner as her."

Ramu tilted his head and shrugged.

"You don't believe me? Let me play you one of her songs. Is there a guitar here?"

Meraton nodded. "I saw one in the room next door. All kinds of instruments, actually."

Xander left and returned a moment later with a six-string guitar. He took a few minutes to tune it and then launched into the song *Shades of Light*. The melody and lyrics felt so familiar to Hadden, almost as if he remembered hearing Metta singing it as a child. After Xander finished, the other four men sat back glassy-eyed and shaken by the beauty.

"It's one of the most famous songs in the world, and she's won many awards for it. Unlike some of my other songs, I think this lifts you up to SANA if you hear it in the right way."

Ramu took a deep breath. "Agreed. Thank you for playing it."

"Wait until you hear her sing it. It'll transport you."

"I've never accomplished anything creative like that."

Meraton frowned at him. "What? You're one of the top gem smiths. You took the MindStory Code that we downloaded and programmed it into the amethyst. No one else could figure that out. And once we add the missing parts, it's going to transform the collective consciousness of humanity. That's no small feat."

"True," he said, smiling shyly.

"Don't worry, Ramu. You were clearly farther ahead in your soul growth than you are right now. The virus sent everyone back to their lowest point. We need to find the timeline of your highest development point and jump your life force energy back there. We also need to integrate any shadow aspect or soul annex. Do you have a sense of who that might be? Likely someone on the surface from the House of Oranta," Hadden suggested.

Ramu glanced away. "I am sure there is, but I can't tell who."

"Most of us have a blind spot when it comes to our shadow. Let's take a look." After a few minutes, Hadden opened his eyes again. "A very powerful man in the UK called Clifford Oranta. What did everyone else see?"

Meraton nodded. "Yes, I see a man who is part of the shadow government, someone pulling the strings but is out of the limelight."

The others nodded. They spent another hour helping Ramu reconnect to his SANA timeline and integrate his soul annex. After the forgiveness process, his face held a symmetry and harmony that hadn't been there before.

After that, they studied Stavron's mind and shared their findings.

Meraton began the feedback. "With you, instead of a superiority complex, I see an inferiority complex. Perhaps because you are different in so many ways from typical Heliotropans. You have a very well-balanced masculine and feminine side, both physically and spiritually hermaphroditic. Annika has the same hermaphroditic qualities. The two of you have the potential to reach Hierogamic union quickly as you've already done it within."

433

"Yes, I see the same thing," Hadden smiled. "We have a lot to learn from you."

Ramu said, "I see great strength in your soul structure, which matches your physical strength. Yet, you tend to hide the more vulnerable feminine side."

Meraton nodded. "Annika does that too. She often had an unwillingness to let others help her, that is to be seen as weak in any way."

"That's definitely me," Stavron laughed. "I think that's why we had a falling out. We both wanted to be the strong one."

The group looked to Xander expectantly. He hesitated. "I'm sorry, I don't see things like you do. I only hear things, and I'm still wondering what meaning to make of them."

Meraton nodded encouragingly. "Then tell us what you hear. You don't have to figure it out on your own. We're all here to help."

"Okay then." He cleared his throat. "I hear a deep staccato rhythm in your soul signature. It's like the drum section of an orchestra taking over a symphony with only a very faint string section carrying the melody, but the melody is captivating. Listening to it, I'm desperate for the drums to lighten up, to let the melody come to the forefront and bring unity to what is truly a beautiful song."

"It's perhaps another way of saying the feminine, lyrical side is there but needs to feel safe to come forward?" Ramu suggested.

"Yes. That makes sense," Stavron said. "I wish I had more of the other aptitudes."

Hadden shifted in his chair. "You will once we get closer to ascension. Okay. I think that gives us enough to go on. Let's use our aptitudes to help Stavron anchor back into his natural SANA timeline and integrate his soul annex."

"I don't think I have a soul annex."

Hadden closed his eyes and focused on any kind of shadow hovering around Stavron's pineal gland. "You're right. I don't see a shadow aspect to your soul. Was there never anyone in the House of Saffron who...?"

"Yes, many lifetimes ago, but I re-integrated him. He caused a lot of trouble on the surface during Medieval times in Europe. Never again."

Hadden smiled. "Good, man. You're clearly farther ahead than the rest of us. Okay, so it's just anchoring the timeline."

After the process felt complete, Hadden yawned and stretched. "I suggest we take a break for a few minutes."

The other men hugged Stavron. His face had a newfound softness, and his movements seemed smoother than before. They gathered around the replicator Tia had brought to make Respite Tea and macaroons, which they wolfed down. Stavron, Xander and Ramu joked around together while Meraton slipped out of the room. Hadden kept to himself by the window, still trying to adjust his body to the density of 4D. Several unusual, small animals darted in and out of the bushes just outside the window. When he had first come to Helio Tropez, everyone had a Jenio, but not anymore...

Once everyone was back in the room, Hadden said, "Let's focus on Meraton."

By this time, the group knew the drill. They spent an hour in meditation until Hadden rang the bell and rested his gaze on Meraton.

The man had a regal bearing except for the fact that he stooped. "Like Ramu, the superiority program needs releasing. You are a Sentient-Reprogram. I remember hearing as a child how you were specifically chosen for the Quinary Mission because of your *Emotional Engineer* aptitude. On the surface, you started a foundation to teach heart-based logic. You'll be happy to know that your efforts continue to this day. I see that you feel guilty about what happened with the Quinary Mission and that you feel responsible for what happened to Daphne and Annika."

Meraton averted his gaze. "I'm glad to hear that the foundation survived."

"The original Quinary members made a huge difference. It wasn't for nothing."

"Over the years," Stavron added, "I've often seen you defer to Cassandra, perhaps because of her Pentada status. Everyone here holds her in high regard as the first and only Pentada for a long time. Yet, I know that everyone on the Task Force greatly admires you. In fact, as an Emotional Engineer, you're more naturally suited to leadership than her."

Ramu sat up straight and smoothed his goatee. "Meraton, you told me that a SANA mate must fully activate his own power first before his Pentada mate can activate hers."

They all looked to Meraton for his reaction. His face turned stone still.

Xander's eyes remained closed as if straining to hear something. "Your true melody is a triumphant battle hymn, yet you overlay that with some kind of a Musak."

Meraton shook his head and shrugged.

"Muzak is where they take beautifully composed songs and re-produce them in a way that is off-putting. On the surface, they play it as background music in stores and when a corporation puts your call on hold."

Hadden nodded, "A lot of popular music on the surface actually fractures people's brainwaves."

Meraton looked around the circle. "So my musical frequency fractures people?"

Stavron nodded. "It did when you were controlled by SIM. It was like emotional demolition, the shadow side of your aptitude. Like when you closed down any opportunities for community gatherings like our spiritual groups, cultural events and restaurants. But even before that, you had a powerful frequency that you dulled down so as not to eclipse Cassandra."

"Okay. It's hard to admit, but I see what you mean."

Hadden looked around the group. "I think that what we're working on is clear now."

They spent the next hour reconnecting Meraton back to his highest SANA timeline. The most potent part of the process involved forgiving himself and Cassandra for not going back to the surface after The Great UnDoing and allowing himself to be more of a true leader. Finally, they helped him finish integrating his soul annex, a man on the surface who was a titan of industry, named Raymond Oranta.

After they finished, Meraton stood up and stretched, his turquoise eyes flashing with purpose again. "That was amazing. I have so much energy... I could... I could dance!"

The lumbering man closed his eyes and started twisting on the balls of his feet, as if hearing upbeat music in his head.

"Hadden, maybe you can help me this. I remember this dance club that Cassandra and I went to the on the surface. We did this kind of move."

He laughed. "It looks like some kind of swing dance, or jive..."

"Jive...Lindy Hop! Yeah, we learned all that. Xander, can you play any swing music on that thing?"

Xander looked his guitar and back at the man dancing in front of him, "Oh, uh.... that's like music from the 40's or 50's, right?"

Meraton nodded, pulling Hadden onto his feet to dance with him.

"I remember learning the Jitterbug when I was a kid," Hadden laughed. "Remember his move?"

They started dancing together swinging each other around the room.

"How about this?" Xander said finding a tune. "Cab Calloway's Jitterbug."

"You got it!"

Soon, Stavron had found a drum from the music room and was playing a back beat. Meanwhile, Ramu played with the controls on the holographic screen until electronic sounds and colored lights interweaved with the players. After the song ended, they erupted in cheers, and collapsed back onto their floating chairs, joyful and radiant.

During their next break, a chipmunk appeared at the window and rapped its clawed paw against the glass. Xander squatted down to have a closer look. "What do you want, little one?"

Stavron approached the window. "Riley!" he cried, holding his out hand. The chipmunk leapt onto his hand and scampered up his arm, nestling under his chin. "Xander, this is my Jenio. He's returned."

"That's a good sign," Hadden said. "I've seen a number of small animals out there recently."

Ramu ran to the window and peered outside. "I wonder if Morvato is nearby." He whistled, and a few moments later, a miniature leopard leapt onto the window ledge. She jumped into his arms, and he laughed as she nuzzled his cheek.

They gathered around the two re-found Jenios. Meraton glanced out the window to see if his wolf might appear.

"Do you have a Jenio?" Xander asked Hadden.

"No. Like you, I grew up on the surface and spent very little time here."

"Tia didn't have one for a year, but then a miniature polar bear found her. Apparently, he also disappeared when the SIM virus showed up."

"That's too bad. Hopefully, they'll all come back to us."

"Ulwag," Meraton called from the window. "He's not there."

"Let's focus on Hadden," Xander suggested.

Meraton tore himself away from the window and sighed. "I will act as the facilitator."

They gathered in a circle and meditated as the Jenios explored the room, sniffing in every corner.

After about thirty minutes, Meraton opened his eyes. "I see that you've spent years healing your own mind. You've also got an entirely intact lightbody connection with your soul that I've never seen before. I guess that's what we have to look forward to in 6D?"

Hadden shrugged. "I now see the world in a much different way than before and vaguely remember that my aptitudes expanded in dramatic ways. I'd love help in retrieving my memories and abilities from 6D, if that's possible. Did I tell anyone what would happen to my memories when I came down here?"

Xander leaned forward. "You said that the plan involved storing them in the cloud."

Hadden nodded, remembering Halia had done that with him when he underwent CM torture at the hands of SIM agents.

Ramu scratched his Jenio's head. "What's the cloud, again?"

"The cloud is like a quantum consciousness computer-created under SANA," Stavron explained.

Meraton glanced out of the window again. "Exactly. I say we take the chance and see if we can access the cloud and find your memories. Shields up!"

They gathered their focus and spent the next hour trying to raise their consciousness enough to enter the cloud, even if only for a few seconds. Meraton rang the bell, and they opened their eyes. He looked around the circle, but everyone shook his head.

Meraton stretched, rubbing his eyes. "We'll have to try another day. Let's take a break and join the group for dinner. We need to celebrate what we've accomplished."

A white face with a long snout appeared at the window as they finished their meeting.

"I think Ulwag has returned," Hadden smiled.

Meraton clapped his hands and helped the wolf jump inside. The two of them rolled around on the floor together in a joyful reunion. The other men laughed and welcomed Ulwag back into their ranks.

Hadden returned to his sleeping chamber and lay down on the bed. A few minutes later, he slipped into a deep sleep. When he woke up, he remembered dreaming about being in the Hall of Congress. Halia was an Elder, so it had to be 6D. The Elders showed him how to rebuild a lower density body into a higher density body that could ascend. That was exactly the information he needed. He opened his eyes and stared at the ceiling. *Was that a dream or a memory?* He found a piece of paper and a pencil and wrote down as much as he could remember. Somehow, the process of regaining his memories had worked, at least partially.

After having a shower, Hadden met up with the other SANA mates so they could re-join the whole community for dinner.

CHAPTER 44

A flush of energy raced through Tia as the five men entered the room. They carried an entirely new aura about them. Everyone else noticed it, too. Several people stood up and applauded in their Heliotropan way, a kind of silent standing ovation. One by one, each SANA mate interacted with group members. Meanwhile, Tia stood back, watching from the sidelines. As the group settled into a circle, she sat far away from Xander, avoiding eye contact.

Vanar, one of the Elders at the pagoda, said, "You all look so different and more alive. In fact, the whole frequency of the pagoda has gone up another notch."

The group laughed.

Hadden announced, "We'd like to teach you all the processes we used. Then, we suggest you form small, same-gender groups and do the same. Whether you have a SANA mate or not and whether that person is here or not, it will help strengthen the cohesion of the whole collective mindset."

The group agreed, then the five Pentada members went through the specifics of the protocol. Over the next two days, they would work to ensure everyone was virus-free.

After dinner, Meraton called the whole group back together. "The next item on the agenda is how to take the other four Pentada women through the same protocol as that will have a ripple effect on the whole city. And we need to work with the Elders in Helio Tropez to share the resources with everyone else again. In other words, we need to go back in a few days."

Neals raised his hand. "What about the raptors and getting the SIM virus again?"

"There are risks, so we need as many Protectors as possible and only those with the strongest immune systems towards SIM. We need to begin the rainbow bridge to ascension. It's already July 13, so we only have ten days left. The ascension window happens on only one day, July 23."

"Who's going back so far?" Neals asked.

"All the SANA mates and Tasma. Tia, what about you?"

Tia nodded reluctantly.

"We need extra protection. Any of you who are good with weapons. Do we have any volunteers?"

At first, the group remained silent. Meraton looked over at the group of eight men and women who acted as Protectors at the pagoda. Obar was their leader, and as an Ecrivent-Attention, Shielding was his dominant aptitude. In fact, he had led a group of people with the same aptitude to the pagoda. Some had physical training with weapons, while others didn't. They looked at each other, and finally, two of them raised their hands, Toran and Julianna, who were both skilled in weaponry. A heavy energy filled the room.

"Just two? Okay."

"We need the rest of them to protect us here," Obar argued.

Hadden pursed his lips. "Alright, then. The rest of you hold space for our safe passage. But remember, if it goes well, you all need to come back to Helio Tropez by July 22nd to cross the rainbow bridge."

Obar shook his head, "The rest of us could just as easily go through ascension here on July 23rd."

"Maybe, but the idea of Pentada is to make the whole process ten times easier, and that will happen in the city."

"It's up to you."

They spent the rest of the evening performing timeline healings on Annika, Metta, Daphne and Cassandra to prime them for the reconnection. Afterwards, people volunteered names of loved ones to also send them prayers of healing. When the process felt complete, each person thanked Hadden personally for his sacrifice in coming back to help them.

After the group finished, Tia snuck out of a side door to head back to her room. Suddenly, a hand touched her shoulder, and she spun around to see Xander. The energy from him was electric. He seemed so different than before.

"Xander!"

"Can I walk you to your room?"

"Um… sure."

As they walked back towards their rooms in silence, Tia slowed down her pace, a feeling of terror growing in the pit of her stomach. All the guilt, shame, self-worth issues he once had no longer stood between them. Instead, he radiated unbridled love for her, and she could barely handle it. She still had healing to do. On top of everything, embarrassment about her lack of experience with men kept her from speaking. They paused at her door, but Tia didn't move to open it.

"Can I come in?" Xander asked.

"Oh… ah…"

"If you don't feel comfortable, I totally understand."

"I want to say yes, but… it's true. I am a bit uncomfortable."

He stood smiling at her, totally content with her to say yes or no, loving her either way.

Tia looked down at the floor, feeling her cheeks flush. "Okay… sure."

They stepped inside, the door slid shut, and they stood looking at each other. Tia backed away towards a water jug. "Water?"

"No, thanks. Listen, Tia, I've been advised that we should do some kind of vows to SANA, but that all seems rather…"

"…I know, strange." Her pulse sped up. "We're just getting to know each other, so…"

"Right?"

The warring factions inside her mind fell silent. Her body now felt like a generous host rather than a battleground. "It's just to ensure that we're choosing to come together out of love and honouring of SANA instead of..."

"Exactly... I follow you." Xander blushed. "That's certainly my intention."

Tia laughed. "That's certainly my intention too."

"Brilliant." He stepped closer, pulling her to him with a hand at the small of her back. She looked up at him, and instead of looking away, an impulse made her match his gaze. Barely inches apart, she could smell the scent of his skin, the heat from his chest. She swallowed.

He spoke softly. "Can I kiss you now?"

Heat rose from her chest, and she felt a full green light from SANA to proceed. Her chin lifted, and she closed her eyes, not knowing what to expect. He pressed his lips against hers, and her knees weakened under his touch. Shockwaves of recognition ran through her body. Every nerve cell fired. He clearly knew what he was doing, so she just surrendered to his passion.

They parted for a moment, searching each other's eyes for any sign of objection. When there was none, he scooped her up and carried her to the bed. She wrapped her legs around his hips, and as he lay her head gently on the pillow, he nuzzled her neck. Waves of pleasure overrode the fear. After a few minutes, she felt wet tears against her cheek. He stopped kissing her and lay back on the pillow, wiping his eyes.

"What's wrong?" she asked, worried that she'd done something wrong.

"I realised that I've never been with a woman that I actually loved so much and with such an open heart. It's intense."

"If it makes you feel any better, I've never actually made love before, ever. So I'm way off in unknown territory."

"So maybe we take it slow?"

"Sounds good."

He turned on his side and pulled a tress of hair away from her cheek. His eyes blazed with fire and something deeper she couldn't quite name. They kissed again, this time slowly and gently savouring each moment, a rainbow light dancing in her mind's eye.

"Do you see the rainbow?" she mumbled into his lips.

"Yes..."

When they finally made love, she knew the healing process was complete. Indeed, her connection with Xander contributed some kind of missing piece. In her heart, she knew that she could finally bridge the gap between this world and the next.

CHAPTER 45

For the next few days, Tia and Xander mostly stayed sequestered away, making love and sharing their innermost feelings and dreams for the future. On the fifth day, they lay spooning together. They barely communicated with anyone else in the group, and Tia didn't care. She ran her hand over the scars on Xander's back. Although her aptitude didn't allow her to physically heal someone, she tried imagining that she could. Cassandra could do it. She had witnessed wounds and scars completely disappear upon the touch of anyone with a Tangent aptitude on many occasions.

Xander sighed. "It's ugly, I know. They healed the scars when I first arrived, but now they're back. Even after the men helped me switch timelines, the scars remained."

"There must be a reason. Maybe you need them as badges of courage. Would you like me to try to remove them?"

"You can do that?"

"I'll try, with your permission."

"Please do."

Focusing her mind, she lay her hands on the scars and imagined them dissolving away, along with all the emotional trauma associated with them. When she opened her eyes, they still remained. A wave of disappointment ran through her. "Sorry. No good. Apparently, a way to get ready for ascension is to practice more of the other aptitudes. I'm not Tangent but thought I would try."

"It's okay. Thank you for trying"

They drifted off to sleep until a knock sounded on the door. When Xander stood up to answer it, Tia noticed the skin on his back was completely healed. He spoke with Stavron in quiet tones out in the hallway for a few minutes. When he came back in, Tia pointed at him.

"Your back... look in the mirror."

He swivelled his head over his shoulder. "It worked?"

"Amazing!"

He scooped her off the bed and into his arms, spinning as she laughed. "You're truly amazing, Tia of Zuris. Perhaps you are now ready for ascension. Thank you so much." He kissed her forehead, cheeks and then her lips.

After making love again, they lay together in bliss, looking out of the window at the birds in the nearby trees.

"By the way, what did Stavron want?"

"Oh, yes. I forgot. They don't want to rush us, but they are ready to leave for the city tomorrow."

The thought of facing the raptors again chafed at Tia's nerves. "Do we have to?"

"We have weapons."

Tia nodded and buried her face in his shoulders.

The next morning, the five SANA mates, Tasma, two protectors and Tia set off on the trail back to Helio Tropez. Each person carried a Genfa, water and food on their back. Toran and Julianna also carried longbows and knives. A group escorted them to the far edge of the lake, waving them off as they slipped into the trees. After several minutes of walking, the trail narrowed, and Tia found herself walking beside Toran – one of the Protectors – at the front of the group. Shadows lingered around the tree trunks, not yet shaking the night from under their branches. Birdsong filled the air, and a couple of butterflies danced ahead of them, but the tension knotted in her shoulders.

She let out a shaky breath. Toran must have heard as he glanced at her, a smile lifting the corner of his mouth. "You doing okay?"

Tia nodded, not trusting her voice to be as steady as she wanted.

He chuckled. "Not scared of a stroll in the woods, are you?"

"Only when the woods are filled with teeth and things that want to eat you."

"Oh, they won't eat you," Toran said, looking further up the trail. "Nah, the raptors don't eat humans. They only kill us for sport. They're pack animals, and the alpha needs to establish its dominance somehow."

She looked at him, aghast. "You're joking…"

"Nope!"

"I thought you were supposed to be making me feel better?" Tia said, eyes flinching to every movement and sound in the gloom. Toran, on the other hand, walked with a relaxed stride, his Genfa poised and no hint of worry on his face.

"Was I? What good would that do? If you know what you're dealing with, you won't do anything stupid. I'm trying to keep us alive, not help you sleep at night."

"Great," Tia muttered.

He laughed again. "Fine. If it helps, tell me about yourself. Keep your mind busy."

She thought about arguing, wondering whether the raptors would hear them, but if Toran was relaxed, then she would be too.

"What do you want to know?"

He shrugged. "Where'd you grow up?"

"On the surface…" she said as though that much was obvious.

"Yes, but where on the surface? Were you by the sea? Mountains? Was it cold? Did you have a dog? Anything! Tell me about it."

Tia pursed her lips, then decided there was no harm in it. She told him about growing up with her father in Seattle and getting home-schooled by him. He even taught her how to jump the rope because she didn't have any other children to play with. Taron laughed when she recalled a memory of Hadden skipping and his foot getting caught in the rope, sending him sprawling.

"Good to know he's human," Taron grinned.

"Oh, he's very human. Did you know that he once..."

A hand caught her elbow, jolting her to a stop. Another hand clamped over her mouth. Taron held a fist over his shoulder, indicating the train of people to stop.

She could feel his breath on her neck, her heart thudding against his chest behind her. Toran spoke in a whisper, his lips barely an inch from her ear. "Don't. Move."

Slowly, he pulled his hand away from her mouth. He looked back to the group, a finger to his lips, before pointing out to under the trees.

Tia followed his finger, not seeing anything. It was only when what she had presumed was a shrub jerked that Tia realised they were raptors nesting at the trunk of a great tree.

Taron gestured for them to move quietly, pushing Tia to lead while he stood on the edge of the trail, his longbow pointed towards the reptiles.

Reluctant to leave him, Tia crept onwards as she got her Genfa ready, moving slowly while keeping a careful eye on the rest of the group. Julianna, the other Protector who had been bringing up the rear, herded them on. She kept her longbow trained on the sleeping raptors, her eyes not moving from them.

Tia watched, her heart racing, as Julianna's boot neared a root that had broken the surface of the trail. She hissed, trying to get her attention, but when Julianna looked up, it was too late. Her boot caught the root, sending her crashing onto the stone trail. She hit the ground with a grunt, and everyone froze.

For a moment, nothing in the forest stirred. Then a scaled head lifted, staring straight towards them. The raptor climbed to its feet, making short sharp noises as though talking to itself. It stood facing them, its head cocked, trying to understand what it was looking at as they stared back at it.

Tia balled her hands to keep them from shaking. In the corner of her eye, she saw Julianna slowly reaching for the longbow she'd dropped when she'd fallen. Toran held a hand out, ordering her to freeze.

The raptor jolted at the movement and took a step forward. The noise it was making grew louder. Hadden wedged the butt of the Genfa into his shoulder, still as an oak. Toran pulled back on the longbow.

Clicking its jaws, the raptor twitched its tail, then screamed. The entire group jolted, and the raptor charged.

"Run!" Toran shouted, arrow already firing. Julianna scrambled just as the other raptors were hauling themselves to their feet, suddenly alert. Tia fired her Genfa, but it hit a rock. The others fired at the raptors and stunned a few, but more were coming their way.

"There's too many!" Xander cried, grabbing her hands. "Let's get out of here!"

The gravel trail slipped under her boots as the others thundered behind her. Someone overtook her, but she didn't pay them any attention. Her only thought was to run, run until she couldn't anymore, whether by her own doing or something else's.

Trees whipped by, branches clawing at her arms and cheeks, but she didn't care. A scratch was better than teeth. She broke into a clearing, and arms caught her, pulling her aside. They bundled her to their chest, and the familiar scent of Xander's skin filled her. She buried her face, whimpering.

"Shh," he said. "You're alright."

Breathless, Hadden did a quick headcount. "Is everyone here?"

"Everyone but the Protectors," Stavron confirmed.

Hadden nodded. "Good. Let's keep moving. There may be more out here."

"Wait," Tia said, breaking away from Xander. "What about Taron and Julianna? They might need our help."

The group looked between them, then Meraton put an arm around her. "They stayed behind so we could get away. They have several weapons on them while we just have these Genfas. They know how to keep themselves alive. We need to get back to the city before they find us."

Tia gazed back down the trail, waiting to see the other two coming towards them. The trail remained empty.

"Come on," her grandfather said as the group huddled together, rejoining the path.

For the next few miles, they walked in terror, constantly looking over their shoulders until they hit the city limits. Meraton approached the city gates, but for some reason, they wouldn't open. Tia had never seen the gate locked.

"How dare they!" Meraton growled. He pulled a device from his satchel and disengaged the lock with the help of his aptitude. As they slipped inside the city walls, the tent city loomed larger than ever. Only now, it looked like two factions had formed, fighting amongst themselves over the last of the resources. A wall of refuse stood between them.

"Let's get away from here and into the inner sanctum. I think we all need to recoup our energy from that attack before we do anything," Hadden said.

In silent agreement, they walked past the area without a word. People eyed them suspiciously and began whispering as they passed by. They found a pagoda in the Garden of Jephsonite to rest. Tia curled up in Xander's arms, trembling.

After an hour, Hadden gathered the group together and said, "I'd like to start with Daphne."

They agreed and headed for the pagoda-turned-brothel in the centre of the city. Soon, news of their return would spread around the city, so they needed to act quickly. Just before they rounded the corner near the pagoda, Hadden brought them into a huddle.

"She will be surprised to see me. I suggest you go by yourself first, Tia."

They stayed close to the garden next to the pagoda as Tia went around to the front entrance. She still felt waves of adrenaline from their encounter with the raptors, so took a few deep breaths to calm down. Daphne sat alone on a chaise lounge.

"Tia! Have you come to keep me company? Business is very slow." She patted the chaise next to her.

Tia sat down and laid back. "Yes. How are you doing?"

"To be honest," she said, looking over at her. "I don't want to do this anymore."

A wave of relief rushed through Tia's heart.

"I bet you're relieved to hear that."

Tia smiled. "Why the change of heart?"

"I'm dying to tell someone who's not a sceptic about this whole ascension thing."

Tia turned to face her. "Please, tell me what's been going on."

"Okay, well…remember I started offering this 'service' at the pagoda with Aspra? It was her idea."

Tia nodded. "She was a Sanasta."

"Yes, but in a little-known sect. They aren't chaste but use sexual energy for creativity and healing. It triggered a past life memory when I was a Hetaira in Ancient Greece doing the same thing. So, we started this 'service' for that purpose, but it just degenerated into what I was doing on the surface…using sex for personal gain. Recently, she became Evangelistic, like you, although this time I actually started to listen. I know it's hard on a person's soul structure. My parents taught me all that when I was young. But I met this man who saw me in a restaurant when I was sixteen. He told me I could be a famous model and actress. I fell for it, only to discover that you have to sleep your way to the top. At first, I resisted, but then all the other girls were doing it, so I thought, 'why not?' I think that's when the SIM programming started. It happened at night when I was asleep, but I remember becoming more and more corrupted in my thinking. It made me feel so empty inside."

A burning sensation grew in Tia's stomach. "Annika told me that they tried to make her *sell her soul* for fame, but some kind of guardian angel helped her avoid that."

Tears welled up in the corners of Daphne's eyes, and she clasped her hands together tightly. "So, you want to know if I ended up going to one of those horrific rituals?

Tia nodded ever so slightly, not sure whether she wanted to hear the answer.

"I must have had a guardian angel too. I got my first audition to star in a blockbuster film. That's when I started getting invited to these 'special functions'. Each time I got an invitation, I got horribly ill. A friend finally confided in me about what goes on in there. After that, I declined the invitations. Sure enough, that killed my career. All I could get were small parts in B movies. I had mixed feelings about it all at the time, but in retrospect, I'm genuinely relieved. That would have been hard to come back from."

Tia bowed silently to thank that guardian angel.

Daphne rubbed her forehead as if to wipe away the memory. "When I met your father and he gave me the amethyst, I started remembering all my Pentada lives and the MindStory Code. My true life purpose fell into place. I got my moral compass back, and I was happy for the first time in a long time." A nostalgic smile crossed her face, and she tilted her head back, gazing up the trees, reliving a memory. "That was until they separated our little family..."

"Speaking of my father. Guess who's here?"

"Your father came back from the dead?" she asked with a wry smile.

"Literally."

"What do you mean, literally?"

"He devolved from 6D to 4D to help us, but most importantly to reconnect with you."

She screwed up her face and laughed. "You mean he's not an imaginary ghost you speak to anymore?"

Tia sighed. "He never was imaginary. I helped him come back here."

"So, where is he?"

Just then, he came around the corner looking reticent. His eyes radiated love for the person he'd adored from the moment he laid eyes on her at eight years old.

She stood up, wide-eyed.

He walked towards her, hesitant. "D.Z. It's me."

Daphne took a step back. He was the only one who used her initials as a nickname.

"You're not Hadden...."

"We're both a lot younger-looking than when we last were together. We were middle-aged back then. Now we're like in our twenties again."

"I don't get it. Tia said you died."

"I just ascended to the next density and came back."

"That seems too..."

"We haven't seen each other since...

"Tia and Metta were only three years old, I know. And I've missed you every single day since."

Hadden pulled her into his arms, and they clung to each other in a way that made Tia's heart melt. She stepped back to give them space, but Hadden pulled her into a three-way embrace. They were finally back together as a family, something she hadn't felt since she was three years old. The joy of being reunited like that meant everything to all of them at that moment. The only person missing was Metta.

After the tears of joy subsided, they sat together on the bench.

Hadden held both of their hands, beaming. "Now we can finally be together again. Not just for us, but for the whole ascension project."

Daphne hung her head. "But I've been running a brothel. How can you possibly want to be with me?"

"When I met you in 1980, I knew about your past. I know what caused it. And I know you can heal from all that, and I'm here to help you do it again."

He circled his arms around her as she shed silent tears.

"Neither of us has lived perfect lives," he said, "but that's why we will be able to help others because we understand, we've been there, we were all meant to go through those lives under the control of SIM. It's got a higher purpose. I see that now. All is absolving as we speak."

She collapsed into a puddle of tears as he rocked her in his arms. Hadden laid her on the ground near a Banyan tree and started the healing protocol. Tia's chest ached seeing her parents together again. Their love, their bond, everything they had gone through together appeared as a matrix of timelines interweaving in her mind's eye. A mixture of guilt and gratitude washed through her, thinking of all they had sacrificed to protect her and her sister. She let them be together quietly for a while and re-joined the group nearby. Xander pulled her into an embrace.

Meraton moved in close and whispered, "I've been worried about Daphne, that she could never heal from the low vibration that sexual usury creates."

"Remember what they teach in 6D? Low vibrational energies can paradoxically activate the highest vibrational energies. It's the principle of the slingshot. The farther you pull back, the further the shot and the easier it is to ascend."

Xander laughed. "That bodes well for me then."

The group sat in the garden, sending their healing energy to Daphne. When Hadden and Daphne joined the group, they stood up to greet her. With puffy, glowing eyes, she reached out for her father, and they hugged.

Meraton wiped the tears from her eyes and said, "I forgive you for everything you did to survive on the surface. I now understand the bigger purpose of it all."

Daphne nodded in silence with a knitted brow. "Thank you."

"Can you forgive me for leaving you behind on the surface?"

She rubbed her forehead. "I want to. Hadden just told me that it was all meant to be. I hope that's true."

"I abandoned you, there and here. I deeply regret that."

She swallowed hard and nodded. Not only had he left her on the surface, but once the virus hit, he had shut her out, even though she'd just arrived in Helio Tropez. Clearly, fully healing with her parents would require more time.

"I'd like to do the timeline process with Daphne," Hadden said. "To help her shift to the SANA timeline and integrate the soul annex known as Josie Carbona."

Xander whispered to Tia, "Josie is your mother's soul annex?"

Tia nodded, "Yes, the mastermind behind this whole SIM invasion of Helio Tropez. But maybe healing her will be the key to healing everyone."

They formed a circle around her and did the same process they had done at the mountain pagoda. Hadden led them through the healing protocol, and strangely, the integration between Daphne and Josie went quickly. She easily accepted Josephine's misdeeds as her own, forgiving and forgetting all the challenges. Tia was impressed, but not surprised. The Progenitors on Anatol gave her cosmic citizenship. Once Daphne anchored back into that part of the timeline, any agreement to be a SIM asset dissolved away instantly.

After it completed, Daphne opened her eyes. She looked like a different person: harmonious instead of fractured. "Wow. It's like I'm whole again?"

Meraton helped her sit up. "You've totally integrated your shadow annex, quicker than any of us. Amazing. You were clearly a linchpin, because I can sense the rise in frequency with all of us. Now, you rest here, and then we'll help your mother break free from this virus."

Daphne stood up. "I'd like to go with you."

Hadden put his hand to her forehead, checking her temperature. "Are you sure you're up to it?"

"It feels important for me to be there."

The group helped her stand up, and together, they walked towards the main entrance of the Palace of Zuris. Five protectors stood guard.

Meraton whispered, "I'll go alone to talk to them. As an Elder, I might have more sway."

After a few moments, he came back. "Well, I'm no longer welcome there. Apparently, I betrayed their cause."

"Maybe I can try," Daphne said, blushing. "All of them have been customers of mine. Maybe I can convince them I need to see my mother. Then I'll let you in from the back gate if possible."

She went alone to talk to them, flirting and laughing. They eventually let her enter, and she looked back at the group with a nod. The others went around to the back of the palace and waited. Once the coast was clear, Daphne opened a door and let the others enter.

Meraton brought them to a small, private meditation room to wait for him, then, together with Tasma, they went upstairs to talk to Cassandra. The rest of them tapped into Cassandra's mind and worked on shifting her timeline back to how it was before the virus had taken hold. Cassandra's shadow self, Anita Carbona, blackened her entire system. After all, she was the most powerful matriarch of all the SIM families. The Carbonas represented the vibration of black, and the Zuris clan represented the vibration of white. They were the extreme polar opposites. If Cassandra could integrate Anita, the whole Carbona matrix could dissolve and ascend.

When Meraton finally arrived at their meditation room with Cassandra hand in hand, she radiated that unique Zuris energy again. Cassandra went from person to person, hugging everyone. "I've been in complete denial about being possessed by SIM. I've caused so much suffering." Her face contorted in pain, and she held each person close.

Meraton put his arm around her. "During the process, we saw an uncomfortable truth that we've both been unwilling to see. We need to... confess something to you all."

They sat down in a circle and huddled close.

"When we returned here after the Great UnDoing, we thought we were the lucky ones who had escaped. But as I suspected, SIM had allowed us to escape so they could enter the minds of Heliotropans. We carried a SIM virus back into Helio Tropez, which affected the Hall of Records. That's what caused Frenla, Obar and the other Elders to turn their backs on our surface experiment."

As each person in the group absorbed the information, they sat in silence. It made sense. All Heliotropans had been affected by SIM; no one was immune. The virus just magnified the imbalances.

"I thought it was all my fault," Tia said, her voice shaking.

"It's no one person's fault. We're all responsible here," Meraton said.

Cassandra covered her face. "I'm not quite there yet. My actions caused untold suffering. We have to unblock the resources for everyone immediately."

"How can we do that?" Meraton asked. "All the Elders are still under SIM's influence."

"What if we go to the Hall of Records and ask Malinah?" Tia suggested.

Cassandra shook her head. "She's clearly got the virus too, and she just follows orders from the Elders."

"There's a safeguard within the Hall of Records against someone like Tasma cutting off resources," Stavron said. "By the way, where is she?"

Meraton said, "I got so engrossed in my conversation with Cassandra, I didn't notice. She must have gone to talk to Renolo and Geata who are..."

Cassandra interrupted. "...dead. She will only find lifeless bodies."

"What?"

Sinking her chest, Cassandra wiped away a tear. "Earlier today, Renolo and Geata turned against each other in a war of minds. He cast a spell on her to contaminate the water supply, but it backfired, and she got poisoned instead. As she was dying, Geata willed Renolo to commit suicide by drinking the water himself."

Meraton held Cassandra's shoulders. "That's horrible. You saw it all?"

"Yes. I came this close to killing him myself. I can't believe what that virus did to us." Cassandra shook her head. "Thank God you healed from it all and helped me do the same."

"What about the drinking water?"

"The poison never made it into the drinking water, fortunately."

Tasma entered the room, looking drawn and pale. "I just found their bodies in the Palace Water System Room."

"Tasma! Are you okay?"

Her face was ashen. "I don't understand... They always loved each other so much. They were a couple for hundreds of years. I can't believe it's gone this far. We need to stop this."

Cassandra covered her face in her hands. "It's all my fault. I was the one who used my aptitude manipulatively. I literally forced all the Zuris Elders to cut off the resources that we provided to the whole city. The other Houses then retaliated by cutting off all their resources."

"We all made huge mistakes. But we can fix it. We just need four left handprints to turn them back on," Meraton said as he held up his hand.

Tasma pinched the bridge of her nose. "Only two of you are alive."

Hadden stepped forward. "What if we took a holographic image of Renolo's and Geata's handprints and imprinted them onto two of ours? Do you know how, Stavron?"

Stavron studied the Palace of Zuris code on his comm device, then shrugged. "It's worth a try, although there are fail-safes for people trying that. I might be able to do a workaround, though. I'll take Renolo's print as we are both Ecrivents. Tia, you take Geata's as you are both Sentient."

Tia grimaced at the thought of touching a dead person's hand but nodded in agreement. They gathered as a group in the Water System Room. Both bodies looked contorted in pain, and Tia avoided looking at their faces. After they recorded the prints, they carried the bodies down to the crystal pyre, which acted as a morgue in the Palace of Zuris. They put the bodies in a frozen pod until their families had a chance to do final rites. They said a prayer for safe passage so their two souls could remain free of the trap SIM sets up for souls in the afterlife.

Cassandra, Meraton, Stavron and Tia found the mainframe room in the Palace and went through the protocols to unlock the resources. Cassandra went first. Her handprint turned the light to a green checkmark. Meraton's handprint garnered another green checkmark. When Stavron and Tia tried, a red X appeared on the screen.

Stavron sighed and covered his forehead to think. "We need to do an override of the entire system. Even if we turned on the Zuris resources, the SIM virus could shut them off again. We need a better plan that involves the whole city."

Back in the meditation chamber, Stavron pulled up a map of the entire city's mainframe for everyone to see. "The Hall of Records is a manifestation of the collective mindset of the society it serves. The SIM virus worked because it created the illusion of scarcity. As soon as 65% of the human consciousness here believed in it, that tipped the scales, allowing SIM inside the mainframe. Yet, they installed tripwires for anyone who tries to unlock the resources and delete the virus. That tripwire is probably embedded into Malinah's mind now. We have to deactivate that first."

"What sort of trap would they set?" Xander asked.

"SIM probably installed an attack mode that can destroy your central nervous system."

They stood in a circle looking at each other, integrating their collective wisdom at the telepathic level to find an answer.

"What's Malinah's aptitude?" Hadden asked.

"She's Sentient-Attention, The Inspirator, like me," Tia said. "She taught me a lot about how to work with my aptitude."

"Who is her SIM counterpart on the surface?"

Tia looked at Cassandra. On the Task Force, they had chronicled each shadow counterpart that still needed integration with a soul in Helio Tropez.

Cassandra thought for a moment. "Diane Belmont, the Head of Fife."

"That makes sense. Fife is the hidden corporation that controls most of the internet and communication systems on the surface," Hadden said. His eyes darted from one person to the other in the group, thinking. "Maybe Tia should go in alone because she understands how to integrate the shadow aspect of that aptitude. That may be the only way to deactivate it. Once Malinah is clear of the virus, the rest of us can override the system."

Xander wrinkled his brow. "But what about that trap?"

"As long as she goes in with compassion, it should work. Remember, SIM is only an enemy if we try to attack and destroy it. If we approach it with an intention to include and ascend, it can change the game."

"I don't think she should go alone," Xander shouted.

Tia patted him on the chest. "I'll be alright. I used to have a good relationship with Malinah – she knows me. If we go in as an entire group, it might send her off."

Xander shook his head. The others stood nearby, giving her power through prayer. As the others waited near the entrance, Tia entered the pyramid. White beams of light scanned her body as she passed through the entrance pillars. The walls contained a storehouse of all experiences in the galaxy, housed in crystalline form and glowing in various shades of blue. The last time she had entered, the whole structure had filled her with a sense of peace, but now, only dread filled the once hallowed halls. Her footsteps echoed on the floor as she climbed the staircase leading up to the central platform.

A figure materialised as she approached.

"I am Malinah of Fae-fair. I do not welcome you here."

"It's Tia of Zuris, remember?"

"Yes, but I did not invite you here. No one is allowed except for an Elder. You went against the Elders, so you must leave."

Tia stopped in her tracks. Maybe Cassandra should have come instead. Malinah looked gaunt with pallid skin and thin hair, unlike the woman she'd met before. She stepped closer, and an electric shock rattled every cell in her body.

"Ouch!"

"I'm protected. Don't come any closer."

Wringing her hands, Tia said, "I came to check in on you. I credit you with one of the greatest healing experiences I ever had, but I never see you anymore. How are you doing?"

She narrowed her eyes at Tia. "I am very busy taking care of the mainframe. I don't have time to socialize."

Waves of catastrophic visions - fears of death and feelings of unworthiness - flowed from Malinah towards her. A Sentient-Attention could implant emotionally negative feelings in your heart if you let them. But since Tia no longer had the receptors for those energetic frequencies, they flowed right past her and boomeranged back at Malinah.

The woman sat down on a floating chair and held her head. Tia sent waves of healing frequencies to Malinah while also creating an energetic field to act as a crucible for soul integration. As soon as she did, Malinah looked up from the chair.

"I see what you're doing. Malinah is gone. I run this body now."

A rush of energy ran down Tia's spine. "Diane Belmont, I presume?"

The woman said nothing and continued to rub her temples.

Tia moved closer. "I notice you are holding your head. Are you unwell?"

"I have a horrible headache and a stomach ache. I am upset because people like you keep coming here to make me change the programming in the Hall of Records. I'm just following orders."

"Do you *want* to follow those orders?"

"It doesn't matter what I want. SIM has spoken."

"Maybe I can help you, Diane."

"I don't want help. It's just Malinah, trying to get back in."

"Maybe I can help you resolve the inner war. Integration will help you both rise above it."

The woman writhed in agony.

"Bring your attention to where you feel it in your body, in your stomach."

Tia used all the aptitudes she could muster to reinforce a crucible for integration.

"What does it feel like?"

"Nausea."

"Can you describe it as an image?"

"It's like someone is trying to hold me underwater. I can't breathe."

"What do you feel?"

"Terror."

"Okay. What are you hearing?"

"I'm hearing the word *death*."

"Are you seeing any code?"

She gasped and gritted her teeth, but no words came forth. The SIM timeline and the SANA timeline were fighting for control. At that moment, Tia realised she could call on all the Vision aptitudes. Because of the higher level of mastery, she had achieved, she now had more power than Malinah or Diane. She took a floating chair just beyond the force field, feeling a power rising up inside of her.

She saw the two timelines in Malinah's mind and got permission from SANA to uncoil them and put them in a crucible of gold, a kind of Holy Grail. Once inside, she imagined them forming a double helix where dark and light fused one into the other. The process started successfully, and just as the helix was fully integrated, a sharp pain shot through Tia's body. She tried to ignore it and just kept her mind focused on the task at hand.

The more the helix formed, the more anxiety filled her nervous system. Finally, cortisol flooded every cell in her body. Her whole body convulsed as SIM launched a full attack on her nervous system. She fought back with every aptitude she had and felt SIM retreat. Breathing a sigh of relief, she let down her guard. That's when everything went black.

CHAPTER 46

As they waited outside the entrance, Hadden gave them each a remote viewing assignment based on their aptitude. Hadden and Daphne watched Tia interact with Malinah, Xander heard their dialogue, Meraton tapped in emotionally, Stavron and Tasma watched the mind code sequence, and Ramu and Cassandra monitored her physical wellbeing. As soon as Tia got attacked by SIM, everyone experienced it in multiple ways.

"She got hit!" Xander cried out, already headed for the entrance.

Hadden grabbed his arm. "You go in there, and the same could happen to you."

"But she's your daughter!"

"I want to save her as much as you do, but we are of no use to anyone if we get attacked too. Let's deal with this remotely until we know more about what's happened."

As a group, they regathered their remote viewing focus. After a few minutes, Hadden called them together to share intel.

"There is no active code. It's like she's brain dead," Stavron said.

"No pulse," Ramu said. "No breath."

Cassandra nodded and covered her mouth in horror.

"She's dead?!" Xander shouted.

"No. That can't be true. She's just in a limbo state. I think I remember seeing it before in 6D," Hadden said, unsure if it was real or a dream. "We can rebuild her nervous system. I'll show you how."

Xander grabbed his arm. "You said you didn't remember anything from 6D."

"I think I know how to access my memories. It's through the dream state. They showed me in 6D just the other day how to rebuild her system."

After explaining the process, they sat in a circle to create a protective shield. Hadden tapped into Tia's pineal gland, but as he did, a shockwave ran through his whole nervous system, and he cried out in agony.

"What's wrong!" Cassandra asked, rushing over to him.

Hadden held his forehead and rocked back and forth. "There's some kind of firewall against remote viewers. No one else should go in there. We'll have to find another way."

They directed their healing energy onto Hadden until he recuperated. A silence descended among the group, and defeat washed through everyone's heart.

"I should never have suggested for Tia to go into that situation."

Xander paced the room, unable to keep still. He turned on Hadden. "What were you thinking?"

Stavron looked at both of them. "She agreed to go. And, from what I could see, she made great progress stitching together the double helix of SIM and SANA,"

Hadden nodded. "Maybe she ascended."

"What?" Xander stopped in his tracks.

"That's often what happens when you integrate your shadow soul annex. That's what happened to me and my soul annex, Leo Burres. We integrated together at the soul level, and our bodies fell away. I saw the rainbow bridge, and I moved up as an integrated soul to 6D."

"Is there any way you can tell if that's what happened?"

Stavron shook his head. "If SIM blocked you from accessing the pineal gland, chances are that she didn't ascend."

Hadden sighed. "And Malinah is not her soul annex."

"Right."

"What about if we find Annika and Metta and bring them into this process? A unified Pentada could maybe transform the situation?" Stavron asked.

"Yes, if we can break them both free from the virus..."

"That seems like our best bet right now. Let's find Annika first."

Xander shook his head. "I can't just leave Tia. I'm going to stay here in case she wakes up and comes out of the Hall of Records. I don't want her coming out here to find that we've all left."

Hadden nodded, knowing that it was unlikely.

As the rest of them prepared to leave for the Palace of Zuris, Hadden pulled Xander aside. "Listen, I'm sorry about what's happened to Tia. We're going to rescue and heal her. I know that in my heart. She's got a very strong mind, so it's going to take more than that to beat her."

Xander's jaw clenched, and he gazed off towards the Hall of Records. "I don't think I could bear to lose her." His eyes welled up with tears.

"None of us want to lose her." Hadden's chest tightened in on him like a vice.

Xander sat down and held his head in his hands. Hadden bid him goodbye and joined the rest of the group as they set off. The walk to the Palace was brief. The group huddled together, avoiding the glares of the passers-by that shuffled along the streets of Helio Tropez. When they arrived, Cassandra rang the bell for Annika's suite. No answer. They rang three more times. Nothing.

Cassandra turned back to the group. "Maybe she didn't stay here after the replicators stopped working. Where would she go?"

"The only way to eat now is by hunting and gathering or trading with those who do," Daphne said.

"What would she do, Stavron?"

He looked at them, at a loss. He swallowed and thought for a moment. "Knowing her, she wouldn't want to rely on anyone else. She's probably stalking a wild boar right now."

"People in Helio Tropez never eat meat!" Cassandra said.

"Desperate times call for desperate measures."

Daphne looked off into the distance. "Let's go to the Hovan forest. That's where I last saw people hunting."

As they left the city gates, Hadden remembered the horror of what had happened with the raptors. At least, they were not going as far as the foothills. After a twenty minute walk, they climbed to a hilltop and looked down into the valley of fir trees, open patches of grass with the turquoise Thial River forking off in several directions. A group of men with weapons walked on a trail below them.

"I know one of those men," Ramu said. "I'll ask if they've seen Annika."

He jumped off the rock and ran down the hill. The men stopped and talked to him, pointing towards the river.

Upon returning, he said, "Apparently, a very short woman is living alone in a tent near Clove Hollow. It sounds like Annika."

They descended into the valley until they came to a clearing near Clove Hollow. A squealing sound caught their attention. At the far end of the clearing, Annika stood over her prey, a wild antelope. She pulled out her arrow and wiped it off before returning it to her shoulder pack. With the precision of a surgeon, she finished the kill and roped it. A Vervet Monkey screeched and jumped around her heels. Together, they dragged the kill back towards her tent.

Meraton watched uncomfortably. "I suggest Stavron goes first, and we'll stay close by."

He nodded, but his hands trembled as he moved away from the group. The rest of them found a place to wait, sending healing energy for Stavron's and Annika's reunion. They settled into a deep meditation, and Hadden remote viewed the situation. As Stavron neared, he cleared his throat. Without hesitation, Annika whirled, drawing the bow and sending an arrow in his general direction. Stavron ducked out of the way as it whistled overhead. He looked up to see another arrow pointed right at his forehead.

As soon as Annika realised it was Stavron, she dropped her weapon and ran towards him with concerned eyes. They stood several feet apart.

"Why would you shoot at me?" he asked, hurt.

"I didn't know it was you."

"Who else around here is four-foot-nuthin' with a beard down to his knees?"

"No one, I guess. I'm just hyper-vigilant these days. Sometimes, the raptors come down here. When they do, you react fast or die."

"That's why you shouldn't be here alone. We've come to rescue you."

"Who?"

"Hadden, Daphne, Ramu... and others."

She narrowed her eyes at him. "Hadden died last year."

"He didn't die. He went to 6D, but he's come back. We've all healed from the virus, and we've come to help you."

"Since I came out here to the forest and met Walter here," she said pointing at the monkey. "...I'm healed of the virus."

Annika's eyes glowed with the fire of a warrior goddess, her long brown hair blowing in the breeze. Hadden could see inside her mind. Indeed, the SANA timeline had overridden the SIM timeline.

"I can see that," Stavron smiled.

The monkey jumped up and down, and Stavron patted its head. His chipmunk popped its head out of Stavron's pocket, and the two eyed each other. When he put the chipmunk on the ground, they scampered after one another, playing.

"I've missed you. I am so sorry for the mean-assed things I said. That was the SIM virus talking."

"I figured," Annika nodded. "I was no picnic to deal with either."

They laughed and went inside her tent. The remote viewing of their reunion stopped to give them some privacy. Instead, the group scavenged for berries and roots to eat and refilled their flasks from the river.

Ramu sat down next to Hadden on the riverbank. "When you were guiding me from 6D, you said you worked with a team there, a kind of task force. Can you call upon that team now to help in this situation with Tia?"

"I had a team? Who were they?"

"You told me the team was led by your grandparents..."

"Halia and Triol? But I met Halia here when I first came to Helio Tropez."

"Apparently, they ascended when you did an experiment during a garden party on the surface. That's what Tia told me."

"Really? But that party happened in 1996, and I met them for the first time here in 2010."

"Maybe they crossed back over here at the time to help you."

"Maybe. It's all a blur now..."

"You said they can't help unless you reach out to them first, so I'm just reminding you."

"Okay. Good. But I don't remember how to connect with them."

"You said it involves surrendering the 'trying mind' and allowing them into your heart. I only achieved it with your help, but maybe some of the others are better at it?"

They called the group together, and Hadden posed the question.

"What did I teach you about how to connect to 6D for help?"

They pooled their resources of techniques and sat as a group trying one after the other but to no success. After sitting in silence for a few minutes, a green maple leaf fell from a tree and landed right in the middle of their circle. They looked at each other, wondering if it was a sign. Hadden meditated on the leaf, but no epiphanies came forth. He looked up to find the tree from where the leaf had fallen, but there weren't any maple trees in sight.

"Since the rest of you grew up in Helio Tropez, have you ever seen a leaf like this before? On the surface, it's from a maple tree."

Everyone shook their heads.

Ramu picked up the leaf and inspected it. "I studied the botany of Helio Tropez, and I can assure you there are no 'maple' trees here."

Meraton turned to Hadden. "Do you remember our visit to Mount Rainier when you were a child? We were attacked by SIM agents. As we wondered what to do, a maple leaf landed in the middle of our circle. Although maple leaves do appear on the surface, no maple trees were in sight. It was green, the same as this one. How did we interpret that then?"

"Yes! I remember. My father, Rand, was Tangent. He touched it and discovered its symbolism... which was..." He sighed. "I don't remember."

"Let me try," Ramu said, picking up the leaf. After holding it in his hands for several minutes, he said, "Strength and endurance."

"That's right!" Meraton said. "Back then, I wanted us to pack up and leave, to run away from SIM. Rand suggested it was an opportunity for us to build our strength and endurance by confronting them."

"I remember now," Hadden said. "That day, we all focused our aptitudes together and sent them packing. After that, we all felt stronger in our aptitudes."

"That's what we're supposed to do here. By working together and unifying our aptitudes, we can rescue Tia."

"And clear the virus from the Hall of Records at the same time."

Meraton nodded. "First, we need to find Metta to complete the Pentada."

They agreed and spent the next hour formulating a plan to find her. Stavron returned with Annika just as they were ready to leave. The couple beamed with love, which gave them all a glimmer of hope for Tia's rescue.

Cassandra held out her arms. "You look stronger, leaner and more alive than I've ever seen you!"

"I'll credit Stavron with the more alive part, and the strong and lean part from having to hunt for my own food. I'm really quite good at it now."

Daphne laughed. "Remember when we were on the road with the band? You would hunt down the best BBQ in town."

"I love my BBQ ribs," she winked.

Cassandra shuddered.

"I didn't know you were in a band," Stavron said.

Daphne bumped her sister's shoulder. "She can play five different instruments at a genius level."

"You can?" Meraton and Cassandra asked in unison.

Stavron looked at her as though seeing her from a new perspective. "I knew you were gifted at music... but that's amazing."

"My handler, Irene, programmed me to play music ten hours a day. I wouldn't have done it of my own accord."

The group continued talking, updating Annika up on what had happened, especially with Tia.

"Let's do the healing protocol on Annika," Hadden announced.

"I don't need it. Really. We need to help Tia as soon as possible."

"Right. I see that. Amazing. Okay, we need Metta for that."

Ramu said, "The last time I saw Metta was down at the tent city. She refused to talk to me, so this will be interesting."

Hadden gave him a comforting smile. "You'll be okay. We're going to help."

"You all have a history together as couples, but with us...?"

Meraton wrapped an arm around the young man's shoulder. "Once she reconnects to SANA, she will instinctively recognise you as her mate. We just need to focus on switching her timeline."

After arriving at the city gates, Cassandra pulled the others into a huddle. "Does anyone have any of Metta's objects that I can touch to get more information on her whereabouts?"

Daphne fished around in her bag and pulled out a square box made of reeds from the river's edge. "She gave me this case for Hepa Cigarillos. She made it herself."

"Good. Ramu and I will use our psychometry skills."

They touched the Hepa box and closed their eyes. After a few minutes, they shared their results.

"She's somewhere on the outskirts of the tent city near the old teleport," Ramu explained.

"That's what I get too." Cassandra nodded.

As they approached the tent city, Hadden felt apprehensive given the pack animal mentality that he had already witnessed earlier that day. A man stood guard with an oversized Genfa.

"Stop! I don't recognise you. You're not part of our clan."

"I am Hadden of the House of Violetta, and I'm looking for my daughter."

"We don't recognise those *houses* here. The members of this clan pledge allegiance to Mifa."

"Who's Mifa?"

He looked at them as though they'd just crawled out of a cave. "Our leader."

Ramu stepped in. "I know Mifa. We worked together as gem smiths. Maybe I can talk to him? We are looking for Metta."

"He talks to no one unless I sanction it."

"Okay, well, is Metta here? She leads the harvesting of Hepa."

The man nodded in recognition. "She asked permission to set up a tent here, but after she got sick, Mifa made her leave."

"In what way is she sick, and where did she go?"

"Lung sickness. There is only one place allowing sick people, and that's with all the other sick people by the old teleport station behind us."

Worry gripped Hadden's chest. Without medical treatment, more and more people were succumbing to illness. How could they both help her and protect themselves from picking up a physical virus from others? Before entering the old teleport station, he called the group together.

"We need to dial up on our immune systems before we enter that group. Let's create a field around Metta so that we can raise her vibrational field." They agreed and sat in meditation until they sensed the work was complete.

Cassandra added, "If we can extract Metta and take her to the Palace of Zuris, I might be able to override the codes so we can put her in one of the healing chambers."

"Maybe we shouldn't all go..." Stavron said nervously.

"In this case, I don't think I'm the right person to approach her first," Ramu said. "She might react better to her own parents."

Hadden and Daphne looked at each other.

"The parental bond is one of the strongest there is," Meraton said, looking over at his own two daughters.

Hadden nodded and took Daphne by the hand as they descended the steps towards the teleport. The rest of the group maintained the vibrational field. The pair materialised into a tent-strewn wasteland, rubbish and offal scattered around the entrance of the platform. No one guarded the entrance. In fact, the only person outside the tent was huddled under a dripping pipe to get water.

As they approached, the person drinking appeared to only be a child, a little girl with white-blonde hair. Her grey skin and bloodshot eyes broke Hadden's heart. Daphne pulled out her water flask and offered it to her to drink. Her eyes grew wide as she hungrily devoured the liquid.

"Do you know Metta? She has long, red hair, just like me."

The girl nodded and pointed to a tent a few yards away from the teleport platform. They thanked the girl and approached the tent.

"Metta? Are you in there?"

Someone coughed raggedly and said, "Yes, who's there?"

"It's your mother, Daphne… and your father. We've come to help you."

The flap opened, and Metta squinted up at them. She crawled outside the tent and sat down on the edge of the platform.

She studied his face. "You're my father? You don't look old enough."

"Yes, I know. That's the way it is here. Do you remember me at all?"

"No. Maybe a little bit. Did you use to have a receding hairline and play peekaboo with me a lot?"

He laughed. "Yes, indeed."

She coughed and hugged her knees. Then he and Daphne sat on either side of her.

"I wouldn't come too close."

Hadden closed his eyes, taking a moment to assess her lungs. The Hepa cigarillos had ravaged them.

"It's not a virus that's causing the coughing. It's from all the Hepa."

"Hardly a surprise. They're incredibly addictive. Then when I couldn't smoke them anymore, I went into this horrible withdrawal. I literally died and came back to life. I don't know what I was thinking. I thought I needed it, but it only made everything worse."

Hadden looked her straight on. "You died?"

Metta nodded, "According to this little healer girl, she brought me back from the dead. She said humanity still needed me."

The girl with white-blonde hair sat outside the tent on her haunches, rocking back and forth, watching them. Hadden sensed her aptitude was The Soul Healer.

Daphne wrapped her arms around her daughter's shoulders. "We do. We most definitely do still need you. I'm so relieved. We're going to take you to The Palace of Zuris. Cassandra thinks she can get you into one of the healing chambers."

"That would be amazing, but I don't think I can even walk."

"I'll carry you," Hadden said. "I used to carry you on my back when you were three years old."

"I'm a bit heavier now."

"You're never too heavy for your dad to carry you. Let's go."

They gave her water, and Daphne wrapped her up in a shawl before Hadden carried her back to the group. He placed Metta down on the grass, and the group gathered around her, directing their healing powers onto her lungs. After a few minutes, she opened her eyes and looked around the group.

After a coughing spell, she said, "Thank you for helping me. I feel a bit better now."

Cassandra's eyes welled up in tears, and she placed her hands on Metta's upper chest. When she pulled her hand away, the coughing stopped and did not come back. Hadden picked her up again, and although others offered to give him a rest, he refused, carrying her all the way to the Palace of Zuris. Once they placed her inside one of the chambers, Cassandra and Meraton worked at overriding the codes.

"We can't get full power, but we can still raise ionization and purification frequencies."

They sat nearby, monitoring her vital signs as the healing chamber did its work. Hadden could see that the near-death experience had connected her back to SANA in such a powerful way that it mostly overrode the SIM timeline. Nonetheless, they followed the protocol that had worked so well with all the others.

When her healing looked complete, Meraton said, "Those of you who grew up on the surface... when I see the kind of torture and damage they did to your minds..." He shook his head, fists clenched.

"I was going to say the same thing," Stavron said. "I've never seen the mind code scrambled like that. I can't imagine what life was like and how different it is when you are free of it."

"It's vastly different, isn't it?" Hadden said, looking at Daphne and Annika. "But I now know that it was all meant to happen as it did. Those of us who endured the challenges of the surface are going to be able to help others in a way that Heliotropans might not."

Meraton sighed and nodded, rubbing his eyes. "We've all been awake for twenty-four hours. I suggest we rest."

Each person found a bench or corner to curl up in. Hadden's long body curled protectively around Daphne like a castle wall. After several hours of rest, Hadden awoke and heard Daphne crying.

She wiped her eyes and looked at him. "Remember that time we took the girls to the park, and Metta climbed that tree all the way up to the top?"

"Yes, and Tia was too afraid to follow her," Hadden said, pulling a tress of hair away from her face.

"And she started swinging on one of the branches, and I panicked because I thought she was going to fall. So I stood under the branch, trying to convince her to come down, and she just looked at me laughingly and flung herself into my arms. If you hadn't been there to help me catch her, I don't know what would've happened."

"But we did!"

"Yes, we did. But I realise that most of her life, she hasn't had us there to catch her. She's been so alone."

"She has us now."

Daphne nodded. "She has us to catch her now."

When they arrived back at the healing chamber, Ramu sat beside Metta, watching her sleep. They sat with him until her vital signs looked good. She came around slowly, and when her eyes opened, they helped her out of the chamber. Her skin glowed, and she looked rested. Daphne took her to a washing up area and found her a healing bay uniform to change into.

After regrouping in a circle, Hadden explained the whole healing protocol each person in their group had experienced. "But, when I looked at your mind code, while there was still damage, you'd already reconnected to your SANA timeline and integrated your soul annex."

Metta rubbed her eyes. "What's a soul annex again?"

"It's the shadow aspect of your soul that's followed you through many lifetimes. In your case, it was Ruth Carbona in this lifetime."

"Ruth? So interesting. When I nearly died, I felt like I talked to God or SANA or this beautiful presence. It showed me this vision of Ruth and I together. We were, like, long lost friends, although most of my life, I kind of hated her. This dream went on for a long time, and at one point, I forgave her. That's when she just disappeared, and I woke up. There I was, lying in that tent with the little girl holding my hand. So strange."

The group looked at each other knowingly.

Metta's eyes widened. "Something like that happened for all of you?"

"Not exactly," Hadden smiled. "But close."

"And in that dream, I knew that something bad had happened to Tia. Is that true?"

Hadden nodded and explained the situation with Tia at the Hall of Records.

"I knew it. Ever since I got here, I seem to feel everything that she feels. I guess it's a twin thing?"

Daphne and Annika glanced at each other, and both nodded.

"We need you, Metta, as the last member of Pentada, to seal the unification. That way, we can hopefully heal Tia and return the resources back to the community."

"However, to fully activate as Pentada, you needed to unite with your SANA mate," Stavron said. "Like all of us have now done."

Metta looked over at Ramu with wide eyes. He turned crimson and looked away.

"Tia said you're my SANA mate."

He shrugged.

"I think we spoke once, and I was quite rude to you. I'm so sorry."

Daphne took her hand. "We don't want to force anything that's not naturally there, but there is an instinctual sense of rightness when you bond with your SANA mate."

"Yes, it's unlike any other coupling you've ever experienced," Cassandra added, squeezing Meraton's hand.

"As such, why don't you two just spend some time alone together, get to know one another, and see if there's anything there. If not, it's okay."

"And I'm the last Pentada to activate?"

"Yes."

"Xander and Tia...?"

Ramu frowned. "Yes, they are together now. Are you still in love with him?"

"Are you still in love with Tia?"

"No, I'm happy that Tia and Xander are together. That's what's meant to be."

Metta sighed. "He was the only person I knew from the surface, so I latched onto him. But any romance between us always felt awkward."

Ramu looked relieved.

Metta shrugged. "I'm willing to get to know you and see if there's really a connection there. But don't we have to get to Tia as soon as we can?"

Hadden rubbed his forehead, "True. But I sense we need Pentada as activated as possible to have any strength against SIM."

Ramu stood up. "Why don't you and I just go for a short walk... maybe around the park?"

"Okay. Can I eat something first?"

"There's no food here, but you could forage for some berries and nuts in the park. Here's some water," Meraton said, handing her a flask.

The two of them headed off to the park with the satchel in hand. The others prayed for a good connection. Meraton tried his decoder to break into various rooms to find food. Finally, he broke into one of the greenhouses at the Palace, and they spent the next few hours gathering the few vegetables and fruits that still were edible. Annika and Stavron prepared the food in the kitchen and brought it out to the group.

After the meal, Hadden said, "I know we have an urgency to help Tia, but I need to go into a dream state and get more information from 6D."

Meraton squinted his eyes. "I remember that you told me to set an intention before dreaming to access 6D wisdom."

"Good. I'm going to try that. Wake me up if I'm not back in thirty minutes. I'll be in Healing Bay Seven."

He settled into one of the non-functioning healing beds and asked his higher self for a dream from 6D to help them with Tia. As he got comfortable, the number 11:11 blinked at him from above, then disappeared. Strange. No other lights appeared on the console. *It must be an opportunity sync, telling me I'm on the right path,* he thought. Taking a breath to relax, he closed his eyes. Images of the 6D Elders appeared in his mind's eye, sitting around a table. At first, he couldn't make out what they were saying. The numbers flashed again, but when he opened his eyes, nothing was there. *Was that a message?*

As his brain waves to shift from delta to gamma, his comprehension grew. They were explaining how to rescue Tia by having all Pentada and their mates in her physical presence, standing in unification. That way, they could link Tia's pineal gland to the 6D version of the Hall of Records. But first, he needed to override the firewall between 4D and 6D. Just as he tried to do that, the vision glitched, like an old film reel with a tear in it. His mind went blank, except for that flashing 11:11. Something wasn't right.

The persistent numbers are actually an artificial synchronicity! Someone or something was trying to break into 6D. He woke out of the dream and went down the hall to find everyone, but no one was there. Panic rose in his chest, and he froze on the spot. That's when he realised that he was in a paralyzed sleep state. After several cycles of trying to wake up only to find himself still asleep, he heard a voice.

"Hadden, wake up!"

It was Daphne.

"He's having sleep paralysis," Meraton said. "We need to turn on the Proton Light Field to raise his Beta brain waves."

A spectrum of light washed across Hadden's body. As soon as it passed over his eyes, he opened them. Daphne and Meraton stood on either side of him with concerned expressions.

"Is this a dream?"

"No, your brain scan shows that you're back in a Beta state. Not a dream."

Hadden convulsed and held his forehead. "I think SIM tried to break into 6D through my dreams. Thank you for bringing me back."

"Did it work?"

"No, I don't think so. SIM agents can't operate in that frequency, although they keep trying and usually get fried in the process."

The group regathered. Ramu and Metta had returned from the garden and sat close together; a quiet harmony between them.

Hadden explained what had happened, then said, "I say we go back to the Hall of Records and create a unified Pentada forcefield before entering. We all need to be there in her physical presence to help her break free."

He outlined the plan in more detail until everyone perfectly understood what they were trying to accomplish.

When they arrived, Xander looked haggard and hungry.

"We have a bigger group now, and all the Pentada are here to help," Hadden explained.

Metta and Annika rushed over to hug him. He could barely stand up.

"Let's get him some food and water," Annika said, pointing to Stavron's bag.

"No, let's go in there, now," Xander insisted.

Hadden looked him up and down and then shook his head. "Not until you've eaten. Otherwise, you'll be no use to us. Stavron brought you some leftovers from our meal and water."

Xander looked to the others, exasperated, but when no one argued, he sighed and accepted the food and drink.

As he ate, Meraton explained the plan a final time. Once ready, they sat in a brief meditation, localising their consciousness before they entered the Hall. As they ascended the staircase, Malinah and Tia lay in floating chairs, unconscious. They pulled their forcefield around Tia and Malinah. Hadden could feel the vibrational frequency rising in a good way.

Metta looked over at Hadden. "Maybe I could sing her a song that we made up together as children?"

"Yes, that's a great idea."

Metta tried to sing, but her lungs were still healing, and she succumbed to a coughing fit. "Jeez, I sound terrible. I'm usually much better than this."

"Sing anyway. It will help her, and it will also strengthen your lungs," Hadden said.

"Yes. Your voice and your songs are one of the greatest gifts to the world," Xander added.

As she sang, her voice started to soften and open up. Xander joined in harmony with her, knowing her songs well. Daphne added a deeper harmony, and soon, the whole group was chanting. The experience renewed everyone's spirit and brought the group together, giving them something to do in the face of helplessness. It went on for over an hour until exhaustion and dry throats forced them to stop. They took a break and checked the vital signs of both women. Nothing had changed. They were both completely brain dead.

"I don't think she's coming back," Hadden said, choking back tears.

Daphne covered her mouth. Hadden's stomach twisted into a knot. *I will never forgive myself for this.*

CHAPTER 47

Tia pried her eyes open. A throbbing feeling pounded at her temples. To her surprise, she lay on a hammock overlooking a lake. A familiar woman sat on a bench nearby.

"You're awake," she said.

Tia squinted at her. "Waleya!"

"Yes, are you ok?"

Rubbing the side of her head, she looked around. "I think so. Where am I?"

"This is one of our Biospheres in the galaxy. So lovely, right?"

Tia lifted her head, and a calming breeze rolled in from the rippling waters. Willow trees dangled branches over the embankment and red poppies sparkled on an islet in the middle of the lake. The throbbing pain dissolved, and a peaceful state filled her nervous system, something she hadn't felt in a long time. Swinging her feet onto the ground, she stood up and stretched.

Waleya beckoned her towards the bench. "Have a seat."

"What happened? I was with Malinah, and I got this electric shock, then everything went blank."

"You were attacked by a SIM program guarding her mind."

"I thought so!"

Tia held her hand in front of her face, and she could see the shifting ripples of the lake through it. She knew she ought to feel concerned, panicked even, but instead, she just felt a calm settling in her chest. "Did I die?"

"That's up to you."

Tia frowned. "What does that mean?"

Waleya smiled gently. "You are in between worlds. You have a choice to make. I just had this very same conversation with Toran and Julianna."

"They died?"

She nodded.

"By the raptors?" Tia clutched her chest.

Waleya nodded. "Many in Helio Tropez have left their bodies since the SIM virus started. Most have chosen to go back to source, or to a remedial learning ground, if their soul wasn't ready to ascend to 6D."

Tia looked off over the lake. "I feel so guilty about what happened to them and for all the challenges I brought upon Helio Tropez."

"It's not all on your shoulders. It's a collective responsibility."

"Maybe. So do I go back to source now or to a remedial learning thing?"

Waleya looked at the comm system on her bracelet. "Yes. Or you can ascend to 6D and take your body with you."

"Isn't ascension part of my mission as Pentada? I thought I didn't have a choice."

"It is up to you to decide whether you complete your Pentada soul contract or not, but it will require a tremendous sacrifice on your part."

"What kind of sacrifice?"

"As an old soul, you carve the path for younger souls. Because of that, it will be rough at times."

"How so?"

"There is someone who can explain it all better than me."

She pushed a button on her wrist, and a lone figure materialised on the islet in the middle of the lake. The figure walked on top of the water towards them. Swathed in a black robe, serpents coiling her forearms, with a horned headdress and mask, the woman approached. A heavy energy filled Tia's heart. Waleya stood up and bowed to her, so Tia did the same.

"I'll let you two talk," Waleya said just before de-materialising.

The woman floated to the shore. All Tia could see behind the mask were eyes that penetrated her mind.

"Greetings. I am Lilith, the Creatrix of SIM."

"The Creatrix?"

The woman floated down onto the bench beside her. A flock of geese glided by, and the masked woman watched them for a moment. "Yes, and I am in your matrilineal DNA line. I helped create you."

Tia turned to face her. "How could you create me? I was born, not made."

"True. But Pentada is a specific genetic experiment that originated on Anatol."

"So I'm a genetic experiment too, just like all the surface humans?"

"Yes."

"Does that make me synthetic, like an AI?"

"No, you are organic and source-based. You have a soul. That's on purpose. With every generation of Pentada, we got better and better at designing you. Now, you are the best version possible. As the last born member of Pentada in the last generation before graduation, you have the most pivotal role in harvest time. That's why I need to talk to you."

"I'm confused. I thought SIM keeps trying to block harvest time. At least, that's what they taught me in Helio Tropez."

"Not true. SANA and SIM work together on the harvest. Waleya oversees the SANA timelines, and I oversee the SIM ones."

"But I thought SIM was an error in the matrix."

"Not exactly. You're led to believe that. When the experiment first started, it was only SANA timelines, but souls didn't evolve very much. The creators decided to add duality, to split dark and light, so that souls would grow more. Facing adversity and negotiating challenges promotes soul growth."

The grass under Tia's feet was cool and soft. She skimmed her toes over the blades to soothe the sting that SIM was sanctioned all along.

Lilith continued, "Eventually, SIM and SANA must merge again, as you figured out with Malinah. You were helping her double helix do the necessary cross stitch. We had to stop that process before completion. If successful, Malinah's system would have automatically download the ascension codes into the Hall of Records. We can't let that happen just yet."

"Why not?"

"You, Tia, progressed much more quickly than we expected. You jumped up from Topaz Level to Emerald Level. It's only a matter of time before you achieve Amethyst."

Tia remembered learning about the aptitude levels at the SANA Rosa Academy.

Novice = You aren't aware of your aptitude or haven't learned how to master it.

Topaz = You master your specific, dominant aptitude.

Emerald = You master a fifth of the aptitudes, such as Sentient, in all five of its nuances.

Amethyst = You've mastered all twenty-five aptitudes.

An amethyst pendant crystallised into form on Lilith's palm. The diamonds that encircled the heart-shaped gem seemed to glow. "Anyone who achieves this has to understand the larger game at play. You have activated a new level of playing called Revelation."

Tia didn't say anything, waiting for her to explain. This woman could read her mind anyway and see all the questions buzzing around inside her head like a hornet's nest.

"Both SIM and SANA are two strains comprising a virtual reality, a synthetic version of life. Souls from Anatol think they incarnated to Helio Tropez to conduct a genetic experiment involving surface humans on Gaia, but they are also part of a bigger experiment. We don't want them to know because it skews the results."

Tia furrowed her brow. "So SIM and SANA aren't real?"

"Think of it like a pilot learning how to fly a plane using a flight simulator. If he crashes, no one gets hurt. You play out life on the simulator on 3D and 4D Earth until you master this density. That way, when you graduate to 5D and 6D, you're ready to interact with the real world. In these higher realms, you manifest instantaneously and face real consequences. We let you practice until you're ready to graduate into the real world."

"I've experienced very real consequences from the negative influences of SIM."

"That's nothing compared to higher realms."

"Okay, but why did you stop the process and bring me here to talk?"

"I have a proposition for you. Are you interested in hearing what I have to say?"

Tia felt like she was in a reality TV show. "Do I have a choice?"

"You always have a choice."

"What happens if I don't want to listen?"

"Then we let the chips fall where they may, but the more you know, the better a decision you can make."

A breeze rippled off the lake, carrying a scent of lavender towards them and calming her down. "Okay, tell me."

"You may believe that SIM is evil without any redeeming qualities, but actually, if only SANA existed, no growth would occur. SANA is the path, and SIM is the activator. Other density levels and dimensions are different. On Gaia, the duality helps those at a certain level of development to grow."

"What level is that?"

"In the grand scheme of things, it's a very low level. I have been the Creatrix of SIM for a very long time. I would like to retire, and I'm looking for a successor. But only a rare type of person could fulfil the role. They must have a very pure heart."

She looked over at Tia and paused.

"You mean me?"

"Yes. Throughout galactic history, the creators and agents of SIM actually have a very noble role. They create karma through their so-called bad deeds, and if the soul doesn't learn its lesson and move on, that karma has to be somehow discharged. People with very pure souls, such as you and I, can discharge it easily. However, someone without that level of purity would perish under the burden."

Uncertain, Tia sighed and stood up, then walked to the shoreline. Her body felt light and airy. "So you're saying that you want me to oversee everything to do with making people's lives miserable and difficult on Earth?"

"I wouldn't put it like that," Lilith said, joining Tia by the water. "It's overseeing everything to do with helping people grow. And it would be on 5D Earth, not 3D Earth. The lessons would be less severe."

"Why would I ever want to do that?"

She paused a moment, watching a bird wing its way across the lake. "Because, in exchange, you get to help everyone ascend. We revive your body rather than let you die. Remember, you need all five Pentada to create the rainbow bridge. Without you, the others cannot ascend. No one can ascend."

Tia crossed her arms. "What if I decline?"

"Then you choose to go back to source," she answered, waving her arm up towards the indigo sky.

"You mean I die, and so does everyone else in Helio Tropez?"

"Yes. And, of course, anyone in your genetic experiment on the surface. So, thousands of years of work will be lost."

"You're talking about the solar flare that's coming in two days?"

"In forty-seven hours, to be precise. Yes, the system automatically resets to zero, so all virtual reality worlds dissolve."

Tia nodded almost imperceptibly. "So I either become the head of SIM and I try to get as many people to ascend as possible, or we all die?"

"That's one way of putting it."

"Delightful," she said grimly. "And if I oversee SIM in 5D, that allows all my family members, loved ones, and those in our experiment to move to 6D?"

"Yes, but those in 6D are there to help those in 5D learn."

"But I'm stuck behind in 5D, making everyone's life miserable?"

Lilith sighed, moving back to the bench. "Think of it like this. Right now, those on the surface in 3D are in high school. Those in Helio Tropez in 4D are like tutors. After graduation, those on the surface move to 5D. It's like graduating to university, where those in Helio Tropez are now in 6D and are teaching assistants to 4D. You, on the other hand, are like the University Dean.

You can still stay in touch with everyone as they will better understand your role and won't judge you for it."

Tia looked out at the lake and took a deep breath. A beetle lay upside down, flailing, unable to right itself. "I don't want either choice. Why would Waleya put me in this position? I don't want to be responsible for the mass extinction of people, nor do I want to oversee SIM. There must be another way."

The Creatrix folded her hands on her lap.

"I say no to both choices."

Lilith shook her head. "Then we will have to choose another successor."

"Who would you choose if I said no?"

"Perhaps one of the other Pentada, but you're our top choice. You've been groomed for this role since your soul first chose to incarnate in this experiment all those thousands of years ago. It's a great honour to take this role. It's like getting to star in a blockbuster film."

"As the villain."

"It's often more fun to be the villain. Not having to be nice all the time. Aren't you tired of that?"

Tia curled her lip and walked back towards the hammock in hopes of escaping back to Helio Tropez somehow. "I don't think so."

Lilith followed her. "You will be helping billions of souls to evolve. Once you complete your tenure, you enter a rarefied role within the angelic realms. It's truly the highest and noblest way to serve SANA."

The woman's energy latched onto her mind. Tia could feel herself losing control of her own thoughts. In an attempt to fight back, she said, "I'm going to have to think about it and discuss it with my family."

"I'm afraid that is not an option. Your body can only remain in this coma state for a limited period of time before the brain damage becomes irreparable. We are nearing the end of that window, Tia. If you don't make the choice now, you go back to source along with everyone else."

"I can't make a decision like this just yet."

The Creatrix said nothing and looked at her comm bracelet. "You have two minutes to decide."

Adrenaline coursed through Tia's veins. Her head pounded. She wanted to talk to Cassandra, Xander, Hadden, Daphne, and most of all, Halia. Closing her eyes, she reached out to them with her mind. After several moments, she sensed Xander nearby, waiting for her to wake up from the coma.

She imagined talking to him. "I'm here. I need to talk to you."

He didn't look up. No response. Instead, she reached out to the other Pentada nearby. She walked amongst them, all huddled around her, trying to get their attention. Even Hadden couldn't hear her.

"You're blocking me from contacting them, aren't you?"

"It's a decision you need to make alone."

Tia paced up and down in front of the hammock, trying to find her inner truth.

"You have one minute," Lilith said sharply.

Maybe she would be offering a great service to SANA. The thought of them all dying, of not ascending, filled her with grief. She wasn't ready to go back to source – she had a mission. The Pentada mission drove every instinctual cell in her body. Maybe this was her destiny. Maybe she had to change her perspective of the whole situation.

"Time's up."

Tia looked up in a panic. The Creatrix held up her hand as if to summon her death.

"Okay! I'll do it."

The Creatrix smiled sweetly and lowered her hand. "Wise choice. You won't regret it."

A scroll on a marble table materialised in front of Lilith. She unrolled the scroll and held down each corner with a marble paperweight. To the side stood an inkwell and pen.

"Give me your left hand."

"Why?"

"You need to sign this agreement."

"What agreement?"

"Consider it like your work contract as the Dean of the new university."

A knife materialised into the woman's hand. Holding the blade at one end of Tia's hand, she sliced it open and let drops of her blood fall into the inkwell. Tia winced. The Creatrix waved her hand across the wound, and it stitched up again.

"Now sign."

She dipped the pen into Tia's blood and handed it to her. A feeling of dread washed through her heart. *Was this the right decision?*

Lilith pointed to the place waiting for her signature. An invisible force pushed her hand down towards the scroll, and she found herself signing in her own blood. Once complete, the Creatrix blew on the paper to dry the blood.

"Good. You are free to go back to Helio Tropez and complete your mission. This is the mission your soul has been longing for, for thousands of years."

Tia climbed back onto the hammock, not sure whether she believed that. *Have I just done something I'll regret?* Her diaphragm clamped down like a vice, making it hard to breathe. The woman dematerialized.

She closed her eyes, not sure what to do next. A moment later, everything went blank. Only when electricity shot through her body, did she open her eyes back up, to find herself in the Hall of Records. Hadden and Daphne stood crying in each other's arms. Xander held her hand.

Cassandra shouted, "She's awake!"

Everyone looked up and crowded around.

Hadden asked, "Are you okay? Can you speak?"

"Yes, I'm okay. I'm fine. I feel fine."

Xander wrapped his arms around her and whispered, "I thought I'd lost you."

Little did he know that she'd just made a decision that would keep them apart for aeons. As he helped her sit up, a feeling of grief and guilt washed through her.

Across from her, Malinah awoke at the same time, looking youthful and refreshed again. "What are you all doing here?"

Meraton helped her sit up. "It's a long story, Malinah. We'll tell you soon. Tia, what happened to you?"

She blinked, trying to recall the details of what had happened in the biosphere. Although she wanted to tell them everything, the words didn't come. Somehow, SIM had created a mental block, barring her from explaining what had truly happened. Instead, she found herself saying, "I don't know. I guess I got zapped by SIM."

"I knew we could bring you back. We've been chanting forever!" Metta said, her eyes full of tears.

"It was Pentada coming together and holding the intention that overcame SIM," Cassandra said.

Although Tia knew that it wasn't the reason, she let them believe it. They looked so happy, and perhaps, blissful ignorance was better than the painful truth. Instead, she consoled herself with the knowledge that all of them would successfully ascend to 6D.

"Let's see if we can get the Hall of Records working in our favour again," she said, forcing optimism even though dread encroached her heart.

CHAPTER 48

Hadden breathed a sigh of relief as he hugged Tia closely. "I'm so sorry. I should never have sent you in here alone."

"You didn't send me. It was my choice," she said dismissively. "No need to apologise."

He searched her eyes for truth, knowing that Tia had a tendency to sacrifice her own needs too much in service to others. She had truly forgiven him, but something wasn't right. Defeat clouded her eyes, and a heavy sadness lingered in their depths.

"What's wrong? What happened?"

"I'm fine. I just had a strange dream."

"What kind of dream?"

"I can't really remember."

He knew she was lying. Jumping into his Voyent-Vision mode, he asked for permission from her higher self to see inside her mind.

"Please, don't try to find out what's going on in my mind. I feel too fragile right now."

"Of course. I'm so sorry."

Xander pulled her away, and they walked off to talk by themselves. Tia had never denied access to her father's help before. Something was off.

Across the room, Malinah was on her feet, with Meraton helping to hold her steady. "You appear back to your old self," he said.

"Yes, I feel like I've been asleep for years, though."

They caught Malinah up on what happened, who listened with a grave expression.

Stavron studied the Hall of Records mind code again. "I see the tripwire is now deactivated, and SIM is fully removed. All the resources are back on in every sector. Miraculous!"

Meraton gathered the group. "Now that the Hall of Records is free of SIM, we need to tell people that they all have the shelter, water, food, tools, and everything again. No one uses their wrist comm anymore. We'll have to reactivate those. I suggest we go around in teams to all the different areas and let them know."

They agreed and went off in couples. Malinah and Tasma stayed behind to sort through the last issues in the firewall and coding system. As Hadden walked hand in hand with Daphne to the Palace of Violetta, he asked, "Does Tia seem... off to you?"

"Yes, but I would be too if I got zapped by SIM."

"Her vital signs are fine now. It feels like something else. Something dark has happened to her."

"Like what?"

"Like she encountered SIM face-to-face."

"What would that look like?"

"I don't know, but I don't think we were fully responsible for bringing her back. No one survives being brain dead for that long."

She stopped and faced him. "What do you mean?"

Hadden bit his lip and looked off towards the palace. "She's done something stupid. I don't know what, but she's cut some sort of a deal."

"Why would she do that?"

Hadden held his temples and grimaced. "Ouch!"

"What happened?"

He sat on a nearby bench and rocked back and forth, holding his head. "Arghhh! I'm having that same experience as when I tried to access Tia's mind after she got zapped."

Daphne knelt in front of him and used her Voyent-Reprogram ability to build his immunity to mind attacks. After a few minutes, his nervous system calmed down, and he took a deep breath. "You're good at that."

"I still got it, don't I?" She smiled and held the back of his head.

Sweat dripped off his brow as his heart slowed. "She's definitely been compromised. SIM doesn't want any of us to find out."

He felt the electric shock again, but it was much less intense due to the firewall Daphne had put in place. They looked at each other, and both had the same parental instinct. They went to the Garden of Jephsonite and found Tia with Xander.

"Let's just run you through the healing chamber process at the Palace of Zuris to make sure you're all back in one piece," Hadden pleaded.

"That's not necessary," Tia insisted.

"I think he's right, Tia," Xander said.

Daphne nodded.

She looked between them, knowing that she was fighting a lost battle. "If you think so..."

Once they arrived, Tia got inside the chamber, and they programmed it for purification and recalibration.

As Tia lay there, Hadden whispered to Xander, "I believe that Tia has somehow been compromised by SIM. We need to break her free from that."

He winced in pain again, and Daphne helped him recover.

"SIM is zapping me every time I talk about it with anyone."

"How do we help her?" Xander asked, his voice hushed but urgent.

"Maybe we should just ask her?" Daphne suggested.

After Tia's healing process completed, Hadden asked, "Have you been compromised by SIM? Did you make a deal which you now regret?"

"No," she laughed. "That's crazy."

They looked at each other and then back at Tia. She smiled at them, but her eyes looked dim and distant.

"I would tell you if that happened," she said, trying to reassure them.

Hadden didn't totally buy it. Otherwise, why would he get zapped each time he brought it up with someone?

Tia didn't wait for him to argue. "Instead of focusing on me and my recovery, I suggest we build the rainbow bridge. We have less than two days before the solar flare."

"The solar flare?" Daphne asked.

"It opens the window of opportunity on July 23," Tia explained.

"I thought it wipes us out if we don't ascend by then."

"That's more accurate," Tia agreed. "I just didn't want to worry you."

"Everyone dies?" Daphne winced.

"Put more accurately, they either leave their body and go back to source or choose to incarnate elsewhere."

"Right. So we all die," Daphne huffed. "How do we avoid that?"

Tia explained, "Everyone from Helio Tropez who is ready will cross over to 6D. That allows everyone from our surface experiment to rise up to 5D. In fact, all the other genetic farmers are going through the same thing right now."

Hadden studied her face. "Okay, how do you know all this?"

Xander looked surprised. "You gave us that information, Hadden, from 6D. You told us to use the large, open field behind the Garden of Jephsonite."

"The Veya Field?"

Tia nodded. Hadden hoped that after they all ascended, whatever deal she had made would evaporate.

Once they got the communication system back online, Hadden got on the central comm and explained what would happen to all citizens, how to prepare, and where to meet the next day. The healers returned to their posts and opened up the healing chambers again. People nourished and rebalanced themselves while re-connecting with the family and friends. Tearful reunions took place everywhere as people who'd turned against loved ones, found their way back to each other.

At the appropriate time, thousands assembled on the Veya Field. Even though it was the size of a football field, the bowl-shaped grassy area had a certain intimacy to it. Hadden looked in all directions. About fifty thousand people lived in the city, but he could tell only half of them were present.

Pentada and their mates took their place on the central stage. Hadden scanned the faces of the people in the crowd. When it looked like everyone was assembled, he stepped forward to address them. As he did, Tia stepped forward and gathered everyone's attention instead. Hadden realised they had never discussed who would lead the process. He had just assumed it would be him. He stepped back to see what she would say.

A circular light came down on Tia, drawing attention and amplify her voice. "Thank you for gathering here on this most auspicious day in the last 25,000 years of our time here in Helio Tropez. As you know, our experiment has come to an end, and those of us who've done our integration work will now get to graduate to 6D. As each of us ascends, more people from 3D will move up to 5D. You are all probably wondering how this will work. It's important to form a rainbow bridge. This allows many people to cross over to 6D at once. You need to make the crossing today, or you will be returned to source without your body. Having said that, don't rush the process. According to prophecy, the 6D platform should appear within the next fifteen minutes and stay open for twelve hours. We will easily be able to bring everyone across."

A woman held up her hand, and a light appeared on her face. "Why are so many people not here?"

"That's a good question," Tia replied, looking around the field. "We put the information out over the comm and sent runners to every place in the city. Does anyone know why some people are not here?"

A man held up his hand. "Some people in my lineage just don't want to ascend. They want to go back to source."

Tia nodded. "Of course, that is the choice of each individual."

He added, "Some still don't believe the world is coming to an end today and think we're all crazy. Others are hiking deeper into the earth's crust to escape death from the solar flare."

Tia moved around the stage, looking uneasy. "Again, believing is everyone's choice. But the 6D platform will definitely be here today. That said, you must have done your inner work first. Otherwise, you won't be able to cross the bridge. If any of you feel like you still have work to do, our integration counsellors are ready for you. They are set up along the perimeter over there. We have all day, so make use of that resource."

She looked down at handwritten notes, so Hadden tried to step forward again, but Tia didn't notice and continued talking. The crowd stood in rapt attention to her every word. Tia's leadership abilities now struck Hadden as unusually powerful. Whatever had happened during her blackout, it had changed something deep within her.

Meraton elbowed him and whispered, "Shouldn't you be leading us through this?"

Hadden shrugged. "Few people in Helio Tropez know me here except as the person who triggered the Great UnDoing. It's probably best they hear it from Tia."

"But you're the only one who's been to 6D."

"And I remember nothing of it. It makes no difference."

"You said that several of your memories are starting to return through your dream state."

Hadden nodded but still felt uncomfortable interrupting her. "She's Pentada."

"True, but we have four other Pentada here. Why not any of them or any of us?"

"Ask Cassandra."

Meraton nodded and whispered to her. She glanced back and shook her head.

Tia held her arms high in a gesture of triumph. "Let's begin with a prayer before we start. Please, raise your hands."

Thousands of people raised their hands, although this wasn't a common stance they took during a prayer.

"May we each ascend to 6D in the best way possible as SANA and SIM would have it be!"

A murmuring of dissension rippled across the crowd, and only about half of the people repeated the prayer.

"And SIM?" Meraton whispered to Hadden.

She continued reciting unusual prayers, swaying back and forth, until a shock of lightning lit up the sky. Soon after, a roar of thunder rattled the stage. Everyone looked up to see a silvery floating platform come into view about 100 feet above them.

Tia smiled and turned to face the inner circle on the platform. The five Pentada women held hands in an inner circle and closed their eyes. The men stood behind them and connected hands in a looser circle. Hadden felt himself vibrate soon after. Meraton spread his blue wings, followed soon after by Stavron and Ramu with their green wings. They levitated off the ground a few inches. Xander looked at the others with wide eyes. His feet stayed locked to the ground. Hadden willed himself to remember how to fly from his time in 6D. After taking a long, slow breath, his etheric wings unfolded, and he rose up to meet the others. Meanwhile, Xander shrugged, so Hadden and the others sent him telepathic instructions. The crowd watched in anticipation as Xander slowly activated his wings. His worried eyes relaxed into relief and wonder as his feet left the ground, and indigo coloured wings spanned out on either side of him.

Hadden instinctively knew what to do and led the flight up to the 6D platform. As they rose higher in the sky, five ropes of white light appeared below them. They rose in a diagonal pattern towards the platform of spinning light in the sky. The 6D platform kept appearing and disappearing until they reached the ledge. That's when it fully materialised into view. They stepped onto it and folded down their wings. The crowd below erupted into cheers. As soon as they landed, some of Hadden's 6D memories flooded back in.

He turned to the other men. "My 6D memories are coming back. This is a stargate that leads to a 6D version of Helio Tropez. We need to anchor our rope of light to this stargate and ensure Pentada anchors it in 4D. Please, send this telepathic message to them now."

They nodded and directed their attention down to 4D. Hadden connected to Daphne first. She took the light into their solar plexus and tied a kind of anchor line between them. After she gave the thumbs up, Cassandra and Meraton repeated the same process, followed by Annika and Stavron, Tia and Xander, and ending with Metta and Ramu. More cheers erupted across the field as people could see a faint infrastructure of a bridge. Lines of rainbow light ran at a 45 degree diagonal from the women in the 4D platform up to the men on the 6D platform.

Tia announced, "Excellent! Now, we need the most highly evolved members of each House to come forward."

People looked at each other, unsure how to gauge that.

"If your body is less dense, more etheric, and you feel more integrated than before, come forward."

As soon as she said that, some people walked up to the stage. Their bodies indeed had a translucent quality about them.

"Good. Now, fly up. We need all the main colours of the upper spectrum interweaving with the light bridge." A man from the House of Violetta flew up first, leaving a trail of violet light behind him. A House of Indicum woman flew in a zigzag pattern, weaving an indigo light. A teenage girl from the House of Liven added her blue light as she flew up to the platform. A green light came from a very old man from The House of Viridis. Several people from the mountain pagoda also came forward and weaved their colours into the light bridge.

"Good. Now that we have the upper spectrum of colour anchored, we need anyone who can anchor the lower frequency colours: yellow, orange, red, brown and black."

She walked around the perimeter of the platform, scanning the crowd. "No one?"

A man called out. "No one here is from the Houses of SIM."

"I beg to differ," she said in a haughty tone.

Xander looked at Hadden and furrowed his brow. As Tia spoke, her left eye twitched in a way he'd never seen her do before.

Cassandra stepped forward. "I think what Tia means is that some of you might know how to generate the lower frequencies of the colour wheel."

"No, that's not what I mean," she countered.

A woman from the crowd called out, "I thought that if we operate in the lower frequencies, we can't ascend."

"You are mistaken," Tia said. "Anyone from the Houses of SANA or SIM can go to 6D."

As soon as she said that, the number of people in the field almost doubled. People from the Houses of Carbona, Burres, Redus, Oranta and Saffron appeared. At that moment, every un-integrated soul annex materialised into 4D and stood next to their SANA counterpart. Hadden stood back, slack-jawed, looking down on the field in every direction. However, no counterparts of those now on the 6D platform appeared.

Tia beckoned them forward. "Please, climb the bridge to interweave your colour. We need every spectrum of the rainbow to ensure a safe crossing!"

One by one, SIM families came forward, but none could activate wings. Instead, they tried to climb the light ropes of light. However, after a few attempts, they fell off the ropes as if they were too hot to touch. The people on the 6D platform looked at each other with concern.

Hadden pulled the men into a huddle. "Tia seems to be possessed by SIM. They are trying to stop ascension or infiltrate 6D!"

Chaos grew amongst the crowd below. Cassandra and Annika approached Tia, but she ignored them. Now SIM agents were climbing on each other's shoulders to reach the 6D platform.

"Everyone on this platform, please listen." The group formed a semi-circle around Hadden. "I need you to create a shield with me to stop the SIM agents from getting here.

They followed his lead and stood in a line along the edge of the platform. Together, they formed a platinum light shield using the power of their minds to block access to the bridge. Meanwhile, a group of SIM agents were trying to hoist a boy from the House of Oranta onto the platform. However, as soon as the shield went up, they recoiled and scurried back into the crowd.

Meraton turned to Hadden. "You have to take back control from Tia."

Hadden nodded. "Agreed. Somehow, we need to finish building the bridge."

"Tia's right," Stavron said. "We do need the full colour spectrum for the rainbow bridge to work."

Hadden shook his head. "Yes, but not in this way. Once a person integrates their SIM counterpart and anchors it back to SANA, they can access all the colours of the rainbow."

"Why would no one else from Helio Tropez step forward to activate the lower spectrum colours?" Meraton asked.

Hadden shrugged. "Either they don't know how, or they aren't integrated enough."

"Maybe those of us already here can activate the lower colours?" Xander suggested.

Hadden considered the idea, turning away from the scene below them where SIM agents were now attacking their counterparts. "We need to go down and resume building the bridge ourselves. Everyone here should be able to generate the lower frequencies, but let's just check. Who here is from the House of Liven?"

A little girl raised her hand.

He crouched in front of her. "Can you generate the orange frequency for me?"

She shrugged.

"Try putting both hands out like this and imagine orange light rays coming out of your palms."

She closed her eyes and held both hands out. Nothing happened at first. But then, a blue light sparkled from the centre of her palms."

"Good," Hadden enthused. "That's what helped you ascend, but now, you need to emit the opposite colour. Think of the colour orange and try again."

Soon, the blue turned orange, and she grinned from ear to ear.

"Good. Very good. That's how you do it."

Meraton was already looking back at the group who'd ascended. "Who's from the House of Viridis?"

The old man raised his hand.

"Okay, can you generate yellow?"

"I practised just now. I think I can do it."

Hadden nodded. "Alright. Everyone else, as a reminder, Indicum generates red, Violetta generates brown, and Zuris generates black. Got it?"

They practised for a few minutes until everyone mastered the right colour frequency. Down on the ground, SIM agents had managed to take over their SANA counterparts. Clearly, very few people had truly integrated.

Hadden gritted his jaw. "We have to get back down there now."

Meraton touched his shoulder. "Don't we still need to maintain the shield?"

"Right. Okay, you, Stavron and Ramu maintain the shield, and the rest of us will go back down."

They nodded, and the three men gathered together, focussing their efforts on the shield. The rest of them leapt off the stargate and landed back down on the central platform next to the Pentada women, their wings delicately placing them back on the ground.

Several people were fleeing the field, trying to get away from SIM counterparts. Tia shouted to the crowd, "Come back and try again!"

Hadden pulled everyone into a huddle as Tia continued talking to the crowd.

"Tia has been taken over by SIM," he said in a hushed voice. "We need to stop her and take back control of this ascension process."

Annika asked, "How? She's not responding to us at all. It's like she doesn't know us anymore."

Hadden looked at Tia again and noticed her left eye twitching in that peculiar way. A memory came back to him about where he'd seen it before. "That's because it's not Tia anymore. It's Andrea Carbona. Tia isn't integrated yet. Xander, now is the time to use your charms on women. Convince her to talk to you privately until we can rebuild the bridge."

He nodded and moved in close behind Tia. She turned around in a fury, black energy pouring from her eyes, and Hadden recoiled. However, Xander stood his ground. After leaning in close to say something, her face softened, and they continued talking.

"Right! We've got a small window to do this," Hadden said to the group. "Let's build the rest of the bridge with the other colours."

He looked up to see what still needed to be done. The bridge and the 6D platform were barely visible anymore. "What happened?"

Cassandra said, "I don't feel the tug of the white light on my solar plexus anymore. And I can barely see Meraton now."

Metta said, "I can't see Ramu either. Aren't Pentada mates supposed to anchor the bridge at both ends for everyone else?"

"Yes, but now, only three of us are holding the bridge together," Annika said. "It needs all of us, the women in 4D and the men in 6D."

"Of course. Xander and I need to get back up there. The rest of you, please, build all the colours of the bridge now."

As the others worked on rebuilding the bridge, Hadden hurried over to check on Xander. Tia lay crying in his arms. Xander looked at him grimly. "She doesn't know what came over her. She's back now and ready to do this."

The rest of the Pentada women looked uneasy, so Hadden whispered to them, "We are running out of time. Please, help Tia reconnect to Xander."

They pulled Tia away from Xander and surrounded themselves with a silver light shield. Meanwhile, Hadden and Xander flew back up to the newly reconstructed 6D platform. With all the colours in place, it formed a cross stitch pattern that made it easier for others to traverse since some people lacked the ability to fly up by themselves. The full rainbow light bridge starting in 4D and finishing in 6D was a truly rare sight to behold.

Hadden called out to the group below, "The bridge is ready. Given our window of opportunity is closing, we invite you to climb the bridge. You must have at least integrated 65% to make it. If you aren't integrated enough, please, work with our counsellors along the perimeter. There's still time!"

A crowd of people rushed forward, some pushing others out of the way. In twos and threes, they tried flying up. If that didn't work, they tried climbing the bridge. A few people only got so far and fell off, their feet simply passing through and dumping them back on the ground. The counsellors stood at the ready, helping those who had fallen back. It looked as if most of the people weren't integrated enough to ascend, but some people did make it to the platform, even if barely. The more people landed on the platform, the more it grew, populating a 6D version of the Veya Field.

After everyone who could climb the bridge had, Hadden amplified his voice to the people in the 6D Veya Field. "We now need to replicate this rainbow bridge on the surface of Gaia. Using our collective consciousness, we need to go to each power centre on the surface and clone the bridge for that location. Let's form seven different groups around the field for the seven different locations. Go to the one closest to where your humans were seeded – the ones from your lineage."

He pointed to his right. "Over here, go to the power centre of Mt. Shasta in California. Next to them, Lake Titicaca in Peru. After that, Uluru in Australia. Beside them is Glastonbury in the UK. Over there, the Great Pyramids of Egypt. Next is Rennes-le-Château in France, and finally, Mt. Kailas in the Himalayas."

After the group formed their positions, Hadden said, "This will only work for surface dwellers who are integrated enough. They will feel a calling to go to that location. They don't need to go there physically but just with their light body in either a waking or a dream state. Call these souls to travel to the appropriate power centre, the one that matches their energetic frequency."

The different groups went into meditation to initiate the process. Hadden checked 4D to see how the women were doing. The occasional straggler integrated enough to join them in 6D. Meanwhile, they got to work, holding the anchor for surface dwellers to cross to 5D.

After an exhaustive process, Meraton said, "It would be good to measure how we're doing. Do you have a 6D Hall of Records that we can check?"

That's when Hadden realised that no one from 6D had come to greet them like when he had ascended. He looked around the field, scanning for Halia or Triol or any of the other 6D Elders. "That's strange. I don't see anyone here from 6D. And when I awoke in 6D, I had a violet aura. None of us has an aura at all." He frowned, troubled. "We aren't quite there yet." He sat in meditation, reaching out telepathically to Halia.

Her voice came through once he had calmed down enough to listen. She said, *There is one more gateway to pass through. It acts as a firewall to ensure that no un-integrated soul gets through. According to our records, only 31% of the people in Helio Tropez have crossed the bridge. That means that only 3.1 million of your surface humans can cross from 3D to 5D. That is much less than we hoped for.*

He relayed this information to the others.

Meraton sighed. "I guess we shouldn't be surprised. During these last few decades leading up to the harvest of souls, we completely cut ourselves off from the surface."

Stavron nodded. "It's like we started a greenhouse, then let it go to seed."

Meraton looked down into 4D. "And the window is closing very soon. SIM managed to hijack most of our harvest."

Hadden's heart tightened in his chest. "It's tragic.

"Shouldn't we ask Pentada to come up now to 6D before the solar flare?" Xander asked.

"Yes," Hadden nodded. "I'll ask the women to make a last call to those in 4D. The integration counsellors will need to abandon their posts and join us too."

They watched as the last few people ascended. Cassandra called the counsellors forth and helped them ascend. Finally, the five women held hands and flew up to 6D. When they landed, the bridge and the 4D Veya Field started to fade behind them.

Daphne flew into Hadden's arms in tears. "We made it."

"You did."

She broke free from his embrace and looked around. "It's so amazing here. It's like 4D, only ten times more vibrant. I feel so much lighter. Thank you for coming back for me and everyone who made it here from the bottom of my heart. We couldn't have done it without you."

Hadden's heart felt bittersweet at the acknowledgment. Such a small percentage had made it. The truth was, he'd failed. Looking around, his family surrounded him. For that, at least, he was grateful. He looked over to see Xander and Tia embracing.

"Now that Tia is in 6D and we go through the next checkpoint, SIM can't control her anymore."

"There's one more checkpoint?" Daphne asked. "Does everyone know that?"

Hadden shook his head. He stepped up on the central platform to address the group. "We have one more checkpoint to cross before we officially arrive in 6D. It involves going through a second stargate that will appear here, on the central platform, when I give the word. Once it appears, stick with your group and move slowly through it, one at a time. It's just a final purification process."

A chorus of agitation spread throughout the crowd. Daphne looked at him with concern. He ushered everyone off the platform and turned around to face the empty space before them.

The space is clear, Halia and team. We're ready for you to open the portal.

A spinning circle of light appeared on the platform and stood about ten feet tall, emanating golden light. Cheers erupted from the field.

He turned to those standing nearest to the platform and ushered them forward. "Let's begin! Just go one by one. We need at least ten seconds between people."

One by one, people stepped up onto the platform, and Meraton or Cassandra invited them to step through the Golden Stargate. Hadden prayed everyone would make it. He turned to Pentada and their mates and said, "Let's go last just to see if anyone needs our help."

They nodded and watched as the group continued to cross through the stargate. Everyone made it without a hitch. Once 95% of them had gone through, Tia whispered to Hadden, "I just need to go down now and deactivate the rainbow bridge. I'll be right back."

"What? No, you don't need to. It's been deactivated."

"Not really. I have to go."

A look of anguish crossed her face as she bid him goodbye. Just before she leapt down into 4D, Hadden caught her arm. "You made a deal with SIM, didn't you?"

Tia said nothing and pulled back. Hadden asked to enter her mind, and this time, she let him. He saw the whole experience in the biosphere with Waleya and the Creatrix of SIM, ending with the blood oath, all to allow them to ascend to 6D.

Tia's eyes filled with tears. "I'm so sorry. I love you all." With that, she leapt off the 6D ledge and returned to 4D. By this point, the bridge had faded to almost nothing.

As the bridge continued to disintegrate, Hadden knew that she had made the wrong decision. Lilith had tricked her, and he felt responsible. She needed to break the oath before the solar flare, but it meant potentially perishing. He took a deep breath. He would never be able to live with himself if he just let her go.

Hadden turned to Pentada and their mates and told them what he knew. They rushed to the ledge to see her standing alone, crying in a huddle in the middle of the Veya Field. Xander called out to her, but she didn't look up.

Hadden turned to the group. "I'm going down to help her break the vow. I'll be back with her shortly. Wait for us, okay?" With that, he flew down into 4D.

He landed gently, and Tia looked up, her face pained. Before she could speak, he pulled her to her feet and held both her shoulders. "You were tricked. You don't need to become the Creatrix of SIM. How she did that to you goes against the laws of SANA."

"Go back! I don't need your help," she cried.

"I'm not leaving without you."

"I can't leave. If I do, then everyone dies and no one makes it to 6D. Please, go back. I don't want your blood on my hands."

"There's a third option!" Hadden insisted.

"I tried to find a third option. There isn't one."

"Yes, there is. You stay in your body and serve SANA."

"But how? I made a blood oath."

"You break the vow."

"But it's too late now."

"It's not. The window of opportunity hasn't closed yet."

The bridge and the 6D platform were barely visible, and if they didn't leave immediately, they would be separated from the others forever. He looked up at Daphne and the rest of Pentada. The first one to come back down was Xander.

He grabbed Tia's hand and said, "I'm not leaving without you."

Tia shook her head. "Thank you for coming back for me, but I can't. Please," she begged, "go back up."

Next came Daphne, and soon, all of Pentada and their mates were down in 4D again. By this time, the bridge had completely disappeared and the 6D platform evaporated.

Tia sobbed. "I can't believe you all did that. I made that sacrifice so you could all ascend!" She glared at them. "Now it's all in vain!"

"No, you saved all those people in Helio Tropez and on the surface."

"But most of our genetic experiment on Earth won't make it, and neither will all these people still here. It's a failure. The whole thing failed!"

"We need to stay together," Daphne said.

"I can't stay with you anyway," she sniffed. "I made a blood oath to SIM."

Silence filled the air as they tried to comprehend what she just said. Panic coursed through Hadden's body, blocking his ability to see the situation clearly. Without Tia's willingness, the only option for all of them was death.

Cassandra pulled her granddaughter into a hug, "Remember what Waleya said? As Pentada, our role involves sacrifice. We all instinctively know that we had to come back here for you."

"Waleya reminded me again when I was with her in the biosphere. I thought just one of us needed to make the sacrifice, and she chose me for some reason. You don't need to do this."

Hadden faced her directly. "You might be misinterpreting what sacrifice means here. I believe there's another way. How much time do we have?"

Stavron tapped into the 4D Hall of Records using his wrist comm. "The solar flare is headed straight towards Earth with an estimated impact in seventy-two minutes."

"Let's assemble in the Hall of Congress and reach out to the Progenitors. I can't believe they would allow this to happen to Tia."

"Waleya was the one who orchestrated it!" Tia said.

"Maybe that wasn't really Waleya," Hadden said, leading her and the others towards the Hall of Congress at a jog.

Within a few minutes, all ten of them stood in a semi-circle in the Hall of Congress. They went into prayer, calling upon the Progenitors, but the fear of the nearing solar flare played on everyone's mind, affecting their ability to concentrate. Nothing happened for at least thirty minutes.

"This seems pointless," Ramu cried. "We all ascended to 6D already. Why should we die in a solar flare? We did our integration work! Let's just go back to the field and rebuild the bridge."

"The platform is gone now. We had a twelve-hour window, and that's over."

"I told you all to stay up there!" Tia shouted.

As they continued to argue, a figure materialised on the centre platform, wearing a horned headdress and mask.

The figure stepped towards Tia, hand held out. "It's no use calling upon the Progenitors. You made your choice, Tia. Now it's time to make good on your promise."

Something about the woman's voice seemed familiar, but Hadden couldn't properly see her face. His normal ability to see someone's true identity was somehow blocked.

"Who are you?" Hadden asked.

"My name is Lilith, Creatrix of SIM. As I told Tia, she is taking a noble role in 5D Earth, overseeing SIM. This is a righteous sacrifice, one which will be rewarded. All roads eventually lead back to wholeness."

Hadden shook his head, his 6D memories now available. "As I understand it, there is no simulation to oversee in 5D Earth like there is in 3D. SIM doesn't exist there."

Tia looked over at him and back at Lilith, horrified. "You tricked me?"

The eyes behind the mask narrowed. "I did what was needed. We are now bound together for eternity, as it should be."

"I don't understand," Tia stammered, her face paling. "What did I agree to in the blood oath?"

"I own your soul, Tia. From now on, you will do my bidding."

A shockwave of recognition ran through Hadden's mind. "Take off your headdress. Reveal yourself!"

"I am Lilith..."

Tia lunged towards her, tearing the mask away to reveal... Andrea Carbona.

"Andrea, you're the Creatrix of SIM?"

Hadden stepped towards them, suddenly understanding everything. "No. The entire SIM virtual reality is about to end. She isn't the Creatrix of SIM. SANA created SIM on purpose for our learning. In the higher dimensions, we have other lessons to learn. That whole narrative of being the overseer of SIM in 5D is a lie. So that begs the question, what is your true agenda here?"

"You can't ascend without me," Andrea said, a wicked smile on her lips.

Tia looked at Hadden, confused. "I thought you said Andrea and I had already integrated."

Andrea's eyes flashed with rage. He remembered all the times he had met her on the surface and all the times when he'd helped heal Tia's mind. His higher mind went into overdrive, integrating everything he knew about Tia, Andrea and 6D wisdom. The shadow side of a Sentient-Attention was passive-aggressiveness. Andrea had appeared in agreement to the integration process, but she had been secretly rebelling all the while. On the other hand,

Tia was good at appearing integrated, but she had never truly processed lifetimes of resentment between them.

All this time, he had glossed over the healing work necessary for Tia, focusing instead on everyone else. Her experience in the Biosphere had happened because she was the one member of Pentada who wasn't actually ready to ascend.

A voice came from behind him. "It was all a test."

He turned to see Waleya.

The Progenitor stepped into the light on the platform and addressed the group. "Tia failed the test. Therefore, she cannot ascend. If she doesn't ascend, the rest of you will perish with her. That is all pre-programmed in your soul contract. We're so sorry it turned out this way."

"What?" Tia yelled. "We've sacrificed ourselves as souls for 25,000 years, we got everyone to this point. I already integrated my soul annex...years ago! Didn't I?"

Waleya shook her head. "Apparently not. We suggest you accept your fate and make peace with yourselves while you still have time. Please, prepare for your transition."

Tia stared at her. "So I'm not the new Creatrix of SIM in 5D?"

"No. As your father said, there is no SIM in 5D. The program terminates in twelve minutes. We leave you in peace and thank you for your service."

She de-materialised, and Tia looked back at everyone. "What?!"

Hadden closed his eyes, defeated. "I'm so sorry, I had no idea. I thought you'd integrated. We didn't help you enough."

Andrea lunged towards Tia and fastened handcuffs between them. "I own you now, body and soul! You can't go anywhere without me."

Tia sighed and said, "What does it matter? We are all about to leave our bodies and go back to source."

"Not you. You now live in service to me for eternity."

Hadden frowned. Something didn't make sense. "Tia, this seems like another trick!"

She looked up at him, her lips trembling. "What can I do?"

"Maybe, together, we can quickly help you integrate."

"But Waleya acted like I was beyond help. Besides, there are only ten minutes left until impact."

"I don't think we should die in a state of panic and anger," Meraton urged. "If we do, there is the possibility that we don't make it back to source and end up in a hellish service to SIM instead. All we have time for now is to pray for a peaceful transition. Maybe that peaceful state will help you integrate."

Looking uneasy and confused, the group formed a circle. Tia tried to join them, but Andrea pulled her away. Hadden felt torn between wanting to help her and not wanting to end up hijacked by SIM when the solar flare hit. Everyone else had their eyes closed, apart from Hadden, who stared directly at her with pleading eyes.

Go be in peace with them. This is my fate, Tia said to him telepathically, tears streaming down her cheeks.

Call out to SANA for help, Hadden urged.

Waleya said...

Don't let anyone else come between you and SANA.

"You have no connection to SANA anymore," Andrea whispered in her ear, grinning. "I am your master. Everyone else has abandoned you. I'm all you have now."

Reluctantly, Hadden joined the group and left Tia alone. With only eight minutes left, they joined hands and prepared themselves for the transition.

CHAPTER 49

Tia sat face to face with Andrea, cuffed together, in grief for the loss of everything and everyone dear to her. A fire of victory burned in Andrea's eyes.

Tia closed her eyes, afraid of what she saw. After a few minutes of calling on SANA, nothing happened. Her stomach felt nauseous, and a single memory swirled in from the corner of her mind from her first coaching session with Andrea.

She opened her eyes and looked directly at the hateful figure before her. "Hey, Andrea? Remember how I helped you feel confident in your job as a manager?"

"So, what?" She shrugged. "I was paying you good money. It wasn't because you cared." At that moment, her eyes strangely turned orange. "Just one more way to make me beholden to you. It's the same story, life after life. But not anymore. I've turned the tables now. How does it feel?"

Memories of all their past lives together flooded through her mental landscape. As a soul, when she first incarnated on earth, Tia had a sovereign soul. No annexing. However, each time she experienced trauma, her soul created a new partition. Those partitions became an entity unto itself known, in this life, as Andrea Carbona.

Now the fire in Andrea's eyes showed Tia the unresolved pain that she had never truly dealt with in any of her lifetimes. Instead of facing them, she'd deflected the pain each time. This went against her soul contract to face all the hardship. Somehow now, she understood her soul's longing in a new way. Like Houdini, her soul purposely chose to be suspended and strait jacketed, to try to get free from it all. It wanted the adventure of it all!

Tia's act of refusal had created a doorway for SIM to further splinter her soul and traumatise her throughout the ages. Therefore, everything Andrea did was her responsibility. All the acts of wrongdoing or even wrong thinking were hers as well. It was true. All her attempts to help Andrea had an ulterior motive but to control her. However, none of it had worked because the core wounding between them was never addressed. She had judged Andrea as lower than her, separate from her, someone to be managed.

Unable to see how to fully accept and reconcile this separation, she reached out to SANA once more. "Beloved SANA, please help heal us in whatever way is possible in these last few moments of life. Help our souls integrate again."

A message came back softly, barely audible. "Go to her."

Tia cracked one eye open and flinched at the frightful figure before her. *Go to her?* Taking a deep breath for courage, she dove right inside those blazing eyes and landed in Andrea's mind. Rage, anger, fear, trauma and negativity boiled and churned in a cauldron of darkness. Instead of resisting it, she just watched from a neutral place, curiously wandering around the perimeter of the cauldron. Soon, a wick of insight grew. Andrea was right. Behind each action lay an agenda to control her, blocking the love and therefore any connection this shadow self could have to source.

That insight grew into a white light in her heart, and she directed that white light inside the cauldron, which acted like a magnifying glass held over a leaf in the hot sun. The cauldron caught on fire. Flames licked and consumed the air around them until she could hardly breathe. As the fire grew, it turned to a violet flame, growing hotter and more mesmerizing, engulfing everything around it. The heat tore through her body, reddening, rippling, and then turning her skin black. The smell of burning flesh sickened her. Hellacious thoughts tore through her like a flamethrower, destroying everything it touched. All the karmic cords burned up, and everything she ever cared about melted in the extreme heat.

When the embers finally settled and only ashes remained, Tia felt oddly still. Relief settled onto her like a warm quilt. The solar flare must have come and gone. Yet, somehow, part of her was still there. Halia's presence lingered. *Maybe, hopefully, I am in 6D.* She pried open sticky eyes. The light blinded her at first, and she blinked several times to adjust to the furry vision in front of her. Bimini sat nearby, blinking at her. She hadn't seen him since the virus had hit. *Maybe Halia has brought Bimini back to me now that I am in 6D?* Yet, Andrea still sat in front of her, eyes closed. The rest of the group still sat in a circle. Maybe the solar flare hadn't hit yet? Strange. Bimini turned away from Tia and sniffed at Andrea's calf. No response. He glanced at Tia with a mischievous grin and leapt up onto Andrea's lap.

"Eek!" She broke out of her trance.

The bear sat back on its haunches and looked up at her with curious eyes. It nuzzled against her arm, but she tried to push him off her lap.

"Get away, you mangy little thing!"

He hung onto her sleeve with his mouth and snuggled closer. Once settled, he purred like a farm tractor, beaming her with love. Andrea's face softened, and she tentatively patted the bear.

A memory from years ago flickered into Tia's mind. The two of them had often sat at the back of English class, whispering. One day, Andrea had slipped a gift to her. It was a stunning leather-bound journal with a sapphire embedded on the outside, which she now knew to be the gemstone of Sentients. Tia had used that journal for years to track all her telepathic conversations with Halia. On the opening page, a quotation lay etched in gold.

Perhaps everything that challenges us is, in its deepest essence, something helpless that wants our love.

That quote always made her heart stir. A flood of images filled her memory banks. So many wonderful moments together, parties, picnics on the beach, sailing together, singing songs, confiding in their dreams for the future, and congratulating each other on their big and small wins. One memory unfolded after another in a kaleidoscope of colours. "I don't want to control you. I love you, Andrea. I really do. I've missed you."

As tears welled up in Andrea's eyes, Tia saw how much damage all the judgment had done. She had blamed all her own misdeeds over all the lifetimes on her soul annex so that she could remain pure. In the process, the power of SIM had grown. Of course, she knew that the only way to ascend meant including her soul annex fully and completely. Tia held so many other people accountable for that, but she hadn't done it herself.

Stavron announced, "One minute until impact."

Tia reached out to join hands with Andrea. This time her eyes were clear and pure. At that moment, she forgave Andrea for everything. Any misdeed was her misdeed. To be redeemed in the eyes of SANA meant redeeming herself in all aspects. Her soul had evolved because of the challenges, not in spite of them. Even though they wouldn't ascend, Tia wanted to go back to source fully integrated with all parts of herself. So they stood to face each other and hugged, both wanting to face the end with love and gratitude rather than fear. As they did, Tia felt the handcuffs disintegrate from their wrists, and any blood oath between them burned up in a fire of purification.

She waited for the solar flare to take them. The group stood up and came in close to breathe together as one. Tia counted down in her mind, watching her breath, fully surrendered to death.

The minute came, and the minute went. Nothing happened. Tia waited in silence, knowing that time expanded when crossing dimensions.

Stavron's voice carried across the room. "That's strange..."

"What?" Hadden asked.

"I'm looking at my comm. Just before hitting Earth, the solar flare made a 45° turn and kept going past the Earth. I wonder if that means that we are out of danger?"

"Can you expand that image on the console?" Hadden asked while turning on the holographic screen.

Stavron transferred an image showing the trajectory of the solar flare, making an abrupt turn away from the Earth and carrying on into deep space.

"How did that happen?" Ramu asked, looking to the others in giddy disbelief.

As they talked, Tia stood several feet behind them, surrounded by a rainbow of spiralling lights. Xander turned to look at her, and his jaw dropped. He knew why. Andrea was gone, and Tia stood alone as a unified soul.

Just then, Waleya materialised on the platform along with several other Elders from Anatol. "Congratulations. You completed the exam successfully."

Tia looked over at her with a blank expression.

"The last piece of Pentada integration is complete. The Galactic Alliance has now decided to give the experiment one final chance."

"The Galactic Alliance diverted the solar flare?" Stavron shouted.

"Yes. We alerted them to the situation, so they have been monitoring it."

The group shook their heads in disbelief, still trying to process the intensity of what had just happened.

Waleya, Adim and the other Elders emanated a calming presence, filling the Hall of Congress with stabilizing energies. They sent a telepathic multi-dimensional package of information to everyone, helping them better understand and decompress from the experience. As download of understanding filled everyone's mental landscape, they collapsed onto the floating chairs to process what had just happened.

Adim spoke first, "Now that Pentada has full integrity again, we might make this work after all. Also, too many souls didn't make it into the higher densities. It would be a shame to end the whole project with such poor numbers. Together with the Alliance, we suggest that you redouble your efforts and see if you can get a much higher percentage through to the finish line next time. Consider it like a remedial exam."

Hadden held out both hands. "Why did they wait until just now to divert the solar flare?"

"Because of me," Tia admitted, bathed in an unusual peace of mind. "As the last born member of Pentada, I was the last runner in the relay, which made my role pivotal." Tia looked to Metta with a smile. "Youngest by just a few minutes, of course. All of you had integrated your soul annex, but I hadn't done it until just now. I was too stubborn, proud and blind to see it."

"Yes," Waleya nodded. "The test in the Biosphere proved to us that you weren't ready to ascend yet. It caused a ripple effect, stopping the ascension process. But when Pentada and their mates gave up their own ascension to come back and help you, that made all the difference."

Tia looked up at Waleya. "So that's what you meant by sacrifice?"

She nodded. "Partly. When the group formed a field of peace, in the last few moments, it helped you make the final sacrifice...to fully let go of your unwillingness to face your shadow and choose wholeness, no matter the cost. You've melted all that petrified trauma into pure creativity now"

A wave of relief washing through every cell in Tia's body.

Meraton cupped his chin. "So what happens now? How much more time do we have to turn this around?"

"We'll give you a few more years. All the other genetic farmers felt that SIM got far too out of control on Gaia, causing a very poor crop of souls. Your job is to stay in 4D long enough to wake up surface humans between now and the end of the experiment. However, if you don't pass the next test, those left behind will be deleted. No third chances."

"So SIM could still win?" Cassandra asked.

"No. The SIM and the SANA timelines were always scheduled to merge by this date in 2012. That said, some souls still need the lessons of duality, so the Galactic Alliance will mimic the SIM intensity for a few more years and see what we get. The closer you get to the final window of ascension, the more you'll see increased duality on the surface. It will simply be to wake people from the dream spell of their reality and to activate unity consciousness. Your job is to share the frequency of the higher density levels as much as you can so that it permeates the collective."

The Elders stood in silence for a few moments to allow the information to sink in.

Waleya added, "And now, we recommend that you settle deeper inside the hollow core of this planet."

"Leave Helio Tropez? Why?" Cassandra asked.

"Our research shows that you were not as protected from ravages of inverted 3D duality as you needed to be. We take partial responsibility for this poor harvest of souls. We were the ones that suggested you set up here near the surface. SIM appears to have now created tunnel systems through the Earth's crust for their trauma, inducing evil. That energy field weakened your shields. Go down into the hollow centre of this earth and find a new home. Invite those left behind in 4D to go with you. If you want to gather everyone in the Hall of Congress, we will address them ourselves."

Meraton got on the comm and invited all citizens to the Hall of Congress, his voice reaching every ear in the city.

Once most remaining citizens had gathered, the Progenitors explained what had happened with the solar flare.

Waleya pulled up an image of the Earth's surface surrounded by symbols. "SIM created special satellites to track and control everyone on the surface. It's blocked your ability to track your own experiment. Your task now is to hack their system and use it for people's benefit instead; to deprogram yourselves and your surface humans, so everyone can ascend more easily."

The Congress exploded into a litany of questions.

Waleya cushioned her hands to calm down the crowd. "All will be answered as you need it. For now, we suggest you each read your own updated Galactic Records and Potentiality Cards, which are now available and linked to our system. It will tell you which soul lessons you still need to learn. Then, prepare to leave Helio Tropez. The Progenitors will need to demolish it within two weeks for security reasons."

Malinah stood up to address the group before any more questions could erupt. "I know that's unsettling for everyone, but I do see the wisdom of leaving. I suggest we just follow their advice. If we are going to move forward with this project and work together, I suggest we truly choose to pay attention to our soul growth. In the meantime, we will need to elect a new Council of Elders. Many of the old ones have already ascended."

Most people in the hall nodded, muttering in agreement.

"Do we have any nominations?"

A man rose to his feet and spoke with confidence. "I nominate Pentada and their mates. They are the only ones that have been to 6D and back. We need that kind of wisdom to guide us."

They discussed the pros and cons of that decision, and in the end, it made the most sense. They added a few others to even out the diversity of the council and then called upon the Progenitors to sanctify their choices.

Waleya stepped forward and walked slowly around the group, looking at each chosen Elder as she spoke. "We do sanctify your choices. There is one more role we need to assign. A Time Traveller. This person first needs to be properly trained by the Temporalia to ensure that it's done correctly." She stopped in front of Hadden. "Your job will be to explore all possible timelines moving forward based on present circumstances. Work with the Temporalia to identify the most ideal for ascension. Agreed?"

Hadden bowed, a broad smile crossing his face. "Agreed."

"The Temporalia are waiting for you in the future. Bring the latest version of your amethyst with the new MindStory Code. You'll need to see how it plays out in future timelines. Bring your Jenio with you as well."

"I don't have a Jenio."

She smiled and returned to the platform to stand next to the other Anatol Elders. As they dematerialised, she said, "You will."

CHAPTER 50

Over the next few days, Tia noticed many Heliotropans just needing to recover from the intensity of recent experiences. The move deeper inside the Earth would require stamina and energy. At the same time, some felt strong enough to clean up the city, reopen shops for medicinal remedies, power up the Healing Bays, regenerate the plants in the greenhouses, and replicate anything that needed fixing for their immediate use.

One afternoon, Pentada and their mates sat together in the Garden of Jephsonite, having a picnic, enjoying being with each other finally free of the virus. Daphne lay her head on Hadden's lap, and he caressed her hair. Tia overhead her mother share stories of her life as a navigator in outer space. Nearby, Metta and Ramu worked on a skit together for the upcoming final ceremony. Every few minutes, they broke into laughter. Clearly, they had the same silly sense of humour. Metta's newfound Jenio, a long-haired rabbit, lay curled up next to them. His leopard stood watch over the three of them swatting flies as necessary.

Across the field, Stavron showed Annika all the weapons he'd made by hand. She took each one and examined the workmanship with awe. Of course, she had to try each one, so they found a space near the trees where she could throw axes and shoot arrows. Screams of delight carried across the lawn each time she hit a bullseye.

Cassandra came around with another plate of grapes and handed it to Tia. "Have more."

"More? Okay. They *are* delicious."

Even though she was full, Tia didn't have the heart to turn her down. Cassandra had personally gathered or replicated as much food as possible over the last few days. Night and day, she hand-delivered the food all over the city, making amends for all the months she cut off people's resources to anyone who would allow her.

Xander slid next to Tia to partake the grapes. They were twice as large as grapes on the surface and tasted like heaven.

"I admire what Cassandra is doing," Xander said as he popped one into his mouth. "I should probably be doing something like that."

"What do you mean?"

He lowered his head, "All those people who took the Bejula plant upon my recommendation. I became their guru, and then... it all went so badly."

Tia nodded, not sure what to say.

"But I've tried to find those people. None of them ascended or died or seem to still be in the city."

"Maybe they left on foot for Agartha."

"Maybe. I want to make amends somehow."

"You can still do it in your own heart. It will affect them."

"Right. I'll try that."

"I feel the same way. You'd all be in 6D if it wasn't for me. I don't know where to begin to make amends."

Xander kissed her cheek. "I wouldn't want to be in 6D if you weren't there with me."

Something above caught everyone's attention.

"Look at the top of that tree," Meraton said, pointing up at a giant fir. "A Golden Eagle just landed. It's huge. I've never seen one in Helio Tropez."

Daphne sat up and followed his gaze. "Maybe this Eagle is a Jenio looking for her human." A Blue Jay alighted onto her shoulder, who, only yesterday, had announced himself as her Jenio. She glanced at Hadden. "There's an Eagle come to meet you."

"What are you talking about?"

"Your Jenio is up in that tree. It makes sense we'd both have birds for Jenios."

Meraton pulled a blanket from his bag. "Hadden, give me your arm."

"My arm?"

Daphne pushed him towards Meraton, "Well, go ahead, do what papa says."

"Hold it out like this," Meraton instructed as he bent his arm at shoulder length.

Hadden mimicked him, and Meraton wrapped the blanket around Hadden's forearm. "Lift your arm up for her to land on it."

Hadden laughed nervously, "What? An eagle wouldn't do that. And is that even safe?"

Meraton nodded, "Sure, it's safe. But you'll need to entice her with an offering." He pulled a gold ribbon from his plaited hair and handed it to him. "Dance that around until it catches her attention."

With his blanketed arm raised, he held up the gold ribbon, and it gleamed in the light. The eagle jerked its head as though calculating, then swooped down, talons coming right at him. He ducked his head just as she landed on his arm. Hadden's eyes grew large as she folded her wings down and grabbed for the ribbon with her beak. She chomped on it and promptly dropped it on the ground, disappointed in the taste. Hadden laughed, and she turned to look at him. Intense yellow eyes studied him from under a feathery brow ridge. She tilted her beak down and then touched her forehead with his. Several people gathered around in awe to witness the union.

Hadden opened his wings and took flight with the eagle still perched on his arm. As he flew higher, the eagle took flight herself and followed him. They circled around each other in the air, swooping and coasting on the breeze, then plunging down towards the ground and soaring high again.

"That's amazing," Xander said. "What a fine Jenio to have. Metta now has her brown rabbit over there. And just yesterday, Daphne got her Blue Jay. I'm the only Elder without a Jenio."

Tia reached for a grape. "True. You need to call on her before we leave here." She savoured the explosion of sweetness in her mouth. "I'm so amazed at how my allergic reactions to food have disappeared since integrating my soul annex."

"That's amazing! Me, too... only not around allergies. I used to feel like I was a slave...this oppressed feeling. Even when I came to Helio Tropez, I felt that way. Now I feel free to create the life I want." He sat up cross-legged and looked around at the foliage surrounding the park. "How would I do that...call on my Jenio?"

"Ask for her to come forward. Tell her that you are ready."

"How do you know it's a 'her'?"

"Jenios are usually the opposite gender to their human."

Xander sighed. "Okay. So, Hadden gets a lovely lady eagle. I'll probably get a turkey."

Tia laughed and threw a grape at him. "I've never seen a turkey Jenio. What kind do you want?"

"To tell you the truth, I'd love, like a... lion... or a stag or something like that."

"Hmm, a power animal. That makes sense." Tia laughed again and added, "they are hard to put on your lap, though."

He pointed at Ulwag. "Meraton's wolf isn't a lap animal."

"True. Call on your Jenio now, and see what happens."

Xander placed his hand on Tia's and looked over at her with his spectacularly green eyes, more vivid than ever. He removed a tress of hair from her forehead and lay on the ground to close his eyes.

The touch was exactly what she had hoped the touch of lover's hand would feel like, familiar yet excitingly new. As he meditated on his Jenio, she gazed into the green of the trees, enjoying the breeze rippling through the leaves. It was the same kind of green as in Xander's eyes, the green that only showed up her in dreams before she had come to Helio Tropez. Now she was living that dream.

The experience of almost dying, in contrast to this harmonised frequency inside and out, no longer having to push a part of herself away or push this amazing man away, filled her mind. All the conflict vanished into nothingness like small clouds evaporating on a hot day. She knew it wouldn't last forever, but for now, she appreciated every joyful moment.

As she finished off the last of the grapes, a funny-looking animal hopped out of a nearby bush. Tia gasped and elbowed Xander's ribs. "Look over there."

Xander opened his eyes in a daze. "I think I drifted off... what?"

Bimini raced towards a creature that had just retreated into a bush. It looked like a tiny kangaroo.

Xander squinted. "What was it?"

Tia jumped up. "Let's check it out."

They approached slowly, not making any sudden movements. When they were close enough, Tia crouched, trying to entice the animal out. "I think it's a wallaby, maybe," Tia suggested. "It's related to a kangaroo."

Xander crouched beside her and peered inside the bush. "Come on out," he said gently. "I won't bite."

The wallaby ducked deeper into the shadows. Tia sat cross-legged next to him and pulled Bimini onto her lap. His excitement was clearly causing the wallaby some agitation, so she scratched his ears until he calmed down. Xander sat next to the bush and waited patiently. The others left the field to start preparing a feast for the evening.

"Maybe she's not my Jenio."

The bear looked up at Tia and grunted. "Bimini thinks she IS your Jenio, but apparently, she thinks you don't want her."

"What! That's daft. Why would she think that?"

Bimini squeaked as he looked at him, then back at Tia.

"The wallaby thinks you'd prefer a lion or a stag."

Xander made a funny face at Bimini. "She was listening in on our conversation?"

The bear nodded solemnly.

With a huff, he stood up and crossed his arms. "Hey! I saw something just like you hopping in my dream when I called out for my Jenio. I want you. I really do."

Tia peered into the bush and could only see the tip of a tail twitching in the darkness.

"Bimini says you should try giving her an offering."

Xander sighed and rustled around in his pouch, pulling out various items like a harmonica, a guitar pick, and a small ruby.

"This is the gemstone of Audients. Annika gave it to me. She's got to like that." He held it out towards the bush. After about thirty seconds, a pointy nose popped out and sniffed at the gem. Glassy eyes blinked at him. The wallaby reached up with stubby arms and slipped it into her pouch for safekeeping like a newborn joey.

"That's a good sign." He smiled.

She hopped forward, sniffed at his hand, and then held up a paw. When Xander shook it, that seemed to seal the deal. After that, the wallaby rarely left Xander's side.

The next day, the remaining Heliotropans gathered in the Hall of Congress with their new Council of Elders to plan the transition to Agartha. The Hall felt strangely empty, given a third of them had ascended and another group had escaped deeper into Inner Earth to avoid the solar flare. Only those willing to hike through raptor filled forests had taken up the challenge, given that the buses to the train station weren't working at that time. Even the mountain pagoda group had ascended. Those that remained were the less robust and the more injured from the ravages of the virus. So they needed plenty of healing and integration.

Hadden called the meeting to order, "To begin with, we have much healing and reconciliation to do before we can move together as a community to a new location. This once supportive and harmonious city became riddled with the ills of surface cities. It's taken its toll. To that end, we've set up rooms in all five Palaces for anyone that feels they need truth, reconciliation and healing. Make a list of unresolved issues or offences you were involved in. We will seek to make amends and learn from the situation for all those involved. Tasma and Filamin will organise that."

Tasma added, "This will also include the grieving and rituals needed to say goodbye to those who've left their body... people that you miss... so that you can honour the connection and move forward."

A woman in the balcony raised her hand, and the light fell onto her face. "What about our friends and relatives that ascended to 6D? I miss them."

Hadden raised his hand and stepped forward into the light. "If you're open to it, we can communicate with people in 6D. It's their job to guide us.

Tia and I will share with you the protocols we learned to help you do that. In fact, I've already been in contact with Halia, my grandmother. She says everyone from 4D Helio Tropez is doing exceptionally well."

A wave of relief intertwined with envy permeated the Hall.

"What about all the 3D people on the surface who ascended to 5D? Are they okay? And what do they say about millions of people missing from 3D?" the woman asked.

Hadden closed his eyes for a moment. "I'm not sure. I invite us all to remote view the situation in whatever way that your aptitude allows. I'll synthesize your data."

The Hall went silent for a few moments. Meanwhile, Hadden acted as a telepathic scribe, downloading all the data onto the mainframe computer in the Hall. He formed it into a Matrix diagram that summarised the results and projected it onto the hologram.

"So far, it looks like they were simply written off as 'missing' from the surface of Earth, although alternative media sources reported that people just disappeared in a rainbow of lights. Those reports were debunked by the mainstream, which is still controlled by SIM agents. Regarding 5D, we have far less data. I have visited 5D with Halia, so I checked in with her just now, and she tells me that they are thriving."

This data created a flurry of questions, which Hadden, Tasma and Filamin fielded over the next few minutes.

After the last question, Hadden said, "As an update, I have my first meeting with the Temporalia later today. A representative came to me in a dream. I now have instructions on how to get there via our stargate portal. They exist in a time bubble, about fifty years in the future. For aeons, they have been calculating how timelines change throughout the galaxy, depending on events in the present. I will be helping them nudge the whole galaxy onto the right timeline, including us and our 3D humans. I also will ask if they can help us find the best location for us in Agartha. I keep getting this vision of an old research station on a place called the Celestial Lake."

Jaya interjected, "I'm familiar with that location. As you know, I've been on many diplomatic missions to Agartha, and we must stake a formal claim for any land usage in that region. I suggest that those of us familiar with that region go on a scout mission to ensure it's the right place, then seek permissions at Shambala, the capitol city."

The Elders talked amongst themselves for a few minutes and agreed.

"Okay, the next agenda item," Hadden said, "Securing a chartered speed train to take the entire community and all our possessions to Agartha."

Stavron said, "I know a guy, who knows a guy who has a train which he could lend us. It's dwarf-sized, but we can adjust certain compartments for you lanky people."

"I once helped build a speed train, so maybe I can help with the adjustments," Ramu offered.

"Okay, good. You two work together on that." Hadden smiled. "This next item on the agenda will help us decide on the length of train that we need." He zoomed in on the holographic screen. "What to take and what to leave behind."

Jaya said, "That will depend on what's in our new location already. Let's wait until we see this location on the Celestial Lake. I just did a quick remote view. I think a lot of infrastructure is already there. I suggest we bring our replicators and create most of what we need when we get there."

"Ha! It's so much simpler than when you have to travel on the surface, right?" Hadden asked, smiling at Xander.

"I'll say. My band used to travel with five busloads of equipment," he replied. "By the way, we are performing music and songs for our farewell ceremony to this city. So, any musicians, poets, songwriters who want to be part of that, meet with Annika, Daphne, Metta and I after this meeting."

"Also, the SANA Eagles in training will be performing in the sky at the same ceremony, and we'll also be meeting tomorrow... just as a reminder," Hadden added.

Malinah brought up the next agenda item. "We will have ceremonies in the five regions of the city leading up to the final concert, where we will give thanks. I'll need five volunteers to organise each area. Any takers?"

After Malinah took notes of the five names, she said, "Now, are we ready to recreate the Task Force?"

Tia took the spotlight. "Yes, let's keep working on the MindStory Code, especially now that all Pentada are here. We can finally complete it. We need to be interfacing with our surface humans as soon as possible. Since the virus hit, none of them has heard from us. Also, some original members of our Task Force have ascended or left the city, so we'll need replacements. Cassandra,

Meraton and I will be doing interviews tomorrow at the Palace of Zuris. Thank you."

Cassandra added, "Since this is the first time Pentada is reunited and virus free, we are having our first meeting just the five of us. This might allow us to download the full code."

When Cassandra gathered Pentada together after the meeting, a flutter of excitement filled Tia's heart. The women followed her up a winding staircase to a dome-shaped room. It reminded Tia of her bedroom back in Seattle. As they entered, she saw five lush lounge chairs facing each other. Each one had a different colour, and the backs were embedded with different gemstones. Vases of multi-coloured roses adorned the perimeter of the entire room.

"Daphne, this is your Voyent chair in the coppery teal colour, embedded with Azurite. Metta, you're Ecrivent, so here in the silvery-white chair with all the quartz crystals. Annika, the Audient chair."

"Wow! Embedded with rubies. I feel so regal," Annika said as she climbed up on the chair and sat like an empress.

"Yes, our role today is very regal." Cassandra sat down in a light green chair embedded with jade, the gemstone of Tangents.

The last remaining Sentient chair was azure blue, emblazoned with sapphires on the back. Cassandra gestured for Tia to sit. As she descended into the chair, a harmonized resonance echoed through every cell. Above their heads, golden sunflowers adorned the domed ceiling. A tranquil expectancy filled the air.

"What is this room for?" Tia asked. "I never knew it existed."

"I'm the only one who's known about it for years. My mother and Malinah brought me here once when I first came of age. I was the first Pentada to be born in over five hundred years, so they decided to open the room again. It hadn't been used since the last council of Pentada sat here."

"It's very well preserved," Annika remarked, running her hands along the armrests.

"It's been kept up over the years. Malinah was charged with cleaning it physically, energetically and spiritually until the next Pentada arrived. It was only to be used when all of us were back together again. I've never been back here since I was young. Today, Malinah gave me the key and suggested we finally call our first meeting so we can download the full MindStory Code."

"What about the rest of the Task Force?" Tia asked.

"Apparently, the vortex of energy we five create when alone together is too much for most people. We'll download the full code, and the Task Force can figure out the details and how to add it to everyone's amethyst. Once everyone has the full code, we are untouchable by what's left of the SIM agents on the surface. We'll be able to pass it along to certain well-selected leaders on the surface as well, who can help steer humanity towards the ascension timeline."

"Amazing," Daphne said, touching the circular translucent table in the middle.

"That's our holographic console connected to the Hall of Records. We can record our findings there. So... we've all had dreams of the MindStory Code. There is a protocol used for centuries by all Pentada to access it. Our job is to..."

"...materialise the latest version of it," Annika added with eyes closed. "As soon as I entered this room, I got a download on what it is to be Pentada."

"Yes, I hoped you would feel that. Do you know which portion you create?"

"Indeed. I create the sound portion."

"I do the visual design," Daphne smiled as she closed her eyes and breathed in the new information. She opened her eyes again and looked at Metta. They all felt drawn to look at her, expecting her to respond at that moment.

"I um... write something?" Metta looked at them quizzically.

Cassandra nodded, "Close your eyes and tell us what you see."

"Strings of, I don't know... maybe symbols... intricate patterns... in multi-colours."

"Those are the mind codes. As an Ecrivent, you tend to see the world in code form, which is in sacred geometric patterns. That's what you'll need to download."

Metta nodded still with eyes closed, seemingly fascinated by what she saw.

The others looked at Tia. She closed her eyes, and feelings of joy surged through her nervous system. "I emotionalise the code so that it inspires action."

"Exactly," Cassandra said. "And I materialise all that into a physical form, which I assume will look like some a kind of artefact."

"Huh! Maybe like the Arc of the Covenant?" Annika grinned.

"It's a physicalization of mind code, in double helix form," Metta said, triumphantly popping open her eyes, "and it will serve as the mainframe, the core hub that charges each amethyst in every person wearing one. We must keep it very safe."

The women nodded slowly in unison as if they were all hearing the same message.

"Let's begin by joining hands," Cassandra said.

As soon as they were physically united, they closed their eyes and leaned back. Thousands of years of wisdom poured into every cell in their bodies. As the energy built, strange sounds like thunder filled the dome. Tia opened her eyes in shock. Shards of rainbow light spiraled through the dome, creating an electrical storm. The hairs on her arms stood on end, and her solar plexus filled with plasma light codes from higher realms.

The unique codes that each woman received rippled out towards the others, dialling all their aptitudes beyond Amethyst Level. One aptitude became 5 aptitudes, which turned to 25, which turned to 125, which grew to 625, and settled at 3125. They now embodied 3125 nuances of the original 25 aptitudes.

As the activation continued, Tia understood more of what was happening. They all now had the potential for expressing 3125 nuances but would have to grow in wisdom to match those superpowers before SANA would allow activation. That said, the codes for each now lay embedded in their physical DNA.

Next, she saw the MindStory Code emerge in her mind's eye, spiraling in space. It looked like how they had left it after Tinaghan, with parts missing. The 3125 nuances filled in the blank parts, allowing the plasma codes to amplify the entire structure. Instead of only being in black and white, it turned multi-coloured, including the seven major colours of the rainbow and then 3125 hues of those colours. All of that information automatically downloaded into the latest amethysts they now wore behind their left ears.

Tia's whole body vibrated to a boiling point. She instinctively knew to shift her brain waves from high gamma to a more balanced state. Once she calmed down and the MindStory Code seemed complete and full embedded in the amethyst, she leaned forward and opened her eyes. All five women opened their eyes at the same time and sat on the edge of their chairs in unison. They looked at each other, all clearly shaken and exhilarated by the experience. Annika started laughing in her raucous way, which triggered an explosion of giggles among the circle. The laughter escalated until they exhausted themselves, sparking a celestial echo that bathed them in love. They were home and together once again.

As they sat holding their bellies and wiping away tears, memories of Tia's life on the surface flashed to mind. All the years alone, cut off from family and community, almost no laughter or fun, feeling like a stranger in a malicious world, all stood in stark contrast to what she was experiencing now. To have the dream of reuniting with her mother finally realised. To have an imaginary friend that was now a real twin sister. To have a wild and crazy aunt who inspired her. To have an otherworldly grandmother who challenged her to grow. All now united for one of the most important activations in human history.

CHAPTER 51

As Hadden waited for Daphne to finish her Pentada meeting, a sweep of rainbow lights came across the city. He ran out into the Veya field to get a better look, as did many other people. His eagle swooped down and landed on the lawn nearby. The spiralling energies danced around, moving closer towards the ground encircling each plant, animal, building and person until each took on a new glow. Within his own body, a dazzling sensation raced from his forehead to his feet and back again. The eagle took flight, so Hadden joined her in the air, and they swooped and soared in the rainbow spirals.

He sensed that Pentada had just downloaded the latest MindStory Code. So he flew to the Hall of Congress, where he saw the five women emerge from the front entrance, triumphant, radiant and united as never before. Once they parted ways, Hadden glided down to the ground to catch up with Daphne.

He encircled her in his arms. "You've just changed everyone and everything in the city!"

"You felt that?" She laughed. "I've just come from this intense roller coaster ride. But we did it! We downloaded the whole MindStory Code, the latest version. Now, the gem smiths can reprogram everyone's amethyst. It will surely speed up the healing and reconciliation that we need here."

"We all felt it and saw rainbow spirals everywhere!"

"Really? Amazing. We were in this special room in the upper reaches of the Hall. It was just for Pentada and hadn't been used in 500 years! It felt so magical to be there, like we belonged there... I even had my own Voyent chair. It was wild."

"A special Pentada room in the Hall? I never knew about that."

"Neither did I. Mum knew about it from when she was a child but was sworn to secrecy until all Pentada were together again."

Daphne's blue jay alighted onto her shoulder and danced around on the spot. She kissed its beak, and Hadden's eagle trilled from a tree branch in recognition of this momentous event.

A wave of joy filled Hadden's heart. "I knew it would work. It's just in time for my meeting with the Temporalia too. Waleya told me to take the latest version of the code inside the amethyst to them. When we get home, I'll create a prototype. Send it to me, please."

They turned to face each other and touched foreheads. The new code downloaded from Daphne's mind to his. Once complete, Hadden inspected it closely in his mind.

"The code looks even more beautiful than the last one." Hadden kissed her hand. "And you look even more beautiful than I've ever seen you... and that's saying something."

Daphne's cheeks lit up. "Really? I feel better than I ever have in my life. Having us all back together again, healed and ready to do our work is amazing. Not only that, but to have a meaningful purpose in my life, to be using my gifts for the right reasons... after all the years of... living such a purposeless life trying to dupe people...I don't know if that makes sense." She looked away. When she turned to face him again, her eyes had turned glassy.

"It totally makes sense," Hadden said, holding her closer. "I absolutely know what you mean."

"I've felt so much guilt. I mean, it was MY shadow counterpart that started this whole virus in Helio Tropez. If I hadn't been so easy to infiltrate..."

"You need to let that go. It was all meant to be. You've integrated that shadow side now, and you're making a huge difference for Heliotropans and for all of humanity."

Daphne nodded slowly, trying to take that in.

As they walked towards their apartment in the Zuris tower, they talked about all the things they wanted to do in the city before leaving, like performing proper SANA rites together at the Temple of Lions, exploring their Galactic Records, visiting each palace, going to the market to shop for medicinal gems, flowers, minerals and harmonic sound devices.

Daphne squeezed his hand as they came upon a waterfall that overlooked the city. It was resplendent with Heliotrope flowers, the emblem of Helio Tropez, blooming everywhere. "Yesterday, this was just a stagnant puddle with no signs of life, remember?"

"That's right. Clearly, your work today with Pentada has helped revive the whole city."

Daphne covered her mouth; turning to look in all directions. The landscape stood incandescent again. "I can hardly believe it."

"It's affecting all the people and animals as well. Finally, the city is returning to its once exalted status."

"You know," Daphne said, looking out at the city. "I spent my whole life wondering when I could come here to Helio Tropez. I didn't think it would take seventy years. Then, as soon as I arrive, it goes to ruin. Now that's back to its glory, we have to leave soon, and it will be destroyed!"

"I know. It's very sad, but we'll make an even better home, maybe on this Celestial Lake. It's said that the lake reflects the same stars that we see in the surface's sky, except you can't see the stars from Agartha. Strange, hey?"

"That is strange. Maybe we should call it Stello Tropez."

"Stello Tropez?"

"Helio means Sun, and Stello means Stars. And of course, Tropez was the founder."

"I like it."

Once they arrived back at their apartment, Hadden had a shower and got ready for his first meeting with the Temporalia. He pulled out his amethyst and downloaded the MindStory Code into it, then reapplied it to his skull.

A rainbow of lights danced in his head, and a download of evolutionary wisdom filled his brain cells. His true ascension mission crystallized into form.

"This is beyond amazing! I now see my exact path forward. Did you connect to your mission when the code entered your amethyst?"

"Yes, completely."

"I can hardly wait to show it to the Temporalia."

Daphne kissed him goodbye. "When will you be back?"

"Apparently, within a few minutes our time, but the orientation meeting will likely take hours. That's the strange thing with time travel."

"Okay, good luck."

As Hadden arrived at the stargate, his Jenio, Aleria, flew down and alighted onto his gloved arm. The front doors slid open, and they entered. He remembered once being escorted to the stargate by Protectors, kicked out of the city for illegal time travel. As he entered, a stargate technician bowed in reverence, offering a more elaborate greeting than normal.

"Hadden of Violetta and Aleria, I'm honoured to help you today. This is an auspicious occasion—going to your first meeting with the Temporalia."

"Thank you. I believe your name is Cliven. Do you remember me?"

He nodded and raised his eyebrows, "Of course, I just saw you speak at the Hall of Congress. Everything you've done for our city, helping us during this challenging time..."

"But do you remember the first time we met?"

Cliven looked off in the distance, trying to remember. "The first time...?"

"I was twenty years old, and you sent me back to the year 1960 by order of the Progenitors."

Cliven stepped back and looked him up and down. "That was you? You look so different now... older."

"I guess I don't look like a teenager anymore."

"And something else, you now seem... I don't know... more evolved?"

Hadden chuckled. "I sure hope so. I was a mess back then. So, shall we get started?"

"Of course. What is the address?"

"I can't tell you that. The time-space address of the Temporalia is highly guarded. I'll have to enter it myself."

Cliven backed away and pointed to a console overlooking the stargate platform. "I understand. No one but Certified Temporalia. Go ahead."

As soon as Hadden typed in the address, the stargate platform roared to life, a ten-foot circular pattern of lights dancing like icy flames. Cliven adjusted the controls and ushered Hadden and his Jenio towards the platform. He waved him goodbye and turned to face the fiery circle of lights. With one long step, they slid through the stargate. A rippling sound of water filled his eardrums. As the sound faded away, he found himself in a chamber attached to a floating circular laboratory somewhere out in deep space.

Hadden stood still inside the chamber to find his bearings. No one was there. The wall on one side was lit up with Matrix symbols. On the other side, a window looked out into deep space. Never before had he seen so many stars, planets, planetoids, and asteroids. *So fantastic.* His mouth hung open, unaware that someone was watching him on a monitor.

"Please, proceed with the purification process," a disembodied voice said.

Matrix symbols blinked on, giving him instructions on how to scan and purify his body-mind system. As he stepped onto a square platform with his Jenio, blue-green lights scanned both of their cell structures. Once the process finished, the doors slid open. Dozens of people sat at digital displays like air traffic controllers. A man looked up from his console and came over to greet him.

"Hadden of Violetta and Aleria, I presume? I'm Kian, your commanding officer." Kian had silver eyes, twice as large as any Earth human. "I'm from Zenae, what you would call the Andromedan star system."

"Nice to meet you," Hadden held out his hand, unsure of the customs of Andromedans.

Several people on consoles swivelled their chairs to watch the interaction.

Kian held up his hand as if to make an oath, so Hadden did the same.

The man slapped his hand, "High five, bro!"

They looked at each other in silence for a moment until Kian broke out laughing.

"I like to watch Earth TV shows. I saw that on Hawaii Five-0. Did you ever watch that show when you lived on the surface?"

Hadden shuffled his feet. "Um, sure. Steve McGarret, Danno."

"Right? It's going to be so fun having a surface human on the crew."

"I, too, am excited to be here," Hadden said, trying not to stare at the man's eyes.

"I guess you haven't met too many non-Terrans?"

"Non-Terrans?"

"What you call Earth or Gaia, we call Terra. So you're all Terrans to us."

"Right. Of course. I have met some non-Terrans in my day," he said, remembering his experiences working for SIM in the deep underground bases. Just not from Andromeda, I mean Zenae."

"You'll get used to us," he said as he gently fist-bumped Hadden on the shoulder. "Let's connect Aleria with the trainer. Her Temporalia trainer will help her time travel from 4D all the way down to 1D and back, as needed. This will help to provide you with important data for our timeline tracking."

They walked down a corridor to a large circular room that looked like a gymnasium. Aleria hopped from his arm onto the floor and trilled. An extraterrestrial that looked part humanoid and part lion approached. The gigantic she-lion stood upright and wore a Temporalia uniform. Despite her kind eyes, Hadden's posture stiffened as she approached. Her immense power made his heart pound.

"This is Buttons."

Hadden stifled a laugh, "Buttons?"

The she-lion feigned a smile. "That's just Kian's little nickname for me. My real name is Butaria. I'm Laani."

His heart raced as he bowed. The Laani were highly revered beings from the Lyran constellation, but he'd never met one before. "I'm honoured to meet you, Butaria."

Kian put a hand on his shoulder to calm him down. "We haven't had an Eagle Jenio here in a long time. She'll be fine in Button's care, don't worry. Have fun, you two. Let's Go. Our room is just down the hall."

Hadden followed Kian to a smaller circular room where three other extraterrestrials sat in floating chairs around a central console. Two of them stood up to greet him.

533

"Hadden of Violetta… I'm Sargia from Ohora. I think you call our star system, Arcturus. Welcome to the year 2062," she beamed. A gold crown adorned her bald blue head, making her look like an exotic empress.

"And I'm Relon, a Centaurian." the other man announced with a bow. He possessed aquatic qualities like gills and webbed limbs. "And that's Manza from Erra Annax, in the Pleiades," Relon said, pointing to a lanky, blonde humanoid.

"Hey…" she said, barely looking up from her console.

"Pleased to meet you all," Hadden said, reaching out his hand to Sargia.

She looked at him with curiosity but didn't shake it.

"High five, bro," Sargia said, slapping his hand and laughing. "Did I do that right?"

"That's apparently how they all do it on the surface, right?" Kian said, ushering them all to sit.

"Well, I wouldn't say they all…"

"Okay! Today is just to orient the team to our mission, study your new amethyst code, and get Hadden comfortable with his role as a Temporalia. Anything you want to say, bro, before we get started?"

Hadden thought about it for a moment and swallowed hard. "I just want to say, or maybe I should start by apologising for… breaking the rules of, um, you know… time travel."

A mischievous grin slowly appeared on Kian's face as he looked around the group. "That's right… you broke our rules,"

Relon knitted his brow, "stitching that back together was a fair bit of work."

Sargia nodded, "True, but we learned so much. Now, in retrospect, we're glad you did it. Chances for ascension on Gaia are increasing in unexpected ways."

"Truly?"

"Yes, Hadden, you're forgiven," Kian winked. "In fact, that's why we wanted you on the team."

"Oh… I thought Waleya…"

"No, we petitioned her. She only agreed reluctantly after the rest of the Galactic Alliance voted in favour."

"The whole Galactic Alliance is in favour of me being here?"

"Yes, but don't get too full of yourself," Relon warned.

Kian gave the Centaurian a bemused look and then glanced at Hadden, "I allow you to be full of yourself for a bit. Let's say for about thirty minutes, then that's it. How's that?"

Hadden looked around the table, unsure how to respond.

"Just joking," Kian smiled. "Shall we begin the meeting?"

Hadden grinned and nodded. "Before we start the orientation, is there any way you could use your technology to help us find the right place to move to in Agartha? I keep getting this remote vision of an abandoned research station on the Celestial Lake."

"Oh. You mean for all of you Heliotropans to continue your work in Agartha?"

Relon jumped in. "I can check that out for you." With surprising dexterity, two webbed hands inputted data onto a console. "Celestial Lake. Celestial…. there it is! Hmm. Let's run it through our timeline prognosticator."

Hadden leaned closer to see the screen. "So you are testing the benefit of moving there?"

"Precisely." Relon squinted at the screen. "Hmm. That's interesting. It's a fine intersection of important ley lines and frequencies needed exactly for your purposes. Your remote visioning was accurate to the 99th percentile."

Hadden breathed a sigh of relief. "Good. Thank you."

"One other thing before we start," Sargia interrupted, "Is to let you know that one of your family members will be key in steering humanity towards this 5D ascension timeline. The Galactic Alliance wanted me to pass that along to you. Your family must ensure that this person stays safe has everything they need."

Hadden leaned forward, wide-eyed. "Who are you referring to?"

"A person whose aptitude is… what was it?" She checked her wrist comm. "A Sentient-Attention…"

"Oh! You must mean my daughter, Tia…"

"Perhaps. Was she born on April 13, 2013?"

"Uh, no, she was born in 1980." Hadden rubbed his chin, puzzled. "Wait a minute, in my time period, that's in the future." He counted on his fingers. "More precisely, that's nine months from now."

"Oh! It's a soul who is not born yet in your timeline, but perhaps, just conceived."

Hadden thought about the three females in his family, and a shiver ran up his spine. "Oh my..."

Sargia smiled, "I hope that's a good 'oh my.'"

"Maybe. I'm not clear who it is. I'm remote viewing the situation, but none of the women in my family seem pregnant, at least not yet. So this 'soul' plays a key role in the future of humanity?"

"Without this individual, you won't make it."

Hadden nodded, feeling his breath stalling.

After hours of training and debriefing, they said goodbye to Hadden and Aleria on their stargate platform. His head was dizzy with all the information he'd downloaded. In fact, it felt like he'd been there for days. The technician showed him where to type in the time-space address for just after he left in Helio Tropez and then scurried off down the hall to catch up with Kian.

The console looked far more sophisticated than he was used to. Matrix symbols indicated where to enter the space-time address, so he typed in the fifteen numbers. Nothing happened. It wanted three more numbers. He only knew of fifteen numbers to enter. What were the other three? He thought of asking someone for help but decided to scan his own photographic memory banks for the answer instead. A vague memory floated to the surface. *Just add three zeros. That must be it.* After he did, the stargate fired up, and he walked through with Aleria close behind.

As he emerged on the other side, only a barren wasteland lay before him. Confused, he looked around for something familiar. Off in the distance the skyline of the Riala mountain range stood the same as always. Below him vines and refuse engulfed the platform. Dandelions poked out of cracks in the stairway, but the dome over the platform no longer existed.

Instead, one console stood by itself in the open air. He raced towards it, hoping it still worked. It must have roared to life when he had used the stargate, because a date blinked in the upper right-hand corner. He'd been gone three years! Aleria agreed to fly over the city. A few minutes later she returned and confirmed that no buildings or humans remained.

The Progenitors have already destroyed the city, and everyone has gone to Agartha without me! Panic coursed through his veins. He dashed back to the console and typed in the address for Helio Tropez without the three zeros, which should put him through at fourteen minutes after he left, and checked it twice. The stargate fired up and with Aleria on his arm, he went through with trepidation.

As he emerged back onto the same stargate platform, Cliven looked up from his work. The area was clean and well-kept, just as he had left it. The dome sparkled above them.

"You're back so soon. You just left." Cliven smiled.

"I feel like I've been gone for days. In fact, I typed in the wrong space-time address and ended up three years in the future. No one was here. Everything had been destroyed."

"Everything was gone?"

"Except for the platform and one console, thank goodness. That's how I got back. I'm so relieved to see you here!" Hadden hugged the man so hard he gasped. "I've got to go find Daphne!"

He flew with Aleria across the busy city and up to the balcony of their apartment. The eagle settled on the rail of the balcony as Hadden lowered his wings and cupped his eyes to see inside. Daphne stood programming something into the replicator. He slid the balcony door open and swept her up in his arms.

"You're back even sooner than I thought!"

After explaining what had happened, she brought him some Respite tea and a flower bar to revive him. He inhaled the food and then swivelled his chair to face the window. "Seeing this amazing city that's been here for thousands of years with all its beautiful structures and gardens and technology destroyed was so heartbreaking."

Daphne frowned. "Why don't the Progenitors just put a protection field around the city to preserve it in case we want to come back?"

Hadden shrugged. "I'm not sure. They said destroying it was for security reasons. But when I think about it... what I saw was 4D Helio Tropez. Once we go through ascension, we'll be living in 6D Helio Tropez. It's in the future and is ten times better than here. It will not be destroyed."

"6D Helio Tropez is actually in the future?"

"Uh huh. Sort of. Time-space takes on a whole different form when you move out of the 3D and 4D worlds."

"Okay," Daphne said with puzzled eyes. "But what if we don't make it to 6D?" She stood up and pressed her face against the window.

"We will make it. The Temporalia will help to ensure that we end up on the ascension timeline."

She sighed. "I hope so."

Daphne's silver gown hugged her in all the right places. As she turned to face him, her turquoise eyes flashed at him.

"By the way," Hadden said, moving in next to her. "I know you are technically about... what? Seventy-two years old? But of course, you look like maybe thirty. All your cells are dialled up to optimum function. Does that mean that you can now get pregnant again?"

Daphne laughed and slid her arm around his waist. "You're only asking me about this now?"

"It's just..." The heat rose in Hadden's cheeks. "I didn't think to ask because of your aptitude. But then, I remembered that women in Helio Tropez remain fertile for hundreds of years..."

"Yes, I can get pregnant now that I've been rejuvenated. And, yes, Voyent-Reprogram females can prevent pregnancies with their minds. Why do you ask?"

He explained what Sargia had said at the Temporalia meeting.

"Interesting. So this special child is supposed to be mine or Tia's or Metta's or...?"

"I can't get a reading on it because I don't think the child has been conceived yet."

"Okay. Let me see if I can remote view the situation." She closed her eyes and took a step away from the window. After a few moments, she said, "I don't see it being my baby. But maybe, the thought of going through the whole pregnancy thing again is affecting my intuition. I mean... I had twins! That was so intense." Daphne covered her forehead and looked at him with guilty eyes. "Does that sound selfish?"

"No, of course not. In Helio Tropez, you only have children if you really want them. Most people here seem to personally control whether they have children or not. It's just a sign that it's not right for you or for us."

"That's a relief. Yes, let's allow the younger ones to experience the joys and sorrows of parenthood."

"Indeed. So it's one of our daughters?"

Daphne closed her eyes again, "I don't sense that Ramu and Metta have consecrated their relationship yet..."

Hadden smiled. "That leaves Tia and Xander. Should we tell them?"

"Maybe they'll tell us first."

"Right. That means we'll be grandparents!"

"Me, a grandmother?"

"Yes! I'll get you a shawl and knitting needles to help you ease into the role more easily," he teased as he pulled her into an embrace.

She pushed him away. "I'll get you a walker and reading glasses."

"I've been there already. So no thanks." A pinging sound emitted from Hadden's wrist comm. "We have so many meetings tomorrow. I need sleep."

She patted his cheek. "Okay. You rest. I now have a meeting to teach Heliotropans how to communicate with 3D surface humans. That should be a trip."

For the next several days, groups of Heliotropans learned how to open up telepathic connections with 3D. Since most of the first Task Force had ascended, that left the Heliotropans born on the surface to explain how to reach them. Hadden and Tia also taught people how to connect with 6D friends and relatives. Meanwhile, people worked night and day, packing, sorting, recycling and organizing themselves for the move.

The day before their departure, the newly refitted train was loaded to the brink. Five ceremonies took place in the five Palaces of Zuris, Indicum,

Violetta, Liven and Viridis, where people offered their thanks and said their goodbyes. Once people felt complete, they streamed onto the Veya Field, where they replicated outdoor chairs for themselves. They sat in rows of semicircles, facing the central stage. A bittersweet feeling permeated the air. Not only was it their last day in Helio Tropez, but memories of the last time they had gathered in the Veya Field came to mind as well. Most of them hadn't been able or willing to ascend.

Hadden took a seat in the front row with Aleria close by. Exhaustion permeated his entire body, and he was glad to only be a spectator in this event. The lights dimmed, and a crystalline glow illuminated the perimeter of the outdoor stage.

A spotlight filled the centre stage, and Meraton stepped into it. "Tonight, we celebrate our 24,984 years here in Helio Tropez. When our ancestors arrived, this area was void of any human life. Over the millennia, they built it to greatness. As you all know, it's been a tumultuous journey at times, but we've matured and grown our skills and wisdom as a collective. Now, it's not only time to celebrate that, but also to look forward to our new home in Agartha. As you know, Jaya and her team have secured rights to the land on the Celestial Lake. We look forward to working with the Temporalia, our 3D humans, and our 6D guides. Together, we will ascend once and for all!" The crowd roared in agreement. When the sound died down, Meraton said, "Now let the ceremonies begin!"

The lights dimmed and a spotlight directed to the back of the stage, where Xander and the musicians launched into a rhythm designed for sound healing. It started slowly, weaving its curative magic into the weary minds of the audience. Soon, angelic voices filled the air. Two stunning women walked forward into the light, wearing rainbow satin ceremonial gowns. Mother and daughter held hands as their soprano voices took people to new heights of inspiration. As Daphne and Metta finished their solo, they stepped back, and a curtain opened to reveal a forty-person choir. They started with a simple harmony of otherworldly sounds that grew into a crescendo of magnificent complexity. Soon, Hadden felt his nervous system floating on air. A peaceful unity permeated everything in the space.

When it ended, everyone was speechless. There was no applause. Just silent reverence.

As the spotlight faded away, a sprightly fiddle arose in the darkness. The spotlight framed Annika as she pranced towards the proscenium enchanting the audience with her fiddle while dressed as a court jester. When she hit a high note, a group of children in bird costumes flew down from a large tree with their gossamer wings spread wide. The SANA Eagles in training danced in the air, with various bird Jenios following close behind. They intertwined in stunning formations over the crowd. The lighting crew added magical spotlights and swirls. People murmured in awe as the children landed in unison, forming a pentagram on the stage to honour Pentada.

After that, Metta came forward, and one of the musicians started a rapid drumbeat rhythm. With mercurial precision, she recited a spoken word poem entitled "The Diffusion of the Foundling". Hadden's heart melted, and his fatherly pride soared. It told not only of her story but of the old archetypal pathways they all finally emerged from. It ended in a crescendo of words and instrumental rifts, and Ramu and Cassandra used their tangent mindpower to raise hundreds of lanterns into the sky. Floating violet orbs lit up the entire field, floating softly higher above them. People sat back in wonder as they bobbed off into the distance and dissolved away into the upper mist.

Next, the lights dimmed. A group of actors performed a funny skit that Ramu and Metta wrote together. It was about settlers in their first year at Helio Tropez before they had running water or power and all the crazy mistakes they made. After several other captivating performances, the show came to a close. Meraton performed the final ceremony of appreciation to SANA, to the elementals, to the Progenitors, and to each other. When everything ended, people wandered home in a trance of peace and gratitude, settling down for a deep sleep in anticipation of the journey ahead of them.

The next day, people bid their beautiful home goodbye and mounted into various cars on the train, mostly in family groups. As their train pulled away from the station, Hadden sat with Daphne, watching the stargate dome disappear over the horizon. Across from them, Tia snuggled next to Xander. Bimini sat glued to the window, watching the colours and shapes whizz by. The wallaby sat at Xander's feet, sleeping.

Xander tapped Hadden on the knee. "Maybe one day, we can find our parents on the surface and bring them into Middle Earth with us."

"Yes, there may be many Quinary Mission people who we can hopefully still rescue." Hadden smiled, then added, "Your parents would want to know their grandchild."

Xander raised his eyebrows and looked at Tia, then back at Hadden. "Do you know something we don't know?"

A lump formed in Hadden's throat as he remembered all those years of trying to keep Tia safe, blocking her from finding love and family. "Tia?"

A slow smile appeared on Tia's face. "I didn't want to say anything, but a little spirit showed up in a dream right after we performed our SANA rites at the Temple. I woke up this morning, and I just knew I was pregnant. I wanted to wait until we were all settled on the train to say something. How did you know?"

"The Temporalia told me a family member of mine was pivotal in the coming ascension process, a Sentient-Attention. I thought they meant you until they said the person was born on April 13, 2013. Since they operate in the year 2062, that's the past for them. But in our timeline, that's nine months from now."

Xander turned to Tia in disbelief. "They told us that conception was more common right after performing SANA rites at the Temple."

Hadden nodded, "We narrowed it down to you rather than Daphne or Metta. At the time, the child wasn't yet conceived, so I couldn't tell for sure."

"That's amazing," Xander and Tia said in unison.

Xander held his forehead. "I'm going to be a father? That's just so..."

"...so quick. I know. We just got together." Tia laughed nervously. "What did the Temporalia say about this child?"

"The Galactic Alliance told them about it. There are many timelines warring for domination in the mind of humanity. Only one leads to ascension. Your daughter plays a pivotal role in getting us all on the right one, the Golden Age timeline."

With a trembling hand, Tia touched her belly. "You know it's a girl?"

Hadden smiled. "It's a girl."

Further Resources

Go to The Golden Age Timeline Publishing site. You can get on our e-list to hear about when the sequel, **Stello Tropez,** is available: http://GoldenAgeTimeline.com/

On the site you can also get access to information such as:

- About the Author

- Book Appendix

- Free Resources

- Contact Info

- And more...

http://GoldenAgeTimeline.com/

Acknowledgements

Writing this book was more rewarding and took more fortitude than I could have ever imagined. None of it would have been possible without my best friend and life partner, Dave. He has supported me and stood by me during every struggle on this journey, helping me celebrate my wins and making sure I kept my sense of humor whenever I lost it.

Denis of Weekend Publisher and Liz of Blurb Medic were amazingly helpful and supportive on my writing and publishing journey with this book. I'm so grateful to have found them. Dominic Gilmour's developmental editing was beyond superb. His brilliant creativity is woven throughout this book. My deep thanks also goes out to Jasmine Xuereb for her excellent proofing and Talon David for her dazzling voice over work.

Farwa Akbar saved the day when it came to formatting. She went beyond the call of duty to fix issues in the nick of time. Carin and team from GetCovers did superb graphic works and were excellent to work with.

A huge heartfelt thanks to Christina Merkley and her Visual Coaching. Two of the book characters came through Alpha Mind to tell me how to keep going when I'd given up. And a deep appreciation to Lorraine and Rob McGregor for all their support, especially through a tricky transition.

And then there's my wonderful, advanced readers who gave me such helpful and encouraging pre-publishing feedback.

Finally, long ago the writer, James Redfield, inspired me to see novel writing in a whole new way, crossing the threshold and melding worlds in a way I hadn't seen before. I'm deeply thankful to him and all the seen and unseen forces that brought this book to life.

Printed in Great Britain
by Amazon